CHARLOTTE VALE ALLEN

THREE COMPLETE NOVELS

CHARLOTTE VALE ALLEN

THREE COMPLETE NOVELS

Illusions

Dream Train

Night Magic

WINGS BOOKS

New York • Avenel, New Jersey

This omnibus was originally published in separate volumes under the titles:

Illusions, copyright © 1987 by Charlotte Vale Allen.
Dream Train, copyright © 1988 by Charlotte Vale Allen.
Night Magic, copyright © 1989 by Charlotte Vale Allen.

This edition contains the complete and unabridged texts of the original editions. They have been completely reset for this volume.

This 1993 edition is published by Wings Books,
distributed by Outlet Book Company, Inc.,
a Random House Company, 40 Engelhard Avenue, Avenel,
New Jersey 07001, by arrangement with Atheneum, an imprint
of Macmillan Publishing Company

Random House
New York • Toronto • London • Sydney • Auckland

Printed and bound in the United States of America

LIBRARY OF CONGRESS CATALOGING-IN-PUBLICATION DATA

Allen, Charlotte Vale, 1941–
    [Novels. Selections]
    Charlotte Vale Allen : three complete novels.
       p.   cm.
    Contents: Illusions—Dream train—Night magic.
    ISBN 0-517-09364-2
    1. Love stories, American.   I. Title.
  PS3551.L392A6   1993
  813'.54—dc20   93-10981
                                    CIP

8 7 6 5 4 3 2 1

Contents

Illusions

For Shirley Van Wagener

One

SHE'D KNOWN JOEL WAS GOING TO DIE. THEY'D ALL KNOWN IT FOR A very long time. But when it finally happened Leigh was shattered. She couldn't seem to absorb it, even though she was there at the end, and saw for herself how, with dreadful ease, Joel simply ceased to exist. While there was a certain, hateful rightness to his death, there was also a terrifying simplicity to it at the last. And she kept thinking it should have been a larger, grander moment somehow. The ease and simplicity distressed her. If he could die this way, after such a long, valiant battle, she had to wonder if there'd been any point to his having struggled as long and as hard as he had.

She was frightened, exhausted, and angry, and the only thing she wanted to do was go to visit her father. She admitted it was an arbitrary idea, even probably irrational. Nevertheless, she was determined to go. She was in sudden, desperate need of a destination.

Once in her aisle seat in the first-class smoking section of the 747, she put a tape into the Walkman, adjusted the volume and the ear phones, opened a book, and tried to ignore everything going on around her. She didn't want to have to speak; she had no desire to communicate with anyone except her father. And she had no notion whatever of what she wanted to say to him, or what she hoped he might say to her.

"You're off on a fool's errand," her mother had declared earlier that day. "No one's ever been able to hold anything remotely resembling a conversation with your father. He'll undoubtedly be up to his thighs in manure; he'll likely give you one of his typical blank stares while he huffs and puffs a bit about the weather; then he'll offer you a glass of cheap

sherry and tell you about the cost of seed, or something equally capti-
vating. I *wish* you'd reconsider, Leigh. This is truly ridiculous."

"He's my *father*, and I haven't seen him in almost thirty years. I *want* to
see him!"

"I know you're upset, dear"—her mother took another tack—"but do
you really think this is wise?"

"I can't give you straight answers," Leigh told her. "I don't *know* if it's
wise. I don't *know anything*."

"It's just that I do worry about you . . ."

"I know that. I worry about me, too. I'll call you from London."

"Please don't do anything foolish," her mother had begged.

"I will try my very best not to."

"It's all madness," Marietta had sighed. "Take care."

"I will try," Leigh had promised.

She'd no sooner finished the conversation with her mother than the
telephone had started ringing again, and she'd wanted to ignore it, let the
machine answer for her. But she thought it might be her mother again,
with some last-minute thought, so she'd picked up the receiver to give a
wearied hello.

At once, Miles had made his pitch. "The last thing you should be doing
is flying off this way, leaving your mother to cope with all the arrangements."

"You just talked to her, didn't you?" Leigh had guessed.

"Yes, but—"

"And if you talked to her, I'm certain she told you she has *agreed* to
cope; she *volunteered* to cope."

"Yes, but—"

"Miles, this is one of those times when I wish you were agent for one of
us, but not both. I loathe all this back-and-forth business, with you rushing between the two of us. It's unfair to everyone."

"Speaking of which," he'd said, "I know it's probably not the best
time, but at the risk of life and limb, dare I ask when, if ever, you intend
to work again, to get on with your life?"

"It is *not* the best time. I may *never* work again. And I especially loathe
it when you start impersonating my mother, sounding like her and trying
to browbeat me with good intentions. Miles"—she had tried to overcome
her exasperation—"I know you mean well. I know you care. But I don't
want to talk to you now."

"All right," he'd backed down. "I know the timing's dreadful. It's just
that we're very concerned about you, Leigh."

"I know that. I thank you for that," she'd said, and put down the
receiver.

Giving up now on her attempt to read, she raised the volume on the

Walkman so that her eardrums throbbed achingly as she looked around the cabin. A few more minutes to takeoff and, with luck, the seat next to hers would remain empty. She'd barely completed the thought when one of the flight attendants touched her on the shoulder. Leigh switched off the music and simultaneously slipped sideways into the aisle so the latecomer could get to his seat.

"Sorry to disturb you," he apologized, passing his overcoat to the waiting attendant.

Leigh gave a slight nod in response, sat again, fastened her seat belt, turned the cassette back on, and closed her eyes. Please, she prayed, not a chatty executive; please not one of those pin-striped wonder boys flying on a company ticket for a few days' business in London.

Finding her place in the book, she tried to force herself to read. It was like being back in school, at a time in childhood when words had been individual entities that hadn't seemed to want to be joined together to make sentences. Simply recognizing random words had been a significant accomplishment, worthy of parental applause. Hopeless. She couldn't make sense of the neatly printed blocks of letters set so reasonably on the page. She closed the book and stared at the back of the seat ahead.

The only reason she'd married the Good Doctor, in whom she'd had only a minimal interest initially, was because she met and was at once taken with his twelve-year-old son. At their first meeting, Joel had made coffee for them and then sat and talked with her about a production of *The Pirates of Penzance* in which he was playing the lead. He'd been so self-possessed, so wise and witty and charmingly confident, that she'd known she'd involve herself with his father in order to spend more time with the son. She'd been open about the selfishness of her motives, and had told Joel about the son she'd lost. He'd loved her anecdotes about Stephen, and had encouraged her to tell all about him. Joel had no jealousy. He was so firmly entrenched in his own identity, even at age twelve, that he was able to hear stories about another twelve-year-old boy and find only pleasure in them.

In view of how little interested the Good Doctor had been in the son of his late wife, Leigh had taken the position that, at the very worst, she and Joel would benefit from one another. And they had.

For just shy of ten years she'd had not only a new model for her books, but also the privilege of watching Joel grow to become even wittier and wiser. Not even his father's eventual outrage had daunted Joel's confidence. Despite the hurt, despite the brief span of the marriage, despite everything, she and Joel had remained close. When Joel "came out," revealing to his father what Leigh had sensed intuitively almost from the start, the Good Doctor threw him out, and refused to see or speak with him even after Joel became ill.

It still infuriated her to think that anyone could be so stupid, so rigid in his thinking that he'd sever himself from his only child simply because that child had not turned out to be interested in girls. It meant nothing to the Good Doctor that Joel had been generous, gifted, and giving. He'd preferred his lovers to be male, and not female. He was, therefore, in his father's eyes, a sickening aberration, a degenerate, a pervert, a disgrace.

Now Joel was dead, and she doubted his father would even attend the funeral. She wouldn't be there either, but Joel would have understood that. They'd been saying goodbye for three years—from the initial diagnosis, through the two remissions, until just two nights ago, when his hand had gone limp in hers and he'd exhaled one long, slow, final time. She'd held her own breath, waiting for him to inhale again, to go on living. But he hadn't. His eyes had ceased to see; they'd gone opaque and visionless. With that final exhalation the humor and inventiveness and energy that had been Joel had left his body. She'd imagined his essence blending invisibly with the air of the room, and she'd breathed deeply as if, if she took in enough of that air, she might take in some significant part of her stepson.

Ten years of running out to catch a late showing of some old movie Joel insisted they had to see; of afternoon concerts at Avery Fisher Hall; of Sunday brunches, and dinners he prepared; of weeks at a stretch in the country where she worked and he tried to do something with the hopeless old furniture, by means of new arrangements, or painted the kitchen a bright grass green, or came into her studio, with coffee and sandwiches, to keep her company while she took a break; of celebrating when an audition turned into a job and he had three days' work on a commercial for a soft drink, or six weeks in an Off Off Broadway production that gave him an opportunity to demonstrate how immensely talented he was. He'd brought his friends along to meet her; he'd come racing across town in a cab, popping in on his way to a party to show her the clothes he'd bought with the residual check from his second commercial. There'd been occasions when he'd stopped by late, after some outing, to have coffee with her and to tell her how angry he was with Jeff over some misunderstanding, or how delighted he was about their reconciliation, or, finally, how exhausted and ill he felt. "I just hope I haven't got the plague," he'd whispered in the waiting room when they'd gone together for his tests. "I've been so goddamned careful."

He'd actually been relieved when the doctor had called them in to give them the results. He'd laughed, and the doctor had stared at him quizzically. "It's a respectable disease," Joel had explained. And when he'd been admitted to the hospital to begin chemotherapy, he'd said, "People have been known to beat it, Leigh. I intend to beat it." But his blood had turned to water, and he'd died.

She swallowed to ease the knot in her throat, and looked around the cabin. Why, with so many empty seats, had they put someone beside her? She felt suddenly furious. They should have known better than to put someone beside her. But at least he hadn't made any attempt to draw her into conversation. And he was, she saw peripherally, wearing an attractive Cartier tank watch and fragrant cologne. A briefcase sat unopened on his knees. The instant the no-smoking sign went off, he lit a cigarette. It smelled wonderful, and she realized it had been quite some time since her last cigarette back at the airport.

Just as she held one to her mouth, a gold DuPont lighter popped up in front of her to light it. She said, "Thank you," hoping she wasn't shouting. Joel was forever accusing her of bellowing when she tried to talk with the Walkman on. She said the words without turning, hoping to discourage further courtesies. She felt very edgy, dangerously full of untapped negative energy. Anything might set her off, and the next thing she knew, they'd be making an unscheduled stop, to put her into restraints before removing her from the plane. She could see herself being dragged, screaming, from her seat. There was a kind of jagged wedge of anxiety inside her chest, just behind her ribs, and when she indulged in imagining the darkest possible scenarios, it felt about the same way it did when she pushed the nail of her little finger into the flesh behind the nail of her thumb: a keen minor pain with the potential for considerable growth.

She'd heard the Albinoni twice, and ejected the tape, assaulted at once by noise—of the aircraft itself, of conversations, of pages turning in books and magazines, of ice cubes and liquids in glasses, of a wailing infant. Airplanes were so damned noisy. Just like hospitals. Hospitals were the noisiest places on earth, what with the announcements echoing up and down the corridors, the efficient-sounding squeak of rubber-soled shoes, various trolleys wheeling here and there, some with medications, some with food, some with mystifying loads of arcane equipment. Joel had never complained, though, about any of it; not when his hair came out, not when the medicines made him violently sick, not even when an acute toxic reaction to the drugs turned his face scarlet. "I'll beat it," he'd told her. "I'm going to beat it." Ah, Jesus! she thought, pushing through the tapes in her carryon bag. I believed you would, Joel. If anyone could have beat it, I believed you would. No one's meant to die a few weeks before his twenty-second birthday. It's too bloody young.

She gave up trying to find a tape, removed the earphones, and at once felt robbed, as if of armor. Why was privacy something one had to erect between oneself and others, like a barricade? It was simply horrendous the way people refused to recognize one's desire to be left alone unless it was clearly signposted by an open book, or headgear hooked up to music, or work arrayed on the tray table. If you simply sat gazing straight ahead, someone was bound to intrude. She was indulging in misanthropy, knew it, and didn't care. Since Joel's death, she'd had to fight an all but over-whelming desire to tell absolutely everyone to fuck off and get the hell away from her. Beneath this desire, rather like the bottom sheet on a well-made bed, was her knowledge of the transitional nature of her present feelings, as well as an ungrudging admiration for the completeness of her alienation, no matter how temporary. She was so deeply, pervasively an-gry, so utterly, desperately grief-stricken, that she wanted, from one mo-ment to the next, to lash out at anyone who inadvertently crossed her path.

She'd only just finished a cigarette and already she wanted another. Why couldn't she quit? Joel had been nagging her for years to give up the habit. It should, she'd long reasoned, have been possible to go to bed one night and wake up the next morning as someone who didn't smoke. If she quit, her lungs would clear in time, her breath would turn sweet as a newborn's, her teeth would stay clean, she'd add years to her life. What for? Who cared?

She turned slightly to take a look at the man with the cologne and the Cartier watch. Late thirties, an impeccably tailored navy suit, crisp white shirt, gold tie pin; clean-shaven, good skin, dark hair, eye color unknown due to lowered gaze, hands resting motionless atop the still-unopened briefcase; no glaring abnormalities, ears and chin well proportioned. He looked young.

Quickly, she lit another cigarette, inhaled, then let her head fall back against the padded rest, considering the issue of age. There was hardly a day, recently, when she didn't, with mild confusion and disbelief, wonder how she could still think and feel as young as she did, yet be as old as she was. Even her mother didn't seem all that old. How did it happen? Eighteen one minute, forty-five the next. It wasn't like catching a cold; it wasn't something that would lay you out for two or three weeks, then be gone. It was there for good, and progressing at an astonishing rate: facial lines and wrinkled knees. Every morning when she ritually bent to touch her hands flat to the floor, if she cared to look, she could have an alarming closeup view of the crepey flesh sagging over the knobs of her knees.

"You're nuts!" Joel had laughed. "You look sensational. You worry about the dumbest stuff. What'll you do, Leigh, when you've got some-thing really serious to worry about?"

"It depends on what you consider serious," she'd replied then.

Well, she certainly knew what was serious now. And she had handled it well. She'd held in the anxiety and uncertainty and fear; she'd been cheerful and optimistic and encouraging with Joel right to the last. They'd even discussed it once, rating each other on how badly or well each had dealt with his illness. "We're both terrific at it," Joel had told her. Now it was over. He was dead, and congratulations for having dealt well were not in order. Now she had moments when the slow decay of her own flesh seemed so ominous she could have sworn she actually smelled it.

The man beside her wore a simple gold wedding band. She had three diamond rings on the third finger of her left hand, two diamond bands on the middle finger of her right, and a large solitaire on the finger beside it. He did have attractive hands, wide and strong-looking. They were the sort of hands she'd always imagined surgeons must have, until she'd married the Good Doctor and relegated that particular fantasy to the trash heap along with the dozens of other fiction-based notions she'd entertained in her lifetime. The Good Doctor had pale, narrow hands that were softer than her own, and almost as small, and far, far cleaner.

"Are you on holiday?"

She turned. She could kill this dead at once, "cop an attitude" as Joel would have said. But she simply couldn't do it, not when she had hours left of having to sit beside him. And she lacked the energy to move elsewhere. Plus, his blue eyes were unexpected.

"No," she answered, her mouth rusty as if she hadn't used it in too long. "Are you?"

"No. I was just," he pointed, "admiring your rings."

She looked at her hands. "Oh. I get married a lot," she said, and then emitted what sounded to her like a grating bark of laughter. He didn't seem bothered. He actually smiled. What was it about his eyes? She was so tired it was difficult to home in on specific thoughts.

"What's 'a lot'?"

"Twice."

"That's not a lot. Four, five, that's a lot." He had a slight accent, but she couldn't place it. The plane was running into some mild turbulence, and he went suddenly sober, saying, "I hate flying. It terrifies me." He gazed at her, as if prepared for either her scorn or her support.

"And of course," she said, fascinated by his visible fear, "you have to fly constantly."

He nodded, still awaiting her ultimate reaction.

"I don't think I've ever met a man who admitted to being afraid to fly," she said, as taken with this thought as she was with the evidence of his fear.

"It's only fair to admit it," he said, looking relieved that she'd chosen not to display scorn, "in case I faint in your lap, or jump up and start screaming uncontrollably."

"You do that kind of thing?" she asked.

"Not so far," he allowed, "but you never know."

"Well, I will consider myself warned."

"You're not afraid?" he asked seriously.

"I'm not fond of turbulence. But afraid? No." Afraid? If anything, she'd gone so far beyond fear she scarcely valued her own life. Take the other night, for example, after Joel died, when she'd been driving around town after leaving the hospital. Some fool in a little car was beside her at the stoplight, just panting to race her. She was in the inside lane; there was a car parked about two hundred yards dead ahead. The lights changed, and she did it: she hit the kickdown switch, and the turbo-diesel shot off, but the guy in the Honda was gunning it for all he was worth and he wasn't going to let her into the left lane; he was hanging in there, nose to nose. Raining, the street icing over, and there they were, the two of them, doing sixty down Park Avenue. She missed the parked car with about six inches to spare, shot ahead and then, in delayed reaction, checked the rearview mirror for police while asking herself what in hell she was doing, while the adrenaline surged nauseatingly through her system and she eased back on the accelerator. The Honda zipped over in front of her before the next red light and stopped, to sit there, its rough idle making the thing shake like a big wet dog. The hotshot behind the wheel had raced the middle-aged woman in the Mercedes, and lost. So now he'd teach her some manners, irritate her thoroughly by just sitting there after the light went green, then crawling ahead perhaps six feet, stopping, then a few feet more, and then, at the last moment, flipping his turn signal and shooting off to the right. Giving her the metaphoric finger. She'd sat through another red light and laughed mirthlessly, thinking they were both idiots. But he was a bigger one because *she* didn't care if she died; he, however, she'd have wagered, cared a great deal, but just didn't know how much. Like most arrogant idiots driving ancient Hondas and trying to prove his social equality and male superiority by having latenight drag races with people who, he believed, considered themselves at least financially above him, he thought he was immortal. She, on the other hand, knew better. She certainly did know better. Periodically, during the past two days, she found herself running that race again, but losing. She could see the Mercedes rear-ending the parked car; she could see and feel the heat of the resulting fiery crash; she could see herself sitting calmly, hands on the steering wheel, as she was immolated.

"There's nothing to be afraid of," she now told the man seated beside her. "You can only die."

He literally blanched, and she felt dreadful for speaking the truth because this man had no doubts about his mortality. "That isn't funny," he reproached her.

"I wasn't trying to be funny," she said. "Just try not to think about it," she advised.

"The more I try not to think about it, the more I think about it. It's a conundrum. I don't suppose you play backgammon?" Again he gave her that open gaze.

There was something about him that was too vulnerable, she thought. It was as if he'd never quite mastered the skill of concealing his feelings, or his need to have those feelings approved. Did she want to spend time over a game with him? They'd be bound to talk. "We could," she said at length, "go up to the lounge. I am assuming you have a board."

"*Would* you?" he asked almost feverishly, as if she were consenting to far more than just a game.

"Backgammon's my weakness," she confessed. She and Joel had, at the last, played daily for hours, until he'd been unable to roll the dice or move the pieces. She'd ended up owing him two million, eight hundred and twelve thousand dollars. "Consider it a gift," he'd grinned at her. "I'm tearing up your markers, toots."

"I am Daniel Godard." Her seatmate extended his hand to her. "This is very kind of you."

"I dislike telling people my name," she said, placing her hand in his. "Call me Leigh."

"What's wrong with that?" he asked, bringing a portable set out of his briefcase.

"I'll tell you after I've had eight or ten drinks."

"You'll be too drunk to tell me then."

"Exactly!" She stood and headed for the staircase leading to the lounge.

"We've got the whole place to ourselves," Dan noted, as they sat on opposite sides of one of the tables. "Couldn't be better. The only thing worse than flying is having to be sociable in forced circumstances."

"I agree. Where are you from?" she asked as he handed her the brown dice and cup. "You have a faint accent."

"I was born in France. My family came to the States when I was nine. And what is *your* faint accent?" he asked with a smile.

"I grew up in England. My mother and I left when I was twelve."

"I think," he said, rolling one die to open—a four to her six; she took the first move—"you sound far more English than I do French."

She shrugged, intent on the game, grateful for the distraction.

An attendant came up to ask if they wanted drinks. Leigh ordered gin and tonic. Dan asked for vodka on the rocks. Neither of them paused in their playing. She couldn't concentrate, though, and lost three games in succession. Conceding the last game, she studied her companion while he cleared the board, and decided he was as bored as she.

"Shall we take a break?" she suggested. "My mind's not on this."

He pushed the board to one side, picked up his drink, and said, "Tell me about your name. I'll have the stewardess bring you nine more drinks."

She lit a fresh cigarette and drew hard on it. "Why are you going to London?"

"I have absolutely no reason. It's merely a delaying tactic. I'm supposed to be traveling in the other direction, but that route means seventeen hours nonstop in the air. By this route, I can fly in fits and starts, and it doesn't seem quite so nightmarish."

"But where are you going?" she asked, curious.

"Thailand." He smiled. "I'll spend a day, or two, or three in London, then pick up a flight to Zurich, or Stockholm, or Frankfurt, wherever; pick up another flight, and then another, until I get to where I'm meant to be."

"It must take forever."

"It does," he agreed. "But at least I don't faint, or jump up and start screaming." He laughed self-mockingly.

"And what will you do in Thailand?"

"I own—owned," he corrected himself, "a mail-order business. I was conglomerated two years ago, but I contracted to stay on for a time to do the buying. What were you listening to before?"

"Albinoni."

"Ah!"

"Ah what?"

"Ah, good. If you'd said Barry Manilow it would've been terrible."

"Why?"

"You know why," he said.

Games, she thought. I'm not up for games. "You tell me."

"Barry Manilow represents a case of mistaken identity," he explained.

"I see. That happens to you often, does it?" Was he some kind of fool who went around judging people by their exteriors and their cassettes?

"It doesn't happen to you?" he countered. "Someone seems a certain way and then, when you become acquainted, they're not at all what they seemed. It was either contrived, or you were seeing what you wanted to see and not what was really there."

"And I seem to be one thing," she said, holding down her sudden anger, "but I may be something else, depending either on my skill at contrivance, or the flaws in your perception?" Another goddamned game, she thought, determined to put a stop to it.

"You seem," he said carefully, "to be many things, none of them contrived. I can't comment on the quality of my perception. It varies, depending on the situation. So," he took a deep breath, "tell me your name."

Because she felt he'd won that round and put her nicely in her place, she told him. "Stanleigh Dunn."

"It's a good name," he said judiciously.

"Oh, *please!* Everyone calls me Leigh."

"I thought you were a man," he said, drawing a leg up and wrapping his arms around it.

"I beg your pardon?"

"My daughter, when she was little, was one of your biggest fans. Still is, as a matter of fact. They're incredible, your books. The illustrations are—phantasmagorical. If I don't get your autograph before we land, Lane will never forgive me." Some doubt touching his smile, he said, "There couldn't be *two* Stanleigh Dunns, could there?"

"God forbid! Phantasmagorical," she repeated. "What a wonderful compliment! Thank you." Since she was predisposed toward people who knew of her work, she found herself relenting in her hasty assessment of this man as a potential games player.

"I've always admired people who could paint, draw."

"How old is your daughter now, Mr. Godard?"

"Lane is almost twenty, *Mrs. Dunn*," he teased. "Do you have children?"

Had he not asked the question, she would have corrected him about the name. Instead, she shook her head, at once reaching for another cigarette.

"You smoke too much," he observed.

"Cigarettes," she said wryly, keeping a grip on her temper, "are my personal punishment and reward." She knew if she sat there one minute longer she'd tell him precisely what she thought of people who liked to comment on the habits of other people they'd only recently met. "If you'll excuse me," she said, "I think I'll try to take a nap." She put out the just-lit cigarette. "I haven't slept in two nights . . ." She stopped, wondering why she'd begun explaining herself to this stranger.

"I'll just sit here, enjoy the quiet, if that's all right with you."

"Of course." She headed for the rear of the lounge where blankets and pillows were stacked. Halfway there, her conscience struck. She stopped and looked back, pitying him for his fear. She considered telling him how little there was to fear, how easily life could leave a person. "Thank you for the game," she said instead.

Distractedly, he replied, "Oh, you're welcome. Thank you."

She stretched out on one of the seats, her handbag on the floor beside her shoes. The instant her eyes closed, she saw Joel, and her anger at the unfairness of it all engulfed her. Pulling the blanket up over her head, she gave in both to the images and to the pain they created. She curled in on herself, her fists wedged against her teeth.

Two

HE DAWDLED OVER HIS VODKA AND WAVED AWAY THE ATTENDANT when she returned, indicating with a finger to his lips the sleeping figure at the rear of the lounge. The attendant smiled her understanding and went away, leaving him gazing over his shoulder at the narrow form, hidden beneath a blanket, of the woman with the man's name. It disarranged his preconceptions to learn that someone with whose work he'd been familiar for so long wasn't the brawny male he'd always envisioned but a thin, crop-haired female with large, suspicious green eyes, a squarish stubborn chin, and an aura of sadness and anger.

It hardly seemed possible, when he thought of those elaborately detailed, otherworldly illustrations populated by nonmenacing monsters, that the woman asleep back there had not only conceived of them, but had executed them with such energy. There were only five or six books altogether, but he was certain that every one of them had won awards. And even though Lane had been sixteen or so when the last one came out, she'd bought it anyway, telling him, "They're not just kids' books, Dad. I'll bet half the people who buy them are grownups. And anyhow, someday I'll have kids and I wouldn't want them to miss out on these. This is *exactly* the kind of stuff kids think about."

Pajama-clad, elfin-faced little boys pushing through the yielding walls of their bedrooms straight into the heart of nightmares that, when confronted, were actually conquerable. Exhausted but victorious, these children returned through their bedroom walls to sleep peacefully, having defeated their worst fears. Sturdy little boys, they slept in rooms chockfull of treasures: mica-glinting pieces of rock, pet turtles, bubble gum cards, rubber bands and crumpled candy wrappers, Matchbox cars; posters and pennants on the walls; dresser drawers gaping open to reveal the chaos caused by small hands searching for favorite T-shirts; heaps of abandoned, inside-out clothing on the floor; bedding half off the mattress; and well-worn sneakers kicked aside, peeking from beneath the bed alongside a battered but much-loved teddy bear.

The completeness of the images was as compelling as their content. And somehow not only the boys, but the monsters as well, were recognizable; all of it rendered so finely, with such an eye for detail that each new book had caused a rush at the stores and received not only review space in the national magazines but a high ranking on their best-seller lists as well.

Dan had never tired of sitting with Lane at bedtime, reading the few lines of text that accompanied each miraculous illustration. The two of them had discovered something new, some previously unseen detail, in the paintings with each viewing. He'd liked the books as much as his daughter had. And now his mental picture of the person who'd created them had been invalidated. Instead of some burly, bearded guy, there was this woman dressed like a diminutive man. Yet the clothes, rather than detracting from, actually heightened her femininity. He reacted strongly to the hint of lace behind the silk shirt, and to the thin wrists emerging from the sleeves of the severely tailored jacket. He found her attractive altogether, with her very pale skin, auburn hair, and angry eyes. It gave him a jab of satisfaction to think that circumstances had put him in the seat next to someone famous. And it was curious to consider that people were merely people until you came to know certain facts about them. Fame, it appeared, didn't necessarily leave a visible stamp.

Lane would be thrilled to find out he'd met Stanleigh Dunn. He smiled, and moved to light another cigarette, thought of the way Leigh had been chain-smoking, and pulled back his hand. He could go days without a cigarette, and usually only had a couple with his morning coffee and one before bed. But flying always had him smoking. There was simply no way he could climb into a plane without a full pack of cigarettes in his pocket and a spare pack in the briefcase. What had she said? Reward and punishment? Interesting way to put it. It used to infuriate Celeste that he could take cigarettes or leave them alone. "It's not fair!" she protested repeatedly. "I smoke thirty and you have one. Why can't *I* smoke just one?"

"I'm not addicted," he'd answered routinely, in time fatigued beyond measure by the conversation. His ability to stay away from cigarettes had evolved into a simile for their marriage: she was addicted, he was apparently uncommitted. Yet they'd remained married, hadn't they? Long after he'd lost interest, in every way, he'd stuck with the marriage. But his presence, his faithfully returning home every night, proved nothing to Celeste. When she failed to derive any satisfaction from taunting him, she turned to taunting Lane, successfully obliterating from her own mind any recall of the teenage antics she'd got up to once upon a time or of the emotional gusts that had turned her into a human storm that raged over anyone who came near.

By comparison, he'd always considered himself bland. He loved his parents, had had a storybook childhood. There'd never been anything to react against, and so he'd merely pretended rebellion for Celeste's sake because she'd been so violently dedicated to destroying whatever bonds existed between her parents and herself. He'd found her entrancing in her role as fifteen-year-old rebel. He'd admired her formidable anger; he'd admired even more her determination to wound her parents by taking risks with her person, with her very life. She had once, to his paralytic horror, jumped out of his car while they were stopped at a railroad crossing and run wildly across the tracks only seconds before a train came roaring through. And he'd never really understood what sort of punishment might be wrought on her parents by the giving of her virginity at age sixteen to Dan. But at that time he hadn't cared in the least about her motives. He'd only been interested in continuing to prove worthy of her time, and in the extraordinary opportunity she gave him to satisfy his cumbersome sexual curiosity. She allowed him to make the transition—in his own eyes—from sordid, hulking adolescence to self-confident young manhood. She gave herself to him in angry awkwardness, and he'd accepted the gift with astonished gratitude and a bursting sense of protectiveness toward her. Inevitably, Celeste got pregnant, and he honored his responsibility by marrying her. He'd been twenty-one; she'd been eighteen. In no way did this honorable act seem to gratify or appease her, and with time he began to see she was incapable of either gratification or appeasement.

He'd been Lane's father for close to half his life and it was one role he'd never regretted. Yet it was his absolute love for his daughter that Celeste had used most successfully against him. She'd mocked him for it, even questioned his manhood; she'd picked and prodded and poked at his love for their child, as if hoping to reveal him either a fraud or a failure. The result was that father and child pulled even closer together. This, in turn, fanned the flames of Celeste's frustration. He'd married a woman who seemed to lack some genetic faculty that would permit her to be happy.

He sighed, then clutched at the rim of the table as the 747 lurched suddenly. He hung on, panicked, for several minutes, anticipating more alarming midair shudders. When none seemed to be forthcoming, he slowly let go of the table and turned to look at the sleeping form in the rear of the lounge. He'd never before confided his fear to a stranger. But he wasn't sorry, even though she'd made that cryptic reference to death.

It wasn't death that frightened him, but the thought of those three or four or five minutes *before* death, when the plane dropped from the sky and panic galvanized the passengers as they realized they were trapped. Imagining that unstoppable descent made him start to sweat and caused his heart to thud sickeningly against his ribcage. He knew that statistics proved he was far more likely to lose his life in a road accident, or at the hands of several infuriated youths in the subway, or even simply crossing the street. But those statistics were nowhere near as terrifying as the prospect of falling through space, sealed inside a huge metal lozenge.

"We'll be serving dinner in a few minutes," the flight attendant said quietly from the top of the stairs. "Will you and your friend be eating?"

"I'll ask her and let you know."

He walked to the rear of the lounge, debating whether or not to disturb her. The other thing about air travel that mystified him was the way one's encounters with people seemed magnified, heightened. Up here, marooned together in the inky sky, people could draw close and exchange the most privileged details of their lives with no fear of criticism or repercussion. As soon as the plane touched down on the tarmac, you pulled away and slipped back into the separateness you put on along with your shoes and your overcoat.

She was entirely concealed by the blanket, except for her right hand which rested motionless at the very edge of the banquette on which she lay. Slowly, he bent to look at her hand, fascinated by the fragility of her wrist. He could span it easily with his thumb and forefinger. It was so fleshless and narrow, so *exposed*. A bracelet would slip right off. He stared at the exposed inner area, thinking he could almost see a pulse beating gently beneath the skin.

He placed his hand gingerly on her arm, saying, "I hate to bother you, but they want to know if you're going to have dinner."

The blanket came away from her head and he saw that she'd been crying. Seeing the evidence of her recent tears struck him in the chest like a blunt-tipped dart, causing him to sit down abruptly while he waited for her to orient herself. She shifted onto her back and looked up at the roof of the cabin as she moistened her lips.

"You probably should eat," he said, studying her. He could see the signs of age in the laugh lines at the corners of her eyes and in the softness of her skin. When she'd smiled earlier, he'd gained an impression that was diametrically opposed to the one he'd had upon first sight. Awake and unsmiling, her eyes were those of a skeptic. But when she'd smiled, she was suddenly younger, impulsive and good-natured. He looked at the slow rise and fall of her breasts and thought she would be astonishing in bed—changeable and surprising and ardent. He wasn't sure why he thought this; it was no more than a hunch. He was finding her increasingly appealing. Part of it had to do with the isolated feeling he had about the two of them alone in the darkened lounge.

"I probably should," she said finally, turning her eyes to him. "Are you always so concerned about the well-being of strangers, or are you relying on me to help get you through this flight?"

He thought a moment, taken aback by her directness. "Probably both," he answered. "Does that make me a pain in the ass? Would you like me to take a hike?"

"It makes you unusual," she said, looking surprised by his strong tone. "Why would you think it makes you a pain?" She leaned on her elbow and gazed at him. Her hair was sticking up on one side in small spikes, and her mascara had blurred the undersides of her eyes. He dropped his defenses, thinking she looked adorable.

Folding his arms across his knees, he said, "I've been known to bring out the worst in people. Good intentions are no guarantee of favorable reactions. We're all supposed to stay inside our stereotypes. If we venture outside, well . . ." He looked at the neckline of her shirt, then away, down at his hands. "There are things we're not supposed to say to people, at least not in casual circumstances. You're supposed to save up your observations for private, persuasive moments. So when it comes to the crunch, you can whip out your most profound thoughts, like American Express Gold Cards, to wow the crowds, and prove you had secret resources the whole time."

She smiled, approvingly, he thought. "I'll tell you something," she said. "Ninety-nine men out of a hundred would've let me sleep here until we landed. And not one of them would ever admit to anything as potentially damaging as your fear of flying." As she spoke, she sat up and pushed her feet into her shoes. "Thank you very much. I have to go repair my face," she said, retrieving her bag from the floor.

While he zipped closed the backgammon set, he thought about the disparaging expression she'd worn while talking about herself. He realized she didn't think she was good-looking, and was again taken off guard. Naive, that's what he was. He could never get over the fact that women had such objections to themselves. Lane was a beautiful girl but she just couldn't see it. And Celeste was the same way. She'd always laughed at his compliments, so that eventually he stopped making them. And years later she'd managed to become almost as unattractive as she believed herself to be. But she'd been a lovely-looking girl, with long, silky, brown hair and wide-set dark eyes.

"You're very pretty," he told Leigh, when they were again seated downstairs. "And when you smile," he forged on, "you're beautiful."

She stared at him for so long he pulled himself tight inside, prepared for an attack. Fear did the damnedest things, made him blurt out whatever was on his mind. Yet she didn't appear angry. If anything, the compliment seemed to make her sad.

"Are you considered legally blind?" she asked at last, with a suspicious little laugh. "You really *are* afraid, aren't you? Or are you simply in the habit of being kind to middle-aged women?"

"You talk as if you're a thousand years old," he said.

"I'm forty-five."

"Never!"

"I'll be happy to show you my driver's license," she told him, still smiling.

"You sure don't look it."

"You haven't seen me first thing in the morning," she quipped.

"I'm sure you look fine. And anyway, it's not that old. I'm forty-two, and I don't consider myself over the hill."

"You're forty-two?" She now stared.

"Uh-huh. A couple of months ago."

"You are living proof that men age better than women."

"Poop!" he said, and laughed.

She continued to stare at him, wondering what could possibly be written on his hidden agenda. The silence held while the attendant served the food, then poured wine.

"This looks above average," Dan said, touching the tip of his knife to the steak. "A lot of times, on short flights, I bring my own food. I'll stop at a deli on the way to the airport and get a sandwich, something I know will taste halfway decent."

"Do you live in New York?" she asked, looking without appetite at the chicken breast on her plate, still mulling over the possible reasons behind his compliments, still working to control the emotions aroused by his compliments. If she wasn't careful, this man's apparent kindness might gut her.

He shook his head. "My office is in the city. We live in Bedford."

"I have a house not very far from there, over the Connecticut line. Mostly for the weekends." She kept talking in order to cover the fact that she wasn't eating. "During the week, I'm usually in the city. My mother detests the country place. She insists the co-op in the city is where I'm most myself. Whatever that is. I've never been especially interested in decor, you see, but since it's such an integral part of her image, she's convinced it has to be part of mine, too."

"What's her image?" he asked, intrigued.

She laughed. "Mother's image is almost as important as her work. My mother, you see, has moments of supreme silliness. She's Marietta Dunne, with an *e* because the *e* lends a certain something to the overall image. You don't know who she is, do you?" He shook his head again, and she continued. "My mother left my father and brought me to New York thirty-three years ago, without a penny to her name. After pawning her jewelry to get us set up in a flat, she rented a typewriter and wrote the first of her romance novels. She sold it, bought back her jewelry, as well as a secondhand typewriter, and started writing as hard and fast as she could. All her heroines are headstrong young virgins between the ages of nineteen and twenty-three. All the heroes are tall, dark, broodingly handsome types with strong jaws who fall instantly, hopelessly, in love with the virgin, and then go through a convoluted series of ill-timed misunderstandings. There's lots of traveling to far and exotic places—which Mother researches personally, sometimes—lots of near-broken hearts, and so forth. They sell by the trillions, and she's become the queen of the romance set—which is where her image comes in. The clothes she wears for publicity appearances are always yellow, and so are the limos hired to take her to speaking engagements. Privately, she lives a life that would give her readers coronaries. She has men from here to there; she looks way better than I do; she enjoys herself to the hilt. She's just simply incredible."

"Do you get along well?" he asked.

"I adore her," she said. "I truly adore her. I think she's the only reason I haven't—" she stopped abruptly, wondering if Miles was right and it was unfair of her to run off, leaving her mother to deal with the funeral.

"Haven't what?" Dan wanted to know, seeing she looked sad again.

"Nothing," she said. "Nothing. Are your parents still living?"

"Both alive and well. My father's a professor at NYU. And my mother just gave up her job last year. She was one of the head fashion buyers for Bloomingdale's. Years ago, in Paris, she was a model."

"What does your father teach?" she inquired, eager to keep the conversation going. She didn't want to have to think about what she'd left behind.

"French, naturally."

"Brothers and sisters?"

"Nope. Just me. And you?"

"Just me." She aligned the knife and fork across her untouched plate of food and picked up her wineglass.

"What about your father?" he asked.

"The last time I saw him was on a visit the summer I was fourteen. I'm on my way over to try to see him again."

"That's a hell of a long time. What was he like?"

"I'm not sure I know. My impression—reinforced in steel by my mother—is of a gentleman farmer. Inherited money, but the house was always dark and stone-cold. I picture him in a tweed hacking jacket and hat, with his trouser legs pushed into a pair of mud-covered Wellingtons;

his face and ears bright red from the cold, and his hands permanently chapped from being outdoors in all weather to supervise the farm activities. Tenants and hired staff did the actual farming." Had he really been soft-spoken and reticent, or was her memory faulty? Describing him had expanded her need to see him.

"So, he has an image, too," Dan suggested.

"Perhaps he does." She looked at him again. "You may be right. And two people with images probably couldn't survive together under the same roof. It's very clever of you to see that."

"Your mother never remarried?"

"Never. She enjoys her gentlemen friends far too much. They give her fabulous presents, take her off on marvelous trips, wine and dine her as often as she'll allow them. And she accepts every bit of it with perfect equanimity. If I had one-tenth of her ability to handle things as they come, my life would be . . . let's just say I envy her that."

"Where does your father live?" he asked, aware that her attention was fading in and out, rather like the reception on a short-wave radio.

"In Warwickshire."

"And you're going up there, when we land?"

"I have to write or phone first. I couldn't just drop in on someone I haven't seen for so long. No, I'll stay in London for a few days while I test the waters." She lit a cigarette, then asked, "Do you ever do things and then wonder why you did them? Dangerous things, stupid things, I mean."

"I'm not sure I follow. Give me an example."

"All right." She paused for a moment, thinking. "I once picked up a man in an airport." She paused again, then went on. "I was married at the time. Well, this airport fellow was unexceptional really, except for his interest in me which, of course, elevated his status enormously." She laughed ruefully. "My interest had to do with reaffirmation of my desirability, et cetera. So, I went with him to a seedy motel, and we did it. Or rather, tried to do it. He couldn't, and tried everything he could think of to persuade me to let him call his wife and have her come make up a threesome. I said, no, thank you very much, and went to the bathroom, had a wash, got dressed, and went home. Later, when I thought about it, I decided I'd been very lucky. He could've been insane, or a murderer."

"I think everyone's done something like that," he said.

"Oh? Have you?"

"Along those lines, uh-huh."

"Did you feel guilty?" she asked interestedly.

"As sin. But for my daughter's sake. It didn't seem to have anything to do with Celeste and me. It felt as if it had everything to do with Lane and me, though."

"I see." She took a sip of wine, thinking. The man had stepped out on his wife, but his qualms had been about betraying his daughter's trust.

"What do you see?" he challenged her.

"I see there's trouble in paradise," she said, and then began laughing so hard she spilled some of the wine down the front of her shirt. Appalled at herself, she went quiet as Dan grabbed his napkin, dipped a corner of it into his water glass, and began blotting the stain.

Realizing what he was doing, he stopped, his eyes meeting hers. He couldn't read her eyes, or gauge her reaction to his small incursion past the invisible wall of her privacy. Jesus! he thought, he'd put his hands on her without even stopping to think about it. Silently, she took the napkin from his hand, and continued dabbing at the stain.

"What's wrong?" he asked quietly. "Is something the matter?"

Her eyes liquid, her voice soft, she said, "If I went slamming out of a room, the good Doctor Jacobson wouldn't dream of coming to ask if there was anything wrong. He would assume it was my problem, and if I wanted him to be aware of it, I'd tell him. You can't imagine how many futile gestures I've made in my life in the hope of getting the right, the needed reaction, just once. And here you are, wanting to know if I'm hungry, if something's wrong; giving compliments, being kind. Are you really real?"

"Sure I'm real," he answered automatically, but without much conviction. He considered asking for her definition of real. Perhaps it wouldn't coincide with his interpretation. Philosophical discussions, even of the most rudimentary kind, were like concentric circles. It made him tired just thinking about trying to define one's "realness," one's state of being. Or was her question simply her way of trying to fend him off? "I'm real," he repeated, then wondered for a moment why she'd chosen to ask if he was real, rather than if he was honest.

"This is ruined." Dropping the napkin on the tray table, she sighed and said, "I think you're the sort of person who always manages to find things to value in other people. Your wife and daughter are very lucky to have you."

"I think the doctor's lucky to have *you*," he replied with utter sincerity, touched deeply by the remark.

Her hand, when she took hold of his, was startlingly cold. "We'll land in London," she said, "and probably never see each other again. But I'm glad you happened to be seated here." As she spoke, she drew closer to him. Then she touched her mouth to his, sat away from him, and released his hand.

Electrified, he sank back in his seat, all his senses thrown into chaos. "I'm glad, too," he managed to get out. It was the truth. She was the surprise reward for an unwanted journey. He'd met this strange, sad woman who'd just kissed him. And he was powerfully attracted to her. His eyes on her hands, he wished he could stop lying, telling her silly, inconsequential lies one after another. But it was too late now. Besides, what harm did they do? A man had to protect himself whatever way he could.

Three

AFTER THE MEAL, THE CABIN WAS DARKENED SO THE MOVIE COULD BE shown.

"I always watch," Dan said. "It helps me pretend I'm not thirty-odd thousand feet up over nothing but water, with nowhere to go but down."

Leigh gave him a vague smile, then fussed with her blanket and pillow, all the while covertly watching as he located the channel for the sound track, his eyes on the screen.

"The most dangerous thing about you, Stanleigh," her mother had once stated, "is your capacity for caring. It's a weapon you use primarily against yourself, to calamitous effect."

Years ago, when her mother said this, Leigh had laughed. Now it seemed to be one of the single most accurate observations her mother had ever made. Because here she was now, inches away from someone she found so attractive she was having trouble thinking of reasons why she shouldn't just put out her hand and stroke him. If only, she thought, ideas and feelings were tangible, items you could look at and turn and touch, life would be so much simpler. You could stack up the blocks and cubes and triangles in such a way that no one could argue with their reality.

She was near exhaustion, and told herself sternly that the affection she seemed to feel for this man was due solely to her state of wearied susceptibility. She was interpreting his complimentary kindness as more than it actually was. And so she closed her eyes to block him out.

Every few minutes throughout the film he turned to look at her. She'd scored a perfect bull's-eye in her observation about his willingness to find good in others. But he couldn't stop himself from seeking it. He was forever seeing hints of treasure where none existed. It was like those

26

rocks in the illustrations of the elfin boys' bedrooms, with glinting bits of mica. Did she really know about that? he wondered. Did she understand the perennial hope that the fool's gold might just once be the real Mc-Coy?

He couldn't stop thinking about that moment when he'd gazed into the disturbing depths of her eyes just before she'd put her mouth to his. For those few seconds, he'd been suspended, caught between pragmatism and his lifelong desire to believe all things were possible. Upon review, he was flabbergasted by how much aspiration one could cram into such a small fragment of time. Yet he'd felt so many things—fondness and anticipation and pure, undiluted hunger. Why was he such a cluck that a demonstrative gesture from an attractive woman could push him to the brink of believing in miracles?

He drank the last of his wine, disgusted with himself. Put him on a plane and he became needy. He was too old to waste his time on daydreams. And yet he was prepared to buy wholesale into a fantasy because an interesting woman had expressed her approval of him with a kiss. Not just any woman, either, but a successful, famous one.

When she awakened, the cabin lights were back on and, beyond the window, a spectacular sunrise was taking place. His passport open in front of him, Dan was completing his landing card. She went to the lavatory to try to do something with her hair, and to add more makeup to the several layers already caked on her face. She looked at her reflection in the mirror and burst into tears, covering her eyes with her hand while her body shook from the force of her weeping. Why had she hacked off her hair? What good had it done anyone to return from the hospital one night and go directly into the bathroom to start chopping off her hair? Nothing proved, no good done; another mess.

She blotted her face with a handful of tissues, then did what she could to fix herself up.

"I thought you might want some coffee," Dan said upon her return. He had a cup waiting for her.

For several seconds she was tempted to ask him if he was trying to kill her with his thoughtfulness and generosity. She felt utterly victimized by his kindness. She managed to thank him, and got herself organized to drink the coffee while filling out her landing card. "How was the movie?" she asked, copying her passport number onto the card. Strive for normalcy, she told herself. Keep all the balls in the air, woman.

"You'll be happy to know Sylvester Stallone is single-handedly killing off the bad guys who menace our lives. Between him and Charles Bronson, it'll soon be safe to ride the subways and go for walks in the woods."

She laughed, finishing the card, then put it and her passport back into her bag. "I keep wishing we could go back to black and white, with plot lines and fade-outs instead of full frontal nudity. There are only so many ways you can show people doing it, and after you've seen those two movies, there's nothing left."

It was his turn to laugh. And then it seemed they'd run out of conversation. She lit a cigarette, then wondered why. Her throat hurt already and another cigarette was making it worse.

Dan tucked his hands into his armpits and looked out the window as the plane began its descent. There was a sudden rumbling in the underbelly, and he swallowed hard, afraid.

"It's just the landing gear being lowered," she said, seeing his fear.

"I know that," he got out hoarsely, unable to look away from the window. "Knowing doesn't make any difference."

She wished she could think of something to say, but you couldn't stop someone from being afraid, just as you couldn't prevent someone from dying, or from behaving badly, or from hating herself. The most anyone could do, ever, was to keep going forward alone. Everyone was separate, for all time. No one fit permanently to anyone else. But she had this goddamned dangerous capacity—or so her mother liked to say—for caring. So she reached over and took hold of his hand, saying, "Listen to me! Nothing's going to happen. We'll land safely, and that'll be that. Don't be afraid just for the sake of being afraid. It's a criminal waste of energy. It's not your time to die. Keep telling yourself that on all those other flights you have to take!"

He held on to her hand in grateful silence, looking away from the window to see that she'd closed her eyes and let her head fall back. He looked out the window again, rescued by her enclosing hand. Once the plane was taxiing toward the terminal, she gently pulled free of him.

He caught sight of her in the terminal, as she was leaving. A porter was carrying her bags and she followed several yards behind. She moved along as if unaware of the people crowded around the baggage carousels, of the others headed toward the exits. To Dan it appeared as if she was dawdling, in no hurry to reach her destination. She opened her purse, got out a cigarette and paused for a moment to light it, then dropped the lighter back into her purse. It was like watching a movie, he thought, and he was the only one aware it was playing.

She arrived at the exit. The porter held open the door for her. She drifted through it. And was gone.

It wasn't the right ending; no movie was meant to end this way, with someone simply going away.

He turned back to the carousel in time to see his own bag come tumbling down the chute, and pushed through the others waiting in order to grab it before it started off on its journey around the treadmill.

In the early afternoon, having bathed and napped for an hour, in clean clothes and fresh makeup, Leigh put on her coat and went out for a walk. She moved through the crowds feeling as if she were pushing her way through fast-drying cement. Loneliness was like cancer eating its way through her system. It was so potent she thought, not for the first time, that it might just be possible to die from it. All those years after she'd divorced Joel's father, she'd never suffered from overexposure to her own company. She'd traveled, spent weeks alone doing this and that, meeting with friends and publishers. Now, she'd plummeted into darkness and only time could bring her out of it. Time, however, was unreliable. It could be weeks, or years, if ever, before she once again found a point to living. She'd come out of it the first time because of Joel. He'd been someone to care about, not a replacement for Stephen, but someone wonderfully unique who'd needed the caring she'd had to offer. Now there was no more Joel, and it seemed too unjust that she should, for a second time, lose a child.

She walked until she grew tired, then returned to the hotel thinking to have a late lunch, but the dining room was closed. She went instead into the lounge, took one of the armchairs by the window, and lit a cigarette as soon as her drink arrived. The gin went directly to her brain. She shouldn't have had it. It had been so long since she'd eaten or slept properly that not only were her clothes loose but the idea of food made her queasy. She was going to have to eat or she'd become ill. And while it was one thing to consider death, it was something else to be ill. She had no patience with her body at those times when it crumbled beneath the onslaught of some virus. So, she would eat. Soon. In the meantime, she'd have another drink, which she would consume more slowly, and she would try to formulate some plans for the coming days.

She glanced around, seeing she was separated from the only other people in the lounge—a quiet foursome—by a wall. It would be some time yet before the room filled for tea. God! she thought, experiencing a resurgence of the agitation that had periodically overtaken her since Joel's death. It was a kind of internal trembling that made everything inside her feel disconnected. What was she going to do? She was utterly devoid of ambition. Eating was too much trouble, as was telephoning her British publisher, as was contacting her father just now, or letting her mother know she'd arrived safely, as was almost everything she could think of. She was going to have to get past this. She couldn't go to pieces now. But God! It was terrible, sitting there with her eyes on the window, hoping no one would come in and find her going out of control. This wasn't some imagined horror, some made-up conflagration to punish her for her failures and omissions. This was real, wasn't it? Sitting alone in the lounge of Brown's Hotel, disintegrating. There had to be something she could do.

Dan looked around his room at the Hilton, depressed. He decided he'd go out, buy something for Lane. He'd take a taxi to Covent Garden and walk through the shops, browse at the outdoor stalls, see all the outrageous kids. When he'd been there a few months earlier, he'd been entranced by the kids with their hair partly shaved and the rest Krazy-glued into astonishing shapes, with clown-white makeup and outfits of studded black leather and chains, skinny black pants and army boots. He'd sat with a drink at an outdoor table, wondering where these people worked, and what their employers made of them.

He went out, got into a taxi, but instead of Covent Garden, he said, "Brown's Hotel," and the driver craned around to give him one of those looks.

"You could walk it in less time than it'll take me to get you there, mate," the man told him. "Five minutes, straight along Piccadilly."

Embarrassed, Dan gave the man fifty pence for his trouble, then strolled the few blocks over to Albemarle Street. Lack of sleep was catching up with him. He knew where the hotel was. He'd been coming to London regularly for years.

There was no answer from her room and he felt absurdly let down. He'd imagined them celebrating the elevation of an airline encounter into an actual friendship. He wrote a note, inviting her to dinner, and handed it over to the concierge. Then he stood looking at the brochures on the concierge's hatch, trying to think what to do next. Like a child, he had a totally groundless urge to cry. Shoving one of the brochures into his pocket, he crossed toward the lounge. He'd go to the bar, have a drink, then head on to Covent Garden.

He stepped into the lounge and there she was, sitting over by the windows with her mink coat puddled around her. She'd changed out of the man-tailored suit into a dress, and the difference was phenomenal. She was attractive now in an entirely different way. She appeared taller, thinner, and somehow less approachable.

As he crossed the room he expected she'd look up and see him, but she was so absorbed in her thoughts she didn't raise her head even when he sat down in the chair next to hers. He unbuttoned his coat, sat back, and openly stared at her. The dress was of soft-looking caramel-colored wool, very simple, and flattering. It emphasized the width of her shoulders and the tapering length of her torso. It also brought out the red in her hair. He decided he liked the pale angularity of her face. And her features, he saw, were slightly asymmetrical, so that, in repose, her mouth had an unusual tilt.

"I tried calling your room," he said, "but I got no answer, so I came in to drown my sorrows, and here you are."

She looked at him finally, and it seemed as if she couldn't decide how she felt about his turning up this way. He stopped smiling in view of her as yet unknown reaction. "I cheated," he told her, "and watched while you were filling out your landing card. Curiosity, I guess. Anyway, I thought I'd call you and we'd get together for a drink, or dinner. Then I thought that was a pretty silly idea because you can't push situations so they'll be the shape you want them to be. I mean, for all I know, you got off the plane hoping you'd never have to see me again as long as you lived." He leaned forward and waited for her to say something.

She shouldn't have been angry, she thought, but she was. Here she'd been praying for something to salvage her emotions, and it came in the form of this man. But he was dressing it up, pretending he was after something more noble than he was. "Men are such dogs," she said with a sigh, "always sniffing around looking for some bitch in heat. I suppose you'd like a drink. We could save time and order from room service." She began pulling her coat out from under her, but when she saw he hadn't moved, she stopped. "You don't want to come upstairs, Mr. Godard?"

"That isn't quite what I had in mind," he said uncomfortably.

"Oh, come on," she chided. "You were so wonderfully honest on the plane. Now you're going to be dishonest, and that's a great pity. You came here because you want to go to bed with me, but you're going to lie and say you only meant to be sociable. Mr. Godard, I'm tired and hungry, and a little drunk from two gins on an empty stomach. I'm so tired that I can't be bothered playing games. If you want to do it, we'll do it. I'm flattered you'd be interested."

He wanted to escape. He also wanted to defend his good intentions. Spotting the waiter peering around the corner, Dan beckoned him over. "We'd like a pot of coffee and some sandwiches, please." The waiter went off, and Dan turned back to her. "Is it possible you could be wrong?" he asked her.

"You have a wife," she reminded him.

"You have a husband."

Pause.

"You don't give a damn that I've got a wife," he said, his eyes narrowing slightly.

"I think perhaps," she said astutely, "*you* give a damn that I've got a husband." What was she doing? she asked herself. Why was she reviving a long-dead marriage? Protection, she decided. However slim, she felt she needed it. There was no need, though, for her to behave the way she was.

Had she already gone so far out of control that she no longer recognized the boundary between acceptable behavior and craziness?

"What are we doing that's so terrible?" he wanted to know, his expression innocent.

"We haven't done it yet," she answered, thinking she was bound to drive him away if she kept this up. And she really had no reason to want to be rid of him.

"Jesus!" he exclaimed, starting to feel overheated, and wishing he'd gone to Covent Garden.

"Why don't you admit it? You want someone to sleep with."

He was saved from having to reply by the swift return of the waiter bearing a tray with coffee and a plate of crustless sandwiches. Dan pulled some notes from his pocket, gave the waiter ten pounds, and waved him away.

"That was good," Leigh said confusingly.

"What was?"

"That bit with the waiter. You care more about people than you do about money."

"Well, of course . . ." he began.

"Don't get defensive," she cut in. "It's a refreshing change."

"From what?" he asked, placing several triangles of sandwich on a plate before passing it to her.

"I've met quite a few men who thought the direct route to either my brain or my money was between my legs."

The remark seemed to him so graphic and so intimate that he had an image of her spread naked on a bed with her legs parted, while some faceless man's hand searched inside her. The image was upsetting but arousing. It stayed with him, gradually fading as their conversation continued.

"What about your husband?"

"He's very successful. My money has never been of any interest to him."

"It doesn't interest me, either. Let's agree to something," he suggested. "You won't talk about your husband, and I won't talk about my wife. Could we agree to that?"

"It may not be possible," she said, rapidly losing her anger. "I'm sorry," she said, looking doubtfully at the sandwiches. "I'm being hateful. It has nothing to do with you."

"You really do think I've got ulterior motives, though."

"Yes, I do," she said quietly. "Because everyone does, and you're no exception."

"You should eat," he said. "Maybe it'll improve your mood. In my experience," he said, pouring the coffee, "most women nowadays want to

be conned. They look forward to the familiar little conversational minuet
we all know is the prelude to a sexual encounter." He glanced at her, read
her objection, and hurried to retrench. "Maybe," he elaborated, "they
don't actually *want* to be conned; they've simply learned to expect it. I
think a lot of women really dread finding themselves locked up in a
traditional situation. Marriage, I think, has become the prerogative of
those young enough to believe they can defy the established code of
failure. Their marriages will last; they're more gifted at commitment than
our generation; they have more talent for life, for careers, for success, for
any goddamned thing you can name. And I have to admit that any group
that can come up with the idea of wearing tennis shoes to and from work
in order to save themselves from possible lower back pain definitely has
the world by the balls. Wouldn't you agree? Would you wear a pair of
Nikes with that dress?"

At this, she laughed, and put her cup down in order not to ruin a second
outfit while in his company. "I don't actually know what that little speech
was about, but you are very funny."

"Why are you giving me such a hard time?" he asked.

"Because I'm old enough to know better."

"I think you play for shock value."

"I don't have the energy to play." She retrieved her cup and drank
some of the coffee.

"You have the energy to be pretty goddamned angry."

"I don't think you realize you're dealing with someone who's not entirely *compos mentis*," she told him. "That's the truth."

"Fine. So what do we do now?"

"I don't know," she said, rattled. "What were you going to do if I
wasn't here?"

"I planned to go to Covent Garden, pick up something for Lane, have a
look around."

"I could go with you."

"Would you like to?" He brightened at once.

"I'll have to change my shoes." They both looked down at her brown
leather high heels.

"I can wait here," he said.

"Come with me. You can remind me what I'm doing. I keep forgetting
things."

Fatigue was doing strange things to her perception. One moment she
felt very tall and terribly thin; the next she felt small and rotund. Daniel
remained fairly constant. What altered was her view of him. He was never
unattractive, but different features caught her attention each time she
looked at him. His eyes were very blue, very clear; then his mouth appeared generous and well shaped; next time, he had good teeth, and fine,

dark skin. In the length of time it took them to ride up in the elevator and walk along the hallway to her suite, she came to a decision, so that once they were inside her room with the door shut, it was inevitable that they should embrace. She closed her eyes and held him. Nothing was ever quite so consoling or more potent than holding another body close to one's own. She lifted her head to look at him, and he did something that removed her completely from the darkness of her mood. He slipped his hands inside her coat, placed them on her waist, and lifted her straight up so that she found herself looking down at him. So pleased was she that she put her hands on his face and kissed him.

"You're so tiny!" he said, holding her aloft. "You weigh nothing at all."

She laughed with pleasure, only a bit disappointed when he lowered her down.

Another kiss, and then they were dispensing with their clothes; an activity punctuated by further kisses and brief, tentative caresses. The laughter was gone. Revealing herself was too serious, too risky; it made her hands shake and her heart flutter. She felt imperiled, put at risk by tidal forces within her over which it seemed she was never going to have any viable control. She had to look away from his eyes, because she despaired of seeing anything but approval there. She had no talent for temporary blindness; even at her most casual, she'd always been horribly serious. That damnable talent for caring was at work again. Because of her seriousness, she most often remained totally silent while making love. Or, to her dismay, she'd say something unintentionally absurd. In this instance, daunted by the firm, healthy-looking body in front of her, she said, "Oh, you're circumcised," and watched him wilt instantly as, with a surge of defensiveness, he declared, "Of course, I am. My father is Jewish. Did you assume because I'm French I'm also Catholic?"

"Not at all." Was this happening? *Why* was this happening?

He pointed at her belly and said, "I thought you said you didn't have any children. That looks suspiciously like a Caesarean scar to me."

She turned her back, bent to retrieve her clothes, then straightened, holding them to her as she faced him again. "I didn't say," she spoke almost inaudibly, "that I'd never had a child."

"Oh, hell! What're we doing? I'm sorry . . ."

"I'll change. If you still want to, we can go out."

"I really am sorry. I don't know what . . ."

"Please!" she cried. "Neither one of us managed to draw blood. Do you still want to go?"

"Well, sure . . ."

"I'll only be a few minutes." She escaped into the bedroom and closed the door.

Not sure what had happened, or why, he stepped into his shorts, pulled on his shirt, and stood doing up the buttons while his eyes remained on the closed bedroom door. He saw and heard himself accusing, and felt sick. He'd overreacted wildly to an innocent observation. Christ! He was going to have to watch himself very carefully.

Dressed, he perched on the edge of the sofa. She was taking more than a few minutes, and the longer she was out of the room, the worse he felt. If she didn't reappear in two more minutes, he'd go over there, knock on the door, and try to explain.

Once the door was closed between them, she found herself folded over her armload of clothing, feeling a complete fool, and trying to tell herself she had no cause. But were they both crazy? She dropped the clothes on the bed, and went to get fresh underwear from the chest of drawers. Her legs felt rubbery as she at last walked over to open the door, fully expecting to find the sitting room empty. But he was still there, seated on the edge of the sofa, with a cigarette.

"That whole thing was ridiculous," he said, the moment she opened the door. "You have to let me apologize."

She leaned against the door frame and said, "If I let you apologize, then somehow I'm obligated to explain, and I can't do that. Let's just leave it be."

"I don't understand what's going on," he said. "I do like you, an awful lot."

"I like you, too. Let's get the hell out of here."

As she was handing her key to the concierge, the man said, "There's a message here for you," and gave her Dan's note.

She read it, then said, "Perhaps by dinnertime, I'll have figured out which of us is really crazy."

"Probably me," he said with a low laugh. "Probably me." He drew her arm through his, and she had the distinct feeling, for a moment or two, that she'd metamorphosed into something rather like a house cat, an animal with nerve endings so close to the surface that the most casual gesture or caress gave satisfaction and reassurance.

"Are you very clever?" she asked, so that he turned and smiled at her. "I have the idea that you are."

"If I was very clever," he replied, "my life would be far less fucked up than it is. I'm not especially clever."

"I think perhaps you are."

"We got so close back there," he said, as the taxi flew around a corner, causing him to slide over against her. "Are we going to have another chance?"

"You're saying you'd like to go through that comedy of errors again?"

"I'm very attracted to you. And if you want the truth, it's been a while."

"You don't sleep with your wife?"

"I don't *anything* with my wife," he confided with a hint of bitterness.

"Daniel, doesn't it ever seem risky to you to admit the things you do? You're afraid of airplanes; you get lonely; you don't sleep with your wife. People just do not go around telling other people things like that."

"I don't think of you as 'other people.' Anyway, I always thought I knew who you were. I had a very detailed mental picture of you."

"You thought," she argued, "that I was a *man!*"

He laughed, shattering the tension, and tilted his head to one side. "I'm so glad you're not. I'm really glad you're not."

She applied a slight pressure to his hand, wanting him to know she was growing fond of him.

"Before or after dinner?" he asked in a whisper.

"Probably before," she answered, able to feel his body's warmth.

He smiled. She closed her eyes. His lips touched against her throat and she started, colliding with his chest. He sat away slowly. "It feels as if I've spent most of my life looking at people going by, seeing things other people never seem to notice, watching the parade from the sidewalk. Every so often, I get the feeling that I'd like to be a part of the whole thing and not just someone stuck on the sidelines noticing all the details." He thought again of the way he'd stood watching her leave the baggage claim area, and that sense he'd had of viewing a movie. The camera could have been anywhere—in someone's briefcase, say, or fitted cleverly into a suitcase.

"Do you always say how you feel, what you're thinking?" she wanted to know.

He retreated a little, his features firming. "It's boring, right?"

"It's definitely *not* boring. Do you find *me* boring?"

"Hell, no!"

"Well, that's something, don't you think?"

He gazed at her for a moment, for the second time aware of a pulse beating—this time, in her throat. Then, as he gazed at her, that image returned of her naked, on her back with her legs parted. "I'm sorry about what happened back there," he told her. "I was way out of line. It was stupid." Everything he said seemed to have an internal echo, so that the words bounced off the interior of his skull.

"It doesn't matter." It was true, she thought. It really didn't matter. She wasn't alone. For a few hours she didn't have to be alone. And perhaps tonight she'd sleep.

Four

THEY LOOKED IN SHOPS ON THE PERIPHERY OF COVENT GARDEN, THEN
in those of the garden itself. Leigh asked to try on a pair of shoes in one
place but when the young woman returned with them, apologized and
said she'd changed her mind. She didn't want or need any more shoes;
she couldn't think why she'd asked to try them, and apologized as well to
Daniel who seemed quite content to go along with whatever she decided.

They moved outdoors and wandered from stall to stall, pausing to
study rubber stamps at one place, dried flower arrangements at another.
Leigh felt they were simply killing time, that he wasn't actually looking
to buy a gift for his daughter. But then he stopped by a display of
handknitted sweaters and began examining them in earnest. Although he
asked for her opinion before he bought the sweater, it was plain he knew
his daughter's preferences and required no assistance. She watched him
pay for his purchase and then moved to one side to wait while it was
wrapped, glancing at her watch before pushing her hands deep into her
coat pockets. It was almost five o'clock. She'd arrived at a point in her
exhaustion where, at present, she felt quite calm.

"If you wouldn't mind," she said when he joined her, "I'd like to
walk."

They set off, and she marveled at her body's ability to function even
when pushed to its absolute limits. "I haven't been awake for this long,"
she told him, "since I was a teenager."

"How long has it been?" he asked.

"Several days. I've lost track."

"What happened, Leigh?"

She knew she couldn't talk about Joel. It was too soon. If she attempted to describe what the past three years had been like, she'd break down. And, besides, it would mean revealing her true status, which she had no desire to do. "I'll tell you a story," she said, and linked her arm through his. "A true story," she qualified, glancing over to see she had his attention. "I got married when I was nineteen. I was madly in love, so I got married. It was very nice. We bought a place in the country. My husband commuted into the city to his job with the brokerage. I stayed at home and sketched a lot, did a few paintings, cooked occasional meals that were inedible, and generally enjoyed myself. We socialized with other young couples; we sometimes had weekends in the city when we stayed at my mother's apartment and went dancing and drinking half the night. We had fun, and I wasn't at all unhappy.

"I had Stephen when I was twenty-one. The timing was right, because I was beginning to get bored, and with Stephen to look after, I didn't have much time to be bored. From the start, everything about him fascinated me. He was so perfectly complete within himself.

"When Stephen was four, I started the illustrations for the first book. I wanted to find some way to capture forever everything about him that was, to my mind, the quintessence of little-boyhood: his prized possessions, his funny habits, his hiding places, his dreams and nightmares, everything. And he was my model, of course. I'd take photographs of him, dozens of them, and then, at night when he was sleeping, or during the day when he was away at nursery school, I'd work him into the illustrations. He was such an imp! And that face! God, he had the dearest face, pointy features and a great, wide smile, sandy hair and freckles and wise-old-man brown eyes. He was forever falling down, coming home with new bruises, cuts scabbing over. While he had his bath every night, we'd take inventory of his latest injuries.

"The two of them wrote their names in the snow in the garden the winter Stephen was six. I'll never forget the way they came in, redfaced and sobbing with laughter, to drag me out and show me what they'd done. Stephen had run out of 'ink,' so Carl had had to do the last three letters for him." She laughed.

"By the time Stephen was nine, if he and his dad went out in the car and were a little late getting home, I'd imagine they'd been in an accident and were never coming back. One part of me was actually relieved at the prospect. I wouldn't have to be responsible; I could go where I wanted, do what I wanted, without having to account to anyone. I had a career, my own money, I'd be able to live unencumbered. I imagined the two of them dead, and my reactions when the police came to tell me, and how I'd dispose of my husband's possessions, and what I'd do with the insurance money. All of it. That was one part of me. The other part of me couldn't breathe. I was so afraid of losing them, of losing Stephen primarily, that I knew my life couldn't possibly continue beyond the moment when I'd be informed they were gone for good. I despised myself for being capable of thinking such thoughts, of imagining them dead. But I couldn't help it. It seemed like something that could very possibly happen. And in a way, it was like preparing myself for the worst, in advance of its ever happening. That way, you see, if anything did happen to them, I'd be ready. I reasoned that you couldn't love anyone as much as I loved Stephen and not, at some time, consider what sort of life you might have without that person.

"So, life went on. I did a second book, and a third, and was working on a fourth. They take quite a long time," she explained. "The actual paintings are two or three feet high by four or five feet wide. That way, when they're reproduced and the color separations are done, you don't lose too much definition. I'm digressing," she said impatiently. "The thing is, I'd become tired of the marriage, tired of being a wife and a mother. If I was going to have to choose, I'd choose being a mother. But sometimes I felt it was miserably unfair to have to choose at all; sometimes I felt as if I wanted to be rid of *every* responsibility to *everyone*. No one running to me to ask where this was, or that was; no one to pick up after; no mounds of laundry waiting to be done; no meals to cook or lunches to prepare. So, I'd daydream, and then I'd feel guilty. And on we went.

"We never had disagreements in front of Stephen. In fact, Carl and I rarely disagreed. I simply wasn't in love anymore; I'd outgrown Carl, as well as the limitations imposed on me by the marriage. I was biding time, seeing other men occasionally on the sly to prove to myself that I was still young, still desirable; I directed most of my energy into Stephen, and the books. We managed to get through another two years, with me hiding out in my studio, living another, different life entirely in my head. I was free-floating, letting my energy and imagination flow unchecked directly onto the canvases.

"I was hardly paying attention when they went out after an early dinner that night. I was putting the finishing touches to the last painting for the fourth book, and didn't want to be separated from the work any sooner than I had to be. So they went out, to the ice rink, to skate. We exchanged kisses, I reminded Stephen to take his earmuffs and his mittens, I smiled, they smiled, we said goodbye, and they left. I worked for another forty minutes or so, and then the phone rang. It was Stephen, calling to say he and Carl had decided to drive into town to see a movie. I said have a good time, hung up, and worked a while longer. At eight, when I imagined the movie was halfway through, I made a pot of coffee, fixed a sandwich, and sat down in the kitchen to eat. Then I took a fresh cup of coffee back to the studio to have another look at the illustration.

"I hope you're not finding this tedious," she said suddenly, and looked at him searchingly.

"No, not a bit," he said, dreading what he sensed was coming.

"It's just that every last detail is so clear, you see. All of it. It's clearer, more detailed, than anything else has ever been. There isn't one minute of it that I don't remember, not a second.

"I started getting ready for bed just before ten. Taking into account that the movie had probably finished at nine, and that Stephen had probably begged to go to Baskin-Robbins for ice cream after, and that it was a twenty-minute drive from the theater, I guessed they'd be arriving home any minute. By ten-thirty, I was sitting in the living room in my night-gown and robe, watching television with the sound turned low so I could listen for the car pulling into the driveway. I chain-smoked, jumping up every few minutes to look out the front window, then went back to sit in front of the TV.

"At eleven, I changed back into my clothes, then called the Playhouse to find out what time the feature ended. I couldn't imagine Carl taking Stephen to the nine o'clock show on a school night, but it was possible. It wasn't likely, though, that they'd stop to have ice cream at that time of the night. So, given that the second showing ended at eleven, I expected them home by eleven-thirty at the very latest.

"By eleven forty-five I began anticipating either a telephone call or a policeman coming to the door. I didn't know what else to do, so I walked back and forth, and went to look out the window every few minutes, and as more time passed, and they didn't come home, I began to feel despair like acid hollowing out my bones so that I got lighter and lighter until the only things holding me anchored to the floor were my Dunhill lighter that my agent had given me one Christmas—it's silver, and quite heavy, you see—and the pack of cigarettes in my other hand. I went back and forth, back and forth, stopping to look at the telephone, then at the window, rehearsing the way it would go, what they'd say when they came to tell me, how I'd react, what I'd say and do; I wouldn't break down or become hysterical. I'd take in the news; I'd do what had to be done step by step. By twelve-fifteen, I had no doubt at all they were dead. I knew it. I *knew* it. They were dead. I was never going to see them again. My heart was triple and quadruple beating, and I couldn't catch my breath, and the slightest noise in the house had me jumping and rushing and exclaiming out loud. The house got smaller and smaller until it was about the size of a refrigerator, and the only two points of reference I had were the telephone and the door, and I was waiting, listening so hard that my ears hurt, and so did my throat from all the cigarettes. I had this dreadful, nonspecific, nonlocalized pain because I knew they were dead and any moment someone was going to confirm it and I didn't know what to do except light another cigarette and keep hurrying back and forth, going over to look out the windows, then to open the front door and stand at the top of the driveway staring out, wanting to see the car come turning in, the headlights swinging in an arc the way they always did, and then Stephen slamming out of the car not wearing his earmuffs or his mittens, while Carl gave his usual lengthy explanation of all the things that had fouled up their plans.

"The call came at one thirty-eight precisely. A very quiet voice on the other end asking me was I Mrs. Dennison. At first I couldn't answer. And then all I could say was, 'Are they dead?' and he said, 'I'm afraid so, ma'am,' and I asked where they were and what I was supposed to do, and he told me. I thanked him and hung up, put on my coat, and went out to my car to drive over to identify them. All the way there, I kept hearing myself asking, 'Are they dead?' and hearing him answer, 'I'm afraid so, ma'am,' and I tried to convince myself I'd misheard; that wasn't what he'd said at all. But he'd said that; it was what he'd said all right. All those daydreams were catching up with me; this was what happened when you had moments of wishing for freedom. If you wished for it, you just might get it.

"The lights bothered me more than anything else. It was so *bright;* there was such a glare in the place. I thought it would've been easier somehow if it had been dimmer, less unrelentingly, garishly, bright. Anyway, I got it done, said yes they were who they were, who they'd been, and they wanted to know if I'd be all right, driving home. Did I want someone to drive me home? I hardly heard them. All I could think was, 'How am I going to live? What am I going to do with my life? I don't have a life anymore. Everything's gone. How am I going to *live?*' I never *wanted* them dead; I'd merely imagined the worst possibilities. Just because you thought of something, because it occurred to you, didn't mean it had to happen.

"Well, one of the officers had the wits to keep me there, get my mother's name and number. They called her and told her, then gave me the telephone to talk to her, and I was like some sort of idiot robot, saying the same bloody thing over and over, How am I going to live? What will I do? My mother said she'd come at once; she'd call my agent and he'd bring her; she'd come as quickly as possible, she said, and asked me to wait for her. Which almost made me laugh, because where was I going to go? Downstairs there were two unbelievably, horrifically shattered bodies. I'd forced myself to look at their faces, because I had to be sure. But I only recognized them by their clothes. You know what happened, Daniel?" Again she looked at him.

"What?" he asked, dry-mouthed.

"It seems there was a young woman from Bedford who'd been seeing a young man from New Canaan, but they'd had a falling-out and split up. So the young lady in question took herself off to a bar to have a few drinks and forget her misery. She had many more drinks than a few, then said goodnight to everyone and got up to go out to her car to drive home. No one thought to stop her. One or two people rather half-heartedly said something to the effect that she was in no condition to drive. But no one took away her car keys, or pulled out her spark plugs. They let her go even though later, at the hearing, half a dozen customers as well as the bartender—who was found guilty of some kind of negligence, I forget whether it was contributory or criminal—admitted she was in an extremely depressed and drunken state.

"She went out, climbed into her car, and drove, at close to a hundred miles an hour, headlong into another car coming in the opposite direction. Everyone died. Instantly, they told me. But what I've wondered for years now is what constitutes the length of an instant. There have been times when I've tried to clock it, to see how long an instant could possibly be, how much I could see and hear and feel and recognize in an instant. Anyway . . ." She cleared her throat, opened her bag, halted briefly while she lit a cigarette, then went on. "I was incredibly controlled. I didn't carry on, or break down at having to see them. I think it was because it had happened in my mind so many, many times that there was a sort of block between what was happening on one level and any possible reaction I might have to it on another. I got through it. One thing after another, I got through it. The funeral, with Stephen's class from school there, singing a hymn. All Carl's friends, and mine. I felt like a witness at the proceedings, wrapped up entirely in the gross unfairness of it: that they could get killed, be dead, leaving me behind to oversee the disposal of their remains. I had to go home and see all the things that had belonged to the other people who used to live there. Stephen's clothes and toys, bits and pieces he'd squirreled away because they'd had some special, secret significance to him, notes from classmates, and notes he'd written. I'd go into his room again and again, determined this time to strip it bare, get rid of every last thing in there so I wouldn't have to see any of it, so I wouldn't have to keep on feeling the sick, sick feeling I had finding his favorite shirt, or three pairs of mittens he'd hidden because he hated having to wear them, so he'd tell me he'd lost them, and I'd go out and buy more, but he'd merely hidden them. I kept finding things, and I'd start feeling hollow again, purposeless, useless, and I'd have to go out and close the door.

"Then, when I thought at last I'd managed to clear out every last thing, that there was nothing left, I'd come across a pair of Carl's cuff links at the back of a drawer, or one of Stephen's socks would turn up in the dryer, and I'd sit down holding the cuff links or the sock, and when I moved to get up again, it would be three hours later and the kettle had burned itself out on the stove, or I'd left the bath water running and it had overflowed. Time had become an immense, elastic vacuum, and I was trapped in it. Oh, hell!" she said, throwing away the cigarette. "You don't want to hear all this. I can't think why I'm telling you."

"I used to try to imagine what it would be like," he said somberly, "if something happened to Lane. I couldn't stand to think about it. I think you're very brave to admit you thought about those things before the accident. Most people wouldn't admit that, even if it was something they'd thought about."

"There's nothing brave about it," she disagreed. "It's simply what I thought."

"Do you blame yourself?" he asked. "I mean, do you feel there was some kind of wish fulfillment?"

It was a good question, she thought. "No, I don't do that," she answered. "I couldn't see that I'd been negligent, or that my daydreams were so potent they could transcend reality. In a way, imagining the loss made me very attentive. There wasn't a day of his life when I didn't tell Stephen I loved him. If I let him go off to school in the morning without saying it, I'd be waiting when he came off the school bus in the afternoon. I'd drag him into the house and we'd wrestle, roughhouse, while I asked him about his day and told him I loved him. He was almost twelve when he died, but he was quite a bit bigger and heavier than I. And very gentle. He had a lovely awareness of his strength, and he didn't want to hurt the Little Mother—that's what he called me. Can't go hurting the Little Mother, he'd say, and then chortle down his shirt front. He had a way of ducking his chin down, and looking up at you through his eyelashes while he went ho-ho-ho down the front of his shirt; or he'd pull the neck of his sweater up over his nose and laugh into the neckline. He had a splendid sense of humor. He needed it, living with me. I was distracted much of the time, my mind on my work, and I'd snap at him if he interrupted, or get angry for no good reason, and then he'd snap right back at me, mocking the way I stood, the expression on my face, the way I articulated each word when I was in a bad temper. He never failed to make me laugh. He knew exactly how to bring me around, jolly me into seeing I was behaving like an idiot.

"My telling the truth doesn't have one goddamned thing to do with bravery," she said, returning to his point. "I've never been brave. If anything, I look for things to hold on to." She became aware that he was holding her hand, and had been for some time. Here she was again, holding on. She wondered if it was obvious to him that he'd inadvertently become the latest of people, things, she instinctively swam toward in the hope of staying afloat just a little while longer. "I almost never talk about any of this," she said apologetically.

"I can understand that," he told her. "I'd probably be the same way. While you've been telling me, I've been having little flashes—you know how that happens?—between words, sort of. I keep trying to put myself into your place in the picture. It's too rough. I can't do it. I *hate* that story. I really hate it. I mean, what about that girl? Weren't you outraged?"

"I felt sorry for her," she said quietly. "I kept thinking about her parents having to come to identify her . . . I don't suppose this is what you had in mind when you came to the hotel."

"I told you: I didn't have anything special in mind. I don't mind listening."

She looked at his profile, and was suddenly apprehensive. He was just a little . . . what? Too good to be true. "I should," she said slowly, "Probably be very careful with you."

"Hell! Don't do that!" he said quickly. "Let's just say fuck it, and be reckless; we'll say and do whatever we want." Why did everything have to have predetermined beginnings and endings? Why couldn't things just happen in their own space and time? Was there really a need for protection?

"I don't trust either one of us enough to be reckless . . ." She trailed off, caught for a moment in the giddiness of fatigue. Everything around her seemed to have come free of its moorings; buildings wavered, people drifted, the pavement undulated.

"Are you okay?" His hand tightened around hers and she looked at him again.

"I need a drink. There's a pub over there." She pointed to the corner. "Buy me a drink. And after that we'll go to your hotel, or to mine. That is, if you still want to."

He didn't move at once; he stood and stared at her, recalling the intensity of his disappointment when he'd telephoned her room and there'd been no response. Nothing ever happened the way you imagined it would. He'd thought of the two of them talking generalities over a drink, followed by dinner; he'd imagined seeing her spread in naked invitation on a bed. He hadn't considered the possibility that she might tell him anything as awful as the story he'd just heard. He'd certainly never considered telling her any of his own true stories. But just now he wanted to throw down hunks of truth in front of her, to see how she'd react to someone else's story. It was an impulse he couldn't bring himself to act upon, yet he could clearly see himself heaving slabs of his own truth around like sides of beef. It made his jaws clench in resistance. He looked away from her to the pub on the corner. There *was* a need for protection.

"Will you buy me a drink?" she asked.

Again, his eyes came back to her. "Sure," he said, in an instant deciding she wasn't someone who overindulged as a matter of course. "Why not?"

As they crossed toward the pub, he asked himself what it was about this woman that had prompted him to pursue her. Her blunt directness irritated him one moment, charmed him the next. Part of the irritation he felt was due to the way she pushed pieces of her personal truth around, possibly as if she sensed his little lies when he told them. And that worried him slightly, because she was clever enough to sort fact from fiction. Of course it was everyone's right to shield himself in whatever fashion he chose. He happened to do it with fairly harmless distortions of the truth, lies that he saw as misleading clues that wouldn't give him away. He hadn't always done it. In fact, now that he thought about it, it was quite a recent habit. Bits of camouflage for concealment. He used lies. And he had a hunch Leigh did it with sex; she used it to sidetrack a man when he seemed to be getting too close to things she didn't want revealed. Fair enough. He varnished facts in one way, she did it in another. Who cared? He didn't. If anything, they balanced each other. All right, she'd thrown him completely by confronting him with the specifics of why he'd come looking for her. He did want to take her to bed. She'd guessed that, and forced him to retreat. He still wanted to take her to bed. She wasn't easy, and the challenge of winning her over was both tiresome and increasingly compelling. He wanted her to capitulate. The odd thing was he was beginning to care. And he couldn't help thinking that caring was potentially the riskiest enterprise known to man. Yet how did you stop yourself?

Five

SHE SMOKED ONE CIGARETTE AFTER ANOTHER, AND DRANK THE GIN very quickly, trying to figure out what she was doing, and why she'd told this man about Carl and Stephen. She was divided between an inclination to tell him all the rest of it, and an impossible desire to retrieve every last word she'd spoken. Staring at her empty glass, a fresh cigarette between her fingers, she examined her feeling of having betrayed two people she'd loved by talking about them to someone she scarcely knew. The worst part of all this was that she wanted to get into bed with this man, to have him put his arms around her, to have him distract her with his body. It was such a hateful cliché, she thought, wanting, in the face of death, to make love, to find some degree of peace no matter how brief-lived it might be. A simple ceremony, an exchange of caresses, and then they'd go their separate ways. There was a decidedly selfish aspect to it, but since they'd both get what they wanted, it would be fair.

"Are you mad at yourself?" he asked. "Do you wish you hadn't told me any of that?"

He was anything but stupid, she thought, her eyes still on the empty glass. "Actually," she said, lifting her head to look into his blue eyes whose dark perimeters looked exactly as if someone had taken a pen dipped in India ink and carefully drawn a fine line around his irises, "I am mad at myself, furious."

"You shouldn't be. Maybe you needed to talk about it."

She opened her handbag, pulled out a five-pound note, and laid it on the table. "Will you buy us more drinks?" she asked, feeling suddenly volatile. One wrong move or word, and she'd go off like a rocket.

"No," he said. "I won't. I'll be more than happy to buy you wine with dinner, even something after dinner, but nothing more now."

"May I ask why?"

"Because you're out with me, because I'm responsible for you *while* you're out with me, because I want to get you safely back to your hotel . . ."

"Where you can safely be rid of me because it's not turning out the way you expected. You came around hoping to get laid, but here I am forcing you to make conversation, instead of just shutting up and doing what you want me to do."

"Jesus! What's wrong with you?"

"You want to be in control of the situation . . ."

"No! I won't buy you more drinks right now because if we *do* do it, I'd like us *both* to remember the occasion. It's too goddamned depressing making love with someone who's drunk."

"Your wife drinks?"

"She *invented* it."

"I'm sorry."

Pause.

"I don't know how we keep managing to do this," she said sadly. "It's my turn to apologize. If I'd had an entire night's sleep recently, I wouldn't be saying or doing any of this. It feels as if my skin's been removed and I'm walking around with the raw flesh exposed. Even the air hurts."

He winced at the description. "I know the feeling," he told her, giving his head a shake, as if to clear it. "Way back when, it was once in awhile. We'd go out to dinner, or to a party, and she'd drink too much, and I didn't mind, to tell the truth, because those were about the only times she'd be interested. But then it got to be . . . she had this prodigious capacity; she could drink so much . . . Christ! She'd sweat booze. And it was like making love to a goddamned duffle bag. And what did it make me, what was I, if I could . . . I felt like a shit because I was still sexually interested in my wife. I'm tired too, Leigh. I haven't slept in a couple of days, myself. And why should either one of us be pissed off if we seem to want to be together? I can't make any sense of that. The way I see it, if I can feel good for half an hour or an hour, if the two of us can have some pleasure, why shouldn't we. *Why shouldn't we?* More and more, I keep thinking maybe that's all there's going to be. Maybe half an hour or an hour's all I'm ever going to get. And if that's it, then I want it. I don't want you to have another drink because I don't want you to turn into Celeste on me. Okay? I don't want to deal with a woman I want who has to be half in the bag before she can do it. Okay?"

"Yes, okay," she relented.

In the taxi, on the way back to her hotel, she remembered and said, "I have to call my mother. I should've called hours ago. She'll be worried."

Once inside her suite, she threw her coat across the arm of one of the chairs, saying, "Help yourself to something, if you want a drink. I'll try not to be too long," then went through to the bedroom and shut the door.

He got himself a Coke from the minibar, popped it open, and sat on the sofa to drink directly from the can. It was one of his habits that drove Celeste wild. So many things he did drove her wild. It took him a lot of years to realize that even if he performed strictly to her specifications there'd always be something that failed to please her, because what bothered her most was his continuing to care about her. Just thinking now about all the years of effort that had gone into keeping Celeste happy made him feel battle-worn and stripped; he felt as if all the blood had been drained from his body by the countless small wounds inflicted by the marriage. As a direct result of so much time spent on failed acts of appeasement, he'd evolved into a man who now told lies for reasons of self-preservation. At best, he gave most people only snippets of truth. He served up concoctions fabricated with great care, stews made of gristly bits of truth hidden by chunks of colorful distortions. He'd become a master chef when it came to preparing entire meals that would fill those with appetites for details and leave them groaning, satiated, and temporarily beyond craving more. He'd come to know the caloric value of items others would discard. And when he stuffed a conversation full of self-protecting camouflage, he almost invariably remembered his father commenting one time on the fact that spare ribs had always been thrown away until the Orientals had turned them into delicacies. Dan had done something similar in turning the lesser details of his life into canapés. He'd been doing it so often, and so well, that even when there seemed no obvious need, he kept on with it. The result was his present inability to deliver up even the smallest portion of the truth without feeling mildly imperiled. Yet he'd told the woman in the other room more about himself than he'd ever told anyone. He'd kept back certain facts, but he'd revealed a great deal to Leigh, and he didn't know why. His interest in her had been minimal until she'd revealed who she was. And learning who she was, discovering he was in the company of someone he'd long admired, had prompted him to be truthful. It was, he thought, very damned strange.

"Oh, Leigh," Marietta exclaimed with a slight quaver in her voice, "I've been frightfully worried about you. You promised you'd ring me as soon as you arrived."

"I'm sorry. I intended to call, then I got sidetracked."

"It was a most distressing day. It really was."

"I'm sorry," Leigh said again, close to tears.

"Are you all right?" her mother asked. "This is not the best connection."

"I'm still functioning."

"Have you been in touch yet with your father?" Marietta's tone was wary.

"Not yet. I'm working up to it. Were there many people?"

"Quite a number. Some lovely young people, really. It went well, all considered."

"I don't suppose Jacobson came?"

"Did you really think he would? No, he didn't come."

"It wasn't a horror show, was it? I'd hate to think I ran off and left you to cope if it was a nightmare."

"It went very well. Jeff read a very moving piece, and several other young people spoke. It was quite a lovely service."

"I should have been there," Leigh said. "I feel guilty."

"Don't!" Marietta said. "There's no need for that. No one could possibly have done more than you did. No one! But are you sure you know what you're doing, darling? This business about seeing Philip . . ."

"I honestly have no idea. I'm just going to get through this, one way or another. Actually, I met someone. He's helping to keep my mind off everything."

"Well, I suppose that's for the good. Try to get some rest. And, please, ring me in the next day or two to let me know what you're doing. I worry, Leigh. You know I do."

"I know. And I'm sorry about not calling sooner."

She had to sit for a few minutes after the call ended, to collect herself. Joel was no more. Jeff had agreed to scatter the ashes into Long Island Sound. "You know how much I love swimming," Joel had laughed. "Don't look that way, Leigh. It's what I want. It really is."

She got up at last, and went out to walk across to the sofa where she leaned down and kissed Daniel on the forehead. "I hope that didn't take too long. We could have dinner downstairs, try for a table close to the fire. Shall I phone and ask if they have one available?"

"How is your mother?" he asked, catching hold of her hand and directing her down beside him.

"Ah, my mother. If only they'd give her the chance, she could run the world. It would be beautiful—legions of unblemished virgins and hardy heroes, concerned only with love. There'd be no wars, no political intrigue, no nuclear weapons, nothing but people earnestly fretting over whether Gregory truly loves Helena, or if he is in fact a cad and simply leading her on. I grew up on my mother's books. Until I was well into my twenties, I honestly believed I would be rescued, like Helena, and Victoria, and Constance, and the others. When I realized that wasn't the way it was going to be, I was very angry, for a time, with Mother. I became most indignant and argued horribly with her because I felt she was simply encouraging generations of girls to believe in fairy tales. It was stupid," she sighed. "If she didn't write them, somebody else would. I suppose the fact is there's a need for those fairy tales." She got the words out, then went silent, menaced again by tears. After a moment, she rose and went to put the Do Not Disturb sign on the outer doorknob, while Dan watched from the sofa. Halfway to the bedroom, she stopped and looked over at him, then continued on into the room. The creak of the sofa springs indicated he was following, and she reached with an unsteady hand to turn off the overhead light. She stood just inside the door, and waited. He came up behind her, and she turned. His hands moved indefinitely, wavered, then settled lightly on the edges of her shoulders, his brows drawing together as he studied her face.

"What?" she asked.

"You seem different every time I look at you."

"So do you to me. We're both punchy. It's probably the best condition to be in." She waited for him to make a move; she didn't think she could take the initiative. She stood there, assailed by slow inner contractions of expectation, and a twisting sensation in her chest that was perilously close to anguish.

"I like you," he said, looking somewhat surprised. "I'm, uh, just having a little trouble getting started."

"Oh," she said, sympathetic. "So am I."

They gave each other shaky smiles, still not moving, and she could no longer bear the tension, so she offered her mouth against his, going forward with the last of her energy and courage, amazed at having found the resources to take the initiative after all.

It was what he'd needed—some evidence of her interest—to begin his cautious examination of the length and breadth of her back. They proceeded, he thought, with an unusual lack of haste. Languorously, she attended to the removal of his jacket and tie, then to the unbuttoning of his shirt. Her motions so mesmerized him that he had to hold her still so he could push his hands past the layers of her clothing to make contact with the sleek warmth of her flesh. Then, again, she stole his attention away with her hands, and with the potency of her mouth. Kissing her was very like drowning; he sank into a stirring darkness wherein he discovered the depths of her appetite and his own. Two minutes, three, then he held her captive to his chest. "Just don't move for a moment, and let me do this," he murmured, taking her out of her clothes before clasping her to the length of his body until she was light-headed and breathless.

It occurred to him—a few seconds' illumination like the flash of a flare —that this half-naked woman he was touching was Stanleigh Dunn; she was *someone*, and he was being allowed to caress her; he actually had his hands on her breasts. He'd never felt remotely like the way he did now, as if he'd been accorded a privilege of exceptional magnitude. He wanted suddenly to be able to touch her everywhere at once, avid for the most intimate knowledge of her. Yet even his greed couldn't force him to move any less slowly. His hands investigated her spine, the flesh tight over her ribs, the tidy span of her waist, the backs of her thighs, while he kissed her throat, her arm, her mouth once again. The pleasure of learning her was too extreme. He frightened himself with the intensity of his desire. He shouldn't have cared about the texture of her skin, or its fragrance; it shouldn't have mattered that her inner thighs were rounded and yielding, and that he was thrilled at having access to her. He'd lost his detachment and was being affected by absolutely everything about her.

This wasn't casual, she thought, stunned by the way he was making love to her. She couldn't move; he held her captive. He appeared to be perfectly content to have her remain as she was—motionless, compliant, open to his inspection. He had control; he could turn her this way or that, do anything he wished. Perhaps he hoped she'd remain passive. The idea frightened her. She freed herself of his embrace to stand pulling air into her lungs in huge gulps. Then she flew at him, to put her hands, and then her mouth, on him. He seemed frozen for a time, almost as if no one had ever done this to him before. Then his hand began to stroke her hair, and she thought frantically, We're too naked. We shouldn't be this naked.

He raised her up and looked slowly at her, his eyes as questing as his hands had been. She found it agonizing to have to stand beneath the weight of his gaze, with a wall of cooling air between them. This was nothing like previous collisions she'd had with near-strangers when, with little or no preamble, she'd closed her eyes and accepted their bodies into hers. Perhaps it was fatigue, or sorrow, or her age, but she was being undone by something she'd thought would bring no more than temporary comfort. It seemed as if she'd lost her prior adeptness at taking without question what was being offered sexually. All at once she was too aware of nuance, of her own dreadful needs and those of this man who was either as dreadfully needy as she, or a consummate artist at manipulation. She suffered his slow, visual examination, powerless to put a stop to it.

Her long pale body, her breasts—fuller and heavier than he'd antici- pated—her vulnerability, made him feel both sad and enormously potent. He couldn't think how this had happened, how they'd argued, and laughed, and talked, and now were skin to skin, exchanging caresses. The pleasure penetrated all his defenses. No one had ever made love to him with such aggressive abandon or such skill. Who was this woman with her spiky hair and grieving eyes, her adroitly experienced hands and mouth? He watched her eyes as his hand moved between her thighs. Her eyelids lowered. He could see a pulse beating strongly in her throat. She swayed slightly, her lips parted. He was astonished to think she'd allow him to touch her this way. But she did allow it. She opened to it.

He maneuvered her to the bed and put her down, then breathed in the perfume, strongest between her breasts. He examined the fine, long bones that formed the cradle of her hips, setting it to rocking gently, undulating beneath his hand. Her arms reached for him, and he let himself be drawn into their circle, sheltered at their apex. He sank into the scented cavern of her embrace, her perfume and motion obliterating everything; he sank into her irreverent ardor, and felt as if he loved her. So quickly, so readily, all sense was lost of where one began and the other ended; definition had no significance. All that pertained was the pulse, maintaining the meter limb to limb, eyes and hands joined; an homage to symmetry.

He was shaken by her continuing silence; she was stricken by his unfeigned interest. Just a short time and each knew the taste and scent of the other's flesh; there was nothing withheld. He rested, still inside her, making no sign he was anxious to be on his way now that he'd had what he'd been seeking. Her body expanded and contracted in slow after-tremors; she lay motionless, savoring the lassitude, her heart gradually finding its more temperate rhythm.

"You can't stay," she said at last. "This can only be for tonight."

"But why?" he wanted to know, unwilling to be separated from her. "We're both on our own. There's no reason why we shouldn't have a few days together."

"There's every reason. We'll have this evening, without complications."

"I have no say in this, do I?" He pulled away, but hung over her as he asked his questions.

"I *can't*. Please take me at my word. I simply can't."

"Do you want me to go now?"

"Oh, not yet," she said, and wound her arms around him to bring him close again. "It's still early. And I did promise you dinner."

He thought of a number of arguments, but had to dismiss them. That's what happened when you told lies; they invalidated your arguments. He gave it up and with a sigh, touched the back of his hand to her cheek, saying, "You have no idea, none at all, how lovely you are. You don't see a bit of it. And you don't believe me, either. I can tell by the way you're trying not to hear what I'm saying."

"Don't," she said. "Let's not say anything." She distracted him again, her clever hands searching, stroking. She wanted only to feel the hard edge of his hip, and the articulate muscle in his thigh; she wanted to trace the deep veins running the length of his arm, and then fold herself into his embrace, seeking oblivion.

Six

"LANE, IT'S ME."

"*Daddy! Where are you?* I've been so worried. Are you all right?"

"I'm fine, sweetheart. I'm sorry about . . . I should've let you know, but I just didn't have a chance."

"But where are you?"

"London. On my way to Bangkok."

"But, Daddy, I thought you weren't going to . . ."

"I know, but I changed my mind at the last minute and decided I should go after all. How are you, sweetheart?"

"Oh, me. I'm okay. It's you. Boy, you can't believe the kind of stuff I've been thinking, not hearing from you for so long. And why London? Isn't that out of your way?"

"Yes and no. You know me." Daniel gave a laugh. "You know I never fly anywhere direct."

"No, I know. I just didn't think you were going, that's all."

"I changed my mind. It's been known to happen."

"Well, as long as you're all right. That's what really matters."

"I'm just fine. How's school?"

"I'm surviving. This semester's a major yawn, except for . . . *God*, Dad! I don't want to blow this call talking about school. How long're you going to be in Bangkok? And when're you coming home?"

"I don't know for sure. A couple of weeks at the outside, maybe less."

"You promise? A couple of weeks and then you'll come home?"

"I promise. I'll be back in plenty of time for Christmas, tons of time. We could go somewhere, if you like. Take a couple of weeks in the sun, the Bahamas or someplace, whatever you'd like."

"If we do go away, would it be all right if Cathy comes with us? I kind of promised her, because her folks're taking a cruise and she'll be alone otherwise. You wouldn't mind, would you?"

"Whatever you like," he repeated.

"Daddy, what's going on?" She sounded suddenly younger, not quite so sure of herself. "I really was getting scared. I kept calling and when I couldn't reach you, well . . ."

Dan could almost see her shrugging, and smiled at the image. "It was very last-minute, babe. I do have one interesting thing to tell you. You'll never guess who I met on the flight over!"

"Who?"

"Stanleigh Dunn."

"Dad! You're joking! You actually met him?"

"Stanleigh Dunn's a woman, Lane. And I not only met her, I got her autograph for you."

"That's amazing! What was she like? Was she nice? Young, old, what?"

"My age, and very nice. I'll tell you all about it when I get back."

"God! Wait till I tell Cath! She'll die! That's too amazing! And you got her autograph?"

"I sure did. Listen, sweetheart, I'd better go. I just wanted to check in. I had a hunch you might be trying to reach me. Call your grandparents, will you? You know they like to hear from you."

"Dad," she said with strained patience, "I've only spoken to them about *sixty* times in the last two weeks. We've *all* been worried."

"Well, now you know I'm alive and well, so you just think about where you'd like to go for Christmas. Okay?"

"Okay."

"Take care of yourself, and call your grandparents anyway. I love you, sweetheart."

"Love you too, Dad."

An officious-sounding woman answered the telephone, and for a moment Leigh couldn't think how to ask for her father. The woman again said hello, and Leigh had to speak or hang up.

"Is Mr. Reid available?" she asked.

"May I ask who's calling?"

"Stanleigh Dunn."

"Oh! Just one moment, please."

Leigh heard the receiver being set down, then the sound of receding footsteps on wood flooring. After several moments there was the distinct click of a door opening, an indecipherable exchange of words, then the return of the footsteps.

"Sorry to be so long," the woman said. "Could you leave a number? He's not able to come to the telephone just now."

"Actually, I was hoping to come to see him."

"Oh, yes? And when did you think you might do that?"

"Well, when might be convenient?"

"Almost anytime, I should think. Had you some specific date in mind?"

"To whom am I speaking?" Leigh asked finally, puzzled by the woman's proprietary tone.

With a laugh, the woman said, "This is awkward, isn't it? I'm Delia, Mrs. Reid. I do apologize for not introducing myself at once. I think Philip would like very much to see you. Are you nearby?"

"I'm in London. I thought if it was convenient . . . how would tomorrow be?"

"You'll come for lunch?"

"If I may."

"We'd be delighted. You know the directions?"

"I'll manage."

"Splendid! Tomorrow then," Delia said. "Looking forward," she said, and rang off.

Leigh made arrangements for a car and driver for the following day, then phoned room service for toast and coffee. In her dressing gown, she went to the window to see what kind of day it was. Rain. She stood looking down at the dull, greasy-looking street, her chest tight from too many cigarettes, her entire body stiff from the previous night's activities.

I'm Delia, Mrs. Reid. Her father had remarried. Delia, Mrs. Reid. Judging by her accent and careful diction, she sounded like the tall, too-thin, bony-chested type who'd wear sensible brogues, tweed skirts, and twin sets; no makeup, long wispy gray hair done up in a bun.

The tray from room service came quite quickly. She signed for it, then sat on the sofa to drink some of the coffee and consume one piece of the toast. She lit a cigarette, refusing to think just yet about last night. If she did, she might relent and telephone Dan at the Hilton. She poured more coffee, smoked the cigarette, feeling the not unpleasant ache in her thighs. Her eyes went to the telephone. Last night had been fantastic; last night had been orgiastic; last night had been such a sexual extravaganza that she could feel heat rising into her neck and face just thinking about it in the light of day.

She hadn't made love so hard, or for so long, or with such *intent*, in years. And now that she thought about it, recalling moments when she'd felt she might literally expire beneath the engulfing waves of almost too much pleasure, she couldn't quite believe she'd actually given herself so absolutely. But she had. She'd made love with someone she scarcely knew, in every conceivable fashion, until she could no longer move and had watched from the bed, through slitted eyes, as he'd crept around the room gathering up his clothes before leaving. And then she'd slept, falling into blackness as silent and unpopulated as a desert in the dead of night. For almost nine hours, she'd slept.

Now it was nearly noon, and it appeared Daniel was going to keep his word. She looked again at the telephone. She smiled, thought of Joel, and was suddenly sad. She tried not to think about him. If she thought about him she'd begin to slide, the way she was now, into an adhesive, cottony substance that threatened to suffocate her. Setting her feet on the floor, she dropped the cigarette into the ashtray, bent her forehead to her knees, and folded her arms over her head. Losing it, I'm losing it, she thought, sitting quite still but floundering. Joel. I miss you. You were so wonderfully special. Every time I opened the door to find you there, waiting, smiling, I had a sense of occasion because you had qualities that radiated; you glowed with youth and optimism and that so enviable belief in yourself. All the dozens of times I opened the door to find you there, with flowers, or a bottle of wine, or a clipping from some magazine, or a plate of something you'd cooked. And you came inside smelling of fresh air and limitless possibilities and you allowed me to enjoy you, the sight of you, your smile, and your audition stories, tales of the cattle call.

She sat up and looked again at the telephone, her arms now wrapped around her midriff. If he'd meant a word of what he'd said, he'd have called, and never mind that she'd said not to. If he'd been sincere, if his feelings had genuinely been aroused, he'd have gone past her words, to make another attempt to convince her.

The telephone rang, and she snatched up the receiver.

"I know we were supposed to hum 'Strangers in the Night' and just walk away," Dan laughed, "but I can't stop thinking about you. Don't be mad. I really did try not to call, but knowing you're there . . . are you mad?"

"I'm not mad." She reached for the still-burning cigarette in the ashtray.

"I can't get a flight out of here until tomorrow morning. Have you managed to get in touch with your father? Did you sleep, by the way?"

"I'm seeing him tomorrow. And yes, thank you, I did sleep."

"Spend the day with me!" he said eagerly. "We'll have lunch, go shopping, or take in a movie, a show, anything you want."

"You're ignoring everything we agreed on."

"Who cares! Let's spend the day together."

"Daniel," she began, then stopped.

"What?"

"I have to care," she said. "I *have* to. I'm glad, though, that you called."

Gently, she put down the receiver. Then, her eyes still on the telephone, she had to ask herself what she was doing. He'd offered, for a second time, an escape route, and she'd refused it. All at once the remainder of the day spread itself before her like a road into infinity. It didn't have to be that way.

She found the number of the Hilton, and called him back. There was no response from his room. She didn't bother to leave a message. Perhaps it was for the best. He could only be a complication in her life. And the last thing she needed, she told herself, going to the bathroom to start the water running in the tub, was an involvement with a married man.

She put the phone down on him, just like that. He was staggered. She'd really meant what she'd said, and intended to stick by it. He'd been so certain, after last night, that she'd change her mind. But she hadn't. With no idea where he was going, he pocketed the room key, made sure he had his wallet, and left.

Tell enough lies, you wind up losing track, not sure what you've said, or why. Sometimes the lies and the truth got hopelessly mixed up, and he couldn't remember which was which. They were thousands of miles away from home; she was the only person he knew nonprofessionally in London; they'd spent hours naked together, but she didn't want to see him. Maybe the previous night hadn't been as exceptional as he'd thought; maybe he was mediocre in every way and was no longer able to differentiate between mediocrity and excellence. Christ! he thought angrily, pushing out of the hotel, to stop on the pavement for a moment before heading down Park Lane.

He stomped along, ignoring the rain and the passersby and the traffic, reviewing the events of the past day and night, deciding that for once in a very rare while he'd told more truth than lies, that he'd given the very best of himself to their lovemaking, and that it was his right, at the very least, to be allowed to state his case. He marched up to Piccadilly, did a complete circuit of the Circus, made an impulsive stop in one shop and then another, then headed determinedly for Albemarle Street.

Outside the hotel he paced back and forth for several minutes before pushing his way inside, going directly through the lobby to the elevator. The Do Not Disturb sign was still on her door. He knocked, breathing hard through his nose, and waited. He heard her call out, "Just a moment," and squared his shoulders, set for a confrontation.

She opened the door, saw him, and tried to shut the door.

"I want to talk to you!" he said, holding open the door with the flat of his hand.

"I don't want to talk to you!" she replied, with both hands trying to push it shut.

"Well, that's too goddamned bad!" He shoved open the door, causing her to reel several feet back into the room. He stepped inside, closed the door, and threw the box of flowers at her. "A little something," he snapped, as instinctively she caught the box. "A token of, as they say, affection. What the hell's the *matter* with you? I'm just trying to be nice and you're treating me like . . . I don't know what . . . a customer or something."

"Can't you take no for an answer?" she wanted to know, a bit frightened by his determination and his irate energy. He was larger and stronger and younger than she, and capable, from the looks of it, of fairly violent behavior.

"Obviously not. I could buy this, maybe, if I believed you didn't like me, but you do. Like me. You did last night. I know you did."

"Last night has nothing to do with today."

"Yes, it does. Listen, Leigh, who's to know if we spend another day together? Who's to know or care?"

She didn't answer, but stood glaring at him, and now he felt like a complete asshole. She looked tired, and her eyes didn't seem quite so large without makeup. She was still in her dressing gown, her hair damp. Somehow, she appeared more accessible than at any time since they'd met. And he was behaving like an ox. She kept staring at him, not moving, not speaking, and he couldn't make the connection between the woman of the night before and the woman now. They seemed completely unrelated.

"You didn't have to hang up on me," he said, hearing how feeble that sounded, and wishing he could disregard the signals and take hold of her. "That's all. As if I didn't even deserve a goodbye. Okay." He started for the door.

"I'm sorry for hanging up that way."

He stopped and turned to look at her.

"I don't want to hurt you," she said, her eyes softer. "I just don't have anything to give you, and you seem to be in need . . . of something." She moved finally, and set the box of flowers down on the coffee table before reaching for her cigarettes. She lit one, then crossed her arms in front of her. "You don't want to know me, Daniel," she said quietly. "People don't really want to know other people. They just want to see new reflections of themselves, or get lost temporarily in someone else. We did that last night: we got lost. That's all there is. That's all I have to give. And surely you have no problem finding willing women to get lost in. You're a very attractive man, and the world is crawling with unattached women."

"How do you know what I want?" he asked. "You don't even give people time to get a word in."

She got sidetracked for a few seconds by his looks, and by the simple fact of his being there. On a purely esthetic level, she was captured by his dark hair and unique eyes; he was a fine-looking man and she couldn't imagine why he was being so persistent, or what it was about her he found so appealing. Her inner voice cautioned her that she couldn't possibly have any sort of a future with someone whose physical appearance made her so self-conscious about her own flaws.

"Go away, Daniel," she said imploringly, tamping down her sexual response to him. "Please. You're a complication I simply can't handle. I do like you. And last night was wonderful. Okay? It was terrific. Truly. I'm sorry I was rude on the telephone. Thank you for the flowers. Please, go away now."

"Could I call you sometime in New York? just to talk, or maybe for lunch?"

"*Daniel!* Don't *do* this, to either one of us! I was rude, and I'm sorry. But you're looking only at the surface of the matter, and not at everything that's underneath. Please, go away."

"This morning," he said thickly, his hand on the door, "I woke up thinking about you. It was the best thing that's happened to me in years." He got the door open, and left. Head down, deflated, his feet and legs heavy, he trudged along the corridor, down the stairs, and out of the hotel. He felt almost sick with sudden fatigue. The one time in his life he'd gone along with his impulses, he'd blown it skyhigh, made a fool of himself. What he wanted now was to go back to the Hilton, have a couple of drinks, and then go to sleep until it was time to head to the airport.

"A goddamned caveman," Leigh said under her breath, watching the door close. She stood finishing her cigarette, then opened the box to gaze at the dozen long-stemmed red roses inside. "A sensitive caveman," she amended. Leaving the flowers on the table, she went to the bedroom to dress, oddly energized by the confrontation.

As she put on her makeup, she reviewed the scene, laughing aloud at the way the two of them had pushed at the door before he'd succeeded in bulling his way in. They were both idiots, she told the mirror.

The rain had stopped. She was just passing Ryman's, had second thoughts, backed up and went into the stationer's to buy a small sketch pad, several fine-point felt-tip pens, two 4B pencils, and a sharpener. With a paper cup of coffee and her supplies, she arranged herself on a bench in Green Park, and began to sketch a bench nearby and, in front of it, the rounded sections of dirt, created by restless feet, that looked to her like bathmats; she went on to a naked tree, its bark oddly dappled; a discarded pack of 555s on the sodden brown grass; a piece of the sky inhabited by restless clouds.

When she stopped, having filled half a dozen pages of the book, her coffee had gone cold, her hands were numb, and the inhalation of a cigarette made her dizzy. She'd spent more than two hours on the first freehand sketching she'd done since her days as an art student. Throwing away the cigarette, she turned to a fresh page and quickly roughed in Daniel's face, the dark hair and light eyes, the assertive chin, the Gallic slant of the bones beneath the flesh. She studied the hasty rendering for several minutes, then decisively closed the book. It was getting dark; the sky was thick with unshed rain. She remained, looking up at the sky, for several minutes more, wondering, as she had done increasingly of late, what possible point there was to her having two homes—both filled with furniture and possessions—and closets full of clothes, some of which she'd never worn, and a life with no purpose. There had to be something, some goal, some interest, someone, to validate one's existence. As always, she returned full circle to her point of mental departure without an answer and only the hope that the visit to her father might provide her with a piece of history, or an incentive, or merely a welcome. Get through this hour, and then the next, and the next, until you've lived out the day.

At Fortnum & Mason she had a gift box prepared of several kinds of tea and coffee and jam, then carried her purchase out into the rain. By the time she got back to the hotel—only a few blocks—the mink was saturated and many pounds heavier. She hung it on a hanger from the showerhead to drip into the bathtub, dried her hair, then went down to the lounge for afternoon tea. And there was Daniel, sitting where she'd sat yesterday, looking like a naughty schoolboy. She couldn't help herself. She laughed, and went to give him a kiss—standing back from herself as she did, amazed by this display that so contradicted her earlier remarks to him—and then to sit with him.

"You're such a fool!" she laughed, pleased by his dogged persistence. "What are you doing here?"

"I was hoping you're a creature of habit. I left another note for you with the concierge, too."

"Inviting me to dinner?"

He shook his head. "Nope. Saying goodbye. I managed to change my reservation, get a flight out tonight."

"Oh!" She opened her bag for a cigarette, unreasonably disappointed.

"I want you to know I'm aware I'm behaving like an asshole," he told her. "You have to believe I don't usually do things like this."

"I believe you," she said. It was true. She did believe him. "Will you stay for tea?"

"If you really don't mind."

"What time is your flight?"

"Seven-forty. I'm going from here directly to the airport. I left my bag with the concierge. Very nice staff here," he said, looking around, as if for examples. "Next time I'm over, I think I'll book in here."

"Well, good," she said awkwardly.

There seemed so much to say that neither of them was able to say much of anything. He stayed an hour, then she went with him while he claimed his bag and the doorman began looking for a taxi. They stood by the foyer doors gazing out at the doorman, natty in his brown frock coat, watching as a cab slid to a stop and the doorman turned to signal Daniel.

Daniel took hold of her shoulders, saying urgently, "For however long it's been—what? Twenty-four hours?—I've felt as if I love you. I know I've been a pain in the ass, but for what it's worth, I'll be thinking about you." He kissed her on the mouth, and she held on, for a few seconds thinking perhaps she was making a serious error in letting him go without so much as her telephone number. But he released her, said, "Goodbye, Leigh," and hurried out through the rain to the waiting taxi. He waved as the taxi drove off and, automatically, she waved back. He had courage, she thought; certainly more than she did. She'd never have been able to admit that, at the last, holding on to him, she'd felt very much the same way. And now there was no possibility of thanking him for rescuing her from the emotional quicksand that had been much reduced simply because he'd given her something else to think about; because, for a few hours in the dark, he'd allowed her to forget everything.

Seven

DELIA, MRS. REID, MATERIALIZED IN THE SITTING ROOM DOORWAY seconds after the housekeeper had taken Leigh's coat. Delia, Mrs. Reid, was, in every way, the antithesis of Leigh's imaginings. Fiftyish, naturally blond, and generously endowed—above average height, ample of breast and becomingly broad in the hips—even her hair seemed incredibly thick in its Gibson girl upsweep. Behind modishly large glasses, her eyes were round and clear and of a perfect cerulean blue. Altogether sunny and stunning, she stood framed in the doorway, looking somewhat cautiously at Leigh. The woman's blatant good health made Leigh feel wizened and haggard. Delia was an older version of the classic example of British beauty Marietta was so fond of using as the heroine in her novels.

"Do, please, sit down," said Delia in a rich plummy voice, having apparently satisfied herself that, physically at least, Leigh represented no menace. "I thought we might have a moment together before you see your father."

Leigh pressed the gift box into the woman's hands with an uncertain smile, saying, "Just a little something. I'm terribly nervous. Do you mind if I smoke?"

"Not at all." Delia slid an ashtray along the top of the square-cut mahogany coffee table until it was within Leigh's reach from the sofa, then sat in the wing chair situated diagonally opposite. She crossed her long, shapely legs, adjusted the silk of her daintily printed dress over her knees, then placed her large, long-fingered hands carefully on the arms of the chair. Her hands, Leigh thought, were somehow out of keeping with the rest of her. They were unadorned but for a plain gold wedding band, the nails short and scrupulously clean. Those hands represented a significant clue to the woman, and Leigh wished she had time enough to decipher it.

"You're not as I expected," Delia said, chancing a smile. "You don't strongly resemble your father, and you look really very young."

Leigh returned the smile. "You're not what I expected either," she admitted, briefly wondering what life would be like for a woman with perfect skin, lapis eyes, Nordic bone structure, a long aristocratic nose, and a mouth that hinted of depthless sensuality. "You must be wondering why I've turned up this way, out of the blue."

"Your father's been hoping for quite some time that you'd contact him."

"He has? I was under the impression he had no interest whatsoever in me."

Delia shook her large, exquisitely molded head. "Nothing could be farther from the truth," she asserted. "However, it really isn't my place to discuss it." Indicating the Fortnum & Mason box on the table, she said, "So good of you. Will you be in England long?"

"I don't think so," Leigh answered, taking a hard drag on her cigarette. She was so nervous her stomach was constricting unpleasantly, and her hands were damp.

"And your mother? She's well?" Delia asked, her pale eyebrows lifting. "Do you know her?"

"We've never met. I do, of course, know who she is. I've even read several of her books. Not quite my sort of thing, but fairly interesting. I understand she's hugely successful."

"Hugely," Leigh agreed.

"I'd best take you along to your father now," Delia said, watching Leigh put out her cigarette with an interest that suggested she seldom had an opportunity to watch someone hold a burning tube of shredded leaves to her mouth and greedily suck in quantities of poisonous smoke.

"I scarcely remember him," Leigh said in a rush. "The last time I saw him was just before my fifteenth birthday. I came for a month's stay, but he was never here." She glanced around the room. "He was busy with the farm, busy with the tenants, busy with this and that. I was deeply disappointed. When I left at the end of the month, we hadn't exchanged more than a few sentences during half a dozen meals we'd taken together. I thought somehow it was my fault, that there was something about me he disliked. How long have you been married?"

Delia was standing now, patiently waiting for Leigh to come with her. "It's dreadful, isn't it," she said, "the way children will hold themselves responsible for the attitudes of their parents. I'm certain there was nothing about you to which he took exception. Twenty-six years we've been married. You had no idea," she said rhetorically.

"None. No one told me. Twenty-six years. Do you have children?"

"Come along," Delia said pleasantly, as if to a recalcitrant child, her hand extended to show the way. "We weren't lucky enough to have children," she said, leading Leigh along the hallway to the rear of the house. "And I was getting rather long in the tooth when your father and I met. He's in the garden room," she explained. "I'll leave you to visit, join you for a cup of coffee in a bit." She paused with her hand on the door, her eyes on Leigh's. "Don't be nervous," she said kindly. "He's really a very dear man."

During the second or two before the door opened fully, and Delia dematerialized as silently as she'd appeared, leaving behind a fragrant floral scent, Leigh was gripped by panic, wondering why on earth she'd come here. She had an intuition that this reunion was going to have unimaginable repercussions.

The so-called garden room had been added since her childhood. Three of the walls were of glass. The perimeters were filed with enormous potted plants, and in one corner was a grouping of rattan furniture with pillows covered in a green and white leafy-patterned fabric. From an armchair, her father rose and came across the room to greet her. Leigh was staring again, as she had at Delia, searching for something familiar about this man. He was taller than she'd remembered, and attractive in ways she hadn't recalled until this moment when she discovered that she did know those deep-set hazel eyes, and that squarish face, and the stubborn jaw so like her own, that shy smile, and even the tentative strength of his hands as they enclosed hers. It was overwhelming. She had the feeling, suddenly, that her ribs were curved inward over a clean, empty expanse that might be filled by the things this man, her father, could say to her.

Keeping hold of her hands, he studied her wordlessly for some time before he spoke. And when he did, his voice too was familiar, low and resonant, the words shaped with precision and delivered with care. "One thought one wouldn't see you again. Then, so unexpectedly, here you are." He didn't smile, but she could see he was genuinely pleased. He was a man, she realized, who rarely smiled, who didn't use what amounted to a facial tic in so many people to illustrate his pleasure. He chose instead to use his eyes, and words. And she couldn't help thinking that if she'd understood this as a child, all their lives might have been very different.

"Come sit down, Stanleigh. Unless," he stopped moving to say, "you find the atmosphere in here overpowering." He gestured at the massed plants that so visibly thrived in the moist warmth of the room.

"No, no, it's fine. This is a lovely room."

"Oh, good," he said, and returned to his chair, his rather stiff, slow gait reminding her of his age. Several newspapers sat on a nearby table, along with an ashtray in which rested a pipe and a number of spent wooden matches. He glanced out at the sodden garden, frowning slightly at the rain splattering against the glass. "You look very well," he said, turning back to her. "Very well indeed. Handsome woman. You've grown to resemble your mother."

"I didn't know you'd remarried," she said, touched increasingly by his diffidence. How could she have forgotten, or failed to know, so many things about him? Or was the truth that, beyond certain fuzzy details retained from childhood and remarks made by her mother, she knew very little about him?

"Years now," he responded, his features lifting with satisfaction at the reference to Delia. "Remarkable woman, your stepmother. Remarkable." Again, he looked out at the rain. "One is most fortunate. Were you aware," he continued in the same tone, "of my efforts to contact you? Was there some specific reason you chose to visit now?"

"No specific reason," she answered. "What do you mean about trying to contact me?"

"One never dreamed," he said quietly, "when you left here that summer that one wouldn't see you again for thirty years. One thought the next summer, or during some school break. Beyond conceiving that you wouldn't return. Mean to say, quite one thing for your mother to do as she would with her life; her prerogative, after all. Quite something else to return my letters to you unopened, refusing me contact with my own child. Can't think why the woman despised me so, although given the circumstances . . ." He trailed off, his eyes somehow magnetically drawn to the rain beyond the glass walls.

"What circumstances?" Leigh asked, bewildered, and remembering now how, when she was a child, her father's manner of speaking had constantly confused her. She opened her bag for a cigarette and lit it. Then, without knowing she was going to do it, she said, "There is a reason, in a way. My stepson, Joel . . . he died a few days ago." She had to stop in order to firm up her grip on her emotions. "We were very close," she went on. "He'd been ill, with leukemia, for nearly three years. When it was over, when he finally died, all I wanted was to come see you. I don't know why. Perhaps it had to do with the dreadful sense of loss . . . I don't know. I wondered, you see, if it was what you felt . . . it suddenly seemed very wrong not to have seen you for so long. As if perhaps a terrible mistake had been made and, unwittingly, I'd helped it happen. Thirty years. We don't know each other. You're married again. The house is completely different from the way I remembered it. I felt," she said inadequately, "I had to see you again." She put out her cigarette and sat back. The only sound was of the rain against the great sheets of glass that were the walls of this hothouse room.

"That was your stepson, you say," her father spoke at last.

"From my second marriage," she elaborated.

"I see. I hadn't known of your first. But I believe I felt fairly much as you say you do." He referred to himself directly as I, not as one, and offered her a slightly apprehensive smile meant, she knew, to be encouraging.

"My first husband and our son were killed in a road accident," she told him, then busied herself getting another cigarette lit. Her throat felt dry and raw, but she knew it was going to be one of those occasions when she smoked nonstop, clinging to illusory support.

"How very tragic," her father said. And there followed another, longer silence while she reviewed that piece of her own history, and he absorbed the impact of gaining and losing both a son-in-law and a grandson all in the space of seconds.

"What's happened to the farm?" she asked at last.

"Came a time when it got to be too much. It's been broken up, parts sold. Retirement," he added unnecessarily. He was seventy years old, after all.

"You must miss it," she said, flooded with sudden sympathy—for both of them. "I do recall how busy you used to be, how much there always was to do."

He nodded, and reached for his pipe, to hold its bowl in the palm of his hand. Leigh thought she knew, all at once, what it was about this man that two so very different women had been drawn to. Certainly he was attractive enough, with his lean height, his plentiful white hair, his Irish tweeds and Scottish woolens; he had the bearing of a man born to wealth and position, as well as that forgivable upperclass affectation of referring to himself as "one." But what appealed about him overall was his aura of kindness. It showed in any number of ways—the prudence in his words and gestures was self-protecting but also intended to spare the sensibilities of others; the intelligence and acuity of his gaze was rescued from harshness by the crinkling of the flesh around his eyes, so that the effect was one of good humor. The smiles he failed to offer with his mouth he gave quite generously with his eyes. Seeing all this, Leigh tried to think why her mother had such tremendous long-lived and ongoing antipathy toward him. He was, very clearly, someone incapable of intentional cruelty. Of course she knew from her own experience how hurtful the unintentional cuts could be.

"What did you mean before about 'circumstances'?" she asked him, certain since he'd created that particular opening he intended to tell her.

"One didn't mean to create a mystery," he said, his diffidence apparently intact. "It was a bit of unpleasantness a very long time ago." He'd no sooner finished saying this when he visibly reconsidered. "That is not strictly the truth," he said, his eyes seeing the window. "It was a frightful jolt, completely unexpected. She confronted me one day, with no warning. Not a hint, prior to then, of what was to come. I was an impediment to her desires, an obstacle standing between her and the life she preferred to live. I was insensitive to her needs, obsessive regarding the farm, less than a satisfactory partner in every area." Meeting Leigh's eyes again, he said, "Perhaps I was rather wrapped up in the farm. Very likely, I was. But I'd gone along believing our life here was a good one. Throughout our marriage, I took my cues from your mother. I realized then that one can live very closely with someone else and be quite unaware of the thoughts and feelings of that other person. I never was terribly good socially, lacked the conversational skills, the dinner table airs and graces that were, by her sights, important. Any number of sins of omission of which I was guilty. Tried and convicted without benefit of what one might call a courtroom appearance. She announced she was leaving and taking you with her. Nothing I could say or do would dissuade her. She wanted an end to the marriage; an end to the 'boredom and bondage' as she called it; she wouldn't hear any argument; one was not allowed to state one's case.

"The agreement stipulated you were to be with me on all your school holidays, but she'd write to say this or that had come up. And, as you know, after two years the visits came to an end. I wrote many times, as did my solicitors. I even made a trip to New York to confront her, but somehow she managed to learn of my presence and left the city in order not to have to see me. There was nothing to be done, so I came home. We tried every means, including a number of threatening letters from the solicitor, but nothing came of any of it. I wrote to you. The letters were all returned. At last I conceded defeat and hoped you'd seek to contact me. And now you have. For that I am grateful."

"Did something happen? I mean, it doesn't make sense. I'm not sure I understand."

"There was a chap in London she was terribly keen on. Perhaps she hoped he'd marry her." He shrugged. "She brooded a bit after that episode. Then she began taking weekends in London, and there were other chaps. One simply couldn't ignore it. It was the sort of thing—rather blatant, and much talked about—that was, after the fact, most embarrassing. I was completely in the dark. I thought we had a good marriage. Then one morning she decided every last bit of it had to be destroyed, so that it could never be resurrected. To this day I cannot think what I did to so turn her against me. As I said, there was no discussion."

"Perhaps," Leigh ventured, "she decided she *couldn't* be married." She hesitated, gauging her sense of loyalty. "My mother," she went on, "likes men, likes to be liked by them. She's always thought I was ridiculous for wanting to be married. She has great contempt for marriage. It feels as if we're talking about someone neither of us knows. I don't think I know *her*, or *you*, for that matter. I didn't know about your letters, or about your wanting to see me. Perhaps things might have been different if I'd known. But in many ways I'm very like her."

"And in many ways, very *un*like her. Understand, please, that I bear your mother no malice. Certainly not at this late date. It's simply that some areas remain puzzling. She refused a financial settlement, yet she left with a number of pieces that had been my grandmother's. They were meant to come to you. Family heirlooms, that sort of thing."

He spoke of the jewelry and Leigh thought of her mother pawning valuable items in order to get the two of them established in New York. Had her mother redeemed those things as she'd said? Just as Leigh was about to assure him her mother still had those heirlooms, the door opened and Delia came smiling in, followed by the housekeeper pushing a trolley bearing a full silver coffee service.

"We've rescued your driver," Delia said, "and installed him in the kitchen. He put up quite a fight, according to Anne here. Insisted on showing her his bag of lunch. Anne, however, has prevailed." As she spoke, she glided across the room to position herself behind her husband's chair. Her hands slid over his shoulders and, in a tellingly protective gesture, she bent to rest her cheek briefly against the top of his head before crossing to seat herself in the chair next to Leigh's. "I know," she said, "the two of you haven't had near enough time alone together, but I'm far too curious to stay any longer in the sitting room alone with my imagination." She gave Leigh a wide, girlish smile. "Has he told you yet how we met?"

Leigh said he hadn't.

Delia looked fondly over at her husband, then laughed. "Men," she told Leigh, "are such fools when it comes to their health. He'd been feeling unwell for quite some time, but kept putting off doing anything about it. I'd just opened my surgery a few months earlier, and it was terribly slow going, everyone apprehensive about the new female GP. In any event, he finally dragged himself in one morning, coincidentally placing his stamp of approval; you know, the country squire seeing fit to put himself in the care of the new physician. Poor fellow had pneumonia. Slung him straight into hospital, and made sure he stayed there. Which, I promise you, was quite a feat. The cows were waiting." She laughed. "The fields were waiting; the tenants were waiting. We kept him tucked away for three weeks, then he went off home grumbling, to see to all those waiting cows and fields and what-have-you. Then, not a week later, he was ringing up to invite me out for a meal."

"She decided," Phil put in, "I needed looking after on a full-time basis. Full time," he qualified, "outside surgery hours, emergency calls, hospital visits, and a week-long spur-of-the-moment trip to the Edinburgh Festival. Fortunately, these days she has a partner, so one sees rather more of her. Of course the telephone still rings at three in the morning, and off she goes to see to someone's granny who's fallen off the loo." He chuckled at this.

The housekeeper, Anne, offered cups of coffee. Then she positioned the trolley for easy access and went out. Leigh lit another cigarette and tried to picture her stepmother in a white coat with a stethoscope around her neck. It was a fairly glamorous image, but one with a lot of appeal. Those hands were a significant clue, after all. Leigh would never in a hundred years have guessed Delia's profession.

"I don't suppose you could come stay with us for a few days?" Delia asked, her hand on Leigh's arm.

"I'm afraid I have to get back to New York," Leigh lied, alarmed without knowing why at the prospect of a long visit.

"There's been a death in the family," her father explained solemnly. "Stanleigh's quite anxious to return."

"Oh, that is too bad," Delia said. "I'm sorry."

Leigh sipped her coffee, wishing she knew what to do, and why she'd lied. She was seated opposite her father, and the feeling she had was of watching an old film with actors who had been familiar to her once but who now seemed slightly mannered. There was this very beautiful blond woman sitting so close that Leigh could almost feel the woman's flesh closing around her. Under other circumstances, these two people would have seemed foreign in every way, but the fact was that the white-haired seventy-year-old retired farmer was her father. And the sweet-natured blonde was his clearly devoted wife, as well as Leigh's just-acquired stepmother. Her long-held view of this man was a concoction fabricated in part by her own time-tempered memories and in part by her mother's ongoing animosity. Both her view and her mother's animosity seemed unwarranted. Setting down her cup, Leigh put out her cigarette, guiltily aware that she'd fogged and contaminated the air of this charming house.

"I'll remember to ask Mother about the jewelry," she told her father, "and let you know. She did pawn some items when we first moved to New York. But I'm almost certain she redeemed them. If they were meant for me, she wouldn't have risked losing them. She's not at all irresponsible."

"One didn't mean to imply . . ."

"It's all right," Leigh cut in. "I know what you meant. It's very difficult," she said, looking to Delia for assistance. "I can't discuss her with you without feeling disloyal. She's been a wonderful mother . . . I mean she's silly and eccentric, and she often talks too much, but she's always

done her best for me. And whatever went wrong between the two of you
. . . well, it really didn't have anything—I don't think—to do with me. I
felt I had to see you, to know you before it was too late . . ."

"We quite understand," Delia came to her aid. "No need to explain, no
need at all. But if you should find your plans have changed, we'd very
much like to have you here. For as long as you'd care to stay."

"Why?" Leigh asked.

Delia looked momentarily startled by the question. Then she smiled
and said, "Because it's your home, after all."

"Oh!" Leigh exclaimed softly, then looked over to see her father nodding his agreement.

After lunch, her father embraced her, said, "Please do come back again
very soon, Stanleigh. It's been good, seeing you," then excused himself to
go upstairs for his lie-down.

Delia said, "Come chat with me for a few minutes before you go," and
led Leigh back to the sitting room, where she picked up a thick manila
envelope from the coffee table. "This is for you to look at at your lei-
sure," she said, giving the envelope to Leigh before sitting with her on
the long sofa. "I know it's been difficult for you, coming here today, but
it's meant such a lot to your father. I hope you'll forgive my saying so, but
you seem terribly angry. I realize that happens when there's the death of
someone close to you, but I can't help sensing there's more to it than that.
Please, don't be angry with Phil. Whatever went on between him and
your mother, it was a very very long time ago. And, as you said, it didn't
really have anything to do with you. You and I may never know what
actually happened. Time has a tendency to distort things, even to change
the way we believe certain events actually played themselves out. I know
it's affected you, but I think you're able to see for yourself what a good
man he is."

"I do see that," Leigh concurred. "And I know marriage can do strange
things to people. I know that from firsthand experience."

"Well, then." Delia smiled, relieved. "So long as you don't hold him
entirely responsible. And if I may offer one small piece of advice, go
gently on your mother. In all likelihood neither one of them is the same
person they were thirty-odd years ago."

"I *am* angry." Leigh was mildly taken aback by the woman's astute-
ness. "Is it that obvious?"

Delia smiled. "There's no harm to being angry. And I quite like angry
people. They have such exceptional energy. I do wish we were going to
see more of you. I would like to get to know you better."

"I'll come back," Leigh promised.

"Good," Delia said decisively. "Good!"

Eight

I
T WAS ONE OF THE VERY INFREQUENT OCCASIONS WHEN HE FLEW IN A
fairly direct line: from London to Hong Kong, from Hong Kong to Bangkok, and from Bangkok to Chiang Mai. He used his stopover hours in
Hong Kong to arrange for his usual interpreter and driver in Chiang Mai,
and they were there waiting when his Thai Air flight landed. A quick stop
to deposit his luggage in his room at the Orchid, and then he was off in
the air-conditioned car to make his visits to Sankamphaeng and Bor Sang.
An hour at each factory to accept the politely offered fruit juice while he
examined the silks and cottons, the paper umbrellas and fans, the lac-
querware and teak carvings, the silver and brassware. He ordered brass
boxes with enameled tops or inset with mother-of-pearl; he ordered sets
of brass cutlery and ornamental spoons; he ordered legions of small,
carved wood elephants, and black lacquered boxes with intricately
painted floral designs in a variety of shapes and sizes; he ordered bolts of
densely woven silk, as well as silk-covered wallets, picture frames, and
notebooks; he ordered the wonderfully smooth boxes whose tops were
decorated with fragments of brown and white eggshell painstakingly set
piece by piece in free-form patterns; he ordered fans and umbrellas of all
sizes, and silver bangles by the gross. He did it all in the space of six hours
on the first day, and another five on the second. He was driven from place
to place through the lush countryside, absently noticing lines of religious
men walking single file along the road in their gauzy saffron-colored
robes, and black-clad women in their oddly shaped straw hats working on
a construction site, and young people driving recklessly everywhere on
their omnipresent motorcycles. He gazed through the car window at the
vast rice paddies, at the astonishing temples—wats—some in ruins, some

intact. It all flew past the car windows, somehow both familiar and first-time new. By the evening of the second day, having spent a restless night in his room at the Orchid, he was at the airport to catch a flight back to Hong Kong.

Once in Hong Kong, installed in a large room at the Peninsula—having gone through the ritual of accepting the welcoming bottle of champagne, the bowl of exotic fruits, the pot of tea; having selected the soap of his preference from the cart wheeled in by one of the bellboys—he was annoyed with himself for leaving Thailand in such a hurry. What he should have done, he told himself, was to spend several days at the Oriental in Bangkok. He thought longingly of the superb hotel and its spectacular view of the river. Dumb. He should have gone there. He could have seen again the Emerald Buddha and the Grand Palace; he could have gone on one of the motor launch cruises down the river to the Floating Market, or to the ruins at Ayutthaya. There were endless wats all over the city he hadn't yet seen, and stores he'd never investigated, strange foods in the street stalls he hadn't tasted. But he'd come hurrying back to Hong Kong as if there were something waiting for him here and, of course, there was nothing.

He'd go out and do some shopping. He wanted a Mont Blanc pen, and he'd find some new electronic gizmo for Lane, and some jewelry, do a little leisurely wheeling and dealing. The best part of shopping in Hong Kong was the bargaining, minidramas in which the vendor played his part with absolute conviction and credible rue at being bested on his price.

He drank some of the green tea, then lit a cigarette and wondered if many people had killed themselves in this hotel. It seemed an improbable place for a suicide. Too many people ringing your doorbell, popping in and out to bring fresh flowers, more hot tea, this-that-and-the-other. He thought of Celeste as he'd last seen her, and immediately sat up to hold aside the curtains and look out at the street, thick with people all with destinations. He looked again at the room and knew he had to get out of there.

He turned right out of the hotel and walked along Salisbury Road, headed toward the harbor and the immense indoor shopping precinct at the Ocean Terminal. He liked Hong Kong, had always enjoyed the multinational crowds, the ceaseless traffic, the countless shops, the tidy good looks of the Chinese, and the music of their unexpected laughter.

Instead of going directly inside to look at the dozens of elegant shops, he went up to the roof of the outdoor parking garage atop the terminal and stood first on one side by the wall and then on the other, gazing at the ultramodern skyline, and at the many ships in the harbor. It was a fantastic city, jammed with people; clothes drying on poles outside the windows of high-rise buildings; double-decker trams zipping along on the Hong

Kong side; cars rushing back and forth between Kowloon and Hong Kong. And over in Aberdeen—he'd gone there only once out of curiosity — there were thousands of people living on junks that looked pretty picturesque until you got close enough to see and smell the sea of garbage in which they floated. The smell was revolting. Dogs and cats sunned themselves or prowled the decks; lines of laundry and people playing mahjongg. The stench had overcome his curiosity, and he'd left there bothered by the difference between the look of the place from a distance and the upclose decay.

He didn't go into the terminal after all, but retraced his steps to Nathan Road where the crowds were even thicker and the sky was filling with neon as the afternoon faded. The signs themselves were art; hundreds of multicolored invitations to buy, to eat, to come look, to see and hear and smell the ceaseless motion of the city. He felt better, and wandered down narrow passages to look into out-of-the-way stalls and tiny shops offering everything from expert instant tailoring to antiques and calculators and cameras and jade and diamonds; anything conceivable. Gold and ivory and pearls; perfume and stereo equipment and Swiss watches. Kowloon was one gigantic shopping center; you could overdose on it.

He bargained in six different shops for the Mont Blanc Diplomat, and finally returned to the first shop to tell the proprietor of the last, best offer, allowing the man to perform his bit of theater as he shook his head, gazed balefully at his merchandise, then with an expression of disgust, said, "Ninety U.S. dollars," and looked as if he'd weep as the words left his mouth. "Cash only," he added.

Dan said, "Sold," and pulled out his money while the proprietor now smiled as he lovingly polished the pen, showed Dan the guarantee papers, then returned the pen to its box and slid it into a padded silk bag. Only then did he accept Dan's money, and write up a receipt.

Farther along the road, Dan sat down with the owner of a jewelry store, accepted the man's offer of a soft drink, and then looked at the ropes of unstrung pearls, the gold chains, the diamonds—set and unset—and the earrings. At a leisurely pace, Dan studied the merchandise before deciding he liked a handmade, unusually set diamond pendant. It was far too sophisticated for Lane, and not something his mother would wear. But he could clearly see himself giving it to Leigh. He could see it so clearly that he began to bargain in earnest for the piece. It was serious haggling, with the owner asking twenty-two hundred American, and Dan coming in at six hundred, an offer that caused the man to reevaluate his initial impression of Dan as another malleable tourist. In the end, they agreed on nine hundred, with the owner providing an appraisal showing the true retail value at just under three thousand dollars. Dan did only token haggling for a fine strand of pale pink pearls for Lane and a seed-pearl choker with an ornate gold clasp for his mother.

When he emerged from the shop it was almost seven and he was hungry. He debated whether to continue shopping for something for his father or to eat. He was too hungry. He'd give his father the pen, and that would solve that problem.

There was a restaurant nearby that he knew from previous visits, and he had a sudden craving for a good Szechwan meal. He worked his way through smoked duck marinated in rice wine and ginger, with crisp rice and many small cups of tea.

By the time he got back to the Peninsula, pleased with his purchases and sated with food, he was ready to try for some sleep. He sat on the side of the bed for a time, examining the pendant. The fact that he'd bought it had to mean he'd see Leigh again. He had enough information to go on. It shouldn't, he thought, be too difficult to find her.

The day was sunny but very cold, and she was glad of the mink as she headed toward the park carrying the package Delia had given her. She still felt drained from her visit with her father the afternoon before, and thought it remarkable that so momentous an occasion had been treated by all of them—on the surface, at least—so quietly, so very socially. They'd all been so damnably British, restrained and polite; very little emotion on display. It had been most civilized, but with undercurrents of not readily identifiable feelings. She knew well enough what she had felt, but she couldn't have begun to state for certain that her father or Delia had felt this or that specifically. It was, she told herself, probably because nothing whatever seemed clear just then. Her feelings were so subject to instant change, so wildly unpredictable, and so extreme, that things she might have found amusing at another time now grieved her.

Seated on the same bench where she'd sat sketching two days earlier, she pushed her hands deep into her pockets as she surveyed the area. Then, turning, she looked behind her at the busy street a few hundred feet away. She did love this city. There was a feeling she had in London that she never had anywhere else. It had to do with the narrow streets, and the monstrously snarled traffic, the double-decker London Reds, the entrances to the undergrounds with their steep escalators, the venerable old shops—and the sense, above all, that rightfully she belonged here. She was of this country; trace elements of its dirt and grandeur and nobility resided in her cells. She was not foreign here as she was everywhere else in the world; this place had been home to her parents and their parents, on and on, back into time. This rambling, architectural surprise package of a city was a part of the heritage she could claim along with her dual citizenship, whatever remained of her accent, her philosophical regard for dismal weather, and her last-gasp sense of humor. Maybe she'd just stay here, she thought, picturing herself installed in a cozy flat somewhere, with a telephone that gave off double rings; picturing herself out to do the marketing with a basket slung over one arm and a scarf to guard her head from the rain; picturing herself climbing into her car at the weekends to drive up to see her father and stepmother. She'd have a coal fire and a cat, and potted plants lining her windowsills. She'd have chilblains, bronchitis, and rheumatoid arthritis. She'd die without central heating; she was allergic to cat hair; and she was a notorious killer of houseplants. So much for that.

She lit a cigarette, then opened the package. It was filled with letters. Across the front of each one, in her mother's hand, was written "Return to sender." They were in date order, all still sealed. She held the rubber-banded packet, profoundly upset by this proof of the small crime her mother had committed against her. She knew that once she opened and read these letters she was going to have to go directly back to New York, because she would be in need of a firsthand explanation from her mother as to why she'd deprived her in such cruel fashion of her father's influence, her father's company, her father's affection.

In advance of the event, she could see and hear herself shrieking at her mother; could see her mother pulling back. Perhaps it would be best to leave it alone, not open these envelopes and see the evidence of a caring she'd been led to believe didn't exist. "Why the hell did you do it?" she could hear herself demanding of her mother. "What right did you have to do that to me, or to him?"

The cigarette tasted foul. She took a last puff, then dropped it on the ground and stepped on it. When she'd come here before, she'd sketched Daniel from memory. He seemed to have been a part of her life for far longer than just a few days. He stood very clearly in her mind; she could see and hear him; she knew his facial expressions and certain habitual gestures he made; she knew the ways in which he made love and the feel of his body under her hands; she knew the sound of his voice and the faint, underlying foreign lilt to his Americanized accent. If she'd asked him to stay on, he'd have done it. Overall, she'd enjoyed his company; she'd liked bantering and arguing with him; she'd liked the look and feel of him. She was right: he represented a complication. Cardinal rule: never become involved with married men. Yet nothing about him suggested the usual guilt and deviousness of a married man. She was aware of the signs and signals. No, this was best. Still, she had to laugh recalling his line about "Strangers in the Night." And there had been that moment when, after they'd made love a second time, they'd stared at each other and then burst out laughing. He'd made her laugh. It seemed noteworthy.

She found her reading glasses—she hated them, convinced they were proof of her decline into old age, and so rarely wore them—put them on and, using her nail file, slit open the first of the envelopes.

It was a voyage back in time, one that took her through the ages of fifteen to twenty-six. Some of the letters contained checks, birthday and Christmas gifts. Undramatic, newsy letters, they represented too many years of thwarted caring. Never once did he make any negative reference to her mother; never once did he express any of the frustration and anger he must have felt. He simply said he hoped she'd receive this particular letter, and that he looked forward to seeing her at any time she'd care to return home for a visit. And if finances were a problem, he'd be more than happy to wire funds. The very simplicity of his declarations undid her. She sat and wept, feeling betrayed by the one person she'd most loved and admired, unable to comprehend her mother's motives. The woman had deprived Stephen of his grandfather, of visits to that great, echoey house and the acres of farmland with the stream he might have fished in the company of his grandfather. And Joel. God! Joel would have gone mad for every bit of it. He'd have checked the plants for spider mites; he'd have admired Delia's decorating; he'd have been out in the kitchen whipping up special tidbits for afternoon tea; he'd have had everyone laughing with his Ethel Merman routines. All the visits that had never taken place; all the emotions that had never known a proper outlet; all the seasons missed. She could only be glad her mother wasn't with her just then, because her rage had murderous proportions.

She put away her glasses, found a tissue to dry her eyes, lit a cigarette, and gave thought to what she wanted to do. It was all fine and good getting from one hour to the next, one day to the next, but she couldn't continue on indefinitely that way. She had too much curiosity left about life, and too much anger—as Delia had so accurately pointed out—to give up and die. So, she was going to have to begin living her life again. But she couldn't merely kill time in the city during the week, then kill more time in the country at the weekends. She had to *do* something. Perhaps Miles would have some suggestions. He was forever calling up with ideas that had popped into his head. Maybe, for once, she'd encourage him.

God damn it! she swore silently, shifting again to look at the city behind her. She wanted to hang on to her anger, yet well in advance of a showdown, she knew her mother would have any number of reasons for what she'd done. And already, a lifetime of actively loving the woman was killing off her anger with her. It was ridiculous. Forty-five years of a life lived with the most dreadful, tenacious optimism. She felt like some uncommon, ridiculous creature, something like a pack rat that hoarded and scrounged, saving up bits and pieces for no discernible reason. Except that in her case the bits and pieces she collected and tucked away all had to do with emotion, and with using those emotions—filips of varicolored feeling—like set dressing. She'd spent her entire adult life attempting to adorn the invisible walls of her existence with portraits of the people she'd loved who'd loved her, as if this documentation could validate an otherwise meaningless era. Plain white cotton she'd turned into embossed brocade by collecting love and weaving it into the fabric spooling off the loom of her life. And what frightened her, now that Joel was gone, was her doubtful ability to find something to substitute for the caring she could never have again. The people she had loved had died, and she was left with big empty spaces all around her that she didn't know how to fill.

Maybe her mother had been right all along in saying how dangerous was her capacity for caring. Getting through the days would have been so much easier without the emotional excess baggage. But how the hell did you stop caring, stop wanting to care? She was such a bloody optimist she even had hopes for some man she'd gone to bed with who was not only married to someone else but who didn't even know her telephone number. What kind of stupidity was that?

And there it was, already happening: She'd shifted her anger from her mother to herself without missing a beat. It wasn't what she wanted. What she wanted was . . . what? *I want my sons back!* she shrilled in mute protest. *I want to keep the love alive.* To lose one son once, all right; it happened. But to lose two! The gross unfairness of it, and now the proof of what her mother had done, had her weeping again. She wasn't sorry she'd made this little pilgrimage. She wished she'd never made the trip. Anger, grief, anger, alternating, taking her up and down, back and forth, like some bizarre circus ride. She jumped up to hurry back to the hotel. She was going to get on the first available flight to New York, to see her mother.

Flying home, Dan berated himself for placing so much importance on a chance meeting, a chance bedding, with this woman. Why was he so bent on pushing the thing beyond its imposed limitations? Buying an expensive gift with the vague notion of tracking her down to give it to her; in the giving, he'd prove the sincerity of his intentions. Crap! All it would prove was his interest. The lies had put him in a no-win situation. It was where he'd thought he wanted to be. Now he wasn't so sure of that. How could he be sure—of anything—when unbidden images of the woman kept insinuating themselves into his consciousness? The images he had of her were so potent, so commanding. All he had to do was half-lower his eyelids, and there was a picture of her, standing in front of him with her shell-shocked eyes and her startled expression as he touched her. What she couldn't have known, of course, was the strangeness he'd felt at discovering this new flesh, so dissimilar to Celeste's. Celeste's bones had hidden themselves beneath overfolding layers of doughy rolls. It had seemed as if her skeleton had been growing smaller while the density of her flesh had been increasing. But Leigh. He'd instantly achieved a sense of the entire woman because of her physical composition, because of the bones lying just beneath the surface of age-softened skin still adhering tightly to its frame. He'd been awed by the delicate weight of her breasts, and the rapacity with which she'd accepted him. And it hadn't been merely a physical acceptance; it had been her emotional appetite to which he'd responded most. Because she'd been right: It wasn't hard to find women. You could find them anywhere you looked. But how often did you come across a woman who could laugh and argue; who was completely her own person and yet, mysteriously, heart-stoppingly, gave access? He admired her talent and her success; he admired her. And she'd removed her clothes, allowed him to see and touch and taste her. Christ! It excited him simply thinking about her.

While he killed time in the San Francisco airport, waiting for his United connection back to New York, he wondered again what he was doing. Those images of Stanleigh Dunn alternated with an image of Celeste as she'd been the last time he'd seen her. It was as if his recall of these two, so different women was doing battle against itself. Right there in the middle of the airport, he felt like breaking down. He didn't want to go back to Bedford; he didn't want to think he was *going back*, and had to keep telling himself there *was no* going back. But prove that to his brain! Convince his memory of that! Impossible! And here he'd paid duty on a diamond pendant he was determined to give to Leigh. Goddamned perverse, going through so much crap with a gift for a woman whose address he didn't even know. To find her, he was going to have to play detective. Or, he could save himself the trouble and just give the damned thing to Lane, or to his mother, and to hell with its lack of suitability. That's what he'd do, all right. He didn't have the time or energy to track down a woman who'd likely be furious—if and when he did find her—not only at having her privacy invaded but at his having disregarded her wishes. They'd agreed they wouldn't meet again, but he was spending half his time planning how he'd find her and the other half pissed off with himself because of the first half.

He was so wrought up over the whole stupid business that he actually arrived in New York having paid no attention to the flight. He'd flown three thousand miles in so preoccupied a state that he hadn't bothered to be afraid. And realizing this as he waited to claim his baggage, he wanted to call Leigh up and say, Look what you've done! I was so busy thinking about you, caring about you, that I forgot to be afraid. He wanted to call her up and say, Listen! I fell in love with you and it's not something I do every day of the week, it isn't even something I've done before, never mind every day, so let's not argue about it. Just see me, talk to me, come to bed with me, and to hell with everything, everyone else. The Good Doctor can go fly; the whole world can take a hike, just don't hang up, okay? Don't hang up.

Christ! He looked around at the other people waiting for their bags to come off the carousel, grateful that thoughts didn't show, that no one could tell he'd really gone over the edge, was into it up to his goddamned neck because he'd sat next to a woman on an airplane who not only happened to be famous but who, a few hours later, had been willing to undress and let him fall into her as if she was the atmosphere and he a sky-diver.

Nine

LEIGH LET HERSELF INTO HER MOTHER'S APARTMENT WITH HER OWN KEY, and walked through looking for her mother. Pausing in the living room, she saw two half-finished drinks sitting in wet rings on the glass coffee table. If her mother had gone out, Leigh didn't know what she'd do with the immense parcel of anger she'd brought along here with her. Continuing on down the hall, she arrived at her mother's bedroom. The open doorway, like a picture frame, contained the image of her mother, nude, sitting astride Laurence whose hands were fastened to her breasts.

Leigh leaped out of the doorway and sagged against the wall, whispering, *"Jesus!"*

The two in the bedroom continued their slow ride, unaware of anything but each other. Leigh couldn't stand it. From just outside the door, she said loudly, "Ask Laurence to leave, please. I want to talk to you!"

Startled sounds from the bedroom, frantic murmurings. Leigh listened for a few seconds before stalking shaky-legged back to the living room to wait, trying to steady her breathing.

Marietta appeared in a silk peignoir two or three minutes later. Six thirty-five in the evening and here she was, damp at the hairline from her activities, flushed in the face and chest, in a peignoir, of all things.

"You really must ask him to put his clothes on and go," Leigh said. "You and I have some matters to discuss."

"What on earth do you think you're . . . ?"

"If you don't mind having him listen in on our conversation, that's fine with me! I need a drink." Leigh marched over to the built-in bar in the far corner of the room and snatched up a bottle of Chivas, the nearest thing to hand. She could feel her mother's eyes boring into her spine, could sense Marietta's deliberating.

"I will be back in a moment," Marietta said stiffly, and Leigh turned to see her sweep away, the peignoir flowing around her like water.

"Love in the goddamned afternoon," Leigh muttered, turning back to the neat Scotch she was pouring into her glass. A swallow, the acid burn, and then, fortified, she threw off her coat, dropped her bag on top of it, and positioned herself in the middle of the room, holding the glass with both hands. "Jesus!" she whispered again, seriously rattled at having caught her mother at the apex of a sexual encounter, telling herself she should have had the doorman ring upstairs to warn Marietta she was on her way up. But who would have thought she'd be engaged in pre-dinner lovemaking?

Five minutes and Laurence came through, paused to collect his coat from the foyer closet and, without a word either to Leigh or Marietta, let himself out.

Her features still flushed, Marietta returned to stand in the living room archway, keeping the peignoir closed with both hands. Striving to maintain self-control, she said, "I am prepared to take into consideration the tremendous strain you've been under recently, but barging in here unannounced to start issuing orders is positively unforgivable. How dare you . . . ?"

"Oh, shut up, Mother," Leigh sighed. "The affronted duchess routine's not going to wash. I want to talk to you. Don't you think you should put on something sensible, like a dress? My God! I always wondered who bought that stuff. I never dreamed it could be my own mother. You look like something Tennessee Williams wrote on an off day." With every nasty word she spoke, she could feel a mounting dismay and guilt at her terrible disrespect; she could also see clearly the effect this was having on her mother. And despite the justification she'd felt upon arriving here, she didn't understand why she was behaving as hatefully as she was. But she'd seen her mother engaged in a sexual act, and the recollection of what she'd seen made her quake. She wanted to scream; she also wanted to heed the inner voice that was insisting it was most unfair of her to carry on this way when her mother had no idea of the reasons why. And on top of all that, the sheer physical presence of the woman was, as ever, monumentally distracting.

Marietta's looks had always managed to sidetrack Leigh, sometimes to Leigh's extreme disadvantage. Because she was an artist both by training and disposition, the way someone looked, the way he or she fit into his or her environment, was an integral part of Leigh's overall vision. She couldn't merely absorb people and settings into her awareness, she had to analyze and dissect those people and settings, breaking them down into their component elements to see how well or badly everything fit. Leigh found her mother alarmingly close to perfect. It was hard to be at odds with someone who so pleased her visual and esthetic senses. Marietta was a Botticelli woman, tall and angular but with surprising voluptuousness. Her skin was so opaline and her hair such a fiery shade of red; her eyes were so large and of such a rare emerald hue; her neck was so long and delicate, supporting the aristocratic sculpting of her well-shaped head; her shoulders were so wide and her waist so narrow; her breasts so fully symmetrical and her hips so tautly inviting that, altogether, even in her mid-sixties, she could literally stop pedestrian traffic. She had been so magnificently created, from top to bottom, that she'd never in her life worn makeup or had to have anything more done to her hair than a regular trim. And her hair was as rich and red now as it had been at age twelve. Her eyes were as clear and revealing as undoubtedly they'd been the day they'd first opened to the air. Her skin was that of a woman half her age. Leigh had believed for a very long time that she'd have been far less critical of her own self had she had someone less blessed, less physically prepossessing as a mother. She'd never been able to accept anyone's compliments on her appearance because she knew she was merely an inadequate, less vivid, copy of the original.

A mother, for example, who'd had a blemish or two during her own adolescent years might not have been quite so vocally horrified when, at age fourteen, Leigh had developed acne. A mother, for example, who as a teenager had spent a few weekend nights at home alone might have been less impatient, more tolerant of the countless Saturday nights Leigh had spent moping about the apartment, praying for the miraculous advent into her life of an admiring teenage male. A mother, for example, who'd had a less than thrilling sexual life might have been more understanding of a daughter who'd confessed, addled with letdown and apprehension, to surrendering to her curiosity one night on the sofa in the living room of the family apartment on Seventy-third Street of a nineteen-year-old boy whom she'd seen only that once and who had never called again. "It is not the end of the world," Marietta had calmly told the then sixteen-year-old Leigh. "Everyone must begin somewhere." It hadn't been what Leigh had wanted to hear; she'd hoped for words of encouragement, reassurance that the future would be brighter and better.

Now here was Marietta holding closed her pale yellow peignoir with a fair, freckled hand, the fabric rising and falling to the cadence of the heaving breasts beneath. Here was the still ravishing Marietta, purveyor of romantic fiction and frequent speaker at conventions of giddy women, with her hair spilling over her shoulders and her bare toes curling into the carpet; Marietta with her ageless face wearing an expression of deep consternation.

"You're a bloody painting!" Leigh cried with reluctant admiration, already halfway undone simply by the sight of her mother. "Why couldn't you have wrinkles and gray hair like other mothers? *I* look older than you do, for chrissake!"

"Is that what this is about?" Marietta asked, a throb in her voice. "You've come here to embarrass me, to rant at me because I don't look like other mothers?"

"No," Leigh conceded, then tossed down the last of the Scotch. "I went to see him," she said, gripping the empty glass as if it offered warmth.

"And he told you scores of sordid tales about me, no doubt, all of which you believe now to be true because you've come pushing in here and discovered me in damning circumstances." The reference to what they both knew she'd seen caused the color to flood upward from Marietta's chest into her neck and face. Leigh thought she looked as if she might actually burst into flames.

"Truthfully, when he spoke of you at all, it was without rancor." She glared at her mother, feeling that morning's reactions gushing back up into her throat. "Why did you return his letters?" she cried. "How could you do that? They were mine. You had no right . . . to let me go all those years thinking he didn't care. He was . . . very dear . . . he was . . . oh, damn!" She was succumbing to tears and couldn't stop herself. "I don't know if I can forgive you!" she got out, choking. "I'd like to know what you thought you were doing, depriving me of my father, deciding for me that he had no place in my life. And what about the jewels? I hope for your sake you still have them. And why, if you *do* still have them, haven't you given them to me? You knew they were intended to be mine.

"God, I wish I could let it all go, just give up and go crazy. Have you any idea how many times I've wished I'd lose my mind so I wouldn't have to be responsible, conscious and responsible, all the goddamned time?" In a plaintive tone, she asked again, *"Why* did you do it?"

Marietta had stopped clutching at the sides of her fussy robe and wrapped her arms around herself. "I knew there'd be trouble if you went to see him," she said recriminatingly. "I *asked* you not to go."

"Tell me why!" Leigh insisted. "This is not the time to play the silly, helpless female."

Marietta's head tilted back and she looked up at the ceiling. The move accentuated the long line of her milky throat, and Leigh understood anew why men lined up for days for the chance to go out to dinner, or to the theater, or into the bedroom, with this woman. It didn't even really matter what she said, or how silly she could often make herself appear. Just to be in her company, to be free to watch her eyes, or to see her smile take form, was something of a privilege.

"I should hate," she said slowly, eyes still on the ceiling, "to think we would find ourselves at permanent odds because of your impulsive decision to go see your father. I should truly hate that."

"Then answer me," Leigh pleaded. "Can't you see I've finally managed to get myself right to the edge? Can't you see that? Maybe I think I'd like to fall into it, just go mad once and for all, but for some reason I keep fighting it, even when the last thing I *want* is to fight it. Can you *see* that?"

Marietta dropped her head and directed her eyes at her daughter. "I can see it," she responded in a tone that signified Leigh had managed to get through to her. "I see far more than you think."

"It's all going to go down the toilet if you don't give me answers. And I'd hate it to happen as much as you. Why? Just tell me why. All I want is to hear your side of it."

"I've never *been* so humiliated!" Marietta railed. "Couldn't you have had the good grace to pretend you hadn't seen? Did you *have* to stand right at the door and begin bellowing? I may be your mother, but I deserve as much respect and privacy as anyone else." The color in her face was growing darker. "You break into my home filled with indignation over events that happened thirty years ago, and begin making demands. Perhaps you've already gone mad. You're behaving as if you have." Her arms reflexively tightened around herself, as if in an effort to hold herself together. "How hateful of you!" she declared. Her eyes filling, she glared a moment longer at Leigh, then crossed the room to slide into an armchair, tucking her feet up under her.

Leigh followed, to stand directly over her so that Marietta had to lean back to look up at her. "One straight answer," Leigh said. "That's all I want."

"Don't hang over me!" Marietta ordered. "I refuse to allow you to bully me in my own home." Putting her hand on Leigh's hip, she gave her a push. "Sit down and try to be rational!"

As Leigh backed away, her mother bent her head into her hand, covering her eyes. Seeing this, Leigh had a moment of panic, believing she'd gone too far. Then, straightening, her mother looked again at her. "He never displayed any affection for you," she said brusquely. "He had no time for either one of us. Whatever it was he felt, he managed to keep it entirely to himself. And when the three of us were together, he seemed to think he had to vie with you for my attention. It was dreadful. I tried many times to make him see, but he wouldn't, or couldn't. Who cares, at this point? I spent thirteen years with him on that godforsaken bloody farm; thirteen years of either being taken completely for granted, or being taken at his whim. At the end, I felt like one of the dairy cows, something he could milk, or straddle, when the mood took him. Don't look shocked! You asked. I'm *telling* you. He saw either one of us only when it suited him, regardless of how much we clamored for his attention. Then, suddenly, after I'd brought you here, he wanted to be your father. I believed he'd forfeited that right.

"You've been deprived of nothing. No one prevented you from contacting him. You could have been in touch with him at any time over the years. You chose not to."

"How could I?" Leigh wanted to know. "How could I when all you've done since the day we came to this country has been to tell me what a worthless joke he was? You killed off any interest or desire I might have had in contacting him. I believed you," she said mournfully. "I believed you, and you were wrong. He did care about me. And obviously he's capable of showing affection, or he wouldn't have the wife he does. He's been married for the last twenty-six years."

She flung this fact into the air like an arrow and saw it hit home.

A moment of widened eyes, parted lips, then Marietta regained herself. "People change," she said.

Leigh went to the bar to pour more Scotch into her glass. She hated whiskey, didn't even know why she was drinking it.

"Don't overdo it," her mother said. "I'm not up to dealing with you inebriated."

"You make it sound as if I drink too much regularly," Leigh countered, replacing the bottle top before lifting her replenished glass. "Unfortunately, I'm not any better at being a drunk than I am at going crazy."

"I loathe self-indulgence," Marietta said. "You're alive and healthy. You have a successful career, when you care to work at it. I know Joel's death has been a great blow, but . . ."

"Don't bring side issues into this," Leigh cut her off. "We both know I've seen better days. I need you to give me a reason not to hate you."

That had the desired effect. Marietta looked so stricken that Leigh's guilt instantly trebled.

"Nothing I've done warrants that," Marietta said, her composure cracking. "I returned a dozen or so letters. Not such a terrible thing, really."

"*I think it is!* I think it was a monstrous thing to do. You *know* I'm not like you, not fabulously self-contained like a Fabergé egg."

Another silence. Then, to her horror, Leigh saw tears begin to slide down her mother's cheeks. "Whatever I am," Marietta protested, deeply wounded, "it's more than mere decoration. How cruel you're being! How horribly unkind!"

"*You* were cruel and unkind, returning those letters."

"Give me one of your filthy cigarettes!" Marietta flung out her hand.

Leigh opened her bag, found the pack, and tossed it over. Then she watched her mother pick up the table lighter, knowing she'd traded hurt for hurt. Her mother smoked only when the stress of a given situation was mounting to intolerable proportions. She lit the cigarette now and inhaled deeply, turning her profile to Leigh as she looked over at the fireplace, tears still sliding down her cheeks.

"You would like to believe that having Philip in your life would have altered events. But you're wrong," she insisted, "completely wrong."

"And what about the men," Leigh pushed on, "the one in London you thought would marry you, and the others?"

Marietta's response took the form of furious laughter. "Is *that* what he told you? How bloody predictable! He couldn't make me happy so there had to be other men in the picture. There *were* no other men. People talked because I escaped for weekends in London. Rumors. There was one man before I married Philip, and none after until I came here. The two of you can't turn me into a trollop just because he failed as a husband and father, and because you've been foolish enough to be intimidated by what you see when you look at me. You've always been duped by the *look* of things. You've spent your whole life in a state of fascination with *appearances*, and *surfaces*, *veneer*. I can't help the way I look. And why you should feel inferior, God only knows. You're a very handsome woman; you've got style and appeal. How you view yourself has nothing at all to do with me, and I will *not* be blamed for things that are beyond my control! I wanted to be free of that man, and I wanted you to grow up without feeling torn between your parents. I wanted my own life. I gambled, and I won. I made a decision to restrict your contact with your father. He was a parent in name only who rarely, if ever, contributed to your upbringing.

"As for my scandalous behavior, it's a fiction. I took up men, on my terms, when I was well into my thirties and had no need of them financially." She took a final puff on the cigarette, then leaned forward to stub it out in the ashtray, the movement revealing to her daughter her bare breasts under the robe. "Why are you doing this, to either of us? I'd have discussed the matter with you at any time, but you never chose to ask. Joel died, and you went off to see that pathetic farmer. Then you come flying back here to make scenes, heaving accusations like crockery. Thirteen years is a very long time to try to make a go of a bad marriage. As you, better than most, should know. Everything I've done here has been with definite ideas in mind. And I rather enjoy being silly. If one is a silly woman, one doesn't have to contend with male competition. I like men well enough, but not so well that I'd be willing, ever, to repeat the experiences I had with your father." She brought her legs out from under her, and sat very erect. "I am well aware you consider me frivolous and essentially lightweight, but I've always been available to you when you needed me. I even, if you will recall, only recently attended to the details of a *funeral service* because you were unable to deal with it. I also loved Joel, but that's not relevant. If I am unlike 'other people's mothers' it is by choice. I've never had any great desire to be like other people. And I cannot for the life of me think why, given your most unique attributes, you'd aspire to be anything but yourself. Excuse me just a moment," she said, and got up and left the room.

Leigh remained where she'd been standing, holding the drink in one hand, and wiping her eyes with the back of the other. She'd been given the truth, which is what she'd demanded. But she'd said and done things she knew were all but unforgivable. She'd made a complete mess of everything.

Her mother returned carrying a small wooden box. "I believe you want this," she said, her words rimed with frost as she placed the box on the coffee table. "I've been intending for some time to give it to you but the occasion somehow didn't present itself. And then, quite simply, I forgot. I apologize for that. As for the rest, you have no legitimate complaints," she said, her arms once more winding themselves around her. "You've been deprived of nothing, nothing. I am too angry to spend any more time with you now, Stanleigh. When things go wrong—as inevitably they do, in everyone's life—you do dangerous, dreadful things. If you're not rushing headlong into marriage with some totally inappropriate buffoon, if you're not sleeping with strangers in between times, then life has no meaning for you because for reasons known only to you, talent and intelligence and good looks aren't enough. To you, Nirvana is a nervous breakdown. And, invariably, after you've done something especially dangerous, you come round here longing for madness. For someone of your considerable intelligence, it's ludicrous. I've always accepted your eccentricities; I've even found many of them charming. But when you invade my privacy, and try to shame me for being merely human after all, you go too bloody far. It's all too obvious you've done it again. You did have a man with you in your hotel room when you rang me. I wish to God you had some equanimity about your sexuality, not to mention some discretion. Don't you think you're getting rather too old for picking up strangers? I think I might prefer it if you did go mad. I suspect it would be a good deal less expensive emotionally for all concerned. I want you to leave now. I've had more than enough of you for one evening. I love you, Stanleigh, but I think all your sleeping with fools has managed to turn you into one." She turned away, then turned back. "And don't forget the family heirlooms," she added caustically. She waited as Leigh put down the glass, collected her coat and bag, picked up the box from the table, and then came across the room. "Don't say another word to me!" Marietta warned. "I am deeply sorry Joel died. He was a lovely young man, and I shall miss him. I am sorry if you feel you lost out on some fairy-tale friendship with your father, and I am especially sorry you felt you had the right to do what you did here this evening, because it is the single most offensive thing you've ever done! We've each had our losses, but not all of us choose to strike out, as a result, at the people who care most for us. Go away now. I need to bathe."

Ten

LEIGH WAS SO ASHAMED OF HERSELF, SO FILLED WITH DISGUST FOR everything and everyone,that all she wanted was to get away and be completely alone. She stopped at the apartment long enough to transfer her bags from the taxi to her car; she dashed up from the garage to clear her mailbox, then returned down to the car, headed for the country.

The driving was fine until she was about halfway home on the Merritt. Snow blew in blinding gusts across the road, reducing what little traffic there was to a crawl. Hunched forward over the steering wheel, she strained to see the road ahead, dizzy with apprehension at the idea of rear-ending some vehicle she couldn't see.

By the time she found her exit, her head, neck, and shoulders were aching. The road conditions were only fractionally better as she headed across Route 124 to New Canaan. Everything was white; the snow reflected the headlights' glare. Her concentration was so intense she nearly continued on through town, but remembered in time that there was no food in the house. She found a deli that was still open, ran inside to buy a few basics, then hurried back out to the car, the wind cutting up inside her sleeves and down the back of her neck as she put the groceries in the trunk.

The driveway was close to a foot deep in snow. No one had come by to clear it. The house itself looked forlorn, alone and dark beneath an unblemished froth of snow. A run inside to turn on the lights and the furnace, then she battled the wind carrying in her luggage and the groceries. Just as she got the door closed the telephone rang, and she rushed to answer thinking it might be Marietta. But when she said hello, whoever was on the other end hung up.

The message light was blinking on the machine. She jabbed the PLAY button and, while she put the food away, listened to a lame explanation of why her driveway hadn't been plowed, followed by a solicitation from *TV Guide*, then three requests in succession from Miles's secretary asking her to call, four hang-ups, a prerecorded solicitation from an insurance company asking her to respond to the following three questions—she fast-forwarded the tape past this—two more requests please to call Miles, an inquiry from a local real estate company asking if she'd be interested in listing the house, another hang-up, and a final urgent request from Miles himself that she call him. She erased the tape, then called the apartment in the city with the remote control, retrieving the messages from that line. Six entreaties to call Miles, an Avon solicitation, three hang-ups. She used the remote to erase and reset that machine, then lugged her bags to the bedroom.

Outside, the wind pushed against the house, and she could hear it creating blow-backs in the fireplace. She'd gone off and forgotten to close the damper. As a result the house was drafty and cold but, luckily, no pipes had burst. Still in her coat, she sat down on the side of the bed and picked up the telephone extension. Marietta answered after the first ring, and Leigh said, "Don't hate me. I hate myself enough for both of us."

"That is not going to do it," Marietta said, enunciating slowly and carefully, as if addressing someone severely perceptually handicapped. "You've mortified me, not to mention Laurence."

"If it's any consolation, I've mortified myself."

"That is *not* a source of consolation. I don't think you need aspire to madness, Stanleigh. I do believe you've finally succeeded in achieving it. I think you're out of control, and if tonight is an example of where madness has taken you, I want no part of it. Just having this conversation with you is upsetting me all over again. I'm going to ring off now."

"You know I didn't really mean any of it," Leigh told her.

"You meant every last bit of it! You may be regretting it now, but you came here determined to create pain, and you did precisely what you set out to do." With that, her mother put down the receiver.

At once, Leigh called back.

Again, Marietta answered after the first ring. Without bothering to say hello, she said, "You're merely compounding the felony. Leave matters alone for now. Have some more to drink, go to bed, take a hot bath, ring Miles, but don't ring *me* again tonight."

"I do love you," Leigh said.

"The only reason I'm even considering speaking to you at some future date is because I believe that. Now, good-bye."

Leigh hung up, then folded in on herself on the bed and closed her eyes.

* * *

Dan simply couldn't make himself go to the Bedford house. He went instead to the apartment in the Village he'd rented six months before but had stayed at only half a dozen times. He wasn't appreciably happier in the city than he was in Bedford, but the apartment did have the advantage of being unknown to his family. He had an unlisted telephone there as well as a bed, a table, two chairs, an AM/FM radio/cassette player, and two lamps. The place was tiny, two small rooms, a kitchen and bathroom, but it did have a working fireplace, and the walls had been taken back to the brick. For these six hundred and twenty square feet of secret living space, he was shelling out thirteen hundred dollars a month. On one level it struck him as ridiculous that anyone should pay so much for so little. On another level he was completely unconcerned. It was only money, and so far money hadn't been able to do anything more than offer basic security and relieve him of the tension of earlier years when he'd worked ceaselessly to build up the business. Now the business was no longer his. He'd been rewarded with more money, and reduced to a glorified buyer. Thinking of that, he couldn't imagine why he'd told Leigh his mother had been a buyer for Bloomingdale's. It was such an absurd fabrication.

He threw his suitcases on the bed, then went to investigate the contents of the kitchen cabinets. Pretty well stocked. If he didn't care to, he wouldn't have to go outside this apartment for weeks. There were rows of cans lining the shelves, and even a big stock of booze.

He put a pot of water on the stove to boil for coffee, then went to get the Manhattan directory, looking first under Dunn, with an *e* and without, then under Jacobson, and finally under Dennison. Useless. Hundreds of listings. He had several Connecticut directories, and reached for the Stamford one, flipping through to the New Canaan listings—the town closest to Bedford—to check the three surnames. An S. Dennison on Crooked Creek. He noted the number, certain it was Leigh's. It sounded like her.

While he poured water through the coffee in the filter, he considered what would happen if he called that number. If she answered, what would he say? He'd hang up, not say anything. But he'd know where she was. Leaving the water to finish dripping, he dialed the number and listened to it ring. Someone elderly—he was unable to tell whether it was a male or female voice—answered, and Dan apologized for the wrong number. Berating himself, he went back to his coffee making.

Carrying a cup of the good, strong French roast, he went to sit down on the floor with his back against the wall to call his parents.

His mother answered in English, but upon hearing his voice switched at once to French, saying, "Daniel, we have been most concerned for you. Have you returned?"

"I'm in town. I got back about an hour ago."

"Is this the way we should anticipate it will be in the future?" she asked. "Do you intend to disappear and then reappear without warning? Lane has been most distraught, telephoning every evening after her classes. Have you any idea what it is you're doing, Daniel?"

"No," he answered honestly. "I can't say that I do."

"Ten days is too long to disappear when one is a parent with responsibilities."

"Lane's hardly an infant," he defended himself. "And I called her from London. She was supposed to tell you."

"She told us. But you only called after being gone four days, with no one knowing where you were. What is going on?" she asked, lowering her voice.

"I told you: I don't know. I went to Thailand, did the ordering. My last official act. I'm not used to having days with no office to go to, no work. I'm not Papa. I haven't retired to my chair and my books and my classical albums. That shouldn't be too difficult to understand."

"No one is accusing you of anything, Daniel," she reminded him. "It's just . . . you are not without options."

"I know, Mama. I just don't know if I want to exercise any of them."

"Are you remaining in the city, or will you be going to Bedford?"

"I'm giving serious thought to getting rid of that house."

"But where will you live? And Lane?"

Patiently, he said, "I'll buy something else, something smaller and more manageable. Maybe a condo. And Lane isn't home anymore, except during school breaks." Having to explain himself exasperated and wearied him.

"Will you talk to your father? He's insisting I give the telephone to him."

"Sure I'll talk to him." At once, he began gearing up to answer more questions.

"When will we see you?"

"How's tomorrow? I'll come for dinner."

"Good. Here's your father."

"Daniel," his father bellowed, "what is it you're doing? Could you explain it to me? Six months ago, I might have understood this, but now . . . ?" Typically, his father ran out of steam and words simultaneously.

"Am I supposed to be keeping to some kind of schedule, Papa?" he asked his father. "Is there a specific time allotted for specific acts and emotions?"

"No," his father backed down a bit. "That isn't what I mean. But you've never done anything like this before. Therefore you must expect we would be concerned. If you tell me all is well, I will accept that. All is well?"

"All is completely fucked up, Papa," Dan answered, feeling like a kid again, and out of his depths. "I can't go back to that house. I, um, I've got a place in town where I'm staying right now. Tomorrow or the next day, I intend to go up and list the house with a local broker. And maybe have a look around, while I'm at it, for something else. That's my first and only priority right now," he said. "Once that's taken care of, I'll have a look, see where I am."

"Have you spoken yet to Lane?"

"Not since I got back, no."

"Don't be upset, Daniel, but she decided she'd like to come with us to Palm Beach for the holidays. Of course," he added, "you know you are welcome to join us."

Dan covered the mouthpiece, turned his head aside, and swore.

"You are upset," his father guessed. "But there's no need. Come with us. We don't leave for another two weeks. That's enough time for you to make arrangements for the house."

"I'll think about it," Dan promised, "but I'm not in the mood for Florida."

"You may change your mind."

"I might. I'll see you tomorrow evening, Papa. I have to go now."

"Daniel," his father said with some urgency, "you know you need only come to us if there is something you want."

"I know that, Papa. I know."

They exchanged goodbyes, and Dan hefted the Yellow Pages into his lap, to skim the listings of publishers. He found the right one, dialed, and asked for the contracts department. Simple. He requested the name of the agent listed on the contract for Stanleigh Dunn's last book, and was given it. He looked up the agent's number, dialed, and said, "I'd like to speak to whoever in your organization represents Stanleigh Dunn." He was put on hold, and then a man with the melodious voice of an actor rather than an agent said hello.

"I understand you represent Stanleigh Dunn," Dan said.

"Quite correct. I have that honor."

"I'd like to get in touch with her. How might I go about that?"

"If you would care to write to her and address the letter to me, I will make certain she receives your communication. Might I enquire as to what this is about?"

"We're old friends," he ad-libbed. "I'm back in town and thought I'd get in touch with Leigh."

"Well, send along your letter and I'll be happy to forward it to her."

"One last question," Dan said. "Is she in town now, or does she still have the house in New Canaan?"

There was a brief silence on the line. Plainly the agent was mulling over the fact that Dan knew about the country house. "I'm afraid I can't say where she is at the moment," he answered. "But you have my assurance I will see to it she receives your letter."

Dan thanked him and broke the connection, dissatisfied. A letter wouldn't do it. It was too easy to ignore a letter. He would have to come up with something more, something that would guarantee him either an address or a telephone number.

All the while he sat sorting through various ideas, a segment of his brain was standing back taking note of his behavior and wondering what it was meant to accomplish. He was avoiding his parents, reluctant to resume his responsibilities; he'd developed an obsession and didn't really want to be free of it because it seemed like the only positive thing he'd felt in far too long. The rest had been performance by rote; doing what had been expected of him; but all the while he'd been going around like a human grenade with a wobbly pin that could be jarred loose by any action that deviated from the expected. He recalled his father's remark about the length of time that had passed and, reviewing his response, he decided it had been truthful. He had no frame of reference, no "priors" as the police liked to say, no previous experience with anything remotely like what Celeste had done, so how was he to know how to behave, or what to do when? He hadn't known six months ago, and he didn't know now. All he did know was that he felt free now from all restraints. And that was because of his meeting Leigh. He didn't give a damn that she was married to someone else. All he cared about was seeing her again. And the more time that elapsed between their last meeting and the present, the more strongly he needed to see her again. It had been six days since he'd left her in the lobby of Brown's Hotel. It felt like months. It felt wrong. It felt like deprivation from some vital substance he required in order to survive.

There was something else he knew, and that was that he was out of control. Instead of sitting there on the floor cradling an empty coffee cup, he should have been calling his daughter. But he had to rein in his emotions first, deal with the small feeling of betrayal he had at Lane's changing their plans without first consulting him. He'd been looking forward to going somewhere tropical, snorkeling clear water with his lithe young daughter and her companion, lazing on a white sand beach while the sun dazed them all into somnolence. Instead, she was going to go with her grandparents to their Palm Beach condominium. And he couldn't go there. He wasn't up to prolonged exposure to his mother and father and their relentless-seeming need to question everything he said and did. They and Lane were the only people to whom he tried never to lie. He omitted, he distorted on occasion, but he rarely lied to them. He just couldn't cope with two or three weeks of being forced to dredge up bits of harmless truth to give to them.

They would have been flabbergasted to learn he'd transformed his mother into a former department store buyer, and his father into a professor. Most likely, they'd have found his choice of careers humorous. His mother was as devoted to Bloomingdale's as she was to his father, but she'd never worked a day in her life. And the only subject on which his father might have been qualified to lecture was Daniel's present inability to perform to standard. International bankers were among the most didactic people on earth, and his father was no exception. Having made a career in money, predicated on the mathematics that accompanied money everywhere it went, his father saw all things on plus or minus scales that in the end were obliged to balance. His emotional life ran along similarly disciplined lines and the closeness of the family had been achieved as a result of his mother's talent for arousing the passion and humor that luckily lay not too far beneath the surface of his banker father's glacial calm. Given all that, there was no way possible Daniel could explain to his father that his recently acquired obsession had managed to shift him out of his six months of suppressed emotion into an active state of feeling. His mother would understand, and so would Lane. But Dan had nothing concrete to tell them. And any discussion of Leigh would not only be premature, it might also jinx the potential he found in the situation.

Leigh had given her mother a week to recover, but it wasn't time yet to call her again. And every time she thought of how they'd gone at each other that night, she wondered if the right time would ever come. That evening seemed to attain more horrific dimensions with every passing day. She could no longer discern which grieved her more, Joel's death or that last encounter with her mother.

She loathed herself so thoroughly she couldn't bear to eat, or to sit still for more than ten minutes; she slept only a few hours a night and when awake devoted herself to splitting the last of the logs and then stocking the woodpile outside the mud room door. She hadn't bothered to go into town for food, and burned occasional pieces of toast which she ate standing at the kitchen counter as she stared at the wind-driven snow that had been falling intermittently since she arrived. She let the machine answer the telephone, and kept the volume at minimum in order not to hear who was calling.

Her isolation was broken by the arrival of the mailman, who trudged up the unshoveled walk from the unplowed driveway with an overnight express letter that required her signature.

"Oughta get that walk cleaned," the man observed, after she'd signed his form. "Someone's gonna go ass over teakettle and sue you good. Wouldn't want that, would you?" He said it pleasantly enough, and she had to agree. After he'd driven off, she put on boots and a jacket and some sheepskin gloves and went out to clear the walk. Two hours later, she parked the shovel beside the front door and came in with her face frozen and her sweater saturated with perspiration. Lighting a cigarette, she remembered the letter, and read it. Then she went to the telephone to call Miles.

"Perhaps," he stormed at her, "you'd be good enough to tell me why you haven't bothered to return my calls. I happen to know you've been there for an entire *week.*"

"I didn't have anything to say to you," she replied.

"Oh, lovely! I don't suppose it occurred to you I might have a thing or two to say to you?"

"No, it didn't."

"Dolt!" he said affectionately. "There are several items on the agenda, as fate would have it."

"Miles," she said quietly, "if you want to talk to me, and you want me to respond, you're going to have to be you, and not my mother. I can tell every time you've been talking to her because you start aping her intonation, her expressions, even her attitudes, until I want to start screaming. It is *not* what I like about you."

He didn't comment, or argue. He simply took a breath and, in the voice he seemed to reserve solely for use with her on those occasions when she demanded it, said, "I have to remind you you accepted an advance for a book you haven't delivered. They're getting shirty, insisting they get either a book or their advance returned."

"I'll send you a check to forward to them. Anything else?"

"You do realize, of course, that it means I have to add back my ten percent?"

"I'll make the check out for the full amount of the advance. What else?"

"No," he said rather angrily, "Just make the check out for the amount you were paid, payable to the agency. I'll have the bookkeeper draw a check for the full amount. Next. You will recall the two gentlemen who took an option on the dramatic rights for *Percival* and subsequently made an outright purchase?"

"I do recall."

"They have put together a book, complete with music and lyrics. And they have called to ask if you would consider designing the production. They feel since you created Percival, you would be the appropriate party to design the sets, costumes, and what-have-you. May I risk interjecting a personal comment?"

"What?"

"I think you should meet with these people. It might be a project that would interest you. If you're not going to do any more books, this could prove an intriguing new direction. What you're doing isn't healthy, my darling. You'll lose your tiny marbles if you don't do *something*. And you've nothing to lose by having a lunch or dinner with these people. They're most anxious to have you work with them."

"I will think about it."

"To assist your thinking, I'm sending you a copy of their book and a tape of the music. It's great fun, Leigh," he said enthusiastically. "I think they may just make it to Broadway."

"Is there anything else?" she asked.

"As a matter of fact, yes. I have here a missive from an old friend of yours. I promised to forward it."

"So, why don't you?"

"Obviously I wasn't about to send along a package insured to the tune of twenty-eight hundred dollars without knowing your precise whereabouts. Also, it came addressed to me with a cover note enclosing cash to pay for the cost of a courier. Furthermore, it would be a waste of everyone's time and money were I to ship this off while you were into playing hermit and refusing to answer doorbells and telephones and the like."

"Who is it from?" she asked, curious.

"Doesn't say. Just some initials on the note and an address downtown. Whoever he is, he's been calling the office first thing every morning for the past three days, asking if the package has been forwarded yet. Diane says he's very pleasant, very to the point. He's also, obviously, very persistent. She offered to take his number and let him know when it was on its way to you, but he declined, said something about it being easier for him to call in."

"Well, I'm here, so you might as well send it along."

"Will do. For fear of sounding like a nag, may I have your word you'll consider this offer? Or are you trying to tell me our splendid relationship is at an end, and I'll have to make do paying homage to your lovely mum?"

"For the time being, you'll have to make do with Mother. I'll let you know when I plan to be in town. And I will listen to the music and read the book and let you know."

"That's all I ask. I'll send the package off tomorrow morning. Take care of yourself, my darling. I miss your aging little pixie face."

"I'm *so* glad I called," she laughed, and hung up.

Talking to Miles had given her a lift. She was actually hungry, and went to the kitchen to look into the near-empty refrigerator. Time to go buy some food and pick up some newspapers. And perhaps later, after she'd eaten, she'd phone her mother.

His plan worked beautifully. The woman who answered the agency telephone was quick to tell him that the package was sitting right there on her desk, waiting to be picked up by Federal Express. He thanked her, replaced the pay phone receiver and turned to scan the lobby. The first two times he'd called from the apartment. But yesterday and today he'd placed his calls from the lobby. Now all he had to do was wait. He bought a newspaper and positioned himself where he could keep an eye on the building entrance, glancing over at regular intervals until he saw the Federal Express van pull up in front. Then, casually, he refolded the paper, tucked it under his arm, and strolled toward the elevator.

Upon emerging at the right floor, he again opened the newspaper, poked the call button, and waited. The Federal Express man arrived moments later, entered the office, and came out again in not more than a minute with the package in hand. Under the pretext of being so engrossed in his reading that he was unaware of the driver, Daniel collided with the man as they both moved to enter the elevator. The collision was sufficiently forceful to knock the package from the man's hands. Dan at once bent to pick it up and, fumbling both with the newspaper and the package, had enough time to read the address before saying, "My fault. Sorry. Here you go."

Dan smiled ingratiatingly and made a show of folding the paper into a tight tube as they rode back down to the lobby. He told the driver, "Have a nice day," and left the building to return to the apartment in the Village where he looked up the address on the New Canaan map he'd bought. Then he took a taxi to the garage on the pier at West Twenty-first Street to get his car, and had no difficulty finding his way to the private road off Route 124 on the far side of New Canaan. He drove on and parked just past the road—which was really only a very long driveway—to look the place over for a few minutes. Then he turned around and headed back to the city.

She lived on Moonstone Lane, in a house he coveted, with a steeply pitched roof and multipaned windows and a fieldstone chimney. And she now had the diamond pendant he'd wanted her to have. He sang along with the music on a Golden Oldies station he found as he drove, right at the speed limit, toward his evening with his daughter.

Eleven

"**D**ADDY, WILL YOU *PLEASE* TELL ME WHAT'S GOING ON?"

"Sweetheart"—Dan smiled at her—"I'm just getting rid of the house. I want to find someplace smaller, maybe a little closer to town." His smile held. The sight of his daughter gave him a pleasure so intense it bordered on pain. Everything about her was so cleanly, fragrantly, sweetly young; her eyes were such a perfect blue and so clear; her hair was so glossy and abundant; her skin had such tone, such resilience. She was his baby girl grown quick and slim and strong; she was the infant he'd held in one hand in proud amazement; she was the stocky six-year-old who played the morning glory in the school play; she was the fourteen-year-old whose room had vibrated with bass-heavy rock music; she was the miraculous end product of his encounters with a woman whose strongest emotion, ever, was self-hatred. "You look terrific," he told her.

It was Lane's turn to take a long look at her father. Nothing showed really, but something was definitely wrong. He was different, had changed in ways so subtle she couldn't pinpoint them. Mostly it was just a feeling she had, a nebulous kind of intuition that alarmed her a little. He didn't appear outwardly altered. His clothes were the same kind he'd always worn; nothing new there: a pair of gray flannel slacks, a pale-blue shirt with white collar and cuffs, red tie with pencil-thin diagonal stripes, charcoal cashmere sports jacket. She loved the way he dressed. He looked like a preppy businessman. There was always something he wore that felt great to touch, like his cashmere jacket today, or a camel's hair sweater she borrowed from time to time. She liked the way he smelled, and his skin, like a baby's, so smooth and pink and perfect. Sometimes, just looking at her dad, she'd get so emotional she couldn't talk because she loved him so much, and she knew the kind of grief he'd put up with from her mother for as far back as she could remember. If she'd ever been asked to choose between her parents—which, in a way she had been, but not directly—she'd have picked her father every time because he was so *for* her, so totally on her side in all the matters that really counted. He'd been the one, her whole life, to sit down with her and talk about the important things, her ups and downs, her confusion, was she too fat or too thin, what schools she'd go to, her boyfriends, everything. He was a really nice man, and he'd always shown her how much he cared about her, how much she meant to him. No matter what was happening in the house—he and her mother could be smack in the middle of one of their horrible fights—he never brought any of that stuff into his dealings with her. He'd even tried, loads of times, to explain what made her mother tick and why she acted like such a spaz most of the time. In a way, it was as if the stuff that went on with him and her mother was a kind of coat, and he'd take it off when he was with Lane. Every so often, growing up, she used to think she could see him putting on that coat, getting ready to deal with some-thing else her mother wanted to fight about. And a few times she'd tried to explain to him how it made her feel to see him shrug his way into that "coat" in order to deal with her mother, how hurt she felt at seeing how hard it was for him. She'd asked him over and over why they stayed together, why they just didn't get a divorce and be done with it. And every time he'd talked about honoring commitments, about moral obliga-tions, about responsibilities. But she'd never been able to convince him that, from her viewpoint at least, he'd done all those things and then some, and there was no need for him to keep on being honorable and obligated and responsible when it wasn't doing any of them one bit of good. She'd known almost all her life that there was no way to please her mother, so there wasn't much point to trying, and that if she had anything important she'd better take it to her father because important things set her mother off in a major way.

"Why won't you come with us to Florida?" she asked again. "You look so tired. You could relax for a couple of weeks and take care of selling the house when you get back."

"You're such a marshmallow," he said fondly, taking her into his arms. "You've been a big softie since the day you were born. You worry too much. You know that?"

"No, I don't, Daddy. I don't worry about anything else the way I worry about you."

"That's my point. I'm an old man, Lanie; I've been around a while. I know how to take care of myself. Just you worry about you. You'll have a great time in Florida. They'll spoil you rotten, as usual, and you'll come back with a great tan and twenty-three new boyfriends."

She laughed and leaned away to look at him. "You're not an old man," she said. "I hate it when you talk about yourself that way. Half my friends think you're the most gorgeous thing they've ever seen."

"So how come they're not all calling, asking me out?"

"Come on! You know what I mean."

"Okay. I'm not an old man."

"Tell me about Stanleigh Dunn," she asked eagerly, and saw an amazing change overtake him. He seemed to glow very brightly for a few seconds, like a camera-flash. Then he pulled back, and said, "You'd have liked her, sweetheart."

"Come on," she said, dragging him by the hand over to the sofa. "I want to hear all the details. How old is she?"

"Forty-five."

"Oh! That's pretty old."

Dan laughed. "Trust me. It's not very old. Aren't you the one who just finished telling me I'm not over the hill?"

"I guess. Go on. What else?"

"She's taller than you, maybe five-seven, very thin, auburn hair, green eyes, English accent."

"She's English? I didn't know that."

"Her mother brought her over here when she was twelve."

"That's amazing. What else?"

"You find everything 'amazing,' " he teased.

"Yes, I do. What else?"

"She's got a good sense of humor." He went on describing Leigh, while an internal voice track simultaneously recited for his private benefit details of a more intimate nature. She's got lovely shoulders, a beautifully tapered back, and her breasts are incredibly soft and full; her thighs are long and smooth and rounded just there; and there's a thin scar that starts below her navel and travels down the exact center of her belly, right the way down; when you kiss her at the base of her throat you can hear her breathing change, just the way it does if you stroke the backs of her knees, or run your fingers very lightly down her sides; her eyes freeze to green ice when she comes, but she doesn't make any sound at all.

"I think you're in love with her!" Lane exclaimed with scary incisiveness, nailing his attention flat to the present tense. *"Daddy!"*

He shook his head, quickly trying to shuffle together a suitable argument.

"You *are!*" she insisted. "I can tell! When are you seeing her again? Will I get to meet her? God! Cath will *shit* when I tell her!"

"Lane," he said sternly, "you can't tell anyone, because it's just not true. It's not happening. Sure I liked her, a lot. But that's all there is to it."

He looked so suddenly tired, so terribly worn out, Lane felt afraid again.

"Talk to me," she said quietly. "We've always talked. I'm not a little kid anymore. I'm almost twenty."

He put his arm around her shoulders and drew her against his side. After a time, he smiled and said, "Do you remember that time when you were three?"

"The Jesus story," she said, and smiled, too.

"Your mother had put you down for your nap, and I came to get you a couple of hours later. And while I was getting you dressed, I asked did you have a nice nap? And you said, 'I didn't nap,' and I said, 'Oh, didn't you? What did you do, then, Lanie?' And you said, 'I went to see Jesus.' And I said, 'You did, huh? And where did you go to see him?' and you said, 'Heaven,' as if it was the most natural thing in the world. So I said, 'What was heaven like, sweetheart?' and you got this indescribably ecstatic look on your face and said, 'It was like cookies.' " He paused and they both laughed. Then he went on. "I said, 'What did you do in heaven, Lanie?' and you said, 'I saw Other Gramma there,' and I said, 'You did? What did you and Other Gramma do?' and you said, 'She gived me ice cream.' And then I said, 'How did you get home, baby girl?' and you said, 'Jesus drived me,' and I said, 'He did, huh? How come he did that?' and you said, 'Because Other Gramma told him to.' " Again they laughed, and his arm was tight around her shoulders. "You've always been the most . . ." He had to stop because he was going to cry.

Lane gave him a minute, then said, "Talk to me, Dad. I can tell this is serious, whatever it is." When he didn't speak, she asked, "Did you spend time with her in London?" He nodded, and she asked, "Did you sleep with her?"

"Lane, I can't *do* this!" he protested.

"I don't see why not. The two of us talked when I started getting serious with Steve. You never once made me feel wrong about it, not the way Mom did. You were the one who got me to go to the Family Planning Clinic; you were the one who discussed the whole abortion issue with me. You're the one I've always come to when something was important. You can trust me, Dad. Maybe I could help."

He withdrew his arm from around her shoulders, and she thought maybe she'd really blown it, trespassed on some kind of parental territorial thing. But he took hold of both her hands and shifted around so he was facing her; he kept his eyes down, looking at her hands. "There are problems," he admitted. "She's married. It sounds like a lousy marriage, but she's married." He finally met her eyes as he went on to tell her some of the lies he'd told Leigh.

"*Why* would you *tell* her stuff like that, Dad?" she asked, flustered.

"I honestly don't know why," he confessed. "I was afraid, I guess. *I don't know.* It doesn't matter anyway. She's married."

"Shit!" she said softly, trying to piece it together. "You actually told her Grandmother had been a *model,* and Grandfather was a *professor?*" She began to laugh. "God, wouldn't they just freak if they knew? It's kind of perfect, in a way. I mean, if I didn't know them, I'd guess maybe Grandmother had had that kind of an exotic past. She has that sort of look. But a professor? That's really reaching, especially the way Grandfather dresses." Her amusement ebbing, she asked, "What are you going to do?"

"Nothing. Not a thing. We met; we spent some time together; it was anything but dull; it's over, and that's that. I want to get the house sold. Once that's out of the way, I'll start thinking about what I want to do with the rest of my life. As for Palm Beach, I'm not in the mood for it, Lane; the cocktail parties every night, the seniors' tennis matches, that whole scene. You don't really mind if I don't come, do you?"

"As long as you're not pissed off with me for wrecking your plans. It's just that I thought about it, Dad, and I really felt I should go with them. They're getting so old, and if I don't take the chance to be with them when I can, I know I'll be sorry later on, when they're not around anymore."

"You're a nice person, Lane," he told her. "I really like the hell out of you."

"Me too you, Daddy," she said, and hugged him hard, worried.

Leigh sat down at the kitchen table with a cup of instant coffee and a cigarette, to examine the package before opening it. Inside was a heavy gold open-ended circle, and affixed to the lower part of the curve, held securely in wide gold claws, was a brilliant-cut half-carat diamond. The pendant was suspended from an unusual gold chain that was heavy and smooth and somehow liquid to the touch. She sat looking at the necklace for quite some time, experiencing a strong, visceral response to its beauty.

The letter read: "Leigh, I know we promised not to be in touch, but I wanted you to have this. I saw it and knew it was for you, that I had to give it to you. The address on the package doesn't exist. It's just some numbers I put there to keep the post office people happy. If you really can't keep it, if it really compromises you, call me at this number, and I'll relieve you of it. I hope you'll want to keep it. I've been thinking a lot about you. All my best, Dan."

Her first instinct was to call and get an address from him so she could return the gift. But her hand didn't seem to want to relinquish its hold on the necklace. And even though she looked over at the telephone on the counter, she knew she wasn't going to call him. At least not about returning the pendant. She wished he hadn't given his number. She could see herself pushing the touch-tone buttons on the telephone face that would connect her with him. To ward off any possibility of this happening, she brought the phone over to the table and called her mother. It had been ten days, time enough.

"Are you still not talking to me?" she asked.

"What sort of condition are you in?" Marietta countered in a voice that said her hair was pinned into place and she was dressed in one of her "working outfits," a simple, belted dress of some lightweight fabric.

"I'm hungry, sober, and sorrier than I can say. If I drive into town, will you let me take you to dinner? Your choice, anywhere you like."

"Miles informs me you're returning your advance. Why would you do a thing like that, Stanleigh?"

"Miles shouldn't be representing both of us, as I've said several thousand times before. He loves gossip too much to be completely fair to either of us."

"You're not answering the question," Marietta reminded her.

"Mother, I have no ambition left, no incentive, and nothing I want to say in an illustration. Why can't you accept that it's over? There aren't going to be any more books."

"It's a sin to waste talent," her mother said very seriously. "You don't have the right to abandon a God-given gift. When I think of all you could still do, it's enough to make me weep."

"Will you let me take you out to dinner tonight?"

"Not tonight, darling, I'm seeing Laurence. Suffice it to say, he has no desire to come anywhere near this apartment at the moment. I'm having to work rather hard to build back his confidence."

Her mother had called her darling; Leigh knew they were past the worst part. Relieved and grateful, she said, "Tomorrow, then. Or are you booked up for tomorrow, too?"

"Tomorrow will be fine. I'm giving the girls a half-day to do some Christmas shopping. You do plan to be here Christmas?"

Leigh hadn't given it any thought, but quickly said, "Of course."

"Good. I'm dictating now, Leigh. I'll expect you at six-thirty tomorrow. We'll have a drink before we go out. I'm encouraged to hear your appetite's returned. You've gone gaunt, and it is not you at your best. Tomorrow, darling," she said, and ended the call.

While Leigh was filling her shopping cart at Walter Stewart's Market, her fingers toyed with the pendant. When she caught herself doing it, she'd stop. Then two minutes later, she'd be doing it again. She couldn't seem to help herself. Daniel Godard was sufficiently interested in her to go to a great deal of trouble to send her an exquisite, expensive gift. He was willing to take risks—or so he thought—to convey to her his thoughts. And she was impressed.

By the time she'd returned home, put away the groceries, and started preparing a casserole of chicken and braised vegetables, she was holding imaginary conversations with him on the telephone. It was almost too easy to picture herself saying in a low voice into the receiver all she'd been unable to confide yet to anyone else.

Daniel, every time I think about it, they die again. Carl and Stephen and Joel, they keep dying, over and over, and the pain is engulfing. It swamps my senses so that when I open my eyes all I see is the blank gray landscape of infinity; all I taste in my mouth is the fineblown sour ash from the chimneys; I can smell nothing else, feel nothing else, think of nothing else but their deaths. For moments here and there, I forget—I did with you—then I suffocate with guilt at having abandoned them.

She wanted to say, Daniel, I don't know why I'm alive and they're not; I don't know the purpose, and yet I keep on living. Why do you suppose that is? Does it make any kind of sense to you? It doesn't to me. I tell myself I'm alive, and therefore I should attempt to work out some sort of future for myself because if you're alive it's what you're expected to do. It's what my mother expects, and Miles. Everyone becomes very impatient with you if you grieve too long, or too visibly, if you don't "snap out of it" the way they'd like you to and stop embarrassing everyone with your ungovernable sense of loss and longing.

She thought she'd say, Daniel, I keep thinking of how good it felt to hold you, be held by you. It surprised me. You put your arms around me, and you seemed so very solid. Lately, I expect people to evaporate when I go to hold them; no one appears to me to have any density. But you did. I can still feel you solid in my mind. The touching, joining, was really very good. But best of all was both of us standing fully dressed and having you hold me. You seemed so glad of the shape and size of me, the *me* of me. Was it illusion?

Had it been real? she wondered. Or was she now, and had she then, been embellishing reality, decorating it with her need?

The telephone rang and he snatched it up, fumbling the receiver to his ear.

"Daniel," she said, "it's such an exquisite thing I haven't the heart to refuse it. But I do wish you hadn't done this."

"No hello?" he said jovially, elated because she'd called as he'd known she would. "No 'is that you'? No 'how are you'? Just a reprimand and a backhanded thank-you?"

"I'm sorry." Her voice was pitched so low he could scarcely hear her. He thought her husband must be close by, so she was keeping her voice down. "How are you?" she asked politely.

"I'm a hell of a lot better than I was five minutes ago. I'm glad you called. I was hoping you would."

"You *knew* I would. I was taught always to be mannerly. It's very beautiful, thank you very much. If there'd been a return address, I would have sent it back to you."

"I guessed that, which is why I did it that way. How are you, Leigh? Did you see your father? How did it go?" It gave him such a good feeling to know details, facts, about her life.

"I'm fine. Look," she said, breaking the rules without having known she would. "I'm coming into the city tomorrow. I could meet you for coffee."

"Where, when?"

She couldn't think how to answer. "It's a problem," she said.

"I understand." He figured she was referring to her goddamned husband. "You could come . . . no. Hell! Wait a minute." He paused in order to give the impression that the number she'd called him on wasn't located at the place where he intended them to meet. He wanted her to think he, too, was taking risks and making special arrangements to accommodate her. "We could meet in the Village," he said, looking around the room. "A friend of mine has a place. I've been keeping an eye on it for him. I stay there sometimes when it's too late to catch the last train." That sounded right, he thought.

"I don't know," she hesitated. "I won't have much time. I'm sorry to be so dithery, especially during office hours."

He was very pleased. She'd assumed, as he'd hoped, that she'd reached him on a direct line at his office. "I make great coffee," he told her. "We can sit on my friend's only two chairs, have some coffee, and talk."

"You know talking isn't what you have in mind."

"Let me give you the address."

"All right. But I really won't be able to stay long. I have a number of errands, then I'm meeting my mother for dinner. Hold on while I find something to write with."

He waited, his eyes now on the bed. He'd change the sheets. And maybe, if there was time in the morning, he'd buy a few things to brighten the place up—some flowers, a framed poster, a small rug for the floor.

"Okay. Give me the address."

He gave it to her, then said, "I just knew you'd like the necklace."

"You were right. I do. I could be there by one. How is that for you?"

"Fine, perfect. I have an early meeting, then I'll go directly to the apartment."

She said goodbye, and he put the receiver down gently, as if the instrument actually contained her.

Twelve

H E WAS WAITING ON THE LANDING, THE DOOR TO THE APARTMENT open behind him. When she got to the top of the stairs he held out his arms, and she walked directly into the circle of his embrace, surrendering to sensation. The world could have stopped right then and she'd have just kept her eyes closed so she wouldn't have to see it go. From the intensity of his embrace and the length of time it was lasting, it seemed he felt the same way. Seconds ticked off an unseen clock while she breathed in his cologne, the scent she remembered, and gave in to small waking dreams with her head against his shoulder, their bodies a single, unmoving line that might be broken only by some ferocious act of nature—volcanic eruption, typhoon—something immense and beyond human control.

He became aware of an insistent little noise behind him inside the apartment and realized it was boiling water splashing over the sides of the pot and hitting the burner.

"The water's boiling over," he said, unwilling to release her. "The water will douse the fire, but the gas'll keep escaping and a couple of days from now when I wake up and strike a match to light a cigarette I'll blow me and everybody else in the building to kingdom come."

"I suppose you'll have to turn it off," she said drowsily, opening her eyes.

"Still, it'll take quite a while for enough gas to accumulate, what with the door being open and so forth."

"Well, that's all right, then."

"The smell of gas is pretty terrible, though. And the neighbors might complain."

She slid away, saying, "I've been told you make great coffee," and wondered how she could sound so at ease when her mouth was dry and her knees were rubbery.

He allowed her to go ahead of him into the apartment, then went to the stove to fix the coffee, watching as she looked around and then, keeping her coat on, sat down in one of the chairs at the stripped-oak table. She lit a cigarette as he poured the last of the water into the filter and turned to find her eyes on him, the fingers of her left hand toying with the pendant. It caused a quickening inside him, as if her hand were on him.

"Wouldn't you like to take off your coat?" he asked, hand outheld to take it from her.

She stared at him as if the question made no sense. Then she shrugged off the mink, letting it fall over the back of the chair. She was wearing smartly cut black trousers, a white silk blouse with black piping around the collar and cuffs, and a pair of flat-heeled black leather boots. "Whose apartment is this?" she asked.

"A friend's," he answered, returning to the stove to pour the coffee.

"Your friend," she observed, looking around, "obviously doesn't live here. I suspect he brings his lady friends here."

Dan laughed as he put a cup down on the table in front of her before sitting opposite.

"Maybe so," he said. "I've never asked. It's handy, and he doesn't use it very often."

"I quite like it," she said, still turned away. "Minimalist style. I've thought for years I'd like to live with tatami mats and pebbles, several meaningful plants." When she faced him again, she was smiling, holding the cigarette to her mouth. "I shouldn't be here."

"Sure you should."

"No, I shouldn't. And how did you manage to steal time away in the middle of the day?"

"That was my last official buying trip I was on," he explained. "I'm now semiretired, or unofficially retired. Something. I've got more free time than I know what to do with. What kind of lies did you have to tell?"

"Nonspecific ones," she answered, trying the coffee. "This *is* good."

"Godards never misrepresent." *We may lie from time to time, exercise evasive tactics, but we never wrongly present ourselves. Except inadvertently, at times when there's only uncertainty.*

"We're not going to make a habit of this, Daniel."

"Of what? Meeting to drink coffee?"

"Of meeting, period. It could create serious problems for both of us. I don't like the feeling I get, sneaking around . . . making complicated arrangements."

"I kind of enjoyed it myself," he said, tilting his chair so that his weight was balancing on the two rear legs. "Danger gets the old adrenaline pumping."

She looked at him, trying to see if he could possibly be serious. "You don't mean that," she said. "You're just as nervous as I am about this." Again, she looked around.

"All right, I am."

To her relief, he brought his chair forward so all four legs were once more on the floor. It reminded her of the way Stephen had liked to defy gravity, sitting tilted in chairs so that whenever she caught him at it, her heart thumped unpleasantly and she had to ask him please not to do it, fearful he'd tip over backward and be hurt.

She pushed back her cuff to look at the time. One-twelve. Somehow they'd already used up twelve minutes. She still had shopping to do, gifts to find for her mother and for Miles, and something to offer as an apology to Laurence. She hadn't even gone up to her apartment but had merely parked the car in the basement garage before coming directly down here in a taxi. She was here, and it wasn't going at all as she'd thought it might. For one thing, it was broad daylight; sun flooding through the gate-covered windows turned the far end of the empty living room into white, mote-filled amorphousness. She wondered if the bedroom also suffered from such an unkind deluge of light. If she went in there to discover more of that same harsh illumination she knew she'd keep her clothes on. It was impossible to pretend, or to hide anything, in bright light.

"Is it dark in the bedroom?" she asked, taking time putting out her cigarette, in order not to have to see his reaction.

"Dark? I don't know." He got up and walked over to the bedroom doorway and said, "I guess it is pretty dark. This room has vertical blinds. Not much else, but it has vertical blinds."

"Good," she said, and brushed past him into the room.

He hadn't heard her move, but all at once she wasn't out there anymore but inside over here, undoing the buttons on her cuffs.

"We don't have very much time," she told him, pulling the shirttails free of her trousers.

"No," he agreed numbly, unable to understand why he couldn't ever seem to control the flow of events when he was with her. Somehow, each time, it was she who set things in motion. The strange part was he didn't mind at all. In fact, it pleased him that she was so in charge of her desire and priorities. But her being rather businesslike now did bother him just a little.

He was still standing in the doorway and, seeing this, she became doubtful. "No?" she asked, stopping with her shirt half off one shoulder. "A change of mind?"

He shook his head and went to put his arms around her. "I don't know why it is," he said, his lips against her soft, cropped hair, "but every so often you make me feel so goddamned sad. I care about you. I'm sorry this feels sneaky and complicated. I didn't think about any of that. Knowing you feel that way makes me feel lousy."

"Don't go overboard," she said lightly. "It's not my first trip away from home."

Now he went from feeling sad to laughing. "Know what I think?" he said. "I think we're both a little crazy."

"My mother would be the first to agree with you. We're having trouble again getting started."

"D'you know, I was so busy thinking about you all the way back from Hong Kong that a good half the time I forgot to be afraid? I was actually in the baggage claim at Kennedy when I realized that."

"You shouldn't be thinking about me, Daniel. This really isn't going anywhere."

"Do you have complete control over what you think?" he asked. "It's pretty good, if you do. I haven't figured out yet how to do that. And why do you keep warning me? It's not necessary. But situations have been known to change."

They were going to use up all their time talking. If they talked too much, he'd become too familiar to her, she'd begin developing frames of reference for him, and he'd start spreading through her life like water. She looked down, fitting together the sides of her shirt.

"Don't give up so easily." He put his hands over hers. "Maybe I'm just a slow starter. And the time constraints are pretty inhibiting. Are you going away for Christmas?" He needed to talk with her; they couldn't just lie down together without first having some conversation. Without an exchange of words, it felt too much like a business deal, as if this was her way of thanking him for the gift.

"No. It's a family affair. Are you?"

"I was supposed to be taking Lane . . . our plans got changed." He didn't want her to think he was without options. "Everyone's going to Palm Beach. My parents have a condo there." Maybe he'd go after all, he thought.

"When do you leave?" she asked.

"I'm not sure. The plan is I'll fly down to join them. When hasn't been decided yet." He was intentionally keeping everything vague.

Talking, and more talking. Either they'd go back to the table, drink their coffee and talk, or they'd get on with this. She put her hands on the sides of his face and kissed him, hoping to get him started. She succeeded. He flew into action, taking her out of her clothes as if he were unwrapping a gift someone had unexpectedly given him. He murmured approving sounds as he stripped away her clothes.

I'm too old for this, she thought. I really am too old for games of any nature; and this is just another, somewhat better game. But Christ! He was, as before, making love to her as if it were his first and last time. And she was reacting like dry tinder held to a match, limbs curling, charred, the heat yielding moisture. How could she be concerned with how it might look, when his burrowing fingers and pretty mouth made her squirm and, responding, reach to stroke him? How could she care about anything more than each moment's heightening liquid pleasure? She wanted to open her mouth and devour him whole, nibbling away at different parts of him until she contained him completely. There was always confirmation, reaffirmation—regardless of how temporary—in the proof of a man's response to her. And here it was. She could shape it with her hands, treasure and nurture it, and, finally, hide it deep within the vault of her body.

There was a moment when, his hands guiding her hips as she sat above him, she thought of how she'd seen her mother doing precisely this, and the shock she'd felt at inadvertently encroaching on her mother's cherished privacy. God, the horror of what she'd done! she thought, losing the rhythm. To be caught in an act as arcane and wanton as this was unthinkable. That moment would exist, standing between her and her mother for the rest of their lives. And it needn't have been that way. All she'd had to do was back away, never letting on that she'd seen. But she hadn't done that. She'd taken what she'd seen and beat her mother over the head with it. Christ!

"What's wrong?" Daniel asked, his hands steady on her hips. "Something's wrong," he decided without awaiting her answer. "Is it me?" he wondered aloud, worried. "I don't know what's what anymore. If it's me, for chrissake, say so! I don't want to go charging ahead, playing blind man. I hate people who do that."

She came forward over him, looping her arm under his head. "Daniel," she said against his neck, "it has nothing to do with you. I just lost it for a moment, that's all. Men lose erections all the time."

"Usually because they start thinking. Thinking and sex don't seem to be compatible. I know how that goes."

"Don't you lose it, too."

They rearranged themselves, and she urged him down upon her. He was heavy. Her bones seemed to creak audibly as she tightened her knees, lifting to recreate their rhythm. Locked into silence again, she sought his mouth, her hands on him, guiding. But it was no good. She really had lost it, although the motions were pleasurable, and she encouraged him, watching as if from a distance the changes that overcame him as he got caught at the last in that final, frantic little race out of himself.

When they were dressing, he suddenly stopped her, sat her on the end of the bed, looked for a long moment into her eyes, then pushed open her thighs and dropped to his knees on the floor. His eyes still on hers, he began teasing her with his fingers, watching until she lost her focus and her eyes grew heavy-lidded. Then his hands went under her and he held her to his mouth.

He went on with it until she was no one, nothing, just a quivering parcel of pure reaction. And she wanted to savor the moment, the piercing perfection of it, but he wasn't allowing it. He continued to hold her, going on and on until it was no longer pleasure but a kind of maddening irritation, and when he gave no indication he'd ever stop, when it seemed he intended to go on and on with this, she became frightened, emitting a small scream as she frantically pushed him away, crying, "Stop! Daniel, *stop!*"

And he stopped, but continued to hold her—his hands fastened to the undersides of her thighs in such a punishing grip she was sure there'd be bruises—until the visible heat left her face and chest. Then he put his head in her lap, and she gazed down at him fearfully, whispering, "We can't do this again. We just can't." She felt afraid, didn't want to say or do anything that might provoke him, because he'd seemed as if he'd wanted to burrow his way into the core of her being. But surely, she told herself, she was misinterpreting. She bent over him for a long moment, shielding him with her body, so he could hear the antic beating of her heart and feel the panic in her hands. Then, abruptly, she sat up, saying, "I have to go!" and pulled on her clothes, rushing here and there in the room, gathering up her things.

"You could use the bathroom, the shower, if you like," he said, in his trousers and unbuttoned shirt, following her to the living room where she snatched her coat from the chair and pulled it on.

"No," she said. "There isn't time. I really must go. Listen to me, Daniel! I can't see you again. This . . . it can't come to anything."

"You don't know that," he began.

"Yes, I *do* know that. I don't know about your reasons, and I don't want you to tell me because I have no intention of telling you mine. You must take my word, believe that there *are* reasons, and I can't see you anymore."

He didn't believe her. He knew all he had to do was take hold of her and he'd be able to change her mind. He did it now: he took hold of her, and kissed her mouth, then said, "I'd be willing to change things."

"Don't! I'm not capable of changing anything. You've had as much as I can offer anyone." Trying to lighten the atmosphere, she threw in, "There's less to me than meets the eye," and gave him a smile.

"I'm in love with you, Leigh. And I don't give up that easily."

She was becoming frightened again. Not only was he refusing to hear what she was saying but very possibly he *couldn't* hear what she was saying, because he was deafened by the noise of his own arguments. "Give it up! Please! I'm *not* in love with you."

"Then why did you meet me here today?"

"Because I wanted to go to bed with you. What does love have to do with it?"

"Not a thing. Nothing. I'm a jerk, that's all. I know you have to go. It's okay."

He was hurt, and she hated it. *"Daniel!"* she cried. "Don't try to blackmail me! You're no more in a position to be in love with me than I am with you. My husband, your wife. Remember?"

"Yup. Nothing wrong with the old brain cells. Memory's intact. The Good Doctor. How is he anyway?"

"I'm going." She started toward the door.

"Leigh?"

"What?"

"I don't think I can give you up all that easily. And I don't think I believe you."

"What? What don't you believe?"

"I think you feel it, too."

"Let me tell you something!" she said hotly. "This is an old, old song, and I know the lyrics to every verse. I can sing it backward and in my sleep. In six months you'll have trouble remembering my name. And if you do remember it, it'll be because you happen to be passing the children's department in some bookstore that has a backlist. After the first rush, when it all dies down, you find out you can't stand the sight of each other, you've got nothing to say, and you start thinking about ways to get out of it. Let it go, Daniel." She gentled her tone. "You're very unhappy just now. I can tell, and I'm sorry. Go home to your family, and let me get on with my life." Again she said, "I really am sorry," then opened the door, and left.

He came out onto the landing as she was going down the stairs. "Merry Christmas, Leigh," he called down to her, leaning over the banister so she had to stop and look up at him.

"Oh, hell!" she laughed. "You're incorrigible."

"Probably."

"Merry Christmas, Daniel." She shook her head, then continued on down the stairs.

In the space of a split second, he decided he simply had to know where she was going. He tore back inside, threw on a coat, pushed his feet into boots, grabbed his wallet and keys, and was out of the apartment and flying down the stairs all in the space of less than two minutes. As he ran he prayed he hadn't taken too long. He hit the street and saw she was just turning the corner onto Fifth Avenue. In a burst of speed, he raced up the street, arriving at the corner in time to see a taxi stop for her. Feeling panicky at the thought of losing her, he leaped into the road, waving his arms to attract the attention of a cab just approaching. The car stopped, Dan jumped into the rear, and told the driver, *"Follow that cab up ahead!"*

"You're kidding!" The driver craned around to look at him.

"I'm not fucking kidding! Keep up with that cab and I'll give you twenty over the meter!"

"You're on!"

His luck held. Leigh's cab hung a left on Eighth Street and another left onto University Place, headed uptown. Riding almost on the bumper of the cab ahead, Dan's driver asked, "Is this Candid goddamned Camera or something?"

"No, no," Dan answered, glad it was a private taxi without the Plexiglas divider. "My wife," he extemporized. "I want to see where she's going."

"Sure." The driver raised his eyebrows, and refrained from further comment.

Leigh emerged from her cab on Park Avenue near Seventy-second Street.

Dan threw thirty dollars at his driver, and climbed out to watch her greet the doorman with a nod as she sailed right inside. This had to be where she lived, Dan reasoned. If it had been her mother's apartment, she wouldn't have made quite the same sort of entrance. How long was she going to stay inside? he wondered, feeling conspicuous. The doorman was giving him the once-over, and anxious not to draw attention to himself, Dan walked past the building to the corner, then crossed to the far side in order to keep an eye on the entrance to Leigh's building.

He walked the length of the block slowly, back and forth, three times before she reappeared. She turned left out of the entrance and started down Park. Keeping half a block behind, he trailed after her, curious to see where she'd go. She cut over to Madison and when she went into a shop, he studied the windows several doors along until she emerged carrying a gift-wrapped package.

She walked, she stopped to enter a total of five shops, and came out each time carrying more packages. She'd been in two antiques shops, a needlepoint place, a jewelry store, and a boutique with handmade lace outfits in the window. He was quite content to shadow her as she headed back to her apartment.

It was four-thirty, he saw, allowing her to get well ahead of him once he'd established she was definitely returning home. He guessed she'd stay inside for a couple of hours before setting out for her mother's. *If* she'd been truthful about her plans for the evening. And what, he thought, if her husband was going to be with her? The last thing Dan wanted was to have to see the Good goddamned Doctor husband. He thought he might be tempted to do something really stupid, like accidentally on purpose bumping into them on the street. No good.

A cab was going past, and he flagged it down. He'd done enough detective work for one day. It was time to go back to the Village, get cleaned up for the final family dinner before Lane and his parents left for Florida. As the cab rocketed down park, he decided he'd have to find out where Leigh's mother lived. If he knew all the addresses, it ought to be possible for him to keep tabs on her whereabouts. Tomorrow, he'd start making inquiries about Marietta Dunne. Right before the holidays would probably be a good time. People weren't so careful at this time of the year.

While he was knotting his tie in front of the bathroom mirror, he had a sudden, alarming, one-step-removed view of his behavior. Jesus Christ! he thought. He was stalking the woman, behaving like one of those psychopaths in thriller novels. No more, he told himself. No harm had been done so far, but if he kept on, letting this thing build into a full-scale obsession . . . no more. And to make sure he couldn't do any more of it, he went directly to the telephone to book a seat on the flight with Lane and his parents. He read out his American Express number, was told to pick up the ticket an hour before the flight time, wished a Merry Christmas, and thanked for flying American.

He didn't want to do it; he wanted to stay in the city in case Leigh changed her mind and called. But he wouldn't. He'd do the sane thing and take her at her word.

He got the tie knotted finally, splashed on some cologne, then went into the bedroom to look at the mess they'd made of the bed. He wanted to lie face down on the sheets and breathe in the smell of her. He *had* to see her again. If he didn't, if she really meant what she'd said, he didn't know what he'd do. The view of the days and weeks ahead with no hope, even of the sight of her, was too devastatingly empty to contemplate.

Thirteen

LEIGH PICKED AT THE SCALLOPS SHE'D ORDERED, WATCHING HER MOTHER eat with her usual gusto, wondering why this woman's hearty appetites—for food, for men, for life—still impressed her so. Yet each meeting with her mother was like the slight twist of a hugely detailed cyclorama that took a lifetime to view in its entirety. She was never bored in her mother's company, irritated sometimes, intimidated other times, but never bored.

Tonight, Marietta was wearing a wonderful dress of buttercup-yellow heavy silk, with a slashed neckline that offered a tantalizing view of her flawless décolletage. The dress was a minor masterpiece of design, with every last detail lovingly hand-finished. The column of Marietta's neck rose like some exotic stalk, offering itself in all its bared vulnerability to anyone who cared to look. Her hair was twisted into a careless topknot, with wisps escaping down the back of her neck: commas of flame along her ivory nape. The woman composed herself each day like a superb collage, with surprising points of interest here and there: a delicate gold chain with a dainty emerald-and-diamond pendant; a pearl dinner ring; clear lacquer on her nails; transparent gloss on her lips; tiny pearl earrings.

"You look heavenly," Leigh complimented her.

"Thank you. You're not eating. Is it not to your liking? We could send it back." Her hand was poised to beckon the waiter. Regardless of who might have arranged a dinner and intended paying for it, somehow Marietta was always the one to whom restaurant staff looked for direction.

"It's all right. I want to tell you something."

"Tell me anything you like. Just, please, don't light another cigarette until I've finished my dinner. It's rather too much like having one's food served on a much-used ashtray. What have you been up to?" she asked.

"It's the one from London," Leigh said. "He's married. I don't know why I agreed to meet him."

"You *do* manage to get yourself into things, don't you? Could this possibly have anything to do with your execrable behavior last week?"

"No, not really. Sometimes, when I have a bad dream or I'm afraid, I wish I was a child again, so I could come sleep with you in your bed the way I used to. I get so tired sometimes, of being an adult."

The waiter came to top off their wineglasses. Marietta gave him a smile and the swarthy man blossomed into well-being like time-lapse photography of a seedling shooting through its developmental stages. He moved away, dazzled. Marietta put down her knife and fork to take a sip of wine before saying, "Everyone feels that way from time to time, Stanleigh. I think one especially feels it when someone you love dies."

"They never feel that way in your books."

"Oh, don't be tiresome. We've been doing so well this evening. I know the contempt you have for my work, but I make no attempt to write about adults. My girls," she said, as if speaking of real people, "are children; they have no pretensions to maturity. That is what makes them so delightful. Every emotion they feel is new; every day is an adventure."

"Even children aren't that naive."

"You think not? My forty-five-year-old child often seems that naive." Marietta sniffed.

"I am at times," Leigh conceded surprisingly, so that her mother regarded her with interest as she popped the last piece of veal into her mouth, then aligned her knife and fork in the center of her plate.

"You may smoke now, if you wish. And perhaps you'll tell me what's happened."

Leigh toyed with her lighter. "It's not that anything's actually happened. I just think I was unwise. Anyway, I told him I wouldn't see him again."

"So what is it that bothers you?"

"Does it ever seem to you," Leigh asked her, "that no one is what he appears to be? I mean, lately I've had the feeling that there's almost nothing that is the way it seems."

"Leigh," her mother began, but was interrupted by the return of the waiter.

"You would have coffee, dessert, Madame?"

Marietta encouraged his recitation of the desserts. Then she wanted to see the dessert cart. The happy little Italian wheeled it over and lovingly pointed out the crème brûlée, the chocolate mousse, the fresh raspberries, the gateaux, the napoleons, the eclairs with mocha cream, and the English trifle. Marietta settled on the crème brûlée topped with the fresh raspberries. The waiter was only slightly crestfallen when Leigh asked just for a double espresso. Marietta's request for cappuccino, however, returned him to his previous ecstasy. He buried the crème brûlée in raspberries, set the overspilling plate before Marietta, then rushed off to the espresso machine.

"He's in love with you," Leigh said with a grin, lighting a cigarette. "You're a shameless vixen."

Marietta flushed with pleasure. "Not shameless," she qualified. "But men do like me. And I do enjoy the attention." Happily, she gazed around. Then, becoming serious again, she dropped her voice, asking, "How *could* you do that, Stanleigh? What were you thinking of? I've gone past being angry with you. But I do feel . . . separated from myself, in a fashion. I thought we understood one another. You were so het up, so enraged. Yet you seemed so very unconcerned with the possibility that *I* might hate *you*. And I did, you know. For a short time, I felt I might never be able to look at you again for creating that vision of me and then forcing it under my nose. How could I be anything but repelled? I know I'm no longer young. I know I must appear ridiculous to you. But I did believe you cared more for me than that. Every morning now, when I'm readying myself for the day, I wonder if I am as ridiculous as you made me feel."

"You could *never* be ridiculous!" Leigh insisted, more ashamed than before. "*I* am, but you could never be. Maybe you were right, maybe I shouldn't have gone to see my father. I don't know. He was very sweet . . . very truthful about what had happened and his feelings. The thing of it is, I believe what you say as well. So, what's true, then? That's what I can't determine."

"Leigh," her mother said quietly, "what I believed to be right at the time may only have been right from my viewpoint."

"What does that mean?"

"Oh," her mother sighed, "I suppose it means that looking at it from your point of view it may well have been a mistake. We all of us make them. If it was a mistake, it wasn't one I made intending to do you any harm."

"I've never thought that was your intention. But I embarrassed you, and Laurence, for no good reason. I love you so much. After the accident, after Carl and Stephen died, I was terrified that something would happen to you, and then I'd have no one. Then, crème past three years, with Joel, it's been the same thing all over again. You were my trump card, you were the one who'd be there. When we had that scene the other week, when I went to the country to hide, the only thing I could think, over and over, was that I'd put you in jeopardy somehow. I'd done something so dreadful, and I thought perhaps I'd be the one responsible for losing you. I need you to be alive and well in the world. What I'm having trouble with is caring about being alive and well myself."

"This is frightening," Marietta said, low. "I really don't want to hear you talk this way, Stanleigh."

"Please just forgive me. I'd rather hurt myself than hurt you."

"*I* would rather you didn't hurt either one of us."

The waiter delivered the double espresso and the cappuccino, saw he wasn't going to be rewarded with one of Marietta's smiles, and busied himself relocating the dessert cart.

"I know that," Leigh said, after he'd gone. "I was feeling sorry for the someone I was thirty years ago, and sorry because, no matter how badly I wanted it, nothing I could do would keep Joel alive. But in the past ten days, I've been thinking things through, wondering if it was unfair of me to depend on Joel the way I did."

"I don't think you were dependent upon him," Marietta disagreed.

"To the extent that I wanted to keep him in my life, I was. There isn't anything really wrong with that, is there?" she asked unhappily. "Is there? I didn't plan my life around him. I didn't keep everything on hold until I knew I'd be seeing him. It was just that I loved him so . . ." She cleared her throat and fiddled for a moment with the coffee spoon.

Marietta looked at her daughter, all at once more afraid for her than she'd been at the height of Leigh's wild behavior. "I wish," she said, "you could see yourself just once, just for a few minutes, as other people see you. You have *everything* to recommend you, but because of your misfortunes you see yourself as a failure. It's very sad, and it's very wrong. I'm your *mother*, Leigh. Don't you know how much I want you to be happy, to have people and things in your life you care about? Don't you know that my one, true fear is that I'd lose you? If I was wrong in what I did, I'm sorry. But it was such a long, long time ago, and you've managed to live through all these years without your father. If you've established a rapport with him, and it gives you satisfaction, then I can only be glad for you. But you really must get back into the world. You've got to pick up and keep going. I meant what I said: it is a sin to waste a talent like yours. And consider this: work could take your mind off everything."

Leigh shook her head. "It isn't the panacea for me that it is for you. And I'm definitely not in the right frame of mind for painting optimistic visions of fantasy worlds."

"Then try something else," Marietta counseled. "Why not consider designing the production for *Percival?* You *have* to do *something!* You must!"

Leigh stared at her mother for a long moment, seeing that Marietta was deeply, visibly, frightened for her. It shocked her to such an extent that she knew, in that moment, she was going to have to make every effort to reconstruct her life if only to please her mother. "Marietta," she said with a smile, "my lovely mum. Do you know that when I was little I used to tell my friends you were a princess?" She laughed softly, with welling affection. "I did. I told them you had magical powers and could cast spells. I used to go creeping with them into your bedroom to show them your closet, with all your magical gowns and dancing slippers. They believed me, too. I'm better now," she said, suddenly, surprised. "I am. It feels as if the cloud is passing. Perhaps," she said, tilting her head to one side, still smiling, "you really can do magic."

The balmy weather and humid air made him very aware of a deepening depression he hadn't acknowledged until his arrival in Florida. The only consolation he had resided in the small pocket diary he carried with him everywhere that had Leigh's Manhattan and Connecticut addresses, as well as that of her agent. Several times in the course of a day, he'd flip through the pages, find where he'd written these entries, and gaze at his own tidy printing, lifted just by the sight of her name. It felt as if his knowledge of these two places were something singular and esoteric. He would read her name, look at the street numbers, and feel linked to her.

In his more rational moments—while he sat on a bench with his mother watching his father and Lane play tennis—he told himself he was in trouble, that if he didn't take some decisive, positive position, he'd wind up in a place from which there might be no exit. He reminded himself constantly of all the things he'd done over the years that had been good, selfless, and beyond the call of duty. But he'd get a long-distance call from the Bedford real estate agent with a too-low offer on the house, and whatever morale building he'd done for himself would dissolve. He was having difficulty concentrating on the dinner table conversations that took place each evening; he was struggling every morning with the question of why he should bother to climb out of the guest room bed, put on clothes, and fake his way through another twelve or fourteen hours. He wasn't sleeping well, and awakened three and four and five times a night to tiptoe through the silent apartment to sit out on the balcony, smoking a cigarette and blinking at the night sky, while his insides churned and his brain tripped over itself with colliding thoughts.

At last, he got some stationery and sat down on the beach to write to Leigh. He knew he'd never be able to send the letter because in it he told the complete truth. He told her about Celeste, and Lane; he told her in detail about his mother and father, who after forty-six years of marriage were still in love and still relished each other's company; he told her about how it felt as if his balls had been cut off since he'd sold the company that he'd worked so long and hard to build; he told her that meeting her had been the single most encouraging event in his life in such a long time that he wasn't sure if he knew anymore how to respond to anything encouraging. He told her just about everything and, in the process, covered nearly twenty pages with his closely written script. And when he'd finished, he sat with his arms folded over his knees and gazed out at the foamy surf wishing he'd told her the truth in the first place. But it was too late now to change that.

After a time he scooped out a shallow pit in the sand, threw in the letter and set it on fire. Then he buried the ashes of his confession with sand and got up to go back to his parents and his daughter, knowing he couldn't have told Leigh the truth because he was too goddamned frightened of ever again trusting anyone the way he'd trusted Celeste. He'd always known it was risky, given her penchant for senseless rebellion, her inability to find happiness and sustain it, but he'd gone ahead and trusted her anyway, because she was, after all, his wife and the mother of their child. And he'd loved her. Jesus Christ! he thought, trudging along the beach. If you weren't very fucking careful, love could kill you.

His mother asked if he'd drive her around while she did some shopping, and he agreed, sufficiently distracted not to suspect her of ulterior motives.

They hadn't been in the car two minutes when she said, "Daniel, I think you must talk to me. You are not yourself."

He looked over at this woman, this person who'd always been in his life, and it was as if he'd never seen her before. Petite, dark-haired, wide-eyed; there was a furrow between her eyes, a down turning to her mouth. He thought the frown unbecoming; if she'd only smile she'd be quite beautiful. Then recognition kicked in, she was familiar again, and her expression was a warning to him that he hadn't been doing nearly as successful a job as he'd thought in concealing his anxiety.

He couldn't think of anything to say, and his mother waited until, at last, he admitted to her some of the things that had been troubling him. She listened thoughtfully, interrupting only to suggest a parking spot, and went on listening after Daniel had turned off the engine and sat with his hands gripping the steering wheel, staring straight ahead as the words gushed out of his mouth.

When he got to the end, his mother took a slow, deep breath and said, "I think two things, Daniel. I think first you should discuss these matters with your father. He understands more than you know. And I think secondly you must take your profits and start another business. Find something that has appeal and begin again. You are still a young man, and you have never been someone who could be content being idle."

"Oh, Christ, Mama! What the hell would I do?"

"Perhaps something different," she suggested. "You are not without resources, and you have an opportunity few are offered. Make a new start with a new enterprise. You *need* to *work*. If you spend all your days and nights thinking only of the past you will drive yourself mad."

"Maybe you're right," he said, letting go of the steering wheel and turning to look at her. "I'll give it some thought."

"And talk with your father, Daniel. Don't forget, he too had to begin again. Not perhaps at your age, but a beginning is a beginning."

He looked again at this woman, marveling at her composure and wisdom. She was the one who'd always taken a hard line with him, insisting he be self-reliant and resourceful, while his father had been the one to philosophize about the vicissitudes of life. Yet it was his father who'd gone into the business world to grapple with the ups and downs of money markets, foreign bankers, devalued currencies, inflated yen, trend-setting deutschmarks, Dow-Jones averages, Standard & Poor's indexes, and the power of the U.S. dollar. Privately, Dan had always believed that his mother, behind their closed bedroom door, had advised his father on every last deal he'd ever made. She might have been fashionable, sociable, and outwardly interested in little more than shopping, but she was also alert, informed, and, above all, vigilantly aware of everything going on around her. Nothing escaped her notice. And he wondered now why he'd thought she wouldn't see through his efforts to appear normal.

"I'll think about it," he said again.

After she'd completed her shopping, and he was carrying her purchases up to the apartment in the elevator, he thanked her. "It's good advice," he said. "I'm glad you got me to talk."

"Men are appallingly bad at talk that has to do with their feelings. You all, every one of you, think you will be made less if you admit to having emotions. Which is why," she concluded with a smile, "you have women. To prod you into confessing."

He kissed her on the top of her head, saying, "I knew there had to be a reason," which made them both laugh.

Christmas Eve, a small group gathered in Marietta's living room for drinks before dinner. Miles was there, resplendent in a black velvet suit, white silk shirt and handknotted red silk bow tie. He'd brought with him his latest client, a young man whose first novel Miles was flogging in a simultaneous submission to eleven publishers. Laurence was there, too, periodically casting uncertain glances over at Leigh as if expecting her to stage another unpleasant scene. And when he wasn't inspecting Leigh, he was looking worriedly at the other two unattached males Marietta had invited. One was a wholesale diamond dealer, a distinguished, silver-haired man with penetrating gray eyes and a large hooked nose. The other was a dapper, younger man of about Leigh's age who owned a smart antiques shop on Madison Avenue, which is where he and Marietta had met. Marietta's long-time senior secretary, Alicia, was also present and had, for the occasion, bought a black Albert Nipon dress with huge, padded shoulders and long sleeves, outsized jet buttons, and a very long, full skirt. The garment hung on Alicia's tall, bony frame with startling effectiveness. Leigh doubted anyone shorter than she, or heavier, could have worn it. Alicia had tied her hair back with a thin black velvet ribbon and even put on some makeup.

Leigh, feeling both doubtful and celebratory, had decided to pay homage to Tina Turner and had worn an Ungaro black leather miniskirt, a voluminous white satin shirt, and black shoes with four-inch heels. She'd put a lot of mousse into her hair, fashioned it into a spiky helmet, and then allowed it to dry that way. Marietta had a fit upon seeing her, whispering, "Go directly to the bathroom and fix that crown of thorns!"

With a laugh, Leigh had said, "Don't be silly, darling! It took me ages to get it this way. It's very trendy."

"You look like an offended porcupine!" Marietta had sniffed, before going off to serve more eggnog to her guests.

Feeling Laurence's eyes once again upon her, Leigh made her way toward him, seeing him stiffen at her approach. He was her mother's most frequent companion, and had been in love with her for better than ten years. He'd gone so far as to divorce his wife in the hope of convincing Marietta to marry him, but he'd yet to succeed. He called her daily from his office and saw her as often as Marietta would allow, which was several nights a week. An eminently successful trial lawyer of fifty-nine, Laurence never missed an opportunity to give Marietta gifts of jewelry, to take her on trips or to the theater, or to ask her to relent and marry him.

"Laurence," Leigh said quietly, approaching him, "I want to apologize. I was very upset, and not thinking clearly. I know it was dreadful, and I am truly sorry." She spoke very softly so that only he could hear, hoping, as she did, that his patrician profile would soften and turn toward her in forgiveness. "The whole thing was nightmarish, and you have every reason to be furious with me. I simply want you to know I regret it."

His eyes still averted, in an equally quiet tone, he said, "I understand how distraught you've been, Leigh. And we're all terribly sad about Joel. I've had time to think it over, and I realize you weren't entirely—responsible." Slowly, he turned to look at her. "It's your mother you upset, more than me. As long as you've made your peace with her, then I'm happy. And anyway," his features relaxed and he gave her a smile, "it's Christmas. We'll forget all about it. Just tell me one thing," he said, eyes again uncertain. "Who is that?" He nodded in the direction of the antiques dealer. "I mean, I know who he is. But who is he?"

She patted him on the arm, saying, "Nothing to worry about, Laurence.

You know my mother. She is the way she is. But she'd *never* give you up."
He smiled again, and she added, "It's the truth." It was. Marietta was all
but addicted to Laurence's style and generosity and attentiveness.

Heartened, Laurence at once made his way across the room to Marietta's side. Leigh watched him go, feeling better, lighter. She was actually
having a good time. Miles was dishing up all the latest dirt, and was just in
the middle of a heavily detailed narrative about Jerzy Kosinski while his
very tall, very thin, very fashionable new young client practically wet
himself over the details. Finishing that story, Miles launched into something he'd just heard about a middle-aged woman who'd written three
million-plus best-selling romances. "Then," he said, hitting his stride,
"the poor idiot took these two young thugs up to her hotel room. She had
such a good time, she had to cancel out on the conference the next day
because she couldn't find enough concealer to cover all her bruises."

"The poor thing," Marietta said crossly. "Really, Miles! I think sometimes you take rather too much pleasure in these sordid little scandals.
How *can* you find that tale amusing?"

Miles grinned, said, "Oops!" and hurried over to give Marietta a kiss
before murmuring an apology only she could hear. The two of them
began talking in undertones, and Leigh went out to the kitchen to help
herself to one of the hot hors d'oeuvres just being placed on serving trays.
She greeted the three women catering the party and turned to go, bumping into her mother who was coming in.

"Just a moment," Marietta said, a hand on Leigh's shoulder.

"What's wrong?" Leigh wanted to know.

"Not a thing," her mother said, and impulsively hugged Leigh to her
breast. "Are you having a good time?" she asked, releasing her daughter.

"I am. And you look ravishing."

Marietta lightly pushed her away. "Go talk to people. Talk to Miles,
see if you can't get him to stop reciting his party pieces. And slow down
on the gin, or you'll be too pied to eat."

"Darling!" Miles called to Leigh as she emerged from the kitchen.
"Come hear this! You'll love it. Nothing seamy or sordid," he told Mari-
etta as she reappeared behind Leigh. "Just a stunning bit of skullduggery.
Come along, Leigh!" he urged, pulling her close to him.

"Miles," Leigh whispered, "no more stories, please. Mother's becoming jittery."

"Oh!" he said, and appeared suddenly downcast.

"You look most elegant," she told him. "And if you'll be you for a
while, I'll stay right by your side and let you whisper all your naughty
stories in my ear. But you have to promise to be you for the rest of the
evening."

He rolled his eyes, saying, "Only for you. And I don't even know why I *do* these things for you."

"Of course, you do. You know exactly why."

"You know," he said, studying her, "you seem somewhat more recognizable this evening."

"No comments, no observations," she warned him. "just fetch me a fresh drink, then come back and talk to me."

He stood looking down at her for a few more seconds, then reached for her glass and went off to the bar. She watched him, feeling recognizable to herself for the first time in a very long while.

Fourteen

"I was just remarking to myself," Miles said, Christmas morning, "how very like your mother you are."

Leigh groaned softly and accepted the cup of coffee he was holding out to her.

"I always," he went on, folding himself into the armchair positioned near the window of his bedroom, "consider myself more than fortunate when you choose to lavish your sublime attentions upon my unworthy person. I merely wonder how I am meant to interpret this long-delayed return of your interest." He drank some of his coffee and watched her run her hand over her hair, an expression of dismay on her face as her fingers came into contact with the mousse-caked remnants of last night's coif. "The bathroom, complete with all mod cons, is where it's always been," he reminded her, "should you wish to avail yourself of the reviving supply of hot water that comes with this rent-controlled mausoleum."

"How can you talk so much, first thing in the morning?" she grumbled, tasting the coffee. "What time is it, anyway?"

"Oh, early. Just gone eight."

"Why are we *awake?*" she lamented.

"Because prodigal Miles wanted coffee and a quiet read of the *Times*. And then, he wanted company, too. I do hope you're not having second thoughts, regrets, that sort of thing," he said. "It *is* Christmas, and I, for one, have cause for rejoicing. A more perfect Christmas morning I couldn't imagine than waking up to find your lissome form next to mine."

She managed to smile at him and say, "Merry Christmas," while absorbing the picture he made in his burgundy silk dressing gown with the curlicued monogram on the pocket in cream-colored silk. He'd showered

128

and shaved, and had obviously been up for quite some time. In contrast, she felt like something small and dirt-encrusted that had just crawled through a camouflaged hole in the earth, groping its way to the surface. She did not, however, feel at all bad.

"And to you, my raddled poppet."

"Tread gently on my ego, Miles. It's the only one I've got."

"I was observing you last evening, while your inimitable mother juggled those three besotted Lotharios with the grace and dexterity of a Wallenda, and I couldn't help thinking that you have a rather tawdry majesty, especially when you get yourself rigged out in leather wrappings and sport truly wicked-looking high heels. And, observing you further this morning, while you slept, was almost illicitly pleasurable." Abandoning the word play, and with it the terribly tony accent, he said, "You really are very like your mother, Leigh."

She found her purse under the side of the bed, opened it for a cigarette, then sat upright again, asking, "Are you being complimentary? And don't you put any grounds into whatever it is you use?"

"Feel free to brew yourself a stronger version," he told her. "Given my advancing age, flawed ticker, and the rest of it, I've been forced to acquire a taste for brown, coffee-tainted water. I know it's awful."

"It is," she agreed. "I wish you'd come sit over here by me. This feels so confrontational. And I'm honestly not up to having you be caustic and witty at this time of the morning. Come sit with me and be sweet, cuddly Miles, instead of Pinter's unacknowledged half-brother."

With a laugh, he got up from the armchair and positioned himself on the bed, carefully arranging his robe before draping an arm around her shoulders, his fingertips spreading over her upper arm. "You've gone very thin since the last time I saw you without benefit of wrapping. And I don't recall you eating more than a few tidbits last night. Which is a pity, because the dinner was divine. And your mother was in rare form. That gown was a triumph. The only other woman I've ever seen who looked as well in black bugle beads was dear Maggie Leighton at the opening night of *Bye-Bye Birdie* back in London in '61. You're not upset, are you, Leigh?"

She patted his small potbelly and said, "No, anything but. You're one of the few men I've ever slept with who's a genuine, uncomplicated delight."

He beamed, and his fingers stroked up and down her arm.

"What did you mean before," she asked, "about my being like my mother?"

"Aaah! Just that I recognize definite similarities. Physically as well as psychologically. The two of you in one room is a veritable feast for the eyes. Of course, I can't picture Marietta in a leather miniskirt."

"You know," she said, cozy against his side, "when you're not playing to the crowd and giving out with your collected stories, I like you better than almost anyone I can name. Why do you do it? Why do you feel you *have* to do it?"

"Everyone has to do it," he said philosophically. "We all have little hats and little faces we put on to help us play out our assigned roles. Every so often we find ourselves having some difficulty getting the hat off. You spend so much time doing business—breakfast meetings, lunch meetings, cocktail meetings, dinner meetings—you simply forget the hat and the face, or they get stuck on. You do it. Your mother does it. We all do it, Leigh. You're hardly the same person in bed that you are at a party."

"No, that's true."

"Of course it is," he said equably. "Conversely, if you spend too much time away from business, it tends to be rather difficult to locate the hat and the face. Which, recently, has been your problem. Last night, and now, seem like a reunion. I've missed you, missed the late-night calls and your surprise visits. I quite liked it," he admitted, "when you'd stop by here after you'd been to the hospital."

"I always felt guilty, as if I was using you."

"Don't be simple-minded, my darling. There's using and then there's *using*. I was flattered that you'd come here. At the last, I wondered where you went."

"I didn't go anywhere. I just drove for hours, or I'd go home and sit half the night drinking coffee, trying to sleep but afraid to in case the telephone would ring and it would be the hospital telling me to come back."

"I understand," he said, and again stroked her arm. "I've been giving a lot of thought lately to what I'm going to do in my declining years."

"You're hardly declining."

"Whatever. I don't much care for the idea of spending the latter part of my life alone."

"Really, Miles?" She shifted to have a better view of him.

"Yes, really. Last year, after that big Five-O bash, I was more depressed than I've ever dreamed it possible to be. There I was, fifty years old, never married, no family, no one to leave behind. I revised my will and had the devil's own time trying to organize my bequests. I sat in my lawyer's office trying to think who I cared to have benefit from my demise and the two people who figured most strongly were you and your mother. I've shared more with the two of you, spent more time with you, than with anyone else. For God's sake, if it hadn't been for Marietta, I'd never have got the agency off the ground. And then you, my undernourished, neurotic little fantasist, with your Newberys and Caldecotts. You really must get back to work, Leigh."

"I can't," she said flatly. "What would you like for your declining years?" she asked him. "Seriously, what would your perfect scenario be?"

"Aaah," he sighed and looked up at the ceiling. "The perfect scenario. You won't hold this against me, for future use as blackmail?"

"Come on, tell me!"

"All right. Someone in my life to look forward to seeing. A big place, with a wing over here for me, and a wing over there for whomever, and we'd meet Tuesday in the dining room for dinner, or Saturday night we'd send out for pizza and watch old movies on the telly. In between times, we'd be off in our separate wings, doing whatever. Trips together, because we enjoy each other's company; outings to the ballet, and so forth."

She listened, nodding her agreement. "It sounds right."

His arm descended and his hand came around to cover her breast. "It could be arranged," he said soberly. "It is, suffice it to say, highly presumptuous of me."

"No, I'm flattered," she told him, touched. "But you wouldn't want to spend time with me, Miles. I've become a complete bore. All I've done lately is chop wood and go for long walks, trying to wear myself out so I'll be able to sleep."

"You don't think you're being just a little hard on yourself? It's only been a matter of weeks since Joel died."

"But I knew it was coming. I knew for months. That's what I don't understand: it wasn't as if I didn't know, hadn't had ages to prepare myself. But when it happened, it was . . . I couldn't believe it."

"One is never really prepared," he said quietly.

Her cigarette finished, she put it out, then nestled against him once more, reluctant to leave. For almost twenty years, Miles had been her agent and sometime bed partner. They'd gone for as long as eighteen months being platonic friends, and then they'd sleep together for a few months before returning to their platonic friendship. He never changed. No matter with whom, or how, he might be otherwise involved, his interest in her was constant. When she was feeling her best, she enjoyed his passion for gossip, his acerbic wit, his predilection for fancy dress, and she liked his looks. He was very tall, and tending now to be jowly; he had merry brown eyes, and a big brushy moustache over well-shaped lips; his smile was wicked and knowing and tended to show his large, very white teeth. He was highly intelligent, the product of the very best British public schools, and of Oxford; and he was always ticking away, just beneath the surface, ready to come up with some thoroughly libelous piece of gossip, or some spurious bit of knowledge. He was irreverent, disrespectful, and charmingly bearlike in bed. Making love with him was always direct and fairly primitive, but he had an abiding concern for his partner's satisfaction and had never failed to make her feel utterly desirable. On the minus side, he had a tendency to ape people, particularly her. mother. And he loved to say outrageous things simply to see what kind of reactions he'd get. Periodically, if he'd just been talking to her mother, or he'd had a difficult day, he'd turn on Leigh in a demanding fashion that had distressed her until she'd learned how to jolly him out of it.

"What are you doing today?" she asked him, her hand going again to his subtle paunch—something about himself he hated but which she liked.

"Childe Harold," he answered, referring to his new young client. "The feast at 4 P.M. Sounds like a horror film," he laughed, fondling her breast. "And you're off to glorious Marietta's, for a Christmas luncheon of flayed pigeons under glass, or something equally bizarre."

"Quail," she corrected him. "I have a gift for you. I'd like to give it to you before I go back to the country. What time do you think you'll be back from Childe Harold's?"

"No later than seven. If you're planning to come back, I'll wait and give you your wee giftie then."

"Are you happy, Miles?" she asked, sitting away to look at him.

"At this moment, excruciatingly. It's always been a mystery and a revelation to me that someone composed almost exclusively of bone and gristle could have such a wealth of breast. I believe I could actually be inspired to devote time creating sonnets to your delectable glands."

"Men are such fetishists," she laughed. "If it isn't breasts it's legs, or asses. Women aren't nearly so stupid."

"They're worse, my darling. Women go about with their heads stuffed full of your mother's addlepated fiction, searching for heroes."

"Shame on you!" she giggled. "Talking that way about your most important client."

"Come back here!" he said, pulling her close to him. "I may represent her, but I've never claimed she was a great literary figure. The truly lamentable fact of present day life is that the majority of people are so technologically addicted, they are so dependent upon their microwaves, their VCRs, their instant replays, that they've not only succeeded in reducing their attention span to about forty seconds or less, they've also acquired an appetite for trash. We live in an era when everything is disposable—overnight celebrities, fast food that comes in biodegradable containers, and books of no content. A good book requires time, and attention, concentration. No one has time. If it requires thought, it's too much trouble. The quick read, with appropriate amounts of badly described fucking done by no-dimensional characters bent on espionage, treachery, or evil of some sort, brings in the big dollars. Granted, your mother has her own genre, and no one *ever* does the dirty deed between the pages of one of her books. But it is what it is, and it is *not* great writing. It is, however, pleasant enough predigested pap; harmless, innocent, and somehow more worthy than a lot of the stuff I flog in the marketplace.''

"I have to go, Miles." She sat up.

"Have I offended you by talking about your mother?"

"No. I just really should go home, wash this jism out of my hair." Again she ran her hands over her head while he bellowed with laughter.

"You've got hours yet," he said. "Stay and play with Uncle Miles." He leered at her.

She sat on her knees and asked, *"Are* you happy?"

"Do you know that I love you, Leigh?"

She shook her head, as if she hadn't heard him properly. "You do?" she replied stupidly.

"I realized it when you married that insufferable gynecologist. I'd assumed you knew how I felt. Now, naturally, I know it was a ridiculous assumption."

"Miles! How the hell could you *assume* I'd know a thing like that? You never said a word, not a single goddamned word."

"I thought you knew."

"Well, I didn't!" she said angrily. "And you wait all these years to spring that on me now? I divorced that man more than *eight years ago!*"

"Does it make a difference?" he asked her.

"Of course it makes a difference! How could you assume I knew? I've always had this—this *respect* for your detachment. And now you tell me you're not detached at all. Do you honestly think I'd have married that idiot if I'd known how you felt? I only married him because of Joel. But if you'd told me . . . God damn it, Miles! I could have had my own child, I . . . now it's too late!"

"After the divorce, you stayed out in the country for almost two years," he said, distraught at her tears. "Then, you'd come and go, in and out of my life, and I thought *you* were the one with the astonishing detachment. And just when I was beginning to think perhaps you weren't quite so casual after all, Joel became ill. For the past three years, you've been unapproachable for the most part. Last night was the first time I felt I'd seen you in *years,* Leigh."

She wiped her eyes with the sheet, then crawled back over to him. "I didn't mean to come unglued that way."

"It's all right. I understand."

"I wish *I* did. I really do have to go."

"Would you like me to see you home?" he offered.

"I'll get a taxi."

He watched her fasten on her brassiere before pulling on the glittery pantyhose from the night before. When she was dressed, she came around the side of the bed to sit on his lap and wind her arms around his neck. Her nose touching his, she said, "For an oversized windbag, you really are very sweet. And I love you."

"Ah, well. For a malnourished crone, you are quite adorable. I'll see you here at seven."

She stopped in the bedroom doorway to ask, "Miles, did you really propose to me awhile back there?"

"You could say so."

"God, Miles! Why would you want to? I mean, you've seen me without my makeup."

"I've also seen you without your clothes. And vice versa. So what?"

"Well, you've given me something to think about."

"While you're tromping around in the snow out there in exurbia, consider a wing of your own. And pizza Saturday night."

She stood a moment longer, then went on her way.

"Did you spend the evening with Miles?" Marietta asked.

"No, I spent the *evening* with you, and your guests. I went *home* with Miles. He proposed to me."

"He proposed marriage?"

"Yes, he did."

"And I don't suppose you accepted?"

"I didn't say, one way or another."

"Hmmnn." Marietta surveyed the table, said, "Forgot the cranberry chutney," and went back to the kitchen for it.

"How many are coming this evening?" Leigh asked. Every Christmas all Marietta's single friends were invited to a buffet dinner.

"Six all told. I had to invite poor Lucinda. She was feeling terribly sorry for herself because Jeremy has business in Paris and couldn't be home for the holidays. I did warn her not to count on him, but she wouldn't listen. It's such a great mistake for a woman her age to place so much store in a man not only twenty-five years her junior but homosexual to boot. She has the idea in mind that she's going to convert him. It's absurd and depressing. But no one should spend Christmas alone."

"Aside from that, how is Lucinda?"

"Lucinda wouldn't be happy unless she was miserable," Marietta stated. "At times she puts me in mind of you."

"Oh, nice," Leigh replied.

"There is some truth to that."

"Well, at least I haven't pinned my hopes on someone like Jeremy. He's such an oily little slug. Why, when there are so many really lovely gay men, did she have to choose him?"

"She gave him her Art Deco platinum-and-ruby cigarette case."

"Christ! Two years ago, she swore she'd never part with it. She just *gave* it to him?"

"It gets worse," Marietta said, positioning the roast potatoes between them. "Not only did she give him the cigarette case, but she's also let him have the Cartier tiara for his show. She'll never see it again, the silly cow, and that piece must be worth a quarter of a million. It's an *original.*"

"Don't tell me any more," Leigh begged her. "I hate stories about women who get desperate and start doing really stupid things."

Marietta gazed meaningfully at her.

"I am *not* desperate, and I haven't done anything really stupid."

"That remains to be seen. Fortunately, you haven't anything monumentally valuable to give away."

"I've got all those so-called family heirlooms. Why didn't you tell me those were mostly marcasite and crystal?"

"You didn't ask. And there are several quite valuable pieces, too."

"I know. But what I can't figure out is how pawning those things gave you enough to get started."

"They didn't quite," Marietta said, telltale color in her cheeks. "How do you find the quail? You don't think it's too dry, do you?"

"No, it's fine. How did you do it, then?"

"I took some money, as well as the jewelry. I should have taken more, but at the time I thought it would be enough. After I'd paid our passage and so forth, it was necessary to pawn the jewels. Philip had his solicitor write a filthy, threatening letter, all to do with misappropriation of funds and wrongful flight. I sent a telegram directly to Philip telling him to call off the solicitor or I'd be forced to retaliate. He refused. I took a loan to repay him. And I retaliated by severing his connection with you."

"Why didn't you tell me this before?"

"Because I didn't think you needed to know that your father was someone who would've seen me in prison for taking what was rightfully mine. Five thousand pounds worked out to approximately three hundred and eighty-five pounds a year for every year of our marriage. Secretaries made more! And I had to see to you, and that dreadful house, and those disgusting, stupid chickens, *and* put up with him! I was eighteen when I married that man. He was handsome and withdrawn and I was young enough and stupid enough to mistake his withdrawal for a rare brand of charm."

"You should have told me," Leigh said.

"For what purpose, pray tell!"

"It helps me understand you better."

"You need that, do you?" Marietta asked.

"Sometimes. Understanding you helps me understand myself."

"I see. Have you picked up any nuggets of wisdom from this sordid little story?"

"Yes, I have," Leigh said impishly. "God! I really do love you. What I have learned, by Stanleigh Elizabeth Dunn: I have learned never to entrust my Cartier tiara to a young man of doubtful sexual persuasion with an unctuous manner and big pockets."

Marietta emitted peals of laughter, then had a coughing fit so that Leigh had to get up and pound her on the back.

Fifteen

"ALMOST EVERY YEAR, FOR AS LONG AS I'VE KNOWN YOU, YOU'VE GIVEN me silly little presents that have some rude significance known only to you. And now you give me something like this. You're starting to confuse me seriously, Miles. It's absolutely gorgeous. I love it."

"I thought last year's ashtray was a bit of genius," he said archly. "Nude reclining in bathtub, her feet tipped cunningly over the edge so you'd have somewhere to rest your cigarette."

"Well, really," she said. "That's exactly what I mean."

"At least I *thought* of you," he said, then asked, "You really like it?"

"I've never had anyone give me lingerie before. Are you quite sure you didn't intend this for my mother?"

"Of course not. Hers is yellow." He laughed heartily at his own humor.

"It's lovely," she told him, holding the pale pink silk teddy against herself.

"I confess that until I bought it I always wondered how women managed to do their business wearing one of those things. I shouldn't have worried. But don't those little snaps tend to irritate?"

"I'll report back to you."

"Perhaps you'd care to model it for me."

"What? Now? I've got to get going. But next visit, if you like."

"I would like. What's so urgently awaiting you in the country?"

"Snow, quiet, room to pace. I need time alone just now."

He sat for a moment stroking the leather of the attaché case she'd given him. "You'll listen to the tape, read the book of the show?" he asked.

"I told you I would, and I will."

"You can't pace for the rest of your life, Leigh."

"I know that. I'm parked in a tow-away zone, Miles. I have to go."

"What about New Year's Eve?" he asked. "What have you got on?"

"Nothing."

"Good. You'll come out with me! Wear something fabulous that you can move in. We'll go dancing."

"You're joking!"

"I am not. Get yourself tarted up, and I'll collect you at seven-thirty."

"Miles, I really don't . . ."

"There's the elevator. I will not take no for an answer. I'll ring you during the week. Drive carefully!"

She stopped at the mailbox at the top of the driveway, leaving the car running and the door open as she cleared the box, then climbed back, dumping the letters and magazines on the passenger seat. Only magazines and occasional bills came to the apartment. The bulk of her mail was delivered here. More snow. And the man with the snowplow still hadn't come. The car crunched through the frozen-over surface of the thick snow, its headlights catching and somehow magnifying the falling flakes. The effect was hypnotic. The night was very quiet, except for the faint whirr of the wind. She closed the garage door and, carrying her bag and the mail, walked back along the tire tracks to the house. She stood for a moment, her hand poised to open the door, listening. Nothing.

Her boots off and her coat hung away, she carried the mail to the kitchen and left it on the table while she plugged in the kettle for coffee. Then she quickly sorted through the mail, tossing the junk ads and solicitations directly into the trash. The magazines to one side, bills over there, and letters here. A large envelope of fan mail forwarded from her publishers; mostly letters from kids. They were, those letters, the best, most rewarding aspect of her work, and she always answered every last one of them by hand. A couple of statements from Miles's office notifying her of royalty deposits made directly to her bank account, with scrawled greetings penned by Miles across the bottom. Something from the Authors Guild, a dozen or so Christmas cards, and a letter postmarked Florida. She knew at once it was from Daniel and wondered, looking around, how he'd managed to get her address. She hadn't given it to him, but he'd obtained it somehow. And that bothered her. Thinking again of the frenzied way he'd made love to her, she was almost afraid to read the letter, and put it off until she'd started a fire in the living room, drawn the curtains, and sat down with her coffee and the fan mail, reading everything else first.

Finally, she slit open the envelope.

"Dear Leigh," he'd written, "I can't stop thinking about you. I meant the things I said, the way I feel. I have to see you again. We have to talk. I've been trying to concentrate on getting a tan, playing some tennis, but somehow everything makes me think of you. Please call me once Christmas is out of the way. Hope you have a good Christmas in the meantime. All my best, Dan."

She had no idea what she'd done with the number he'd sent along with the pendant. And right then, all she felt was upset at his having discovered her address. The letter served to add to the reservations she'd had at their last meeting and to strengthen her resolve not to see him again. But his asking her to call reminded her of the telephone and she went to the kitchen to see that the red light was flashing on the answering machine. She hesitated, reluctant to hear the messages for fear of learning that Daniel had also managed to get her unlisted number.

"Don't be ridiculous!" she told herself, and hit the PLAY button.

Three hang-ups, another call from *TV Guide*— didn't those people ever give up?—a message from her old school chum, Dolly, berating her for being such a rotten friend and ". . . How come you never call me? Seriously, I'm very sad about Joel, and imagine you must be down in the dumps. So, call me, okay? We'll get drunk and reminisce. Happy Christmas, Stannie, and please call when you get home. It's been too long, and I miss you."

The tone. Then Miles saying, "New Year's Eve, you unreliable strumpet. Be sure to write it in your diary. And let me know at any time if you're interested in having a wing of my estate. Call me in the interim if you're bored, or out of sorts, or in the mood to hear the latest, a positively juicy item I've only just heard. Be a good little tartlet, and don't forget to listen to the tape and read the book." His voice changed, and he said, "Forget all that, and call me when you get in, will you?"

While she was waiting for the machine to reset, she wondered about the recent spate of hang-ups, hoping they had nothing to do with Daniel.

"You took your sweet time," Miles said. "I was beginning to think something had happened."

"I was looking through my mail. I simply forgot to check the machine. Are you going to start keeping tabs on me?"

"Not at all. I just wanted to tell you last night was very nice, Leigh. And I'm absolutely serious about New Year's Eve. Don't disappoint me. I'm planning a fantastic night."

"You're serious about all of it, aren't you?" she asked him.

"I believe I am, yes."

"Why, suddenly?"

"Because I don't want you rushing off getting yourself involved with yet another fool without at least knowing how I feel about you. That way, if you do get involved elsewhere, I'll have stated my case. And *please,* look over the *Percival* material."

"I will consider everything," she told him.

Dan truly had intended to stay the full two weeks, but by the end of the first week he was so agitated, so restless that when the call came in from the real estate agent with a decent offer, he jumped at the opportunity to go back and deal in person with the negotiations. He told the agent he'd counteroffer by that evening, and quickly booked a seat on the afternoon flight to New York. He told Lane and his parents that some business had come up, as well as an offer on the house, packed his bag, kissed everyone goodbye, and got a cab to take him to the airport, refusing his father's offer of a ride.

Once on his way, he felt infinitely lighter, less antsy. And on the flight back, he several times got out his address book to look at the listings he'd made for Leigh. It amused him to think that, with the glut of mail over the holidays, he might actually get there in advance of his letter. She'd really be surprised.

One problem he could foresee was his apartment telephone. He'd have to get a machine so he wouldn't miss any calls, although the only call he cared about was the one he was sure to get from Leigh. Turning to the blank pages at the back of the little book, he started a list. He put "answering machine" at the top, followed by "moving company" with a question mark. If his counteroffer was accepted, he'd have to do something about clearing the house; he'd also have to start looking in earnest for another place. That meant trekking around with real estate people, and he didn't even know what he wanted, except to be nearer to Leigh. New Canaan had a number of advantages, not the least of which was that Connecticut had no state income tax. All the signs were positive.

Thinking about her and that house on Moonstone Lane, he had to wonder if she wasn't lonely there, out on such an isolated piece of property. The nearest neighbors were at least a quarter of a mile away. He hadn't been able to get a full view of the house, so it was possibly larger than it had looked, with only its side and part of the front visible from the main road. The garage was at the end of the long driveway, separated from the house by about a hundred yards. It was a two-car garage, but he'd seen only the Mercedes. The Good Doctor had probably dropped the second car off at the station when he'd taken the train to his office in the city.

She didn't have any kind of a marriage, he thought. Not only did she seldom refer to her husband, but she seemed to come and go when she chose, without consulting anyone. Look at the way she'd come to meet him. And the way she'd made love with him! No one with a good marriage did the things she did.

Christ! he chided himself. Since when had he become an expert on women and marriages? His only firsthand experience was his own fucked-up marriage to poor fucked-up Celeste. He closed his eyes and saw her, and the panic started pounding in his chest. For a second or two he couldn't seem to open his eyes and he thought he might start screaming. Then his eyes shot open and he gasped for air, frantically filling his lungs as he tried to erase that view of her, all the blood, so much of it; that blood like screams without volume.

He dried his hands on his handkerchief and gulped down the drink he'd ordered, a double vodka on the rocks. Why was it getting to him now? That's what he couldn't understand. He'd been just fine at the time. He'd handled the whole thing dispassionately, proud of himself for not coming unglued. What a jerk he'd been, to think he could get through something like that without turning a hair!

Neither his parents nor Lane knew all the details; he'd spared them that. And Celeste's father had passed away more than a year before, so he hadn't had to know. The only people he'd talked to had been the police, and that hadn't, strictly speaking, been talking. It had been a case of responding to questions, reciting facts. He hadn't really *talked* to anyone, and maybe that had been his big mistake. Maybe if he'd discussed it with his father or his mother, maybe if he'd told some people what it had really been like, it wouldn't have kept coming back at him now, giving him night sweats, making him feel so constantly on edge.

But there was Leigh. She was the positive side to all this, and thinking of her gave him a lift. He knew she cared. She was afraid to admit to it because of her doctor husband. But they'd work it out. Maybe he'd drive out, see the real estate agent, and then go by and look at Leigh's house. If only he had her number, he'd be able to call her up and they'd talk. They had a lot of talking to do. There had to be some way to get her number. But how? He went back and forth over ways and means, and suddenly, there it was. It was tricky, but not impossible.

"You *cannot* back out!" Miles said. "I knew, left to your own devices, you'd change your mind. But I won't have it, Leigh. If I must, I'll come out there and get you. This is pure, divine inspiration, and under no circumstances will I allow you to deprive either one of us. *Leigh!*" he implored her. "I've wanted for the last hundred years to live out this particular fantasy."

"My God!" she said, impressed by his pleading. "Just what is it you've lined up?"

"It's a delicious surprise. I guarantee you'll have the best time ever."

"You've got me so curious, I suppose I'll have to come."

"Oh, wonderful! Wear your frothiest creation. You have my word, it won't be out of place. I'll collect you at seven-thirty sharp. It's going to be such fun!" he crowed, sounding years younger and breathless with excitement.

She hung up and wandered back to the living room to open the curtains. The room smelled of last night's fire, and cigarette smoke. It looked shabby and she thought she really should get new carpeting and have the furniture reupholstered. Nothing had been done in here in fifteen years. The sofa and armchairs were all saggy-bottomed, the fabric worn right through in places. Maybe that would be her New Year's resolution: to do over this room. She'd have the house spruced up, and very possibly she'd do the production design for the musical.

She'd been prepared to hate what had been done, but the dialogue was spare and right in keeping with the original. And the songs—sung on the tape by the composer and lyricist—were cheery but not saccharine, and pretty catchy. For the past couple of days she'd been going around the house humming fragments of the melodies, Percival's theme in particular. She had, the previous evening, gone to the bookcase to get a copy of the book, studying the illustrations with an eye to how they might translate into stage sets.

In the bedroom, she looked through the closet. Nothing suitable here, but there was an evening gown in the city she'd worn once, about ten years before, to a charity ball the Good Doctor had wanted to attend. The dress had been hanging in a fabric bag in the closet ever since. And if she remembered correctly, the matching shoes were there, too. It was starting to feel like fun, and she unearthed the box with the jewelry her mother had given her to see if there was anything that might go well with the gown.

By two, she was ready to go. She carried her overnight bag to the car, thankful the snow had finally stopped so she wouldn't have to worry about road conditions. While she waited for the engine to warm up, she decided she'd tell Miles that evening she wanted to do the production design.

Dan couldn't believe it! She came out of the house carrying a small suitcase, opened the garage door, disappeared into the darkness inside, and five minutes later reversed the Mercedes and drove off.

He was torn between wanting to follow her and his need to get her telephone number. A few seconds and the decision made itself. Her car was out of sight. She drove very fast, and he made a mental note to talk to her about that. It was dangerous to drive too fast on these back roads, with so many blind turns.

He made himself wait fifteen minutes before he got out of his car, checked to make sure no one was around, then ran down the driveway to do a quick tour of the perimeter of the house. Through the kitchen window he could see the telephone and answering machine on the far end of the counter. But he couldn't read the printing on the dial.

All the doors and windows were locked. The mud room door was a snap, though. He just pushed his MasterCard in between the lock and the frame, jiggled the knob a couple of times, and the door opened. Perspiring heavily, he ran to the side of the house to see that the driveway was still clear, then he raced back and let himself in.

It wasn't at all the way he'd thought a house of hers would be. The kitchen wasn't, anyway. He'd have loved to take a good, long look around, but it was too risky. He left his wet shoes in the mud room, then went into the kitchen and looked at the phone. The center circle of the dial was blank except for the area code; 203 in large print, and then nothing. He was stunned with disbelief. Maybe the number was on the extension. He ran into the bedroom, spotted the extension on the table beside the bed, and got to it to find this dial, too, was blank. "Shit!" he muttered, returning to the kitchen. He stood, the kitchen clock ticking very loudly, trying to think. She wouldn't have her own number listed in her address book. And he couldn't see any address book around. He stared at the telephone and the answering machine beside it. Then, on impulse, he went over and pressed the outgoing message button on the machine. Her voice came on giving the number, followed by a message. Quickly, he noted the number in his book, reset the machine, made sure the signal light came on, then rushed back to the mud room.

There were different-sized coats and jackets hanging from hooks on one wall of the room. Above them hung a variety of hats. Opposite were a washer and dryer. And a stack of freshly done laundry, folded and waiting to be put away. Without thinking, he snatched the first item from the top of the stack, pushed it into his pocket, stepped into his shoes, and let himself out.

He was about to run back up the driveway when he stopped and looked to see his footprints disappearing around the side of the house. Breaking into a sweat, he realized he was going to have to do something about them. There was a shovel leaning beside the front door. He grabbed it and made a circle of the perimeter of the house, smoothing fresh snow over the impressions he'd made, following his tracks all the way to the cleared walk. Then he returned the shovel to where he'd found it, looked again to be sure the footprints had been erased, and fled back to his car, amazed at how easy it had been.

Someone really ought to talk to her about those locks, he thought, as he drove off. If he could break in so easily, anyone might. Checking his watch, he saw that the whole thing had taken less than seven minutes, although it had felt like hours. But he'd done it. He'd been inside her house, got her phone number, and something else—what was it he'd taken? he wondered, reaching into his pocket.

Some kind of slip, he decided, taking a hasty look. He'd examine it more carefully once he was out of the area. He was due at the real estate office in New Canaan in twenty minutes. The Bedford house was sold, pending the usual inspections and mortgage approval, and at an excellent price.

It seemed as if the broker wanted to know everything. Before she'd even consult her book of listings, she had to have information, specifics, so she could narrow down the number of places she'd show him. He was annoyed and overheated, and reached into his pocket for his handkerchief, almost pulling out Leigh's slip before he realized what it was. He glanced at the agent, hoping she hadn't noticed. She hadn't. But things were getting out of hand. What the hell was he doing, breaking into someone's house and stealing her undergarments? Did he really think Leigh wasn't going to notice the thing was missing? Or that someone had gone to the trouble of smoothing out the snow around the entire perimeter of her house? Had he moved anything, touched anything she might notice? Jesus! He was getting so worked up he could hardly concentrate on what the agent was saying.

"I have two very special condominiums I think might suit you," the woman said. "We'll go in my car."

They *were* very special, Daniel had to agree. Where had his mind been when she'd asked all those questions and he'd supposedly given answers? Special to the tune of nearly half a million for one, and just under four hundred thousand for the other.

"These are a little out of my price range," he told her. "But you're headed in the right direction."

"What is your ceiling, Mr. Godard?" she asked him a bit impatiently. "Perhaps I misunderstood."

She was such a bitch, Dan thought; she was acting as if she didn't believe he could afford anything in this town. Why was she being so miserable?

"I don't want to go higher than three," he told her. Three hundred thousand for a goddamned apartment was a lot of money, by anyone's standards. And six percent commission on a sale like that was a sweet eighteen thousand. Not a bad day's work for someone who only had to drive around town and show her listings. There was no need at all to be bitchy. Especially when, these days, you couldn't tell how much money anyone had by the way he dressed.

"Fine!" she said, flashing a quick, icy smile. "I have three other listings in that range that are also very special. Slightly older buildings, but lovely."

They drove through town, and he found himself becoming increasingly disturbed. By the time she was showing him through the last of the apartments, he was so distracted he could barely feign an interest in seeing the master suite and the two-and-a-half bathrooms. He said, "I'll have to think it over," and suffered while she drove him back to the office. He promised he'd be in touch, then jumped into his car and nearly rear-ended someone by starting to reverse without first checking the rear-view mirror.

He was driving, but he didn't know where he was going. All at once he was so exhausted he knew he couldn't make the trip back into the city. He needed to stop, to lie down and sleep. Resigned, he turned the car around and headed back to Bedford. He'd sleep on the sofa bed in the den, he decided, his hand in his pocket, buried in the silk teddy.

Sixteen

MILES STOOD, HIS HANDS CLASPED IN FRONT OF HIS CHIN, HIS breath held as he gazed at her, momentarily lost for words. He had never seen her look as heart-stoppingly beautiful as she did that night. The dress, of black taffeta, was strapless and ran in a line just below the tops of her breasts. Beneath the line were two rows of wide ruffles. Then the fabric wrapped itself tightly around her torso just to the waist, where it descended from dozens of tiny tucks into a full, sweeping skirt banded at the bottom with two more rows of ruffles.

Her hair was completely concealed beneath a close-fitting black net cap covered with sequins and beads in a feather design. With her hair covered and her high forehead bare, her eyes looked very large and very bright; her cheekbones were prominent; the shape of her face had startling definition.

"Leigh," he said at last, "you're simply beautiful."

"Oh, no," she tried to push away the compliment.

"You are," he insisted.

"Miles," she said, smiling, "you're very sweet." She began to turn, and he stopped her, his hands on her arms.

"Just once," he told her, "believe that it's you, and not someone being kind. Now," he released her. "Are you all set?"

"I borrowed Mother's evening cape," she laughed, caught up in his excitement. She grabbed the floor-length black satin cape from the chair and shook it open to reveal its brilliant egg-yolk yellow lining, then fastened it on at the neck and pushed it back over her shoulders so that the lining showed. The cape framed the bare expanse of her pale skin above the black gown. Her only jewelry was a large citrine pendant in a Victorian setting of curling silver leaves and flowers.

He couldn't stop looking at her, admiring not only the very flattering outfit, but this new version of the woman he knew. "I've never seen you in party gear. You realize that? We'll have to do this often. When I think of all the parties we could go to . . . this is going to be even better than I'd hoped."

"Where are we going?" she asked him.

"It's a surprise. No questions, please."

He'd hired a limo. The liveried driver snapped to attention as they came out of her building and, with a bit of a bow, held open the door.

"I'm getting very curious, Miles. You do look most elegant. Even black patent evening pumps. I've never seen *you* all rigged out in a tuxedo. You look edible." She leaned over to nuzzle her nose into his neck, then sat away to light a cigarette. It surprised her to discover she felt very strongly about him. Until Christmas morning, when they'd had that conversation, neither of them had attempted to put words to their relationship. Since then, intermittently, she'd found herself thinking about him. And now, all at once, it seemed she cared far more than she'd suspected. She wasn't sure of herself, or her timing, and so tried to put her emotions to one side. "Mother's going to the Plaza," she said, "with Laurence."

"Yes, I know."

"You do?" She looked around at him.

"I do have occasion to talk to her."

"Fairly often, from the sound of it."

"Almost daily, as it happens. Recently, we've talked rather more than usual. She's been, to say the least, rather concerned about you."

"I've started feeling better, since Christmas."

"That is undoubtedly because I've taken you under my amply endowed wing."

"It is, is it?" She smiled at him.

"I have decided you need guidance out of that slough of despond in which you've been mired."

"And you are my self-appointed tour guide?"

"Until such time as I am directed otherwise. Put that out!" he told her. "We're arriving."

As she pushed the cigarette into the ashtray, she looked out the window, asking, *"Where?* I don't see a thing."

"Paradise on the second floor," he replied. "Roseland."

"How fantastic! I've always wanted to see what it's like."

"You will love it," he declared.

The mirrored ball in the ceiling revolved, sending shards of white light over the dense, whirling crowd, while the big band onstage played Glenn Miller classics.

"I do love it!" she laughed, as he moved her about the floor.

"My secret passion," he confided, leading her with effective ease. "I was the too-tall, too-thin—if you can imagine it—out-of-place youth who hung about the local *palais-de-danse* and won the hearts of every young female within a fifty-mile radius. Every weekend while I was at Oxford, I polished up my shoes, slicked down the hair I then had in abundance, and went to loiter with intent while I eyed the likelier of the ladies. There are times when, if I close my eyes, I can see those girls in their best frocks, and hear the music. Those are some of my happiest memories."

"I'll want to come here all the time. It's like a time warp, Miles. All the beehive hairdos and crinolines, anklestrap high heels. And the makeup; so much bright-blue eye shadow."

"Forgive me," he said, "but are you not the same woman who came out disguised as Billy Idol a short time back?"

"Point made."

"All of us here are devoted to the dance, and to the music."

"Thank you for bringing me," she said seriously. "I'm having a wonderful time."

He kissed the tip of her nose, then said, "This city is the most terrifying and the most fabulous on earth. I know of places that simply couldn't exist anywhere else. Yet you risk your life to get to them. Twenty-seven years I've been trying to make sense of why I'm here. But every time I think of living anywhere else, I start traveling down a mental list of the things I'd miss, and I know it isn't time yet for me to leave. Undoubtedly, I'll wake up one morning to find there's no list at all. Then, I'll retire to the country."

"To the estate, with the wing over here, and the wing over there."

"It does exist," he said. "I have some property, with a dilapidated farmhouse on it."

"I didn't know that."

"Don't be naive, my darling. I don't blurt out everything. And I'd remind you the two of us have only very recently begun to communicate again in any reasonable sort of fashion. A drink?"

"I'd love one."

Everything seemed extraordinary. He led her by the hand off the dance floor, and she felt secure and cosseted simply because he had hold of her hand and was leading the way. She wondered if making love with him would be different now, and experienced twinges of excitement at the prospect.

"Who was the old friend, by the way?" he asked, after their drinks had been served.

"What old friend?"

"The one who rang me, then sent along the insured package."

"Oh! Someone I met on the flight to London."

"I see," he said.

She thought he looked hurt as he turned to watch the dancers for a minute or two.

"You didn't give him my address, did you, Miles?"

"Shame on you!" He turned back to her. "You know better than that. There is no one on my staff who'd give out any personal information at all about any of my clients. Why?"

"I had a letter from him, at the house. It bothers me. I can't think how he got my address, and I don't like the idea that people could easily find out where I live, start pestering me."

"You wanted to dip in and out of this chap's life like some convenient pool. But he's smitten, and he's pursuing you. Have I got it about right?"

"Why are you so angry?" she asked him.

"I'm not angry at all," he said, with an exaggerated lifting of the eyebrows and widening of the eyes that only served to underscore the fact that he was indeed angry.

"You are," she insisted.

"Never mind that. Why are you so concerned that this chap's managed to get your address? Have you done something foolish, Leigh?"

"I don't think so. I slept with him twice."

"Bestowing your favors at random again."

"Miles! You're being unpleasant and peculiar, not to mention insulting. If you want to know the truth, the only other person I've slept with in the last two years is you."

Hearing this, he softened and became apologetic. "Is that the truth?" he asked, reaching for her hand. "Honestly?"

"Honestly."

He held her hand to his mouth, and gazed at her. "You're my only one, too," he admitted.

"Why?" she asked him.

He kissed her knuckles, then her palm. "No one else interests me."

"I think I want to design the production, Miles. I love the songs. I can't stop humming the melodies. And they've been very clever and sparing with the dialogue."

"That makes me happy," he said, smiling now. "It really does make me happy."

"Why have you never married?"

"Why?" he repeated, closing both his hands now over hers and holding it captive on the table in front of him. "Why?" He looked around, listened for a moment to the band, then returned his eyes to hers. "Come dance with me," he said. "We've only got another forty minutes before we move on, and we can just as easily talk while we dance."

He directed her back onto the floor, wrapped his arm around her waist, put his cheek to hers, and said, "Twenty-five years ago, you were Marietta's fractious, married daughter. The first time I saw you is as clear in my mind as if it were yesterday. I'd stopped by the apartment for a drink with your mother. We were sitting in the living room going over the terms of a contract, and you came flying in, all full of yourself and vibrating with energy. I remember looking up thinking, 'What the bloody hell?' and feeling my stomach drop at the sight of you. You were what, twenty? Didn't look more than fifteen or sixteen. And you had that astonishing mane of burnished copper hair, and those great calf's eyes of pale green. You were long and skinny and electric, and couldn't have been anyone but Marietta's daughter. I'll never forget it. Your bell-bottom trousers and a paint-smeared sweatshirt, dirty fingernails. You were in and out in five minutes.

"When your mother told me you were married, I couldn't believe it. For one thing, you didn't look old enough. And for another, it simply wasn't *fair*. But that's the way things were. There was nothing to be done about it.

"A couple of years after that, you had the first book done and I offered to represent you. And a couple of years after that, you invited me, and I quote, 'to reaffirm your desirability.'"

"God!" she laughed softly. "I really did say that, didn't I?"

"You did indeed. And I was only too happy to oblige you. So," he took a breath, "we embarked upon our curious affair. Now you see her, now you don't, for the next six or seven years. Until the accident. Then, when I should have stated my case, I didn't, and you married that overpaid vagina inspector. Mercifully, that didn't last too long. But by then, I'd decided to take things as they came because it seemed fairly clear I'd left it for too long. And anyway, I thought I'd become adept at being a bachelor. No shortage of invitations, no shortage of company. And when the mood suited you, I'd be available. I've only ever thought of *you* as someone I'd consider attempting to live with, and you seemed—after that last go-round—to prefer being on your own.

"Then, as I told you, after that depressing bash last year, I started thinking about my life and came to the conclusion that I'd probably blown it for good and always. But if I ever again had the chance to state my case, I would, and in no uncertain terms. Soooo," he wound down, "finding you there in my bed on Christmas morning, I decided to play fast and loose with my own poor shriveled ego and tell you that you still excite me, in all kinds of ways, and that despite all the nonsense, I adore you, you cantankerous little hen." He lifted his head to look at her, and asked, "Was it that bad a story?" as he put a finger to her cheek, caught a tear and licked it from his finger.

"I remember you that first time," she told him. "You were sitting on the sofa with Mother, and your legs were so long that your knees were up almost to your chin. And I thought you were far too young to have that great big moustache; I thought you'd probably grown it hoping it made you look older." She sniffed and smiled up at him. "This great oaf sitting there in his three-piece suit, with his terribly upper-class accent, and his excruciatingly good manners. You jumped up and shook hands with me. Remember? And I started laughing. I don't even know why, really. I just thought you were trying so hard to be mature and competent, and underneath all that, you weren't really sure what was going on. I guessed right off you'd been to bed with Mother. You had such a guilty look. I liked you, Miles." She rested her head on his shoulder. "You made me wish I'd met you, and not Carl, first.

"I'll tell you a secret not even Mother knows. No one but the Good Doctor knows. Because it was part of the agreement." She raised her head and met his eyes. "The reason I got so upset when we talked the other morning . . . I agreed because of Joel, you see, because Jacobson had him and categorically didn't want any more children. But I thought it wouldn't matter. I'd have Joel. So I agreed, and he had one of his colleagues do it. He claimed it was unethical to perform surgery on one's own wife, but he had a colleague who would take care of making sure there'd be no possibility of my having any more babies.

"It was supposed to be a simple, little procedure. But it went horribly wrong. Infection set in, and they had to take me back into surgery. By that time, the infection had spread so far the only thing they could do was remove everything. I told myself I didn't mind. Because I'd be going home to Joel. Well, as we both know, Joel is no more. I'm not really sorry, Miles. Not about Joel. But when you said what you did, and I thought about how different things might have been . . ." She left the rest unsaid, and returned her head to his shoulder. After a few minutes, she said, "I cared far more for you than I ever did for Erik Jacobson."

"What about now, Leigh?" He'd stopped moving, and they'd become an island around which the other dancers eddied. "What about now?"

"Maybe," she allowed. "Maybe. But I need time. It's still too soon. I still cry without warning. I'm still finding things of Joel's in the apartment, and at the house. I do love you, and part of it is because I know you now. It probably wouldn't have worked back then. But I do know you now. Give me a kiss, Miles."

Dan couldn't sleep. He lay on the sofa bed in the den in the dark, his eyes open, his brain almost audibly clicking and whirring. At last, he turned on the light, got up, and went through each room of the house, turning the lights on as he went. Years of history crowded in on him as he recalled all the birthday parties at which Lane had sat there, at the head of the table, in the dining room. Paper hats and party horns, gaily wrapped gifts, triangle sandwiches, ice cream, and cakes with candles. Family dinners of silent, epic duration while Celeste sat and glowered at him and Lane, defying them to choke down their food in her presence.

Her anger was like a coating that lay heavy on the walls of every room. If he put out his hand, he was sure he'd feel it, hot and sticky, like her blood. He was aware of her presence as he pushed past the swinging door into the kitchen and stopped with his hand on the light switch, blinking in the fluorescent brightness at the white appliances, the bare counters and polished floor of black and white tiles. The plants on the windowsill had long since died, but no one had thought to dispose of them. He stalked across the room, opened the cupboard under the sink, found a large green plastic bag, and dumped the desiccated plants into it; knotted the top, opened the back door to admit a burst of gelid air, and heaved the bag out beside the bin enclosure. The raccoons and neighborhood dogs wouldn't bother with this particular trash.

He slammed shut the door, locking it, then marched out of the kitchen leaving the lights on. Into the living room to glare at the furniture, wondering how they could have called it a "living" room when neither he nor Lane had ever voluntarily set foot in the room for fear of disarranging the magazines so artfully positioned on the table behind the sofa, or of inadvertently pushing a chair or a pillow out of place. This was Celeste's showpiece, with the needlepoint fire screen, and the never used tuxedo sofa, the polished brass candlesticks, the standing brass lamps and crystal ashtrays. Jesus! All these years and no fire had ever been lit in that fireplace because the smoke might have discolored the pale-green walls, or an ember might have burned a hole in the pale-green carpet, or the smell of burning wood might have buried itself in the draperies. He hated this room.

Upstairs, he stood in the middle of Lane's bedroom, studying the rock posters on the wall, blow-ups of last year's superstars—Boy George, and Frankie Goes to Hollywood, and Cyndi Lauper. Stuffed toys surveyed the scene from the top shelf of the bookcase to which they'd been relegated some years earlier. The lower shelves were crammed with old school textbooks and paperback novels. *To Kill a Mockingbird, There Must Be a Pony, The Catcher in the Rye,* volumes of Shirley Jackson and Raymond Chandler, and *A Separate Peace; Your Turn to Curtsey, My Turn to Bow*—all books he'd read years ago himself, titles that had the warmth of familiarity.

This was the only room in the whole fucking house that had experienced a life, that had shaken with music and telephone conversations and crowds of girls giggling together over the school yearbook, with its muzzy class pictures and cute comments.

He turned off the light, shut the door gently, and moved along the hallway to the master suite. This was where he'd been headed all along. This had been his destination for twenty-one years. And had he only known it, he'd never have said yes, never have said I'll be honorable, I'll be responsible, I'll do the right thing, the supposed only thing. He'd have locked himself into his boyhood bedroom and refused to come out.

Barefoot, he padded across the carpet, sucking in his breath as he went, his shoulders rigid with tension as he arrived at the bathroom and stopped, gearing himself up. Fear like bile rising into his throat, he reached inside and flicked on the light. Of course it was immaculate. The place had been completely scrubbed and repainted. But he could see it all nevertheless, just the way it had been, the way she'd intended him to see it. The blood pooled on the floor by the sink, splatters leading over the floor to the tub.

His eyes moved across the room and came to rest on the tub. He was folding inward, trying to contain the horror. Right there, that was where she'd abandoned herself finally, leaving the remnants behind for him to find, knowing—she'd had to know—she'd at last succeeded in attaining the reaction she'd been seeking all her life.

Sliding down, boneless, he sat on the floor, trying to understand what she must have been thinking while she did it. No "hesitation marks." The police, the officials had spoken so knowledgeably, as if they'd dealt with similar scenes of carnage so often they'd lost their capacity to react. Long, purposeful cuts, they'd told him. The length of both inner fore-arms, around both ankles. And then, as if dissatisfied, it appeared she'd gone berserk, slashing at herself; she'd left the fouled single-edged blade on the edge of the sink before lifting her lacerated limbs into the tub, to immerse herself in the water that overflowed, spilling down the porcelain to inch across the floor. All tucked into herself, as if shielding those torn arms, the ravaged breasts and belly and thighs, she'd closed her eyes and gone dreaming while the blood ceased its humming in her veins and swam outward in thick, swirling strands to blend with the water; an embryo returned to its liquid medium. They'd never, the cool officials admitted, seen quite such an *angry* suicide; never seen anyone so *flayed* by her own hand. Which was why they had to ask so many difficult questions.

He wept, great shuddering sobs, and crawled out on his hands and knees, to collapse on the bedroom carpet until his body ceased its spasm. He shouldn't have come here, no matter how tired he'd been; he should have gone back to that safely impersonal little apartment where he had no difficulty sleeping, where the bedclothes still bore Leigh's scent. This place no longer belonged to him; it had never been his. In sixty days it would be overrun by the new owners' three small children; their ebullience would kill off Celeste's ghost. Arrangements would be made for movers and packers to come here and deal with the collection of worldly goods Celeste had so avidly acquired. But then what?

He sat up. There was no point in wrapping and packing when he wanted none of this, and only Lane's things had a future. He'd get rid of it all, sell it. He never wanted to see any of it, ever again. He and Leigh would get their own things, new things, comfortable things, things without prior history. They'd shop together, mutually agree on their selections.

Back downstairs, he closed up the sofa bed, returned the pillows and bedding to the den closet, then went into the hall bathroom to shower. He steeled himself to return upstairs to the closet where he stripped his clothes from the hangers and dresser drawers, packing everything in suitcases and some cartons he brought up from the basement. Then he carried it all out to the car, filling up the trunk and most of the back seat.

When he was done, and he'd taken everything—the photo albums and framed pictures, income tax papers from the desk in the den, and the Braun electric coffee mill from the kitchen—he was so dizzy from lack of sleep he was seeing double. But he wouldn't stay in this house. He put on his coat, wound a scarf around his neck, went out to the car, and started to drive.

A knocking sound awakened him. Jerking upright, completely disoriented, he turned, and opened the car window.

"See your driver's license and registration, sir?" the police officer asked politely.

"Sure." Dan wet his lips and popped open the glove compartment for the registration, then got his wallet from his hip pocket to pull out the license. While the officer went back to his patrol car to check the documents, Dan looked through the windshield to see, with a start, that he was parked on Route 124, opposite Moonstone Lane. Jesus! he thought. What if she'd come home and seen the car, called the police?

The officer returned, passed the papers back to him, and bent down with one hand on the roof of the car, asking, "You all right, sir?"

"Oh, I'm fine. Just felt too tired to keep driving, so I thought I'd pull over, grab a little shut-eye for a few minutes."

The officer's eyes went to the boxes on the back seat. "Moving, huh?"

"That's right. Shifting some stuff from the old house."

"Helluva way to spend New Year's Eve," the officer said. "Drive carefully now. And don't forget to buckle up. Good day, sir."

Dan got the car started, remembered to fasten his seat belt, then pulled cautiously off the shoulder onto the road. A glance in the rearview mirror confirmed that the officer was standing by the patrol car, watching him go. Dan drove on, checking the mirror every few moments, until he'd gone a good five miles and the road was deserted in both directions. It was six-forty. He'd slept for almost four hours out there on the road where anyone could have seen him. What bothered him, when he remembered as he was taking the on-ramp to the Merritt, was that he'd forgotten to do what he'd gone there for: the damned silk thing was still on the passenger seat. The cop must've seen it and wondered if Dan was one of those creeps who liked to masturbate into women's underwear.

"Jesus!" he said aloud, easing his foot down on the accelerator. Not only hadn't he put the thing back when he'd had the chance, but a goddamned cop had seen it. He was going to have to be very, very careful from now on.

Seventeen

"I REALLY WISH I KNEW WHY YOU INSIST ON FLEEING BACK TO THE COUNTRY every time, without fail, just when I'm enjoying your company most. We have before us a four-day weekend. What is so urgently awaiting you out there, in the hinterlands?"

"Nothing, especially. Why don't you come with me?" Leigh said. "We could go over some of my ideas for the production. I've made a few notes, some rough sketches."

Miles sat, silently contemplating the logistics. "I suppose," he said at length, "I could bring my car and follow you there."

"You could also drive up with me. I'll put you on the train Sunday night."

"No good. It wouldn't be so bad if it was a direct run, but I loathe making that change in Stamford, hanging about on the platform, hoping the express is going to be on time. And it never is. I will come, but I'll bring my car."

"You're an elitist snob," she teased. "The truth is, you don't like being mistaken for a lowly executive."

"I see nothing wrong with elitism," he said loftily. "Some of my best friends are members of the elite."

"I'll give you Joel's keys, and you can meet me at the house."

"Perfect."

She found the keys in the kitchen drawer and gave them to him before they went down to the garage to get her car. She dropped him in front of his apartment on Fifty-ninth Street, explained that she'd stop along the way for some groceries, then headed across town. The traffic was light, the day mild and sunny. She felt really very well as she played with the

156

dial on the radio until she'd located Joel's favorite station. The old show tunes connected her to Joel, and she was able to think about him without feeling bereft. Nostalgic, lonely for him, but no longer anguished. She had, with Miles's help, taken another small step away from the darkness of her grief.

Since she knew none of the stores in New Canaan would be open, she took the thruway instead of the Merritt, in order to stop at one of the markets she thought would likely be open in Darien. It was a minor but necessary inconvenience. With Miles in the house for four days, she was going to have to offer him something more substantial than coffee and burned toast.

Because there was so little traffic, she couldn't help noticing the dark-blue BMW that seemed to be keeping pace with her. She looked into the rearview mirror every so often to see that it was still behind her, and wondered idly why it didn't pass. Then she got caught up in the music and forgot about the other car until she was leaving the thruway at the Darien exit. When she put on her turn signal, so did the BMW. The car stayed behind her right through town, keeping a short distance back. It was there when she turned toward the shopping center after passing under the railroad bridge, but when she pulled into the parking lot, the BMW drove on past, and she promptly forgot all about it.

She filled a cart, actually enjoying herself. These new moments of all but mindless pleasure seemed remarkable to her; they were proof of her slow but steady return to life, and when she recognized the moments she became increasingly optimistic, as well as mildly guilty at leaving her sorrow behind. Yet she knew this was the way it had to be, and she accepted it.

Miles had already arrived. His car was in the garage, and he came out of the house as she pulled in, to help carry the bags inside. As she was about to open the trunk, she noticed a dark-blue car going past on the main road. She thought to mention it to Miles, decided it was nothing more than coincidence—Connecticut was crawling with BMWs, Benz's, and other imported cars—and said nothing.

"Very domestic, this is," Miles commented, helping to put away the groceries. "Very suburban, and very twee."

She leaned against the counter, lighting a cigarette. "Good or bad?" she asked him. "Sometimes I find it hard to decipher your cryptic little observations."

He closed the refrigerator door, saying, "It's a pleasant change. I always forget how quiet it is outside the city. It's also been quite some time since I've seen you in your alternative environment. While I was waiting, I had a look around."

"Snooping!"

"No, merely a look around. In view of the deplorable condition of the rest of this place, I have to assume Joel did over the kitchen. It's the only room that's had any attention paid to it. Speaking of which, your light's flashing." He indicated the answering machine, and stayed by the refrigerator as she walked over, carrying her cigarette, to push the PLAY button. He liked the way she moved, the way she held her cigarette; he liked it that even the smallest things captured her attention, so that the directness of her movements led to periods of stillness while she studied an object, or listened to something. She'd sail purposefully across a space, then halt all motion while she concentrated her attention. Now, for instance, she stood with one hand on the counter and the other, with the cigarette, in midair, her eyes on the machine as the tape rewound. He was also perennially intrigued by the kinds of things that caught her attention. He attributed her eye for the unusual to her being an artist, but unlike other artists he'd known, Leigh could be highly articulate about how the things she saw and heard affected her.

He was so taken by the look of her in this setting that it was a few seconds before he homed in on the voice on the tape. Then, his focus shifted to her face, to see she looked agitated and confused.

"I decided," the voice said with a forced little laugh, "that you must've lost my number. Which is why I haven't heard from you." A change of tone, the voice going deeper: "Leigh, I have to see you. Please call me as soon as you get in. There are things we really have to talk about; important things." He gave a number, then said goodbye.

The tone signaled the end of the message.

Then, "It's me again. I forgot to wish you a happy New Year. Please don't forget to call me as soon as you get in."

The tone, followed by five short beeps, signified the last of the messages.

"Jesus!" Leigh said, and hit the RESET button. "Now he's got my number. How the *hell* did he get it?"

"I take it," Miles said, "that's your airplane playmate."

"It's *not* amusing!" she said sharply. "First he manages to get my address. Now he's got my telephone number. I feel as if I'm under siege. Obviously, I'll have to get a new listing."

"Why don't you simply tell him, nicely, of course, that you're not interested?"

"I've already done that. Clearly, it's made no impression whatever. Do you want a drink, or some coffee?"

"You want a drink," he could see. "Why don't we have coffee instead? It's still a bit early to hit the sauce."

She held the cigarette under the faucet, doused it, then threw it into the garbage bin under the sink. "Could your ticker handle a decent cup of coffee?" she asked, grabbing the kettle to fill it.

"My ticker is capable of handling any number of things."

"Yes, but what about real coffee?"

"Even real coffee." He gave her a smile, but she didn't notice.

She opened the cupboard over the stove, got the Chemex pot, threw a paper cone into the filter, then half-filled the filter with the fresh-ground dark roasted coffee she'd just bought. Her movements were now jerky, jagged, reflecting her irritation.

"Is there something wrong with this guy?" he asked, curious.

"I don't know *what's* wrong with him! He certainly doesn't understand a 'no' when he hears one. I want to change clothes. Come keep me company."

"I'd like to remind you you did promise to model a certain undergarment."

"The fashion show's scheduled for later on," she told him, trying not to take her upset out on him, but having trouble holding it in. It gave her the jitters to think Daniel had somehow managed to secure both her address and telephone number.

He sat on the side of the bed while she threw open the closet doors, watching as she collected a pair of jeans, a plaid shirt, a heavy sweater, and a pair of wool socks.

"I'm sorry to go on and on about it," she said, tearing off her clothes as if they were contaminated, "but I'd dearly love to know how he got this number. I mean, what's the point to being unlisted if just anyone can get hold of your number?"

He let her talk, thinking she'd run herself dry on the subject if he simply listened without commenting. She kept on, speculating on the possible ways in which Daniel might have obtained her number, while she hung away the outfit she'd been wearing, then pulled on the casual clothes. By the time she was dressed, rather than running dry, she'd worked herself into a tight-lipped state of near-hysteria. She went quiet very abruptly and stood gazing at the framed picture of Joel on the dresser top.

"We could take a drive later, go to see the 'estate,' if you like."

"What?" She turned to look at him.

"It's not too far, over near Brewster. I thought you might care to see my dilapidated holdings."

"The coffee," she remembered, and went shoeless back to the kitchen.

He got up to follow and arrived in time to see her lighting another cigarette, before lifting the kettle to pour water into the filter. She seemed, at best, only peripherally aware of him, and he told himself the wise thing to do would be to take himself off to the living room with one of the manuscripts he'd brought along. No point to crowding her, he reasoned; if she wanted to talk, she would. He opened the new attaché case she'd given him, got a manuscript, then stretched out on the sofa with his head propped on the arm, and started to read.

A few minutes later, she came in carrying two mugs of coffee, the cigarette clenched between her teeth. She placed one mug on the coffee table within his reach, and the other on the mantel. Then, squinting against the cigarette smoke, she pushed crumpled newspapers under the grate, positioned three logs, and struck a match to get the fire going. It was something he'd seen her do many times, but he watched her over the top of the manuscript, trying to keep up with her mood swings. She was no longer as visibly agitated, but deeply pensive, as she reached for her coffee, at last removed the cigarette from between her teeth, and sat cross-legged on the floor to keep watch on the fire.

As had happened not infrequently during the many years he'd known her, he found himself moved and softened by her upset. "Are you feeling sad, Leigh?" he asked.

She gave a slow nod of her head, allowing almost a full minute to go by before saying, "I did warn you. I'm not the best company just now, full of unpredictable ups and downs."

"I don't require entertaining," he said, and went back to his reading.

She drank her coffee and chain-smoked, from time to time poking at the fire to rearrange the logs. She liked the heat, and smell, and noise, of the fire; it soothed her, made her drowsy. Like a poultice, it drew at her anger and apprehension and sadness, until her shoulders relaxed and she felt calmer. She gazed into the fire, appreciating the many different colors it produced, almost mesmerized by the glow. When at last she shifted to look over at Miles, she saw he'd fallen asleep. The manuscript was in danger of sliding off his chest.

She got up and put the pages on the coffee table, then watched him sleep, feeling her affection for him returning. He was too long for the sofa, and didn't appear especially comfortable with his head and feet propped on the shabby arms. His presence, though, altered the room, made it look less neglected, less abandoned.

Redirecting her gaze to the window, she saw odd snowflakes drifting down, and the sun casting blue shadows on the undisturbed snow coating the lawn; its surface was so smooth it looked lacquered. Her mood lifting, she thought she'd get the teddy and put in on to show him. She went to the mud room for the laundry and carried it to the bedroom. No teddy. She was sure she'd put it through the delicate cycle with the other under-garments. Maybe it was still in one of the machines. She went to check. Both the washer and dryer were empty. She double-checked, then went back to the bedroom to search every drawer in case it had been put away with the socks or the shirts. It hadn't.

Puzzled, she reviewed the teddy's whereabouts since Miles had given it to her. She'd brought it here along with her other Christmas gifts. She remembered setting it to one side; she preferred to launder anything new prior to wearing it, in order to get rid of any sizing the manufacturer might have put in to keep the item from losing its shape. She could see herself setting the wash cycle, adding the Woolite; she saw herself timing the dryer and setting the dial to air-dry the lingerie; she knew she'd taken care to fold the garment and set it on the top of the pile. So where was it?

She went again to the mud room, looking around, even craning far over to look down between and behind the machines. Nothing. Was she becoming forgetful? she wondered, making a slow tour of each room of the house, even looking under the beds and checking all the wastebaskets.

"The damned thing's simply disappeared," she told Miles, sitting on the coffee table and patting him on the arm. "I've been over every inch of this house, and the teddy's gone. You haven't seen it, by any chance, have you?"

He roused himself, turning to lean on his elbow. "You can't find it?" he asked dopily, not quite awake. "Did you leave it in town?"

"I brought it here. I washed it. It was with the other laundry, right on top. Now it's gone."

"What about your cleaning lady?"

"I haven't had her for months. I didn't want anyone around."

"Well," he said, "that *is* odd." He sat up and smoothed his hair with both hands. "Undoubtedly, you'll find it at the apartment. Miles has to go to the loo." He gave both her knees a squeeze. "Why don't we go for a drive?" he suggested, on his way to the bathroom. "Get some fresh air, see how the old estate's faring."

"Only if we take my car. You can drive it. I'm really not up to a long ride in a vehicle with no springs, hundred-year-old shocks, and a heating system that's equivalent to having someone lying on the floorboards breathing on one's ankles."

"We'll take your car," he laughed.

Abstractedly, she set the fire screen into position, then carried the mugs to the kitchen. It niggled her that she couldn't find the teddy. She knew damned well she'd washed it; she knew exactly how she'd folded it so that the embroidery on the front was uppermost.

"Just going to put on a sweater," Miles called from the bedroom. "Won't be a tick."

She simply couldn't stay up, and was peeved at herself. How long was it going to take before she could sustain her moods? Pocketing her cigarettes, she found her keys and bag, then went to the mud room to pull on her old Frye boots and Joel's sheepskin jacket, all the while looking around, hoping to spot the teddy.

Miles reappeared wearing a pale-blue pullover and a pair of loafers. "It's about thirty minutes from here," he told her, noticing she'd slipped into a different frame of mind. "Thirty minutes there, thirty to look around, thirty back, should make it around six. Then a nap before dinner, perhaps a cuddle with Uncle Miles. You'd rather not go."

"It'll be dark soon. Why don't we wait and go tomorrow? Would you mind very much?"

"I do not mind." He helped her out of the jacket and returned it to the wall peg while she got out of the boots.

She turned and wound her arms around his waist, hiding her face against his chest.

"Poor old Leigh," he commiserated, resting his chin on the top of her head. "Why don't you tell me about this Daniel person. You have my promise I won't be judgmental. I think perhaps you should talk about it."

"I'm such a mess," she said, her words muffled. "Driving home today I really was smug, thinking what terrific progress I'd made. Stupid, stupid."

"Rubbish," he said fondly, and looped her arm through his as they went back to the living room.

While she added another log to the fire, he dropped into the armchair nearest the fireplace. She went to sit on the floor before him, with her back against his legs, her eyes at once drawn to the fire. "His name is Daniel Godard. His father teaches French at NYU. His mother was formerly a fashion buyer for Bloomingdale's. He had some sort of mail-order business, but it was bought out two years ago. He has a daughter, Lane, who is evidently a big fan of my books, which is how, he said, he knew who I was. His wife, Celeste, has, from the sound of it, every problem known to man, from alcoholism to frigidity. He's forty-two, very good-looking, and terrified of flying. And that is how we got into conversation. We hit some turbulence and he turned positively ashen.

"Once we landed, I thought I'd seen the last of him. But he'd spied on me while I was filling out my landing card, and came to Brown's that afternoon. To make a long story short, by six we were in bed." She twisted around to cross her arms on his knees, her expression apologetic. "I was in appalling shape, Miles."

"Go on," he said. "I told you, I'm not going to judge any of this."

"Well, there I was, sitting alone in the lounge, quietly going to pieces, and he arrived to save the day. So, we had our little what-have-you, and I said very firmly I wouldn't see him again, but back he came the next day. Finally, he left to go on to Bangkok, I believe. And that, I thought, was the end of that. Except, he ferreted you out, and sent along the gift, with his number. It was not the sort of gift one could ignore. At least I couldn't. So I rang up to thank him and before I knew what I was doing, I'd agreed to meet him."

"And you slept with him a second time," Miles filled in. "And again, you told him you wouldn't see him. And again, he didn't believe you."

"That's exactly right."

"I don't suppose I'd have believed you either, my darling."

"I did *not* give him my address or my telephone number. I told him categorically I would not see him in future. He frightened me," she admitted.

"How?"

"Sexually. I won't go into the lurid details. Let's just say there was an undercurrent that alarmed me, and I decided I really didn't want to risk seeing him again."

"Risk? Kindly go into the lurid details. *How* did he frighten you? You're fairly intrepid, you know, my hedonistic little love slave. When you confess to being alarmed, I think it's very significant."

"Are you mocking me, Miles? I swear I'll do you an injury if you are."

"I'm completely serious," he assured her. "You know I can't resist coining endearments. Do tell me. Seriously."

"He didn't want to stop. That's all. It was as if he intended to keep on with it until one of us died. And I thought it might be me."

"Literally?"

"Oh, I don't *know*, Miles! I'm talking about a feeling, not anything tangible or literal. There was something about him that was just—desperate. I felt terribly sorry for him because he seemed, at moments, so dreadfully unhappy. But there was more to it than that. I had the sense," she said slowly, thinking it through, "that as close to the edge as I thought I was, he was very much closer. As I say, it was simply a feeling."

"But a frightening one."

"Yes."

Miles thought for a time, automatically running his hand up and down her arm. Whenever they were together, he was drawn to touch her. "I think," he said, "Monday morning you should make arrangements for a new listing. It might even, you know, Leigh, be wise to consider staying in the city for a time, until he's given up hounding you. You don't think he has the New York number, too, do you?"

"I don't know. I'll go check that line, see if he's left any messages." She went to the kitchen and returned inside of two minutes to say, "No messages."

"Inconclusive," he said, thinking aloud. "Perhaps he knows you're here."

"Don't!" Her eyes widened. "I don't need you to alarm me further, Miles."

"Sorry." He looked at his watch. "Time for a drink. Gin and tonic?" he asked, rising to go to the trolley by the dining room door.

"Uh-huh," she answered. "Christ, Miles! All the men I've known over the years, not one of them's ever kept on after me. Why now? I'm not up to this. I'm really not."

"So, don't stay here," he said, carrying the ice bucket out to the kitchen. "Come back into town and stay with me, or with your mother. Wait it out. He's bound to quit eventually."

"It's so damned irritating!" she railed. "I can't imagine a woman doing this sort of thing."

"Oh, no?" he said calmly, returning with the full bucket. "Obviously, you've never seen a minor masterpiece Clint Eastwood did called *Play Misty for Me*. Women most certainly do do things like this. I wish you'd stop believing unpredictable behavior is the exclusive domain of men. I've had women hound me after I've tried, in the nicest possible fashion, to break off with them. There was one who persisted for an entire year before she finally gave it up. For twelve long months I didn't dare answer my telephone at home. I screened every call through the answering machine. And, suffice it to say, I had to tell Diane not to accept any calls from her at the office. In the end, she did quit. But I promise you I found it every bit as unpleasant as you're finding this. He will stop in time. It may take a while before the penny drops, but he'll stop. They always do." He gave her her drink and a smile, saying, "These things happen, Leigh. It's a fact of life. And, actually, you've been bloody lucky it hasn't happened to you before now. You'll get a new telephone number; you'll spend some time in town; and he'll give it up and leave you alone."

"What happened in the movie?" she asked, then tasted her drink. "Come sit with me by the fire. Bring the sofa pillows, if you want to make yourself a nest."

He laughed. "Strike you as an oversized bird, do I?"

"Only sometimes."

He stretched out on his stomach, his chin propped on one hand, and tried to sketch in the details of the film. "It's been ages since I saw it, so I don't remember it all that well. Eastwood was a disc jockey with a late-night show. And this woman kept calling to request 'Misty.' Somehow, they meet up and go to bed. Next thing anyone knows, she has a full-fledged obsession. I recall it got very gory at the end, and she was carted off after running amok with a knife or scissors or some such. The point was, he got involved because he entered into what he thought would be nothing more than a one-nighter. Interesting, rather Gothic, morality tale, that illustrates quite well that women cannot lay exclusive claim to the role of victim. Not," he added, "that I see you that way."

"I should hope not." She shivered and moved closer to the fire. "I never dreamed it would get so out of hand. He was there when I needed someone . . . something. And I suppose I did give him mixed signals. Let's not talk any more about it."

"Well, you're welcome to come hide out in the mausoleum with me." He rattled the ice in his glass, then said, "I can't for the life of me think why I'm down here in this horribly unnatural position." He pushed himself into sitting position, took another swallow of his Scotch, then set the glass on the coffee table. "Fancy a cuddle? Why not come over here and let Uncle Miles drool all over you?"

She laughed, set aside her drink, then knee-walked over the carpet to give him a kiss.

"One of the things I like best about you," he told her, draping his arm around her shoulders, "aside from your truthfulness, is your brain." He tapped his finger lightly against her temple. "You are a truly intelligent being. What I never cease to wonder at, though, is how someone so truly intelligent can be so naive about the implications of her actions. I promised not to judge, and I'm not going to. I think this happened because you were, and are, having the devil's own time trying to stay steady. And I know how that is. You think you've come out of it; you're actually able to laugh, and hold a rational conversation. Then, wham! You're up to your eyebrows in pure blackness and it's hard to breathe, let alone talk, or laugh, or do any of the dozens of everyday things you've got to do."

"How do you know that?" she asked.

"Luckily," he said, "I was young. The young are so much more resilient. I believe the older you are, the rougher it is."

"But what happened? How young were you? Miles! What haven't you told me?"

"Nothing alarming," he said, giving her a kiss on the forehead. "Don't overreact," he said kindly. "I'm not going to tell you a horror story. It's not even a terribly uncommon tale. I was nine, the youngest in the family, and was evacuated to the country. A raid wiped out the rest of them, mother, father, and two older sisters. I was old enough to suffer, and young enough to be able to go forward."

She shook her head sadly. "How old were your sisters?"

"Sixteen and eighteen. I was one of those 'surprises' that came long after they thought they were done with nappies and feedings and so forth. For a time I had three mothers, really, not counting various aunts, and a lovely gran. Perhaps that's why I've always liked women so much, having my early years surrounded by them. Believe it or not, there are times when I still feel lonely for them. Lovely girls, my sisters."

"Somehow I've always thought your family was all over there. Miles, I am sorry. How very sad for you."

"It wasn't so bad, really," he said. "I lived with my Uncle James and Aunt Caroline, my mother's sister and her husband. It wasn't in the least Dickensian. They were very good to me. Their son Geoff and I attended school together. We've stayed in touch." As he talked, he drew her gradually closer until she was seated in his lap. "There was a fairly sizable estate. Uncle James was the executor." He was about to go on when something—a movement?—caught his eye, and he looked over at the window.

"What?" Leigh asked, at once aware of the sudden shift of his attention.

"Nothing." He told himself he must have imagined it. "I've lost track of my narrative thread. It's difficult to concentrate with you purring away here like a great, tawny cat."

"I'm too warm now," she said, and sat away to pull the sweater off over her head.

"I interpret that as an invitation," he warned her.

She didn't say anything but simply kept her eyes on his.

"Well," he said, "since there's no objection . . ." Lazily, he began to undo the buttons on her shirt. "I suppose it must have something to do with all the fresh air and country quiet."

"What does?"

"My renewed interest in your anatomy."

"I think it has more to do with opportunity, which is something you've never been able to resist."

"Whatever." Adroitly, he unhooked her bra and, with a sigh, closed his hand over her breast. "Lovely," he murmured approvingly. "Give us a kiss, love. We'll have a bit of a cuddle, then see to dinner."

Made serious by his persuasive hands, she tilted her head back to kiss him. His mouth brushed back and forth against hers, lips grazing, before coming to rest. She liked the way he kissed. He was never presumptuous, never invasive, but always progressed gradually toward the heart of a kiss, and its expanding potential.

His mouth moved to her throat, then to the rise of her breast, and then to her nipple. Her body gave a small responsive leap, and she laced her fingers over the back of his head to hold him to her, as she extended her legs in a pleasurable stretch, her eyes closing.

Eighteen

AN UNLOADED THE CAR, DUMPED ALL THE BAGS AND BOXES IN THE middle of the apartment living room, then went downstairs intending to return the car to the garage. He found himself headed uptown instead. He badly wanted to see Leigh. He had left her a couple of messages, but it was too soon to expect her to call back. He parked halfway down the next block on the same side of the street as her building, and settled in to wait. He couldn't even be sure she was there. But her car hadn't been at the house in New Canaan, so the chances were better than even that she'd come by the apartment at some point—assuming she planned to head back to Connecticut. Of course, she might be spending the entire weekend in the city. He hated not knowing her plans. It made him feel left out, and diminished in a way, as if he wasn't important enough to be told what she was doing. Naturally, she was in no position to do that, what with the Good Doctor probably hanging constantly in the background, keeping tabs on her. Once the doctor was out of the way, neither he nor Leigh would have to go through any more of this crap. In the meantime, he thought he'd keep watch for a while, on the off chance she turned up. He felt purposeful, and quite comfortable, waiting. He had the radio turned on low, and every half hour or so he started up the engine to warm the car's interior.

While he waited, he ran down all the possibilities: she might already have made an early start back to the country; she might not emerge from the apartment—if she was in fact in there—for several days; she was probably with the Good Doctor—a notion that bothered the hell out of him. He wanted a look at this guy, wanted to see what kind of man could take a woman like Leigh for granted; what kind of man didn't bother with

167

good locks on his doors to ensure his wife's safety, didn't bother to be aware of his wife's comings and goings.

He smoked a cigarette, cracking open the window to keep the air circulating in the car, his eyes on the building entrance. Good thing it was a holiday. The streets were pretty much deserted. Wednesday, but it felt like Sunday. Quite a few offices in town were staying closed right through Monday. All in all, it was very damned fortunate he had so much free time now to devote to Leigh. Any other time in his life he'd have been too busy—with the business, with trying to keep Celeste on an even keel, with keeping his parents up-to-date, and with making sure Lane had everything she needed. The timing couldn't have been better.

At twelve-ten, he saw the Mercedes nose out of the garage entrance on the side of the building. With bursting excitement—glad he'd thought to keep both the side and the front of the building in view—he put the BMW into gear and pulled out, getting close enough to see there were two people in the car. Seeing this started an electric buzzing in his chest. He was finally going to get a look at the Good Doctor.

The Mercedes headed down Park to Fifty-ninth and pulled over in front of an older, medium-rise building with a number of doctors' offices on the ground floor. The passenger door opened, and Dan saw the Good Doctor climb out. The man bent to say something to Leigh, then shut the car door and went into the building.

So that was the husband. There wasn't time now to think about it. He had to pay attention to tailing Leigh. It was a cinch, really. Once he figured out that she was headed over to the East Side he fell back, letting a few cars get between them. He stayed maybe a quarter of a mile behind, noting she drove fast and well, signaling without fail every time she changed lanes. He admired the way she handled the big sedan. She was a decisive driver, maintaining her speed, obviously relaxed behind the wheel. Celeste, when she'd been sober enough to drive, had been the worst: easily rattled, lacking a sense of direction, frightened by the power of the car. "It's *you!*" she'd accused regularly. "I drive just fine when I'm by myself. I know you're watching every last thing I do, and it makes me so edgy I can't do anything." The truth, of course, was she was simply a lousy driver.

He kept up with Leigh along the Bruckner, all the way to the New England Thruway exit. He was not far behind when she left the thruway at Exit 11 in Darien, and let his speed fall under the limit as they took the Post Road through town. He expected her to keep going to the start of 124, but she turned right immediately under the railroad bridge, and he had to cut over from the left lane—fortunately no one was on his right—to make the turn.

It would be too obvious if he followed after her into the shopping center parking lot, so he kept going, reversed in the driveway of the outdoor market—closed for the winter—and went back to cruise the lot until he spotted her car. He parked a couple of aisles over, then hunched down in the seat to wait, feeling even more purposeful and keyed up. He was doing things he'd been seeing all his life in movies and on television, but until now it had never occurred to him that he'd absorbed a hell of a lot of information on how to play sleuth.

Half an hour later she came out of the market pushing a cart. She unloaded the bags, returned the cart to the market entrance—he gave her points for that; it was something he always did, too—then got back in the car. He tailed her, staying a half mile or so behind, right the way to her house, and cruised past the top of the driveway just as she was about to open the trunk of the Mercedes. He hadn't timed that too well, and hoped she hadn't spotted him. He'd seen the second car in the garage, which meant the Good Doctor had decided to spend some time at home for a change.

He was anxious for a closer look at the doctor, but that wasn't going to be possible in daylight. After sundown, though, he'd be able to sneak up to the house and see what was going on. Only a few hours until dark. In the meantime, there were a couple more things he wanted from the Bedford house.

In the light of day, the house didn't bother him so much, and he even wondered, for a few minutes, if he wasn't perhaps making a mistake getting rid of it. No going back now, though, he reminded himself. And he'd made one hell of a profit on his initial investment. Besides, there was no way on God's earth he could ever bring Leigh here. No. The two of them would start fresh, with someplace new.

He got his toolbox from the garage and stowed it in the BMW's trunk, then let himself in the side door, surprised to hear the telephone ringing. He wondered if it could be Leigh, remembered she didn't have this number, and thought maybe it was the real estate agent with the latest news on the sale. Or maybe it was Lane, or his parents. He hesitated, reluctant to speak to anyone. He'd just spent a week with his family, and right now the only person he wanted to talk to was Leigh. Besides, the agent wouldn't be calling him on New Year's Day, would she? He hesitated too long, and the ringing stopped. Relieved, he went to the den to get several items from his desk.

Sitting behind the desk, he considered Leigh's husband. The man was not what Dan had expected. He was big, over six feet, and solidly built. Expensive black topcoat, no hat, moustache; he'd moved with authority, giving the doorman a slight nod as he'd gone inside. Big stupid bastard didn't know what he had, and it was too late to change anything. All Dan had to do was get her off somewhere quiet where they could talk, and he could make her see she was wasting herself, wasting time and potential and emotion. He'd make her see.

He thought about things she'd told him, about other affairs she'd had, about the look and feel of her in bed, and knew she'd understand there was no need to do any of that anymore. He'd keep her happy, keep her satisfied. It was what she wanted. She was just afraid to make the break. He knew how that was. But once the decision was made, things became very easy. Making the decision was the big step. All right, so maybe Celeste had made that decision for him, in a way. It didn't matter; what mattered was his making that decision now, for Leigh.

All at once, he remembered the piece of lingerie in his coat pocket; he fished it out and laid it on the desk top, with his fingertip tracing the embroidery on the bodice. He laid his head down on the cool silk and closed his eyes. Then, reluctantly, he sat up and opened the top drawer for the scissors. It was a shame, but he really had to destroy it. He couldn't go around with the thing in his pocket.

When he was finished, he folded the pieces into a sheet of paper, and dumped it into the garbage in the kitchen. Before he left, he'd put the garbage in the bin outside. Tired and hungry now, he fixed a can of soup and ate it out of the pot along with a handful of crackers. Then he rinsed the pot, put it in the dishwasher, wiped the crumbs off the counter, and, yawning, decided he'd take a nap. He opened the sofa bed in the den, got the bedding from the closet, pushed off his shoes, and lay down.

When he awakened, it was dark; almost five. He'd slept longer than he'd thought he would, but felt better as he went into the hall bathroom to shower and shave.

By six, he'd parked about a quarter mile past Moonstone Lane, on a gravel shoulder at whose apex sat a row of mailboxes. There wouldn't be a mail delivery, so it was a good place to leave the car. There were no outside lights on at her house, but the living room windows glowed invitingly. He ran quickly, lightly—he felt unbelievably weightless, and somehow powerful—down one of the tire tracks in the snow on the driveway, dropping low as he left the track and cut diagonally across the lawn. He crept to the side of the house and, with extreme caution, raised his head until he could see through the window, instantly jerking out of sight when he spotted the two of them sitting on the floor near the fireplace. He'd unwittingly placed himself directly in the Good Doctor's eye line. Luckily, he hadn't been seen. Ducking below the window, he inched along to the second of the three windows, that would allow him to take a peek inside without placing himself in view.

Pressing tight to the wall of the house, he rose up on the far side of the window, then inched forward until he had an unimpaired view of that portion of the room. Immediately, he was livid at having to watch that son of a bitch in there pushing himself on Leigh. Dan could see she didn't care for it. She gave in though, took off her sweater, and lay across the bastard's lap like a rug, closing her eyes so she wouldn't have to see. Poor Leigh. He had to get her out of this situation; it was rotten.

He knew he shouldn't be watching, but he couldn't look away, a twisting spurt of anger overtaking him at the sight of that oversized, heavy-handed prick mauling her, sucking on her like some immense infant. Jesus! It was so goddamned wrong! She was being forced to perform. And he had to give her credit, he thought, the anger robbing him of much of his lightness; she was playing it out very damned convincingly. He had a moment or two of doubt, wondering if she really was acting. But no. He could tell it was a performance. Still, performance or not, he had to restrain himself from smashing through the window, or running over to kick in the door when the son of a bitch pulled her jeans halfway down her legs and then worked his hand between her thighs. He had Leigh half-naked in his lap. The two of them were going to do it in front of his eyes, and he had to drag himself away from the window because if he saw one more second of what was going on in there, he'd kill the bastard.

He raced back up the driveway, panting hard, his arms and legs pumping, fists clenched. He had to put a stop to this, get Leigh the hell out of that situation. He threw himself into the car, got the engine going, then floored the accelerator, sending gravel rattling against the undercarriage as he flew halfway across the road, reversed in a fury, then shot off, shifting from first directly into fourth, back toward Bedford. His temples were pounding, his lungs heaving, his eardrums vibrating noisily. *No more of this!* he ranted silently, hitting sixty, then seventy, when the road straightened. He'd get her out of there; they'd talk; he'd rescue her.

He had a great deal to do, a tremendous number of things to do, and not a lot of time in which to do them. Most likely it would take the better part of the night to get everything done. But that was all right. He felt huge, bursting with untapped energy, his brain busy ticking off details on a mental list.

Even in the country, without the clanging of delivery trucks and garbage cans being emptied at 5 A.M., Miles couldn't hang on to his sleep. It eased away, leaving him alert and ready for the day. It had always been that way, but he didn't mind. He used the time in the city to get paperwork done before leaving for the office. He was able to wander at a leisurely pace around the apartment, doing this and that, having breakfast and a read of the paper while the noise on the streets gained in volume. He liked mornings. They made him feel young, for some reason. He'd always been able, in the light of morning, to make sense of things that had seemed somewhat indecipherable during the night; he found a clarity to the world and to his life with the advent of each new morning that often was just beyond his reach in the dark.

For a time, he watched Leigh sleep, liking the sight of her at rest equally as well as he enjoyed visually measuring the economy or generosity of her movements when awake. Altogether, he liked her. He doubted that would ever change. No one else he'd known, male or female, was such a blend of contradicting qualities; no one else could be as painfully serious, or give herself so wholeheartedly over to sheer nonsense. He found her entirely irresistible, as much now as twenty-five years before. And his being here now was the most encouraging thing that had happened since Joel had taken ill, when she'd cut herself off from everyone and everything but the death that was taking place inside of someone who, by rights, should have had a long, rich life. It wasn't surprising that Leigh was having such trouble coping with the loss of Joel. Joel had been a rare and remarkable young man, one it was impossible to dislike. He'd had a natural zest, a limitless enthusiasm that embraced all things, new and old, as well as people and events, and most especially Leigh. She'd been his staunchest ally, his devoted mother, and his willing friend; she was the only mother Joel had known, and there'd never been a moment when he'd minimized her importance. She'd been his anchor, his confidante, his greatest admirer. And he'd rewarded her, in his unique fashion, with a filial regard and a comprehension of her complexities that was nothing less than outstanding in one so young. They'd understood each other perfectly, even when they'd disagreed. Joel had accepted her infrequent criticisms, her brief-lived affairs, and her advice, with an intuitive recognition both of his own good fortune and of her wisdom. That Joel had died was a true tragedy. But that he, Miles, was being received back into her life was, perhaps, a result of that tragedy. And he thought, not for the first time, how very odd and convoluted were the paths along which one's life could lead.

He would surprise her, he decided, and prepare breakfast. While the bacon was spitting under the broiler, he went to open the front door on the off chance she was still having the *Times* delivered. No such luck. He was about to close the door when he noticed footprints in the snow; two sets of them cut across the lawn. Leaning out, he saw where the snow had been trampled between two of the front windows. Bemused, he closed the door and went into the living room to look out at the impressions in the snow, then turned around to study the interior of the room, first from the near window, and then from the far one. Both afforded a clear view of the fireplace end of the room. He *had* seen something last evening. That very slight movement hadn't been his imagination. Someone had stood outside and looked in at them. The hair on his arms rose, and he rubbed his forearms.

Returning to the kitchen to check the bacon, he decided not to mention it to Leigh. What he would do was increase his effort to persuade her to spend some time in the city. Obviously, it wasn't a good idea for her to remain alone here. But if he didn't point out the footprints, or tell her he'd seen a shadow in the window, wouldn't he be doing her a frightful disservice?

He filled the kettle and put it on to boil, becoming progressively angrier at the idea that someone had been watching when they'd made love the night before. What kind of man sneaked around looking in people's windows? Bloody disgusting! he thought, opening the refrigerator for the eggs. Once the breakfast was ready, he'd wake Leigh, they'd eat, then they'd drive to Brewster. And he'd broach the subject somewhere along the route.

She came in, belting her robe, as he was buttering the English muffins. "The bacon woke me," she said, pouring herself some coffee. "Miles?" She leaned over the counter to look at him. "Is something wrong? You look a little peculiar."

He should have known her special radar would pick up on his mood. "I *feel* peculiar," he admitted, wiping his hands on the dish towel. "At first, I wasn't going to say anything. But then I saw that would be sheer bloody negligence, to say the least. Leigh, you cannot stay here on your own. I'm going to *insist* you come back to the city with me. You can stay at your place, or with your mother, or even with me if you like. But I absolutely will not allow you to remain here."

"Why, for heaven's sake?"

"I want to show you something." Taking her by the upper arm, he led her to the front door, opened it, pulled her over the threshold, and pointed. "What do you make of *that?*" he demanded.

It wasn't possible to overlook the footprints. She followed their trail to the windows then back to the driveway. It could have been an oil delivery. The tank was buried somewhere over there. But the company didn't make deliveries on holidays, except in emergencies. And besides, they'd filled her tank the previous week. She recalled taking the delivery slip from the mailbox at the top of the driveway. Those prints in the snow hadn't been there yesterday when she'd arrived. She'd have noticed them. Which had to mean they'd been made sometime last night.

"You've got a peeping Tom!" Miles declared, pulling her back into the house. "I *thought* I saw something last evening but I told myself I was being fanciful. Clearly I was *not*. Someone stood out there and looked in at us. Think about this for a moment, Leigh! You could scream your heart out in here and no one would hear you. If I have to *carry* you out to the car, if I have to bind you hand and foot, I am not leaving here without you."

"I need a cigarette," she said, and freed herself from his grip to go get one.

"You *need* an *alarm system*," he called after her, "and some *protection!* Not a bloody cigarette!"

"Stop bellowing at me," she said quietly, returning from the bedroom with her cigarettes. "It's hardly *my* fault that someone's decided to start looking in at my windows. And I'm not stupid, Miles. Do you seriously think I'd *want* to be here alone, knowing someone's watching me? You're fighting all by yourself. I wouldn't dream of spending any more time here than necessary. In fact, I'll pack and leave with you this afternoon. I'll call Tom in town and get him to look after the place while I'm away."

"Call the local police, too, and have them start patrolling the house. Breakfast is ready," he said curtly. "I'll dish up."

"My God! You really do think I'm stupid!" she accused.

He stopped, pulled himself together, and turned back to her. "I don't think anything of the sort, actually. I'm taking it out on you because I opened the door to see if you were having a newspaper delivered these days, and what do I see but tracks in the snow! You're anything but stupid. But you *are* very damned vulnerable here, and that makes me edgy, which in turn makes me angry. I apologize for my less than gracious way of displaying my concern for you. I love you. The very *idea* that any harm might come to you . . . well."

The telephone rang. They both started, then turned to stare.

"I'll let the machine answer," she said, with the feeling that things were suddenly closing in on her.

They waited until the machine clicked on, followed by a silence while the outgoing message played, then Marietta's voice said, "Leigh, you can't have gone out this early in the morning. Are you there, darling?"

Leigh went to pick up the receiver, at the same time pressing the RESET button. "I'm here. How are you?"

"I am perfectly well. How are you? Is Miles with you? I rang both your numbers and concluded you'd gone off together."

"You should try your hand at detective novels," Leigh laughed. "He's here."

"Well, that's lovely. It's high time the two of you started taking each other seriously. I have nothing of significance to say. I simply wanted to know how you are, and if you had a good time last night."

"We had a wonderful time. Did you?"

"The Plaza," Marietta said sadly, "is *not* the splendid hotel it once was. It's gone downhill, and badly, I'm sorry to say. But it was a most pleasant evening. I won't keep you."

"Miles has talked me into coming into town for a while. I'll call you this evening when we get back."

"What a good idea! Are you going to do *Percival?*"

"I think so, yes."

"Better and better! I couldn't be more pleased. I'll ring off now. My love to Miles."

Leigh hung up to see Miles had put the food on the table and was waiting for her to join him.

"How is your mother?" he asked.

"The Plaza has gone downhill."

"Poor Marietta's always the last to know," he said, and laughed.

Leigh drank some of her coffee, thinking. It had to be Daniel who'd come looking in the windows. What a bizarre thing for him to do! And it really did have to be him. It was exceedingly unlikely that anyone else would take such a risk. It irked her that he'd violate her privacy in that fashion, but mainly she felt sorry for him. Something was dreadfully wrong in his life and whatever it was, it was driving him to do things that were, she was certain, very out of character. No matter how she turned the pieces, she couldn't see him as a particularly menacing figure.

"You're not eating," Miles said. "I'm becoming terribly bored by your not eating."

"We can't have that, can we?" she countered, and dutifully picked up her knife and fork. "I think it was Daniel, Miles."

"I must say you're being very damned calm about it. It doesn't *bother* you that he's got your address, your telephone number, and now he's started peeping through your windows?"

"Of course, it bothers me. But . . . I don't know. I'm not sure what I think, or how I really feel. There's something so very very sad about him."

Miles reached over and stole a strip of her bacon, then sat munching it while she ate some of the scrambled eggs. He was about to offer his opinion on the matter when there was the sound of a car pulling into the driveway. He craned around toward the door as Leigh got up and went to the window to see a dark-blue BMW pull to a stop at the foot of the walk.

An alarm went off inside her head at the realization that it had been Daniel following her from the city yesterday. She said, "Oh, no!" as he now got out of the car and came striding up the walk.

"Who is that? Is that this Daniel person?" Miles asked from the table.

"Damn it all! What is he *doing* here? This is ridiculous!" She backed away from the window and looked over at Miles as the doorbell sounded. "Let me handle this, please. I'll get rid of him." She cracked open the door and said, "Daniel, what do you think you're doing?"

"I want to see you, Leigh. We have to talk."

Miles got up from the table, saying, "What the bloody hell is this?"

Leigh turned, her hand upheld to stop him, as she said, "Daniel, please leave. This is difficult and embarrassing."

"*What the hell do you want?*" Miles thundered, pulling the door fully open to confront the younger man.

"She doesn't love you!" Daniel informed him.

"Oh, for God's sake!" Leigh interjected.

"Are you out of your mind?" Miles pushed forward, attempting to shift Leigh to one side, out of harm's way.

"*Don't touch her!*" Daniel exploded, and drove his fist solidly into Miles's middle.

Leigh screamed.

Miles gagged, and bent double. But Dan wasn't finished. His fists began pounding into Miles, delivering uppercuts, crosscuts, body blows, as he shouted out Miles's unworthiness, reviling him for forcing himself on Leigh.

"STOP IT!" Leigh screamed, pulling at Daniel. "STOP IT! *He has a bad heart! You'll kill him!* WHAT DO YOU WANT?"

"I want to *talk* to you!" Daniel huffed, letting up on Miles. "I want you to *come* with me!" He panted, hanging over Miles, who was on his knees now, struggling to catch his breath, his face purple.

"Don't hit him again!" she begged. "Let me get my coat. I'll come with you, and we'll talk. Will you just let me get my coat? Please, don't hit him anymore! Miles?" She moved to go to him, but Dan pushed her away.

"Get your coat!" he ordered. "I'm taking you out of here, away from this son of a bitch."

She ran to the closet for her coat, keeping her eyes on the two men, terribly afraid Daniel would actually kill Miles, who had sunk all the way to the floor now, his face still dark as he drew in wisps of air. Pushing her bare feet into the first available pair of boots, she got the coat on and ran back, anxious to help Miles. But Daniel took hold of her arm and dragged her out of the house and down the walk toward the BMW.

Upon arriving at the car, he became apologetic and strangely formal, saying, "I'm sorry, Leigh, but I'm going to have to ask you to ride back here."

She didn't know what he was talking about, didn't even want to hear him. She was too worried about Miles, and turned toward the house, afraid he'd been seriously injured.

Dan was opening the trunk of the car. She turned to gape at him, suddenly, finally, afraid. Was he actually telling her he wanted her to get into the *trunk* of his car? She took a step away. "I'm not getting in there!" she said, and took another step, looking again over at the house. She'd thought she'd sit with him in the car for a few minutes, they'd talk, she'd convince him he was behaving irrationally, then she'd go back inside and see to Miles. But he was actually coming after her, determined to get her into the trunk. He put his hand on her arm and she flung it off. "I am *not* getting in there! Don't be ridiculous!"

"Please don't fight me, Leigh," he said quietly. "If I thought I could trust you not to try to jump out of the car, there'd be no problem. Normally I wouldn't dream of asking you to do this, but I'm very afraid you'd try something, and I wouldn't want to risk your getting hurt. Please." His hand closed around her wrist. She yanked futilely against his grip.

When he saw she intended to go on resisting, he said, "If you don't do as I ask, I'll kill the son of a bitch. I really don't care, Leigh." And as if to prove the weight of his threat, he lifted his other hand to reveal the tire iron he'd just removed from the trunk and had been keeping by his side, out of her view. The sight of it stopped her.

"All right," she relented. "Just promise me you won't harm him any more than you already have."

"I give you my word. Now come on." He drew her to the rear of the car and she looked into the trunk, her heart giving a frenzied leap as she saw he'd placed a blanket and some pillows inside. It looked to her like a coffin.

"What *is* this?" she cried, pulling back.

"I only want you to be comfortable. Come on. Climb in. I'll give you a hand."

Unable to believe this was actually happening, that she'd get inside, and he'd shut the lid on her, she lifted one leg over the rear bumper—surely to God something would happen to put a stop to this lunacy!—then the other. She looked around. Maybe a car going by on the road . . .

"Lie down, Leigh," he told her. "You'll be all right."

She didn't want to lower her head. As long as she kept looking around, there was the possibility of someone coming to help, something . . .

"Lie down!"

She had to turn on her side and bend her knees in order to fit into the space.

"Don't worry, Leigh," he said. "I'll drive carefully."

Oh, Jesus! He was really going to do it. Gently, he pushed closed the lid, and she was trapped in the rubber-smelling, pitch-black, cramped space. She heard the car door slam, then felt the vibrating roar of the engine as it started. Then the car was moving. Even though she knew it would do no good, she put her hands flat on the lid and pushed hard. Useless. She was locked in. And he was driving away. What about Miles? God! He had to be all right. Where was this man taking her? What if he intended to kill her? What if he meant to trick her by making it seem as if he was driving away when what he was actually planning was to go back into the house and murder Miles? *God!* Nothing must happen to Miles. He gave his promise he wouldn't harm Miles. But what if he decided to kill *her* if she didn't do what he wanted?

Nineteen

E KNEW THE CONTENTS OF THE NOTE BY HEART. THEY RECITED themselves to him when he least expected it. Her voice, sounding sixteen or seventeen, read the words she'd written on that piece of her expensive stationery. She'd had to have paper from Tiffany's, with her monogram in the corner, supplies for letters she never wrote—except for thank-you notes now and then to his parents or hers, for some nightmare of a dinner or some gift they'd given her.

"Dear Danny"—her voice filled the car's interior—"I'm completely sober right now. It's not my favorite thing, but that doesn't matter. I feel so sad, Danny. I've been feeling this way for so long that I don't know how anything else feels anymore. I don't really blame you. It's just that you've always had such high ideals, such impossible expectations. You set standards and because you could meet them, you wanted all of us to meet them, too. But I was never you, Danny. I was always just me, but you wanted me to be you. I never liked being me, it was hard, so hard, especially when you didn't seem too happy with the me I was, either. We agreed on that, didn't we? Neither one of us was happy with me. I'm just so tired. It'll be better this way. I'm sorry. Celeste."

He hated it! He didn't want to have to hear this. He turned up the volume on the radio. His foot pressed down on the accelerator. He made as much noise as he could, but it was like a loop, and he couldn't stop it playing. "Danny, it'll be better this way." She'd had to blame him, had to blame his standards, his expectations. Christ! He'd given every last thing he had to the effort, to making it work. But she'd never be clear, never say she wanted or needed this or that; she'd never give him a clue to help him find out what would turn her around. It was his fault. Hers too. But his fault. Not now. Not now.

He upped the volume even more on the radio, but kept an eye on the speed.

Gradually, she came to believe she was suffocating. The darkness, the smell, the vibrations, enveloped her until she wondered if this was going to be how she died, locked into the trunk of a car driven by a man out of control. The space was getting smaller and smaller, and she closed in on herself, bringing her knees up to her chest and winding her arms tightly around them as if this might make her physical self more manageable.

Claustrophobia. That was the name of this feeling. The word now had a dreadful new meaning. She'd scoffed once upon a time at hearing of people who grew panicky in confined spaces, in elevators, for example. She was appalled to think she'd disbelieved, doubted the truth of so foolish-sounding a concept. She had no doubt about it now: it was an absence of light, and tainted, diminishing quantities of air, and a monstrous confinement. She kept her eyes open, blinking repeatedly, as if this might clear the darkness and bring light. She examined with her hands the walls of her cage, looking for something, anything. There was nothing. Daniel had removed even the spare tire from the trunk. Her hands moved over the rough, prime-coated metal, touching every ridge, every die-stamped indentation. Then she tucked her hands between her thighs, listening to her heartbeat in her ears. The vibrations were making her nauseated, as was the rubber smell, underlaid with traces of gasoline and carbon monoxide. Where was he taking her? The ride was going on and on interminably. Each time the car slowed, even fractionally, she thought perhaps now they'd stop. But they went on, the engine noise rising to a higher note as the revolutions became faster, and music from the car radio seeped in through minuscule crevices, bass-heavy and pulsing.

The car was tightly sprung, taking every bump and pothole with a hard snap of its taut suspension. And she felt all of it right through to her bones as she was shaken and thumped in direct correlation to the condition of the road. A large pothole. The wheels sank into it; her body lifted, then fell on the hard metal bed of the trunk. Fluid kept filling her mouth; she swallowed repeatedly; her throat worked nonstop as she swallowed the bitterness. She tried not to smell the odors or taste the metallic air, but her fear of being smothered kept her mouth open wide. She prayed the motion would stop soon because she was going to be sick. The coffee and eggs she'd eaten were threatening to gush from her throat. She had to close her eyes at last, to concentrate on holding down the nausea. Her fingers laced together between her thighs, eyes closed, she tried to focus on controlling the sickness. But it was gaining, and hours, days, were passing as every last pebble, pothole, and wrinkle in the roadbed made its direct impression on her body.

This would be what hell was like. You didn't know you were going there; you simply spent eternity in the process of transit; confined in reeking darkness with only your dissociated thoughts to comfort or confuse you. Maybe she was already dead.

The car left the highway, and she could hear street sounds, cars honking; there was the stop-and-go of an intersection. The music from inside the car was turned down. Sudden accelerations and decelerations. It was the abrupt starts and stops that destroyed her best efforts. Her stomach overturned and she retched, frantically turning her head toward the rear of the trunk in order not to soil herself. But in turning so suddenly, so blindly, she struck her head sharply on the trunk lid and helplessly vomited all over herself, collapsing back on the pillows with involuntary tears leaking from her eyes and blood oozing from her scalp. She was so thoroughly, unremittingly ill that, for the present, she was incapable even of thought. All she wanted was an end to the punishing entrapment.

He pulled up in front of the building on West Tenth, locked the car, then hurried to open the trunk, stopped cold by the sight of her. Her face, under trickles of blood, was dead white with a greenish tinge around her mouth and nostrils. Her hair was sticky wet and clung to her skull. Her eyes had sunken into dark hollows. And she'd been sick all down the front of herself. The robe hung open under the fur coat, leaving her all but naked. She stared so fixedly, she lay so still, he thought for one horrific moment she was dead. Then, her pupils dilated, and she blinked against the light.

He glanced up and down the street. No one around.

"Jesus, Leigh," he whispered, maneuvering her to a sitting position, trying to think how best he could lift her out of there. "I'm sorry. I never thought . . . Jesus!" Leaning forward, he got his arms under hers and around her back, and pulled her out, her legs dragging painfully over the metal lip. He had to hold her upright while he got the trunk closed because if he let go of her, she'd collapse. She shoved him away, and he grabbed for her, thinking she'd been faking him out, but she staggered to the curb and, holding on to a lamppost for support, vomited into the gutter, then stood hanging on to the post, her head lolling.

"Let me get you inside," he said, draping her arm around his neck and getting a firm grip around her waist. "We'll get you cleaned up. I'll make you some tea to settle your stomach. Come on now, Leigh. Try to walk."

Drunkenly, she wiped her mouth with the back of her hand, trying to get her legs to function properly. They wanted to buckle, and she thought she'd like to sit down on the stairs and stay there until the dizziness went away and her stomach stopped leaping convulsively. She'd never felt so sick. It was so dreadful, so absolutely complete, that it preoccupied her utterly, rendering her temporarily unconcerned with her whereabouts. Tea. He'd said something about tea, and it sounded right. Tea, and someplace to lie down; perhaps a bathtub filed with tepid water. She reeked of vomit; the smell of it caused her to start retching again when they were halfway up the inside stairs. He stopped, waiting. But her stomach was empty now. Her body shuddered its way through a series of dry heaves that left her incapacitated. She started to slide away, but Dan kept hold of her, turned her around and slung her over his shoulder. The motion heightened her dizziness, and she shut her eyes in order not to have to see the stairs behind them telescoping mountainously.

Inside the apartment, he set her on her feet, a steadying arm around her, while he locked the door.

"I want a bath," she got out. He heard, picked her up, and carried her through to the bathroom, sat her down on the toilet then stoppered the tub and got the water going. As the tub was filling, he took her out of the coat and her boots, saying, "It never occurred to me it'd make you sick. You have to believe that. You'll take your bath and I'll fix you some tea. It'll calm your stomach. Okay?"

She didn't answer, but simply gazed at him from her sunken eyes. He could not believe an hour or so in the trunk had had such a devastating effect on her. Daunted, he took refuge in practicalities. "I'll sponge off your coat and the robe. They'll be as good as new. I've got some cleaning stuff in the kitchen." He busied himself putting her things just outside the bathroom door; he tested the water and, satisfied, turned off the taps. "Come on. I'll help you in."

Lacking the energy to question or protest, she allowed herself to be lifted into the tub. She sank into the water—hotter than she'd have wished—and watched him inspect her robe before folding it over his arm. "Try to relax," he told her. "I'll be back in a couple of minutes. There's shampoo, and soap. And I put a fresh washcloth there, on the rim. Everything you need."

It registered: he'd planned for some time to bring her here. This was his apartment, not that of some friend who was out of town.

Her eyes seemed all she was able to move. They turned to take in the details of this bathroom she hadn't seen on her previous visit. There was no shower curtain or hooks. The mirrored door to the medicine cabinet had been removed. The shelves held a plastic container of Johnson's baby powder and one of baby oil, several bars of soap, two toothbrushes and a tube of Crest, roll-on Ban, and alone, on the top shelf, a bottle of Vol de Nuit, her perfume. The sight of it disturbed her; it symbolized something. What? Did he think she'd dab perfume in the bends of her elbows and knees in some fantasy performance? Did he think the perfume would make her feel at home here? What the hell *did* he think? She hadn't the remotest idea. Her stomach ached; her throat burned; her mouth tasted foul. She lay unmoving in the water, still feeling the motion of the car. Her eyelids kept wanting to close, and she had to force them open. She needed her wits about her, but her attention span had suffered and been abbreviated severely by that ghastly ride.

Dan reappeared carrying a white mug. "Here's your tea, and some aspirin." He approached the side of the tub and squatted to be at eye level with her. "Drink this, and take the pills, then soak for a while." When she failed to respond, he said, "Poor Leigh. I guess you need a hand." He rolled up his sleeves, reached for the washcloth and the soap, began lathering the cloth. And then he bathed her.

She was both eased and offended by his casual control of her. She told her body to reject his hands; told herself to get hold of the soapy cloth and fling it in his eyes, blinding him, so she could get the hell out of there. But her circuitry seemed deadened, as if someone had thrown a master switch somewhere. She couldn't do a damned thing but watch as he washed her the way he'd undoubtedly washed his daughter a hundred times or more in her childhood. He had that parental way of holding her, of applying the lathered cloth to the parts of her body, and then efficiently rinsing away the soap. He even slid his arm under her neck, supporting her head while he gingerly shampooed her hair and inspected the gash in her scalp. He did it all in no time flat, then eased her down into the water, stood up and dried his hands, saying, "Try to drink the tea. I'll be back in a couple of minutes to help you out of there."

He went away. She didn't care. She managed to lift the mug, managed to get it to her mouth and swallow some of the now lukewarm tea. Her stomach received it, accepted it, seemed to be subdued by the liquid. He'd added sugar, and almost immediately she felt a degree of energy returning. She sat up slightly higher in the water, holding the mug to her mouth with both hands, sipping steadily until the tea was finished and her belly seemed obscenely swollen from the several ounces of liquid.

Returning the mug to the side of the tub, she held very still, listening intently. Only a clock ticking—the same one she'd heard the last time. Where was he? Maybe he'd gone to move the car. He'd double-parked. He couldn't just leave it that way. He'd have to move it. That was likely what he'd gone to do. With newfound strength, she got herself out of the tub, took a towel from the rail and, wrapping it around herself as she went, tiptoed out of the bathroom. Glanced into the bedroom. Empty. He'd gone out. Her coat had been sponged clean and was draped over the back of one of the two chairs, her boots standing to one side. Throwing off the towel, she pushed her feet into the boots, pulled on the coat, then rushed to the door. It wouldn't open. She turned the deadbolt, twisted the doorknob, but still it wouldn't open. Why? What? She looked over the door and saw, about eighteen inches above the deadbolt, another lock, of a variety she'd never before seen. It had an odd-shaped keyhole. She ran her fingers over it, bewildered, trying to think how to open this smooth-faced cylinder, defied by its unusual keyhole. This had to be a lock that opened from either side, and he'd gone off after securing it from the outside. He'd imprisoned her in this apartment. She couldn't believe it, and whirled around to search for an alternative exit. There were two windows in the living room, with the gates she'd noticed on her earlier visit padlocked over them. Same in the bedroom. Beneath the vertical blinds was another window, another padlocked gate. The bathroom had no window. Knowing it was useless, she nonetheless went to each of the windows to yank on the padlocks. Thick, solidly locked. She stood there, trying to think what to do when she heard footsteps on the stairs. Thinking it might be Daniel returning, she returned the coat to the back of the chair, positioned the boots as she'd found them. The footsteps went past.

Picking up the towel, she padded back to the bathroom, her sugar high dissipating. She moved to pull the plug in the tub, but stopped. Let him do it! For spite, she threw in the aspirins, and then the mug. It hit the surface of the water, tipped, slowly filled, and sank to the bottom, striking the porcelain with a small clunk.

The telephone! She went through the place—which took only a minute or two—finding jacks, but no phone. Not in the closets, or the kitchen cabinets, or the refrigerator. He'd removed the telephone. She was so frustrated, she wanted to start screaming. And thinking of screaming, she remembered Miles saying she could scream her heart out and no one would hear. God! What if Daniel's beating had triggered a heart attack? What if he were lying there at her front door, dead? Damn Daniel! What the hell did he think he was doing? This was insane! He'd locked her into this goddamned apartment, taken out the telephone. She didn't even have any cigarettes.

Neither did he. Another search showed he had plenty of food and liquor, but no telephone, no cigarettes, and nothing sharper than a butter knife, not even a pair of scissors or a razor blade. The place had been cleared, as if in anticipation of a suicide. There wasn't even a pot or frying pan that weighed more than a few ounces. What did all this mean?

He'd been gone at least half an hour, she estimated, unable to locate that clock whose ticking could be faintly heard everywhere in the apartment. There was a ghetto blaster, and she wanted to find a news station, but first she was cold. She was also feeling dizzy again, and sick to her stomach. She opened the closet in the bedroom. Slacks, rows of suits, sports jackets, shirts, but nothing casual. She put on one of his shirts, a pair of his boxer shorts she found on the closet shelf, and a camel's hair sweater. Then she sat down at the table with the ghetto blaster, wondering if she was about to hear of herself as a news item. Woman abducted by stranger. Author kidnapped from breakfast table. Agent murdered by unknown assailant; author sought.

Keys fitted into the locks; she froze. The door opened, and Daniel stepped inside. His face was masklike for a moment. Then he smiled, and said, "You're feeling better. Good. You're probably hungry. I picked up some stuff at the deli on my way back from the garage. I have a place over on the pier where I keep the car. It's very reasonable, even if it is a little out of the way." He chatted, as if she'd just dropped in for an impromptu visit, while he hung up his coat, then carried the bag from the deli behind the counter that separated the kitchen from the living/dining room.

She turned off the radio. "I need a cigarette."

He stopped what he was doing and looked over at her. "You really don't, Leigh. I've been meaning to talk to you about it. You smoke way too much. It's very bad for you. So, we're both going to quit. I got rid of all the cigarettes, including the pack I found in the pocket of your robe. I'm afraid I had to get rid of the robe, too. Never mind. I'll replace it. It'll be easy. You'll see. The nicotine's out of your system in seventy-two hours. After that, it's only a matter of kicking the psychological addiction. The cilia in your lungs actually become activated after seventy-two hours; they start working again, clearing out the garbage. Three days, that's all. It's pretty incredible, when you think about it." He'd never been able to convince Celeste. And she'd made such a fuss, finally shouting at him, "I'm *not* you! I'm not filled with endless purpose. I *like* smoking. At least it's something that's all mine!" He carefully folded the brown paper bag, then put it in one of the drawers, saying, "We'll kick it together. Just don't think about it."

"You are out of your goddamned mind," she said quietly.

His eyes when he looked at her were, for only the briefest moment, filled with madness. For that moment, he looked capable of rage, and of the violence she'd seen him inflict on Miles. "Don't say that, Leigh," he rebuked her, his eyes normal again. "I adore you. I'm not out of my mind. I *had* to do something. I couldn't stand you being with someone who doesn't treat you properly, someone you don't love. It's so obvious you don't care about that man."

The words were right there in her mouth. All she had to do was explain who Miles was, confess she'd lied about being married. Although she wasn't quite sure why, she decided it would be best to allow Daniel to go on believing Miles was the Good Doctor. "What is your plan, Daniel?" she asked him. "Do you even *have* a plan? Or are you merely intending to keep me locked up in here forever?"

"Plan?" He seemed muddled. "No, I don't have a plan. I mean, I wanted to see you. I wanted to bring you here. I had to get you away from him. I couldn't stand seeing the way he . . ." He stopped, unwilling to admit he'd spied on her.

"You stood outside the house last night and watched us," she said, trying not to think about how much she wanted a cigarette. "How could you do that? Have you any idea how it makes me feel to know you watched us making love? When I *think* of it . . . my God! It's such an offensive thing to do, Daniel. *All* these things you're doing, they're such violations. Can't you *see* that? Surely you can't want me to feel as invaded as I do."

He watched her lips move, hearing Celeste say, "I could have been someone decent, Danny. But I've never been able to be the way I thought you wanted me to be. Danny? Are you even listening?" He shook his head, and smiled. "You look kind of cute in my things, Leigh. I wish I could let you keep them on."

He came out from behind the counter and stood close to her. "I really can't let you do that." He held his hand out to her. "Come on, Leigh. Come with me."

"Where? Why?"

"We're going into the other room."

"What if I say no, Daniel? What if I say, to hell with you? What if I say, I'm not going to do one damned thing you want me to? What then?"

He regarded her with an expression of infinite sadness. "You don't want to fight me. I've got the Good Doctor's address on Fifty-ninth. And your mother's, too," he lied. "I don't want to hurt anyone, but if I have to, I will."

It chilled her. She took another tack. "What about your wife? And your parents, your daughter? Isn't someone going to be wondering where you are?"

"I'll be in touch with them," he answered, some doubt touching his features. "I'm away pretty often, traveling. They're used to it." His hand was still extended to her. When she remained stubbornly seated, ignoring his hand, he said, "You have every right to be pissed off with me for the ride I gave you. I'm sorry, and I mean it. But you've got to come with me. Please don't fight me. I hate fighting all the time. I'm worn out from it."

"Just answer one question. Tell me what you hope to gain from this."

"You. I want you. I know you care for me. It was there, right from the start, on the plane. I intend to convince you to make the break, get yourself out of that marriage. Once you see that, then we'll be on our way."

"And if I don't see it, you'll harm my family. Daniel, can't you see that threatening my family won't make me care for you?"

"You *already* care for me. The way you let me . . . the way you . . . I know you care. Whatever it takes, I'll do it. *Whatever* it takes."

There it was again in his eyes, that madness. It made her skin go cold, seeing it. How much proof did she need? she asked herself. She'd already seen him use his fists on Miles. All she had to do was picture Marietta unwittingly opening the door to this man . . . she got up and brushed past him. Once inside the bedroom, she waited to see what he'd do.

"Take off the clothes, Leigh."

Oh, no! she thought. But could she refuse? Perhaps if she made love to him, played it out, she'd get him to trust and believe her. Then she'd be able to get away from this place. She could see no alternatives. So she removed the clothes, and he returned them to the closet. He opened a box he got down from the shelf, saying, as he did, "Lie down."

When she saw what he meant to do, everything in her protested. While she didn't doubt what he'd said about going after Miles or her mother, until this moment, she hadn't thought he'd actually harm her. She could only wonder at her stupidity. And if she struggled with him over this, he'd subdue her; she hadn't the strength to protect herself.

She couldn't help it. She began to cry when he took hold of her wrist and fastened a long, institutional-looking canvas restraint around it. She tried to sit up, her limbs rigid with resistance, and he said, "Just lie still, Leigh," while he fastened the other end of the canvas to the leg of the bed frame. One wrist, then the other. She held herself stiff, but it did no good. One ankle, then the other. She gazed at the ceiling, swallowing against the fear, the indignity, the excruciating inhumanity of this act he'd committed against her, strapping her to the bed frame like a sacrificial victim in some grotesque, demented ritual. She was spread on the altar of his choosing, agonized at being so gapingly on display, at this nonphysical rape. The humiliation robbed her momentarily of her ability to speak, or to look at him. She shut her eyes, but it didn't help. The humiliation sang in her ears, pumped in her lungs, churned in her belly. How could this be happening?

"Daniel," she whispered, forcing herself to look at him in the hope that he'd see and comprehend her suffering, "don't do this, please. I'm not young. I don't have the strength for this. Please!"

He didn't see, didn't comprehend. She could read the desire overtaking him, and had to wonder what substance in him craved this kind of power, this degree of control. Even her tears failed to affect him. He undressed, put away his clothes, and left the room. She heard the shower go on, and even though she believed it was useless, she began to rock back and forth against the restraints, encouraged when the bed moved slightly. The frame was on casters. The bed could be rolled. With every last bit of her energy, she threw her body from side to side, succeeding in moving the bed somewhat more to the left. She rested a moment, listening for the sound of the shower. Still going. A deep breath, and she began again. The bed rolled a bit more to the left. Then a bit more. And suddenly, miraculously, the tension of the bindings on her left wrist and ankle eased. He'd wrapped the canvas around the legs of the frame and her rocking had freed her. Two seconds and she was up, pulling wildly at the restraints. Ten more seconds and she was in the living room, snatching up her coat as she flew to the door, her hand reaching out to the key that was now in the lock.

The impact when he landed on her was so tremendous it knocked the air from her lungs as he sent her crashing into the door. He grabbed her by the back of the neck and threw her halfway across the room, then came after her as she scrambled on her hands and knees toward the door. His hands in her armpits, he lifted her to her feet, kicking the fur coat aside. She saw his arm pull back but had no time to defend herself. His fist approached with almost invisible speed, made stunning impact with her jaw, and there was an instant of utter silence before the blow registered, and she felt herself falling.

Twenty

HE HIT HER. THERE WAS AN AUDIBLE CRACK AS HIS FIST CONNECTED with her chin. Her eyes rolled back into her head, and she fell. He was so jolted by his own actions that for a time he seemed to become disconnected from himself and from her, and could only watch as she fell, her body bonelessly toppling. She lay in a heap on the floor; he was rooted, immobilized. *Danny, why don't you give it up, go out and find yourself someone who'll be the way you want her to be? It'll never be me. Don't you know how that makes me feel, Danny? I'm always going to fail. So what's the point to trying?*

His vision seemed to clear, enabling him to see all at once the bruises on her back and legs, the scrapes on her shins where her legs had dragged as he'd lifted her out of the trunk. He was inflicting injuries on this woman; he'd actually struck her with his fist, when all he'd wanted was to be with her, to be close to her, to show her how very much he cared for her. Why couldn't it ever be right? Why did things always get so screwed up?

He picked her up and carried her to the bedroom where, very carefully, he positioned her on the bed before going to the kitchen for ice. He took half a dozen paper towels, folded them over a handful of ice cubes, then returned to the bedroom where he stopped to think.

He deeply regretted using force on her, but he couldn't see he had any alternative. If he didn't bind her in some fashion, she'd keep on battling him, keep on trying to get away. And he couldn't let that happen, not before he'd had any reasonable kind of chance to make his points. There came a time when your voice just had to be heard. You couldn't keep on indefinitely, hoping gestures, displays of kindness and thoughtfulness,

189

would make an impression. All he wanted her to do was try to see things as he did. It wasn't such a lot to ask.

He lifted each corner of the bed and removed the casters. Then he returned her wrists and ankles to the restraints, before testing the bed to make sure it no longer rolled.

She came to, knowing instantly he'd tied her up again. He had, however, undergone some minor form of metamorphosis in the interval, because he was stretched out beside her on the bed, holding an ice pack to her jaw as he told her, over and over, how shocked and sorry he was.

"I've never hit anyone, ever, before today," he was saying. "None of this is the way I wanted it to be, the way I pictured it. You have to believe that. I care so much for you, and seeing you last night, having to see that bastard touching you . . . I knew it was all wrong to watch, but I couldn't . . . I . . . there are so many things I want to tell you . . . why is it always so damned hard to get the timing right, to get in every-thing that has to be said?" He lifted away the ice pack to see the condi-tion of her jaw. It didn't seem bruised. Letting the pack fall over the side of the bed, he moved closer to her. "They're not so tight this time. There's enough slack so you can turn on your side to sleep. I had no idea you were so badly thrown around in the back of the car. You should've said something. But I'll try to make you feel better." He sat up and reached for something. It was the baby oil. "This'll help," he told her, and poured out some of the oil on his palm, put aside the bottle, and coated his hands.

Her eyes followed his every move, as she tried to find some thread of logic in the things he said and did. He seemed to alternate between differing aspects of his personality, as if feelings he'd suppressed for a lifetime had all at once started fighting for precedence in their right to expression. In order to try to deal with him, she kept having to put aside her attempts to make sense of this situation. Despite the fact that there were only the two of them here, it was hard to keep track of the many and varied themes that appeared to worry and distract him.

Starting at her right foot, he began massaging the oil into her skin, all the while keeping up a rambling monologue that didn't entirely divert either one of them from what he was doing with his hands. She couldn't get a fix on her feelings; couldn't sustain her fear, or her anger, or her confusion. Nor could she prevent herself from responding on a purely primal level to certain of his acts—first his bathing her, now this very sensual laying on of hands.

"It's late in the day, everybody tells me, to be reacting. And I keep telling them I can't help it. I think of all the things I did wrong, and part of me believes I was responsible; it was my fault. Another part of me says, no. It was fifty-fifty. I don't know." He reached for the bottle, poured more oil into his palm, then went back to work, on her thigh now, lifting to get to the underside of her leg. "She was angry the whole of her life. Nobody ever knew why. We'd get together and talk about it, her parents and me. But we couldn't figure it out. It was as if cylinders in her brain were constantly misfiring; or maybe she kept short-circuiting. Whatever it was, the most she could manage, ever, was a day or two when she'd be up and happy and involved. Then, down she'd go, and she hated everyone and everything, and most of all herself. Christ, how she hated herself! Hated her face, her hair, her legs, the shape of her breasts, her hands, her feet, her teeth. Consuming, lifelong hatred. It was her full-time occupation, hating herself. And when I came along, what could possibly have been more natural than hating *me* for *not* hating her." More oil, then his hands rubbed, stroked, rubbed, her belly, her waist, her buttocks; rubbing, stroking. "When Lane was born, I thought maybe that would be the magic. Someone new, someone perfect. Celeste couldn't possibly hate her own baby. But she did. Hated her. The baby cried; the baby messed her diapers; the baby was hungry; the baby had colic. Celeste hated her. 'Here's your child!' she'd say, furious, and practically *throw* Lane at me. How can she hate an infant? I wondered, and looked at this perfect little girl, trying to understand. But I couldn't. I just couldn't. Lane was beautiful; she was our child. So, I took her over. The minute I came through the door in the evening, I was busy with Lane, getting her fed, getting her bathed, getting her ready for bed, getting up for her night feedings; first thing in the morning, I was up to put her into a clean diaper, heat her formula—and later on, the little jars of cereal—feed her and put her back into the crib before I left for the office. Most of the time there was some babysitter from the service with the baby when I got home from the office. And Celeste would be up in the bedroom, on the bed with a drink in her hand, watching the soaps, or some old movie, just waiting to recite this long list of grievances she had. I decided it was postpartum depression; she'd get over it; just give her time and room enough, and she'd get over it. But she managed to go from the postpartum depression into general depression without missing a beat. And from there, it was Celeste's state of being: she was depressed." *Danny, how can you talk about me this way, to someone who doesn't even know me?* "I'm sorry."

Leigh watched and listened, willing herself to disappear, to evaporate.

More oil, and gently he shifted her onto her side to smooth the oil into her back and shoulders, down her arms, rubbing, rubbing; his hands curving over her buttocks, down the backs of her thighs, her calves, then up again to ease her onto her back once more, with a pause for additional oil so he could knead it into her breasts and over her belly to her inner thighs, where one hand stayed while the other spread itself over her breast, and he stared first at his hand on her breast, and then down at the hand wedged between her thighs, and he lost track of what he'd been saying and thinking because he was so completely captivated by her glistening body that he had to come nearer to see close-to every last detail of her construction—the deep-blue veins that traversed her shoulders and ran beneath the bluish-white skin the length of her arms and surfaced on her breasts like tiny, irregular roads leading to the delicate buds that collected at the tips. Her breasts were, to him, as soft as the dreams he'd had as a small child, and as tantalizing. Her belly was flat but cushiony, bisected by that thin scar that disappeared down into her groin, down, to hide behind silken red-brown hair that contrasted so startlingly with the milky flesh coating her bones. He had to rest his face on that inviting cushion of flesh, pressing his lips against the promontories of bone that sheltered it, dipping his tongue into the hidden knot punctuating that too-tempting expanse. He longed to sleep with his face pressed into her belly, his one hand covering her breast, his other curved into her groin. But it was a fleeting desire, of no significance; he was driven to touch her, to slip his fingers into the heated elastic interior of her body, to withdraw to investigate the secrets contained within the folds of her flesh; pushing, probing, until the body beneath his hands shifted in response, lifting, spreading.

Hadn't he known? he thought deliriously, leveling himself between her thighs to touch and taste, to submerge himself in sensation, ecstatic at proving once again, to both of them, how strong was the bond between them. Here was the proof: she was dissolving in undulating invitation, her thighs tensed, her belly quivering. He'd prove to her how well he knew her, how right they were together; he'd make her see that the balance could be attained, that the sense lay not solely on one side or the other but precisely in the middle.

She listened attentively to all he said, hoping for some inadvertent clue that might provide a way in which she could deal with him. But he seemed so genuinely infatuated with her that he was unable to sustain his thoughts. He'd hit her; he'd actually knocked her unconscious. Now her head hurt terribly, the dizziness had returned full force, the massage had evolved into a full-scale lubricious assault on her body, and she was not free to reject him. She was tied to a bed—granted, the restraints were looser than before, but she was a captive nevertheless—and this man could do anything he fancied to her; he'd deprived her of her right to consent, he'd deprived her of her freedom, and now he was depriving her of control over her own body.

She steeled herself, determined to remain detached; she would be stone, she would feel nothing. She would not react. This man had beaten Miles, dear, dear Miles. This man had abducted her from her home and forced her to ride in the trunk of his stinking car; he'd physically harmed her; he'd strapped her down and humiliated her to her very soul; she would feel nothing. He put his mouth on her, his hands and tongue played over her, and she told herself she would remain cold; she would feel nothing. The last time they'd been together, he'd made love to her in this same manner, and had refused to stop; he'd gone on until the pleasure he'd given her had devolved into a gruesome form of pain, but still he'd refused to stop. She would feel nothing. Yet, if she didn't contribute actively, didn't play out an affectionate charade with this man, he would strike her again, hurt her in ever more serious fashion until she ceased to exist. He would kill her. She trembled. From fear? Reaction? She would not feel. She would not. But, God! Here he was again, making love in that heartbreakingly doomed fashion, a supplicant worshiping at a shrine of his own creating, and he was causing her to feel a grating mix of base sexual pleasure, mounting fear, and pity; she could not prevent herself from feeling.

He laid himself upon her defenseless body, he slid his hands under her and held her open like a book he might read; he sighed and pushed himself fully into her in one rending motion that made her heart pause; and then, like a lone shipwreck survivor clinging to a fragile bit of wreckage, he pressed kisses on her lips and throat, he licked her eyelids and her chin, as he rode the outgoing tide and sang hymns of his own composing in the hope of salvation.

His body remained heavy on hers, motionless, still solidly lodged within her. She turned her head aside, overcome by sudden loathing for him, and for herself. Had she not been tethered, she'd have thrust him away; she might even have tried to hurt him, to inflict some small measure of retaliatory pain. There were excuses for his behavior, perhaps; but she had none. He'd invaded her, and her odious body had betrayed her, had gone over to the enemy like some avid, independent camp follower. He'd abraded her senses, forcing her—physically, at least—to feel. And she'd felt everything, *everything;* she'd even been aware, during an instant of sudden stillness, of his release within her, that deluge of additional heat blanketing her interior. She'd been momentarily awed, and then bludgeoned by dismay and thoughts of death. He might not be intending to kill her, but he might, inadvertently, succeed in causing her death. Just now, she had an almost indecent yearning for freedom of any kind, even death. To have this confinement continue, to suffer through more of his sexual forays, would make her despise herself so totally she'd have no desire left to live. He was compelling her to look at herself from his critically disseminated viewpoint, and she knew now, too agonizingly well, what her mother had meant when she'd spoken of feeling separated from herself. Leigh had thought she understood at the time. She realized now, laboring to breathe under this man's weight, that she hadn't understood in the least. And, seeing this, she began to weep again, wishing she could right the terrible wrong she'd done her mother. It was far more than having had a firsthand viewing of her mother's still strong sexuality. It was far more significant than the one-step-removed beauty that the artist she was had perceived—there was, without doubt, an ethereal beauty to a voluntary act of love, especially when engaged in by a lovely, willing woman and an eager, caring man. No, she'd have been in safe territory, they all would have been, had she hoarded her private image instead of flinging it back at her mother. Very few people, if any, could withstand the shock that came with having their most intimate, most voluptuous moments infringed upon by outsiders. She'd done it to her mother. Now Daniel had done it to her. And, like a child, she wanted her mother, wanted the comfort and forgiveness and sympathy only her mother could give her. Perhaps she'd never see her mother again. This thought accelerated her weeping.

Daniel became aware of the change in her breathing, the cadence of her sadness. He withdrew from her, and was taken aback by the way his departure appeared to cause her pain. Her body seemed to shrivel, her flesh rippling as if he'd slowly pulled a long knife from her interior; her nipples tightened; the hair on her arms rose; the tendons in her throat gained alarming definition; she shivered, and tried to shield herself with her elbows and knees but because of the canvas ties she could only bend inward slightly.

"Daniel," she said, her voiced deep and cracked, "you must listen to me." Her eyes when she turned them on him, were hollowed and dark. "If you don't untie me, if you don't trust me, at the very least, not to try to run out of here without any clothes, I will lose my reason. I truly will go mad. You don't want that, do you?"

"But there's slack, you can move some. And it's warm enough in here, but if you're cold . . ."

"*Daniel, listen!* You're taking away everything I need, all the things that allow me to have any feeling for myself. If you strip me of *everything*, I can't live. Surely you can understand that. It's not so very complicated. You have my word I'll stay with you. I won't fight you. But you've got to untie me. I feel ill. I have to use the bathroom. Please, undo these things and let me go to the bathroom. Please!"

Without another word, he went around the bed, kneeling to release the restraints. Then he took them from her wrists and ankles, and stood rolling the strips, asking, "Do you need help?"

"No, thank you. I can manage."

"You'll have to leave the door open," he began.

"I will close and lock the door," she said firmly. "I must have *some* privacy. Do you intend to witness my every last act?"

"You can close the door, but don't lock it."

"Thank you. May I wear one of your shirts?"

He shook his head. She didn't push it, but stood up unsteadily and walked out to the bathroom. The dizziness rushed back with being upright, and she had to keep her hand on the wall to prevent herself from falling. Being on her feet also caused a gush of fluid down her thighs, and the feel of it, the smell of sex, nauseated her. She got inside the bathroom, reached automatically to lock the door only to discover he'd removed the locking mechanism. Hopeless. Her stomach rose, and she vomited the tea into the sink, then hung over the basin, quaking. She really was too old to sustain much more abuse; perhaps she would die, after all. She rinsed her mouth and the basin, then sat on the toilet feeling as if some frenetic aging process had overtaken her and was racing through her system, burning out nerve endings, dimming her vision, dehydrating her cells. More fluid left her body. Her interior felt battered, scalded. She got the shower going, then climbed into the tub and sat beneath the water, hoping to God Miles hadn't been seriously hurt, that his heart was strong enough to withstand the beating Daniel had given him. She wanted him alive; she wanted her mother alive. If they were out there, beyond that locked front door, she had an objective: to get back to them, and to make good on every last error or omission she'd ever made. She'd find some way to erase from her mother's mind that dreadful image Leigh had forced her to see. And she'd tell Miles, finally, how deeply, how long-lastingly, she cared for him.

Dear God, but she'd been a fool! All those years of coming and going, arrivals and departures, in and out of his life; she'd been waiting for him to make some declaration of caring and intent, as if it mattered who instigated the making of declarations. Anyone looking at her life would have interpreted it the way Miles had, would have withheld whatever pronouncements he might have rehearsed dozens of times. She'd lived for years and years on the surface of situations, taking flight at the slightest hint of anyone's need for more of her than she was willing to give. She'd elected to show the very best of herself only to her two sons, because her two husbands, and the many lovers in between, hadn't displayed the elusive qualities she'd sought without actively knowing of her quest. And all that time, if only she'd stopped to look, she would have seen that he'd been there all along. Miles was the one who'd accepted her from the outset precisely as she was, without qualification, without hidden plans to alter her to suit more closely his specifications; he'd been happy to have however much of herself, her body, her thoughts, her emotions, she cared to offer. And instead of giving him the most and the best, as he deserved, she'd played out the game, on and on, bedding strangers, investigating strangers, even caring for strangers. And why? Because men were not to be trusted. They left you in your childhood, abandoned you for mysterious, never-stated reasons; they died and left you to try to find ways to fill the emotional gaps; they elicited frightful promises and made you put your mark on the agreement in blood and tissue ripped from your insides; they used you for purposes so vague, so muddled and indeterminate, that the only possible defense you had was to remain a stranger yourself, offering only inadvertent glimpses of what lay beneath your misleading surfaces. But Miles had been constant; Miles had been faithful in his heart; Miles had offered pleasure, and protection, and even a home. Christ! What did it take to make her see and value what had been there for so long?

And now that she thought about it, it was likely she was the only one *not* to see it. Certainly her mother had known for ages, had made numberless references to the very unique qualities Miles had. And Joel. Joel had teased her, saying, "Give the poor guy a break, Leigh. He sees pure gold when he looks at you. I sure as hell wouldn't pass on someone who looked at me the way Miles looks at you. That doesn't happen too often in a lifetime." And what had she replied? Something flip, something silly, something witty, to cover the hesitation underneath, the fear not quite buried, of investing one more time in one more man.

The door opened and Daniel was there, looking in at her, with his hand on the knob.

"GET OUT OF HERE!" she shouted at him, covering her breasts with her hands, drawing her knees up. "YOU GAVE YOUR WORD YOU'D LEAVE ME ALONE IN HERE!"

"Just wanted to make sure you're all right," he defended himself.

"LEAVE ME ALONE!" she screamed, her eyes and mouth and nose filling with water. "JUST LEAVE ME ALONE!"

He backed away. The door closed.

She sat under the stinging spray and cried noisily, her hands still clasped protectively over her breasts. She really didn't want to die.

"They have absolutely nothing to go on," Miles was saying. "There is no French professor at NYU by that name; nor has there ever been a buyer at Bloomingdale's of that name. Undoubtedly, there is a daughter, at some college somewhere. But it could take *years* to check every college roster in this country. The message he left on Leigh's machine was erased by your call. We did find a sketch of the man that Leigh made. The police are circulating it throughout New York, Connecticut, and New Jersey. There's also a bulletin out on the car. The snag is we don't have a license plate number. There are a fair number of Godards in the Manhattan directory, and they're all being canvassed. I think," he said slowly, "we have to make some sort of statement to the press. It may be the only hope we have of getting anyone who's seen or heard anything to come forward. I can't think what else we can do." He raised his hands in a defeated gesture, and waited to hear what Marietta would say. He'd never seen her in a condition remotely like the one now. There was a furrow between her brows that seemed to have materialized overnight. Her natural pallor now appeared waxy, even unhealthy. She hadn't bothered with her hair and it hung to her shoulders, which had an uncharacteristic slump. She'd found a package of cigarettes someone had left behind, and was smoking one as she listened to what Miles had to say.

For her part, she winced inwardly at the varicolored bruises around his eyes and along his jaw and cheekbone. His face was lumpy with swelling on one side, but he'd declined her offer to have the housekeeper fetch him some ice. He had repeatedly beat his fists together over the past two hours, furiously blaming himself for his failure to keep Leigh safe. "Gone to bloody seed," he'd insisted. "I was useless, a damned great bag of wind, puffing and blustering. He ran right over me like a train."

"It is not your fault," Marietta had several times absolved him. "*No one* could have anticipated anything like this."

She smoked the cigarette, made queasy by the inhalations, trying to come to grips with the facts. "If you believe it might do some good, I don't think we have any choice. Perhaps you could write a press release, handle this for me. I couldn't possibly deal with reporters *en masse*. Or even individually. I simply want to stay here, close to the telephone. You don't think he'll harm her, do you? Why is he doing this? Is it money he's after? And if he is, why hasn't he made any demands? I simply don't understand the purpose of his taking her."

Miles closed his eyes for a moment, biting back on his instinct to state unequivocally that he would kill the man if he harmed Leigh in any way. His eyes open, he said, "He seems to care for her. One can only hope."

"Miles, more than anyone or anything else, I love my daughter." She extinguished the cigarette, then said, "Until two days ago, I never fully appreciated just what Leigh's been through, her losses, the anxiety, the pain of grief, the protracted mourning. I'm ashamed to admit there were times when I was most impatient with her; I was convinced she was being self-indulgent, wallowing in her sorrow, anointing herself in it. The deaths I've experienced have been appropriate, somehow, or not directly connected with me. My mother, my father, they were well into their eighties when they died. There was a naturalness, an inevitability to their passing. I was fond of Carl; I was devoted to Stephen and to Joel. But they were *Leigh's* connections, *her* bonds, and only incidentally mine. This loss is mine, entirely mine. The dread, the speculations, the fear . . . I cannot *bear* the thought that I might never see her again. And I simply cannot stop thinking of all the occasions when I failed to praise her, or to compliment her; when I failed to work harder to understand her, to display all the love I've always had for her. Please do whatever has to be done. In the past two days, I've come to see that nothing, really, will ever again have any value without Leigh. In two days, I've come to recognize how very well, in fact, she handled those losses. I have nothing like her resilience. I have nowhere near her degree of courage. I'd prefer to be alone now, Miles," she said regretfully. "You'll ring me later?"

"Of course."

"You'll forgive me if I don't see you out."

"Of course."

He got up, crossed the room to press a kiss on her cheek, then made his way to the foyer, hearing behind him Marietta's deep, painful-sounding sigh. He really would, he vowed, kill that man if he harmed Leigh.

Twenty-one

S HE WORDLESSLY REFUSED HIS OFFERS OF FOOD AND DRINK, AND LAY ON the edge of the bed, her eyes to the wall. He gazed at the knobs of her spine, at her naked haunches, then went to cover her with the blankets. He thought about tying her up again, decided it would be all right for now; he wasn't going anywhere, and neither was she. She was giving him the "silent treatment," but he was used to that. It never lasted very long.

She didn't want to talk, had nothing it was safe to say. If she said anything at all, it would lead to more attempts on her part to determine some logical course to his actions, and logic had nothing to do with what was happening. She wanted to go home; she wanted her mother; she wanted to be assured of Miles's well-being; she wanted the familiar safe haven of Miles's embrace. She could feel Daniel's eyes, but would not acknowledge him. She shut him, and this place, and her entrapment, out; she closed her eyes.

He went to the kitchen to make coffee, then sat at the table with a mug and listened to the radio with the volume very low so as not to disturb her. When he looked in again on her, she was asleep. Periodically, he went to check on her, but she hadn't moved. Finally, he ate. Then he climbed in on the far side of the bed and, after watching her for a time, went to sleep.

She slept right through until the afternoon of the next day, and he thought she'd probably go on sleeping if he didn't rouse her. He sat on the side of the bed and put his hand on her arm, softly saying her name. She didn't stir. It alarmed him. He shook her, spoke her name loudly, and her eyes opened. She looked at him blankly, without recognition.

"You have to eat, Leigh. I've made you something. Don't go back to sleep. Come on. I'll put the food on the table."

He got up and went to the door. Her eyes tracked him. Nothing had changed. She was still here. She reeled into the bathroom, used one of the toothbrushes to clean her teeth, then went to sit at the table, drawing her knees up against her chest, and wrapping her arms around them. Her vision was blurry. She felt strangely distanced from everything. "I want a cigarette," she said, ignoring the coffee he put in front of her.

"Drink your coffee and don't think about it. Food'll be ready in a minute."

She reached for the mug, and had to use both hands to lift it. She couldn't believe how weak she was. Her body felt as if it was going to topple off the chair. She drank some of the flavorful coffee and, keeping hold of the mug for its warmth, she watched him, busy in the kitchen, radiating health and energy as he put food on two plates. He was dressed in navy slacks and a pink shirt with white collar and cuffs; he was clean-shaven, his hair damp-combed. She was naked. She felt like an animal, and despised him for making her feel that way. How dare he treat her like some uncommon form of house pet! Putting the mug down, she got off the chair, went into the bedroom to snatch one of his shirts from its hanger. She buttoned it on, then returned to the chair and her coffee.

"You can wear it for now," he relented. "But I can't let you keep it on." He spoke most temperately, as if what was taking place was in no way out of the usual. It ignited a fuse in her chest.

"Why don't you kill me now?" she said with cold rage. "You must have a knife hidden somewhere, or a blunt object, something you could use. Why don't you just do that, Daniel? Get it over with quickly. It would be infinitely kinder than doing it by inches, the way you are. Here," she held out her wrists. "Get a razor blade and open my arteries. I'd prefer to die fast than go through any more of this."

His eyes went round. He dropped the plates. He began to shake as if palsied. His head vibrated back and forth, back and forth, in some form—she thought—of denial. Tears streamed down his face. As she watched, her anger shunted off to one side by this astounding display, he lost control.

"How did you know?" he asked, between gulping sobs. "You knew! Did you know? You didn't know. How could you know?" He put his head down on the counter and wept like a child. She'd never seen anything like it. But she recognized the emotion, and the recognition drew her out of the chair and around behind the counter.

"Daniel, I'm sorry," she told him, a sympathetic hand on his heaving back. "That's what happened, isn't it? I'm so sorry."

"I told myself it was good, it was over, it was better, we weren't going anywhere, not for years and years, it was better. *It wasn't better!*" he cried. "I tried so hard, I did, I know I did, I tried but nothing was ever right or good, she couldn't be happy, and I tried so hard, *I tried*, but she did it, it was my fault, my fault!"

She tried to transmit her sympathy through her hand on his back. But he raised himself abruptly, his arm flying out, catching her across the face. "DON'T PATRONIZE ME!" he shouted. "DON'T THINK I'M SO STUPID I CAN BE CONNED!" A second blow drove his fist between her breasts and sent her colliding with the refrigerator door. Slipping in the spilled food on the floor, her feet went out from under her, and she fell, her lungs in spasm. She couldn't breathe. If she let her panic take precedence over her common sense, she knew she'd asphyxiate. Hold on, hold on! she told herself; don't struggle, don't try to breathe, just concentrate on getting your throat to open; don't panic; wait for everything to right itself. It'll be okay, okay. She let what air remained in her lungs escape slowly, slowly, and at last there was an inner relaxing; she was able to draw in tiny sips of air. She took shallow breaths, overcoming her instinct to pant, her eyes never leaving him. His stance was simian; his shoulders were hunched forward, his fists held tightly at his sides. He looked ready to administer more blows. If she said the wrong thing now, he'd almost certainly go on striking her. Oh God! What was the right thing to say to him? What would keep him from delivering more blows, further injuries?

"Daniel," she whispered, "how can you treat me this way when you know I love you?"

He grunted, and wiped his face on his shirtsleeve, his eyes red-rimmed.

"I love you," she whispered.

He made a disbelieving noise, but his eyes stayed on her.

"I love you, Daniel," she told him again.

He threw back his head and roared at the ceiling. It made her skin crawl, but she changed neither her expression nor the tone of her voice. His eyes returned to her.

"You know I love you," she repeated, breathing slowly, steadily; each inhalation bringing pain. Something in her chest felt broken. He'd struck her so hard; it had been like a brick thrown at her at great speed. "I love you," she insisted. "You've been right all along. I can't deny it."

He fumbled with his trousers. She wanted to, but didn't dare close her eyes. He fought his way out of his trousers and his shorts, then he threw her down and fell upon her, tearing the shirt out of the way, stabbing blindly against her until he located where he wanted to be and pushed into her, oblivious to everything but his need.

She didn't struggle; she didn't help; she tried not to cry out, tolerating the pain of dry flesh driving within dry flesh. If you fight him, you will die, she told herself. Whatever he does, whatever happens, don't fight him! You can live through this; you can. It hurt. He wanted to rip her to shreds;

the knowledge transmitted itself through the ugly thrusting, the grinding of his bones against hers.

It was over. He rested for a moment, then pulled abruptly out of her. She gasped, feeling her eyes bulge at the pain. God oh God God! As if nothing extraordinary had happened, he put his clothes back on, went to the sink for the sponge and began cleaning the floor. She sat up slowly, trembling hands trying to cover herself with the shirt. Her eyes never left him; she feared doing anything that might provoke him. There were fragments of broken crockery all over the floor, several splinters were embedded in her feet and the backs of her legs. She looked at her legs, then at Daniel scooping food up with both hands and dumping it into the garbage. His lips were moving; they shaped inaudible words.

"I have to go to the bathroom, Daniel."

"So go!" he snapped without looking at her, busy setting the kitchen to rights.

"I wouldn't leave you if it wasn't necessary."

"Go on!" he said impatiently. "And get that fucking shirt off, the way I told you to!"

Without a sound, she pulled herself upright, hesitated long enough to pull shards of porcelain from the soles of each foot, then limped off to the bathroom, leaving a trail of blood.

She kept looking over at the door, expecting him to come bursting in, but he left her alone to catalogue her injuries and sort through her thoughts. She could only be grateful now that he'd removed the bathroom mirror. She didn't have to see herself. It would have heightened her fear, she knew, to see the bruising she could feel with her fingertips on her jaw and cheek, the healing gash on her head. The area between her breasts was already starting to turn blue; breathing was agonizing, as was any but the smallest movement of her arms and shoulders.

Fortunately, none of the cuts was deep, but several of them didn't want to stop bleeding. And inside, dear God! Inside it was as if he'd taken rough-grade sandpaper to her. She was swollen and raw. Using the toilet brought tears to her eyes. *I want to go home go home want to go home.* Soundless litany; soundless tears. Eyes traveling over the walls, the ceiling, searching for something, anything. She was taking too long; Daniel was bound to come after her. Pull back the tears; push away the little girl's recitation; prepare to deal, to do whatever has to be done in order to get through this.

She almost forgot to take off the shirt, remembered just as she was about to open the door, and removed it. Naked again.

She went to sit at the table, knees tightly together, feet flat on the floor, hands in her lap: a portrait of obedience and contrition. He was at work, preparing more food. She sat very still, thinking how far away and long ago it was since Christmas. And Miles, who knew most of her secrets and all her imperfections, quirks. Miles, whom Daniel had struck so hard half a dozen times, with such rage. Miles with the tricky heart, and the periodic EKGs, and the cautionary lectures from his internist. Had Daniel killed him? She told herself no. You couldn't kill someone so easily. Yes, but you could; if Daniel's blows, his assaults on her body were anything to go by.

He brought her a plate of food, and she thanked him. He was calm again as he sat opposite and poured two glasses of red Mouton Cadet. She gave him the best smile she could manage as she picked up her knife and fork, then looked at the food. The smell of it repelled her. Some kind of frozen fish filet in a white sauce, with bright green frozen peas, and frozen hash-browns shiny with cooking oil.

"Eat, Leigh," he said, back again in his reasonable mode. "You really must eat." He held out his glass, said, *"Salut!"* and tasted the wine.

She murmured, "Cheers!" and took a sip. She would eat, and drink, and then, she was certain, she would be sick. Setting down her glass, she cut into the fish, raised the fork to her mouth, inserted the fish, began to gag, stopped, waited, chewed, and swallowed. The fish fell into the well of her stomach to swim on the shallow surface of the wine. She cut, chewed, swallowed, drank more of the wine. She would not think about how much she craved a cigarette, or about her nakedness, or about his eyes taking bites out of her exposed flesh; she would eat the oily potatoes, the slimy peas, the fish that tasted faintly of iodine.

He looked over at her midway through the meal, and found himself disconnected again, and profoundly frightened by the situation he'd created. Poor, lovely Leigh; he'd taken away her clothes; he'd made those bruises on her face and chest. He'd subdued her, and she'd at last admitted to her true feelings for him. But why the hell did it have to be such a contest? Why did they have to go through such turmoil?

As he gazed at her, she seemed suddenly foreign, and he wondered who she was. Who was this woman sitting so quietly, eating the food he'd made for her, drinking the wine he'd poured into her glass? Her hair was short instead of long; she was very thin, not rounded and billowing; her eyes were green, not brown. *You never see me the way I really am, Danny. If you could just once see me, really see me, maybe then you'd let up a little on both of us.*

Well, he could hear that, all right. He wasn't crazy. He knew damned well this wasn't Celeste. Celeste was where she'd wanted to be, where she'd taken herself. Christ! Goddamned mind games. It annoyed the hell out of him.

But who was this woman? Sure, he knew her name. She just didn't look all that familiar. She wasn't young. Maybe he hadn't been aware of it before, but he could see it now. Her skin wasn't as tight to her bones as he'd thought, and her breasts had undoubtedly been higher even a year or two earlier. The texture of her skin lacked the elasticity of youth. Yet she'd been created wonderfully well, and he craved her softness, the feel of her under his hands. Having her there, being able to look at her, was wonderful, just wonderful. And she'd at last declared her love for him. Everything would be all right now. He adored the shape of her head, the breadth of her shoulders, the symmetrical bounty of her breasts; he loved her accessibility, and the knowledge that she was there for him, solely for him. And she loved him.

After the meal, he said he had to go out for an hour. "You can listen to the radio, if you like. Do you want me to get anything for you?"

Inspired, she said, "I need Tampax. And some cigarettes?"

"No cigarettes. Are you expecting your period?" he asked, looking fascinated. "I hadn't considered that. Do you take birth control pills or something?"

"Pills," she fabricated smoothly. "They're at the house."

"Well, if you're expecting a period, it's not likely you're going to get pregnant. But that would be okay, too." His eyes turned vague for just a moment. "Anything else?"

"Some sort of antiseptic, for the cuts."

"Okay. I won't be long."

"Oh!" she called after him. "Perhaps a newspaper?"

"Sure," he agreed, and went out, locking both the deadbolt and the strange mechanism above it.

While he was gone, hoping to appease him, she cleared the dishes and loaded the dishwasher. Then again she limped through the apartment looking for something she might use on the locks, or the padlocks on the window gates. The butter knives were no good, too thick to insert between the door and the frame. She tried the foil containers from the frozen food but they were too malleable, useless. In the midst of her searching, her stomach gave stabbing warning signals and she had to run to the bathroom to be sick again.

Chilled, she put on her fur coat, guessing she had perhaps thirty-five minutes before he got back. She went over every inch of the apartment, but found nothing. At last, she peeled a banana and gagged it down while she sat at the table and went from station to station on the ghetto blaster, hoping to hear some news item about herself. Nothing.

Hearing footsteps outside, she hurried to put her coat back in the closet, then sat again at the table to play with the tuning dial, looking for Joel's favorite station. It distressed her that she couldn't find it. She turned off the radio and went to push aside the verticals, looking out at the windows of other apartments across the way. She felt invisible. Maybe she could find something to smash the glass; she'd stand there and scream until someone saw her; they'd call the police. The key turned in the deadbolt and she moved back to the table, her heart beating too quickly, as if he'd almost caught her in the act of screaming.

Dan put down a brown paper bag containing Tampax, a small bottle of iodine, and the day's final of the *News*. He hung away his coat, then carried what looked like a toolbox into the bedroom. While she skimmed the paper, he began banging and hammering. In the fifteen minutes it took her to go through the paper twice, he completed whatever he'd been doing in the bedroom and came back out carrying the toolbox. He unlocked the padlock on one of the gates, slid it aside, opened the window, put the toolbox outside on the fire escape, then closed the window and the gate, and secured the lock. The keys went into his briefcase which he snapped shut. The case had a combination lock, she saw. But it was something that could be opened even with a dull butter knife. Hope shifted in the pit of her stomach. Or was she about to throw up the banana? She sat listening to WQXR, maintaining her pose of external calm. The banana stayed down. But she was exhausted. She'd only been awake a few hours, yet she was ready to sleep again.

"I'd like to lie down, Daniel," she told him.

"Sure," he said, and got up to go with her to the bedroom. "There's a slight change," he told her, indicating the metal loop he'd fastened to the exposed-brick wall. "We'll let the leg restraints go for the time being, but I have to make sure you stay in one place." With that, he bound her wrists with one of the canvas straps, and secured it to the loop in the wall. He left her plenty of slack so she could turn over, but not enough to allow her to go beyond the foot of the bed.

Again, she lay facing the wall. He sat and stroked her, smoothed her hair back from her face, then stroked her some more, his gestures becoming bolder; he fondled her breasts with greedy possessiveness. She couldn't believe he wanted more sex, but it appeared he did. "Daniel," she smiled at him, "I can't just now. I'm feeling very crampy."

"When are you due?" he asked.

"I've lost track. Anytime, I should think."

"Well, we'll try again later," he said, and to her enormous relief, he covered her, turned out the lights, and left.

Being trussed up this way wasn't quite the indignity being spread on the bed had been, but it was ignominious nonetheless. Fine points. The freedom to close her legs, to shut some part of herself away from his eyes, restored a tiny portion of the self-respect he'd stolen by tying her legs apart. Just thinking of the way she'd been strapped to the bed made her begin to perspire, as the heat of degradation merged with her anger and fear.

She told herself she couldn't afford to waste time or energy on being angry. She needed to think how to handle this. He'd "collected" her, as if he'd read the Fowles novel. Now he was rewriting the book, adding twists and sexual variations, while she was preoccupied with thoughts of the death of the captured butterfly.

Well, she was no goddamned butterfly, and she had a fully functioning brain. There had to be certain advantages she could claim—recreating a menstrual cycle for herself was one. She'd insert a tampon first thing in the morning. While it didn't guarantee he wouldn't devise other ways and means of using her, it might give her some time to mend internally.

Oh, *God!* she thought, for the moment losing her ability to think calmly and rationally. She wanted to be out of this place, away from this man. People had to be looking for her. Unless Daniel had killed Miles. If he had, it might be some time before Miles was found. And then no one would have any idea what had become of her. Perhaps Miles was dead, and it was assumed that she was, too. If Miles was dead . . .

Daniel appeared in the doorway, silhouetted against the light from the living room. He'd lost all trace of the simian stance he'd had earlier in the kitchen and seemed more like the Daniel with whom she was most familiar.

Seizing hold of the opportunity, keeping her voice hushed, she said, "Daniel, on a purely practical level, there are things I'm going to need." He remained in the doorway, listening. "Much as I hate to admit it, I do have my vanity, and there are all sorts of creams and lotions I use. If I *don't* use them, I'll start to look like a used tea bag."

She gave a little laugh, and wondered at herself, at her resources. He laughed with her. Encouraged, she went on. "My electric shaver and my cosmetics. *Tweezers,*" she laughed. "I don't think you'll care very much for the sight of me dried out and hairy."

He stood thinking, then said, "I can fix that," and left the doorway.

If he went out—perhaps to buy a few things for her—she'd have a go at the screws holding the hinges of the gates to the window frames, using the edge of the butter knife. She examined the hinges in her mind, reaching three of them, with three screws in each. It wouldn't be very difficult, or take very long, to remove nine screws. Then she'd be able to push aside the gate, open the window, and get away down the fire escape. Her coat and boots were in the closet. She'd find a taxi, have the doorman at her building pay the fare. God, God! She was fifteen minutes away from home, if she could just get out of this small-scale prison, away from this frighteningly disturbed man.

He came back, carrying something. She couldn't make out what. Then he turned on the light and she saw he had a towel over his arm, and in his hands a basin of water, soap, a sponge, an orange Bic disposable razor, and the bottle of Vol de Nuit.

"Stand up a minute, Leigh," he instructed. Afraid to refuse or to question him, she did. He spread the towel over the sheet, as she watched with mounting apprehension. "Okay," he said. "You can lie down again now."

Keeping her hushed tone, she asked, "Daniel, what are you doing?"

"Don't worry," he told her. "I'm not going to hurt you. Come on. Lie down."

Jesus! Her pulse speeded up. There was no way on God's earth she was ever going to be able to anticipate the circuitous turns of this man's thinking. She stretched out on the towel while he put down the basin, then freed her hands. At once, she rubbed her wrists where the canvas strap had impaired her circulation, her eyes never leaving him. Maybe he intended to pry the blade free of its plastic casing and do as she'd suggested: open her veins. She could only hope he hadn't succumbed quite that thoroughly to his madness.

He sat two thirds of the way down the bed and lifted her legs across his lap. He lathered the sponge, soaped one of her legs, then picked up the razor. Working slowly, deliberately, he began to shave her leg. She wanted to laugh; she didn't dare.

By the time he'd sponged and dried one leg and started on the other, she'd relaxed. He really wasn't going to hurt her. If anything, this was somewhat more bizarre, but equally as comforting—at the outset—as the massage had been. He had moments when he seemed acutely aware of the more esoteric aspects of femaleness.

He derived such pleasure from attending to her, from his responsibility for her well-being, that he never wanted this time to end. When he'd shaved clean each leg, he smoothed the baby oil into her skin, from her ankles to the tops of her thighs; he applied dots of the perfume to the insides of her ankles and at the backs of her knees. Then he sat with her legs resting across his lap and looked at her groin, then at her arms. She didn't shave her outer arms. Fine, golden hairs. Celeste had despised her body hair, had shaved her arms as well as her legs. Her body had always been smooth as a baby's. He looked again at Leigh's groin, a stirring in his belly. He said, "Open your legs, Leigh." Her eyes widened. She didn't move. "Open them," he told her.

"What are you going to do?" she asked, aware of the pulse beating hard in her throat, and at her temples. So quickly, in an instant, she felt once more imperiled.

"Just relax, and don't worry," he crooned, urging her knees apart.

"Jesus Christ!" she whispered, putting both hands between her legs. "Daniel!"

"You'll like it," he told her, and plucked away her hands. "I'll be very careful. It's something I want to do."

"Daniel!" her voice was pleading.

"You have to trust me," he insisted.

It was true; she did. She had no choice.

"Lie back and close your eyes," he told her.

She did as he wished, feeling the perspiration collect and trickle down her sides. It lasted an eternity, while she kept motionless, her fists pressed into her eyes, terrified he'd slip and slice into her with the razor. He scraped and lathered, paused to clean the blade, lathered and scraped some more. He told her to bend her knees. With reluctance and dread, she obeyed. More lathering, more scraping. She tried to control the shaking that started somewhere in the center of her body and spread outward in waves.

He lifted the lower half of her body and removed the towel. The sheet felt refreshingly cool. She exhaled with relief and was about to open her eyes when his bare, oily hands began the subtle attack she'd known all along was coming.

His fingers slid over her. He used both hands, watching himself, then glanced up to see her biting the side of her hand as he succeeded in gaining access to every part of her. And then, with her caught, impaled upon him like a glove of flesh, he had to bend his head to taste and explore her.

He delivered her a new brand of pain, then placed a layer of vile sexual stimulation on top of it, causing her to writhe impotently, which heightened the pleasure as well as the pain. He didn't overextend it this time, but took her right to the limit, nudged her over, then played witness to another loss of herself, keeping her impaled until the last of her tremors had ended. Then he withdrew his hands, and gently straightened her legs, and she thanked God it was over, feeling, in the aftermath, agonizingly distended by his acts. She also felt emptied, wrung dry. If he'd just leave her alone now, she'd sleep—possibly for days. But when she opened her eyes, it was to find him at her side, expecting her to perform. And if she didn't do as he wished, he'd either strike her again, or worse, force his way inside her and do further damage. So she got down on her knees, and she did it. He caressed her hair, and said over and over, "I love you." She did it, and forgave herself for wanting to survive so badly that she'd set aside her pride, her dignity, any and all caring she'd ever had for herself. She did it. And gagged. Then ran, still gagging, to the bathroom.

After that, he allowed her to sleep.

Twenty-two

"ARE YOU ALL RIGHT? WOULD YOU LIKE ME TO COME?" MILES ASKED anxiously.

Marietta sounded just a little older every time he talked to her, and that was on an average of half a dozen times daily for the past four days. This afternoon her voice was weary as well as older. "I can't do a thing," she confessed, as if her inactivity were a crime. "I've asked the girls not to come in for the present. Except for Alicia, who's been so good, screening the calls, keeping people away. Did you find anything?"

"I went through everything in the house and the apartment. Luckily, I had Joel's keys, so I didn't have to bother with the manager at her building. Marietta, I went through every pocket of every last garment she owns, her handbags, her luggage, the studio, her desk, every last drawer and cupboard in both kitchens; even the wastebaskets. I've looked *everywhere*. Either she destroyed the letter he sent her, or he managed to get it back from her when she saw him. I don't know. It's maddening. I know I saw a return address on the package I forwarded to her, as well as the letter with it. Diane doesn't remember, either. Federal Express, of course, only has our address on the label. I was so hoping . . . I can't think what else to do. And the police, well, it's simply laughable. Every department points at some other department, insisting it's their jurisdiction. The general assumption is she's been taken out of state. However, since there's no *proof* of that, the Connecticut police are spinning their wheels and the FBI can't be called in. And the New York police argue that since no one can be certain she's in New York State, let alone the city, they can't do anything more than they've already done—which is bloody little. No one has anything to go on. When they ran the computer

check on the flight manifest, it turned out Mr. Godard had paid for his
ticket in cash. Therefore no credit card number, therefore no mailing
address. They've asked Scotland Yard to try to track down his landing
card, but evidently it's a process that can take as long as ten days. It's as if
the man never existed. I *imagined* him. And since I didn't actually *see* him
force her into the car, there's even the possibility that she went with him
voluntarily. The pendant is untraceable, of foreign origin. It's been two
days since we gave the release to the press. I thought by now perhaps
there'd be something. I honestly don't know what to say. It's the most
frustrating . . . I don't have to tell you. I'll stop by later. I have a meeting out of the office at four. I'll be with you by six."

"Oh, good," she said, sounding dazed.

"Have you slept?" he asked, concerned.

"The odd hour. I'll see you at six, dear," she said, and put down the
phone.

He hung up, wishing he hadn't any business demanding his attention.
Every hour he spent away from his effort to locate Leigh added to his
guilt and his fear. Four days. It seemed like months, years. He looked
repeatedly at his watch throughout each day, confused and bothered by
how slowly the minute hands moved. He'd collected all the items Leigh
had given him over the years and sat examining each one in turn, recalling
the occasion of its presentation, and what they'd said to each other, what
they'd done before and after. For hours, he'd retrieved near-lost moments, to study and treasure them. And then he'd returned the gifts to
the places where they normally resided, with the sudden fear that he had,
perhaps, held some sort of private memorial service in advance of the end
of her life; perhaps he'd been wrong to look at and hold those items she'd
once looked at and held; perhaps, by his actions, he'd sent mistaken
messages into the atmosphere that might find their way to her. Everything felt wrong, smelled wrong, tasted wrong, looked wrong.

He tidied his desk top now, dreading this last meeting of the day, with
a good, young editor whose inscrutability would, Miles knew, be insufferable. Tolerable at any other time, but not today. But he couldn't post-
pone. He'd sold the man a book, he'd accepted his commission, and he
had a moral obligation to the author to stay in the ring and keep bobbing
and weaving.

He sat with his head in his hands gazing at the blotter, trying yet again
to come up with something he might have missed. The package and its
accompanying letter had been the only clues he'd so far come up with,
and his disappointment at failing to find either the wrappings or the letter
was so acute it made him feel ill. He kept going back in his mind to New
Year's Eve, and the way he and Leigh had danced at Roseland, when he'd
achieved a state of happiness it seemed he'd anticipated all of his life.

They'd been inches away from a commitment. He'd believed utterly that another few days or weeks, and she'd have been willing, at the very least, to make alterations in their living arrangements. Perhaps she'd have agreed to sell the New Canaan house and move her belongings to his place outside Brewster. He couldn't think now why he'd described it to her as dilapidated when, for more than eight years, he'd been going up on weekends and holidays to oversee the kitchen renovations, the installation of two new bathrooms, the replacement of the roof, the repainting of the exterior, the double-glazing of the windows, the decorating of the interior. He'd gone to garage sales, scouring the local papers for ads, picking up odds and ends, occasional antiques in good condition; he'd shopped for months to find just the right sofa, the most comfortable chairs. Every spare cent he had had gone into the house. And it was very near to being the way he'd envisioned it at the outset. All along, it had been his intention to show it to Leigh, to offer it as a lure, to induce her to take up residence in the far bedroom with the onetime lean-to he'd had converted to a north-light studio. He'd created his version of the perfect environment for her, with a refinished and lacquered brass double bed, an Edwardian dressing table and matching chest of drawers; there were flowing white curtains on the windows and dusky rose carpeting on the floor that complemented the flower pattern of the white-ground handmade quilt he'd bought for the bed. He'd left the brick floor of the studio as it was, merely having it scrubbed before putting down a large square straw mat. Bamboo shades on the studio windows and over the sliding doors to the garden, as well as on the skylight he'd had cut into the roof; there was even a small sitting area with a white wicker rocker and matching table.

The house was the surprise he'd planned for her ever since the day she'd announced to him she was divorcing the Good Doctor, having finally legally adopted Joel. That very same day, after leaving his office, he'd gone to the garage for his car and made the drive out to the country to look at the house, picturing her in it. Not once during those years had he ever considered it a fruitless enterprise. He'd always believed a time would come when she'd stop skipping out of reach every time matters threatened to turn serious. She wasn't a frivolous woman, he'd told himself; she'd been badly burned, and was fearful of being burned again. To her way of thinking, it was less hazardous to indulge in casual affairs. What had never failed to bemuse him was her inability to see that she was every bit as enticing to men as her mother. They seemed to spot her from a distance and gravitate toward her, perhaps sensing her singular gift for giving. Because even at her lowest ebb, she always gave far more than she took away with her. Yet in all the years he'd known her she'd never accepted as truth his compliments, his praise, his eagerness to show to her her own beauty. She just couldn't see or believe it. But she cared. Marietta was spot-on on that score: Leigh's greatest talent, and greatest weapon against herself, was her ability to care. She'd cared about some man on a flight across the Atlantic, and it had detonated in all their faces. Hell! he thought miserably. She *had* to be all right. He'd come to pieces— he could feel it, incipient as a cold—if any harm came to her. He, too, had spotted her from the distance and been drawn to her. But unlike the others, he'd placed his faith in time and circumstance and the conviction that she'd turn one day and realize he'd been patiently waiting. Patience did not necessarily provide rewards. And time now felt like an enemy.

He swiveled his chair around to look out the window, remembering the costume party he'd had one year. Joel had been fifteen, he recalled, starting to smile as the details of the occasion came back to him. What a splendid party that had been! Joel, in a long, dark wig, his makeup perfect, had come as Hedy Lamarr, rigged out in evening gear with high heels. He'd been the hit of the party. And Leigh. He reached for his handkerchief. Joel had done Leigh up as a French courtesan, with a white, powdered wig and a rented gown; powdered cleavage and decorative beauty patches. She'd been so lovely, Miles had found it hard to breathe, looking at her. White, the dress had been. And white the stockings and the shoes. And later on, after she'd sent Joel home with Marietta, she'd showed him the corset. Laced down the back, and white, too. Ruffled white pantaloons. He'd sat and gazed at her, dazzled.

Lane was sprawled on her bed trying to study for a psych test when Cath came charging in without even bothering to knock.

"Wait till you see this!" Cath told her, waving a newspaper. "I nearly *shit* when I saw it."

"What?"

"I was at the chiro's this afternoon, for my back, you know. And there's always hundred-year-old *National Geographics* and shit like that in the waiting room, or weird magazines like *Runners' World;* stuff you'd never read if you weren't stuck there. Anyway, there's this whole stack of old newspapers, right? So, if it's a choice between *Runners' World* or the old papers, I'm going for the papers. So, anyway, I'm sitting there, just looking at the pictures, about to turn the page, and that's when I saw it. *Look!"* Cath had folded the paper to the article and scrunched on the bed beside Lane, tapping her finger to point it out.

Lane took the paper and read the short AP piece, feeling weird. She knew in her bones her dad had something to do with this. She didn't want to believe he could do anything so warped as kidnapping someone, but she did believe it. The last couple of months he'd been getting stranger and stranger, and every time she saw him he was so kind of out of it that it made her want to put her arms around him and hold him, as if he were a little kid, and promise him everything was going to be okay. He made her feel like crying all the time because she could tell he'd lost his center.

"Your dad met her, right?" Cath was saying, taking the paper from Lane and rereading the story. "Didn't you tell me he got you her autograph?"

"Right," Lane said quietly. "He did."

"And now she's been abducted! That is just too amazing!" Cath declared. "Don't you think?"

"Yeah," Lane agreed. "Amazing. Can I keep that?" she asked, reaching for the paper.

"What? Oh, sure. Bet you'll want to show your dad, right? God! Won't *he* freak?"

Lane didn't respond. It was her turn to reread the piece.

"I thought you'd be totally amazed," Cath said, frowning at Lane's subdued reaction.

"I am. It's just that I've got this psych test day after tomorrow, and I've really got to study."

"Right," Cath said, getting off the bed. "So, fuck off, Cath. Right?"

"Yeah. Okay?" Lane gave her a smile she didn't feel. "I absolutely have to go over the stuff, or I'll blow the course. Thanks a lot for showing me this. It's pretty amazing, all right."

"Call you tomorrow," Cath said a bit doubtfully, at the door.

"Okay, Cath. Thanks a lot. Really."

"Yeah." Cath went out and shut the door.

Lane read the story a third time. Then she got her wallet, put on her coat, and went out to the pay phone down the road. She didn't want to call from the phone in the hallway, where anybody could hear. She felt shaky as she punched out the number for the Bedford house, then gave the operator her dad's AT&T credit card number. The phone rang and rang. She let it go twenty times before hanging up. Then she punched out the Palm Beach number, recited the credit card to another operator, and worked out what she wanted to say.

Her grandmother answered, and Lane had to get herself together and sound cheery as she said hello and how are you, then listened to her grandmother say she was fine, and so was her grandfather. And how was she?

"I'm fine," Lane told her. "Have you heard from Daddy lately?" she asked, trying to keep it casual.

"He hasn't called you?" her grandmother asked, at once sounding disturbed.

"No," Lane admitted, "and I'm getting kind of worried. I was hoping maybe you'd heard from him."

"Not a word since he left us. It seems to be becoming a habit: he vanishes for days, and then reappears."

"Not for this long," Lane said. "It's eight days tomorrow. The longest he's been gone before this was six days. I'm worried about him," she allowed. "If you do hear from him, will you call and let me know? Sometimes it's hard to get hold of me here, I know."

"Of course," her grandmother said, sounding shocked that Lane would think she wouldn't. "You are all right, *petite? Tu as besoin de quelque chose?*"

"No, I'm okay, Grandmother. Give my love to Grandfather. And *please* call me if you hear anything."

"Of course," her grandmother said again.

It didn't feel right. Nothing felt right, and hadn't since her mother had killed herself in the upstairs bathroom. It creeped her out even to think about taking a razor blade to her veins. She'd always known her mother was a borderliner, but she'd never thought Celeste would actually kill herself. And Lane had a hunch she hadn't been told the half of it. Because if her father was anything to go by lately, it'd been a major number, her mother's last act. Lane just knew it'd been so bad it'd thrown her father totally for a loop.

He'd seemed okay at first, when he'd called to break the news. She really hadn't felt much of anything except sad for her father because despite the fact that Celeste had been a major bitch forever, he'd loved her. The woman had been a boozer, a bitch, a total embarrassment—Lane had stopped inviting kids to the house when she was twelve—and nothing like a mother. If it hadn't been for her dad, Lane would probably have run away when she was fourteen, because the woman just would *not* get off her case. There wasn't one single thing Lane had ever done in her whole life that her mother had liked. Lane couldn't make the slightest move without setting her off. Her mother hated Lane's hair, her clothes, her friends, the way she sat, stood, walked, talked, ate—every last thing about her. Lane couldn't remember even one time when her mother had hugged her or kissed her or even smiled at her. All the hugs and kisses and smiles Lane had ever received had come from her father and her grandparents. Back when she was little, she used to try to do things to please her mother, to make her happy. But by the time she was eight, she knew it was a total waste of time. And she decided it wasn't her fault if her mother didn't like her, because everybody else did and told her so, which meant it had to be something about Celeste, and not anything that was wrong with Lane. So, she'd stopped trying, and did her best not to rise to it when her mother had a fit about something or other; she'd ignored Celeste or pretended she didn't hear. And when her dad asked if she'd maybe like to go to boarding school for grade nine, Lane had said, You bet, for sure, absolutely, but I'll miss you, Dad. And he'd said, 'It has to be better for you than this, sweetheart,' and she'd known what he meant. He didn't have to say any more than that, because he'd always known how things were. What she'd never been able to understand was why he'd stayed married to Celeste, how he could claim to love her even when she turned into a total slob and was blotto by eleven in the morning. But he did, and he stayed, and he wouldn't hear one bad word about his wife, not from anyone. And by the time she was seventeen, Lane thought she had a fix on both of them, and it made her sad. Because it really was as if her dad was in love with this girl he'd known in high school who'd gone off and left this other woman behind in her place, and he was spending his entire life trying to find the girl from high school inside this other woman. And Celeste, in one of her rare, lucid moments, had really rocked Lane by saying, "He can't see that that girl was never real. He made her up, then wanted me to become her. I tried, but how do you turn into someone else? I did try. It was just too hard."

That first year in boarding school, Lane had come home during the school breaks. But after the second time, when Celeste threw a fit because Lane talked on the phone too long with Cath, and pulled the cord right out of the wall before starting to pound Lane over the head with the receiver and her dad had to pull Celeste off, Lane spent all her school vacations with her grandparents. And aside from that afternoon the summer she was seventeen when she'd sat out on the terrace with Celeste, watching her mother smoke one cigarette after another, her hands trembling, while she eyed the drink on the glass-topped side table and tried not to go for it because she wanted to have some kind of sensible conversation with Lane, and actually managed to be a real person for a couple of hours, the next time she'd seen her mother was at graduation, and Lane had made a major effort to be nice and polite and everything, but Celeste was so bombed you could smell it from six feet away and everybody was staring at her because she could hardly stand up straight. She'd looked years older than Lane's dad, and Lane had felt so sorry for the both of them that she'd stuck with them the whole time, right up to when they left to go home. Then Lane had gone back to her room and cried until she threw up because she'd hated the whole scene so much, and she didn't want to feel sorry for her mother, but she did. That whole afternoon was the first time—maybe it was because Lane was eighteen, and sleeping with Steve by then, and not a kid anymore—that she could see the walking, talking tragedy that her mother really was, that her dad had helped Celeste become. Looking at Celeste—which was what Lane had always called her, never Mother—was like looking into this big, dark tunnel that had no light at all, not even a hint of it at the other end. If you went into that place, you'd never come out again. It was scary as hell. And if it hadn't been for her dad, maybe Celeste would've been someone else and okay; or maybe she'd have been locked up somewhere a long, long time before. But nobody ever did lock Celeste up, and she never did get a fix on things, so she went and offed herself. And it blew her dad's brain. The past couple of months he'd been like someone dangling from a high wire, afraid to hang on and afraid to let go. He blamed himself for Celeste, and Lane knew why, and knew there was never any way to do the right thing every time, not for anybody, and he was taking on too much of the blame because even Celeste had known that the things he'd always said and done were from the heart and never out of meanness or spite. He just didn't have any of those things in him. Which was why Celeste worked on him the way she did—because it was the only area where she had a fighting chance of coming out even. They were two people who shouldn't ever have been together. But they were. For twenty-one years. And if Celeste hadn't finally ended it, they'd have been together forever, with her dad trying and trying with no hope ever of succeeding, and Celeste resisting and resisting, with even less hope.

Back in her room, she went through the article one more time, deciding a whole lot had intentionally been left out. The story hinted that the police knew who'd abducted the author, but weren't releasing all the facts. They quoted comments by the guy who'd been with her, her agent, and gave his name as well as that of Marietta Dunne, who was the mother.

Lane sat on the bed, holding the newspaper on her lap, touching her fingertips to the kind of blurry newsphoto of Stanleigh Dunn that didn't really give you any idea what the woman actually looked like, and tried to think what to do.

Miles was on his way out the office door on the afternoon of the sixth day, when he overheard his receptionist saying, "I'm sorry. He's not available at the moment."

Miles signaled to her, mouthing Who is it?

Diane said, "Just a moment, please," into the mouthpiece, and put the caller on hold as she referred to the name she'd jotted down on her pad. "Lane Godard?"

Miles reacted as if he'd touched a live wire. "I'll talk to her!" he said. "Put her through." He flew back to his desk to grab up the telephone. "This is Miles Dearborn," he said breathlessly.

"Mr. Dearborn," a young voice said, "you don't know me. My name is Lane Godard. I just yesterday saw the story in the paper. The thing is, my father told me he met Miss Dunn on one of his flights."

"Yes, I know that," Miles said urgently.

"Well, when I saw the item in the paper . . ." She hesitated, then went on. "Mr. Dearborn, I think maybe my dad has something to do with this."

"He most definitely has something to do with this," Miles said, keeping his voice steady. "I'd very much like to see you, talk with you."

"I'd like that, too. I'm calling from Vermont. I go to college here," she explained. "But I've got a car, and if I leave now, I could make it to New York by about eight or nine tonight, depending on the traffic."

"I'll meet you. Tell me where."

"Mr. Dearborn, do the police have to be involved in this?"

"We can discuss that."

"Okay. My grandparents have an apartment on Fifth Avenue. That's where I live when I'm home from school."

"Fine. Give me the address. I'll meet you there, let's say at eight-thirty."

She gave him the address, then said, "I don't really know if I can help you. Nobody's heard from my dad in a week and a half."

"Drive very carefully," he told her. "And we'll talk this evening."

Excited at this break, Miles quickly called Marietta to tell her. "It may come to nothing, and it may be something. I'll keep you posted."

"Come here directly after you've talked to the girl," Marietta told him. "I don't care how late it is."

Lane made another call to her grandparents, to let them know she was taking some days off from school and was on her way to New York. She didn't mention anything about her father or Stanleigh Dunn. She didn't want to say a thing to them until she'd spoken with Mr. Dearborn and heard the whole story. Once she knew the facts, then she'd have some idea what to do.

"You've got to understand," Lane said. "Whatever my dad's done, it's because he's been totally wrecked since my mother committed suicide almost seven months ago."

Miles sucked in his breath and sat back, stunned.

"Would you like something to drink, Mr. Dearborn?" Lane asked. "There's everything in the bar. My grandparents entertain a lot."

"I would, actually. Scotch and water would be lovely. Thank you."

She went to fetch his drink and he tried to relate this very forthright, obviously distraught young woman to the man who'd erupted into Leigh's house and begun using his fists. She was wholesome, in a low-key punk fashion that was uniquely well suited to her. About an inch or two over five feet, she had long, glossy brown hair fastened to sit askew on top of her head; round, questioning eyes; olive complexion. She was dressed in skin-tight black trousers and what looked to be combat boots, a man's dress shirt with a pleated front, and over everything was an outsized burgundy wool cardigan festooned with a variety of rhinestone brooches.

One of her ears sported three pierced earrings, the other merely one. The effect was most pleasant. He thought she looked like nothing so much as a feisty little elf. She was tiny enough to look good in the gear. And she had an effervescent quality that even her present distress couldn't disguise. This young woman had a natural exuberance coupled with visible intelligence. Her eyes challenged; she listened closely to whatever was said; and she had no fear of silences. Miles liked her. He simply couldn't connect her to her father, except for her eyes. They both had the same brilliant blue eyes, ringed darkly around the irises. In the case of the father, the eyes had been most disconcerting. The daughter's eyes were a triumph of sheer beauty.

She came back with something clear for herself and Miles's Scotch, sat close by on the footstool that was the partner to the chair Miles occupied, and went on with her explanation. "My dad told me he'd lied to Miss Dunn about my grandparents, about what they did. My grandfather retired two years ago. He was in international banking. And my grandmother has never worked. He told me he didn't know why he'd said those things. But I knew, kind of." She looked down at the glass in her hand, then raised it to her mouth. From the way she drank, Miles knew the beverage was nonalcoholic. "He's always told basically harmless lies. It was sort of his protection, his camouflage; he told people things that were meant to make everything look okay. My mother was crazy," she said flatly, turning those exquisite eyes once again to Miles. "From what I've heard over the years, she was always crazy, right from the time she was a kid. But she was the only woman Dad ever knew. They started dating in high school. She got pregnant, and he married her. I was the pregnant part," she said with a little smile. "Anyway, she started hitting the sauce when I was born, and she just never stopped. The couple of times she tried drying out, she was so totally insane that it was actually better when she was drinking. The booze kept her kind of vague. But sober. Boy! I mean, she'd pick a fight with me, or with my dad, over absolutely anything. When she was on the sauce, she'd be so out of it that the fights never lasted long. Sober, they went on for days. I mean *days*. She'd start in on Dad the minute he walked through the door and keep it up all the way through dinner. I'd hear them still at it when I went to bed. And next morning, she'd be following him down the stairs, still shrieking away at him. I don't know how he stood it. I honestly don't. But he put up with it. It was like he came home every night hoping for miracles. He'd come through the door with a big smile, ready for things to have turned around. Naturally, they never did. Because neither one of them could hear what the other one was saying. And that was the whole problem, right there. They were in love with two different people, these dream images they'd made up for themselves back in high school when they were kids. He was okay, because he had control over every other area, you know? But all she had was the house, and me. And she couldn't control me, she couldn't make me into the way she wanted herself to be. Because I wasn't like her. I don't know if you can follow that. Celeste thought she could say what she had to say through me, and if I said the words, then maybe Daddy would finally hear. The problem was she'd forgotten a long time ago what she was trying to say. And anyway I didn't want to be *her*, I wanted to be me. Dad, at least, always knew who I was. He could see what was going on with Celeste and me, and he could tell she was totally disconnected from me; like she didn't have any parental switches anybody could turn on, so I was either going to be her alter ego, or I was competition. When she stopped trying to program me, I became the full-time competition. Until Dad sent me away to school. That was when I was fourteen. Until then, it was a war. Mostly between the two of them. Really, between Celeste and Celeste. You know? Nobody understood her. So she had contempt for everyone, and especially Dad. Jesus Christ! He was this jerk who didn't have the brains of a pineapple; he was weak; he was stupid; he was worthless. She even, this one time, made insinuations about how maybe the two of us, me and my dad, had something sexual going on. I went totally berserk. I was going to kill her. Dad had to drag me out of the house and walk me up and down the road for an hour to get me cooled down. Imagine *saying* a thing like that!" She looked at Miles, seeking confirmation of the horror of the accusation.

"I can't imagine it," Miles said quietly.

"Right! She was out of her fucking mind. Sorry for swearing. But you can imagine what it was like for me, trying to figure this whole thing out for years and years. Well, what happened was, back last June I finished up my first year at college and went on a cruise with my grandparents. I like to spend as much time with them as I can. They're pretty elderly, you know. So anyway, we sailed on the twelfth. Dad came to see us off with champagne and flowers, the works. Then he went home and found her. I know it had to be pretty bad, and that he didn't tell me or my grandparents anywhere near all of it. It *had* to be bad, because the whole bathroom had to be done over, the walls, the floor, all of it. We got a ship-to-shore call from him and flew home from the next port for the service. Closed casket, and then a cremation. I thought he was taking it really well. You know? I mean, I kept looking at him, waiting to see cracks. But he seemed okay. He went back to work—he had six months left of his contract with the big company that bought him out—and made his buying trips; went away and came back all right. The only thing different was he wouldn't go anywhere near the house. He stayed here with us, then he'd take another trip for two or three weeks, and back he'd come.

"Then, at the beginning of November, no, wait, it was Thanksgiving, that's right, we were in the middle of dinner with the turkey and the rest of it when suddenly I could see Dad was all choked up. He was sitting there, holding his knife and fork, staring at his plateful of food, and he started to cry. I felt like dying," she said, her voice gone small. "I love my dad, Mr. Dearborn. He's the best father anybody could ever have. I mean that. He's decent, and kind, and good to people. He was good to that poor crazy woman for twenty-one years. I can't believe he'd ever hurt anybody, not on purpose. And if he's done this, the way you say he has, it's because he doesn't know what he's doing. He's not who he's always been. And it's because of what my mother did, not because he's a sicko or anything like that. You *have* to *believe* me."

"I do believe you. But—forgive me—he beat me stupid and kidnapped someone I love very much. It's rather difficult to be as sympathetic as I might under other circumstances."

She stared at him, taking in the bruises on his face, her eyes filling. "My dad did that to you?" she asked.

"I'm afraid so."

"Oh, shit!" she whispered. "I'm getting so scared. I feel like I'm going to wet my pants. Excuse me a minute," she said, put down her drink, and ran out of the room.

When she returned a few minutes later, she said, "If anything happened to my father, I don't know what I'd do. I really don't. I can't even *think* about it."

Miles reached out to put his hand on her arm. "I feel precisely that way about Leigh," he told her.

"But she's married." Her brows drew together in confusion. "Dad told me that was the big problem: she's married."

Miles shook his head. "No, not for many years."

"I don't get it. None of this makes sense."

"Your father told Leigh *he* was married. You're right: none of it makes sense. There's someone I'd like you to meet. May I use your telephone?"

"Oh, sure. It's over there." She pointed out an extension on a table near the living room door.

Marietta had pulled herself together for the meeting. She'd pinned up her hair and, for once in a very rare while, had applied a bit of makeup to relieve her pallor. She sat very quietly, smoking a cigarette, and heard Lane out.

Lane repeated what she'd told Miles, unable to take her eyes off the woman seated opposite. She was kind of old, and she looked really upset, but she was the most beautiful woman Lane had ever seen. And all the time she was talking, Lane kept wondering what Stanleigh Dunn must look like—that newsphoto was nothing, a dud—if her mother was this beautiful. The whole thing was getting to Lane really badly now that she'd heard Mr. Dearborn's story, and she'd told both him and this amazing woman all about her mother and father. She felt as if she was on the verge of losing everything in the world that had ever mattered to her, and she didn't know what she could do to prevent it happening. She told all of it, even some things she hadn't told Mr. Dearborn, because she didn't want to disappoint this woman who paid such close attention and seemed so incredibly sympathetic. Lane couldn't imagine having a mother like this. It would have to be like the miracle her dad had always hoped for.

"I'll do anything I can," she promised them both, winding down. "I know it's probably hard for you to see from your side of it, but I'm as scared for my dad as you are for Miss Dunn."

"I'm able to see that," Marietta said kindly, very taken with this outlandish child with the extraordinary eyes. It seemed inconceivable to her that a man who could foster such loyalty and love in his child would do harm to Leigh. "I think," she said judiciously, "your father's very fortunate to have a daughter like you."

That tipped it. Lane covered her face with her hands and started crying. She felt sorry for absolutely everybody. Here her father was a kidnapper, of all things. And these people were being so decent and understanding. She accepted the handkerchief Miles offered, blotted her face, and stood up, saying, "I'll keep this and send it back to you clean. Okay?" Then she went over to where Marietta was sitting and before she knew what she was doing, she was on her knees with her head in the woman's lap, crying all over again, and saying, "I'm sorry. I'm really sorry. He's not a bad person; he's really not. He's just had *such* a bad time; it's been *so hard* for him. If you knew him, the way he really is, you'd know he'd never intentionally hurt anyone."

Marietta put her hands on Lane's face, looked into her eyes, and said, "You are not responsible for what your father's done. Whatever happens, remember that. Will you remember that?"

Lane nodded dumbly.

"If you don't wish to stay alone in your grandparents' apartment, you're more than welcome to stay here."

"I'll be okay," Lane said, thinking she should probably feel embarrassed at making such a total Gumby of herself, but she didn't. These two people weren't about to blame her for her father's actions. Somehow that made matters worse. Maybe Celeste had taught her to expect blame, she thought; also it was the one thing she knew really well how to deal with. She got up, again mopping her face with Mr. Dearborn's handkerchief. "I want to go up to Bedford and look through the house. The thing is, if I find anything . . . what I mean is, I'll help any way I can, but I can't stand the idea of bringing the police in on my dad. So maybe"—she looked first at Miles and then at Marietta—"we could try to do this without involving them. I mean, I know maybe they'll have to get into it in a big way, but maybe they won't. You know?"

"I understand," Marietta said. "It would suit everyone if this could be resolved privately."

"Right. So, I'll check it out and let you know if I get anywhere."

Marietta got up to see her to the door, waiting while Lane shook hands with Miles.

"I meant what I said," Marietta told her in the foyer. "You are *not* responsible. The people we love very often do inexplicable things. Those things don't necessarily reflect on *our* actions. You're a lovely girl, and your mother was something of a fool. Anyone would be proud of you."

"You're so nice!" Lane cried, and gave Marietta a hug. "I've got your number and you've got mine. I'll call you either way, and if I don't find anything at the house, we'll get together tomorrow and try to think what to do next. Right?"

"Right," Marietta agreed, returning the hug. "You've had a very long drive. Go home now and try to get some sleep."

Lane stepped away out of the woman's embrace. And maybe it was because of all the emotion and talking about things she'd never before had an opportunity to tell anyone outside the family, and maybe it was the scariness of the whole situation, but she looked into Marietta's terrific green eyes and said fervently, "I'd've given *anything* to have a mother like you!" Then she bounded off down the hall, and Marietta closed the door.

Twenty-three

*L*EIGH HAD LOST TRACK OF TIME. DAYS BECAME NIGHTS, BECAME DAYS; and the more time that passed, the likelier it seemed she might never again see her mother, or Miles, if he was still alive. Daniel's blow to her chest had been more damaging than she'd thought initially. The bruise between her breasts was a deep purple-red area, from which threads of livid color traveled outward. While externally there was no particular tenderness, internally she ached. And it was most acute when she attempted to eat. Daniel presented her with food. She swallowed as much as she could. Most often, within minutes, her body rejected what she'd consumed. He prepared cups of tea and coffee, swimming with cream and thick with sugar. She drank the liquid, gaining temporary energy from the sugar, then becoming dizzy and weak-limbed after the sugar high ended. Daniel believed she was faking it. He didn't actually say it; his actions and facial expressions did. Because his own health was unimpaired, he couldn't see that anything occurring could possibly make her ill. Therefore, it had to be a ploy, a sign of her weakness like her less frequent requests now for cigarettes.

She remembered, with rekindled hope, the letter Daniel had sent with the pendant, giving his telephone number. Surely, if Miles were all right and found that number, the authorities would be able to trace the address. But her hopes collapsed when, alone and unfettered for an hour while Daniel went out on one of his mysterious errands, she put on her fur coat and found the letter in the pocket. She sat on the floor of the unfurnished living room, huddled inside the coat, and wept with frustration and despair. Then, pulling herself together, she returned the letter to her pocket, went to the kitchen for the butter knife, and began working at the screws threaded through the hinges of the steel gate over the far window. It was slow going. Only the very tip of the knife was thin enough to fit the slot on the screw face. The knife slipped constantly out of the groove, but she kept at it, finally managing to loosen all three screws in the bottom hinge. Then, because Daniel was due back at any moment, she quickly gave each screw several turns back into the wood of the frame so her efforts wouldn't be noticeable. The knife rinsed and returned to the drawer, her coat back in the closet, she shut herself into the bathroom to sit in a tubful of hot water, the heat drawing some of the hurt out of her cuts and bruises.

Several of the cuts had become infected, their perimeters inflamed and red. She applied the iodine, tears springing to her eyes as the brown medication seared the liquid rims of the cuts.

On her first try, she couldn't insert the tampon. She was too swollen. She needed some sort of lubricant, but she couldn't find the baby oil. Perhaps Daniel had used it all during those sexual preambles. For her second try, she accidentally managed to tip over the bottle of Mazola cooking oil he'd left on the counter. In the bathroom under the pretext of washing her hands, she coated the applicator tube with the oil, and was able to position the tampon inside her. While she was washing her hands, she wondered at the degree of madness in this apartment, and its contagion. Surely to God, what she was doing was every bit as deranged as the majority of Daniel's actions. And if she ever did get away from him, was she going to be rational? What was rational? She was no longer certain. She simply knew she had to do anything and everything in order not only to keep whatever grip she could on her sense of herself, but also to discourage Daniel from surrendering to his unpredictable spurts of brutality.

She believed now one truly could die in captivity. But she had no intention of giving up her life without using every last resource she had. So she went about the apartment, slowly pacing the living room back and forth at Daniel's urging—like a convict in the yard—trying to keep her body functional, trying to hold on to the last shreds of her dignity, parading naked, back and forth, back and forth, with the damned Tampax pushed inside her like a bullet in a gun chamber, the string dangling irritatingly between her thighs. She hated him; she hated herself. She felt increasingly capable of murder.

Daniel had stopped bringing newspapers; he'd removed the batteries from the ghetto blaster and stored them in his briefcase. More tantalizing than anything else was her discovery of the telephone, sitting out there on the fire escape, wrapped in a plastic bag, beside the toolbox. She stared and stared at it, thinking she could reach through the gates to smash the glass, but it was beyond her range. There was no way for her to get to it.

So it sat, inches away, with a steel gate and a sheet of glass between her and the freedom one call would bring. She wasted perhaps ten minutes hanging on to the gate, staring out helplessly, all but shattered by her mounting frustration. Then she went back to work, and as she struggled with the unyielding screws on the second hinge, her eyes went repeatedly to the telephone. She could feel the instrument in her hands, could see herself plugging it into the jack in the living room just over there, could hear herself speaking quickly into the mouthpiece, summoning help. But she couldn't get to it.

On the evening of the second day of wearing the tampons, he came into the bedroom and said, "Take it out, Leigh!"

For one dreadful moment, she thought he'd somehow discovered her lie, and couldn't think what to say or do.

"Take it out," he said again. "Don't be embarrassed. I really don't mind. It's not so bad; it's even kind of warm. We'll have a shower after. I want to be inside of you."

"Daniel, I can't. Please, don't ask me to do this."

"You're being silly."

"No, truly, it is embarrassing. It's very private. I'd prefer not to. Come lie down, and I'll make love to you."

"I don't want to be in your mouth," he said petulantly. "I want to be *in you*. Just go and take it out!"

"Daniel, I'm not up to it. I don't feel well. Let me make love to you now, and tomorrow I'll be well enough to do it properly."

"Take it out!" he insisted, his eyes darkening.

All her resolve to be cautious, to play by his rules to keep him appeased, vanished. She simply broke. It was as if something inside her head had been stretched too thin, and it snapped. "FUCK YOU!" she screamed, and smacked his face hard, first with one hand, then with the other. Scrambling onto her knees on the bed, she struck him as hard as she was able with her fists, screaming all the while. She wanted to kill him.

For a moment, he was so taken aback he could only sit there, with his arms raised to ward off the blows. Then he realized someone might hear her; he had to shut her up. He caught hold of her wrists, hissing, "Shut up, shut up!" but she was shrilling at the top of her lungs, face bright red with the force of her screams. He slapped her. She broke free and slapped him back, still screaming. He was beginning to sweat, panicky at the thought that someone might be home in one of the other apartments and hear the noise and come pounding at the door demanding to know what the hell was going on in there. And he couldn't have that. So he dragged her forward, put one hand around her wrists, and clamped the other over her mouth. But she didn't stop, the volume was merely reduced. "Shut up!" he warned, forcing her down, his knee across her midriff. "Shut up, shut up! You'll spoil everything!" She went quiet; he relaxed his hand fractionally but kept it over her mouth. Then her teeth sank into the side of his hand, breaking through the skin, biting deep and hard until the pain was excruciating. Her legs thrashed, her knees banged against his ribs, her whole body was fighting him, while her teeth threatened to meet in his hand. He did the only thing he could think of: he wrapped his free hand around her throat and pressed down on her windpipe, harder and harder, until her jaws unclenched and he could get his hand free, until she stopped thrashing about, until her eyes were bulging from their sockets, until she went limp, and her eyes closed.

Absently, he wiped his bleeding hand on the sheet as his breathing quieted. Then he saw she didn't seem to be breathing, and a new panic exploded inside his head as he pressed his hand under her breast, unable to feel any heartbeat. "Oh, Jesus!" he cried, and pinched together her nostrils, pulled open her mouth and began breathing into her, mentally counting. He pushed air into her lungs, then pressed his joined hands into her heart, counting, counting, tears dropping from the end of his nose, terrified to think he'd killed her when all he'd been after was to stop her screaming. She *couldn't* die. Not Celeste and Leigh, too. *Breathe!* he begged her. Breathe! And then her lungs seemed to flutter, and he heard the air rushing into her mouth. It made a whistling sound as she drew it in, in, then slowly out; a rhythm was established. He held his shaking hand under her breast to feel her heart beating slowly, steadily, and cried loudly, open-mouthed, unaware that he was making almost as much noise as she had.

Unable to stop shaking, he covered her with the blankets and lay down, holding her tightly, terrified at how close they'd come. What was he doing? What? He no longer knew. She shouldn't have defied him; she shouldn't have attacked him that way. Why couldn't she allow him to love her without feeling the need to do battle every inch of the way? There was no need for it. Why wouldn't she see that? If she'd just do what he wanted her to do; if she'd just eat and let him take care of her; if she'd just stop trying to direct him away from where he wanted to be, it would all be perfect. But she couldn't do anything the way he wanted her to, and she kept challenging him. She could eat, but she refused merely to get back at him. And she could've taken out the goddamned Tampax, but she wanted him to beg. When was she going to stop all of it, and give in? What difference did it make if she had her period? It was nothing, nothing. He loved her, but she was making everything so goddamned, unnecessarily complicated. Maybe it was because she had nothing to do here, and she was bored. He'd taken the batteries out of the radio, but couldn't remember now why. There was no TV or newspapers. He hadn't even thought about getting her any books or magazines to read, or maybe some pencils and a sketch pad. Sure, that was it. She was putting up such a fuss because she was bored. He'd go out and get her some magazines over on Eighth Street, some drawing supplies, maybe some candy or something. And, for a change, he'd bring back a pizza, make a salad and some garlic bread, open a bottle of the Chianti. A change of pace would do the trick, give her something to do, something to look at, something different to eat.

When she woke up, she knew she was alone. She'd come to recognize a certain stillness to the apartment when Daniel wasn't in it. Even sitting motionless in a chair, his presence sent electric currents into the air. She lay, feeling deadened. He might as well have tied her up again because she was as shackled by exhaustion as she was when he bound her wrists with the restraints and attached the canvas to the loop in the wall. Her legs felt numb. The ache was still there in her chest and she could scarcely swallow. Her hands were battered from their brief fight, and her head throbbed, her eardrums hurt. She'd fought him, and he'd choked her until she'd blacked out. Why, when she knew how incendiary he was, had she put herself so at risk? Stupid. Bloody stupid. He wanted complete capitulation. She'd have to give it to him, or next time she really might die. She'd come too close this time. She could still feel again the undiluted terror of being unable to breathe, of his hand bearing down down down, closing her throat. God! The fear, the utter agony of having no air to breathe, the protesting shudder of starving lungs, the disbelief and panic causing every bodily system to shut down. She couldn't quite believe she'd actually lived through it, that she'd been as near to death as she had without going all the way over into the darkness on the other side.

She was profoundly aware now of her breathing, of the action of her lungs with each inhalation. It seemed miraculous that her heart continued to beat, that she could flex her fingers if she wished to, or even turn her head. She hadn't died after all, and she would take no further risks. She would obey him absolutely, regardless of the nature of his requests. She would not disagree, or defy, or argue, or strike out at him; she would be precisely what he wished her to be: an obedient slave. She would loathe it, but she would save herself. He wanted her; she would find the strength to go to the bathroom and remove the tampon. If he questioned her, she would supply some credible lie. She would permit him access to any part of her he cared to claim; she would allow herself to be used. This would not last forever. Common sense dictated her time of entrapment would be limited. It wasn't possible to hide out in the middle of Manhattan with a captive indefinitely.

She could, of course, start a fire. But in the event the fire went out of control, she might suffocate, or be burned alive. No good. She could smash the windows through the gates in the hope of attracting attention. But being Manhattan, it was likely no one would pay any attention. She could take a couple of cans from the kitchen cupboard and pound on the front door with them. But there was little traffic in and out of this building, almost none during the day. The other tenants were nine-to-fivers, and Daniel now went out only during those hours. In the evenings, he remained with her, insisting she sit at the table and keep him company while he fixed a meal, or changed the bed linens, or acted out his sexual fantasies upon her body wherever they happened to be when the urge overtook him. The most she could do was keep on working at the screws on the gate hinges. If she could get them all loosened, she'd only have to wait for him to go out again, then put on her coat and boots before pulling the gate free of its moorings, opening the window, and climbing away down the fire escape. But for now, her first priority was to return her body to a state of accessibility. How he could derive satisfaction from using her in the ways that he did, she couldn't comprehend. It had to do, as she'd first suspected, with power, and his lack of it with his late wife. And, in a peculiar way, it had to do with her old favorite pastime, reaffirmation. She didn't want to understand him, but in many ways she did. It was both a useful tool and an extreme disadvantage, because understanding of what had tipped him over the edge made her more sympathetic than she should have been. Even locked into combat with him, she sensed the disbelief he felt at his own actions. It was as if the Daniel she'd met on the flight to London was also locked up in some small place, struggling against the Daniel who had, for the time being, taken charge of his thoughts and actions.

She was able to sit up, but had to remain on the side of the bed for many minutes until what felt like vertigo ebbed. It was the same when she gained her feet. She had to lean against the wall for support, then take many small steps around the perimeter of the room, groping her way to the door, until she was out and working toward the bathroom.

He had brought more aspirin, at her request, and she tried to take some but couldn't swallow. She was obliged to crush several on the rim of the sink with the bottom of the bottle, then lower herself painfully to lick up the acidic powder before washing it down with handfuls of water. She felt ninety years old. Even the slightest movement required concentration and involved some degree of pain. After removing the Tampax, she sat on the toilet with her hands resting on her thighs, very aware of the bones beneath her palms. She was shrinking, her tissues dissolving. After—what?—seven days, eight, locked up here, she'd eaten practically nothing —sips of tea and coffee, bites of unbuttered toast, half a banana. Her stomach was becoming distended; the knobs of her knees had hideous prominence, as did her hipbones and elbows. And, feeling about with her hands, so did her shoulder and ribs. Back rushed her terror. She had to do something, take in some nourishment, or her body would cease to function. She was in far worse condition than she'd thought. Perhaps she'd been here not just days, but weeks. She couldn't recall.

What to do, what to do? She thought of Joel, closed her eyes and saw him, her wonderful son, tall and handsome and smiling. Stephen stayed forever young. But Joel had grown to manhood, with wide shoulders and great, long legs. He'd shaved; he'd worn cologne; he'd known love; he'd given love. He'd had style, and humor; he'd had kindness and wisdom; he'd had the best sense of fun and occasion. His father had despised him, had refused even to see him when he knew Joel was dying. "He wouldn't come, would he?" Joel had guessed from the look on her face when she'd come back from the pay phone in the hospital waiting room. "Oh, well," Joel had said. "It's his loss. Right, toots?"

Joel. He'd been everyone's favorite waiter at the restaurant where he'd worked nights. He never forgot anything, delivered food and drinks with a flourish, never intruded but gave special service. And everyone adored him, gave him huge tips, and returned asking to be seated at his station. He'd looked very smart in his black tuxedo trousers, white shirt, and black bow tie. He'd played out his role with pleasure and effectiveness. "Just don't, please, come eat here," he'd begged her. "They put the leftovers back into the pots. They use the pieces of bread you leave on your plate to make croutons. The kitchen floor would turn your stomach. There are mice under the fridge. And they use whatever's left in the wineglasses to make their salad dressing. If you or the Grand Duchess"— which is what he'd called Marietta for years—"ever show up here, I won't be able to *save* you. You'll be eating recycled food."

Joel. He'd been her model for *Percival*, and for *Dolldance*. He'd been her best and closest friend, her cheerer-upper, her lovely boy, her grown-man son. She could almost hear him telling her what to do, whispering into her ear.

She heard the front door open, but didn't move. She continued to sit on the toilet, shivering with cold, but unable to get up. She listened to Daniel bustling about, putting away his coat, doing this and that, then his footsteps crossed the living room floor to the bedroom. A pause. She waited. The bathroom door opened.

"Why are you just sitting there that way?" he asked, not sounding angry, only confused.

"I can't get up. I'm sorry. I can't." Her eyes and nose had started to run. Her head hung. Talking hurt her throat. Her voice was no more than a whisper, barely audible.

He thought she looked like a skeleton somebody had propped up in the bathroom for a joke. He wondered why he hadn't noticed it sooner. "Are you doing it on purpose?" he asked from the doorway. "Are you starving yourself to get back at me?"

"No," came her all but disembodied reply. "I can't eat."

He wasn't sure. Yet he could feel himself leaning toward her.

"You have to help me," she whispered, turning sunken eyes on him. "Help me."

He could see every last vein in her body, especially across her chest, and in her lower arms. She looked like some kind of anatomical chart, with even the capillaries visible in the bends of her elbows and around her ankles. She was completely without color, blank white, except for those alarming dark-blue veins that seemed too close to the surface of her skin, and the intense bruising between her breasts. Her eyelids, and beneath, also looked bruised. Her lips were cracked and split. The flesh beneath her cheekbones dipped into hollowed shadows. The shape of her skull was clearly discernible under her matted hair. And along her jaw, and around her throat, were more discolorations; cuts and scrapes on her legs; fading, yellowed areas down the length of her back. He went over and lifted her, most alarmed by her lightness. She seemed to weigh nothing, as if her bones contained only air.

He carried her to the bedroom, saw that the sheet was wet, and had to set her down on the floor while he stripped the sheet, got a fresh one, and put it on. After he'd encased her in the blankets, he was about to go when her hand reached to stop him. Curious, he looked at her. This was all very strange.

"Daniel, listen to me." She wet her lips, tugging on his sleeve—a small, ineffective gesture, but one that made him sit down beside her. "*Listen!*" her wispy voice pleaded. "Daniel, I know you're in there somewhere, and I know you care about me." She had to stop for a moment. Speaking was agony. "Daniel, are you listening?"

He nodded, his eyes on hers.

"I'm dying, Daniel. If you don't help me, I'm going to die. Is that really what you want?"

He didn't say anything, but she thought she saw his eyes relenting.

"When Stephen was an infant, he was very ill with bronchitis, got dehydrated and weak, nothing would stay down. The doctor had me give him an electrolyte liquid. Go to the drugstore, Daniel, tell them you have a sick child, ask for something with electrolytes." She stopped again, swallowing in an effort to ease her throat. "Even Gatorade," she whispered. "Joel used to drink it when he ran. Ask the pharmacist. Please! Don't let me die, Daniel. You can't want that. Please?"

"Oh, Leigh," he said unhappily, his eyes glossy with tears. "I *don't* want that. I'll take care of you. I will. Please don't die. What is it? Electrolytes? I'll get it for you. I'll go right now. I'll hurry."

He got up and ran out without bothering to stop to put on his coat. He locked the door, then took the stairs three at a time, to hurry over to the drugstore on Eighth Street; back where he'd just come from. Oh Jesus! he thought, pounding along the icy, slippery pavement. Don't let her die! I really don't want that. Electrolytes electrolytes. Christ! What if they'd never heard of the stuff? What if it was some kind of coded message, and they'd hear it and know he had her locked up in the apartment? No, that was nuts. Electrolytes. Had to be real. Who was Joel? He didn't remember her mentioning anyone called Joel. Maybe it was the Good Doctor's first name. No, she'd called him Miles. But, wait a minute. He slowed to a walk. That agent, *his* name was Miles. It hadn't been her husband at the house. It had been the agent. The son of a bitch he'd seen her with, the two of them half-naked on the living room floor, it hadn't been her doctor husband, but her *agent.* So where the hell was her husband?

What does that matter? he asked himself, turning the corner on Tenth. So she had other men. None of that had a thing to do with right now. *She's going to die if you don't bring back this electrolyte stuff. How about two dead women on your conscience? That'll be good, Godard. Two of them, and you'll never sleep again; there won't be anywhere you'll be able to go. Is that what you want?* No! No!

Danny, you're not a bad person. I've never said that you were. But maybe I am, Danny; maybe I'm the one; and maybe this is never going to work because no matter how much you love me, no matter how well I know that, you only love the person you think I am. No one could ever love the person I really am. Let me go, Dan. Just let me go. Do us both a favor.

He began to run again, got to the drugstore, and raced to the back counter where the pharmacist was busy typing a label.

"Be with you in a moment," he told Dan.

"Listen!" Dan couldn't wait. "My baby, my daughter's very sick. I talked to the pediatrician. He said to come in and ask for an electrolyte liquid. She's got bronchitis, can't keep anything down. My wife's scared silly because we're from out of town, just passing through, and don't have a doctor here. *Please!*"

The man stopped typing and peered at Dan over the tops of his bifocals. "Hang on," he said, and went over to the shelves to pick up a quart-sized brown glass bottle. "Take it easy," he told Dan, giving the bottle a shake, then setting it down while he looked up the price. "How old's the baby?" he asked, running his finger down what looked to be an inventory list.

"Three months. She's so goddamned *little.*" It was the truth. Leigh was disappearing, dwindling away.

"Four times a day, couple of tablespoons."

Dan paid, thanked the man profusely, then clutched the bottle to his chest and went running out, back along the ice-slick streets, afraid he'd fall and smash the bottle and Leigh's life liquid would drain away; he ran as fast and as carefully as he could to get this stuff to Leigh, so she wouldn't die.

And Celeste's voice, he could hear it, clear and young, told him, *It's a good thing to do, Danny; the right thing. I know you've always tried your hardest.*

Twenty-four

*L*ANE DIDN'T SAY ANYTHING TO HER GRANDPARENTS ABOUT WHAT WAS going on. She didn't want them to know what her father had done, and she had the idea that they might not ever *have* to know if she could be the one to find her father. She had to admit it was a pretty remote chance that, even if she did find her father and Miss Dunn, the police wouldn't be involved. But she believed that if she could be the one to locate them, the entire matter might be resolved without either her grandparents having to know or the police being dragged into it. It was pretty iffy, but she believed it. She'd find them; then she'd take care of her dad, look after him, make sure he got glued back together.

The problem was, she couldn't find one single thing that was of any help to her. She drove up to the Bedford house to discover a note on the kitchen counter from a real estate agent begging Mr. Godard to call immediately. Lane phoned the woman, who explained that the sale was all set, the buyers' mortgage had been approved, and she needed Mr. Godard to sign various documents. Lane promised to have her father call, then went to the den to go through the desk.

It looked as if her dad had cleared out a lot of his papers. And the ones he'd left behind were mostly old tax returns, paid bills, business correspondence, birthday and occasion cards she'd given him; and a big brown envelope full of drawings and stories and stuff she'd done when she was really little. He'd saved all her funny stick-doll drawings, and pages of printing. "You're the marshmallow, Dad," she said aloud, returning the stuff to the envelope, "not me."

There had to be a clue somewhere. He couldn't've just vanished without leaving something, even unintentionally. And that's when it hit her.

233

She opened the bottom drawer of the desk again and pulled out all the files, piled them on the floor, and began to go through their contents.

He had to hold Leigh's head up to give her the liquid. Then he fed her some mashed bananas. She could only get a small amount down, but it was a start. And she was so grateful that it made him feel the way he had when Lane was a baby and he'd spooned cereal into her tiny pink mouth; when he'd bathed the baby, and dried and powdered her, before pinning on a clean diaper. He'd had a sense then that came back to him now of the singularity of his responsibility to this other being who was so completely dependent upon him for her survival. He'd cherished both the infant and his responsibility. Lane had established for him his sense of his own worth. It was very similar now, attending to Leigh.

After he'd fed her, he brought a basin of water and gave her a sponge bath, then patted her dry. Already he thought she looked better. He brought in the things he'd bought earlier—the hyacinth plant whose blossoms were just opening to emit their pungent perfume, the half-dozen magazines, the art supplies, and the now-cold pizza. He set the plant down on the floor near the bed so she could see and smell it; he positioned the magazines and art supplies nearby so she could reach them. Then he sat on the floor with his back to the wall, and ate wedges of the cold pepperoni-and-mushroom pizza while he talked to her.

She could see a change. It was as if her approach to the entryway to death had shocked him back, at least part way, to his senses. He was nowhere near as in control of himself as he'd been at their first meeting, but he was less angry, and overwhelmingly upset and apologetic. What struck her most strongly was the impersonal way in which he was describing what had to have been a true horror, and she understood that only by distancing himself verbally, and in his visual recall, could he even approach thinking about it.

"I couldn't let Lane or my parents see her," he was saying. "Not in that condition. *No one* should've had to see her." His eyes were opaque, as if he were reviewing the details from the vantage point of many miles and many years away. "You don't," he went on, "think about death in that context. I mean, we all think about getting old, dying someday. You read stories in the newspapers, or you turn on the network news, and there's the latest atrocity. But it has nothing to do with you. You react to the sight of body bags, and the closeups of shattered glass and blood spills. Television really removes you from things, and it shows you so much gore that it loses its impact. It's such an ongoing part of everyday life . . . it comes to you live at five, or from the Eyewitness News Team at six, or from Tom Brokaw or whomever, at seven . . . that the news doesn't seem like the news unless there's a story in there somewhere about the latest skyjacking by lunatic terrorists with causes nobody knows about, or hundred car pile-ups on some expressway, or an earthquake in some remote country, or some outspoken deejay who's gunned down getting into his car. You become inured to it. It's like Stallone and Bronson and Eastwood and Norris; all those guys playing 'might is right' and blasting people to shit if they come up against resistance. Bodies right, left, and center, and everybody buys that. The kids line up for days to see these 'good guys' kill off their enemies with submachine guns. As if that's the way to handle people who get in your way. The thing is, you just get used to death as a form of news or entertainment. So, when you come home and go upstairs to your bedroom and you happen to look over and see through the bathroom door that there are what look like puddles all over the floor, and you very slowly put down your briefcase, and very slowly walk over to the door to look inside, and you see what you see, you want to believe it's another news item. But you know goddamned well it's no movie, and not the network news. It's for real, and it's not some foreign diplomat, or five hundred strangers on some airplane, it's your thirty-nine-year-old wife. It's this person you've known since she was fifteen. It's this woman you had a baby with, this someone you've been trying to know for more than twenty years who never *wanted* to be known because the only thing she believed was her own was the secret to her identity. That's who it is. Except that she's not there anymore. She's gone away and left behind this body she's eviscerated; she's ripped this body to pieces with a razor blade, then cut its throat, and left it curled up in the bathtub, floating in thick, dark red liquid, for you to find. And a note." His mouth remained open but no more words came out. He stared and stared at that faraway scene, as his hand put down the half-eaten wedge of pizza, then came up to hover for a moment before covering his eyes.

He cried like a small child locked out of his house. It was terrible to see, and terrible to find herself reaching out in sympathy to him. But how could she not seek to console him when she knew that pain so well? She whispered, "Daniel," and held out her arms to him, and he huddled against her, and wept so desolately that she had to weep with him, aware of the wrenching irony of the situation, but momentarily unconcerned. She was incapable of ignoring his suffering, even if it had driven him over the brink of the madness that resulted in her being there. She even regretted having exaggerated the extent of her physical disability, despite its having been the key she'd needed to unlock him.

She held him and tried to kiss away the hurt the way she'd kissed Stephen's boyhood cuts and scrapes, the way she'd tried, at the outset, to console herself in this man's arms. The human touch, fundamental and necessary as water, was the most and best she could offer him. And she wondered at herself, at her capacity to disregard, even temporarily, what had gone before. But she could; she did. People would think *she* was the mad one. But what did anyone know, really? It all came down to losses, one way or another, and trying to find some way to deal with them. And it helped, it did help, as she well knew, to hold on. So she held him, and mourned for Stephen, and for Carl, for Joel, and for Daniel's dead wife. She applied herself to the task of amelioration, consoling him with kisses, with the touch of her hands, with her mouth, with the length and depths of her body, enveloping him in her sympathy in order to ease the pain. She directed him to where he'd wanted all along to be, then rocked him in the cradle of her thighs, whispering assurances that everything would be all right, he'd see. It would. "You'll see. It will. You'll see, you'll see."

Lane finally manage to get through to Cath.

"Where *are* you?" Cath wanted to know. "*Everybody's* been looking for you."

"I'm home. Listen! I don't have much time. You know that friend of Davy Kaye's, the guy he knows who's a major hacker?"

"Right. What about him?"

"You've got to get me his number. I have to get in touch with him."

"Why? What's going on?"

"Cath, I can't go into it now. You've got to get me his number, or get him to call me. I'm at the house, in Bedford. I'm gonna stay right here by the phone. I don't care what you're doing, drop it and get Davy to call the guy and either get me his number or ask him to call me collect. Will you do it, please?"

"Well, I guess."

"Cath, it's so important! It's probably the most important thing you're *ever* going to do. Call Davy right away, then call me back. Okay?"

"Okay."

"Leigh, who's Miles?"

She shifted a bit to one side to have a better view of his face. "Why?"

"Who is he, Leigh?"

"Miles is my agent."

"And he was the one with you at the house."

"Yes."

"Not your husband."

"No."

"And who's Joel?"

"Joel was my stepson, actually my adopted son. He died two days before you and I met."

"I didn't know you had a stepson. How come you never mentioned him before?"

"I wasn't aware that I hadn't."

"You *never* mentioned him."

"I was very distraught, Daniel."

"That's okay. But if Miles is your agent, and Joel was your stepson, then who's the Good Doctor, and where is he? Why was your agent with you at the house?"

"The doctor is Erik," she answered, not sure if telling the truth now might not set him off again. He seemed more himself than at any time since he'd taken her out of the house. "Miles was with me," she said carefully, "because I asked him to be there."

"Am I stupid? Is there something missing?"

"Daniel, I've been divorced for more than eight years."

"So why the hell did you tell me you were married?"

"Why did *you* tell me *you* were married?" she countered.

"I don't know. I was scared."

"I can't say that I was scared, but I was extremely upset. I loved Joel dearly. I was having a terrible time accepting his death. You, of all people, should have no problem understanding that. I didn't want to become involved, so I simply told you I was married."

He rolled away from her and lay on his back looking up at the ceiling. She kept her eyes on him, wondering which way he'd go.

He let out a long, long sigh, then, with disbelief, said, "We didn't have to go through one bit of this, not a bit of it. Jesus! We both lied. And *look* where it got us! *Jesus!*" He sat up, asking, "Why do you sleep with so many men? Why do you do that?"

"I don't know. Perhaps because it makes me feel attractive."

"You need to sleep with a lot of men to know that?" He looked dumbfounded. "You don't know it any other way?"

She couldn't give him an answer; she didn't have one.

He dropped back down, and turned to look at her. "You're the only other woman I've ever made love with, except for Celeste."

"Oh, Daniel, it was *all* lies, wasn't it?"

"Why did you say you had your period when you didn't?" he wanted to know.

"Think for a minute about what's been going on here, and then ask me that question again."

"You didn't *want* me?" he asked, childlike once more.

"You didn't give me a choice."

He stared at her, and in the silence she thought she heard that clock ticking somewhere. Where was it? He brought up his hand to look at it. It was obviously infected.

"We should clean that," she whispered. "Put some iodine on it."

"Doesn't matter." He lowered his hand, for a few moments aware only of its throbbing heat. "I can't let you leave," he said finally.

"Of course you can," she said calmly.

"No, I can't. You'll have me locked up; they'll throw away the key."

"Daniel, whatever happens, you have my promise I won't do that."

"I'd be a cluck to buy that, Leigh. I just *can't* let you leave."

"You also can't keep me here forever. I'm already ill. If this goes on very much longer, I won't make it. Look at me, Daniel! Take a good look!"

He did. And, as before, it was impossible to argue with the reality. He'd abused her in many ways, and it showed. He shook his head back and forth.

"Have you been in touch with your family?" she asked.

Another shake of his head.

"I imagine they must be very worried about you. Don't you think you should get in touch with them, let them know you're all right?"

There had to be a catch in it somewhere, but he couldn't spot it. What she said made sense. And he felt guilty as sin for neglecting Lane. She was probably worried sick about him.

"You should at least telephone and talk to them," she suggested. "And then perhaps you could let someone—my mother or Miles—know that I'm all right, too."

"No," he said, the recognizable Daniel starting to recede. "You'd better have some more of that electrolyte liquid."

"All right," she agreed, and gave up for the moment.

"Hi! Listen, thanks so much for calling me back. I really appreciate it. Look! I've got this major major problem and you're the only person I could think of who maybe could help. See, what it is, I've got this telephone number. Right? What I need is for you to find out the address for me. No, no. It's nothing like that. Look, can I be straight with you? My dad's in some trouble, and I'm trying to help him. The number's his, see. And if I can get an address to go with it, then I'll be able . . . what? No way. I've got the phone bill right here in my hand. I wish it *did* have the address. No, my dad's having this other number billed in on our regular phone. So, like in with all the other stuff on the bill, there's a separate account for this other line. I swear, it's the absolute truth. It's *very* important. Ask Cath. She'll tell you I don't mess with weird shit. *Please!* . . . Oh, sure. Like I can see me calling up the phone company business office and laying this on them. They'd buy it about the same way you are. No way. Listen, I *know* you could get into major trouble. I'll *pay* you. Whatever you want. Well, I don't know. What's fair? Sure, okay, fine. A hundred's fine. How long will it take? Really? Shit, that's fantastic! No, okay. No, right. I'll wait right here. Thanks so much. Really. Thanks."

"There's no reason why you shouldn't stay with me," Dan was saying. "None. Not one single reason. If you care about me, what difference does it make?"

"The difference comes back to the matter of choice. And there isn't any involved in this. Can't you see that?"

"No. No, I can't. No husband, no wife. No reason not to stay with me. I need you here. I *need* you, Leigh. I'm looking after you now. You're already starting to look better after just a day and a night on that stuff. A couple more days and you'll be feeling stronger, and then maybe you'll want to look at some of these magazines, or maybe do some drawing." He could see he wasn't winning her over. It gave him an ache in the gut, because he was trying so goddamned hard to convince her. Or was it himself he was trying to convince? Things were very mixed up. "If you love me, if you're telling the truth, then what does any of it have to do with choice? I just can't trust you. I mean, I know if I leave the door unlocked, if I open the gates on the windows, and then go out for half an hour, when I come back, you'll be gone. I don't want to *lose* you."

"You won't lose me," she told him, hating being forced to be so dishonest, and trying to ignore the cloying fragrance of the hyacinths. "I don't see why, after all we've been through together, you don't even trust me enough to let me sleep one night without tying me up. Do you plan for me to sleep this way forever? You can't imagine how dreadful it is, Daniel. You'd be miserable if I did it to you. You'd be miserable if I came bursting into the bathroom when you were in there, or if I took away your clothes while I kept mine on. What will make you trust me? Tell me, and I'll do my best to prove I'm worthy of your trust. Just tell me what you want."

"Stop pushing at me!" His voice rose. He glared at her, holding his injured hand in the palm of the other like an earthbound sparrow. "I can't stand it, being pushed at constantly! This is the way it has to be! Don't back me into a corner where I have to make my points by hurting you! I *can't stand* hurting you, but you force me into it."

"All right," she sighed, and turned away from the sickening perfume of the hyacinths she didn't dare ask him to remove.

"Hi! You *got* it? Oh, Christ, that's amazing! What? I've got a pen and paper ready. I'm all set. Okay. Yeah. Right. No, I've got it. The minute I get back to school you'll have your money. Thank you *so much*. You'll never know what this means to me. What? Well, sure, I guess. No, okay. That'd be cool. Wait a minute, I'll write it down. Right. I'll call you for sure, first thing. We'll get together. Great. Thanks again, Ralph. Really."

She put the phone down, then said, "No way, asshole. The money's *all* you get. What an amazing nerve!"

She dialed the Manhattan number, and let it ring twenty-five times before she hung up, confused and disappointed. She'd been so sure her dad was there, that he'd pick up and she'd be able to talk to him. Had she made some mistake? Was this number a new office her dad had opened and hadn't told her about? No way. An office wouldn't have an unlisted phone; it would have a company name, not just her dad's. It had to be where he was. She wanted to get in the car then and there and drive into the city, but it was too late. By the time she got there it would be close to midnight and no way was she going to go playing detective in the Village at that time of night, not to mention the problem of parking the car, or the creeps who only seemed to come out after dark. What she'd do was keep trying the number until midnight. Then, if there still was no answer, she'd try again first thing in the morning. And if no one answered she'd drive into town and go to the Village. It was possible he was there and just not answering the phone. Maybe he'd unplugged it. If he had Miss Dunn with him, he wouldn't want people calling, or maybe he wouldn't want Miss Dunn to have a chance to call the police or something.

Shit! She didn't want to think he was capable of stuff like that, but she had to believe what Mr. Dearborn had told her. And she'd seen how beat up he was. It was all so scary, so totally Twilight Zone. She couldn't imagine her dad hitting anybody, but Mr. Dearborn wasn't someone who'd lie. You could tell that about him; you could tell a lot about him by the way he'd talked about Miss Dunn—Leigh, he'd called her—he'd said her name so sort of sadly, as if the worst thing he could think of was that he'd never see her again.

And Miss Dunn's mother, she'd been ready to hate Lane at the beginning, and all because of Dad. But she'd been so incredibly fair, offering to let Lane stay there with her, and even being so nice about Lane crying all over her lap. The whole thing was one gigantic, scary mess, but it was going to be over soon. She absolutely knew it.

She went upstairs, going past her own room to her parents' bedroom, to put on the light and then go to look at the bathroom where it'd happened. In a way, she almost wished she'd seen it for herself. Maybe if she had it would've been more real to her than it was, because she just couldn't picture it, couldn't come up with any kind of an image of her mother to put into the frame. The whole thing was such a major waste—Celeste spending her entire life being miserable and taking it out on everybody; her Dad breaking his ass to turn it all around and make it into a fairy tale with everybody happy; and her growing up being her own mother, and sometimes being mother to her dad, too. She'd tried forever not to be resentful about the fact that she'd never had anybody play mother to her, except for Grandmother who was really kind and generous and everything, but not a mother. She just couldn't stop thinking how amazing it would be to have a mother like Marietta Dunne.

She tried the Manhattan number once more before she went to bed in her old room. She let it ring thirty times. No answer. She set the alarm for eight. That way, she'd get back to the city, stow the car in her slot in her grandparents' garage, then go downtown to that address on West Tenth Street.

"I have to go out for an hour," Dan told her. "So, if you have to go to the bathroom or anything, go now."

"Why? What do you mean?"

"Do you want to use the bathroom or not?" he asked impatiently, finding the situation very heavy going for some reason this morning. He felt tired of it, tired of having to keep track of everything.

"Yes, I do."

"Okay. Make it fast."

"Daniel, what's so urgent?"

"I've got things to do," he said, standing with the canvas strip in his hand, waiting for her to stop wasting his time and go to the bathroom. He'd suddenly remembered he had to sign the sale papers for the house, and he wanted to call the real estate woman and get her to courier them down to him. It was risky, having someone come to the door, but he figured he'd just put some tape over Leigh's mouth or something, keep her out of the way and quiet until the coast was clear, and then that matter would be completed. He'd considered driving out to Bedford to get it all done, but he didn't want to take the chance of leaving Leigh alone in the apartment for the three or four hours that would entail. He'd use the restraints to keep her out of the way and quiet now for the hour or so he'd be gone. He'd go out and call the agent, then he'd zip up to midtown to his bank. He wished he hadn't resisted getting a bank card all these years. With a card, he could've got money out of some local machine. But he didn't have one, so he was going to have to hike up to his branch on Madison and Forty-sixth. Christ, but she took ages in the bathroom! Just like Celeste. What was it with women and bathrooms and the amounts of time they could spend in them? Back when he and Celeste had first been married, she used to sit on one side of the basin with her feet on the other while she put on her makeup. She'd stopped it after Lane was born. And, in a funny way, he'd missed the sprinklings of powder and eyeshadow that had tinted the backsplash.

"Come on!" he called from outside the door. "I've got things to do, Leigh. I can't wait around all day out here."

"Then why don't you go?" came her muted reply.

"Come on!"

She opened the door asking, "Is there some reason for your waiting?"

"I want you in the bedroom." He turned on his heel, the canvas unfurling from his hand.

"You're not going to tie me up and leave me alone here," she protested. "What if there's a fire? What if something happens? I'll be completely helpless, Daniel. I can scarcely make myself heard. I'd be incinerated if there were a fire. I wouldn't be able to scream."

"Nothing's going to happen." He grabbed her wrists, threaded the long end of the canvas through one of the reinforced slots, made sure she had just enough room so her circulation wouldn't get cut off, then secured the end to the loop in the wall. "I'll be an hour, and hour and a half tops. Nothing," he repeated, "is going to happen." Christ, but he was fed up with this whole thing!

"This is cruel, Daniel," she reproached him. "I thought you were going to look after me."

"I am. But for now I want you to stay in here. I'll make it up to you," he promised, with no idea, as he spoke the words, how he'd ever be able to do that.

Resigned, she turned her head away. She felt his eyes, felt his desire to say something more, but he didn't. After a few seconds, he left. The front door opened and closed; the cylinders turned first on one lock, then on the other. She wondered if he'd discovered that she'd loosened the screws on the window gate and that was why he'd left her tied up. Dear God! Was this *ever* going to end?

Twenty-five

FTER HE LEFT, LEIGH LAY LOOKING AT THE METAL LOOP FASTENED to a steel plate, through which four screws penetrated into the brick wall. She tugged experimentally, then yanked hard with the full weight of her body. Nothing. She got up off the bed to sit on the floor directly in front of the loop, thinking it wouldn't be too hard to free herself. The canvas strip was elaborately knotted into and around the loop, but if she used both her hands, she'd be able to undo the knots. Since he'd previously only tied her up this way while he was present in the apartment, she'd had no opportunity to examine the setup at close range. Now that she did, she saw, with a darting excitement, that all that was involved was untying the strip. She positioned herself even closer to the wall and extended her hands, then stopped. If he returned to find her free, he might suffer another enraged spasm and strike her, or choke her again.

She didn't know what to do, and tried to guess how long it might take her to get loose. Ten or fifteen minutes perhaps. Another fifteen or twenty to work on the final screws on the iron gate. It could be done. She might actually be out of this place within as little as half an hour. She had to try.

As Lane expected, no one answered when she dialed the number first thing the next morning. She hurried to dress, then ran out to the car only to find that it wouldn't start. When she turned the key in the ignition the engine groaned like someone trying to lift a big rock, then went dead. "Shit!" she cried, pounding the steering wheel with her fist. She had to get to the city. Of all the times for the battery to die! Knowing it was useless, she waited a couple of minutes, then tried the starter again anyway. This time, not even so much as a groan. Why had she left the car

243

outside instead of putting it in the heated garage for the night? The garage. She looked over at the closed double doors. Her mother's car was still in there. Her dad kept talking about selling it, but hadn't so far done anything about it. Its battery was probably dead, too, after all this time. But it was worth a try.

She had to go through the house because she didn't have either the automatic garage door opener or the key for the manual one. She entered the garage through the kitchen door, switched on the overhead light, and stood looking at her mother's dust-covered white Lincoln. Celeste had practically never used it, even though she'd always liked to drive and was a pretty decent driver when she was sober. It kind of bothered Lane to touch something of Celeste's, but her sense of urgency overcame her reluctance, and she opened the driver's door to see that the keys were right there in the ignition. Crossing the fingers of her left hand, she reached out and turned the key. The engine coughed a couple of times. She gave it a little gas, the engine caught, she eased off the accelerator, and the car sat idling. "Great!" she said. "Great!" and felt a totally surprising burst of warmth toward Celeste.

The real estate woman sounded overjoyed at hearing from him. "I was beginning to wonder," she said, with a giddy little laugh. "But then I heard from your daughter, and she said you'd be in touch."

"You what?" Dan asked her, his grip tightening around the receiver.

"Your daughter saw the message I left for you, and called me yesterday. She said she'd ask you to contact me."

Dan couldn't think for a moment. What was Lane doing at the house when she was supposed to be up in Vermont?

"Mr. Godard? Are you still there?"

"I'm here."

"We need your signature . . ."

"I know that. I'll give you an address. Send everything down by courier. I'll sign the papers and get them right back to you. Don't worry," he added, before she could object. "I'll pay for the courier."

"That'll be fine. Now hold on just a tick while I get something to write with."

She actually put him on hold; he couldn't believe it. What the hell was *wrong* with everyone? And why wasn't Lane at school where she belonged? He listened to the static on the line, growing more and more annoyed, while better than a minute went by before the woman came back on the line.

"Sorry," she said. "Another call came in. Now, what was that address?"

Jesus! he thought. He felt like telling her to forget the whole thing, but he couldn't do that. So he took a calming breath, then gave her the address. He had to repeat everything, and by the time the call ended, he'd worked himself into a temper and wondered if he should put off going to the bank until Monday. But, checking his billfold, he saw he was almost out of cash. He flagged down a cab, noting the time. Twenty after ten. He figured he'd get back down to the Village by eleven.

Lane made it to her grandparents' apartment by nine-fifty, was out on the street looking for a taxi by ten, and in front of the brownstone on West Tenth Street by ten twenty-five. She paid the driver, then stood on the sidewalk studying the building, getting up her nerve. Maybe her father wasn't even here. But she had nothing else to go on, and nothing to lose. She walked up the front steps, looked at the row of bells on the outside of the door. One bell's name slot was empty. She pressed that button, and waited. Nothing. She pressed it again, and waited. Still nothing. She gave the door a push and, to her surprise, it opened. She passed into the hallway and stopped at the foot of the stairs, listening. Not a sound. Burglars' paradise, she thought. Six bells, one without a name, second from the top. The place had a garden entrance as well as this one. If the bells were in height order, that meant second from the top had to be on the second floor in a three-story building.

She started up the stairs, checking the doors as she went. No numbers. Two doors on the second floor. She went to the far end of the hall. Blank. She came back to the door nearest the stairs. A handlettered card in a brass slot. She turned and went back to the door at the far end.

Leigh heard the buzzer go; her head jerked up; her heart lurched. The buzzer went a second time. She got up and walked as far as the restraint would allow, which was to the foot of the bed, to stop, straining forward. There was the sound of light footsteps coming up the stairs. God! Someone was coming here! Had they finally found her? She strained further against the canvas strap, trying to get closer to the door. There was a quiet knocking.

"I'M IN HERE!" Leigh gave her shout as much volume as she could muster. "CAN YOU HEAR ME?"

The knocking grew louder. "Oh, God! They can't hear me! I'M IN HERE!" The tendons in her throat felt as if they'd break from the effort she gave to making herself heard.

Lane thought she heard something, and put her ear close to the door. "*Is somebody in there?*" she called.

"YES! YES! CAN YOU HEAR ME?"

Lane pressed closer to the door, her hands flat on either side of her head, able to hear what sounded like whispering from inside. "*I can just barely hear you!*" she called back. "*Is that Leigh?*"

"YES!" Tears came to Leigh's eyes. "YES!"

"This is Lane! I'm going to go call Mr. Dearborn, then I'll come back. I'll be back as fast as I can. Did you hear?"

"YES!"

"Okay! I'm going now."

The light footsteps ran away down the stairs. Leigh sat abruptly on the foot of the bed. The girl was going to get Miles. Miles was all right. The two of them were going to get her out of here. It was over. Over.

Lane rummaged through her bag for the paper with Mr. Dearborn's number; found it, dropped a quarter in the slot, pushed out the numbers. Busy. Busy? She disconnected, dropped the quarter again, redialed. Busy. No way! She jiggled the arm, threw in the quarter for a third time, got the operator and asked her to try the number.

"You can dial that number direct," the operator droned.

"I know. I want you to check it."

"One moment."

Silence. The number tones. Busy signal.

Then, "That line's busy."

"It can't be. It's a business phone. Could you *check* it please, to make sure it's really busy and not out of order?"

"Just one moment, please."

The line went vague and fuzzy, the way it did when you got put on hold, and Lane waited, tapping her foot, her body feeling as if it was going to start jumping up and down, jiggling around.

The operator came back. "There's a problem on that line."

"Oh, hell! Thanks." Lane hung up, then dialed again, just once more, on the off chance it was a mistake. No mistake. Busy busy. She fingered her quarter out of the slot, ran to the curb and scanned the street for a cab. Nothing coming. She started to run toward the intersection. The subway would be faster than a cab. She'd hop on a train, go to his office, get Miles, bring him back down here. But what if he wasn't there. He *had* to be there! No way was she going to call the police on her dad, no way.

There was a long line at the bank. Daniel looked around at the other customers—businessmen, secretaries, a woman in a fur coat. His eyes stayed on the woman for several moments, then moved on. Tellers behind the counters, special service people, a guard, a woman in a fur coat with high-heeled black boots. The line inched forward. The woman was over at the counter, talking head to head with a young woman behind the counter. So many people, so many. Everyone on this side of the counter in heavy coats and boots, scarves wound around their necks. The floor wet with tracked-in slush, brown muck. The guard stood by the door, hands folded in front of him. The line moved forward another foot. And it seemed, all at once, as if all these other people were performing in different little scenarios. They were all very separate, very distinct. Again he looked at the woman in the fur coat, her back to him. He, too, was separate, and visible, alive. It shook him to think of his state of being, of his validity as a unit, a man, a person, someone independent and autonomous. Until that moment, he'd lost sight of something very basic: that every last creature stood alone, and was allowed the right to function alone, or in concert with others, at his choosing. It seemed incredible. Yet, standing there in the bank, looking at the woman in the fur coat, he was all but overwhelmed by guilt at the realization that he had willfully, abusively, deprived another person of that fundamental license. Down in an apartment in the Village that no one else knew about, was an important woman whose importance had been taken away from her—by him. What he'd done in forcibly removing her from her home and installing her in that small secured fortress was an offense of such epic proportions that it actually stunned him as he waited in the queue, inching closer to the person who would provide him with the funds that he'd come for in order to perpetuate the crime he was committing against Stanleigh Dunn. It was so wrong, so monstrously wrong, that he simply couldn't think why he'd done it, or what he'd hoped to accomplish.

Standing there, holding his withdrawal slip, with only two other people left in front of him in the line, he felt so much a criminal that he was sure the other customers had to be able to see and smell it, like some foul aura he radiated. Standing there, patiently waiting while the female customer now at the counter engaged in what looked like it would be a lengthy transaction, it occurred to him that he was in terrible trouble. And if he took action, he could prevent the trouble from becoming worse. He looked again to the front of the queue, then at the broad, overcoated back of the man ahead of him, and asked himself what he was doing. It wasn't too late to set some of it to rights.

He broke out of the line, shoved the withdrawal slip into his pocket, and hurried out to the street. A taxi would take too long. He started running along Forty-sixth Street, toward Lexington and the subway. He had to get back down to the Village and set Leigh free, end this crazy thing he'd done. He sprinted along the sidewalks, darting around people, fused on reaching his destination. He had to return to Leigh all, or at least part, of what he'd taken from her. A stitch in his side, he breathed through his mouth, maintaining his pace, ignoring the pain, seeing—with each yard he covered—more of the scope of his actions. And the more he saw, the more convinced he became that he was out of his mind; he'd gone completely crazy. Maybe he was coming back from it now, or maybe this was merely a temporary remission. It didn't matter. The only important thing was getting back to the prison he'd created, to free his prisoner. He wanted it so badly that his throat worked and his eyes swam; his fingers pressed tightly into his palms; his heart pumped deliriously; and his head felt crammed with the broadening ramifications of his mad acts. He was out of his goddamned mind. He'd probably be spending a fair portion of his future in a jail somewhere, while Lane and his mother and father tried to deal with the facts of what he'd done. He saw himself being carted off in handcuffs; saw himself being incarcerated, interrogated. He deserved it. Christ! He'd tied her up and gone off without even bothering to give her any more of the electrolyte drink. If she died, he'd be a murderer. He felt as if his bowels had turned to ice water. A murderer. Maybe somebody had come while he'd been out, kicked in the door to find this dead woman, naked and restrained, in the bedroom. Christ, Christ! He'd never wanted anyone dead, not Celeste, and not Leigh. He didn't want anyone to die. And Lane! What would she think, finding out that her father had done something so completely insane? He got a token, pushed it into the turnstile slot, and paced back and forth on the platform, his eyes on the tunnel, willing the train to hurry.

The sound of the door opening awakened her. She sat up, using both fettered hands to keep the blankets around her, and was taken aback by the sight of Daniel, red-faced and out of breath, rushing into the room to begin undoing the canvas from the loop in the wall, while declaring, in highly agitated fashion, the shame he felt at his actions.

"I'll get you out of here," he told her. "This is crazy. I don't know what the hell's been going on, but I'll get you out of here before I do any more of it. I don't have the right, *nobody* has the right to do something like this. I know you'll never forgive me, and you shouldn't. I'm just so goddamned glad you're still alive, that I haven't really hurt you badly. Leigh," he cried, struggling with the knots, breaking into tears. "I never *meant* any of this to happen. Honest to Christ, I didn't. I'm not in love with you, Leigh. I don't even know who you are. And I know you've only been saying the things you have to protect yourself. The things I've done to you! Jesus! It's like I keep sliding in and out, and I've got to get you out of here before I slide back again." He finally got the knots undone, then bent to release her wrists, stopped by the sight of her abraded skin, his tears proliferating. "I'm *sorry!*" he wept. "I'm so goddamned sorry!" Gently, he put her hands down, saying, "I'll get your coat, your boots, and take you home."

He went out to the living room and was about to open the closet when there was a knock at the front door. He went rigid. More knocking. And then he heard Lane call out, "Daddy? Are you there?"

Lane. He took a step toward the door, then stopped.

"Daddy?"

Ah, Lane! He lowered his head, swamped by misery and self-disgust. Too late, too late!

"Are you in there, Daddy?"

He began moving to the door. Leigh came out of the bedroom, her eyes on him as she reached into the closet for her coat and pulled it on. He undid the top lock, then the bottom one, visibly shaking from head to toe. His hand went to the knob, and he turned it.

The door opened and there was a moment of silent tableau. Miles saw this man and, beyond him, Leigh. The sight of Leigh, her condition, ignited Miles. He threw himself at Daniel, prepared to beat him to a pulp.

"Miles!" Leigh begged, running over. "Don't hurt him! Please, don't!"

Miles let go of the man, and looked uncertainly at Leigh. He wanted to take hold of her, to get her out of there, but something else was happening, and she was compelling him to see it. She took hold of his hand and clung to it, but her eyes were not on him. And he turned to see what it was that had her so in its grip.

Dan looked at Lane, who was standing out in the hallway staring wide-eyed at Leigh. Her hand came up to cover her mouth as her eyes turned questioningly to her father.

Leigh let go of Miles's hand and moved forward. Daniel shrank out of her way, flinching in anticipation of curses or blows.

Lane couldn't move. Her feet and legs turned to cement, she watched, weighted down, as the woman with large, sunken eyes in a face that, beneath the bruises, was almost gray, came toward her. Lane took it all in: the marks on Leigh's throat, the rubbed-raw areas on her wrists, and all she could think was that her father had done those things to this woman. *Her father.* It was so much worse than anything she'd imagined; way worse. Her dad had hurt this woman, hurt her badly, hit her, and done God only knew what else.

The two men stood apart, both of them watching Leigh.

Leigh went to the girl and wordlessly drew her close. The girl came willingly, burying her face in the luxurious fur, quivering, afraid. Leigh held her tightly and whispered, "Don't hate your father for this. Help him, but don't hate him." Her arms brought the girl closer still, and Lane burrowed against her, eager for her words, for her forgiveness. "Nothing will happen," Leigh promised. "Nothing. Thank you," she said inadequately. "You've been very brave; I'm so grateful."

Miles nodded in agreement, not at the words he couldn't hear, but at this display of Leigh's instinctive knowing and generosity. Then he put his hand on her shoulder. "I'll take you home, Leigh."

"Don't hate him," Leigh whispered fervently. Then she released the girl and let Miles take her out of there.

"Should I take you to your mother's?" Miles asked in the taxi. "A doctor? Perhaps I should get you to a doctor?"

She shook her head, reluctant to turn away from the window and the exceptional scenes of life on the streets. Even the freezing rain seemed remarkable. "Take me to my place," she whispered, turning inside the circle of his safeguarding arm. "I can't let Mother see me this way."

"Oh, Leigh, are you sure I shouldn't get you some medical attention?"

"I'll be all right," she insisted, pressing herself closer to him, very cold. "I thought you were dead. I didn't know. Will you stay with me?"

"Sshhh. Of course I will." He held her hand in silence for the duration of the ride, trying to quell the frantic action of his heart.

She looked around, finding everything different, altered. Miles reached to help her out of her coat, emitting a shocked gasp at finding her naked under it. He made angry noises in his throat at seeing how emaciated she was, and how battered. He scooped her up, declaring, "I'm putting you straight to bed," and carried her to the bedroom.

He pulled back the blankets, set her down, then stared, exclaiming, "What the bloody hell!"

"What?"

"Did that sick bastard do that to you?"

"What?"

"*That!*" He pointed at her groin, indignation and outrage making his ears ring.

"That," she repeated, and raised up on her elbows to look down at herself. "That." She looked at him, then again at herself. "It makes me look much younger, don't you think?" She fell back laughing so hard that tears came to her eyes. And then she broke.

He held her, while sobs throttled her, wrenching their way from her throat, and she tried to tell him how she felt. "I was so afraid he'd killed you. I couldn't think how I'd go on if he had. I was so afraid for you, so afraid."

"It's over now," he told her. "Over."

After a time, calmer, she said, "I keep thinking perhaps I won't know how to be free anymore, Miles. Nothing looks or feels quite right. I'm so frightened." She began to tremble, and it so unnerved him that he said, "If you won't have a doctor, then you must have your mother."

"Please, don't call her! I don't want her to see me this way!"

"Leigh, don't you realize she'd rather see you 'this way,' than dead? *We* were so afraid *we'd* lost *you*. I'm going to call her. She'll know better than I what needs to be done here, Leigh. I'm out of my depth. The most I can do isn't good enough."

"He said if I didn't get into the car, if I didn't ride in the trunk—he made me ride in the trunk, Miles, it made me so ill—if I didn't do it, he said he had your address and hers, he'd come after you. I'm so glad you're alive, Miles!"

Keeping hold of her hand, he picked up the telephone on the bedside table and dialed Marietta's number, spoke to Alicia, then waited while Marietta came to the phone.

Miles said, "Hold on a moment, Marietta," and put the receiver into Leigh's hand.

Leigh got the instrument to her mouth, and said, "I need you. I . . ." She couldn't say anything more.

"I'll come at once," Marietta said, and broke the connection.

"She's coming," Leigh told him wonderingly.

"I know." He replaced the receiver and touched his hand to her cheek. "I'll get you a nightgown."

She watched him open the drawer and select her favorite long-sleeved granny gown. He held her, got the gown on her, then tenderly eased her down again.

"Thank you," she whispered, clutching his hand. "I do love you so, Miles. I think," she said, then paused to moisten her lips. "I think we've been very foolish, you and I."

"No," he began to disagree, but her eyes were closing. "With all my heart, I love you."

Her eyelids lifted, and she smiled at him. "You're so romantic," she teased. Then, growing serious, her eyes beginning to close again, she said, "I'm not going to die, after all." As sleep overtook her, she wondered if she'd actually spoken the words aloud.

After

I T WAS A PERFECT SPRING DAY, PLEASANTLY WARM. THE SUN SHONE UNIMpeded through a cloudless blue sky. There was an easy breeze with a soft edge that held the scent of newly cut grass. Leigh sat in a wooden lawn chair in the rear garden, her hands resting on the arms, her head supported by the broad back slats. Her face turned to the sun, she breathed deeply and slowly while mentally taking stock. All in all, she felt physically well. The damaged ligaments in her chest had taken the longest to mend, and with each breath she drew she still expected to feel the protesting soreness in her chest. But it was no more now than a faint echo. She wasn't yet accustomed to the loss of pain, and thought how very strange it was that one could come to rely on discomfort, as if its existence were proof one was actually alive.

She was also unaccustomed to living without cigarettes, and often dreamed of smoking. When she woke up, she looked around guiltily for the evidence, not completely certain dreams couldn't transcend sleep. Of course, there was nothing to be found, except the lowgrade, continuing longing she had to hold a cigarette to her mouth and fill her lungs with pungent smoke. Daniel had forced her to give up cigarettes, but she didn't want to take them up again. She thought more often, with more yearning, about cigarettes, than she did about anything or anyone except Joel. And Daniel. There was no fear attached to her thoughts of Daniel, but rather a sense of wonder coupled with disbelief that those ten days had, in fact, been real.

It was strange to think of that time and to relate it to the way she was occasionally startled by sounds or shadows, by the recreation in her dreams of certain scenes that caused her to surface with her heart pounding and sweat soaking into the bedclothes. There were moments in the dark when she was suddenly convinced it wasn't Miles with her in bed, but Daniel. She even came to, some mornings, to find she'd slept on her side with her wrists pressed together, as if bound.

At random moments, heat would overtake her, and she felt again the humiliation she'd suffered at being tied to the bed. These were the bad times, when she'd mourn for the woman she'd been prior to the experience, because she doubted she'd ever again feel one hundred percent free, or safe. There would always be some part of her brain that stubbornly held on to the experience, arbitrarily pitching images at her. She didn't take them well. She cringed, and sought distraction. She despaired of the grating anxiety that turned her lungs to punctured sacs unable to contain sufficient air; of the shame of having been seen, and examined, and used.

Everyone was kind. Miles paid close attention, waiting for signals, encouraging her to talk, controlling his reactions so there'd be one less thing with which she'd have to cope. Marietta was attentive but not overly indulgent. Once satisfied Leigh had sustained no debilitating injuries, either psychic or physical, she took to treating her in the old, accustomed way—exhorting Leigh to get to work, to get up and get out, to stop being so indecisive. "It was nasty; it was sordid and hateful, but it's over," Marietta told her. "But if you dwell on it, it will *never* be over."

Leigh felt fairly confident that externally she revealed a little less of her feelings about the incident each day, while internally she tried to deal with those feelings. She was working on the production design for *Percival*, had already completed the scale model of the stage, with the flats and the revolve, as well as watercolor sketches of the finished set and the costumes. She'd been attending rehearsals, to study the cast as they moved about the rehearsal hall on the West Side, in order to keep the designs appropriate to the individuals who would have to perform in them. And after this weekend she'd be staying in the city to oversee the making of the costumes, as well as the preparation and painting of the sets—which were, in most cases, large-scale reproductions of the original illustrations. She wanted to be present as all the pieces came together, in case there were problems with the lighting, or the way the costumes fit against the flats. She was enjoying it. As her mother had said, there was pleasure in work; there was progress and satisfaction, and a sense of ineffable rightness. Work was good; work preoccupied her; work kept her darker thoughts at bay for long periods of time. Miles was also good, and with him, there was progress and satisfaction. He was attentive and loving and, of course, still the old Miles, with his passion for lurid tales and for gossip. And when he and her mother and she were together, Miles and Marietta bickered and fussed, and she sometimes thought that if one hadn't known of certain events, one would have been unable to perceive any alteration in their behavior. But everything was subtly altered. Marietta continued to see Laurence and her other men friends, but was spending more evenings at home alone. She claimed it was because she was overworked, or desirous of her own company, or had a need for thinking time. Leigh thought the truth was that Marietta had looked into an abyss, and it had badly frightened her. She could no longer dance with her previous abandon. None of them could. And it was sad to think that Daniel's actions had wider-reaching effects than anyone could ever have dreamed. Marietta's new stay-at-home policy was one example. Miles's tendency to be overly solicitous was another. He kept on asking Leigh did she need this, or want that, until she had to say, "Miles, I'm not crippled or impaired in any way. And if you don't stop treating me as if I'm made of glass, I swear I'll go stark raving mad. I liked you far better as a bear." He frowned, then said, "Well, in that case, I have things to do. So, I will see you later," and off he went, smiling, to make a number of telephone calls.

It was all slightly odd and anticlimactic, as if, had she suffered more extensive injuries, they'd each have been better able to cope with her. But the damage was primarily inside her head, in her thoughts and feelings, her hesitations and reactions, and that was an area she was able to keep out of sight. So, with a sigh and a slight shake of the head, the three of them picked up and went on with their lives.

Some nights she dreamed of Daniel; she saw again his astonishing black-outlined irises, and heard his laughter or his sobs, and felt a new emptiness inside herself, as if some vital organ had been removed without her knowledge. No matter how she tried, she couldn't get to the root of this particular emotion. She knew it had, in some measure, to do with the dependency he'd compelled her to feel and to display; it also had to do with his inability to be responsible for his acts, and her understanding of that. In all her thoughts of him, he was an abandoned little boy, caught up in a bewildering emotional circus that exits from which always seemed to close before he was able to reach them. And she couldn't help wondering if the Daniel who emerged, ultimately, would resemble either of the other Daniels to whom she'd been exposed, or if he'd be someone completely different. Certainly, *she* was different as a result of her prolonged and intense exposure to him. Locks on bathrooms had to lock. Yet even when they did, throughout her time in the tub, or the shower, or at the sink, she kept expecting the door to fly open. Her bed had to be well away from the walls of the room. And she'd removed the frame from beneath it. The sight of an innocent towel loop in the ladies' room of a restaurant disturbed her so much that she ran from the place. Small things: like driving through the city and glancing out the car window while stopped at an intersection to notice police gates across a pair of windows beneath which was a fire escape; like the scent of hyacinths; like a man coming out of an office building wearing a pink shirt with white collar and cuffs; like a nude mannequin in Bendel's window, awaiting clothes with a fur coat draped around its shoulders. Things no one else would take notice of caused an interior clutching, dried her mouth, made her nervous.

She lowered her head now, and looked around. She felt drowsy with the heat of the sun soaking into the wool of the cardigan she'd put on over one of Joel's favorite shirts. She looked at her hands: dark smudges of soft lead pencil, several nicks from the mat knife, flecks of dried paint. She returned her hands to the flat arms of the chair, and raised her feet to look at the old Bass loafers she'd found while they'd been packing up the New Canaan house. Teenaged feet. It amused her to think that if she were viewed from the knees down, she might pass for someone young. She let her feet return to the grass, her eyes caught by the forsythia bushes, their tips full to bursting, ready to reveal the yellow flowers within. The land sloped gently downhill to the gravel driveway and then rose again, cutting off the view of the road. At night, the silence was like an additional blanket she pulled over herself; it was thick and soothing, without secrets. More often now, she slept long nights, to find the morning spread sumptuously in every direction. She could slide open the glass doors of the studio and walk barefoot across the chill damp grass to see what new growth had occurred overnight; or she could stand and marvel at finding that some small internal area had healed itself while she slept, leaving her fractionally safer and less fearful. Some mornings she thought perhaps her time with Daniel would, one day soon, like her periods of mourning, lose its sharp edges and become just a vague interlude, a time between times; an experience bracketed by other, equally if not more important experiences. She would never forget it, however. And it sometimes surprised her that she'd survived, because Daniel had given her such a craving for her own death, such hunger for an ending. But she'd chosen to fight and to survive, because she'd had enough of death, and wanted life. She'd chosen not to press charges, and it had been a good choice. Daniel had committed himself for treatment, had temporarily signed away his freedom. The act seemed to Leigh singularly appropriate.

They'd traveled together to such extremes, to such remote regions of human experience, that it didn't seem likely that anything would ever again be quite so terrifying, or so personally revealing. There were times when she placed the experience under the microscope of her analytical skills and saw, with a shudder both of revulsion and fascination, that her brain and her body had been induced to suffer seismic convulsions, not all of which were without pleasure. It was hateful to acknowledge the pleasure, but it had existed. She could only view it as some sort of flaw in her psychological makeup that she could have derived pleasure from one single moment of her imprisonment, yet she had. So what did that make her? And what did it make Daniel? She wanted to know. She thought that if she did know she might be able to respond more fully to the many good moments in her present life.

She heard the car turn into the driveway before she saw it. Tires on the gravel. She got up from the chair and walked over the grass along the side of the house as the car came to the top of the driveway and stopped. The engine was turned off and the silence, like a lid, closed over the space where its noise had been. The door on the driver's side opened, and Leigh descended the slope to the driveway, breaking into a smile, her arms swinging open in welcome. As her body hurried forward to make good the welcome, her arms closing around this dear, eccentric, lovely young woman, she thought perhaps she knew, after all, what her time with Daniel had made her.

"I'm so happy to see you!" she laughed, reveling in the moment.

"You look amazing!" Lane exclaimed. "Your hair's getting so long! And I love that shirt!"

"Come inside!" Leigh took her by the hand. "Mother and Miles are waiting to see you. But first I want you to see the 'amazing' studio Miles has made for me. And I want to hear about your father and your grandparents and school."

"This place is incredible!" Lane said, marching along at her side. "I love it. It's huge. Did you finish everything, the sets and costumes and everything?"

"All but the last-minute changes." Leigh stopped. "How is your father?"

"Way better," Lane said soberly. "Really way better. But he doesn't think he's ready to come home yet."

"He will be," Leigh said, putting an arm around Lane's shoulders as they began walking again. Suddenly, she felt very much better herself, because she had an answer of sorts. And it suited her reasoning.

"Are you going to marry Miles? You really should you know, Leigh. He's just gonzo over you."

"Gonzo?" Leigh laughed. "I'm carefully considering all the pros and cons. They tend to weigh rather heavily in his favor." Stopping again, she turned Lane toward her and looked her over. Ribbons and vests and a T-shirt under what had to be one of Daniel's shirts, a gypsyish brilliant-red skirt; odd clips in her hair, bracelets halfway up her arm, and army boots. "Will you let me take some photographs of you?" she asked.

"Oh, sure. D'you love this? Check it out!" Lane did a turn on the grass, the skirt ballooning around her legs. "Come on!" She pushed her arm through Leigh's. "Where's this amazing studio?"

"Just over here."

Her time with Daniel, Leigh thought, going arm in arm over the grass toward the back of the house, had been the long, attenuated labor that had returned her to motherhood. And here was the end product, the living, lively child. It made sense, really, if you thought about it that way.

Dream Train

DEDICATION

This book is for Claire Smith,
who not only "parented" its conception
but served as midwife through a difficult birth.
My gratitude and affection are limitless.
You are, quite simply, the very best.

ACKNOWLEDGMENTS

There are many people who helped in many ways before, during, and after the writing of this book. Some of them are: Sam MacDonald of Air Canada, who was a terrific flying companion and who shared with me the frightening story of her apartment fire; John Reeves, photographer extraordinaire, who patiently answered all my technical questions; Archie MacDonald, valued friend, who assisted with the background research on the Orient-Express; Bruce Hunter, master of the telex, who invariably sorted things out; Mariolina Franceschetti of the Italian Cultural Institute, who unearthed the details of the Special Law for Venice; Renato Piccolotto, chef for the Venice Simplon-Orient-Express, who took me through the stages of food preparation for the train; Giovanna Paschero, operations supervisor for the VS-O-E, who spent hours with me at the depot at Scomenzera explaining the logistics and maintenance of the train; Dr. Natale Rusconi of the Cipriani in Venice, who extended exceptional hospitality; Paola Starace, who gave friendship as well as assistance; Adrian Denham, chief steward on the VS-O-E, for creating a singular opportunity to allow me to ride in the locomotive of the train; Antoine Cadier, train manager, for his help in general; Mariana Field Hoppin and Denny Davidoff, for providing information and good company; my editor, Judy Kern, who is blessed with humor and patience, for her suggestions; the train staff of the VS-O-E, who were kind and accommodating; Caroline Boyle of marketing (U.K.), who made my travel arrangements and answered many questions; CIGA Hotels, Venice for their help and hospitality; and, finally, James Sherwood, whose wish it was to have a novel set on the new Orient-Express, for the trip of a lifetime and an unforgettable experience.

One

THE NIGHT BEFORE SHE WAS TO LEAVE VANCOUVER, JOANNA DREAMED again of the fire. She was back in the bathroom, the only place in the apartment she'd been able to get to, with foul-smelling oily black smoke snaking in through the gap between the bottom of the door and the frame; she was back in that little room soaking towels in water before pushing them up against that dangerous gap, all the while screaming for help, hoping the neighbors above or below would hear and call the fire department. Over and over, she'd screamed, *"I don't want to die in here!"* while pounding with her fists on the ceiling, the walls, the floor, praying to be heard and rescued. No one came. Minutes were hugely elastic, ballooning into immeasurable portions of time. She kept on screaming and pounding on the ceiling and walls; there was nothing else to do. When she dared put her hand to the bathroom door, it had grown hot. The fire was eating away at it on the other side. Mouth dry, throat raw from screaming, heart racing, she turned on the shower and aimed the spray at the door, then with her toothbrush glass began splashing water around the room while her voice, automatically now, pleaded with Sally who lived upstairs, and with Jean and Barry who lived downstairs, to call the fire department, to get people to come and save her. Her life had been reduced to a small, highly flammable package she wanted to keep intact.

Forcing herself awake, she sat up in the dark hotel room, her body slick with the sweat of fear, shattered anew at the near loss of her life, and at the actual loss of years of work. The destruction of her clothes, keepsakes, furniture had been upsetting of course. But the ruin of her files of prints and negatives and slides had been a permanent injury. She'd lost moments of time; corners, fragments, features of faces, scenes and events.

Her personal vision up to that point had been wiped out by the fire. It was a monumental loss. In some ways what she'd produced in the eight years since the fire was better—more clearly perceived, more profoundly graphic; yet she knew she'd never be able to duplicate the innocence and enthusiasm that had given those early efforts their uniqueness. She often wished—if for nothing else than comparison—she could review those lost photographs, lay them down beside her present efforts and try to track her personal passage in life through the people and scenes she'd chosen to represent a particular day, a time, a mood, or a feeling. The odd print turned up now and then: someone had admired a picture, so she'd made an extra print; the someone called up out of the blue and in the course of conversation mentioned the print; elderly magazines in the waiting rooms of various members of the medical profession upon whom she had occasion to call—she'd come across a piece of her own work and gasp with pleasure at the discovery. She had no qualms whatever about stuffing the magazine into her handbag and taking away retrieved bits of her life.

After a time she switched on the bedside light. Almost eight. There was no point in trying to go back to sleep for the twenty-five minutes left before the alarm went off. She sat back against the headboard, thinking about what had preceded the fire: those four years with Greg. It had been a game, more or less, with both of them playing out preassigned roles. He was the one meant to garner laurels, to harvest crops of success. He was the one who was supposed to shinny up the corporate ladder in a dazzling, spotlit climb. And she was supposed to have been entirely supportive and nurturing during his ascent. It gradually drove her crazy. She refused to accede blindly to his wishes or to surrender her right to her ambition, so they kept their separate apartments, even though it was accepted that they were a couple. There had been times when she'd disliked being known as the other half of Greg. Yet because she'd always been uneasy about her personal attributes, she'd stumbled along with him through the retrospectively clichéd ups and downs of their time together, until the fire.

He'd always had a casual disregard for the things her growing success provided. He'd put his shoes on the furniture; he'd broken a vase she'd carried on her lap all the way from Hong Kong, and couldn't understand her being upset at its destruction; he'd even tapped his cigarette ash onto the floor of her new BMW rather than using the ashtray; after the first year he'd eaten her food without comment; he'd slept in her bed and used her body, also without comment. He'd infuriated her. When they'd argued about his transgression of the moment, he'd invariably pretended innocence, claiming not to understand what it was that had set her off "this time." And the implication that she was someone too readily set off heightened her anger with him. By the time of the fire she'd actively loathed not only Greg but herself for continuing to be involved with him. It was something she simply couldn't understand about herself—her remaining for so long with someone who, once past the initial stages of the romance, had displayed so little approval of any aspect of her.

All it took to end the whole affair was a spark, some ashes from one of his cigarettes fallen down the side of the sofa—he'd had the ashtray perched on the arm, another of his habits that had maddened her. The spark had smoldered for hours, long after he'd gone home, before erupting into flames that had gutted the apartment and reduced to ashes all evidence of her flourishing career, as well as every memento of her past. It was pure luck that she'd been too tired that day, after shooting a cover feature for *Connecticut Magazine*, to lug her equipment up from the garage. So she'd left it locked in the trunk of her car. Those items, and the film from that day's shoot, were all that remained of her equipment. Everything else had been incinerated.

When the fire chief came to talk with her at the hospital, where she was well into the process of detoxification, and he'd revealed to her his findings—that the fire had, without question, started in the sofa—she'd refused to see Greg again. Yes, it had been an accident. But it was one caused by his seemingly permanent disregard for her, and so she couldn't forgive or absolve him. She hadn't even been able to speak to him because had she said anything at all, considering her years of accumulated anger and her ultimate outrage at his being responsible for the fire, she might well have killed him. She'd had repeated visions of strangling him, or running him down with her car; she'd stabbed him, shot him, poisoned him; she'd humiliated him publicly and *then* stabbed, shot, or poisoned him. She wanted him dead and gone, as dead and gone as all the work of her life to that point.

When he'd telephoned, she'd said, "Stay away from me! I don't want to see you or hear one word from you ever again!" Her voice had been low and foreign and tremulous with rage. She'd put down the receiver with a shaking hand and stared for a long time at the ceiling, wondering if she was being unfair, deciding maybe she was, but any more of Greg and there'd be nothing left of her to salvage.

The fact that he took her at her word and made no further attempt to make contact proved once and for all his lack of feeling for her, which only further depressed her. If she could spend four years with a fool like Greg, what was *she*? No matter how many times she went back over the time with Greg, she failed to find any satisfactory explanation for her involvement. She'd been sifting through the clues to her own identity ever since, but still hadn't any viable answers. Her inability to come up with answers in the matter of Greg no longer bothered her to the degree it had in the immediate aftermath of the fire. But every so often—late at night or en route to some assignment—she couldn't help looking back and speculating on the subject. All she knew for certain was that the fire stood as one of the two milestones in her life.

The second was the death of her mother two years ago. She had no nightmares about Lily. And when she thought of her, it was as she'd always been and not as the shrunken cadaver she'd become at the last. Her father and her younger brother Ben—always called Beamer by the family for reasons long since forgotten—and she had all prayed, near the end, that Lily would go soon.

It was, however, one thing to crave an end to someone's suffering and quite another to have a life without that someone in it. With Lily's death, it seemed Jo lost still more fragments, corners, exposure-tested strips of her own past. There were also new questions for which she periodically struggled to find answers. Lily had been her mother, after all, and the most influential person in Jo's life. Lily's absence, the silencing of her voice, left Jo feeling oddly empty-handed. She'd always thought a time would come when she and Lily would sit down together and review their history and, in the process, at last enable Jo to make sense of all sorts of things that continued to bewilder her.

She looked again at the clock. Eight-twenty. She got up and went to the bathroom to shower, leaving the door open as she always did now. Her flight wasn't until eleven, but it took her at least an hour and a half of a morning to assemble herself for the day. She liked to linger over coffee while reading the local newspaper, dipping toast points into her coffee cup, eating mechanically as she absorbed details of the latest front-page disasters, scandals, atrocities, and weather predictions. The news was eternally so bad that, by comparison, she felt quite well. Her health was good, her career hummed along; she was free of having constantly to consider the moods and preferences of anyone else. She set her own pace, often made her own travel arrangements, worked out her articles according to the degree of interest a project aroused in her. She'd left Manhattan after the fire and bought the condominium in Rowayton (on the garden level so she could escape either through the front or the rear patio door in the event of a fire. And when traveling, she refused to stay above the fourth floor in hotels; upon arrival she at once checked the location of the fire exits). She had a home, yet she rarely lived in it.

For six to eight months of the year, for two weeks here or a month there, she made nests of hotel rooms, setting out her coffee and portable one-cup coffee maker, the family portrait she'd taken while still in college, her notebooks and pens, her stock of film, the heavy camera bag, the books and research materials needed for the assignment, her Walkman and the detachable microspeakers. She'd check in, take a few minutes to distribute her bits and pieces, and at once the hotel room would seem less sterile, more familiar. She'd recently begun to dislike hotels, and it took more and more effort to rid them of their sterility.

She'd been in Vancouver for four days doing a feature on Expo 86 for *Worldview*, a trade travel magazine that featured her work two or three times a year. She was considered a dependable source of high-quality photographs and clean prose that didn't suffer from too arch a personal viewpoint. She approached every project with an open mind, prepared to be pleased and enlightened. The result was an increasing number of plum assignments: covers for *U.S. Travel*, for *Gourmet*; features with photographs for everything from *People* to *Architectural Digest*. There were jobs that were strictly photographic, and some were purely journalistic, but the majority required both photos and text, and these were the ones she most enjoyed.

Expo had been one of the really good assignments. The pavilions were clever, even exciting; the grounds were immaculate, the employees friendly, the color-coding of areas well-designed and effective, as were the trains and monorail; the nightly fireworks display complete with laser light show and music had turned her into an eight-year-old, open-mouthed with delight as, through the lens of the tripod-mounted Nikon, she'd watched the bursting flares in the night sky reflected in the water below. She had a hunch that one of her time-exposure fireworks shots might make the cover, although it was often impossible to predict what might make an editor's heart tick over. There were shots she'd been positive would be snapped up for covers that were passed over in favor of less tricky or less exciting exposures.

Anyway, this job was done, and she was looking forward to going home, to eating food she prepared herself, to going upstate to the place in Kent where her parents had moved after her father's retirement, to see her dad and Beamer. She'd been on the road longer than usual, having come to Vancouver directly from a job in San Francisco and, before that, one in Nashville. The last year or so, her assignments had been one on top of another, which meant she had to do her writing in hotel rooms on rented typewriters. She couldn't seem to bring herself to say no, to turn down offers of work. The result was the feeling that she was somewhat less than real, like some arcane form of processing machine, something that absorbed information, captured the visuals on film, then assembled everything into a readily digestible format and sent it off by courier either to her agent or to the publication in question, depending upon the particular protocol. Time off, time to herself, had become, at age thirty-six, vital and elusive.

A number of times of late she'd referred to herself as the mobile cipher, the invisible eye, the sponge in the corner soaking up details and bits of trivia. It sounded amusing, people laughed; but Sally, who was still a close friend, had a couple of months earlier said, "I'm beginning to think you have no idea who or what you are anymore, Joey. You talk as if you're middle-aged and ugly, as if no one in his right mind would find you interesting or attractive. I'd like to remind you that you're still young, and very goddamned attractive. I hate it when you talk about yourself that way." With an encouraging smile, Sally had gone on to say, "People do see you, you know. Whatever you may think, you're definitely *not* invisible."

Sally's remarks had made an impact, because she'd begun to feel vaguely uneasy, even afraid. There were moments when it seemed as if she were actually fading, like a color negative left on a sunny window sill. She felt out of step with people's attitudes and values. She also felt something of a fraud, because most of the people she met encountered her professional self. This was the Jo who, with confidence bred of experience and technical skill, could keep conversations afloat and be sincerely engaging. But without an assignment backing her up, without the camera, the personal self seemed to be in trouble. Her presence anywhere seemed validated by her career, and without her professional credentials to back her up, she not only lost confidence, she also feared she had nothing of interest to say to anyone. She'd arrived at a juncture where she better than halfway believed the Jo who wore the professional hat had taken precedence over the Jo who didn't. And the only consolation she found nowadays was in the small rewards she gave herself at the conclusion of each assignment: clothes, a piece of jewelry, cassettes or books or videocassettes. Things just didn't feel right.

As usual she was too early for her flight, and settled into a phone booth to check in with her agent in New York.

"Did you get my message already?" Grace asked.

"What message?"

"Are you home? Where are you?"

"I'm at the airport in Vancouver. I fly out in an hour."

"Well, listen, kiddo! I've got some great news."

"What?" Jo asked warily. Great news usually translated into another job, and all she wanted was to go home.

"It's the assignment of a lifetime, Jo. They're all set to go. The guy they had lined up to do it rolled his car day before yesterday on the Jersey Turnpike. Nothing major, but he's not going to be going anywhere for a while. I just happened to be over talking to Harry Harris at *Travelogue*, and he was in a total panic, asking did I have anyone who could jump in at the eleventh hour. Of course, I told him you'd be free, and he was ecstatic."

"Oh, God! What is it this time? Bora Bora, or down-home cooking?"

"If I knew how to work a camera, kiddo, I'd do this one myself." Grace took a breath, then said, "It's the Orient-Express."

"The Orient-Express? I thought that shut down years ago. Does it still run?"

"Sweetheart, it runs and then some. You'll catch the train Sunday morning at Victoria Station in London, and ride it to Venice. Then five days at only the most sensational hotel in Venice, the Cipriani. Then a return ride to London. The Italian Tourist Bureau's involved, too, and they'll be laying on a couple of things for you. The hotel's PR director will have all the info. The hook is a great ride followed by a stay at a great hotel. Say yes, and let me call Harry back."

"Wait a minute! First of all, how long is the train ride? And what do I need? Give me a little something more here, Gracie! I can't just change my plans and agree to this without a bit more input."

"I'll telex Henry in London and tell him to air out the guest room. You know he loves having you stay with him. So that's no problem. When can you get over there?"

"I've *got* to go home, Grace! I mean it. I've been on the road for the last hundred years. I want to see if my place is still there; I want to see my dad and my brother; I want to do my laundry." She paused, then said, "You already said yes, didn't you?"

"Uh-huh. You can't turn this down, sweetheart. Cover feature, plus whatever material Harry doesn't use, he says we can shop elsewhere and that includes all the foreign rights. This could be good for half a dozen markets. Top-dollar fee. And, come on, Jo! The *Orient-Express*! I know people who'd kill to ride that train, me included. Black-tie dinner, the Alps, fascinating people. Then, there's only the most gorgeous city on earth waiting for you at the other end."

"I never have been to Venice," Jo said consideringly.

"Go catch your plane. I'll talk to you tonight, with the details."

"What about the airfare to London?"

"Prepaid executive-class ticket's waiting at Kennedy. Call me the minute you get home. There's a lot of stuff to go over before you leave."

"I love having about ten minutes' notice that I'm heading off to Europe. What kind of kill fee?"

"Fifty percent. Think about it on the flight back. You're perfect for this one. I'll bet by the time you call me later you'll be out of your mind with excitement. Gotta go, another call. Think about it!" she said again, and hung up.

Think about it! Jo looked at her watch. She had plenty of time to walk through the terminal to the bookstore, just to see if they had anything on Venice or the Orient-Express. Nothing on the train, but a Berlitz guide to

Venice she paid for, then popped into her handbag before making her way to the departure gate. The nonslip strap of the heavy Lowe-pro camera bag bore down into her shoulder, and she thought longingly of the visits she'd planned to her chiropractor. Now she'd be lucky to see him once before she left. *If* she decided to go. Mentally, she went through her wardrobe trying to think which clothes might be right.

Oh hell! she thought, starting to smile. Of course she was going to go. How could she possibly turn down anything as intriguing and exciting as a ride on the Orient-Express?

Two

THE APARTMENT SEEMED TOO QUIET. THE PICTURES ON THE WALLS were misaligned—proof that the cleaning lady had been there in Jo's absence. Everything felt odd. She had to stop every few minutes and look around, trying to decide what was wrong. Usually, coming home was like arriving at a good party. This time it was as if she'd wandered by mistake into someone else's house.

She opened the windows to let the humid breeze move through the rooms, then stepped outside onto the deck. In the afternoon silence, a family of ducks sat as if dazed on the surface of the pond. The grass had just been cut and the smell of it was powerful. She stood breathing in the scent, looking first at the ducks bobbing on the pond, then at the dissolving clouds.

Although she sometimes missed the frantic pace and perennially menacing atmosphere of Manhattan, overall she'd come to prefer living in Connecticut. The silence at night was broken only by the clacking rattle of late trains passing on the tracks that ran near the lower part of the condominium complex; during the day, if she cared to take a stroll over the grass, she might hear the concert pianist practicing, or someone's stereo, or the laughter and splashing of kids up at the pool. Ordinary, everyday sounds for the most part, the background music she'd grown up with and that, as a teenager, she'd longed to escape. And for those five years when she'd lived in the city, she'd harbored a certain smug satisfaction at having discarded her suburban background. She'd acquired a new and different set of survival skills; she'd grown street-smart and proud of her ability to navigate the subways. She'd concentrated on her work, had done it so well that she'd established a good reputation and earned enough money to buy the BMW which, in truth, had been a frivolous and wildly expensive toy. Keeping it garaged in the city had cost almost as much as the rent on her apartment. In the end, she'd moved the car up to her parents' place, reregistered it in Connecticut, and Beamer had used it more than she had. Until the fire. Then she'd escaped back to the sub-urbs, using her savings for the down payment on the apartment, and the insurance money to pay for the furnishings and new camera equipment.

She'd been grateful for the quiet of Connecticut. Now, suddenly, it made her uneasy. Everything seemed skewed. Why, if everything was going so smoothly and so well, was she standing outside on the deck watching half a dozen sun-dazed ducks instead of busying herself with all the things she'd promised she'd do once she got home? No answer.

She sat down, her thoughts shifting to London, and to Henry. She had to smile, remembering their first meeting almost ten years before. She'd gone along to his office shortly after her arrival in London, geared up to meet someone middle-aged, very British, and stuffy. Gracie had only said, "You'll like Henry," and had smiled rather significantly, which had led Jo to expect the worst. Every time someone declared two strangers would like one another, the two in question seemed destined to despise one another on sight. But in this case, Gracie had been right.

Henry hadn't been middle-aged or stuffy. He'd greeted her warmly and they'd gone off to lunch, during which he'd chatted companionably, smiling often, while she kept her professional hat fixed firmly in place. He had been very British, perfectly correct in his dealings with the restaurant staff. Yet his correctness had been offset by his enthusiasm for her work and by his habit of meeting her eyes straight on and nodding approvingly whenever she spoke. Gracie had been right: She did like him. She more than liked him, finding him sweetly appealing in his three-piece suit and starched shirt. He had lovely manners, an absurd sense of humor, and a talent for making the person he was with feel important.

"I'd love to have one of your photographs," he'd told her as the meal progressed.

"Anything in particular?"

"I haven't seen it yet," he'd said. "But I'll know it when I see it."

"You will, huh? Any clues as to what it might be?"

"Not a one. I'll be quite forthright about it, however. No fear. I'll ring you, or write to say I'd like a print of this one, please. So be prepared."

"Oh, I will." She'd smiled at him. "I'll be living in a state of suspense from now on."

He'd looked at her for a long moment before saying, "Oh, don't! I'd hate to think of you suffering, waiting for the dreaded declaration. No, it'll be painless, I promise. I'll simply see what I want and inform you.

Since Grace sent over the samples, I've been most curious about you. I expected you'd be fat, for some reason."

"Fat!" she'd laughed. "Why fat?"

"Don't know. Something to do, I think, with how very—*comfortable* your photographs are. I envisioned you waddling happily along, spotting something that took your fancy, then clicking away. Needless to say, I'm delighted you're not. Fat, that is. Anything but, actually. And younger, too, than I'd imagined."

"Fat and old. I'm going to have to take a good long look at my stuff. Maybe somewhere inside me there's a middle-aged fat lady." She'd thought, looking at his smiling mouth, that she'd have liked to kiss him. His proximity and his comments and the look of him made her somewhat giddy, and she'd wondered if perhaps he'd inspire her to give up Greg. She didn't at all mind the prospect.

"You know," he'd said a short time later, "I'm about to buy a house. In Chelsea. When next you visit, possibly you'll come stay in the guest room. I'm sure it would be much more comfortable, not to mention less expensive, than a hotel. And I think you and Brenda would hit it off nicely."

"Who's Brenda?" she'd asked, hoping he'd say his sister or cousin.

"My fiancée."

"Oh!" Her giddiness had gone, along with her budding romantic interest. She'd returned to the hotel after the meal feeling like an idiot for having been prepared to become involved with him. She'd chided herself for being too fast off the mark, and had conscientiously shuffled her emotions like an old deck of cards, thereby relegating Henry to his proper place as business associate and friend.

She never did get to meet Brenda. By the time he'd moved into his house, he was no longer engaged to her. Jo got into the habit of staying in his guest room whenever she visited England, always glad to see Henry, safe in her acknowledged involvement with Greg. And Henry had been wonderfully kind, most solicitous, when she stayed with him a few months after the fire. "You're well out of it," he'd said. "I never did care too much for the sound of that fellow."

She'd been so grateful for his sympathy and understanding that she'd never thought to ask why he'd said that. Of course, he'd distracted her with laughter, and outings to the theater; and he'd assured her she could do far better for herself. He had, in fact, instinctively said every last thing she'd been wanting to hear. Dear old Henry. It'd be good to see him; he'd make her laugh.

She shook her head, went inside, and called her father.

"Are you home, Joey?" he wanted to know.

"I got back an hour or so ago. But I'm leaving in a few days for London. I was thinking maybe I'd hop in the car, come up to see you and Beamer tomorrow."

"Oh, hell, Sweetcakes! We're leaving in an hour for Fishers Island. Didn't you get the message I left on your stupid machine? Christ, but I hate those things!"

"I haven't listened to my messages yet. How long are you going to be at Fishers?"

"A week. The Fullers wouldn't take a no. They've got some female they want me to meet." He laughed. "Everybody and his cousin's got some woman they think'll just fill my bill. How long are you over in London?"

"A couple of weeks at least. I'm doing a feature on the Orient-Express."

He whistled, then laughed again. "Ver-ry nice. Don't suppose you want a traveling companion?"

"I wish. How's everything? How's Beamer?"

"Right as rain. Your kid brother's bitching about wasting valuable time so he's dragging his computer and a whole mess of work along with him. He'll probably spend the entire time in his room, with the poor Fullers' telephone hooked into some system or other so he doesn't miss out on any hot offerings. He'll be a millionaire any minute now. Hey! Make sure you send me a postcard from the Orient-Express. I've always had a yen to ride that train. Does it still go to Istanbul?"

"No, just to Venice."

"Just Venice. Will you get to spend any time there?"

"Five days."

"Maybe I'll cancel the Fullers and come with you," he joked. "I haven't seen Venice since the war. I hope for your sake it smells better now than it did then."

"I'll call you when I get back," she promised. "Give Beamer my love, okay?"

"Okay, Sweetcakes. Have a good time. And don't forget my postcard!"

She hung up and went to unpack her bags.

While the first load of clothes was churning away in the washer, she took the camera bag into the second bedroom, which doubled as darkroom and storage area. She lifted out the camera body and the lenses, and all at once she just had to get out. Grabbing some film from the refrigerator, she shoved everything back into the bag, ran out, and jumped into the car. She felt panicky as she reversed out of her slot, her whole body tensely coiled. The only cure she'd discovered for this malaise, or whatever it was, was to get out and shoot some film.

She drove, the tension easing almost immediately as she was visually soothed by the physical beauty of the area, and ended up at Weed Beach in Darien. She found a slot, pulled in, picked up the camera bag, and headed across the lot to the far end of the beach.

There were many mothers with young children, rows of impossibly lithe teen-agers in advanced stages of tanning; radios and cassette players created pockets of music; the air reeked of mustard and of coconut oil. The hot, heavy air hung like a transparent, shimmering curtain.

She walked slowly along the rocky shore, looking out at the boats on the Sound, then down at the crusty tideline. Her attention was caught by something she couldn't at first identify but which was, upon closer inspection, a paperback book that had been taken out on the tide, then washed back in. The cover was long gone; the sun had dried and curled the pages, turning it into something like an extraordinary marine flower. Fitting the telephoto to the camera body, she dropped to her haunches to take several shots of her find.

Then, caught in the rhythm, freed and eased by the complicity existing between eye and camera, she opened the lens full to photograph some of the sailboats. With the glaring sun and wide-open aperture, the final shots would seem as if they'd been taken late in the day.

She moved on to a close-up of some odd, stunted bushes; then bits of debris tangled in the seaweed at the tidemark; a medium shot of the slow-moving queue of children patiently waiting to buy Popsicles at the snack bar.

Forty minutes, twenty-four black and white exposures, and she was trudging back through the sand to the car. It was too hot to sit in at once, so she stood looking around, waiting and thinking through the idea that she was not only unprepared to go rushing off on another assignment, she was also very nervous about it. She'd thought she'd come home, putter around the apartment for a few days before going upstate to see her family; she'd thought she'd bring her photo files up to date, and spend some time in the darkroom. Instead, her family was unavailable, she had just enough time to do a little background research before repacking and flying off to London for another of her of-late increasingly awkward sojourns at Henry's house with the redoubtable Suzanne hovering in the foreground and making it clear by means of certain facial expressions that she was less than thrilled at having Jo there.

Jo's prior relationship with Henry meant nothing to Suzanne. Neither did their professional dealings. Jo was another woman and therefore a disruption and a threat. Henry either failed to see or chose to ignore the heaviness in the atmosphere during these visits, and Jo had been planning to stay elsewhere on future trips. But this assignment had come up so suddenly that it simply hadn't occurred to her to get Grace to inform Henry not to expect her. More fodder for her uneasiness. Well, if it got to be as heavy as her last stay, she'd move to a hotel. As fond as she was of Henry, his taste in women was doubtful at best. Brenda had sounded bad enough; Suzanne had absolutely no sense of humor. How could a man like Henry live day after day with a woman who wouldn't recognize a joke if it was lit up in neon? Henry's women made Jo frustrated and sad; they all seemed so—*second-best*, as if he was making do until the one he really wanted came along. And that was ridiculous, because Henry had everything to recommend him. But there he was with Suzanne. God! How could he stand her?

During the flight to London her anxiety returned. It seemed she was doing everything wrong. Why, for example, had she put aside the Nikon at the last minute and packed the Pentax body and lenses? The KX was old and she hadn't used it in years. She should've told Grace she wasn't up to this, but she'd hardly protested at all before letting herself be overcome by the romantic idea of riding the world's most famous train. And "idea" was the key word, because all she'd managed to find on microfilm at the library were a couple of magazine pieces with some interesting facts about George Pullman and his American cars, and about Georges Nagelmackers, who'd created the original Compagnie International des Wagons-Lits. She'd Xeroxed both the articles and brought them along. Aside from this she'd rented a few movies with Venetian settings. And that was the sum total of her research. She hated feeling so unprepared, and wondered if maybe her professional hat was starting to slip. If so, she was in serious trouble because, without it, she'd have nothing going for her.

And what if she hadn't brought the right clothes? The dinner on board was supposedly a gala event, with the passengers in twenties-type finery. She'd packed a two-piece beige silk outfit that was smart, but not especially festive. Maybe she'd buy something dressier in London. But then she'd get stuck with a dress she'd likely never wear again. Come on! she chided herself. There's not a thing wrong with your clothes; there's not a thing wrong with the Pentax. Everything will be fine.

Henry had left the key to the flat in the flowerpot outside the door, as always. She let herself in and discovered a package on the floor addressed to her, with a Post-it note from Henry attached saying he'd be out for the evening but wouldn't be late, and the guest room was ready for her.

She carried her things into the cozy, familiar flat, trying to pinpoint what was different. Certain items—knickknacks, several pictures—were missing; so was the overpowering scent of Suzanne's perfume. Just to be absolutely sure, Jo ventured down the hall to the master suite, where she opened the doors to the wardrobe. Only Henry's clothes. Suzanne, obviously, was gone.

"Great!" she said aloud. "Great!"

Feeling much better, she settled in the guest room.

The package contained a four-color brochure, one booklet titled *Passenger's Guide to the Venice Simplon-Orient-Express*, another on the Bournemouth Belle and a glossy dark blue folder stamped TRAVEL DOCUMENTS. The entire package was impressive: the glossy dark blue luggage tags and stickers, the Sealink boarding card, the itinerary typed on beige paper with chocolate trim, a beige card bearing the VS-O-E logo reading: "We have pleasure in enclosing tickets for your trip to: Venice. The check-in is at: 10.00—Victoria Station." Handwritten.

She went through everything feeling as if she'd been given an exceptional gift. The presentation was elegant, and personalized in a way no airline ticket ever could be. The *Passenger's Guide* was loaded with information, including histories both of the Pullmans and of the Continental carriages.

She was starting to get excited, and even more concerned about her clothes because, according to the guide, "You can never be overdressed on the Venice Simplon-Orient-Express." She'd consult with Henry. He had great taste; he'd know if her clothes were right. And now that godawful Suzanne was out of the way, maybe they'd be able to sit and talk together, in their old comfortable fashion. Suzanne was gone! God! It was too terrific. Maybe she'd have a chat with Henry about his peculiar taste in women and find out why he kept taking up with such wretched types. Sure. Then he'd follow suit by asking what self-destructive impulse had prompted her to stay with Greg for four long years. Game, set, and match. Maybe they both had lousy taste in partners.

Her unpacking done, she wandered through the flat, admiring anew Henry's taste in furnishings and the lovely Victorian details of the place. He lived on the ground floor and rented out the flats on the second and third floors. The rooms were large, with high molded ceilings, everything painted white. The furniture was chunky modern, upholstered in soft gray fabric, with clean rounded lines and down cushions. No clutter, just a few large potted plants, an assortment of antique brass miniatures on a round mahogany table near the front windows, several compelling watercolors, and the large black and white piece of Jo's he'd loved on sight. "This is the one!" he'd announced. "I must have it. If you don't give it to me, I won't be held responsible for the consequences. They'll find my poor shriveled body—after days of searching—huddled in the doorway of the Quali-Print shop where, as everyone knows, you have access to their darkroom. You wouldn't want that on your conscience, would you?"

"God, no, Henry! I'll go back this very moment and have them do you up an eleven-by-fourteen on archival paper. Your poor shriveled body," she'd scoffed. "It'd take more than just days to get you to that state."

"All right. After *weeks* of searching, they'll find my poor *semi*-shriveled body. Better?"

"Better."

"Truly, Jo," he'd said, studying the contact sheet with a magnifying glass, "this is divine. What a clever girl you are!"

He'd looked at her with such overflowing admiration that for a few seconds she'd been tempted to throw herself at him and bite him on the neck. She'd liked him so much just then her teeth had ached slightly with a sudden brief desire to take large bites out of him.

The shot he'd chosen was one of her own favorites, a hand-held exposure of four old women seated on a park bench. They were smiling and talking, their hands busy with knitting. The foliage all around served as a lacy frame that contained them perfectly. Like most of her best work, the shot had been done on the spur of the moment, one afternoon here in London after leaving Henry's office. She stood back from it now, deciding there was a good deal of Henry's influence in the final product. Henry was such a staunch fan of her work that he never failed to inspire her to go right out and find more subjects for more photographs that would prompt more of his open approval.

There was another note from Henry on the refrigerator door. It read: "Eat and drink. In anticipation of your arrival, I've taken the highly unusual precaution of stocking the larder. I don't expect to be later than ten, so try to stay awake for a drink and a natter and the latest gen on the assignment."

She put on the kettle, then opened the refrigerator to laugh aloud at the sight of a roasted chicken with yet another note attached, this one to a drumstick. "Eat me, Alice," it read. She wasn't hungry, but tore off a small, crisp piece of skin to nibble as she looked out the kitchen window at Henry's lovely garden. She'd been promising herself for years that she'd one day sit Henry down in his garden and photograph him amid his flowering bushes. This time, she vowed, she'd do it. She'd get him out there in some of the ratty clothes he kept around for his gardening sojourns, and she'd shoot away until she had exactly the view of him she wanted. It'd be a shot that showed the contrast between his proper British gentleman image and his off-time, faintly crazy, soil-tiller persona. He'd be smiling his rather devilish smile, the one that showed his teeth, and he'd have dirty hands and knees. And, of course, he'd be wearing his "plimsolls," as he referred to what she called sneakers, with his toes poking through.

All at once, she was neither thirsty nor tired. It was only nine-thirty in the morning and the sun was shining. Her spirits considerably lightened, she grabbed the camera bag and her purse, pocketed the keys, and let herself out.

The streets of Chelsea were quiet at this time on a Thursday morning, and she walked along looking at the houses, pausing to take a shot of a row of pastel-painted terraced dwellings, each with its own tidy patch of garden at the front. As she neared the river, she saw a black woman pushing a child in a stroller and heard the woman singing softly. Her voice floated like a butterfly, tilting and directionless, on the fragrant air. Jo was captivated, especially when she got close enough to see the woman's broad, beaming face and that of the tiny Oriental child in the stroller. There was a picture here she wanted; she was also intrigued by the pair. Curiosity and confidence pulled together; knowledge of her abilities gave her a physical and psychological certainty. It came to her every time like a sense of well-being, enabling her to say and do things she was never able to do without the camera in her hands.

Slowing her pace she said, "Good morning," and the woman turned to offer her an unsuspicious smile.

"Is it a boy or a girl?" Jo asked, elated by the huge black eyes the child had fixed on her.

"Girl," the woman answered. "Her name's Mai-Ling. Ain't it, darlin'?" She placed a caring hand on the child's head.

"God, she's adorable!" Jo said, overwhelmed by those immense eyes. "How old is she?"

"Seventeen month. She's a little ting, but soooo smart. Smart, ain't you, darlin'?"

"Are you from Jamaica?"

"You been to Jamaica?" the woman asked avidly.

"Not yet. But I've always wanted to."

"Where you from?"

"Connecticut."

"You visitin'?"

"I'm going to Italy on Sunday, then I'll be back for a week. Work," she explained.

"What work you do?" the woman wanted to know.

"I'm a photojournalist."

"Ah! So that's how come you got the camera, huh, and tings bulgin' in the pockets."

Jo looked down at herself, and laughed. "Would you let me take your picture?"

"What you tink, Mai-Ling? You want dis lady take your picture?"

The child broke into a great smile, revealing her tiny new white teeth —four on the top and four on the bottom.

"Mai-Ling wants a picture," the woman announced.

"If you could just stand right where you are," Jo said, "that'd be great."

"What you gonna do with a picture of the two of us?" the woman asked, amused. "Big ugly black woman and little Mai-Ling?"

"You're not ugly!" Jo said, holding the camera away from her face. "You look wonderful, real. The two of you are beautiful."

"You tink so, huh?" The woman now smiled again, revealing a mouthful of large, startlingly white, perfect teeth. The child, who'd been tracking the conversation, chose that moment to turn in the stroller and put her little hand on the much larger black one that held the stroller's strut. Jo felt that interior leap of excitement that came when she knew an exposure was going to be perfect, adjusted the focus, and got the picture. She quickly took three more shots, then put the lens cap back on, saying, "Thank you very much."

As they started along the street, Jo said, "My name's Joanna. What's yours?" and saw herself back at school, making this same introduction at the start of every September.

"Me, I'm Florella. You goin' put our picture in some book?"

"Oh, no. It's just for me."

"You go takin' pictures of all the people you see?"

"Sometimes I think I'd like to, but no. Have you been in England a long time?"

"Twenty-two years," Florella answered. "Long time. I was here till I was fourteen. But my people they hatin' the winter, so they save up, and we all go home. Me," she laughed, "I save up eight years, workin' chambermaid in the hotel, and come back. I like the winter. An' I like this child here!" She stroked Mai-Ling's glossy black hair and the child at once swung around to offer her an adoring smile. "I got seven of them I cared for," she explained. "Some're grown big now. They come to see me. You have children?"

"No."

"You should," Florella laughed. "Then I come care for your babies."

"I'd love that!" Jo told her, able for a moment to picture a rollicking household populated by happy, noisy children shepherded by this affable woman.

They'd arrived at the Embankment, and Jo said, "I'm going to stay here for a while. If you give me your address, I'll send you prints of the pictures."

Jo got out her notebook. Florella recited her address, then said goodbye and pushed Mai-Ling's stroller off along the waterfront. Jo watched them go, then turned to survey the view.

Brightly painted tour boats were headed down the river, to the pubs along the route, or to Hampton Court. She took shots of the boats, then turned to focus on the street. People were passing and she held still, waiting for them to move on. She waited and waited, and suddenly realized that the figure blocking her view had stopped and wasn't moving. Lowering the camera, thinking to go around this impediment, she heard laughter, looked up, and saw Tyler.

Three

"THIS SIMPLY ISN'T POSSIBLE!" HE EXCLAIMED, GRINNING AT HER. "BUT it must be. It is Joanna James, after all!" With that, he gave her a hearty hug, then stepped away, saying, "I'd know that camera anywhere! How absolutely incredible!"

"I couldn't imagine," she laughed breathlessly, "why some idiot was blocking my shot. This really is amazing!"

"Are you in town for a while? What are you doing? Are you going to be free to have dinner with me, Joanna?"

"God, I'd love to! When?"

"How about this evening?" he said quickly.

"Sure. That'd be fine. I don't believe this!"

"I'm not sure I do, either. Where are you staying? Christ! Let me find something to write with." He patted all his pockets, his eyes never leaving hers.

"I've got a pen," she offered, getting it from her bag. "I'm staying at my agent's place." She wrote down Henry's address and telephone number, tore the page from her notebook and handed it to him. "Do you live around here?"

"I'm just on my way to Surrey, but I'll be back to collect you at six on the dot and we'll have dinner. I have quite a number of questions I want to ask you, but right now I must run. I'm spending the afternoon with my son." He put his hands on her shoulders and gazed at her as if stunned. "The last thing I ever imagined happening," he told her, then laughed again. "This is just too fantastic! Six o'clock, all right?"

"Definitely!"

He released her, gazed at her a moment longer, said "Later!" and went loping off across the road to his car.

She stood rooted to the spot until he'd driven off. Then, too distracted to take any more photographs, she started back toward Henry's house, marveling over this utterly unexpected turn of events.

She'd met Tyler three years earlier when she'd done a piece on crossover productions—American shows that went to the West End, and British companies that came to New York. It had been a major piece involving extensive interviews both in New York and in London, and Tyler Emmons had been one of the British in New York. An unpretentious man with an impressive acting and directing resumé, he'd agreed to an interview, declining her offer of an expense-account lunch and inviting her instead to a Sunday dinner at his sublet apartment in the West Sixties. After a cheese-and-mushroom omelette, salad, French bread, and a bottle of pleasantly woody-tasting Spanish red wine, she'd photographed him in the kitchen as he prepared coffee. The interview had continued over the coffee and then, suddenly, they'd found themselves making love on the living room sofa. Since she wasn't in the habit of going to bed with her subjects, or with men she'd only just met, she'd made a point of treating the event as an accident, and went on her way determined not to think any more about him. Luck and Gracie prevailing, she'd accepted an out-of-town job shortly thereafter and was able, with distance and time constraints, to remain detached.

Her detachment, however, had suffered considerably when, upon arriving home after a three-week absence, she'd found a desiccated floral arrangement outside her front door and several messages from Tyler on her answering machine. The third and final message had given his London address and telephone number, and an expression of his regret at not seeing her again before he left. She'd dutifully entered the information in her address book but made no attempt to contact him on subsequent trips to London. He was married, and she'd always had a horror of finding herself involved in a sordid affair as the "other woman."

She'd also always had trouble understanding men, the things they did, and why. And for reasons still unclear to her, she'd dealt all her adult life from what seemed to be a disadvantaged position with them. With women, too, for that matter. She could interview anyone, she'd often said; but she found "just talking" hard. She also failed to see the prettiness men claimed to admire in her. If anything, being a so-called pretty woman was a help professionally and a hindrance in private life. The men she'd known intimately seemed to have been more interested in the shape of her face than in any intelligence she possessed. Being in love could be hazardous to one's health, like smoking or drinking too much. She told herself it was preferable to remain detached and in control. And so she'd written off their intense interlude as an accident, but that hadn't stopped her from thinking about Tyler from time to time with something like longing.

That evening had been memorable, she thought as she retraced her steps to Henry's house. The two very brief affairs she'd had since had only fused her attention on that single session with Tyler. She'd eaten his food, asked her questions, taken his picture, removed her clothes, and lay down with him. Then he'd insisted on seeing her safely to her car, waiting until she was inside with the engine going before heading back to that apartment whose details and dimensions were even now indelibly imprinted on her brain. And on those occasions when she happened to be over on the West Side in the city, she'd think of Tyler and that apartment. In her mind, he'd never left. Everything remained precisely as it had been on that Sunday evening.

He'd been so unlike other theater people she'd interviewed, so unlike other men she'd met. And, actually, *he'd* removed her clothes, which had made her feel desirable. Being expected to undress herself reduced her interest and desire, making what was about to happen seem more like a medical examination than an exciting encounter. He'd undressed her; he'd praised her; he'd made love to her with an attitude of privilege that had moved and disarmed her. He'd been so attentive and so interested in everything about her that she'd fled from the prospect of finding herself locked into a hopeless romance with him.

In the guest room, she stretched out on the bed for a nap, trying to imagine why fate had conspired to put Tyler back into her life. It was purely happenstance. Yet wasn't it funny how, until she'd seen him again just now, she'd remembered everything about him but the way he looked. Other people, even some she'd seen only once, stood very clear in her memory, especially her mother. She could effortlessly resurrect a portrait of Lily that was perfect even to the faint down that was visible on her forearms in strong sunlight. She could close her eyes and see her mother full-face or in profile, her pointed chin and deep-set gold-brown eyes, the massed weight of the hair at the nape of her neck. Beamer looked so like her that sometimes, seeing him, Jo wondered if their mother hadn't managed to relocate herself after death in her son. He even had Lily's same slow judicious delivery of thoughts and opinions, her same sudden ability to break into motion or laughter. He also had a talent for efficiency and neatness that was Lily to the core. Lily would have fifteen people in for dinner, and when Jo went off to bed, the living and dining rooms would be chaotic with dirty dishes, half-empty wineglasses, overflowing ashtrays; the counters in the kitchen would be lined with pots and pans and sticky wooden spoons; the carpet would be crunchy with the crumbs from French bread. Yet no matter how early the next morning she awakened it would be to find everything immaculate, the counters clean, the sinks empty, the carpets freshly vacuumed, as if no one had cooked or served four courses of a meal to noisy, invited guests. That was Lily.

Jo thought she was more like her father, cautious with her emotions, yet committed utterly to the people for whom she cared. Both she and her father were fiercely devoted to home and their concept of it. It had been her father who'd gone about the house with a proud proprietary air, pausing to admire the way, for example, the sun filtered through the fronds of a Boston fern set on a column in the bay of the dining room windows. Often he'd come home from the office to tie on an apron and prepare the dinner. And when Jo and Beamer had been small children, it had been their father who'd overseen their nightly baths, heard their prayers, then tucked them in for the night; while Lily, preoccupied with plans for some forthcoming dinner party, or with some piece of needlework she was in the throes of designing, came in at the last when the children were barely awake to touch her lips to their foreheads before drifting away, leaving behind the fragrance of Chanel No. 5.

Lily, tall and thin and enigmatic, still drifted through Jo's thoughts, a piece of tramlined canvas half-painted in her hands, one of her husband's white shirts, its sleeves folded above the elbows, holding the light, her long legs pushing against the air. Lily, the old-fashioned, wistful-seeming debutante, had in fact been a model of independent progressiveness; it had been she who'd spotted in Beamer an early and powerful talent for mathematics. She'd come home one afternoon, calling for Beamer to come help her unload the many cartons filling the back of the station wagon: She'd bought him his first computer. And it had been Lily who, in spite of her husband's protests regarding the unsuitability and expense of the gift, had given the seven-year-old Joanna her first 35-mm SLR camera. "I think you need this" was what she'd said when giving the gift into her daughter's hands. "You're visual. I know you, and this is who you are."

Well, Jo was who she was, all right. Lily had certainly known about that. With her camera, or in the darkroom, Jo knew exactly what she was doing and who she was. But without the camera, or outside the darkroom, she was having trouble. There were those times of invisibility, when she felt that her eyes were the only part of her that were visible or functional, when she couldn't imagine why anyone would want to spend time with someone who'd become quite so boring or remote as she could manage to be.

Maybe, she thought, turning on her side as sleep overtook her, she was doing too much, or the wrong kinds of things; maybe she was spending too much time alone, although she did enjoy the apartment and was forever shifting the furniture to find arrangements that better pleased her eye. When she thought of the place, the image she had was of herself in the chair in front of the fireplace, her feet on the ottoman, and snow falling beyond the sliding glass doors. The sky was that deep blue-gray of twilight, and the trees surrounding the complex were black filigree against the night.

Tyler. It was just incredible. . . .

She heard a quiet tapping at the door but couldn't get herself sufficiently awake to respond. The tapping stopped and she allowed herself to slide back into the welcoming depths of her sleep. Then there was a weight on the side of the bed and a light touch on her arm, and she forced her eyes open to see Henry sitting beside her.

"Hi, Henry," she said dopily. "I thought you were out for the evening."

"Hi, Jo. The client canceled." His hand remained a moment longer on her arm, then was withdrawn. "How are you?" he asked softly, as if she were still sleeping.

"I'm fine. How are you?"

"Splendid, thank you. Your friend's waiting. I've given him a drink."

"Oh, my God! What time is it?"

"Five-fifty. He's early."

"Shit, Henry! I think I'm in a coma."

He laughed and again put his hand on her arm. "Take your time. I'll entertain him until you're ready."

"Oh, thank you." She yawned hugely.

He stood up and headed for the door. Halfway there, he turned back to say, "Good to see you," and smiled—very meaningfully, she thought— before going out.

Ten to six. She jumped up, at once understanding Henry's smile— she was half-naked, having slept only in her underpants—and began trying to get ready while at the same time trying to determine how she felt about having held a brief conversation with the man while in a state of near nudity. God! She just couldn't think about it.

Shaky with fatigue, her hands were unsteady as she tried to do something with her hair, abandoned her attempt to put it up and allowed it to hang, then smudged on too much eye shadow. The lighting in the bathroom was dim, flattering; in stronger light she imagined she'd appear overdone. She should've put Tyler off until tomorrow evening. But wasn't it lucky Henry's client had canceled; otherwise no one would've answered the door and Tyler would have gone away wondering why she'd stood him up.

Dressed, she picked up her bag and hurried through to the front of the house, slowing as she approached the living room, to study Tyler in conversation with Henry. The two were standing near the fireplace, drinks in hand. They couldn't have been more different. Tyler had a small bald spot at the crown of his head and had cut his hair very short as if to show he not only knew he was losing his hair, but didn't give a damn. He was taller, thinner, and not as young as Henry. He was, she recalled, in his late forties, although he didn't look it.

Tyler was casually dressed in a pair of blue trousers and an open-necked long-sleeved white shirt. Henry, shorter and somewhat heavier, wore his usual three-piece suit—this one of pale gray. His shirt was white with a pencil-line gray stripe; his tie was of charcoal-gray silk. His hair was closely cropped but abundant. His mustache and beard were neatly trimmed; he had color in his cheeks; his eyes were very clear and very blue; he looked healthy, successful, and amused, as if by some private joke.

She stopped just inside the doorway and waited. She felt awkward, and loathed the feeling she occasionally had of being unequal to certain situations. Her talent and credentials got put on hold and she became someone who automatically stood to one side to observe the proceedings. She blotted her damp palms on a tissue as she waited for the men to notice her.

It was the shifting of Henry's eyes in her direction that alerted Tyler to her presence—and it also reminded her that Henry had, only minutes ago, gazed approvingly at her bared breasts. She blushed as Tyler turned, smiled, said "Aaahh!" and came to kiss her on both cheeks in the Continental fashion that always threw her off guard—the first kiss being expected, the second disconcerting. Henry, she saw, watched with interest and, Jo thought, with something like a proprietary air.

"You look so well, Joanna," Tyler was saying. "It really is wonderful, seeing you again."

"You look very well yourself," she said, feeling like a parrot, and wishing Henry weren't there to hear this inane dialogue.

"A drink?" Henry asked from over by the fireplace.

"I don't think so, thank you, Henry. Not on an empty stomach."

"Something nonalcoholic perhaps?"

"Nothing, thank you."

"Well, in that case." He downed the last of his drink, then said, "I'm off. You know where the key is, Jo dear. Good to meet you, Tyler." He shook hands with Tyler and patted Jo on the shoulder as he passed her. "Lunch tomorrow," he told her. "I'll see you at the office at twelve-thirty."

"Okay. Bye, Henry."

Tyler put his glass down on the coffee table, saying, "I thought I'd give you dinner at my place, if that's all right with you."

"Sure," she agreed.

Outside, he held open the passenger door of his car. "It's a fair distance," he told her, waiting to make sure she got her seat belt properly fastened.

"Whereabouts?" she asked.

"Near Camden Passage. Do you know it?"

"Vaguely. Where all the antique shops are, right?"

"Right."

He drove very fast, whipping in and out of the traffic, passing between cars so closely she just knew they were going to crash. The speed and his aggressive passage along the narrow streets made her nervous. At last, she ventured to say, "I'm afraid I'm a very bad passenger. Would you mind slowing down a bit?"

He glanced over, and for a moment she thought he might take this as a criticism and be offended, but he said, "Sorry, not thinking," and eased back on the accelerator. "I'm not a very good driver," he apologized. "I tend to get distracted, don't think about what I'm doing." He smiled before redirecting his attention to the traffic. "Yours, you'll be happy to know, is not the first complaint. Better?"

"Yes, thank you."

"It really is good seeing you again, Joanna. I thought perhaps I never would."

"How was your visit with your son?"

"Much the same as always. At twelve years of age he has far more important things on his mind than a dreary afternoon visit with old Dad. He was in that dreadful state of being torn between his sense of obligation and a burning need to know the West Indian cricket test scores. We each did our duty, had a walk and some sandwiches at the local pub, brought each other up to date on the events in our lives, then said goodbye. He's a decent boy; heart's in the right place. I love him utterly, hopelessly, stupidly, and try not to let either of us take advantage of my affection for him."

"You have just the one child?"

"Didn't know I had any, did you?" He grinned over at her mischievously.

She smiled, admitting, "No."

"You look sleepy," he said sympathetically. "Jet lag's such a bitch." He glanced again at her. For a very pretty woman, she had no conceit. As a result the impression she'd made initially, and made again upon him now, was contradicted by the way she presented herself. She looked most sophisticated, dressed smartly; altogether she was very nicely assembled.

But her self-effacing, quiet manner, along with her shy smile made her infinitely less formidable than she seemed at first sight. She had warm brown eyes and an exquisite complexion. She was also a superb photographer. He considered the shots she'd done of him to be the best ever. He felt they reflected the man he was, rather than the projection of an image he wanted others to see.

"So what are you doing now?" she asked him.

"Just opened with a nice little four-hander I've directed. Comedy-suspense-whodunit. With luck, it'll have a decent run. Not *The Mousetrap*, but it has potential. Good script; cast's better than all right; fair notices. I don't, however, care any more for the business than I did when we met."

"Doesn't seem as if you do," she agreed.

"It's a bloody great relief not to have to put a face on it for you. Most of the time one's bouncing about raving what a marvelous thing it is, what a super cast, what smashing sets. It's such shit! Never mind that! Tell me about Joanna and what you're doing here!"

"I'm doing a piece on the Orient-Express."

"Oh, lucky you!"

"I guess. It doesn't seem altogether real to me. It probably won't until Sunday morning when I'm actually getting on the train. For some reason I'm very worried about this job."

"Do you usually worry?"

"Sure. About every job, although lately I seem to be getting worse." She looked over, taking quick mental snapshots: His face was freshly shaved, angular, his cheekbones high and slanting, his hazel eyes slightly hooded; strong nose, generous mouth, high forehead. He was a handsome man, one Americans would call rugged. She couldn't think what the British equivalent might be. He was easy to talk to. It was as if they'd seen each other only days before, and her reactions to him were almost as they'd been at their first meeting. There was a place inside her that was especially vulnerable to him, as if long ago he had, in advance of their meeting, reserved a spot in her emotions so that when they met she'd have the sense she did of always having known and been aroused by him.

"Perhaps you need a break," he suggested, "some time to yourself."

"Maybe so." Suddenly, she recalled Henry sitting on the bed beside her, his hand on her arm as he talked softly in the darkened room. Good to *see* you. She suffered another brief spasm of embarrassed confusion and felt her face grow hot. Why had it seemed as if the two of them had played out that scene before? Why had it felt, for a few seconds, as if the next logical step would be Henry's slipping into bed with her?

"Here we are!" Tyler announced, pulling up on the wrong side of the street behind a van.

She looked out to see trim white rows of houses lining both sides of a street that was, by London standards, unusually wide. And the houses were larger than those she'd looked at this morning in Chelsea; spacious two-story dwellings most of which had, from the look of them, been recently renovated.

None of what was happening had been planned, and little of what she'd planned—ever—seemed destined to happen. For a moment she wondered if she was entirely awake, or if she wasn't somehow caught in the unraveling threads of a dream.

She felt a bit guilty about Henry, and wondered if he was bothered by her failing to spend her first evening in town with him. But he'd had plans. And they'd been canceled. So where had he been going? He hadn't said. He'd just effected a smooth exit and gone off. Was he seeing a new woman? she wondered. She hoped not. She didn't think she could survive one more of Henry's women. He had the worst taste, really. After Brenda, there'd been Gillian, one of those awful, horsy British women who smell of oats and leather. She'd lasted about six months. Then there'd been a lull of a year or so before the advent of Francesca, who came and went in less than three months. Then, for about two years, Henry hadn't seen anyone in particular. Jo had stayed with him three times during that period and they'd had good, long, heavily conversational visits. It had all ended with Suzanne, who wound up staying for—what? Four years? Jo had privately feared Henry might actually marry her. But now she was gone. No more Suzanne. Thank God Henry hadn't married her.

"Jo?" Tyler tapped her on the arm. "I said we're here. Are you awake?"

"Oh, right. Sorry."

He held open the door and she lifted her leaden body out of the car.

Four

TYLER'S FLAT WAS BELOW STREET LEVEL, AND SURPRISINGLY MEDITER-
ranean. Running the full length and width of the house, it had terra-cotta-
tiled floors, stark white walls, an ultramodern open-plan kitchen that was
separated from the living room by a serving hatch, and two large airy
bedrooms. The furniture was minimal and plain: a sofa, half a dozen huge
floor pillows, a coffee table, and a wall unit in the living room; an immense bed, side table, and wardrobe in Tyler's bedroom; a single bed,
chest of drawers, and wardrobe in the other bedroom, which was obviously his son's when he came to visit. The bathroom was also very modern, with a heated towel rack, a tub as well as a shower, and a bidet
alongside the toilet. On the walls of the long hallway that ran from the
front door through to the living room were framed posters of plays and
films in which Tyler had appeared or which he'd directed. The only
adornment gracing the living room wall was a large, exquisitely rendered
oil painting of a country scene. Its frame was of ornate scrolled gold-
painted wood, and bore a brass plaque giving the name of the artist and
the title. The artist was Joseph Mallord William Turner.

Jo looked at the engraved name, then stood away to study the painting
again, experiencing a flutter in her chest as she took in the details of the
placid country scene above which, in the distance, darkening clouds gathered menacingly. Her reaction had two distinct levels: The first was composed of awe, even reverence; the second was one of recognition, not of
the painting itself but of childhood afternoons spent at her grandmother's
farm.

Her father's parents had lived on what had been, early in the century, a
working farm. By the time they'd bought the place, the fields had been

reclaimed by wild grasses and weeds. It had been the James family's country home during the early years of their marriage and, after her grandfather's retirement from his law firm in Manhattan, their full-time residence.

Jo barely remembered her grandfather, who'd died when she was five, but she'd adored her grandmother, who'd stayed on at the farm until her death at ninety-two, when Joanna was thirty. And the view from the wide verandah of the old stone house had been very like the one in the painting on Tyler's wall. Looking at it revived the joy of her visits to her grandmother, the summer months she'd spent at the farm as a child. She'd walked with her grandmother through the fields in the late afternoon, feeling the sun on her shoulders and the dry warmth of Granny Emily's hand as they'd made their way at a leisurely pace toward the stream that cut across the northwestern corner of the land.

Granny Emily was the most generously open-hearted person Jo had ever known, a woman prepared to love every newcomer on sight. Smiling, wide-eyed, with tremendous natural enthusiasm, she'd created for Jo some of her happiest memories, the majority of them consisting of revelatory moments when her grandmother pointed out some example of earthly splendor or made some quiet observation about the ways of the world. It was her grandmother who taught Jo how to *see*, to take note of everything around her—the life beneath the wild-growing grasses as well as that beneath the surface of the stream. Always saying "Hush now, look!" she directed the child to be still and to allow her eyes to absorb all the details that might otherwise be missed. There had been many occasions when Jo had sat in one of the wicker porch rockers beside Granny Emily, the two of them silent as they watched a storm approach over the fields. "It's not here yet," her grandmother would say when Jo thought perhaps it was time to go indoors. "Wait awhile and watch." And sure enough, it would take another ten minutes or more before the rain spread itself over the house, forcing them inside. They would sit together on the sofa in the warm-seeming circle of light from the old standing lamp and go through Sears, Roebuck catalogs from fifty years before that Jo had discovered in a box in the attic. "We had a brass bedstead like that when I was a girl," Granny Emily would say of an advertisement. "Twenty-two dollars was a fortune back then. Imagine that!" Or they'd giggle together over the corsets tied onto wasp-waisted women who seemed, in the illustrations, to have no difficulties breathing. "Be glad they've done away with those contraptions," Granny Emily told her. "I'm sure it's why we all dropped like flies, fainting dead away of a summer afternoon."

Granny Emily's heart simply ceased beating one night, according to the nurse-companion who spent eight years with her at the last. "When I go," said Peggy, who'd also adored Emily, "I'd sure like it to be that way. Just close my eyes at the end of a good day and sleep my passage into heaven."

Dragging her attention away from the painting, Jo turned toward the kitchen, where Tyler was uncorking a bottle of wine. I could live here, she thought, and said, "This is a great apartment."

"It has its drawbacks," he said, but without intensity.

"You even have a lovely little patio," she noticed, looking out past the French doors.

"It's bloody cold in the winter," he explained, coming over to give her a glass of white wine. "And there's a drainage problem out there." He inclined his head toward the patio. "On the plus side, there's a laundry room, as well as several other storerooms I haven't quite decided what to do with. And it's wonderfully cool in the summer. It's also, incidentally, tripled in value since I bought it three years ago. This area's gone very trendy. It was in a transitional stage when I moved in. Used to be mainly West Indians here back in the sixties. Now it's chock-a-block with the British version of yuppies. Come sit down, Joanna."

He sank down on the sofa, propping his feet on the coffee table. "I'm afraid you're about to learn the truth about me." He smiled at her.

"What truth?" she asked, joining him.

"Aside from stews in winter, I can't cook much more than omelettes. And if I recall correctly, I dazzled you the last time with one of those."

"That's all right. It was terrific."

"Thank God!" He laughed softly, then took a swallow of wine.

"Is it a real Turner?" She shifted around for another look at the painting.

He, too, looked, then smiled and leaned across to kiss her cheek.

"You are such a dear little person" he said affectionately. "It is indeed real. My great-grandfather spent rather a large portion of his inheritance to acquire it. My son will own it one day, and, with good luck, his son after him. It's all any of the men in the family have had in the way of a fortune to pass along."

"I'd say it was a lot."

"I feel that way," he agreed. "Of course, at twelve, Jeremy would prefer to think he'd inherit the Jaguar. I had to explain to him that if I dropped dead tomorrow, by the time he was of an age to drive, what he'd inherit would be a rusting great pile of scrap metal. He had the idea the car would get parked in the garage alongside his mother's and would simply be there, waiting for him. That was assuming I was going to drop dead in the very immediate future." He laughed. "I honestly think he was a little disappointed about that."

"There's nothing wrong with you, is there?"

"Not a thing," he assured her, "beyond the usual ravages of advancing old age."

"You're not that old. It's very nice out there," she said, her eyes again on the patio. "Do you use it much?"

"Not so far this summer, what with the show. We were supposed to have a provincial tour, but the plans were changed and they let us open early because a theater came available. How pretty you are, Joanna."

"Oh, no," she said quietly, automatically, still looking at the patio, liking the disparity of the shadowy enclosed area and the still-light sky above; rich, trailing vines crept down the walls from some unseen garden above. There was something mysterious, even faintly ominous about the damp-looking cement patio floor and the darkly green potted plants massed in one corner.

"Oh, yes," he insisted equally quietly, taking hold of her hand and thereby drawing her attention back to him. "Lovely dark eyes," he said, his hand lifting to touch her cheek, "beautiful skin."

She sat immobilized, listening, waiting, breathing slowly, cautiously. She was fascinated by his interest in her.

He studied her for quite some time, trying to work beyond her denial of prettiness to its actuality. She was, he thought, the embodiment of prettiness: her heart-shaped face enclosed by the in-curving sweep of her thick brown hair with its razor-edged fringe falling just to her eyebrows, its darkness contrasting wonderfully with her pale, flawless complexion; her eyes wide-set and perfectly round, long-lashed and almost black; her nose small and well placed, her mouth deliciously bowed, her chin daintily cleft. He had, from their initial meeting, very much liked the look of her. He wondered if he'd ever commented to her on how strongly she reminded him of Louise Brooks as Lulu. He didn't think he had. It was the hair, mainly, that blunted cut, longer than Lulu's but otherwise the same. And the expressiveness of those eyes, the uptilting corners of her mouth. A dear little person, with a dear little face. And, as he well remembered, a most mature expressive little body; narrow-hipped, small-waisted, with beautiful breasts that were absolutely symmetrical and not too large for her frame.

He knew she was watching him, but for the moment he was too absorbed in studying her, and deriving too much pleasure from the act, to break the spell. He wanted just another few seconds to remind himself of the details, of the appeal of her somewhat stubborn chin and her slightly lowered eyelids. He found even her makeup—a touch of color in her cheeks and around her eyes—rather touching. And what fascinated him most was the dichotomy between this quiescent creature silently sitting next to him and the woman she was when working. The two seemed unrelated. In repose, she didn't appear to be capable of the work he knew she did—especially the photography.

Again he touched the back of his hand to her cheek, watching as he did the way her eyes widened oh-so-subtly in response.

"I saw this woman this morning, taking photographs down by the Embankment, and I thought, 'How like Joanna she is! How very like Joanna.' Then I came closer, and you turned and pointed your camera in my direction, and I thought, 'My God! It is Joanna!' And I told myself it simply wasn't possible. There I was in Chelsea for a breakfast chat with the show's producers. I'm rarely in Chelsea, and rarely first thing in the morning. And who should I see but the one woman on earth I truly thought I'd never see again." His hand stroked her cheek and she thought, irrationally, that he must be a good father because he had a gentle touch, a personal touch, as if he was a man who demonstrated his fondness through his fingertips and open palm. "Joanna," he said softly, taking his caress to her hair.

Her response to his approach was immediate and spontaneous. She was simply ignited. His hand went under her skirt, his mouth opened on hers, and she couldn't think at all. Dazed, she watched him undo her blouse, watched him apply his hands to her breasts, and felt she might stop breathing altogether. He whispered, "Jesus Christ, Joanna!" and reached under her skirt with both hands. She lifted, helping, then closed her eyes and clutched his shoulders as he slid to his knees on the floor and held her to his mouth. Incendiary caresses; then he moved abruptly away from her and she opened her eyes, a maddened accomplice, to see him rising in front of her. Dragging her with him, he sank down on one of the floor pillows, pushed her skirt out of the way and brought her down on his lap, both of them tugging at his trousers. Panting as if they'd just run a race, his hands on her hips brought her forward; he surged to meet her, held her steady, made an entry into her body that was smoothly triumphal, then directed her into a demented dance that ended with noisy finality, followed by sudden silence. She lay against his chest with her head on his shoulder, formless and deadened as if he'd found some hidden zipper through which he'd removed her skeleton.

"I've been wanting to do that for three years," he said, almost angrily, holding her very tightly. "Why the hell did you run away from me in New York?"

She shook her head, unable yet to find her voice, and wondered why she'd allowed this to happen. He'd closed in on her so quickly she hadn't had time to think. It was exactly what he'd done in New York.

"I thought you didn't care, Joanna. I thought perhaps it hadn't been as rare and delightful as I'd thought. You flew away and didn't respond to my flowers or telephone messages. I was inept, or heavy-handed, or had completely misread the signs. I thought I'd made an utter ass of myself."

"No," she said quietly. "None of those things. *I* thought it was casual."

"Oh, I see. Three years later, it turns out you think I'm one of those casual fuckers, so cocky and confident I'll have any woman available."

"That isn't what I thought."

"But how was I to know that? I could only interpret your silence as disinterest, or possibly disgust. It had to be that I'd repelled you, this grunting, sweating, middle-aged man trying to prove himself of interest to a sweet young woman."

"It wasn't that way at all. Is that how you think of yourself?" She found the strength to sit away and look at him.

"Not as a matter of course. But in recent times, yes. I spoke to you on the telephone and agreed to the interview, thinking you'd be another half-assed journalist intent on self-promotion. Then you arrived and you were nothing of the sort. You were so keen, so bloody aware of externals, so gentle and unassuming, and so totally unaware of yourself. All the while we talked I kept looking for the chinks in the performance, but it was entirely real. You hadn't the least idea how adorable you were. And it hasn't changed."

"Tyler, you were *married.*"

He stared at her for a long moment, then gave a bitter-sounding laugh. "No," he told her. "No! Not only did you think I was a casual fucker, you thought I also casually fucked around on my wife. No, no, no!"

He held her face in his hands and said, "I've been married. Twice. My first was a qualified disaster that ended some fourteen years ago. And my second, my poor second marriage, it . . . What happened to it? It was euthanized about five months before you and I met. Neither of us wanted it to end, Joanna, but it had to be put to sleep, rather like a big old family pet that had outlived its ability to do more than eat from its bowl and dream for hours at a stretch in front of the fire. I was devoted to Dianne. I believe it was mutual. God only knows, we went through the wars together. But it all just slowly, sadly trickled away. We outgrew our need for each other. It was *over* when I met you, Joanna." He withdrew his hands from her face and waited for her response.

She couldn't, for a moment, meet his eyes. She shook her head, and the movement caused her hair to swing forward over her face, leaving strands caught in her eyelashes. She didn't want to consider the implications of her flight three years before. It was too humiliating, evidence of her fearfulness and her inability either to trust her own instincts or what she seemed to see without a lens to look through. She'd run away, believing she'd made a bad judgment call. She didn't ever want to be some man's well-kept secret.

"I thought it was because I was there, I was handy and willing," she confessed. "And then afterward, the flowers and all, well, you were just being nice because that's the way you were: nice. It was the kind of thing I thought you'd do."

"I see. Well," he smiled at her, "I am nice. But not *that* nice. I was very taken with you. It seemed not to be reciprocal. A fine kettle of fish, wouldn't you say?"

She smiled at him. "My grandmother used to say that."

"Did she now?"

"Yes, she did."

"Are you going to run away again, Joanna?"

"I don't know. I don't know what's happening."

"What's happening," he said, "at this very moment, is pure, requited, unadulterated bloody lust." He underscored each word so carefully, so dramatically, that she had to laugh.

"I'm not completely stupid, Tyler. That part I definitely understood."

"Good! Then understand this: I am forty-nine years old, and my past history is against me. I admit that absolutely. I'm in no position to make rash promises, so I will do my utmost not to promise you anything I can't deliver. I'm also in no position to make expensive emotional mistakes, nor would I ever wish to hurt you in any way. I haven't the foggiest where this is headed, and I have no intention of pushing one way or another. I would simply like both of us to give it a chance, see where we get to."

She remained very still, wishing, just for once in her life, she could manage to integrate the two too-distinct halves of her self so that her decisions, when she made them, would be rooted in a confidence born of age and experience. Maybe it was never going to happen. Maybe she'd spend the rest of her life relying on her career to give her credibility. She hated the thought of that, even despaired of it. She'd permitted Greg to persuade her into four years of turmoil. All she knew for certain was that never again was anyone going to push her into a commitment about which she had doubts. And she was far too tired at that moment to make a decision about anything.

"What you said before, about the way what happened made you feel. Was that really the truth?" she asked, looking at the remains of their meal on the coffee table.

"Actually, it was somewhat less than the whole truth. If anything, I understated it. I think we all have these snapshots of ourselves we carry about in mental portfolios. We see ourselves as this or that, and we behave in ways we think are commensurate with those images. Then, when things don't go quite as we'd imagined they would, it seems those pocket snaps are invalidated, inaccurate. I was embarrassed," he conceded. "I was under the impression that you and I were at the brink of something very good. Then, a few weeks later, I felt like the biggest fool, self-deluding, out of touch, *old*. I'm not able to speak for other people, but when that sort of thing happens, I've a tendency to reexamine events and my part in them, and to decide I missed something or performed less than brilliantly. Possibly, it has to do with having spent the better part of my life either acting or directing actors, playing out roles while trying to keep a grip on who I really am. Most actors, you know, simply aren't home. They're grateful to the theater or to films for allowing them to slip into a persona that seems to fit for a time. I've always had a vested interest in being myself. It's why I've got rather a lot of contempt—intermittently, I admit—for acting."

"Then why do it?" she asked.

"It's the family business," he said with a smile. "My father and mother were both in the theater. Mother gave it up when she became pregnant with my sister, but Father stayed in it to his death. The only one of the three children who didn't go into the business is my brother Michael.

"It seemed eminently reasonable to me as a child that I'd follow my father and older sister into the theater. I made my first appearance at age seven in *A Midsummer Night's Dream*, and that was that. It wasn't until I was in my mid-twenties and married to Elizabeth, my first wife, who happened to be a hugely successful film actress and considerably older than I, that it occurred to me that pretending to be other people for money was an absurd way to earn a living. It suited Elizabeth perfectly, because her entire existence was a masterly performance. But I began to feel a fraud, and dishonest. Plus, I'd always loathed the more humiliating aspects of the business: the rigged auditions, the repeated call-backs, the necessity of burying one's native intelligence in order not to offend some director.

"On the plus side, nothing is quite so thrilling as a production that's all of a piece, when everything works and both you and the audience get caught up in the singular magic of a successful production. It's the hook that keeps you coming back. I would rather, however, be a photojournalist."

"Oh, no you wouldn't," she disagreed. "I think maybe we all wind up where we're supposed to be."

"Perhaps. But what you have, what you do is tangible, readily marketable. You're also highly gifted."

"It's strange, you know," she said, thinking back. "When I came to interview you, I was having a lot of trouble because I couldn't get any kind of a fix on you. There didn't seem to be one definitive, distinctive 'attitude' that was intrinsically you. You know? And then, when you got up to make the coffee, you unbuttoned your cuffs and rolled up your sleeves, and there it was."

"There *what* was?" he wanted to know, liking very much the change that overtook her when she talked about her work. She became articulate, confident, even forceful; she seemed to acquire crisper edges and stronger definition. She knew what she was about, didn't grope for words, didn't hesitate; she just allowed her visions to acquire tangibility.

"It. You. I knew who you were because of the attention you paid to grinding the beans, even to warming the coffee pot. I'd never seen anyone warm a coffee pot. It was so *idiosyncratic*. I had the picture then, in my mind. You know? And once I've got that, then actually taking the photograph becomes secondary."

"Are you aware," he asked her, most curious, "that you change when you've got a camera in your hands? It's true. I remember so vividly the way you actually seemed to alter physically. You were like a dancer, bending or stretching to frame the shot you wanted. I can still see you crouching in the corners of that kitchen, clicking away at me and murmuring to yourself as I tried very hard to pay attention to the normally simple routine of making a pot of coffee. Just a little unnerving it was, my dear, witnessing your transformation from soft-spoken, polite interviewer to aggressive, self-assured photographer. Altogether impressive, it was; changing lenses, adjusting the focus, moving closer, then away. I swear, it was as if the camera was some vital prosthetic device and with it in your hands you became suddenly complete.

"I mean to say, I found you pleasant enough during dinner. But the moment you opened your bag to take out the camera, you became positively compelling, electric. Like a sprite, you darted here and there, watching me through the viewfinder, your body sinuously insinuating itself into impossible spaces. And while you were snaking about the place, making me feel more of an observer than a participant, I might add, I was suddenly, seriously attracted to you. All at once, I noticed your hands, and the shape of your face, your ankles. I thought I'd like nothing better than to have you around for months so that I could watch you lose yourself to a process I seemed to know."

"How?" she asked, her head tilted to one side. "I don't know what you mean."

"Your description of the mental processes you go through to take your photographs isn't so very different from directing, you know. Both have to do with visualizing something and then attempting to make good on what you've seen."

She stared at him appreciatively, finding that receptive place inside herself expanding. "I think you're right. I'll bet if you tried, you'd probably take good photographs."

"That's your obsession, my dear. Mine has to do, if you will, with *tableaux vivants*. Similar, but different."

If she wasn't very careful, she thought, she'd fall in love with him. Then she wondered why that would be a bad thing. She knew very little about him, except what he was revealing to her now.

"Did you go to theater school, Tyler?"

"Learned by doing. School of trial and error."

"Maybe" she said tangentially, "no one's ever really completely happy."

"On a professional level," he answered soberly, "I think that would be deadly. If one grows satisfied, one's work tends to become stale. Satisfaction breeds smugness and a certain brand of fear. If you succeed at something, if it works well once, there's a tremendous temptation to keep on doing things that same way, over and over. When you take that route, you lose your freshness, your spark, the excitement generated by risk-taking."

Risk-taking? Was that what she did? She didn't think so. "I'm very tired, Tyler." All at once, the last of her energy was draining away. "Do you mind if I use your shower?" She was horrified by the idea of returning to the Chelsea house, possibly encountering Henry, with the evidence of her love-making with another man still wet on her flesh.

"Oh, terribly," he laughed. "Of course I don't mind. Come. I'll fetch you a towel." He held his hand out to her. "I've talked your ear off and here you are, poor dear, with your bloody jet lag."

He opened the door to the linen cupboard, removed a large sunflower-yellow towel and gave it to her, saying, "This is a good color for you, I think. I'll just clear away the dishes while you bathe, then run you back to Chelsea. You have everything you need?" he asked, his hand on the door.

"Yes, thank you."

He went out and she stood holding the towel, wondering why it was that things never happened when you were ready for them.

Five

"WHEN WILL I SEE YOU?" TYLER ASKED, HIS HAND ON HER ARM preventing her from leaving the car. "You can't just fly off without making a definite date for us to meet."

For a few seconds she couldn't think. Then she said, "Saturday. But it'll have to be an early night. I'll be packing, getting ready to leave Sunday morning."

"Saturday it is." He smiled at her, but she seemed preoccupied. "Is something wrong, Joanna?"

"Tyler," she began, then stopped, turning to look at him. "Tyler," she started again, "don't count on me. What I mean is, I don't know how I feel, and I never do know until I've had a chance to back away a bit and think things through."

"I see," he said stiffly.

"No, you don't," she disagreed. "It has to do with me, Tyler, not so much with you. I can't go into it right now. It's late and I'm falling asleep on my feet. We'll talk on Saturday. Okay?"

He stared into space for a moment, then turned and smiled, saying, "Of course. I'll see you to the door."

"No, that's all right." She leaned across the seat to give him a quick kiss. "I like you a lot. I liked you three years ago, and I like you now. The person I have the problem with is me. What time Saturday?"

"Six?"

"Great. I'll see you then." She got out, walked to the door, fished the key out of the flowerpot, and let herself in.

Henry called out "Hello!" from the living room, and she walked inside to see him sitting in one of the armchairs, his tie loosened, a glass of white wine in his hand.

"Hi, Henry." She leaned against the door and looked in at him. He seemed happy to see her and beamed at her from the depths of the chair. One of the things that appealed to her about Henry was seeing in his face the schoolboy he'd once been. Despite his sophistication and his always proper style of dress, the schoolboy aspect was, to her mind, one of the most likable parts of Henry. He consistently looked as if he'd just emerged from a barbershop, with his hair trimmed in a side-parted style that had lately come back into fashion. His mustache and Vandyke beard were meticulously maintained yet the sight of them made her smile involuntarily because they seemed like a disguise the boy had adopted in order to make himself appear more mature.

"Could I get you a drink?" he asked. "A glass of wine?"

She shook her head.

"A cup of tea?"

"No, thanks. I've got to go to bed. I can hardly keep my eyes open."

"Poor you. Have a nice evening?"

"Uh-huh. How're you? Everything okay?"

"Everything is splendid, thank you. Business as usual. Run along to bed now, and I'll see you at the office tomorrow."

"You love being an agent," she said. "How does someone get to love being an agent? All those writers calling up to complain."

"Not quite. It's certainly not boring. *You're* not boring and you're one of those writers."

"Henry, I'm one of the most boring people I know."

"Shame on you," he chided. "You certainly are not."

She sighed, then said, "I should've turned this one down. I have an awful feeling it's going to be a disaster."

"It'll be sublime. I wish I were going."

"I wish you were, too," she said, surprising them both.

"Very kind of you." He saluted her with his glass before taking another swallow of wine. "I thought you were off to bed."

"I am. You're so sweet, Henry. You really are. All those notes!" She laughed softly. "Eat me, Alice. Honest to God!"

He gave a self-deprecating shrug.

"You know something?" she asked, desperately sleepy yet anxious to continue talking with him. "You always remind me of a naughty schoolboy. It's what I see when I look at you."

He laughed hugely, then exclaimed, "You've caught me out! That is precisely and specifically what I am. *Hart Minor!*" he declaimed in a low rumble. "*Step out into the corridor and remain there until sent for!*" His laughter grew, sending tears to his eyes. "Hart Minor! You are in disgrace! We do not draw rude pictures in our copybooks! You will see me after class! *Hart Minor*, you are doomed to failure; you are utterly without redeeming graces! You are a filthy, disobedient little slug!" He wiped his eyes on his shirt sleeve. "I was an appalling schoolboy, forever going about with food stains on my jacket, tie askew, blots on my copybooks; sent time and again to Coventry for transgressions against the established decorum. On my last day the headmaster declared it wouldn't in the least surprise him to read one day in the newspapers that I'd been sentenced to Wormwood Scrubs for some truly heinous act against humanity. Christ!" Again he blotted his eyes. "I haven't laughed this hard in decades."

"What is 'Minor'?" she asked from the doorway, quietly captivated by his performance. He'd obviously been sitting drinking wine for some time. He wasn't anywhere near drunk, just nicely uninhibited.

"When you have two or more boys in an English school with the same surname, the younger or the one with lesser standing becomes minor."

"Oh! I thought it was like junior."

"No."

"I take it Suzanne's gone."

He nodded.

"D'you— miss her, Henry?"

"Not bloody likely. Do you miss what-was-his-name, Greg?"

"No, but that ended years ago. And you were with her for ages."

"History. It's better than five months since she left."

"I used to get the impression she wasn't fond of you having your clients stay here."

"There was," he said with a philosophical air, "a great deal Suzanne wasn't fond of. In the end, I wasn't especially fond of *her*."

"But don't you miss having someone around?"

"Yes and no." He set his wineglass down, got up and came across the room. "Are you aware that your eyes keep dropping shut?" He raised her chin with his cupped hand. "I think we'd best put you to bed, Jo. Come along." He took her hand and led her along the hallway to the guest room. Like a zombie she allowed him to direct her, feeling safe with Henry as she rarely did with anyone else. She stood and watched him straighten the bedclothes, then fold them back invitingly. "There you go," he said. "All you have to do is climb in, close your dear eyes, and go off to Noddy Land."

She laughed but didn't move. "I'm wondering," she told him, "if it's possible—to sleep standing up."

"Possible but not comfortable. Are you going to be able to manage?"

"Oh, sure," she answered, still unmoving.

He stood watching her. Again her eyes began to close. Amused, hands on his hips, he said, "This will never do. You'll ruin my reputation as a hotelier. Imagine having to put the guests to bed!"

Her eyes opened. "What?"

"Don't plan on this as a regular service. Smart top," he said, somewhat hesitantly approaching her.

"You like it? It's Claude Montana. Cost about the same as a small car."

He laughed. "Snaps. Thank God!"

"*Story of O* wardrobe," she quipped as he got her out of the blouse, then unzipped the skirt.

"You're supposed to help," he protested, daunted by her undergarments.

"Never mind, Henry. Just point me in the right direction."

"You're not drunk, are you?" he wanted to know, propelling her over to the bed.

"Only had two glasses of wine." She bumped into the side of the bed, turned and abruptly sat.

He gave her a little push and she obligingly lay down. He covered her with the blankets and watched as she moved beneath them. Then her arm emerged and she dropped her underwear over the side of the bed.

"You're supposed to tuck me in and give me a goodnight kiss," she told him.

"I'd like to remind you I am not your father."

"Hurry up!" She extended her arms straight up in the air and he bent to kiss her on the forehead. "Thank you," she murmured. "You smell good." She closed her eyes again, at once feeling the hum of jet engines in her body.

While he watched, her body visibly settled into a deep and immediate sleep. Stifling a laugh, he turned off the light and tiptoed out to return to his chair in the living room and the last of his wine.

An insistent mechanical beeping roused her. She opened her eyes, trying to figure out where she was and what was making the noise. The only thing on the bedside table, aside from a lamp, was a portable radio. She picked it up and held it as it continued, like some peculiar robotlike little creature, to give off its offended beeps. She pushed and pressed all its buttons and finally succeeded in silencing the alarm. Returning the clock-radio to the table, she saw the note Henry had left stuck to the lampshade. "See you at twelve-thirty. A most enjoyable performance last night. Your hotelier in good faith, H."

She smiled and sat up.

In the guest bathroom there was another note, this one stuck to the mirror. "Hope you're planning to have dinner with me this evening.

Unless you have another date, you'll have to. In your absence, I ravished the Eat-me chicken. Cheers, H."

She laughed, peeled the Post-it from the mirror and dropped it into the wastebasket.

Henry kept her waiting for almost twenty minutes. Sitting in the reception area, she began to wonder if his keeping her waiting for so long meant something. It didn't feel right. The receptionist appeared intentionally to avoid Jo's eyes, and as more time passed all sorts of negative possibilities occurred to her: Henry was miffed at having had to put her to bed last night; something had gone wrong with her assignment and he was frantically trying to set it right before he saw her; he was angry with her about Tyler for some reason. She'd never had a date come to pick her up at Henry's house. Maybe he hadn't liked that.

By the time he emerged from his inner office, she just knew she was in trouble of some kind. This conviction was compounded by his failure to apologize for keeping her waiting, and by his curt greeting, which consisted only of a nod. His face was tight, even angry, and he remained silent as they left the building together. Her reaction was to draw herself together inside, and to harbor a mounting anger of her own. Two men now, in the space of just hours, had pressured her in some way. Was it something about her that made them behave this way? She couldn't see that it was.

Without bothering to say where they were going, he walked very quickly, cutting in and out of the midday crowds, toward the restaurant he'd booked into for lunch. His pace and continuing silence heightened her anger. She looked into the faces of people they passed, seeing colors and styles of dress she liked, and wished she'd brought the camera. She'd have preferred to be wandering around taking pictures rather than trying to figure out why Henry was behaving as he was.

And what kind of an idiot was she? she demanded of herself, hurrying to keep up with his wild dash along the streets. She had to be some kind of jerk to give in so easily—the way she had last night, for example, with Tyler. It made her squirm to think what a pushover she was. And there it was! She'd been anticipating this rush of self-hatred since leaving Tyler the night before. It was what she'd tried to warn him about: she was unreliable, except where her work was concerned.

There was a short queue at the restaurant and they had to stand in the foyer with half a dozen others while the hostess seated the earlier arrivals. Jo couldn't look at Henry. He could go to hell. She'd reserve a hotel room for her return stay after Venice. She'd get the article done, then go home without seeing Henry or Tyler. She didn't care if she never saw either of them again.

"What's the *matter* with you?" she snapped finally. "I don't think I want to eat with you, Henry. My grandmother always said you should never eat with people you don't like or who make you uncomfortable. Right now, you're making me very uncomfortable. You haven't said a word to me, just marched me along here."

He looked totally taken aback by her outburst. His eyes stayed on her, but she could tell he was hoping no one was listening. She could also tell he was trying to come up with something to say to her. When he didn't speak, she said, "That's it! I'm leaving!" and turned to go.

She got all the way out the door and onto the street before he caught up with her, catching hold of her arm.

"I am sick and tired of accepting weird shit from people that makes me feel as if I did something wrong I'm supposed to know about, but don't. You kept me waiting for ages, Henry, then you came out and you might as well have snapped my leash, just expecting me to trot along after you. I shouldn't have come to stay with you. In fact, I'm going to go get my stuff right now and check into a hotel. I'm so *tired* of being expected to understand everything." She stood glaring at him, ready to storm off.

"Joanna, I'm sorry. It's been a perfectly foul morning, and I'm afraid I simply wasn't thinking."

"Go to hell, Henry! I have foul mornings every day of the world and I still manage to be polite to people."

She was so angry her face was scarlet. "Look," he said placatingly. "If I've been rude, it was completely unintentional, and I apologize most sincerely."

"I'm also tired of people not thinking. I don't need this. I *really* don't need this. You were so darling to me last night, Henry. I was totally wiped out and you were an angel. But that was last night and you'd had your wine and were nicely oiled. Now it's today and I'm just another pain-in-the-ass client."

"That is most assuredly *not* how I think of you," he said emphatically. "I apologize for keeping you waiting, and for not speaking to you. I *wasn't* thinking; I was distracted. Please, let me give you lunch and we'll set things to rights."

"I don't want to eat with you, Henry. At least, not in there."

"Fair enough," he said quickly, gamely. "We'll go somewhere else."

"Forget it! I'm not hungry. Why do men *do* these things, as if women aren't people, don't deserve the same courtesy you give each other? All you guys slapping each other on the backs, all so full of it. I *hate* men. With all my heart, I hate men!"

"Aahhh, now!" He smiled at her. "You know you don't really hate me, Jo. Now, I've apologized, and rather nicely, too, I think. I refuse to accept your thesis that men are more polite to each other than they are to women. At least I, for one, don't subscribe to that policy. You've scolded me thoroughly; I am abject. I propose that I pop into one of the take-away places along here, get some sandwiches, then we'll sit down somewhere safely neutral where I will tell you about my morning and you will confide to me the real reason for your anger."

Accepting her failure to reply as agreement, he hurried into a take-away place and returned in a few minutes carrying a white paper bag.

"There are some benches just along here," he told her.

Luckily, there was an empty one. She chose to sit as far from him as she was able. Smiling inwardly, he doled out the contents of the bag—two cheese-and-chutney sandwiches and two containers of tea—then, as he unwrapped his sandwich, he observed, "I've never known you to be temperamental. I am very sorry to have upset you. I truly don't know what I was thinking of, treating you in that fashion. Sometimes, I think we do and say things, behave in certain ways because no one thinks to stop us. In that regard, I may be rather spoiled. Certainly no one in the office would dare say a word. I am, after all, their employer. But, Jo, I do believe you trust me. Otherwise, I think you'd have said nothing." He gazed penetratingly at her for a moment, then continued. "If that trust didn't exist, you wouldn't have blasted me quite so thoroughly. We tend to display our true feelings only to those from whom we believe we'll receive an honest response. So now, why don't you tell me what's upset you."

She looked away. The untouched sandwich sat on her lap. She could feel the July heat beating down on the top of her head, soaking into her clothes. She despised herself.

Failing to get any reaction from her, Henry, between hungry bites of his sandwich, said, "I'll enlighten you about my morning. I began the day with a light step, cheery and optimistic. Arrived at the office, and within mere minutes, the crises began. First came the telex having to do with the loss, the actual, physical loss, of a manuscript that was being sent by courier from one of our authors to his publisher. It's been missing for *six* days, and the damned book's already behind schedule. Then, not one but two authors rang up to point out errors we'd completely missed in their contracts. *Then*, the bank manager informed me that a very substantial check we'd paid in from a supposedly highly reputable foreign publisher had bounced sky-high. On and on, climaxing with an hysterical editor screaming—and justifiably—over an author's having removed all the editorial flags from a manuscript, thereby incapacitating the poor editor. Minor madness. You look especially pretty this morning. The sun's turned your hair quite red. You must forgive me, Jo. Surely you know I'd never want to upset you in any fashion."

"How come hardly anybody tries to anticipate the effects of the things they say and do?" she asked, still not looking at him. "I practically kill myself trying not to step on people's feelings, to be thoughtful and considerate. And I wind up every single time feeling steam-rollered. Never mind *feeling* it, I *am* steam-rollered. I just go along and let myself be used because I don't have the brains or something to say 'Wait a minute!' Nobody gives you any time."

"What's happened, Jo?"

"You'd think I was old enough to know better. I like the light," she said confusingly. "Maybe I'll go back to your place and get the camera."

"You haven't eaten, and you haven't said you accept my apology."

"I'm really not hungry. And I do accept your apology, Henry. I can't tell you what happened. It would be tacky and indiscreet, especially since I haven't actually figured it out for myself yet."

"It might help to talk about it."

"I've got to stop letting these things happen to me. That's really what I'm angry about. Anyway," she took a deep breath, "I should go back. I've got notes to make about the train."

"If you're certain. You will have dinner with me, won't you?"

"Oh, sure. Why not?"

"Don't make it sound like a chore, Jo. I'm really very fond of you, you know."

"Since when? You've never shown one bit of nonprofessional interest in me in ten years. Are you sure you haven't decided to be fond of me because of Tyler?"

"That's nasty!" he accused.

"You're right, it is. I'm sorry. I don't know about you, Henry, but I think I'd rather take photographs of the world right now than get bogged down in the middle of it. Honest to God. You have no idea how nice people can be when you're on a shoot. They'll get out of your way, stand back and watch respectfully for ages. Most people think you're doing something really special and they admire that."

"That's because you *are* doing something special. I've only seen the end result, of course, but I imagine people are able to see quite readily that you not only know what you're on about but that you're very bloody good at it, to boot. It is not, however, possible or healthy to stay forever on the outside looking in. Sooner or later, whether or not we much care for it, we're bound to get involved. And it's up to you to control your own life. Now, I won't preach any more at you. But humor me: Eat."

She unwrapped the sandwich, stared at it for some moments, then picked up one of the quarters. "You're being too nice," she complained, most of her anger lost. "How can I keep on being mad when you're being so reasonable?"

"You can't."

She looked over to find him smiling at her.

"Can you?" he coaxed, anxious to be back on good terms with her.

"No." In spite of herself, she had to respond to his smile. "Why do I like you, Henry?"

"Because I represent the quintessential best of British manhood."

"Oh, right! How could I have forgotten that? Silly me."

"Eat that, Jo dear, before it goes stale."

"The best of British manhood," she scoffed.

"You have an impressive temper."

"Thank you."

"You're welcome."

Six

"GEORGES NAGELMACKERS WAS STRONGLY IMPRESSED BY THE AMERI-can, George Pullman. Pullman's first car, Pioneer, influenced every luxury train coach for nearly half a century. Nagelmackers' meetings with Pullman renewed his interest in his dream of a transcontinental European express."

She put down her pen, giving her eyes a rest while she considered what she'd been reading. Pioneer had been too big and too heavy to be used on the rails existing at the time, so it had sat on a siding for months, a great big beautiful curiosity—until the assassination of President Lincoln. Then, Pullman had offered his carriage to Mrs. Lincoln to carry the president's body. The rails along the route were widened and Pullman's creation moved into history. How, she wondered, had he come up with that idea? Had he done it out of some genuine desire to be of service to his country, or had he made the offer knowing that both he and the carriage would benefit from the attention it was bound to receive on its stately journey? Probably both. Pretty damned clever of old Pullman.

She looked again through the article, trying to find a hook upon which she might hang her own piece. Yes, there was the tie-in between the train and the hotel, but the article needed a viewpoint and she didn't have one yet. Undoubtedly, she would find it once she'd actually been on the train, and it wasn't normally something she worried about in advance. Yet here she was, worrying about it, and thinking it a shame that the dates were a little off, otherwise she could have tied the inaugural run of the Orient-Express on October 4, 1883, to its "second start" on May 25, 1982. Maybe she could use that anyway. She chewed on the end of her ballpoint pen as she scanned the list she'd made of important facts. It all sounded so removed and dry, so unreal. "The Train of Kings, the King of Trains." Maybe that had impressed people a hundred years ago, but nowadays not a whole lot was impressive—to anyone. People had seen and done it all; the most remote places were accessible and a lot of folks had the money for the fare. What could she possibly say about this train that hadn't already been said dozens of times before? Hers certainly wasn't the first piece to be written on the VS-O-E.

Agitated, she got up and went to the kitchen to put on the kettle. While she waited for it to come to a boil, she stared out at Henry's beautiful garden. A long, narrow enclosure, it was surrounded on three sides by high brick walls. Down the right-hand side and along the rear wall Henry had planted tiers of flowers and shrubs, with tall perennials rearmost and low-to-the-ground annuals front-most, and careful attention paid to color. On a circular bricked area halfway down the garden sat a round white-painted metal table and four graceful chairs. A red-and-white-striped Cinzano umbrella sheltered the grouping from the sun. Trees from the neighboring gardens provided shade in the early morning and late afternoon, casting dappled patterns over the grass and flowers.

She wondered if she, like Katharine Hepburn in *Summertime*, might take a humiliating spill in some polluted canal, or be pursued by some fabulously handsome Rossano Brazzi–type Venetian. Oh, sure! That kind of stuff only happened in movies. And hadn't Hepburn developed some kind of permanent eye infection from taking that movie dive into the canal? And why had the Hepburn character gone scurrying home to Ohio or wherever instead of sticking around for more of Rossano? It would've been a different picture altogether if it had been written by a woman, without the corny symbolism of fireworks in the night sky and an abandoned shoe on a balcony. Still, there were moments that were horribly, painfully accurate, like that scene with poor Katharine sitting all by herself at a table in the piazza, watching all the twosomes go by.

The movie hadn't been at all the way she'd remembered it. She'd forgotten about the stunning blond older woman who'd owned the pensione, and the darling little boy who'd followed Hepburn everywhere, getting her to buy feelthy postcards, and trying to sell her pens and stuff. God! That little boy would have to be in his forties now. And Hepburn was pretty near eighty. The amazing thing about movies was the way everyone in them stayed the same age forever. Only the audience got old.

The kettle had boiled and shut itself off. She turned it on again while she got down a mug and a teabag. She happened to glance up as she was about to return the tea canister to the cupboard, and there was another note from Henry.

"Biccies in red tin. Your favourites with the dark chocolate. Courtesy of H. Hart, Hotelier."

She laughed. It wasn't possible to be angry with someone who left notes all over the place. Did he do it for everyone who came to stay, or only for her? She couldn't recall his ever leaving notes for Suzanne, but he may have done at the beginning, and Suzanne may not have been amused. She'd had absolutely no sense of humor, Suzanne. Maybe someone that beautiful didn't feel she needed one. "Who knows?" Jo said aloud, pouring water over the teabag in the mug. Beautiful women were so intimidating. Suzanne had been, for damned sure. And Jo had always wondered how Henry could treat her so matter-of-factly, as if there wasn't anything special about her. For her part, Jo had never been able to think of anything sensible to say to the tall, coolly blond, alarmingly elegant woman. Perhaps it had been because Suzanne had seemed less than interested in anything Jo might have had to say to her. She'd been polite, inquired nicely after Joanna's health, asked did she have everything she needed, then gone on her way—to talk on the telephone in her frightfully-frightfully voice, or to speak in an urgent undertone to Henry in the privacy of their bedroom, or off on one of her astounding shopping sprees. The woman had private resources that were apparently limitless, and she'd thought nothing of spending three or four hundred pounds for a pair of shoes, or a scarf. Jo had been stunned speechless on one occasion when Suzanne had displayed for her—like a teacher with a small child—her acquisitions of the afternoon: two Hermès scarves, a pair of Ferragamo boots with a matching satchel, a "divine little bangle" from Cartier, and an assortment of Chanel cosmetics. Jo had looked over at Henry to see his reaction to these purchases, but he'd seemed only mildly interested and definitely unimpressed.

Then there'd been that time when Jo had been awakened by the sounds emanating from the bedroom down the hall. Suzanne and Henry had been doing something in there—bumping into the walls and furniture, their voices raised but their words indistinguishable. To escape them, and the memory their noise triggered, she'd put on her coat and boots—it had been winter that visit—and had gone to sit on the rear steps gazing sleepily at the frozen garden, waiting it out until they finished their fight, or their love-making, or whatever it was they'd been doing.

According to Henry, Suzanne had left shortly afterward. Jo imagined she'd probably taken up with some duke or earl with a "divine little pied-à-terre" in Belgravia. What a bitch! Jo liked most women, found them almost always willing to talk, to confide, to share, and it distressed her to meet someone like Suzanne, who was a woman only anatomically but not in disposition. So, the big question was: What had Henry seen in her? And what did he mean when he said he was really very fond of Joanna?

Carrying her tea, she opened the kitchen door and sat down at the top of the rear steps. It was time to confront her feelings about what had taken place with Tyler.

On a night some thirty years before, Jo had awakened very abruptly, very completely, and had sat in her bed blinking in the darkness, trying to think why she was awake in the middle of the night, when she heard the sounds she then understood had seeped through the layers of her dreams. From down the hall, the sound of her parents' voices came sliding around the edge of her bedroom door, which always stood slightly ajar in order to admit a sliver of light from the chandelier on the landing, which stayed on all night.

She'd crept over to the door, holding her breath, listening to the altered yet recognizable voices of her mother and father as they growled at each other, heaving what seemed to be accusations back and forth. She'd been unable to make sense of the occasional words that came clearly, intact, down the length of the hallway. There'd been a lull and then, to her horror, she'd heard a cry, followed by the unmistakable sound of her mother's weeping.

Very afraid, Jo had gone running silently barefoot along to Beamer's room to find her three-year-old brother crouched among the pillows at the top of his bed, chewing on his fists. She'd climbed into bed with him, whispering, "It's okay, Beamer," and settled down with her arms protectively encircling him. "Go to sleep, Beamer," she'd whispered in the tone she'd heard their mother use a hundred times. And he had. Pressing his wet face into her shoulder, he'd closed his eyes and gone to sleep, while Jo lay holding him for a long time, until the house was quiet and the only noise was of the wind pushing against the windows.

The next morning, just before boarding the school bus, Jo had turned to her mother to ask, "What happened last night? It woke up me and Beamer." And her mother had looked alarmed, saying, "God, Joanna! Don't ask me now! The bus is waiting. I can't answer you now. Ask me again when you get home from school." She'd urged Jo onto the bus, then stood at the foot of the driveway until the bus turned the corner and Jo couldn't see her anymore.

When Jo came home from school, Lily was in the kitchen, busy with preparations for one of her dinner parties. She let Jo sit in a corner and lick various bowls and spoons, and Jo forgot to ask again. She did remember on subsequent days, but somehow it was never the right time to ask. So she didn't get an explanation. And it wasn't until many years later that an answer of sorts came to her quite by accident, one afternoon in Manhattan. But by then it no longer mattered—at least that's what she told herself—because she was well beyond childhood and innocence, and she no longer trusted people as she once had, with the exceptions of her grandmother and Beamer. Everyone else was suspect. And Greg, whom she'd trusted as best she was able because she'd told herself she'd spend her whole life alone if she didn't trust someone, proved to her that she'd not only misplaced her trust but also was not the best judge of men. She seemed rarely able to understand their intentions.

Henry had made her admit she trusted him. And he was right: She did. She'd never in her life blasted anyone who'd upset her. But she'd sure as hell blasted Henry. And then he'd made her laugh. He could always make her laugh. Right from their first lunch together he'd known how to elicit her laughter. Tyler, by comparison, made her head ache slightly with some of the things he said; it was as if she was required to match his intensity, and she wasn't sure if she was either willing or able to do that. Tyler was thirteen years older than she, lived in England, and traveled almost as much as she did. His love-making had been tidal, seismic, determined. She'd been swept away. His intensity had overcome her. Yet everything had taken place on a primal level; her brain had had nothing to do with it. She hadn't had much opportunity to laugh. And with daylight, she had to wonder how she could have done the things she had the night before. She despaired of having revealed herself so nakedly, of having applied herself to Tyler's body like someone seeking life-sustaining liquid. Christ! She put her head down on her knees and closed her eyes. She truly did like the man. She also liked Henry. Now, out of nowhere, Henry claimed to be fond of her. And when he'd said that, the spot inside her she'd thought to be reserved for Tyler had expanded in anticipation. She couldn't help thinking of her initial and immediate attraction to Henry ten years earlier, and how foolish she'd felt when he'd spoken of his fiancée.

She'd met both Henry and Tyler professionally. And she knew how differently she dealt with people on that level. Maybe they were both operating on the assumption that that was the real her. Then there was Greg, who'd been, at the last, indifferent to her both personally and professionally. Maybe she had nothing to offer anyone, on any level. God! It was so hazardous to care for people. How could you ever be sure what was real?

She raised her head and drank some of the tea. She couldn't see Tyler tomorrow night. She needed some distance, and time to do her work. She went inside to the telephone, and held her breath as the double rings on the other end started. A click, then Tyler's answering machine came on. Relieved, she waited for the tone, then said, "Tyler, it's me, Jo. Look, I'm really sorry, but I'm going to have to cancel out on tomorrow night. I'm way behind on my notes for this job, and I've got to get organized before I leave Sunday morning. I'd love to get together with you when I get back, so call me in a week. Okay? Talk to you soon. Bye."

* * *

"So," Henry asked as they walked along the Embankment after dinner, "did you go out and about with your magic camera this afternoon?"

"As it happens, the magic stayed in its bag. I got caught up in reading about the train, and by the time I stopped, it was too late. I had to take a shower, get ready for dinner."

"I take it you're feeling somewhat more relaxed about the job now that you've had a chance to do a bit of homework."

"Somewhat."

"Good. We've had the most marvelous weather this summer," he said, breathing deeply of the balmy evening air. "Some of the shrubs have flowered three and four times. I've been able almost every evening to sit out of doors with a drink and something needing to be read. Even fixed myself dinner once and ate it in the garden."

"What did you 'fix?' " she asked, well aware of Henry's lack of culinary skills.

"Bangers I grilled with my very own hands, and some salad. Very nice it was, too. I detect a mocking tone in your voice."

"Oh, heaven forfend! Did Suzanne cook?"

He laughed. "*Suzanne? Cook?* Good God, no. She simply fetched in hampers from Fortnum and Mason, or some other favored emporium. Cooking would've destroyed her manicure, or undone her permanent wave, or something equally disastrous. She did, however, brew up the occasional pot of tea. She even, once, actually warmed some croissants in the oven. Talked about it for days after, she was that proud. Suzanne, my dear Jo, was the most purely ornamental human being I've ever known; programmed from birth to be decorative above all. And you and I must both admit that she succeeded admirably in that department. For a fairly brainless, entirely superficial, primarily self-interested creature, she was nevertheless a wonder to behold. Especially, I might add, without benefit of clothing."

"It sure doesn't sound as if you liked her much, never mind her physical charms."

"Hard to ignore those," he snorted, "but, honestly, I didn't."

"Then why ever did you stay with her for so long?"

"I couldn't think how to ask her to leave," he admitted. "She seemed quite content to stay, and I thought it would be cruel of me to ask her to pack up her Guccis, her Zandra Rhodes frillies, her Chanels, and all the rest of it, and bugger off."

With a laugh she said, "That's not how it was. Was it?"

"Not quite. It was remarkable, Jo, truly. I'd come round a corner, or walk into the kitchen, and there she'd be; and it was mind-boggling to think that this beauty, this satiny, peachy, luscious-looking creation actually lived and bathed in my home, and even took off her clothes and allowed me to be something alarmingly like a dirty old man. It did actually feel that way at times," he confessed, looking over to gauge her reaction. "I mean to say, it did seem as if I were taking advantage of a child. Her interest in matters sexual was negligible. My interest in her evaporated fairly quickly in view of that. So." He cleared his throat, saw Jo wasn't going to say anything, and went on. "I never for a moment thought of it as anything more than temporary, but there's no other word but 'fascinating' to describe her habits, and her mannerisms, and her behavior. What would have been gross affectations in anyone else were the *bona fides* with Suzanne. It was, at times, like living with some dotty Kay Kendall character. No matter how she annoyed me, no matter how long she tied up the telephone, or the bathroom, no matter what silliness came out of her pretty mouth, I was perpetually fascinated. When she finally, rather archly, confronted me to say she was leaving, that she was bored silly by me, by my clients and houseguests, by my tedious three-piece suits, by my unspecial automobile, and by my pedestrian attitudes to all things she considered important, I was only mildly disappointed, and tremendously relieved. I thought what a pity it was that the world's longest play was going to end so anticlimactically. All the expensive frippery went into her matched set of Louis Vuitton bags. A chauffeur appeared to carry the bags out to a waiting Daimler, and she was off. Didn't leave behind so much as a hairpin. Farewell, Suzanne, adieu." He swung out his arm in a theatrical gesture, then laughed softly. "What a twit!"

"Did she really say all that about you?"

"Oh, indeed. And a great deal more. Fetched me up good and proper, she did," he whined in Cockney tones. "I was that broken up, I was. Sat right down and drank meself an entire bottle of Pouilly-Fumé for consolation."

"No, really. Did you care?"

"Not terribly, although no one likes to be accused of being boring. It's the same as being told you're sexually inadequate."

"You think so?" she asked interestedly.

"Yes, I do, actually."

"Wow, Henry!" she exclaimed suddenly. "I just thought of the most amazing thing. You know that movie, *Summertime*, with Katharine Hepburn, the one in Venice?"

"I know it, yes," he answered, wondering what on earth this had to do with the subject at hand.

"Well, her character's name in that movie is Jane Hudson. And in the movie *What Ever Happened to Baby Jane?* that character was Baby Jane Hudson. That's absolutely amazing. I wonder if it was some kind of send-up or something. I mean, the Hepburn movie was in 'fifty-five and Baby Jane was 'sixty-two. I can't see the connection, though."

"God in heaven, Jo!" he laughed, his expression one of mixed amusement and disbelief. "How do you *know* these things?"

"I don't know. I just love movies. When I'm home, sometimes I'll rent eight or ten of them for a weekend. I love the visuals, the setups, the weird camera angles. And the stories, of course. When we were kids, my mother would drop me and Beamer off at the theater while she went shopping, and we'd sit there, the only two quiet kids in the whole place while the rest of the kids hurled popcorn boxes at each other and shouted all the way through the movie. We both loved it. I still can't stand it when people talk through a movie."

"I'm not fond of it myself," he said, watching her stop and look at a boat chugging up the river toward the City. Going to stand beside her, he said, "Have you resolved your difficulties of this morning?"

"Not really," she said quietly. "Maybe I'll never resolve them." She turned to look at him. His eyes were a very clear blue in the fading light, his rounded face most pleasant to look at. He was wearing another of his three-piece suits, having bathed and changed upon returning home. "I'll bet you don't own a single pair of jeans," she challenged.

"You win that wager; I do not. I am not one of those tall, lean American men who are singularly well suited to those garments. I am evolving into a portly British type who's most at ease in clothes that don't cling to his every crease. Does this mean," he asked, "that I will never measure up in your eyes, Jo?"

"Oh, sure, Henry. How could I ever be serious about a guy who doesn't own a pair of Levi's? I mean, really."

"Pity," he quipped.

She stared at him. "Are you joking, Henry? You're joking, right?"

"Not altogether. Would you care to go somewhere for a drink? Or would you rather have coffee at home?"

"We could have it in your garden," she suggested.

"Lovely. I even laid in some cream, knowing you take it in your coffee. And fresh-ground beans. I'll allow you to make it. Your brew is far better than mine."

"You just don't put in enough coffee, that's all."

"I could put in half a pound per cup and I'd still serve up something undrinkable."

"When I get back from Venice, I really want to take some shots of you in your garden."

"Whatever for?"

"Because it's something I've always wanted to do, but this is the first time I'm getting the chance. I mean, I couldn't very well pose you in the garden with Suzanne hanging around looking disdainful."

"Contemptuous, I think," he corrected her. "That would be more her style."

"How could you stand her? I'd really love to know that."

"It wasn't all that difficult." He took her arm as they crossed the street. "And you, for example, didn't appear interested."

"*Me?* What d'you mean, me? What do I have to do with anything?"

"Quite a good deal, actually."

"Henry!" She stopped on the pavement. "What're you *talking* about?"

In answer, he kissed her on the side of the neck, then stood looking at her.

Suddenly unsure, she said, "Is it because of Tyler?"

"What?" His eyebrows drew together; he looked mystified.

"Nothing," she said, realizing this display of his interest hadn't a thing to do with Tyler.

"I've always found you most appealing, Jo. I was under the impression you knew that and had chosen long since to keep our dealings on a strictly professional basis."

"I *didn't* know that," she told him, starting to walk again.

"My mistake," he said without inflection.

"I didn't say it was a mistake, Henry. I just said I didn't know."

"Well, now you do. I hope I haven't embarrassed you."

"Why would that embarrass me? It confuses me, but it definitely doesn't embarrass me. I seem to manage to do all the really embarrassing things to myself."

"Are you involved with this Emmons chap?" he asked, striving for just the right note.

"Not 'involved.' I've slept with him twice. I don't think that constitutes involvement." Since he'd felt free to make the sexual references he had to Suzanne, she felt equally free to discuss Tyler. Yet hearing her own voice make this declaration was like listening to some woman she didn't know, but about whom she had enormous curiosity. "I've wondered for a long time," she went on, "why it is that making love has to mean something. And I've also wondered why I'm incapable of doing the things I do without fearing repercussions. It should be possible to go to bed with someone and forget all about him the next day." No matter what she did, or how much she wished she could change it, the expression of some man's interest in her was a serious matter, something she was unable to treat lightly. This was a discussion unlike any other she'd ever had with Henry, and beneath the words yawned a potential that alarmed as well as drew at her. She'd been avoiding Henry's appeal for years for all sorts of reasons. Now there'd been a subtle shift in their dealings with one another and she felt it only fair to warn him.

As they entered the house, she said, "I know what I'm like, Henry. I mean, I'm very good while it's all happening. I'm wholehearted about it; I even build imaginary houses that the two of us go to live in. But then I wake up and I know none of it's real, and that it's time to get the hell out."

"How sad," he said sympathetically. "How very sad that you should feel that way. It's not the way I'd have thought of you."

"Oh, Henry, you really are very sweet, such a kind and funny man." She was so very fond of him, she just had to put her arms around his neck and look closely at his eyes before kissing him on the mouth. To her surprise, he seemed to take her interest in him very seriously. Without another word they went hand in hand into his bedroom where, the silence holding, they went about the business of removing their clothes. They were both so intent, she thought, and yet so unusually comfortable together that she wasn't at all bothered by the need to undress herself. It was as if they required these few moments for final, private consideration of what they were about to do, so that if either of them changed their minds they'd have a clear space in which to say so.

There was no mind-changing. Once they were naked together on his bed, she drew him avidly into her embrace. She'd wanted to do this for ten years. She just hoped neither of them would end up being hurt.

"I could very easily fall in love with you," he told her later, his voice breaking the stillness in the room.

"I live three thousand miles away, Henry, and I come to England two or three times a year."

"It doesn't have to be that way," he said reasonably, stroking her hip, and wondering why this had been ten years in the happening. How dismal! he thought, to have lost years of such exceptional pleasure.

"I don't know if I want to change anything." At once, she saw herself attempting to consolidate her belongings; stacks of cartons waited to be filled as she tried to decide which of her possessions were dispensable.

"Will you hate me in the morning," he asked cannily, "as you hated Tyler?"

"I didn't plan any of this, Henry. Maybe I'm having some kind of breakdown. I honestly don't know what's happening to me."

"Perhaps it's something that happened a long time ago and it's just now catching up to you."

She looked at him leaning on his elbow at her side. "Henry Hart without the three-piece suit." She smiled and took her hand over his shoulder, down the length of his arm.

"Joanna James in the flesh." He returned her smile. "And very nice, too."

She pulled him close and held on, as if the weight of his body could protect her from her thoughts.

"You're my first, you know," he whispered against her ear.

"Your first what?"

"My first American, of course." He ran his fingertip around her ear.

"And you are the quintessence of the best of British manhood," she laughed, wrapping her arms tightly around him. "The things you say, Henry."

"All to keep the conversation flowing. There should never be unseemly lags." He raised his head in order to look at her. "This is very nice," he observed. "Are you having a lovely time?"

"You make it sound as if we're at a cocktail party."

"Oh, good gracious! You mean we're not?" His head swiveled around, as if realizing they were at the center of a crowd.

Her chest heaved, and instead of laughing she was suddenly on the verge of tears. To get past it, she gave his beard a tug and raised herself up to clamp her mouth over his.

Seven

SHE MANAGED TO USE UP THE BETTER PART OF SATURDAY MAKING notes and reorganizing her luggage. The camera bag was ready to go, and she'd remembered to retrieve her supply of film from the refrigerator. She was beginning to get excited about her ride on the train, imagining all sorts of intriguing people, fabulous clothes, luxurious service, attentive staff.

Periodically during the day, she went into the kitchen and looked out to see Henry in the garden. In an ancient pair of khaki walking shorts, a threadbare white shirt, with worn-through espadrilles on his feet, a tatty straw hat on his head, gardening gloves and shears in hand, he weeded and pruned, watered and fed. At one point she was sure she heard him talking to the plants, then decided it was his portable radio.

As long as he remained in the garden and she was free to watch him through the window, she was able to view events dispassionately. After knowing each other for ten years, they'd made love, and he'd admitted he could fall in love with her. And instead of responding positively, she'd hedged. Standing in the kitchen, watching him through the window, she cared so much for him it made her feel like weeping. But when he knocked on her door just after five to say, "I'm for the bath, Jo. Have you made plans for the evening?" she felt unreasonably apprehensive. She had to fight off her instinct to throw open the door and let him reassure her or make her laugh.

"I'm afraid I have," she lied through the closed door. "I'm sorry, Henry."

"Fair enough," he said, sounding not in the least bothered, and went on to his room.

321

Having told this lie, she was obliged to delve into her suitcase for a change of clothes and, once dressed, to leave the house. Henry called out to her to have a good time, and she felt like an idiot as she went to catch the number 22 bus to Piccadilly. She crossed the Circus with a crush of tourists and studied the theaters as she went along Shaftesbury Avenue, ending up buying a ticket from a scalper outside the Palace for *Les Misérables*.

Her seat turned out to be a good one, right on the aisle in the center of the orchestra. Since she was early, she had plenty of time to read the copious program notes and to admire the theater, with its cupid lighting fixtures at the base of the first balcony and its marble-and-onyx columns.

She was unprepared for the emotional intensity of the production, for the memorable music, or for the epic and unforgettable depiction of heroic lives and deaths. As she sat, holding a tissue to her eyes, the music clutching at her like beseeching hands, she saw herself wrestling with her mother for possession of a plastic container of prescription capsules. She'd been fourteen at the time, and had come home early from school because she'd been feeling uneasy. She'd walked home and let herself into the house, gone upstairs, and arrived in the bedroom doorway to see Lily's reflection in the mirrored bathroom door. She couldn't have said why, but she'd known her mother was going to take all the pills and kill herself. It had to do with the way Lily had stood there studying the container, the concentrated manner in which her hand gripped it.

Jo had put down her schoolbooks and walked through the bedroom, stopping in the bathroom door. "Give them to me!" she'd said quietly, causing Lily to start and to stare round-eyed at her as her hand closed tightly around the container. And then they'd struggled physically, Lily sobbing "No, no!" as Jo, with superior strength and determination, bruised her mother's wrists and, in tears, broke Lily's grip on the vial. "I *need* them!" Lily had begged, trying to stop Jo as she'd removed the lid and emptied the capsules into the toilet. They'd both stood and watched as Jo flushed the toilet and the capsules went swirling down the drain—Jo panting, Lily weeping mournfully. "*I* need *you*!" Jo had shouted at her mother then. "It's not fair!"

"You don't know a goddamned thing about what's fair!" Lily had shouted back. "You don't know a *thing* about *anything*!"

"You don't really mean it," Jo had told her. "How can you want to die?"

"Oh, I want to," Lily had insisted with stunning negative power. "I can want to and I can really mean it. And what are you doing home?"

One question, and they were back into their roles as mother and daughter.

"I didn't feel well."

Lily had at once put the back of her hand to Jo's forehead, and in that moment, Jo knew it was over. Lily had abandoned her death plans. And if she'd ever formulated any others, Jo never knew of them. It didn't matter whether or not she did because she'd left Jo with an ineradicable memory and even more unanswered questions. All Lily said then was, "Don't tell your father or Ben about this, please."

And Jo had said, "I wouldn't." Then she'd collected her schoolbooks and gone along to her room where, exhausted, she'd at once fallen asleep.

She wept through most of the performance, then stood and applauded until her palms were stinging as the cast took their curtain calls. She felt wrung-out and as exhausted as she had that afternoon twenty-two years before when she'd done battle to keep her mother alive.

After stopping in the foyer to buy a cassette of the original cast recording, she went reeling back along Shaftesbury Avenue to get the bus to Chelsea. She felt pried open, too vulnerable as she walked up the road to Henry's house, picked the key out of the flowerpot, and let herself in.

The lights were on, but Henry didn't call out as was his custom. He didn't say anything until she walked into the living room to see him sitting in one of the armchairs with a glass of wine in his hand. The TV set was on, but the volume was turned very low. He turned and looked over at her. "Hello. Nice evening?"

"Yes, thank you."

"Had rather an interesting chat with your friend Emmons," he told her. "Most interesting, actually. Care for a glass of wine, Jo?"

"Sure, okay. I'll go get a glass."

"Aren't you curious," he called out after her, "to know what we discussed?"

She paused in reaching for a glass and leaned on the counter with her eyes closed. Please don't let there be a scene! she intoned mutely, then got down a glass.

"Lovely stuff, this." He examined the label on the bottle for a few seconds before pouring some of the wine into her glass. "Cheers! Do come sit down."

Apprehensive, she perched on the edge of the adjacent armchair and tasted the wine, keeping her eyes on him. "What did you do, Henry?"

"Ate leftovers, watched rather a good American film on the tube, talked on the blower for a bit. Nothing tremendously thrilling. And what did you do, Jo dear?"

"Went to see *Les Misérables*."

Growing animated, he said, "Isn't it stunning? Christ, but I adored that production. I could go once a week, every week, for years. I have the album here somewhere." He got up and walked over to the shelves that housed the stereo and his record collection.

"I've got the cassette, if you want to hear it." She pulled it from her bag and held it out to him, but he was already on his way back to his seat and seemed not to have heard her.

Retrieving his glass, he shifted around to look at her, his expression one of infinite sadness. "Are you playing some sort of game, Jo?" he asked mournfully. "It really does seem as if you are." He looked away. "A very pleasant chap, Emmons. Of course, I've seen quite a number of his productions, films. Decent actor, a shade contrived now and then, but very decent. He's under the impression you're avoiding him. I can't think why he chose to confide in me, although he couldn't possibly be aware of the irony of the situation. I could hardly tell the man I had the impression you were also avoiding *me*. I don't believe I've ever had a conversation remotely similar. It wasn't at all as embarrassing as I've always imagined that sort of conversation to be. In any event, no one's accusing you of anything at all, Jo dear, but an explanation of some sort would appear to be in order. Of course, if you feel you don't have to, well, then of course you shouldn't."

"You're a little drunk, Henry."

"No, I'm a middle-sized fellow, only slightly drunk, to be precise." He laughed, then went back to looking sad. "I felt very bloody sorry for poor Emmons. He's besotted with you, obviously. Half the men in London evidently are besotted with you. Naughty of you, Jo dear." He waggled his finger at her, then smiled very sweetly. "None of my business, actually."

"That is true," she agreed, then sat quietly for a time, drinking the wine and considering what, if anything, she wanted to say. "Okay," she said at last. "Here's the truth. Okay?"

"Okay," he agreed.

"I don't know how much I care about either one of you. I made love with both of you, and I think I'd like to sleep with you again tonight—which is neither here nor there, really. There's this tape in my head that says if I don't hurt you or Tyler, one or both of you will probably hurt me in some way. I looked at Tyler's apartment—he has an honest-to-God Turner, if you can imagine that—and I thought to myself, 'I could live here.' Then I look around here, and I think, 'I could live here.' When I go home, undoubtedly I'll look at the condo and think, 'I could live *here*.' I sound like a goddamned fruitcake, but I want to tell you exactly what's on my mind right this very moment.

"I picture myself with Tyler, or with you—either one, it doesn't matter which for this scenario—and I imagine hearing low angry voices in the night, but this time one of those voices is mine. And I don't *ever* want to be one of the people behind the bedroom door, hissing out my fury in the dark to someone who only likes me because I have no goddamned shame, because I'm willing to use all the parts of me that make pleasure, because men only seem to want you to shut up and receive, and if you question or resist in any way, they'll burn you down, destroy your history. Now, Henry, does that sound like any kind of game you know about?"

Sobered, he answered, "Yes and no. It's definitely not one I'd be interested in playing."

"Good!" she snapped. "Neither am I."

"I've been tactless and now you're angry with me."

"I wouldn't say tactless, and I wouldn't say angry. I don't see you being asked to explain yourself to anyone. Does this strike you as fair?"

He shook his head. "It does not."

"Right!"

"I apologize," he said humbly, then smiled brightly. "Would you really like to sleep with me tonight?"

"I'll fix you some coffee while you go take a cold shower." She got up and made to go to the kitchen.

"You may find yourself with a very alert drunk," he cautioned.

She had to laugh. "You're making out you're farther gone than you are. I've seen you truly pissed once or twice and you're not even close yet. Don't try to con me, Henry."

"Let's compromise and say a *tepid* shower, shall we?"

"Go on. By the time you're finished, the coffee'll be ready."

She didn't hear him come into the kitchen, and jumped when his hands closed over her hips. "Don't *do* that! You scared the daylights out of me."

"Pish tosh! You're made of sterner stuff than that." He lifted aside her hair and kissed the nape of her neck.

"How old are you anyway, Henry?"

"Let's just say you and I are contemporaries."

"Fine. Let's just say that. Your coffee's ready."

"While I was in there, splashing away to humor you, I gave some thought to what you said. I'm most intrigued by your sense of yourself as 'shameless.' "

"You are, huh?"

"Yes, I am. Not that I discount any of the other, highly interesting things you had to say. But for the moment, I'd like to concentrate on your so-called shamelessness."

He turned her around, tugged her blouse free of her skirt, popped open the buttons, and then with one finger unhooked the front of her bra. At once, she crossed her arms over her breasts. "I rest my case," he said quietly with a gentle smile, giving her a kiss on the forehead. "So much for the 'shameless' Joanna James. Given the chance, I could probably disprove a fair number of the other statements you made. I do recall that during your last stay here, Suzanne and I had one hell of a row late one night. If that was what you were referring to, I'm very sorry you had to be a witness to that ugly scene. I don't think I've ever behaved so badly, either before or since, as I did at the last with Suzanne." He paused a moment, trying to gauge her reactions. She continued to stand with her arms crossed over her breasts, her eyes fastened to his. "I'd find myself," he went on, "attempting to introduce some thread of sense into one of our arguments, and then I'd stop and ask myself what in hell I was doing arguing with the woman in the first place. It was pointless and futile, but I rose to the bait at least a dozen times before I gave up and just allowed her to rant and rave over some mythical injury she'd suffered, until she wore herself out. Her complaints and accusations were groundless, not based on anything I'd said or done, but rather on my countless sins of omission, my greatest sin being my failure to have inherited, as she did, vast sums of money. So, if you heard any of that last battle, I apologize. In my own defense, I'd like to say that the most compatible people have been known to disagree; they do argue and raise their voices at one another. It doesn't mean they've stopped caring for one another; it means, purely and simply, that their opinions don't happen to coincide on every issue. And most of the time it's an effective way to clear the air, to get rid of some of the animosity that can build up when you've had rather a lot of exposure to one another. Don't hide, Joey," he said, unwinding her arms and holding them away while he gazed at her.

He called her Joey, spoke her name so meaningfully that she was drawn into his mood. She was also moved by the way he seemed to care for her. She was seeing new aspects of him almost hourly, and here, now, was another. Her face and neck aflame, she watched him closely, aware all the while of the possibility that someone in one of the neighboring houses might be looking in at them. There was an element of risk, even of exhibitionism in what was happening between them, and something inside her was both thrilled and alarmed. Henry had released her arms and was pushing the blouse and bra off her shoulders. He unzipped her skirt and tugged down both it and her slip. She wondered how far he intended to go, and how far she'd allow him to go, as she breathed in the aroma of the coffee and the scents of the bath soap and shampoo he'd used. His hair was damp, his skin moist. She was held for a moment to his chest as he lifted her, then he set her down on the edge of the table. Now her back was to the windows and she felt fractionally safer, shielded from view. Her eyes never left his; she tracked his every movement until he bent his head to her breasts. Then, involuntarily, she whispered, "Oh, God!" and had to clutch at the edge of the table to prevent herself from toppling over. When he raised his head, the cool air rushed over her, heightening the sensations he was creating. Their eyes locked again, he placed his hands firmly over her thighs and stood motionless for a minute, two. She moved first, and then his hand slid forward, probing, reaching. His eyes widened, as if to see her reactions more clearly. She saw his pupils dilate, his lips part slightly as she opened. Her hand rose and fastened to the front of his robe; she pulled at the fabric, signaling, and, his eyes still wide, his face came near to hers, then nearer. Someone in one of those houses could be watching as she spread herself on the table, then closed around Henry's hand, his mouth on hers, his beard and mustache soft against her face, his belly smooth, hairless, gently rounded under her delving hand. Oh, yes, she was shameless, she thought, closing her eyes at last, unconcerned by the possibility of spectators, concerned only with stretching to broaden the pleasure, with perpetuating it. Shameless, she reciprocated stroke for stroke, her hands hidden by the robe, as curious to know his limits as she was to know her own. She could feel his muscles bunch and tighten beneath her hands, could feel her own power in the increasing pressure of his mouth and the strength of the hand that continued to grip her thigh before relocating to her breast. They were going to do this beneath the ceiling lights, framed by the windows and door, right there in the kitchen with the coffee still fragrant on the stove and the loud hum of the refrigerator. I could fall in love with you, too, she thought; maybe I fell years ago and relegated the case to the file of situations hopeless or lost, boggled as always by the logistics, and by past history. She was lifting off the table in her eagerness, her python thighs ready to devour him as she got open his robe and stroked him forward. He was strong, she thought, stronger than those three-piece suits would have led one to believe. His hands went under her, holding her steady while she strained to absorb him. Her body wanted to slide away across the smooth tabletop, but he wouldn't allow it. Like some outrageous circus act, she was brought upright once more, her ankles locked like iron around him. An oversized baby cradled to his shaking chest, she was in his arms and laughter was spewing from his lips. "I'm sorry," he laughed, damp circles under his eyes, his lips dipping into the curve of her neck. "This is too bloody slippery! And besides, I don't have the balls to finish this in here." The laughter ebbing, he carried her into the bedroom where, with her help, they got his robe off before turning serious again. "You're marvelous, Jo," he murmured, taking her down on his bed. "Bloody marvelous!"

She kissed the rim of his ear, then whispered, "If you stop again, I'll murder you in your sleep."

She dreamed again of the fire, so vividly that she could feel the heat all down the left side of her body. It burned. The hair on her arms was singed. She'd die this time. No one would come. She wanted to move, to escape the flames that were wrapping themselves like burning bandages around her disintegrating flesh. This isn't real! she insisted, the truth reaching through to the part of her brain that manufactured dreams. She could wake up; she could.

With a start, she came to. The heat was still there down her left side and, turning, she found its source. Henry lay glued to her side, his body generating the warmth her sleeping self had interpreted as fire. Gingerly, she eased away a few inches and at once her skin began to cool.

She lay looking at Henry in the early morning light and thought, with mounting affection, that he was a gentleman even in his sleep. He didn't thrash or snore; he simply allowed rest to come to him. A lock of hair had dropped onto his forehead, accentuating his schoolboy look. She smiled down at him.

The breeze entering through the window soothed her, distancing her from the dream. She continued to gaze at Henry, savoring this rare guilt-free opportunity to consider him. His body pleased her. She saw him at that moment in shades of black and white and gray gradually coming clearer the way a print did in the developer bath. Henry was shorter, more solidly built than Tyler. Tyler had the physique of someone always hungry; Henry's body was well fed, sleek. Tyler's limbs were longer, leaner, less visibly muscular; his hips were shallow, bony. The cushion of flesh extending from Henry's middle to the tops of his thighs was an area without hollows. When she'd joined with him and they'd sat facing one another, they'd joined completely, touching everywhere. They were well matched physically, she and Henry. While their striving together lacked the frenzy of her love-making with Tyler, she felt more an equal participant with Henry and less a recipient.

Ah, if only it could stay this way, she thought, daring to let herself love this man for these few secret minutes, while the only sounds were the hum of the refrigerator and the tap-tapping of the metal loops at the ends of the drapery tiebacks. If only there were no memories, no previous experiences to interfere with the natural flow of emotions. But she wasn't young, she'd long since left home, and she'd learned not to trust the part of her that craved the thrust and heat of men. She loved them best, she thought, from a distance. Still, Henry slept so sweetly, with such touching munificence, his palms resting gently open to accept gifts or dreams.

At eight forty-five she telephoned from the kitchen for a taxi. Then she put her bags by the front door and went to keep watch through the living room window. She didn't want the cabbie ringing the bell and waking Henry. She'd talk to him when she got back from Venice, as she would Tyler. Or maybe she'd never speak to either of them again. She couldn't concern herself with personal situations just now. She had to flip that professional switch and be ready to take notes and photographs, to absorb everything she was about to see.

The taxi came within fifteen minutes. With her bags stored up front beside the driver and the window lowered to admit the morning air, she sat back feeling relieved to be moving away from her involvements with Henry and Tyler, and very keyed up about the train. She was tremendously excited, eager for a look at this famous conveyance. She'd never dreamed she'd get to ride on the Orient-Express. She could scarcely sit still during the short ride to Victoria Station, and felt her heartbeat accelerate as she paid the driver, then opened the door to find a porter waiting to take her bags.

"They're departin' from platform 2 this mornin', I do believe, Madame. Right this way, if you will."

This was it! The adventure was beginning! As they entered the great vaulted station, she couldn't prevent herself from smiling. It was too terrific! There'd be fascinating people from fascinating places. Perhaps she'd even meet some of them.

She followed the chatty porter across the station to the far platform, expecting the train to be there, waiting. But it wasn't. No train, no passengers. There was, though, staff at the check-in area. She was unreasonably disappointed.

"There you go, luv!" The porter swung her bag onto a luggage platform set between two portable waist-high check-in stations fronted with the beige and brown Orient-Express insignia on their uppermost portions, and by the glossy blue and gold-crested Wagons-Lits insignia below. After tipping the porter, who wished her a happy trip, she presented her packet of travel documents to one of the smartly suited young women behind the counter.

While the young woman read the letter of introduction, Jo pumped herself back up again, reminding herself that she'd have an entire week free of complications, free of Henry and Tyler. It really was a relief to be out of all that. And maybe she'd be able to make sense of what had gone on during the past few days, not to mention the peculiar overlapping of her personal misgivings into her professional behavior. The train trip would sort things out, she was convinced. There was something about trains—even crummy commuter trains—that allowed your thoughts to form more clearly.

"Ah, yes," the young woman said. "We're expecting you, Miss James. The train manager's been told you'll be traveling with us today. If there's anything at all you need, be sure to let him know. You'll be in Lucille," she went on, consulting a clipboard before making a note of Jo's assigned seat number on a small card. "We do hope you'll enjoy your trip."

Jo thanked her, accepting the seat designation, and asked, "What time does the train actually arrive in the station?"

The young woman glanced at a large clock suspended from the platform overhang. "Within the half-hour, I should think. You are rather early. The station buffet has quite decent coffee, if you'd like to wait there."

"I was told I'd be able to board in advance of the other passengers to get some pictures."

"Oh, certainly. I'll have a word with the train manager and we'll make certain you have an opportunity to do that. You'll have about half an hour or so. I'm sorry it's such a short time, but the Pullmans are in constant service."

"That's okay." Jo looked around. Still no other passengers. "Maybe I will go have some coffee."

"It's really not bad at all. Just over there." The young woman pointed to her left. "If you're back by nine-forty, you'll have tons of time."

"Thanks a lot."

"My pleasure."

Jo queued up in the buffet, got coffee and a buttered roll, then carried her tray to a single table occupied by a young man reading the *Observer* and asked him if the other seat was vacant. He indicated it was, and she was glad to sit down and loop the strap of the heavy Lowe-pro bag over the back of her chair. Every table in the place was full, mainly with young people, all reading.

The coffee was good. She ate the roll quickly, realizing she'd eaten very little in the past three or four days. She'd engaged in a great deal of strenuous sexual activity, but she'd missed a fair number of meals. Which was why her suit felt so loose. She looked out at the station as she drank the coffee. It really was too bad she'd arrived so early. This enforced wait made her realize how sleepy she was, and how bewildered. But she refused to think about Henry or Tyler. According to her watch, the train would be arriving in about fifteen minutes, and she intended to return to the platform in about ten to take some shots of her fellow passengers— the others probably knew better than to arrive too early—and of the train itself as it pulled into the station.

With a jolt, it occurred to her she'd forgotten to take her birth control pill, and fumbled around inside her purse, found the container, poked out a pill, and discreetly put it into her mouth. A swallow of coffee and it was done. No chance of creating a little Tyler or a little Henry.

She thought of the determined way Tyler had come at her on the sofa, the way he'd dived under her skirt, and heat rushed into her face. Then there was Henry, displaying a surprising lusty streak in his kitchen. And what the hell had she been doing? Men didn't make love to invisible women. That was part of it, a not insignificant part of it, now that she thought about it. But, God, the whole business was so messy and complicated! More than anything else she was relieved to be leaving it all behind. She gulped down the last of the coffee, hooked both the camera bag and her purse over her shoulder, and hurried back to the platform.

There were now half a dozen or so people at the check-in stations, all with those small totally automatic cameras, and all, apparently, with Louis Vuitton luggage. Positioning herself against the wall beyond the velvet cord separating the area from the rest of the platform, she got out the Pentax, adjusted the aperture for the very low light level, and took several shots that showed the passengers, two brown-coated baggage handlers, and two security officers who checked each new arrival with metal detectors. Security was minimal, just the personal check by the guards. None of the luggage was inspected.

She relocated near the steel gate that prevented people from wandering down the length of the platform. Almost ten. The train would be along any time now. Turning, she saw a fair-sized crowd waiting to hand over travel documents to the calm, polite young women in charge of the check-in. Several groups of Orientals, quite a number of people who looked British, not many Americans—which was a surprise. She'd expected the majority of passengers to be American, but it was a thoroughly mixed group. And the number of Vuitton bags was proliferating at an amazing rate. Her old Hartmann had a kind of shabby nobility among all those new-looking cases.

Looking out along the branching network of tracks, she was anxious to see the train, and set to take shots of its arrival. It was awkward that her suit didn't have any handy pockets into which she could pop her spare lenses, but she'd guessed correctly the importance of being well dressed for this trip. Everyone was expensively but conservatively turned out; the men in suits, not a woman in trousers.

10:03. The train was approaching. Her sense of adventure rushing back, she watched the engine through the telephoto until it was in range for a good shot. She framed each exposure so that the clock and platform number were visible in the upper left-hand corner, and switched to the 50-mm lens as the train came to a halt, to get shots of the white-jacketed waiters and stewards as they emerged from the carriages and came down the platform to the front of the train where they stopped to confer with the check-in staff. The men were immaculately groomed in navy trousers with gold stripes down the outsides, white jackets with navy lapels sporting gold VS-O-E insignia pins, gold-braid epaulettes, navy bow ties on crisp white shirts; several wore short white gloves. This was great! She worked quickly, changing back to the telephoto for some close-ups, then a few medium shots of the gleaming brown and beige carriages, each with a crested name plaque: Audrey, Cygnus, Perseus.

She moved to the still-closed gate to have a word with the train manager.

"Ah, yes," he said, admitting her onto the platform and offering his hand. "Good to have you with us. You're in Lucille, seat 14. If you'd care to, you may go through the carriages now. It should be another fifteen or twenty minutes before the passengers begin to board."

She was about to thank him when someone tapped her on the shoulder, and she turned to see Henry smiling at her, holding out a single red rose in a paper cone. Her reaction to the sight of him was fifty percent disbelief and fifty percent delight. It was touching of him to go to this trouble; it was also an impediment to the work she had to do.

"I thought I'd come see you off," he said somewhat shyly. "Couldn't resist having a peek at the train, too."

Her delight won out. "You're so darling, Henry!" She gave him a kiss, accepted the flower, then said, "Come with me. Okay? I want to leave the camera bag in my seat before I get some quick shots of the interiors."

"May I? I don't want to get in your way, but I really would love to see." She was, he thought, more self-possessed and businesslike than he'd ever seen her, and he couldn't help but be aware that she might construe his turning up this way as an unthinking, even feckless, gesture.

"Come on," she urged, and started along the platform looking for Lucille. "In here, Henry." She turned to be sure he was following, then stepped inside, dazed with pleasure at first sight of the interior of the parlor car with the tables set for lunch—white linen, crystal goblets, silver vases of fresh carnations, blue and white porcelain.

"Isn't it fabulous!" Henry exclaimed, looking more the schoolboy than ever. "I'm sick with envy, Jo."

"It's wonderful," she agreed, finding her seat and setting the Lowe-pro bag down on its flowered velour upholstery. She put the rose on the table, dropped her lenses into her shoulder bag, then backed away to take several shots of the tables with the sunlight glinting off the silver and crystal.

Keeping his distance, Henry watched, captivated by this first-time viewing of her at work. She held the camera, her eyes slightly narrowed as she judged the light, the angle, the composition, then lifted the camera, made adjustments, and took the shots. She so visibly knew what she was doing, was so completely in charge of herself, that she appeared to him for the first time neither young nor tentative. She also seemed taller, thinner, and extraordinarily concentrated. He didn't know which intrigued him more, the train or this new aspect of someone he'd thought he knew well. In the few minutes it took her to photograph the interior of the car, his assessment of her underwent a profound and radical shift, and he was at last able to make better sense not only of her but of his long-time attraction to her. He was charmed, impressed, and mildly daunted.

"I won't stay, Jo. I know you've got a lot to do." He watched her turn and remember he was there, and knew he was right to get out of her way. Just as he disliked having someone sitting on the far side of the desk when he was attempting to conduct business over the telephone, he could tell she was torn between politeness and an urgent need to get on with the job at hand.

"Thank you so much for coming to see me off," she smiled at him, "and for the rose. I'll walk back with you," she offered.

"Oh, no need," he assured her. "Have a wonderful time. And don't forget my postcard."

"I won't." She gave him a quick hug and a kiss. He'd bathed and shaved and donned one of his three-piece suits—a navy one that darkened the blue of his eyes—to come see her off. "Really, Henry, thank you for going to all this trouble." She gave him another kiss. "I'll see you in a week. Okay?"

"Okay, Jo." He stood a moment longer looking around, then walked quickly away.

"God!" she whispered, feeling enormously pressured by the time constraints. *"God!"*

Almost at a run, she went to the head of the train and began, hastily and methodically, taking pictures of the various interior details of the five parlor cars and three kitchen cars: brass luggage racks, tulip-shaped glass and brass overhead lights, the mosaic lavatory floor of Cygnus, the Greek dancing girl marquetry panels in Ibis, the marquetry floral frieze and burr wood panels of ash in Ione. The detailing of each carriage was remarkable, she thought, taking close-ups of the light fittings and of the different styles of luggage racks, of the pullman crests, and the pink-shaded table lamps. It was like going back sixty years in time, to when the majority of these carriages had originally been completed. Audrey had carried the Queen, the Queen Mother, and the Duke of Edinburgh to review the fleet in 1953; Cygnus had been reserved for use by visiting heads of state; Ibis had been part of the Golden Arrow; Perseus had been used in Winston Churchill's funeral train; Phoenix had been the Queen's favorite carriage; Zena had been used in the film *Agatha*. Each carriage had a unique and fabulous history.

By the time she got to the end of the train, people were sitting, nibbling the nuts and olives on each table. She found her way back to Lucille and looked appreciatively at the lace seat-back cover as she pushed the Lowe-pro under the table. Three women were already in place at the table at the far end, and a late-fortyish English couple were at the table for two on the opposite side of the aisle to Jo. Keeping the camera close to hand, she got out her notebook, made a few quick notes, then finally unwrapped Henry's rose and breathed in its perfume. The train hadn't yet left the station, but she felt as if she'd already done a full day's work. She'd never before had to do so big a shoot in so little time.

"Just made it!" Tyler announced, all but skidding to a stop at her side. "Thought I'd come to see you off," he said, setting a gift-wrapped box on the table beside the rose. If he saw the flower, he neither questioned nor acknowledged it. He stooped to kiss her just as she was getting to her feet, and the top of her head smartly connected with the underside of his chin.

Both of them apologizing, flustered, she smiled at him, staggered that he'd not only come to see her off, but that he'd also dressed for the occasion in slacks and a sport jacket, even a tie. Here she'd been smugly thinking she'd managed to get away from both of them, and they'd both showed up. She couldn't begin to think what it all meant.

"It's sweet of you to come," she told him, directing him out of the carriage and onto the platform, wondering why she'd been painting such unattractive mental pictures of him. He was very good-looking. And she'd forgotten how his voice seemed to rumble out of his chest and vibrate inside hers. There were women who'd do anything for a chance at this man.

"Almost missed it," he said, indicating the cleared platform. "I wanted you to know I was disappointed about last night. I was very much looking forward to seeing you again, Joanna."

"I'm sorry, Tyler. I just couldn't make it."

"Well, never mind." Taking hold of both her hands, he asked, "You'll be back when?"

"Next Monday."

"Promise you'll ring me as soon as you get back?"

"Sure." She suddenly wondered if the other passengers were watching through the windows. She hoped not.

"Off you go, then." He caressed her hair briefly before giving her a pair of those Continental kisses she never seemed prepared for.

"God!" she laughed nervously. "Just give me one sensible kiss before you go, will you? Every time you do that I feel as if I'm dancing a waltz while everybody else is doing a tango."

He laughed and obliged with a kiss on the lips, then another on the top of her head.

"Better," she said, taking a step back into the carriage. "Thank you for coming, Tyler."

"Enjoy yourself! Oh, what's your hotel?" he remembered to ask.

"The Cipriani."

"Lucky you!" He waved, then started off along the platform, turning to wave once again before going through the gate.

She returned to her seat and looked at the package Tyler had left sitting beside Henry's rose. For a second time, she picked up the rose and sniffed at it. The train began to move. She looked out the spotless window to see the daylight beyond the station approach. Reaching for one of the black olives, she bit into it as they left the station behind and the rails spread wide like the gigantic veins of some immense metal organism.

Well, she thought, now she'd finally managed to leave both men behind. Then she turned to look around, just to be absolutely sure.

Eight

THE WAITERS CAME ALONG OFFERING CHAMPAGNE. JO WOULD HAVE loved some, but had to decline in order to remain clearheaded.

"No?" The waiter looked positively crestfallen. "Perhaps some juice, or mineral water?"

"Water would be great, thank you."

Cheered by this simple request, he went off.

The three women at the far table seemed to be having a fine time, laughing in bursts, their conversation animated. Jo couldn't help being aware that she was the only person in the carriage, possibly on the entire train, traveling alone. She concentrated on her notes, taking occasional photographs through the window—of people at work in their allotments, of the Queen Anne's lace and wildflowers standing above the ivy blanketing both sides of the track. She knew she gave the impression of someone with a job to do. The camera, notebook, and pen were her validation. She also knew the three women had noticed her, and were speculating quietly, curious about what exactly Jo might be doing. Silly as it might have been, the familiar cadence of their American accents was comforting. It was one thing to go on a shoot or assignment in some remote location, but it was something else altogether to find herself a passenger with a purpose on the world's most famous train. And the temptation to abandon herself to the sheer pleasure of the experience was a strong one. Yet the majority of the people she'd so far seen appeared determined to remain outwardly unimpressed, as if they were accustomed to such attentive service and so unique a means of transportation. Of course, it was a train. But not just any old train. This was eleven million pounds worth of a scrupulously restored train, and the staff at least seemed fully aware of that fact.

336

Beckenham Station, Shortlands, Bromley South. She wrote down the names, recapturing her long-time fondness for this country. England was, to her mind, a place where truly eccentric people could be left alone to flourish. You could, like Henry, spend five days a week being a business-man and then, at the weekends, put on clothes the Salvation Army would've rejected, and spend six hours on your knees in the garden, talking to your annuals while plucking encroaching weeds from the pe-rimeters. And no one would think it odd or unusual. In the setting of his own creating, Henry was perfectly placed, entirely comfortable. The very first time she'd seen the house, he'd taken her on a tour that had ended in the then rubble-heaped garden.

"I have plans for this garden," he'd told her with a visionary's zeal she'd found lovable.

"You do, huh?" she'd teased him.

"I certainly do. And just remember, you skeptical American upstart—and don't think for a moment I'm unaware of your lack of reverence for that venerable institution the British Garden—that one day you'll be assigned to photograph what I create here for *House & Garden*."

"I'll beg for the assignment, Henry. I'll throw myself at the editor's knees and plead to be allowed to photograph your garden."

"Why is it that Grace's clients are all so irreverent? None of Dearborn's people—whom I much prefer"—he'd sniffed in mock offense—"are nearly so lowbrow."

"That's because most of them are English, Henry. And I'm not in the least lowbrow. I mean, just because I'm not delirious with excitement over the prospect of your garden doesn't mean I won't grovel for the chance to shoot it."

"I may not even allow you to *sit* in it. No doubt you'd leave aban-doned Kodak boxes in the grass, litter the place with chewing-gum wrap-pers."

"I don't even chew gum!" she'd protested.

"I expect you'll take it up just to annoy me."

She'd stared at him for a moment, wondering if he could possibly be the least bit serious, and he'd started to laugh, saying, "Had you going, didn't I? Just for a moment, didn't I? I could see you wondering if I'd finally gone right over the edge and was actually serious. Admit it! You were thinking I'd gone round the twist, weren't you?"

"Of course, I wasn't," she lied, her face flushing.

"Ah, Jo dear," he'd sighed still smiling, "I do enjoy you."

She'd thought for a moment he was going to kiss her, and she'd waited to see what he'd do, all the while imagining how she'd ask Greg to leave and the pleasure she'd derive from that. But nothing happened. Henry had looked at her for a second or two more, then looped his arm through hers and said, "Come along and see the flats. The tenants haven't moved in yet, and if I do say so myself, they've turned out very nicely."

The waiters were coming by again, this time offering red or white wine to accompany the lunch, and Jo accepted half a glass of the red from a need to celebrate the occasion. There had never been and would never again be another job like this one. A sip of wine, then she unwrapped Tyler's gift. A package of Terry's All Gold chocolates. He couldn't have known that she rarely ate chocolate, but she was pleased nonetheless by the gesture. Putting the box to one side, she gazed again out the window at blocks of houses with neatly clipped lawns, laundry billowing on lines, flowers leaning over fences, the flowing brick arches of overpasses. How could Tyler possibly know her likes and dislikes? Altogether, the time they'd spent together didn't add up to one full day. She was acquainted with his sexual skills, and the intensity with which he displayed them, and she was more than a little susceptible to his fervent demonstrations. But that was all. It wasn't very much.

Orpington Station, Knockholt, Dunton Green.

A few months back she'd done a photographic essay on an author of children's books who'd designed the production being mounted of the adaptation of one of her books. Jo had driven to the place just near Brewster, New York, where the woman lived, to photograph her sitting in a chair outside at the rear of the house where the snow had been as umblemished and glossy as the frosting on a cake. The author lived with her agent, who'd hovered in the background the entire time Jo had been there, as if concerned that Jo might suddenly whip out a gun and start firing. She'd found his protectiveness endearing. He'd obviously cared very deeply for the woman. She wondered idly if Henry knew her.

A wide bowl of dark mushroom soup with a sprinkling of fresh parsley was set before her. Then came Scottish smoked salmon stuffed with prawns and celery in mayonnaise, new potatoes, and a salad of tomato, cucumber, and melon. The food was very light, simply delicious. She ate slowly, appreciating the subtle flavors.

The sun glanced off the brass base of the pink-shaded table lamp. The interior of the carriage hummed with now-muted conversations and the musical notes of cutlery striking against porcelain. As the meal progressed, she felt increasingly cosseted, especially when the train manager stopped by to ask how she was enjoying herself and if there was anything she needed.

"Everything's wonderful," she told him. "But I do have a couple of quick questions, if you don't mind."

"Certainly."

"How many passengers are you carrying today?" she asked.

"With those we'll pick up in Paris, one hundred and thirty-eight."

"And what's your maximum?"

"One seventy-five, ideally."

"D'you get about the same number on the return trip?"

"Usually fewer northbound. It's something we're working on," he explained, "trying to get more passengers originating in Venice."

"Why is that?"

"Well, Italians tend not to take their holidays in Britain. That's one thing. And it would seem a larger number of people start from London with Venice as their ultimate destination. As I say, we're working on it."

"Do you usually get a lot of Americans?"

"Oh, yes. The Americans do enjoy the train."

"And you run all year?"

"We shut down for six weeks from mid-November to the end of December, then start up again for New Year's Eve."

"That would be fun," she said, imagining being inside the cozy train as a winter snow was falling beyond the windows. "I guess that's it for the moment."

"Anything else, please don't hesitate."

"I won't. Thank you."

She set aside the notebook as the waiter arrived with a huge tray of orange-and-Cointreau profiteroles in chocolate sauce. Her appetite had been satisfied, but she couldn't resist tasting the dessert. She found the sauce a bit too sweet, but the coffee was good and strong and she gratefully accepted a second cup while refusing the offer of a liqueur.

Sevenoaks Station, Tunbridge, Paddock Wood.

Sheep grazed in a field; a passing British Rail train was a noisy blur. She felt herself being lulled by the motion and the intermittent sunshine. The three American women were laughing again, and Jo looked at Henry's rose lying beside her coffee cup. It was a nice setup, the coffee cup with a lipstick imprint, the rose. She arranged it a little more precisely, then prepared to take a shot, aware of the three women's silence as they watched her, one of them murmuring, "She's taking a picture of the flower. Did you see . . . ?" Jo didn't hear the end of what the woman said, but suspected it had something to do with the fact that not one but two men had come to see her off. And rather than feeling elevated at having had such attention paid to her, she was chagrined, and didn't know why. No time to think about that! She got up to go have a look in the other carriages, to see what her fellow passengers were up to.

In one of the compartments in the next carriage, a couple sat reading newspapers, ignoring both the scenery and each other, as if they were riding a commuter train home after a day's work in the city. How blasé, Jo thought. But farther along, a group was standing in the passageway looking out the windows and chatting happily about the food and the scenery and the exceptional service and wondering aloud how much they might tip the staff upon arrival at Folkestone.

Hearing mention of Folkestone, Jo looked out the window to see they were already approaching their destination. She turned and hurried back to her seat to reorganize the camera bag, returning the lenses to their cushioned compartments. Notebook safely stowed, she took a five-pound note from her wallet to give to the waiter when she left the train. Her festive mood increased as the train came to a stop, sat for several minutes, then reversed into Folkestone Central.

As she stepped down onto the platform, she realized with a pang that she'd left both Henry's rose and Tyler's chocolates on the table. And there was no time to go back for them. She had to get shots of the passengers being directed by VS-O-E staff to the Sealink Ferry.

On board, they were shown into a private lounge. A vast carpeted area with deep chairs and settees, it had a bar, and display cases at the rear contained items for sale in the duty-free shop. The staff offered tea or coffee, drinks from the bar. Jo arranged herself in an unoccupied area near one of the windows and sat for a few minutes taking in the details. She didn't want anything to drink and it seemed it would be a while before the ferry departed. She decided to go up on deck to have a look at the famous White Cliffs of Dover and get some fresh air. Lack of sleep was starting to catch up with her.

A couple of men with little automatic cameras were already at the rail, aiming at the view and snapping away. For some reason, those cameras annoyed her. Maybe it was because ownership of them convinced people they knew something about photography—although she hadn't actually had anyone espouse that theory to her directly. Her annoyance stemmed from the fact that the cameras made taking pictures too easy, so people were no longer quite as impressed with professional photography as they'd once been. Or maybe the truth was she resented the high quality of the end product, work done entirely by the camera without the need for extra lenses or any degree of skill on the part of the owner. Secretly, there were times when she longed to rid herself of the load of gear that dragged down her shoulder. And as if in defiance of that shameful longing, she carried with her everything conceivable she might need, from a minitripod, to several cable releases, varicolored filters either to enhance or reduce available light, and the three lenses without which she couldn't work effectively: the telephoto with the macro setting, the medium wide-angle, and the 50-mm. She did have a fisheye, as well as a teleconverter that doubled the length of the telephoto or 50-mm, but she disliked having to adjust the aperture to compensate for the distortion and reduction of light caused by the converter.

With the Lowe-pro bag at her feet, she leaned on the rail and looked out at the water and cliffs. The sun had decided to stay out, but the light was peculiar, diffused, rendering the view fuzzy and remote. But some shots of the other passengers pointing their automatic Nikons and Minoltas and Kodaks at the scenery would be good. She sat on one of the benches, got out the Pentax and a fresh roll of 400 to reload, her eyes feeling gritty. She'd have to find someplace in Venice to print up the roll she'd already shot so she could have prints made from the slides to send to Florella.

There were now five men at the rail, and two women standing back wearing patient expressions as they waited for the men to finish. A good vignette, Jo thought. But as she raised the camera, the wide-angle in place, everyone—as if on cue—shifted out of her way. They'd all been watching her. To cover herself, she left the camera bag on the bench, got up and went to the rail to make a couple of uninspired exposures before going back to sit down.

A number of people emerged from the VS-O-E lounge to stroll along the deck. One couple caught Jo's eye. The man was dressed in a suit, hand-tailored but subdued. The woman, however, was sporting a brilliant green leather outfit, the skirt so tight she could only take tiny steps in her four-inch heels. The suit jacket was closely nipped in at the waist, then flared widely over her ample hips. Screaming, teased red hair, masses of heavy jewelry, and a lot of bright green eyeshadow. Amazing! Jo thought. The suit must have cost a couple of thousand dollars, was probably Italian-made, and would've looked fabulous on someone several inches taller and forty pounds thinner. Jo was delighted. All the other passengers she'd seen were so low-key that the woman stood out almost violently among them.

Bitchy, very bitchy, she admonished herself. She was probably a very nice woman; she just had no clothes sense. One of those people who equated an outrageously expensive price tag with quality and high fashion. And what about you in your little black linen suit? she reminded herself. Perfect for church on Sunday. Talk about conservative!

Back in the lounge she spotted several sets of honeymooners. One young woman nestled against her new husband, her head on his shoulder. The pair were exceptionally good-looking and well-dressed. He was tall and dark with perfectly proportioned features, aristocratic in a rather Edwardian-styled light gray suit; she was also tall, with long strawberry blond hair cascading over her shoulders, and not a bit of makeup. Her dress was of pink Indian cotton, with a long full skirt, a prim lace-covered collar, and short puffed sleeves. The two were visibly at ease with one another, as if the ceremony they'd recently gone through had been no more than a pause for formality during a long ongoing love affair.

Another honeymoon couple nearby seemed, in contrast, light-headed as they laughed explosively and often, periodically clutching at each other's arms as if to be certain they were actually in the same place together.

The three American women were over near the bar, having coffee and reading magazines. Strange Muzak tapes of sixties tunes played softly; the ship's movement was scarcely noticeable. Just as Jo was about to doze off, an announcement advised passengers to present their passports to the French officials at the office opposite the duty-free shop. She roused herself and pushed out through the lounge doors to join the line.

It took only a few minutes, then she went to have a look at the duty-free offerings. She picked up a spray bottle of Chanel No. 5 eau de toilette, paid for it, dropped it into her purse, and returned to the lounge, where she unwrapped the bottle, sprayed her throat, then breathed in the fragrance of her mother. As she stared out the window at the glassy Channel, she tried to think why she hadn't bought her usual perfume. Then her thoughts shifted as the scent brought back an image of Lily at her dressing table, putting the finishing touches to her hair and makeup. Jo had been sitting on the end of the bed, watching. Satisfied, Lily had reached for the familiar clear bottle with the black top to place the ritual dabs of Chanel at the base of her throat and behind each ear. Then she'd stood up, smoothing the skirt of her dress. Black it had been, Jo remembered. Black silk, with quite a low-cut neckline that had made Lily's skin look slightly blue.

"He's late again," Lily had addressed the mirror. "Don't you have homework to do?" She'd turned to look at Jo.

"Mother," Jo had said with tried patience, "I'm a junior, for Pete's sake. Don't you think I know when and how much homework I've got to do?"

"Sorry," Lily had said curtly. "Where's Beamer?"

"*He's* doing *his* homework."

"What about dinner?"

"I'm taking care of it. Everything's ready to go. It's not my fault Dad's late."

"No one's suggesting it is." Lily had looked down at her shoes, then again at Jo. "I don't remember being so prickly at sixteen."

"I'm not 'prickly.' If anything, you're the one."

"Why is it," Lily had asked quietly, "that children speak to their parents in a manner we simply wouldn't tolerate from any other living soul?"

"Because children have to behave well for other people. Parents are the ones who have to put up with us the way we really are." Jo had smiled at her, going across to pluck an imaginary piece of lint from the shoulder of her mother's dress. "You look divine. And you know you love me."

"There are times," Lily had relented, "when it's quite a challenge. Where the *hell* is he? We're going to be late. I *hate* being late."

"He'll be here."

Jo had gone off downstairs to take the casserole from the oven, calling out to Beamer, as she went, to come and eat. The two of them had sat at the kitchen table, eating and looking over periodically at their mother, who paced back and forth in the living room, stopping every few moments to look out the front window before continuing her pacing.

They were concocting chocolate sundaes and Lily was still pacing but with a drink in her hand now, when the telephone rang. Jo and Beamer had stared at each other, waiting to see who'd answer. Lily picked up the extension in the living room, and the two of them continued to stare at each other.

"He's up shit creek without a paddle this time," Beamer had whispered. "She'll *kill* him."

"Sshhh! I'm trying to hear what she's saying."

They listened, but Lily wasn't saying anything.

"Five bucks says he missed the train," Beamer wagered, still whispering.

"Sshhh! Wait!"

From the living room they heard Lily put down the receiver. At once, they went back to the melting ice cream and the container of Hershey's chocolate sauce, the torn-open bag of crushed walnuts. The whole time they were fixing the sundaes they kept expecting Lily to come in and rant about the latest excuse. But she didn't. She sat for a time finishing her drink. Then she walked purposefully into the kitchen to put her glass in the sink, announcing as she did, "I'm going out. Make sure you clean up after yourselves in here. Don't stay up too late. And, Beamer, if you don't clean up that room and get all that crap off the floor, I will throw every last thing in there in the garbage. And believe me, I mean it. Joanna, try to limit your telephone conversations to less than three hours." She'd whipped the keys from the hook by the garage door, picked up her handbag from the counter, and sailed out.

After she'd gone, Jo had looked at her sundae, decided she didn't want it, and dumped it down the disposal. "You'd better clean up your room, Beam. She means it."

"I never thought she'd actually go without him," Beamer said, stirring the chocolate sauce into the ice cream. "There'll be a big fight tomorrow."

Jo had stood over the sink gazing at the mess of uneaten sundae.

"There won't be any fight," she'd said, feeling a little sick. "Neither one of them will say a thing."

Beamer came to sit on the counter beside her, still stirring his ice cream. "I'm never getting married," he'd said, taking an experimental taste.

"Sure you will," Jo had told him.

"Nope. I never will. You wait, you'll see. I absolutely will never get married. It stinks."

"No, it doesn't," she'd said, feeling miserable now as well as sick. "Some day you'll go crazy over some girl and that'll be it for you."

"I might go crazy over some girl, but I'll never marry her."

"Oh? And what if you want to have kids?"

"I'm not having kids, either."

"For Pete's sake, Beam! You're not even thirteen years old. You can't say things like that."

"Sure I can. I'm *saying* them. I've spent better than twelve years with the two of them. That's plenty for me, thanks a lot."

"You don't understand."

"Oh, and you do, right?"

"Maybe," she'd said. "They love each other, Beam."

He'd finished the last of his sundae and turned to look at her. "Looks more like hate to me."

"You just don't understand."

"Okay. But I'm still never getting married." He'd hopped down from the counter, nudged her out of the way, and got a plastic garbage bag from under the sink. "I'll go clean up my room. I don't want her coming in and throwing out all my good stuff."

He'd left then, and Jo went back to gazing at the mess in the sink, thinking, This isn't the way things are supposed to be.

Turning away from the window, her eyes came to rest on an elderly, distinguished-looking couple opposite, separated from her by an unoccupied banquette. The woman smiled; Jo smiled back. With a hand held to her mouth, the woman indicated she was sleepy, and Jo nodded her agreement. The woman's husband was unaware of the communication between them, his attention on a stack of folders he was reading closely, peering down at them through bifocals.

There was something about this couple that at once aroused Jo's interest. They were in their seventies but seemed—regardless of the woman's mime of fatigue—more alert and aware than the majority of the other travelers. They were dressed simply, but extremely well, he in a summer-weight suit of beige wool with a white shirt and Liberty cotton floral tie, she in a tidy cotton shirtwaist dress with a white cardigan whose trim matched the dress fabric. They were both above average height, had exemplary posture, and had obviously been a startlingly handsome pair in their youth. It was easy to imagine the impact the two of them must have made some years back upon entering a room together. They seemed accessible, and Jo hoped she might have an opportunity to get to know them.

More lulled, she let her head fall back against the seat and closed her eyes.

Anne watched the young woman across the way close her eyes, and said softly to her husband, "What a lot of equipment she has, Jimmy. Did you see?"

"See what?" he asked without looking up from his reading.

"That dear girl with the camera across the way, the one traveling on her own."

Jimmy glanced up and looked around.

"Directly opposite," she said in an undertone. "I saw her on the platform at Victoria, taking photographs. Then she boarded before everyone else. I think she's doing some sort of photographic essay."

"Hmmmn." He returned to his brochures.

"She does so remind me of Lucia. That same shining hair and lovely, open features, great dark eyes. It must be awkward, being on her own. Lucia did so loathe traveling alone. I don't think I'd care very much for it."

"I expect she's accustomed to it," he commented, for the moment abandoning his brochures to look over at Jo. "Does rather resemble Lucia," he agreed. "Fallen asleep, hasn't she? Bit more petite, but there's a definite resemblance."

Anne looped her arm through his and the two of them sat gazing at the sleeping Joanna. Anne sighed. Jimmy automatically patted her hand. "Done rather a splendid job on the old train, wouldn't you say? Looked much as it did when I rode the Bournemouth Belle as a lad."

"You're not disappointed, then?"

"Should say not. Undoubtedly, they've done an equally bang-up job on the Wagons-Lits."

"Oh, undoubtedly." She gave him an affectionate smile, then looked again at Jo. "If she's on her own at dinner, perhaps we should invite her to join us."

"If you like," he said indulgently, and again patted her hand.

Jo was awakened by another announcement, this one informing those in the lounge that they would be disembarking once the other passengers had cleared the ship. She straightened and smoothed her skirt, trying to come fully awake. Most of the others in the lounge looked a little dazed. She wondered how she was going to make it through the rest of the afternoon, and the evening; she also tried to think how she could possibly photograph every aspect of this journey without, at some point, appearing totally obtrusive. Were she just another paying passenger and not some-one being paid to do a job, the sight of some woman jumping up every few minutes to take pictures would irritate the hell out of her.

The female staff, having changed out of their serving aprons and put back on their brown suit jackets, began herding the passengers out of the lounge. Their trip up and down the various aisles and corridors only took a few minutes. And just over there was the train. It was wonderful, simply wonderful: the blue carriages spotless and shining, a staff member stand-ing on the platform outside each carriage to assist people in finding their compartments. Jo unearthed the tag she'd been given at Victoria, and was pointed toward the appropriate carriage.

The cabin steward introduced himself, then escorted her to her com-partment. "If there's anything at all you require, Madame, please let me know. I'm Mark, and I'll be bringing your breakfast in the morning. What time would you like to be awakened?"

"Eight, please."

Her suitcase was already in the compartment. She stopped in the door-way and looked in, admiring the space that would be hers until the train reached Venice. Gleaming polished wood with a tiger-lily marquetry de-sign. To the right, curved doors concealed what she knew from the guide was a wash basin. Everything had been arranged like a painting, with bottles of Evian water and drinking glasses positioned in metal loops fixed to a corner of the wall to the right of the window; a copy of the Orient-Express magazine open on the table beneath the window, with a folder of stationery and some leaflets positioned precisely in the center; an ashtray with a small blue box of matches; lace covers on the seat backs; bolsters at each end of the seat; padded hangers; scrolled metal luggage racks; an upholstered stool; a discreet array of buttons on the wall at what would be the head of the bed when the compartment was made up in its nighttime configuration—to summon the steward, or douse the lights, or turn on the night light. This was, she'd been told, one of the four sleeping carriages that had been air-conditioned, and the air was crisp, even nippy.

While she was standing there completing her visual inspection, the maître d' came by, clipboard in hand, to ask which seating she would prefer at dinner, early or late. She chose early. A note was made of this, and she was given a discreet chit with VOITURE LAQUE DE CHINE printed on the top, and her seat number written in.

She used the wide-angle to photograph the compartment, then opened the pair of curved doors to see they were mirrored inside. Thick white towels with the gold-embroidered VS-O-E logo were folded into a rack; more bottles of Evian water; a shiny blue plastic container of bath soap, as well as hand soap in the now-familiar dark blue glossy cardboard; racks to contain her cosmetics; and the tiger-lily motif had been painstakingly hand-painted above the basin and below the mirrors on the doors to lend continuity to the decorating theme.

Crouched at the extreme end of the seat, wedging herself tight against the window, she got a shot of the basin area, then sat down and looked at the closed and locked doors directly in front of her that someone in the next compartment was trying to open. She smiled, wondering when they'd realize that the doors didn't conceal a closet or some secret locked room but did in fact open to double the space if a large party were traveling in adjoining compartments. The jiggling and pushing kept on for several minutes, then abruptly stopped. During this time, Jo hefted her suitcase onto the seat and got out her clothes for that evening as well as for the next day, hung them on the hangers provided, put her cosmetic bag by the basin, then closed the suitcase and tried to get it out of her way. It was too large to go onto the overhead rack, and if she pushed it under the small, fixed table, there'd be no room for her legs. At last, she placed it against the pair of locked doors and propped her feet on it; it made a handy ottoman.

While she found the compartment exquisite in design, and thought it would be very comfortable for two people sitting side by side, she couldn't imagine what it would be like for two adults attempting to dress or undress, or to sleep in such limited space. And speaking of sleep, where was the second berth hidden? Probably, the rear of the seat cleverly lifted up, or something. She made a note to ask the steward about it.

The train was moving. She sat by the window, looking out every few moments, while she flipped through the Orient-Express magazine. It had been left open at a double-page painting that illustrated the route from London to Venice: a bold black line punctuated by red circles at London, Folkestone, Boulogne, Paris, Basel, Zurich, the spur to Chur, St. Anton, Innsbruck, Bolzano, Verona, Venice. The painting was nicely done, depicting the Tower of London in the upper left-hand corner, then snowy Alps, and a gondolier mid-canal in the bottom right-hand corner. Sixteen hundred-odd miles.

Next she opened the small portfolio to look at the postcards and writing paper. Everything she'd seen so far was tastefully discreet and of top quality. She got out her notebook and pen to jot down a few facts. Passengers were requested not to take the towels, since the stewards would be charged at journey's end for missing items. Passengers were also asked not to drink the tap water, hence the stock of Evian.

She paused to consider the contrast between this train and the ones she often rode into Manhattan. Those commuter trains were so totally *plastic*: orange molded seats, booze posters, seats supposedly designated for the disabled and elderly that were invariably occupied by those neither old nor handicapped. And the view in the immediate foreground was of garbage littering both sides of the track and, nearer to Manhattan, derelict buildings with tin sheeting over the windows. This, she thought, running her hand over the plush seat fabric, was the zenith of train travel: windows without so much as a smudge on them; fittings that shone from regular attention; staff anxious and evidently happy to see to one's every need. If there was something she wanted, say from the cabin-service menu—some Beluga caviar perhaps, and an aperitif—all she'd have to do was press the call button and someone would come at once.

A quiet tapping at the door roused her. It was the maître d' who with an apologetic smile said, "Perhaps Madame was not aware of the time change. We are now at the second sitting."

"Time change?"

"Yes, Madame. One hour ahead. I have taken the liberty of rebooking, since I am certain Madame would not wish to miss dinner."

"Oh, thank you. I'll be right there. I'm awfully sorry."

"Not at all, Madame. There is no need to rush. You did wish to dine, yes?"

"Definitely. I really appreciate this. I'll be along in a few minutes."

"Very good, Madame. I hope," he smiled congenially, "you had a good sleep."

She'd managed to sleep for close to two hours. She got the shades drawn over the windows and then, trying to keep her balance, hurried to change clothes. She'd have liked to shower but there were no bathing facilities on board, aside from the basin in each compartment.

Fifteen minutes later, feeling half-assembled, she slung the camera bag over her shoulder and took a final look at herself in the mirrored doors. She hadn't ever had that consultation with Henry about her wardrobe for this trip. A pity. She wasn't at all convinced the two-piece beige silk was dressy enough.

When she emerged, Mark, the steward, was in the corridor.

"I'll lock your compartment now," he informed her. "If you plan to stay late in the bar car, I'll give you the key. Otherwise, just come and I'll open the door for you. And could I have your passport, please?"

"Oh, sure." She ducked back inside, found the passport, gave it to him, then had to stop to ask, "Which way is the dining car?"

"To your left, through the bar car. Enjoy your evening," he said pleasantly.

On her way down the corridor, holding on to the walls for support, she looked into the lavatory at the end of the carriage. Gleaming dark wood paneling, marble counters, bevel-edged mirrors; the room was pristine, scentless.

The entrance to the bar car was being used as a display area for VS-O-E gift items. Ties and scarves were draped over the brass handrails; photographs showed other available items. The car was full, the noise level high. People stood at the bar. White-jacketed waiters deftly carried trays of drinks to those seated in the armchairs and settees. A very large man in a tuxedo sat at the grand piano to the right of the bar area, playing innocuous renditions of old standards. Most of the male passengers were in tuxedos; the majority of the women wore evening dresses. Jo didn't see anyone in twenties-style gear, but there was one standout couple: a Japanese pair; he was perhaps in his early fifties, wearing a well-cut tuxedo and dress shoes with heels built up a good two inches; his companion, much younger and stunningly beautiful, had on a white silk kimono embroidered with white and gold threads, and a scarlet obi. The kimono looked as if it had never been touched by bare hands. The silk was matte, flawless, liquid as milk. The young woman, with her sleek cap of thick black hair, had captured the attention of the majority in the bar car.

As Jo picked her way through the crowd, people greeted her with smiles; a number said good evening. People were talking across the aisles; there was much laughter; the atmosphere was entirely festive—a party on wheels, whizzing through the night. Jo returned the smiles and the greetings, got to the far end of the car, and managed to open the door without either hitting anyone or falling off-balance in her high heels.

The maître d' greeted her at the front of the Chinese carriage as if the sight of her gave him great pleasure. With a demibow followed by a flourish, he said, "This way, please, Miss James," and showed her to a table for two halfway along the carriage. She sat down facing another empty table for two, then looked around to find people at nearby tables smiling at her. She smiled back, suffering through one of those piercing moments—like the one poor Katharine had had alone at her table in the piazza, watching all the couples go by—when her status as an unaccompanied woman was close to unbearable. She felt as if a small rock were lodged at the bottom of her stomach and her insides were churning around it in protest. Rather than invisible, she felt too conspicuous. It took someone, she thought, with great self-confidence to ride this train alone. It was a vehicle meant for twosomes; it required another person to whom one might turn to comment upon the people, the clothes, the food, the wine, the service. She busied herself organizing the camera bag under the table, notebook and pen close to hand. As she did, she wondered how many women had boarded this train alone, convinced they'd have magical, romantic encounters only to discover, as she was in the process of doing, that the presence of so many pairs could be dealt with in one of two ways. Either one toughed it out, concealing one's disappointment, or one made an attribute of one's aloneness and elected to respond positively to the curiosity and attention paid by those with sufficient generosity to extend welcoming smiles. Well, she'd smile and have a good time, she told herself, because there was no point in succumbing to the lure of self-pity. She smiled at the handsome elderly couple she recognized from the ferry, then picked up the gold-tasseled blue menu to read the offerings.

Escalope of sea bass with caviar and vodka to begin, followed by a fillet of beef sautéed with truffle sauce, spinach flan, and spring vegetables in a light puff pastry.

The waiter came to ask if she cared for something to drink.

"Some water, please."

"You would like *eau minerale*, or Perrier?"

"Mineral, please."

"Very good, Madame."

The car was a work of art: black lacquer panels with predominantly green designs of shrubs and trees, bits of color here and there in tulips, birds nesting in a tree, the red rooftops of a pagoda; more highly polished brass; dusky pink and white upholstery on the armed dining chairs, a complementing fabric in the curtains gracefully looped back from the windows.

Her eyes again met those of the elderly couple and it appeared they were about to speak to her when the attention of almost everyone in the car was drawn to the latest arrival, being shown to her seat by the charming Giuseppe, the maître d'.

The latecomer was a woman whose presence seemed to generate electricity. Somehow unaffected either by the motion of the train or the knowledge that she was being watched, she moved fluidly on very high heels, leaving in her wake a wonderfully rich fragrance of exotic flowers. She was wearing a black evening suit, exquisitely cut to show off her small waist, slim hips, and long, shapely legs.

Along with everyone else, Jo watched her take her seat at the facing table. An exquisite-looking woman, she had long almost black hair, pale skin, and dramatic makeup that accentuated her round light blue eyes and sensual mouth. She lit a cigarette, then shrugged off her jacket to reveal a white lace camisole top underneath. Beautiful shoulders and arms; her skin looked as if it had been polished, the tops of her breasts enticingly revealed above the scalloped lace. Jo was mesmerized. This was the sexiest woman she'd ever seen. She told herself she really had to stop staring so blatantly. But just as she thought this, the woman looked up, studied Jo for a moment, then smiled before turning to speak to Giuseppe, who'd lingered by the table as if he too found the newcomer riveting. He bent his head, listening intently, then straightened, nodded, spoke, listened again, nodded once more, and approached Jo.

"Mademoiselle," he said in an undertone to Jo, "wonders if you would care to join her for dinner since she sees that you are both alone."

Jo looked over at the woman, who smiled again at her, and underwent a moment of anxiety, unable to imagine what she could possibly find to talk about to someone so beautiful throughout an entire dinner. She felt the coil binding of the notebook under her fingers, collected her professionalism, and returned the smile. Think of it as an interview, she told herself.

"I am Lucienne Denis." The woman offered her hand as Jo sat down opposite with her notebook and camera. "Much better not to eat alone, eh?"

"I couldn't agree more," Jo said and, taking hold of the woman's hand, introduced herself.

Nine

"Excuse me just for one moment," Lucienne said, and picked up the menu to scan the wine list. Then, without bothering to look around, she made a lazy gesture with her hand that at once brought Giuseppe back to the table.

"We will have the St. Émilion," she told him, then asked Jo, "You will have some wine?"

"I'd love some, thank you," she answered, to Lucienne's obvious satisfaction.

"So," Lucienne said, retrieving her cigarette from the ashtray, "what is it you are doing with all this?" She indicated the camera and notebook.

"A travel feature for an American magazine."

"You're a journalist, eh?"

"Primarily a photographer. Do you have a career? That's a wonderful suit."

"You like this? Good. I like it, too. You are interviewing me, eh?"

Jo flushed. "Not really. Just curious."

"No matter. My career . . ." She paused to take a final puff on the cigarette before putting it out. "I have a bistro in Paris. Chez Lucienne. You know Paris?"

"Not very well. I don't get there often, but next time I do, I'll be sure to come to your restaurant."

"Ah, well, you will have to make a reservation four or five weeks in advance."

"Really?" Jo was impressed.

"I make exceptions," Lucienne said with amusement. "If you are

352

planning to be in Paris, you telephone to me and arrangements will be made. It helps," she laughed, "to know the owner."

"Are you from Paris?"

"No, Canada."

"Oh, really? Where in Canada?"

"I was born in Quebec."

"I love Quebec City," Jo told her. "I was there about four years ago, to do a feature. It was one of the best times I've ever had. Where in Quebec did you live?"

"We lived in the bush, eh, far from anywhere. My papa, he worked with the lumber company."

"I can't imagine you living in the bush," Jo said. "You give the impression of someone who'd know her way around a city, who'd never lived anywhere else, especially not in the bush."

"You think so?" Again Lucienne smiled. "Why do you think this?"

"Oh, well, your clothes, for one thing, and the way you wear them. I don't know. Just everything about you. You seem very urban."

"Urban?" Lucienne looked puzzled for a moment, then laughed. "I like this. Urban," she repeated. "My parents they send me to a Catholic boarding school in Quebec City." She made a face. "At sixteen I ran away."

"My God! Where did you go?"

"I worked in a bowling alley. Very exciting." Again she made a face.

"And then what?" Jo asked, anxious for details.

"You are very curious, eh?"

"Always," Jo admitted disarmingly. "Do you mind?"

"No, I don't mind. Other people, I think maybe they mind?"

"Sometimes," Jo allowed.

"Me, I don't mind. I leave there to go to work in a restaurant, save my money, because I have decided I want to go to Paris. When I am twenty, I work on a ship and go to Paris."

"What did you do on the ship?"

"Ah! I cook, for the crew. A terrible job, very hot. You have been on a ship?"

"A couple of times."

"This was a—cargo ship. That is right, cargo?"

"That's right. Were you the only woman?"

Lucienne laughed again. "No. There were four. I would not go to be the only woman."

"It sounds like you've done some pretty amazing things."

"Maybe so."

The waiter came with the wine, opened the bottle, then awaited

Lucienne's approval. She sniffed the cork as well as the neck of the bottle, studied the label, then said, "Good." The waiter exhaled as if a crucial test had just been passed, and poured a small amount into her glass. Again she sniffed; then she tasted; then nodded. Happily, the waiter poured the glasses full.

"*Salut!*" Lucienne touched her glass to Jo's, and drank.

The red wine was very dry, very smooth.

"Did you ever get in touch again with your family?" Jo asked.

"Oh, yes. I was very angry with them, you know, for sending me to live with the nuns. But once I am free, I write to them to say I'm happy now, everything is okay."

"And what about your restaurant? How long have you had it?"

"When I am twenty-eight, I start my bistro. *Et voilà*, the rest, it is history. So"—she lit a fresh cigarette and shifted the direction of the conversation—"you will be staying in Venice?"

"For five days, at the Cipriani. And you?"

"You have been before?"

"No, never."

"You will *adore* it! The Cipriani is very fine, very good cuisine. I stay also at the Cipriani. I am to be married soon in Venice," she announced, having decided she liked this young American woman with all the questions.

"That's terrific! Congratulations."

Rather than appearing elated at the prospect, Lucienne seemed offhand. "You think it's good to be married?" she asked, as if Jo's opinion was of importance. "You are married?"

"No. The staff seems to know you." It was Jo's turn to redirect the conversation.

"I like the train," Lucienne said simply. "I come quite often to meet with Paolo in Venice. Sometimes, if he has business, he comes back with me to Paris. You like this train? It is your first time?"

"Yes, and I love it. It's fabulous."

"Yes." Lucienne looked around with a pleased, even proud, air. "When you are at the Cipriani, you will meet Renato. He is the chef who prepares the food for the train. You speak Italian?" Jo shook her head. "No matter. You will meet him, see how they make the menus."

"How do you know him?" Jo asked, finding this far easier than she'd anticipated. Lucienne wasn't at all difficult to talk with; she was, in fact, most responsive. At this latest of Jo's questions, her gleaming shoulders lifted in a delicate little shrug. "I am impressed very much with the food on the train, so I ask who it is who makes the menu, and when I am in Venice, I go to the hotel to meet this man, see his kitchen. He is young, but very good. Very modern methods they have for preparing the food.

Then," she laughed, "very traditional method for taking food to the train. It travels by boat. Old and new together. Very good."

Listening to Lucienne, Jo couldn't help thinking what a good thing it was that she'd had no preconceived notions about this journey, because every aspect of it so far had been unexpected. She couldn't imagine any other set of circumstances that would have placed her in the company of this beautiful yet agreeably accessible woman. Lucienne struck her as quintessentially French, with that impeccable flair for clothes, and the dramatic features, that French women seemed to have genetically. She was, Jo imagined, someone who probably always looked good, even when climbing out of bed first thing in the morning. She also had the ability to make Jo feel as if her opinions and impressions were of significance, so that rather than being intimidated as she'd feared at being in the company of someone who attracted so much attention, she actually felt very much at ease, as well as grateful for the woman's spontaneous invitation to join her. She was also glad to have no particular need to wear her professional hat. It was an easy pleasure to share in the give-and-take of thoughts and information with someone so surprisingly forthcoming.

The waiter returned, asking if they were ready to order.

Lucienne retrieved the menu, studied it for a minute or two, then said, "I will have the smoked salmon." In an aside to Jo, she said, "I am not in the mood for sea bass."

"I've never had it," Jo replied, "but they served seafood for lunch. I think I'd prefer a salad, if that's possible."

"Certainly, Madame." The waiter noted their selections. When satisfied there were no other substitutions to the set dinner they cared to make, he went off.

Jo again looked around the car, noticing two middle-aged blond American women, both in beaded evening dresses, who seemed to be having a grand time. They clinked their wineglasses together, laughing. Farther along, waiters were presenting two sets of honeymooners with bottles of wine, making inaudible explanations as they did. Jo watched as the wine was poured and then both young couples raised their glasses in the direction of the elderly couple across the aisle from Jo. She turned to see the older pair lift their glasses in a toast to the newlyweds.

They were a remarkably attractive twosome, most distinguished, and Jo could just picture them on a tea plantation in Kuala Lumpur or some other exotic locale. He had the look and bearing of someone accustomed to being in authority. And his wife had the manner of a woman who'd dealt efficiently and well throughout her life with household staff.

Noticing that Jo was watching, the woman leaned over to say, "We spent our honeymoon on the train, you see. And Jimmy's very sentimental."

"Not at all," Jimmy disagreed. "One simply doesn't have honeymoons every day."

"We're celebrating our fiftieth anniversary," the woman went on, unfazed.

"Oh, that's wonderful!" Jo looked over at Lucienne and the two of them drank a toast to the couple.

Lucienne smoked her cigarette and watched her dinner companion talk with the old English couple, finding this American woman most engaging. Initially, Lucienne had thought she was perhaps in her late twenties, this Joanna. But upon closer inspection, she raised her estimate to the early thirties. She was not in the habit of inviting strangers to dine with her, especially not women who invariably sought, in some fashion, to compete. Joanna not only seemed uninterested in competition, but was openly complimentary, and her admitted curiosity was charming because of the interest she showed. Qualities, perhaps, of a journalist. But Lucienne saw something more. This Joanna was well groomed, her clothes were very good, but altogether she had an aura of gentleness and a sense of fun that made her appear younger than she was. Studying Jo as she continued her conversation with the English couple, Lucienne decided her new friend had a veritable gift for engagement, for compassion. This, in Lucienne's experience, was rare. But Joanna very much liked people. And as if to confirm this mute evaluation of Lucienne's, Jo now swung into conversation with the two blond American women who seemed most eager to confide to her the difficulties they had had in bathing and dressing for dinner in their shared compartment. Lucienne sat back, lit another cigarette, and was content to watch Joanna charm everyone with whom she spoke.

"We fell all over each other," one of the women declared with a laugh.

"She's not just kidding. We deserve prizes for getting dressed, I'll tell you."

"I was wondering how two people would manage in a compartment," Jo said with a smile.

"It ain't easy, sister," the first woman said. "But we wouldn't've missed it for the world."

The first courses arrived then, and to Lucienne's amusement, Jo said, "This is so beautiful, I just have to get a shot of it," and proceeded to take a picture of her salad.

"This is something you do often?" Lucienne asked as Jo was putting away the camera.

"I'm afraid so. It's the sort of shot editors love. And so do I. Even if they don't use this particular exposure, I'll look at it sometime when I'm going through my files, and it'll remind me of the entire evening. I'll think about that darling couple celebrating their fiftieth anniversary by sending wine to the newlyweds, and I'll remember those two women from New York. And of course I'll remember you. Did you hear what they said, the two women?"

Lucienne shook her head.

"They're doing the 'Big Three': the Concorde, the Orient-Express, and the QEII. The trip of a lifetime." Lowering her voice, she said, "I'd bet anything the two of them were show girls once upon a time. I can just see them in some nightclub, all done up in skimpy little costumes with feathers and spangles. Can't you see it?"

"Maybe," Lucienne allowed. "Or dancers, eh?"

"They have that glamorous look. Anyway, I'll remember them, and the fact that you're on your way to get married."

Lucienne frowned slightly and started on her smoked salmon. "I am not so sure," she admitted after a few moments. "Six years I have been saying 'not now' to Paolo. Then, in April when he was in Paris, I said, 'In July.' Now it is July and I think maybe it is not such a great idea."

"Why not?"

Lucienne gave another delicate little shrug, wondering as she did why she was revealing so much to this woman. Yet why not? What could be safer than a discussion with someone you met on a train, someone you might never see again? "It is very complicated," she said. "I am thinking this moment about Chez Lucienne, about my regular clientele, and about the chef who is very temperamental. I am hoping they will do the deposits correctly. Too many things."

"And if you don't do everything yourself," Jo said sagely, "you can't be sure everything's being done right."

Lucienne's eyes widened. "Precisely! You are this way?"

"I don't know." Jo thought about it. "Maybe I am. Sometimes I'm not altogether sure what I'm like. And the only person I have to worry about is me."

"So maybe you are this way after all."

"Could be," Jo said, quickly eating the lightly dressed salad that had been arranged like a flower, with cuts of avocado intersecting leaves of curly lettuce. "Don't you want to get married?"

"Sometimes I think yes, sometimes I think no. You are happy with your life, eh?"

"Yes and no."

"I am the same." Lucienne took a morsel of smoked salmon into her mouth, drank some of the wine, then gazed appraisingly at Joanna. "You are—*mignon*," she smiled. "You understand French?"

"Only a little."

"You are gracious. This is not a usual quality of young women. I am very happy to meet you."

"Thank you," Jo said quietly. "I'm happy to meet you, too. I was starting to feel conspicuous, and you rescued me. It's very kind of you to invite me to join you, and very kind of you to say such nice things."

"It is not kind. The truth is not a kindness."

"No," Jo spoke slowly. "But how many people even know what the truth is, let alone tell it to other people?"

"Ah, yes. Well, I am in agreement with this."

"D'you mind if I ask you something?"

"Already you have asked me everything," Lucienne smiled at her. "I don't mind."

"Doesn't it bother you, traveling alone?"

"No. I prefer it."

"Why?"

"Because it is an occasion when I have no need to think of other people. It is a time only for myself."

"That makes sense."

"But of course it does. You must always take the time to be with yourself, enjoy your own company. You dislike to travel alone?"

"Not usually."Again Jo looked around. Most of the others were finished with their main courses and were being presented with dessert. Everyone seemed to glow. Much laughter, the throb of conversations beneath the perpetual noise of the train itself, the chimelike music of cutlery against porcelain, clinking glassware. It was like a dream, or a scene from another era; it was unlike anything else with which she was directly familiar. She thought again of the way both Henry and Tyler had showed up to see her off, then looked at the woman opposite and decided she preferred her present company. It was what she needed just then. She was able to be herself with Lucienne in ways she couldn't be with either man. Maybe it wasn't possible to be completely one's self with any man unless you were so sure of your identity, your priorities, your needs, that others lacked the power to influence you. But was that entirely true? What about Lily? *Who was it who put a camera into your hands and said, "This is who you are?"*

"What is it that you think?" Lucienne asked.

"Sorry. I was thinking that nine times out of ten women are easier and more satisfying to be with than men."

"Some women. Some men. But I will drink a toast with you on that!" Lucienne said, and touched her glass to Jo's. Then, pleased with themselves, they laughed.

The food was superb, and both of them made small appreciative sounds as they ate, then laughed some more, and drank more of the wine.

"This is so great!" Jo said happily when the waiter brought their dessert, an iced meringue with three different kinds of fresh red berries.

"You are not going to take a photograph?" Lucienne teased.

"Nope. I'm just going to eat it. I love fresh berries. I love this train!"

"After," Lucienne said, "we will go to the bar car. This you will love, too."

The bar car was only half full now, the atmosphere rather subdued. It took only a moment, once they were seated, to see that the cause was the corpulent pianist, who was playing a rather somber version of "Autumn Leaves." He finished the piece with a rippling arpeggio, then sailed into a medley of Viennese waltzes. It was all wrong, the first element of the trip that was totally out of synch.

"I have not seen this one before," Lucienne said. "Usually, the music is very lively, eh? People sing, they dance. Not like this."

A cheery young waiter came over and Lucienne ordered a cognac. On impulse, Jo asked for Grand Marnier. She'd already had several glasses of wine, and realized belatedly that she'd allowed Lucienne to pay for it. "This is my treat," she told Lucienne. Her reward was a sudden smile that seemed composed of equal parts pleasure and surprise.

The three American women Jo recognized from Lucille and from the ferry were seated directly behind the piano player and were trying, without success, to get him to play something a little more upbeat. Opposite the three women were the two blond widows Jo was still convinced were former show girls. A French couple with a young son of perhaps ten or eleven sat in stony silence.

"What d'you think?" Jo asked Lucienne, quietly indicating the French pair. "I think she's his third wife, at least, and the boy's his only son. He has the name, but she has the money. She hates him for having the name, and he hates her for having the money. The boy wishes they'd get a divorce so he can stop tagging along with them everywhere they go and just stay home and hang out with his friends."

As Jo made up this history, Lucienne studied the family, and when Jo had finished, she nodded once slowly and said, "That's good. I like it. Now tell me about the four there."

Jo looked where Lucienne indicated, taking stock of two American couples, Texans, from what she could hear of their accents, and probably parents traveling with their daughter and her husband. The daughter was a billowy, curly-headed blonde in a frilly, fussy, full-skirted dress; her husband was in a navy suit, very Ivy League, and looked thoroughly bored. The mother was a petite, good-looking blonde, exquisitely dressed in white silk, and the father was in black tie.

"Okay," Jo said. "The father is in oil. The mother's been taking night courses at the university for the last couple of years, working on her master's in something esoteric, like, say, medieval history. The chunky one's her daughter, and the guy with her is her husband. The parents are old money, at ease and discreet. The daughter managed to snag a husband, probably by telling him she was pregnant. She's never done a thing in her life except spend her parents' money—and she's very good at that. The husband probably works for the father and likes the parents but can't stand his wife and would do anything to get out of the marriage, but he likes to spend their money, too, and doesn't want to give it up, so they're stuck together. The daughter's a real piece of work; she's the kind who'll drive around a shopping center for hours until she finds a parking place right in front of the store she wants to go to."

Lucienne laughed, saying, "You are too terrible. Did you also make some story for me when I came to the dining car?"

Jo blushed. "Actually," she confessed, "I thought you were some French film star, but I couldn't think who."

"I like that," Lucienne declared. "I don't mind to be mistaken for a film star. Do you see the little Japanese in the very beautiful—what do you call it?"

"Kimono."

"Yes. Now, I tell you my story. You see he is very much older. And this is not his wife. He wears a wedding ring, but she does not, eh? He has the company in Tokyo that makes the machines to answer the telephone, and she is the one who sits at the reception to greet visitors. He buys her the clothes and takes her always when he travels, so that everyone will think he is a very great man with a most beautiful young wife. He thinks no one can see that he has special shoes to make him tall. You see this?"

"I did!" Jo laughed behind her hand.

"Ah, look!" Lucienne said. "See these two!"

Coming up the aisle was a very slim woman in a perfect beaded and scalloped twenties dress that was sleeveless and had a scooped neck. Around her neck and hanging almost to her knees were several ropes of pearls, and her hair was concealed by a beaded cloche; even her shoes were right, with sculpted heels and rounded toes. Her partner was wearing a white tuxedo, white shirt, and white bow tie.

"They must have shopped for months to find those clothes," Jo said admiringly. "I'd love to get a shot of the two of them, but I wouldn't dare. It's too intrusive."

"You are wise," Lucienne approved.

"More like experienced," Jo said. "There are times when you just can't jump up and start taking pictures."

"Something is happening." Lucienne tapped Jo on the arm.

The piano player was rising from his seat. There was a sudden conference among the three American women and then the oldest of them slipped onto the bench, flexed her fingers, and started playing show tunes. The other two at once began singing along, and the car sprang to life. Others began to clap and to join in the singing.

"This is better!" Lucienne said happily. "She is great, eh? And the one who sings, not the tall dark one, but the *petite* in the gray, she has so much fun. You see?"

Jo directed her eyes to the woman Lucienne had spoken of, an attractive woman with high cheekbones, large eyes, and tremendous energy, who sang out in a good strong show voice; she laughed gaily and applauded with enthusiasm between numbers. "I can never remember the words," Jo said, her eyes still on the singer, who had a long neck and very short boyishly cut dark hair. Diamond rings on both hands, as well as diamond earrings, yet none of it was ostentatious. Her outfit was like a Pierrot suit, the top with several layers of ruffles around a wide drawstring neck, the trousers fitted at the waist and hips but loose in the legs.

"She reminds me of someone, too," Jo said, "but I can't think who."

People sang and clapped along; more drinks came; drinks were sent to the singers and the woman at the piano. Then the two women were not only singing, they were, in seeming defiance both of gravity and the lurching of the train, dancing in the aisle while the others cheered. Jo and Lucienne clapped, too, and there was a moment when it occurred to Jo that she'd had a great deal to drink, and she looked around, hoping she wasn't disgracing herself. But no. Everyone seemed happy.

The French woman took her young son off to bed, the husband trailing reluctantly after. Then, not five minutes later, the husband returned and joined with the two women dancing in the aisle. The sullen-looking young Texas woman and her blue-suited husband got up, too, as did one of the honeymoon couples.

"There will be trouble," Lucienne said in an undertone. "Did you see that? He has taken the wife and boy to bed, now he returns. She is the type who will not be happy with this. She is one who will blame the two women who sing and dance."

"How can you tell?" Jo took a sip of her second Grand Marnier.

Lucienne made a knowing face. "It is not so difficult when you are accustomed to dealing every day with many people."

"You really love it, don't you?" Jo guessed. "Is your fiancé expecting you to give up the restaurant when you get married?"

"He doesn't say it, but I think it is what he hopes."

"And you don't want to do that."

"I don't think I am *able* to do it," Lucienne sighed. "I make decisions late at night sometimes, eh? It is quiet, Chez Lucienne is closed, and I am alone. Then I make decisions, because I am tired, because I am soon to be forty, because it has been a long day. But in the morning, I think forty is not so very old, and I am not tired, there is work to do, and I have great pleasure in the work. You have not been married ever?"

"No. I used to think it was inevitable, that I'd do all the things I wanted to do, and at the end would be marriage. Now I'm not so sure anymore. I mean, I'm not unhappy the way I am. I love my work, just the way you do. And for the most part, the men I know only seem to be interested in my willingness to sleep with them. Who I am, the way I am, none of that's a big part of what they want somehow. Maybe I'm not explaining it all that well. I don't usually have so much to drink."

"I think you explain it *very* well," Lucienne put her hand on Jo's arm. "You are most truthful. It is a long time since I talked with a friend."

"Me, too. I'm the same way you are about making decisions at night. The one thing I know for sure is that it doesn't matter what I tell myself after the sun goes down, because when it comes up again, everything'll be different."

"Yes," Lucienne said softly.

The piano player had returned. The three American women were preparing to leave, as were the majority of the others in the car. Jo looked at her watch to see it was almost twelve-thirty.

"I had no idea it was so late," she said. "I think I'm going to have to go to bed now. It's been a very long day."

"Then you must go," Lucienne smiled tiredly.

"Thank you so much for asking me to join you. I've had a terrific time, really terrific. Maybe we could have lunch together."

"That would be good."

"Okay. Well, I'll see you in the morning." Jo picked up the camera bag.

"*Bonne nuit*, Joanna."

"Thanks again."

Stopping at the bar to pay for the drinks and to tip the young waiter, Jo looked back down the length of the carriage to see Lucienne light a cigarette before lifting her cognac. The half-dozen or so remaining passengers were all covertly eyeing her as they got ready to leave. From this distance Jo was again struck by her new friend's glamour, by the feline grace of her posture, by the exquisite structure of her body, by the beauty of her pale skin, dark hair, and light blue eyes, and also by the unseen barrier that seemed to hold her locked in isolation. For a few seconds it seemed to Jo as if she'd never seen anyone so visibly cut off from others simply by dint of her physical beauty. She was tempted to go back and stay until Lucienne was ready to go to bed. But then Lucienne seemed to decide that the time had come. She finished the brandy, stubbed out her just-lit cigarette and reached for her bag.

Jo hefted the Lowe-pro onto her shoulder one last time and started back toward her compartment.

Ten

WITH THE SHADES DRAWN OVER THE WINDOW AND THE BED MADE up for the night, the dimensions of the compartment seemed much reduced. It was also extremely cold, and she got down on her knees, pushing past the stool and her suitcase to close the air vent. The motion of the train also seemed more pronounced, throwing her off balance, so she had to undress in stages. It took quite some time before she was finally in her nightgown, with her clothes hung away.

Face clean, teeth brushed, she was eager to climb between the crisp sheets. The night light above the bed cast a cobalt-blue glow, allowing her just enough light to see potential obstacles, and she lay down, at once even more aware of the train's motion. Recumbent, she became a part of the train, her entire body sensitive to the track bed. She wished she'd thought to bring on board some Dramamine, or even her Valium, because with the undiminished cold of the compartment and the lurching rush of the train over the tracks, she was very uncomfortable. But her medications were in the bag she'd checked through to Venice.

It was odd to think how readily she'd slept earlier, and how difficult she was finding it now. If she didn't get some sleep, she'd be a wreck by the time she got to Venice. But the more she yawned and thought about how tired she was, the less able she was to get to sleep. She turned from side to side; she even tried switching off the night light but had to turn it on again at once; it was simply too unrelentingly dark without it.

She drifted on the surface of sleep, and her thoughts were drawn toward Henry. In that state of being neither asleep nor awake, he once more acted out his passion, while she was both observer and participant. She watched and responded to the descent of his hands as they shaped her breasts, measured the span of her waist and hips; her appetite grew as he displayed his approving pleasure. She noted his surprise as she revealed her inability to be passive or detached. They surprised each other, she saw from her vantage point of distance. Henry's approach to her was direct yet refined; like an avid botanist examining the intricacies of some peerless floral specimen, he delved ever deeper into its core until, jubilant, he found its heart behind closely-wrapped concealing petals. And having uncovered the mystery of his hybrid treasure, he was respectful, even reverential. He had responded to her with whispered expressions of elation as if, like her, he also had never mastered the art of being casual.

Then there was Tyler. His approach had little to do with discovery, but almost everything to do with claim-staking; placing his territorial stamp on what he craved. His view was generalized, not specific. He appeared to have a talent for cloaking his true feelings by using a lifetime of theatrical training and experience as a scrim. This gauzy fabric could be lowered at a moment's notice to soften the landscape of his vulnerability. His love-making had been self-directed, an activity meant to display his masterly technique and determination. It had been impressive, breath-taking and, ultimately, impersonal. Tyler had taken her over; Henry had encouraged her to be aware. The two men had talked on the telephone and Tyler had revealed more of the state of his emotions to Henry than he had to her during the hours they spent naked together. Why was it men could find some fashion in which to communicate to each other, but not to women? Or was it she who had the reservations, the difficulties, the lack of trust?

She continued to drift, thoughts and images floating into range, then away, for what felt like hours. She remembered an afternoon—a Sunday, it must have been—when she and Henry had walked through a fine mist of winter rain all the way to Westminster Bridge. She'd left the camera back in the guest room because of the mist, and was feeling especially empty-handed, so she'd put her arm through Henry's. And he'd reached across to pat her reassuringly on the hand. The gesture had taken her off guard and she'd turned to look at him, but he'd been looking straight ahead. So she'd decided it had been an automatic gesture on his part, and she'd been angry with herself for being someone who constantly sought meanings where none existed.

"Is something wrong?" he'd asked her. "Are you cold?"

"No." She'd given him a bright, false smile. "I'm just fine, thank you."

His eyes had stayed on her then, and he'd said, "Someday, Jo, you'll tell the truth when someone asks you how you are. And then, to your utter astonishment, you'll find you get precisely the reaction you were seeking."

"What?"

"Nothing. Forget it. I have a splendid idea," he'd announced.

"What?"

"I think we should have tea at the Savoy."

"God, Henry! I'm not dressed for that."

"You think not?" He'd looked her over. "What's wrong with the way you're dressed?"

"The Savoy? They'll throw me out on my ear."

"Oh, on your ass, possibly. But never on your ear."

She'd laughed, and he'd reached out and pinched her cheek.

"You're such a twit, Jo. They'll just think you're another rich American tourist."

"Yeah. But I'll know I'm not."

"Well," he'd sighed. "I suppose it'll have to be a cuppa at some caff, then. Someplace where you'll fit right in."

"They'll be tickled to death to see you in your little three-piece number."

"I'm sure they will. Lend a bit of tone to the establishment. Tell you what. We'll compromise, and have tea and crustless sandwiches at the Ritz. We'll tell them you're blind. I'll whisper something to the effect that the poor girl thinks she's wearing her best Chanel. They'll go along. We British excel at closing our eyes to the indiscretions of the handicapped."

"Hell!" she'd laughed again. "If I'm going to be blind, let's go to the Savoy."

"Good girl!"

Gradually, she was aware of the train slowing to a stop. At once, she fell asleep, only to awaken a short while later when the train started up again. This continued throughout the night: she'd sleep when the train stopped, and come awake when it started up again.

She'd finally settled into sleep when the steward knocked with her tray. With an inward groan, she sat up, got the door unlocked, and said good morning to Mark as he slid the tray onto the table beneath the window. She then raised the shades partway to find it was raining, which meant she'd be unable to take any shots of the scenery. And that was just fine. She'd spend all the time she wanted drinking the fresh-squeezed orange juice and some of the coffee from the thermos flask; she'd sample the croissants and brioches and taste every one of the small jars of jam and marmalade. And she'd save the *International Herald Tribune* to read in the bar car. Her eyes felt too gritty, she was too tired altogether, to concentrate on reading just then.

Gazing out the rain-drenched window at the mountains—they were passing through Switzerland—she thought longingly of a hot bath or a shower. The two widows from New York had been quite crushed to learn there were no bathing facilities on board. Jo knew from her reading that there wouldn't be any. Nevertheless, it would have been good to immerse herself in a deep tub of water and scrub away some of the travel grime. But there was only the basin, and she badly needed to bathe. So she got out of her nightgown and, holding on to one of the mirrored doors for support, managed a sponge bath. It helped, as did having daylight enlarge the compartment. She no longer felt in need of medication; she was merely tired.

Dressed finally in black cotton slacks and a short-sleeved black shirt, carrying her purse and the camera bag, she made her way to the lavatory at the end of the carriage. It was again spotless. She was impressed.

Upon emerging, she came across Mark feeding pieces of wood into a small boiler at the end of the carriage just beyond the lavatory.

"What is it you're doing?" she asked as he laid the last of the wood on the fire before closing the paneled door.

"This heats the bathing water," he explained. "We use charcoal and wood." He opened a lower door to show her a store of bags of both.

"That's amazing! How often do you have to feed the fire?"

"Peak usage hours. Before dinner when we leave Boulogne, and again in the morning, then before lunch. We try to anticipate the need and keep the boiler stoked. The passengers," he confided, "sometimes get rather cross if there isn't enough hot water, especially first thing in the morning."

He was happy to stand there for an extra minute while she got a picture. She thanked him and went on to the bar car, which, with morning, had been transformed into a kind of salon. The gift items were back on sale, and several people were inspecting them. The waiters were serving juice and coffee; people sat reading newspapers; and the corpulent piano player was at his post, his music more appropriate in daytime than it had been the night before. There were couples and quartets here and there, either staring out the windows or talking quietly. Fresh flowers were on the bar and the piano top, and the air bore no trace of the previous night's tobacco smoke. This car changed character, depending on the time of day or night and on its occupants. But whatever its character, it was clearly the focal point of the train.

From a seat about two-thirds of the way down from the bar, she took in the details: cream-painted ceiling with dark wood strips, and two recessed areas adding height; dark paneling down the sides; the upholstery on the armed chairs and settees was predominantly taupe, with a paler shade of taupe in the scrollwork design; the carpet was in shades of muted green with hints of red in a curling leaf-and-flower design; in front of the settees were oblong coffee tables that had held drinks last night and now held cups of coffee; the curtains were a dusky pink, held at each side by tasseled cords; here and there were more of the pink-shaded lamps; brass handrails were regularly spaced the length of the car; and at the far end, to the right was the bar and to the left the grand piano.

Luke, the sweet-faced young waiter, came to ask what she would like. She ordered coffee, then set the camera and lenses in front of her on the fixed, round-edged table. It was still raining. She'd have to get shots of this scenery on the return trip when, with luck, the weather would be clear. She looked down the carriage again to see the fiftieth-anniversary couple entering. As they approached her, she said good morning.

"Oh, good morning! A pity it's raining," the woman said brightly as they settled opposite. "I expect you could get some quite wonderful photographs of all this."

"I'll be going back to London on the train," Jo told her, "so I'll have another chance."

"Ah, good, good," her husband said quietly, listening in on the conversation as he aligned his reading matter on the table.

"May I ask what it is you're doing?" the woman inquired.

"I'm writing a feature on the train for an American travel magazine. Primarily, I'm a photographer, but quite often I do cover articles, which means I do the photographic work as well as the writing. I'd rather just do the photos, but economically it's more practical to do the entire piece."

"How very interesting. Jimmy's quite keen on photography, aren't you?" She turned to her husband.

He had to shift slightly sideways because the space beneath the table wasn't sufficient to accommodate the length of his legs. "I prefer black and white, actually," he said to Jo. "I find color photographs rather distracting. When it comes to color, I'd much rather study paintings."

"Which is what he'll be doing throughout our stay in Venice," Anne added.

The waiter brought Jo's coffee, then, with a little bow, said, "Good morning, Sir James, Lady Arlington. You would wish something?"

Jo watched as Sir James asked for tea and his wife said she'd like some coffee. She felt like a child, awed at being with members of the British peerage, and for a few moments was rendered speechless.

"How rude of me," Lady Arlington said, correctly interpreting, and charmed by, the surprise widening Jo's eyes. "I am Anne, and this is Jimmy."

Jo told them her name, then admitted, "I'm really impressed. I've never met anyone with a title."

Anne laughed. "Hardly impressive," she said, thinking again how very like Lucia Jo was. "It's Jimmy's title. I merely tag along."

"Oh, but even so," Jo said. "To be Sir and Lady, it's so—storybook."

"How very dear of you," Anne said. "I'm afraid we're most ordinary, except for Jimmy's passion for the Venetian artists, and the Italian school in general. He'll most likely walk my feet off in Venice, taking me to out-of-the-way churches to show me works by Titian and Tintoretto and all the others."

"It's not your first trip to Venice, is it?" Jo asked them.

"First in fifty years," Jimmy said.

"We spent our honeymoon in Venice," Anne elaborated. "This is our second trip." She looked lovingly at her husband. "He's always been reluctant to return for fear of having his first impressions altered."

"But the paintings, the artwork, will still be the same, won't they?" Jo asked him.

"We'll know soon enough," he said with a smile.

"And how long will you be staying in Venice, Joanna?" Anne wanted to know.

"Just five days."

"One can see quite a great deal in five days," Jimmy said. "A number of must-sees, of course. Splendid works in Santa Maria del Giglio, including several Tintorettos; then there's the Gothic church of Santo Stefano; and—"

"I should write all this down." Jo grabbed her notebook.

"Most assuredly," Jimmy agreed. He repeated the names he'd already mentioned, then went on to include, "Santa Maria della Salute which, among others, has a number of Titians; then, of course, you simply must see the church of San Trovaso, and San Sebastiano; and, very important, San Nicolò dei Mendicoli; San Giacomo dell'Orio; San Simeone Grande; San Silvestro." He named half a dozen more churches, then wound down, saying, "Not to mention the Accademia, and all the galleries."

"You see what I mean!" Anne laughed. "I have my work cut out for me."

"You certainly do," Jo agreed. "How long are you planning to stay?"

"Several weeks," Jimmy said. "After fifty years, one really shouldn't rush through the city."

"I wouldn't think so." Jo gave him a smile, and he stared at her for just a moment, then returned it.

"Where will you be staying?" Anne asked her.

"At the Cipriani."

"Oh, so shall we!" she said. "You must dine with us one evening."

"I'd love to. Thank you very much."

"Actually, we were about to invite you to join us last evening, but we noticed you struck up an acquaintance with that most attractive French woman."

"Isn't she gorgeous?" Jo said. "She'll be staying at the Cipriani, too."

"In that case," Jimmy said, "we'll have to give both of you dinner."

"She's going to be getting married in Venice," Jo explained.

"Now, that's a pity," Jimmy said, and laughed when Anne slapped the back of his hand. "She is a rather fabulous creature."

For her part, Jo found these two rather fabulous. Sir James, Jimmy, was very tall, perhaps six foot two or three, with a full head of lustrous white hair, a broad forehead, wide-set blue eyes, a long well-modeled nose, high slanting cheekbones, and a relaxed mouth. This morning he was wearing navy trousers, a long-sleeved white shirt, a sleeveless cotton V-neck pullover in a Fair Isle pattern of misty blues and greens, and a jaunty light green bow tie. Anne had on another shirtwaist dress, this one of emerald green polished cotton that pointed up her fair skin and green eyes. She was shorter than her husband, about five six or seven, and wore her hair in a loosely waved bob that came just to below her ears. Again Jo couldn't help thinking what a striking pair they must have made fifty years ago, riding this train on their honeymoon.

"How," Jo asked them, "does the train seem to you fifty years later?"

"They've done a bang-up job!" Jimmy declared. "Have you noticed," he said, turning toward the window, "that even the smallest round-headed screw is of brass?" Turning back, he said, "Have to say I'm impressed. They haven't messed about with her, trying to add bits and pieces to placate those who come along expecting to find three-piece suites in every compartment. No. It's just as it was, but actually better. I don't recall there being a grand piano." He smiled. "But it's a jolly nice touch. Had a word with the train manager last evening about it. Wondering, you know, how they managed to get it inside. Took the legs off, you see, then brought the beast in on its side when the carriages were separated."

"I was going to ask about that," Jo told him. "I was wondering myself."

Luke came with Jimmy's tea and Anne's coffee, and in the lull Jo noticed that the interior of the car was growing lighter. She looked out to see that they were moving away from the rain, and automatically raised the camera. Chalets sat here and there at the base of the mountains; a river of impossible, Caribbean, blue appeared around the next bend; a sawmill with tidy stacks of lumber beside a brick retaining wall that backed onto the riverbank; a covered bridge; fields of flowers. Suddenly, the land dipped far below the tracks, spreading into a lush green valley surrounded by mist-enveloped mountains; on the rain-slick roads of a village, a man with an umbrella stood alone near an intersection watching the train go past; gliding through a town, past a block of low-rise apartments, and there was a man out on his balcony with a video camera set up to film the train's passage; on again into the countryside, where an elevated highway clogged with traffic sliced cleanly across the shaved sides of hills; red-roofed white-painted houses set like Lego bricks in graduated clusters climbing a hillside; a stone castle perched precariously at the edge of a mountain; tall spires of narrow churches poking above the treelines; an old steam locomotive parked in the garden beside a quaint little station hung all around with baskets of pink flowers; snow-covered peaks visible behind low-hanging clouds; dense stands of fir trees dwarfing a chalet positioned in a clearing; the elevated highway reappearing far above the train, curving off into the distance; a black-roofed white church halfway between the track and the highway; the sky thick with roiling gray and white clouds; sudden shafts of sunlight falling like spotlights to illuminate an isolated farm with fields whose shapes conformed to the strange configurations of the land; a small castle with two crenelated towers.

When she paused to reload, she noticed that Jimmy and Anne had gone and that the car had grown quite full. Diagonally opposite were a French quartet—three women and a man. The women all wore heavy gold jewelry—Cartier watches, thick link bracelets, necklaces, brooches. Farther along two young couples Jo hadn't seen before sat slouched in gloomy silence. One of the men, heavyset and in need of a shave, had on a Walkman and sat staring straight ahead, his legs sticking out into the aisle. The other man was in the midst of paying Luke for some drinks; the two women with them were whispering together, looking around from moment to moment as if fearful of being overheard.

The three French women were watching Jo load the Pentax, and she smiled at them, then returned her attention to the passing scenery. The clouds had pretty well dissolved, but the sun hadn't yet fully broken through. She looked at the rain-spattered window, then raised her eyes to the sliding glass panels above the fixed section of the window. Inspired, she stood up, pushed apart the panels, and found she was just tall enough to hold the camera steady in the open space.

For the next hour she stood by the window, periodically taking shots of some of the most spectacular scenery she'd ever seen. Luke came by now and then to offer her more coffee, and to warn her twice that they were approaching tunnels.

At last, cramped from standing for so long wedged between the table and her seat, she parked the camera and walked up the car to stand by the bar and chat with the young waiter.

"You like to take the pictures," he observed. "You make book on the train?"

"Not a book. Just a story for a magazine."

"Oh! You like the train?"

"It's wonderful. Do you like working on the train?"

"Is very good," he nodded vigorously. "Nice peoples. I like it."

"How long have you been working here?"

"Three year. You take my picture?"

"Yes, I'll take your picture."

"Good," he said. "Is good."

She went back for the camera, then waited at the bar while her model served some drinks. The barman smiled at her. She smiled back. In spite of her lack of sleep, she felt extremely well and very happy. The trip so far had been highly pleasurable, and she still had Venice ahead of her.

"Where I stand?" Luke asked, returning.

She posed him against the bar so that the available light from the window hit him full on, then waited for his wonderfully sweet smile to take form before she made several exposures. She tipped him for his attentive service, said she'd see him later, and started back toward her compartment.

Returned to its daytime mode, the space no longer looked quite so confining. After stowing the camera bag on the luggage rack, she hefted her suitcase onto the seat to repack her clothes from the previous day. That done, she sat down to look out the window, wondering where Lucienne was. It was less than half an hour to lunch and there'd been no sign of her. She'd probably slept late. And if she had, then Jo silently congratulated her.

No point in procrastinating. It was time to do her notes. She began to jot down all the details she could remember of the night before and of this morning. She'd been at it for about fifteen minutes when suddenly a small, very round Japanese boy of about eight bounced into the doorway. Knees bent, body slightly crouched, chubby hands clutching an automatic camera held by a strap around his neck, he stood grinning so hard at her that his eyes all but disappeared into the creases of his face. He was dressed in a white short-sleeved shirt with epaulettes, black shorts, black knee socks, and black lace-up oxfords. He continued to hold his pose in the doorway, his feet firmly planted, hands on the camera, his face looking permanently creased into that rather bizarre, faintly maniacal grin.

Jo said, "Hi. What can I do for you?"

He shook his head, smiling all the while, cemented in place like a little Buddha. Then a tiny woman, obviously his mother, in a black and white polka dot silk dress came scurrying along the corridor—Jo could hear her faltering steps and exclamations of distress—appeared in the doorway, and at once began laughingly scolding the boy in Japanese. To Jo, she said, "Sorry, so sorry," and offered a smile very like the one still plastered to her son's cheeky face.

"Oh, that's okay," Jo said, and watched the woman maneuver the boy out of the compartment and down the corridor. She could hear her high-pitched voice and tinkling laughter diminishing as they reached the end of the carriage.

Jo returned to her notes.

". . . bar car warm; people buying from boutique, having coffee. More families have arrived—trio of gorgeous small blond giggling kids; the scenery like melting pictures; 2 Amer. men playing backgammon; fluffy overweight young Texas woman talking at bar with Antoine, train manager, in loud voice, asking about 3 women last night, suggesting they're schoolteachers on vacation. Antoine concealing shock, tells her 1 is well-known author (thought I recognized her), other 2 important publisher and B'way producer. Bar car core of train nerve center, natural draw for passengers to meet and covertly study each other; many tunnels, sudden utter darkness enclosing car; people talking softly in Fr., and pianist plays on—'Blue Danube' often; 1 Fr. woman with huge solitaire surrounded by baguettes; 2 of the blond children go to sit behind pianist on ottoman, elbows on knees, listening; staff constantly offering service, assistance; lunch to be in 2nd dining car, 'Étoile du Nord.' L. right about Fr. couple from last night. Husband talking to little boy, wife livid, thin-lipped with anger. When the 3 Amer. women come through, wife gets up very pointedly and leaves carriage. The 3 women exchange looks, greet man and boy, and sit in far corner whispering, then laughing. Intrigue. Almost no sleep, hours staring in dark thinking about H. and T., with the feeling I must . . ."

Abruptly, she stopped, closed the notebook, recapped her pen, and washed her hands before setting off for the dining car.

Eleven

GIUSEPPE ASKED HOW SHE WAS ENJOYING THE TRIP AS HE SHOWED THE way to her table. "Mademoiselle Denis will take lunch with you?" he asked.

"I thought so, but I haven't seen her this morning. Maybe I'll go ask her. Do you know which carriage she's in?"

"I will find this out," he said.

While she waited for him to come back, she took a few shots of the interior of the car: marquetry panels of urns of flowers, surrounded by dark wood trim; beveled mirrors set into the partitions; brass overhead lamps with tulip shades; deep green upholstery fabric on the chairs; a swirling floral-like design on the dark reddish-brown carpet; fresh flowers on every table and the usual array of polished crystal and silverware.

Giuseppe gave her Lucienne's carriage and compartment number. She thanked him, said, "I'll be right back," and returned through the bar car, the staff car where the employees slept for three or four hours during the trip, on through her own car and into the next. At the far end she found one of the stewards.

"I was wondering if you've seen Mademoiselle Denis this morning."

"She is still in her compartment, Madame. She did not wish to be disturbed earlier."

"Oh!" Jo looked along the corridor, wondering whether she should disturb Lucienne now.

"But that was much earlier," he added.

"Okay. Thank you."

With the decided feeling she was about to intrude, she went to knock at Lucienne's door. Hearing a response, but unable to decipher it, she said, "It's Jo. May I come in?"

This time the answer was clear. "Come!"

Jo opened the door. It was dim inside, the shades still drawn. In a long pink T-shirt, Lucienne lay curled up in a tight ball on her side on the bed.

"Are you all right?" Jo asked, at once concerned. Lucienne's face was waxy and white, her eyes darkly shadowed.

"Will you give me please some water?" she asked, and Jo at once opened a bottle of Evian.

Propping herself on an elbow, Lucienne accepted the glass and drank down the water. "Thank you." She put the glass back into Jo's hand before pushing herself up to a sitting position. "It is better now," she said. "Please sit."

Jo sat. "What's wrong?" she asked.

"I have this stupid thing, endometriosis. You know what this is?"

"Yes I do, actually," Jo answered. "It's very serious. Have you been to a doctor? Obviously, you have. But I mean, do you have anything to take for it?"

"I hate pills, and I hate doctors. Always, right away, they want to cut you open, take everything away. The pain is now," she said dismissingly, "because my period comes today or tomorrow. Then the pain will go away." She wound her arms around her knees and looked at Jo appraisingly.

"I was hoping you'd have lunch with me. When I didn't see you, I thought I'd come . . ." she trailed off.

"Mignon." Lucienne smiled and lightly touched two fingers to the underside of Jo's chin. *"Tu es très gentille, très attentive."*

"You really should see about it. You wouldn't necessarily have to have surgery. There's medication—" She stopped because Lucienne was shaking her head.

"Already, I am much better. Also I am hungry. I will dress and we will eat, eh? You go, and I come in a few minutes."

"Are you sure?"

"Absolument, I am sure."

"If you're nervous about it, I'll be happy to go with you to a doctor when we get to Venice. It's really not good to ignore it."

"I know. You go now. Tell Giuseppe I come to join you."

"Okay." Reluctantly, Jo left her.

Back in the dining car, she looked over the menu (steamed deep sea fish and scampi with rock green beans; lamb medallions with zucchini flowers; green beans rolled in bacon; roast potatoes; white peach charlotte; Colombian coffee), then exchanged greetings across the aisle with Jimmy and Anne, with the two New York widows, and with the trio of women the frowzy babe from Texas had wanted to believe were schoolteachers on vacation.

Inside ten minutes Lucienne appeared looking so fit and elegant in aquamarine slacks and a matching silk shirt that Jo could hardly believe this was the same woman she'd found ashen and agonized less than half an hour before. With her blue eyes sparkling, her hair casually twisted into a knot on top of her head, she didn't look as if she'd ever had an unhealthy day in her life. Nestled in the neckline of the shirt was a diamond pendant; gold loops in her ears; a man's Rolex on her wrist; white leather ballet flats. She breezed in, bringing her wonderful scent and, again, the attention of everyone in the car.

"Not too long, eh?"

"Incredible," Jo replied. "I could spend three days working on it and I'd never look one-tenth as good as you do."

"Pah! You are young. You have no need for work. You look very fine as you are." She turned to order two glasses of white wine, then stopped the waiter. "This is Gian Paolo," she told Jo. "Gian Paolo is passionate about the train. He has the biggest collection anywhere of Orient-Express—memorabilia. This is the word?"

"That's right. You do?" Jo asked him. "How come?"

Shyly, Gian Paolo said, "Because is only one, Signorina," then excused himself to fetch the wine.

"He adores the train, and being able to work on it. Charming eh? Giuseppe has told me every time the boutique has some new item to sell, Gian Paolo buys it for his collection."

"That's great. I'll have to get his picture, work him into my piece. You know, I haven't encountered anyone who works on this train who isn't happy as Larry."

"Who is Larry?"

"It's just an expression."

"So somewhere," Lucienne said drolly, "is a happy man named Larry."

"Somewhere."

"So," Lucienne asked, "what have you done all morning, take pictures?"

"Uh-huh, dozens."

"Very beautiful, the mountains. Good for the spirit to see all this." She looked out the window. "We come soon to Innsbruck. At the Brenner Pass we will get another engine, another engineer."

"How many times have you done this?"

"Perhaps six or seven, maybe more. When I grow tired of Chez Lucienne, and the staff, and the patrons, the chef and the suppliers and the banker; when I grow tired of everyone, I come on the train, make a trip to Venice for three days, or five days, or so. Then, when I am no longer tired, I go back. It is a little gift I give to myself. And what is it you give to yourself, Joanna?"

"I don't know. Movies, I guess. And music. Books. I just finished reading a biography of Diane Arbus. Are you familiar with her?"

"No." Lucienne sipped at her wine, then lit a cigarette. "Who is this?"

"She was a famous American photographer who took strange pictures of strange people. According to the book, she was pretty strange herself. She committed suicide when she was forty-eight or -nine. Anyway, toward the end of her life she was mostly taking pictures of—freaks, I guess you could say. The thing that got me was she used to sleep with most of her subjects. I mean you'd have to see her work to appreciate just how weird the idea is of sleeping with some of those people. It made me think of those primitive people who didn't want to have their photographs taken because they believed their souls would get captured inside the camera. You know? Well, she seemed to be trying to get inside people's souls by sleeping with them and then taking their picture. It really bothered me. Not that I'm prudish, but it's so strange to think of giving a part of yourself to someone in order to take away an image. Maybe she was trying to punish herself. She came across in the book as very needy, very dependent. I don't know. I can't really figure it out. Maybe it's my viewpoint that's off-kilter. All I know is that what you shoot is reflective; you make statements about how you see things, and how the things you see affect you. I've only once made love with someone I photographed, and I still don't know how I feel about it."

"It is my experience," Lucienne said, "that very often you cannot get to the friendship with a man until you show them the sex will not be good, or important. So, you sleep with them because it is what they want and then, like children, they are satisfied and you are able to be friends."

She spoke so matter-of-factly that Jo had to wonder why, in her own life, sexual issues loomed so largely. Obviously, this was one area of Lucienne's life about which she had absolute equanimity.

"What's your fiancé like?" Jo asked after Gian Paolo had presented them with their first courses.

"Oh, Paolo," she said. "He is *very* Italian, but also very American. He grew up in New York until the age of thirteen. Then his family brought him back to Italy. He is a child of—privilege. This is the word? A family of much money."

"That's the word."

"Good. So, they have much money, and now Paolo has the money and is head of the family. The family," she elaborated, "do not care very much for this marriage. I am too old; I am not Italian; I have no line."

"You mean lineage?"

"Yes. I cannot make children to preserve the name."

"Why not? Lots of women in their forties are having babies these days. You're not so old."

"Perhaps not," Lucienne sighed. "But I have this stupid sickness. To make children, they say to take many pills for many months and after that *maybe* everything is okay. I hate pills."

"Would you like to have children?"

Lucienne looked away, considering. "Sometimes, again at night, I think it would be good. But when I think again at morning, I think this would be madness. Paolo is young, eh? And I think he would like the children." She gave one of her delicate little shrugs, and turned back to her seafood. "All things are complicated. We will see."

"How young is he?" Jo asked.

"Thirty-two." Lucienne laughed, showing her small, very white teeth. "My little boy. His mother and sisters are horrified he wishes to marry someone so *old*."

"Eight years isn't that much of a gap."

"To them, Mignon, it is the Grand Canyon!" She laughed hugely, enjoying herself. "To me, it is nothing; less than nothing. Ah! Here are your friends!"

"Don't wish to interrupt," Jimmy said. "Just wanted to invite the two of you to join us for dinner this evening."

"That's so nice!" Jo said. "You haven't met Lucienne. Sir James and Lady Arlington, Lucienne Denis."

Jimmy shook her hand, then Anne did, saying, "We've been admiring you. I do hope you'll be able to dine with us."

"I would adore it," Lucienne declared. "I am enchanted to accept."

"We'll book a table, say for eight?" Anne looked first at her husband then at the two women.

"That's fine," Jo said.

"Thank you so very much." Lucienne tilted her head in a graceful gesture of acceptance.

"We'll leave you to finish your meal," Anne said, taking her husband by the hand.

"The lamb's first-rate," he told them. "First-rate."

After they'd gone, Lucienne wanted to know, "How do you know them?"

"We just met."

"Everyone likes you, I think," Lucienne said. "I think this is so."

"Don't I wish."

"You don't think people like you?"

"Not everyone, that's for sure."

"Then they are foolish. You are very"—she searched for an appropriate word—"engaged, very interested in all things. You are one, I think, who cares."

"D'you mind if I ask you something?"

Lucienne grinned at her. "More questions, more curiosity." She shook her head indulgently. "Ask me something."

"Why did you invite me to join you last night?"

"Ah! Why? I have not ever done this before, but I look at you and think to myself, This one, she is being very brave. But the eyes are of the child in the corner, èh? I think you are very young, very fragile. I think you will be interesting, not difficult."

"I'm definitely not young."

"No, not so young as I think. But very interesting. I never have a dinner companion who makes photographs of the salad," Lucienne laughed.

Gian Paolo came then to remove the plates, and Jo remembered to ask if he'd mind her taking his picture.

"I would be happy, Madame," he said proudly.

"After lunch?"

"Yes, Madame. You would, um, give to me one copy of your photograph?"

"I'll be glad to. Will you be making the trip back on Saturday?"

"Yes, Madame."

"Great. I'll get prints made while I'm in Venice and have them for you on Saturday."

"You see," Lucienne said, "everyone likes you. Royalty comes to invite you to dine; people wave to you from all corners."

"But that's just be—"

"It is because," Lucienne said firmly, "you have the eagerness—for all things, I think. And also because you say and do how you feel, and this makes others feel better in themselves. It is a little sad maybe you don't know this about yourself, because others can see it, eh? Giuseppe and Gian Paolo and the Royal Family and the two—*veuves*, the widows, and the three who sing, all see it. You must begin to think more of yourself, Mignon. You have a lover?"

Color surged into Jo's face, but she answered, "Yes and no. I don't know," she faltered, thinking how best to explain the tricky situation with Henry and Tyler. Luckily, the two widows stopped at the table at that moment to say hello.

"Isn't the food divine?" said the one.

"We just stuffed ourselves," said the other.

Jo introduced Lucienne and the first of the women leaned down and in a confiding tone said, "I want to tell you I said to May here last night when you came into the dining car, I said, 'May, is that the most stunning woman you've ever seen, or what?' And May here, she said you had some nerve, walking around with her body." The woman laughed heartily.

May gave Lucienne a guilty smile and said, "Don't mind Liz. She always blurts out whatever she's thinking. But I honest-to-God wouldn't mind being able to wear something like that black suit and look as good as you do in it."

Lucienne accepted the compliment, saying, "I will tell my *couturière* what you have said. She will be very happy. I might ask a question?" she inquired.

"Oh, sure," said May.

"You have been dancers, eh?"

The two women turned to look at each other, then burst out laughing.

"That's the best! You think we look like dancers? I *love* it! Liz here works for the New York City Board of Education. And I'm in business thirty-six years. Dancers! God love you, that makes my day! That's the best yet!"

"Enjoy your lunch," said May. "See you later."

"See!" Lucienne exclaimed when they'd gone. "Because I am with you everyone is friendly."

"You mean they wouldn't have spoken to you otherwise? Sure they would have. I would've been willing to bet they'd been show girls."

"No one has been so friendly when I have come on the train before," Lucienne said. "This is different because you are here. You jump up to take your pictures; you speak with everyone, ask many questions. And everyone is gratified, because you are having a happy time and you show it to all. And you are very charming, very pretty. Everyone responds to you. Most of the others, also me, we are soigné; we think perhaps it is déclassé to show we have a happy time. They should have you to ride the train all the time, then everyone would speak with everyone else and not worry about appearing naive. Ah! Here is Gian Paolo!"

Jo wolfed down the tender pieces of lamb, quickly cleaning her plate, then saw that Lucienne had eaten almost nothing.

"You should eat," Jo told her.

"I am not so hungry." She lit a cigarette, then drank some more of her wine. "I will eat later, when we dine"—she gave Jo a mischievous grin—"with your royal family."

"They're very dear people." Jo laughed, then explained. "I'd decided he was one of those characters in a Somerset Maugham story, with a tea plantation. And here he turns out to be *Sir James*. Of course, I don't actually know what he does, or did, so I could still be right. And she reminds me in a way of my mother. She's older than my mother would be now, and not really like Lily. I can't explain it. Have you any brothers or sisters, Lucienne?"

"One brother, older."

"Me, too. One brother who's younger."

"And your mother, she died?"

"Two years ago. She had stomach cancer. It took her a long time to die, a long, long time. I forget sometimes that she's not there anymore, that I can't phone her, or drive up to show her a couple of batches of slides, or the latest prints; I can't sit with her and ask her what she thinks about this or that."

"You were close with your mama?"

"I wanted to be, but we weren't ever really close. We just, eventually, got to be friends, I guess."

"My mama, she is close always with my papa, but not with Louis or with me. Me, I am close with Louis. But I don't see him so very often. It is strange with families, eh? All different, all the same. Me, I never cared to have my own family. Chez Lucienne is my family. My staff, they come to me with their troubles, their amours. My clientele, they confide to me exceptional facts of their lives. I have little time for anything else."

"Except for Paolo," Jo reminded her.

"Paolo, yes. I have in my baggage a marriage dress. I look at this dress and I think, Lucienne, you are crazy! What is it that you do with this dress? I think," she measured out her words, "maybe I do not believe in marriage. You believe in it, Mignon?"

Almost inaudibly, Jo answered, "No. I did, when I was little. I really did. All through my childhood, it was like something religious. You know? It was this miraculous reward you got for being female. Then, gradually, I stopped believing. And so did Beamer, my brother. When he was twelve years old, he told me he'd never get married. He swore it. At the age of twelve. I'll never forget that night. I kept thinking there had to be something I could say to get him to change his mind, but I couldn't come up with anything. Nothing."

"And now he is married?" Lucienne asked.

Very quietly, Jo said, "No. He's thirty-two years old. He's had more women than I could possibly count. But he's not married."

Lucienne watched as Jo turned to look out the window, and wondered at the younger woman's sudden and profound sadness.

"Why does this make you so unhappy?" Lucienne asked her. "Perhaps it is right he doesn't make a marriage."

Jo slowly turned back. "Maybe, but I'm not so sure. Even though I knew my mother was going to die, somehow I thought there'd still be a chance for us to talk. She'd tell me things, explain—" She stopped abruptly. "I'm sorry. I didn't mean to get into all that."

"But I *asked* you to get into it," Lucienne said.

"You know something? What you said before, about people not taking the time or making the effort to talk to you? Well, I think *they* all missed out, because *you're* very charming and sympathetic. And kind, too. I'm glad as hell you asked me to have dinner with you."

"Thank you. Now, finish for me what it is you wanted to say. I think it will be good for you, eh?"

"I'm not even sure I know what I was trying to say. It's just that ever since she died, I've been having this feeling, off and on, that I'm invisible."

"Invisible? You mean that no one sees you?"

"Sort of. I know it's ridiculous, but I think I was always waiting for her to tell me her side of the story. My mother was someone I knew for thirty-four years, Lucienne. And never, not once, did she ever explain a single thing she did."

"And you needed this explanation?" Lucienne was puzzled.

"I thought I did."

"But, Joanna, why does this make you invisible?"

"God! I sound like a mental case. I think," she said carefully, "it's because it was Lily who defined me, who decided one day who it was I should be. And I accepted it without question. But maybe I'm just something Lily made up, another version of her."

"Is that what you are?" Lucienne asked. "I think not," she went on. "I think you are who you have made yourself to be. But perhaps your mama she didn't say it was good; she didn't say it makes her happy. And if she is the one who decides for you, then she should be the one also to say it is a good decision. Yes?"

"You mean approval? She should've given her approval?"

"Yes."

"God!" Jo said. "Maybe that's it. I'm going to have to think about that."

"It shouldn't matter to you what anyone says, Joanna. Only what *you* say."

"You're right. You're absolutely right. Thank you."

"For what?" Lucienne wanted to know.

Jo gave her a smile. "For letting me talk about it."

"Ah, well," Lucienne said with a sly smile. "Perhaps I will make you listen sometime to things I would wish to say."

"Fine. Happy to."

"*Alors, ça suffit*. Now we have coffee, eh?"

Twelve

AFTER LUNCH LUCIENNE WENT BACK TO HER COMPARTMENT TO PACK, promising to meet Jo later in the bar car. Jo, having eaten both her own and Lucienne's dessert and feeling glutted, watched Lucienne, who'd eaten almost nothing, go off. The woman gave no external sign whatever that she was feeling less than perfectly well. While admiring Lucienne's style, Jo was bothered by her refusal to seek medical help for a very serious ailment. Her old friend Sally had had endometriosis and she, too, had encountered a doctor whose first and only suggestion was that Sally have a hysterectomy. But Sally had kept looking until she'd found a doctor who didn't believe that the solution to every problem with the female reproductive system was simply to remove the offending organs. This doctor put Sally on a course of uninterrupted oral contraceptive pills for close to a year. The purpose of the pill-taking was to inhibit ovulation, which would kill off the endometrial tissue implants and relieve the pain. It worked. Granted, Sally didn't have a period during that time, but she said with a laugh it was no great loss, and since she very much hoped to have a child someday soon—if she could just find a suitable father—it had been a most reasonable and humane treatment. "Course, he says it could start all over again any time," Sally had said. "But it's almost three years and so far so good."

Jo's thinking was interrupted by the arrival of Gian Paolo for his photo session. She took his picture alone as well as with Giuseppe and several of the other waiters, promised prints for each of them, then left for the bar car. Maybe she'd phone Sally from Venice to get the name of the pills she'd taken. If she had the generic name, maybe Lucienne's doctor could obtain them for her. It had worked for Sally. Maybe it would work for

Lucienne. The pain, Sally had told her, was unimaginable, agonizing. Jo couldn't bear the idea of anyone's suffering that way, especially after having seen her mother, near the end, bite right through her lower lip to keep from screaming.

The car was deserted, except for Anne, who was sitting alone smoking a cigarette. Jo went along to say hello.

"Do sit with me," Anne said. "Jimmy's having a lie-down. And I'm behaving like a delinquent, sneaking a cigarette. He loathes it when I smoke, so I encourage him to have regular naps." She laughed, then said, "I saw your friend pass through just a moment or two ago."

"She's going to pack."

"Oh, I see. Would you care for something to drink?"

Luke had come hurrying over and stood at attention, hoping to be of service.

"I'd love some coffee," Jo told him.

"You take more pictures?"

"Probably."

He shook his head like a grandfather pandering to the whims of a small child as he went to the bar to fetch her coffee.

"He's so cute," Jo said.

Anne took a long, obviously satisfying draw on her cigarette. "He has the face of a naughty choirboy. I recall finding the Italian men most attractive years ago. But back then I found most men attractive. It used to make Jimmy dreadfully apprehensive when I admired another man. He took it as a minor personal threat. He has, I'm happy to say, long since grown past that. But every now and then I suspect his overt fondness for good-looking women is his own little effort at retaliation. Men are so easily undermined, don't you find?"

"I guess they are," Jo agreed, watching and listening closely. Without her husband, Anne seemed quite different, more forceful but no less pleasant. It was as if being on her own, however temporarily, allowed her to be entirely herself without the need either to accede to her husband's wishes or to make any of the daily compromises—in behavior, in attitude, in opinion—that were an ongoing part of any marriage.

Jo knew she behaved differently in the company of other women than she did with men. Look at the things she'd said and done with Henry and Tyler! Granted, she'd been more herself with Henry, but that had been because Tyler seemed to have performance expectations. Nothing explicit, just hints. And, too, regardless of his claims of dislike for the theater and its practitioners, he was one of them. Even he admitted his entire life had been geared toward performance.

"Would you allow me to show you something?" Anne asked, reaching for her handbag.

"Sure I would." Jo finished removing the camera and lenses from the Lowe-pro, slipped the bag under the table, then waited, curious about what Anne wanted to show her. It turned out to be a photograph.

Anne removed it with care from a large well-worn but still handsome Cartier wallet. She held the photograph for a moment, looking first at it and then at Jo before passing it across the table.

Jo accepted it but didn't look at once. She was trying to read the expression on Anne's face, but couldn't. All she knew was that being shown this picture was highly significant. And when at last she did, she knew at once why. With an interior shiver of alarm and suspicion she had to study the shot for some time before she was convinced she wasn't looking at a snapshot of herself.

"Quite something, isn't it?" Anne said softly. "I've had the same reaction since first seeing you on board the ferry."

"Who is it?" Jo asked, pushing aside her things to make room for the coffee Luke set down in front of her.

"That was Lucia." She took another look before returning the photograph with the same exaggerated care to her wallet. "My daughter. She died two and a half years ago. She was thirty-two." She saw that her cigarette had burned itself out in the ashtray, and lit another.

"What happened?" Jo asked in hushed tones, wondering what it was about this train that inspired such intimate conversations. It had something to do with the isolation, and with the compression of time.

"Drug overdose," Anne said flatly. "She finally succeeded in doing what she'd spent more than half her life attempting to do: She found a way to escape reality altogether."

"My God! I'm so sorry. It must've been an awful shock, seeing me on the boat."

"Actually," Anne smiled, "it was rather wonderful, like seeing Lucia as Jimmy and I had always hoped one day we would. You have a remarkable resemblance to her. She was taller, and frightfully thin. But all in all, it's quite uncanny."

"Do you have other children?" Jo asked, sensing the woman's need to talk.

"Two sons, one in Singapore, the other in Vancouver. Lucia was the youngest. It simply shattered Jimmy. He was devoted to her. I'm afraid I wasn't ever quite so blind to her considerable problems, which were apparent to me from the time she was six or seven. It's impossible, of course, to say why, or what specifically her anger stemmed from. It has been suggested that the difficulty of her birth and temporary oxygen deprivation might have had something to do with her behavior. It's academic now. But by the time she was twelve, I knew we were in for a most difficult time with her." Suddenly apprehensive, she said, "You don't mind my telling you this? I do hope it's not an imposition."

"No, not at all. I'd really like to hear about it."

Again, Anne smiled. "I knew you'd have a sympathetic nature. And I was made certain of it last evening when you accepted that lovely, lonely woman's invitation to her table."

"Why would that make me sympathetic?" Jo asked, mulling over Anne's perception of Lucienne as lonely. Were other people aware of nuances she failed to see? The last thing she'd have thought of Lucienne was that she was lonely. "It might just make me someone who's overly curious, or unable to turn down invitations."

"Oh, I think quite a number of people would have found some pretext for refusing. In my experience, the majority of women are thoroughly intimidated by the good intentions of those we view as more attractive than ourselves. I've always thought truly beautiful women had to be the loneliest people on earth. And as for you," she smiled, "you may very well be overly curious, or unable to turn down invitations, but I sincerely doubt that's the case. I've been watching you," she admitted, "and it's been most interesting to see how people are drawn to you. That may have something to do with *their* curiosity. And mine," she added. "There's something quite seductive about a single woman—at least in this environment—constantly making notes and taking photographs. There is always the possibility you might actually be making notes about the very people who are watching you."

Jo gave a little laugh. "I swear it's this train. I can't think of another place where we'd all be spending so much time checking each other out. Or getting to know people in quite the same way." She paused, looking at Anne's hands, which were long and very well cared for, the hands of a much younger woman, markless and manicured and adorned only with a wide wedding band and an eternity ring of quite large round-cut diamonds. "I'd like to hear some more about your daughter, if you feel like talking about her."

Anne gazed at her for a moment before speaking. "I think," she said, "among the parents of those with children who abuse substances of one sort or another, ours is a fairly commonplace tale."

"I don't know much about it."

"Oh, the details differ, naturally. But the basic outlines are alarmingly similar. In Lucia's case, when she was old enough to articulate her grievances, she informed us that our lifestyle, our manners and values and pastimes, were all worthy only of her contempt. She had no idea what she'd have preferred as an alternative; she simply knew we were decadent establishment fools with tedious friends, outdated values, and primitive notions of sexuality." She shook her head. "The irony of that last bit of scathing invective wasn't lost on Jimmy or me, but we weren't about to reveal to her the intimate pieces of our history together in order to alter her opinion of us. Especially since everyone was so against our marriage in the first place.

"You see, when we met, Jimmy was married to someone else. Miserably unhappy, but determined to make a go of it. He's an honorable man, and when he gives his word, he's committed. He'd been married for six years, and what he wanted more than anything else just then—I'll tell you in a moment of his previous disappointment—was children. Bertie used all sorts of tactics to avoid the issue, and him. At that point, he was twenty-eight. I was eighteen. And positively wild." Again she smiled, and raised her eyes to Jo's. "By the standards of the time, I was quite simply ungovernable. My parents were at their wits' end, and threatening to send me off to a cousin with a ranch in Australia. By today's standards, I was most innocent. But fifty years ago, my dear, I was considered a devil." She laughed, as if pleased by her rowdy past. And Jo smiled encouragingly. "In any event, there I was in London, casting about for ways to escape the family yoke, counting down the days before I'd be shipped off to the outback. My parents insisted I accompany them to what I knew was going to be a tediously dull dinner, but I couldn't find any way to avoid it, so I went. And there was Jimmy. What a glorious man he was then! I fell in love with him instantly, on sight. I knew he was married—Bertie was right there, after all—but I simply did not care. It was, I might add, entirely mutual. We looked at one another across the room before dinner and there was an extraordinary recognition. Is this all terribly boring?" she asked suddenly.

"God, no!" Jo said quickly. "Not at all."

Anne's eyes stayed on Jo while she tried to think what had prompted her to tell all this. She hadn't ever, with so little compunction, revealed quite so much to a comparative stranger. But the resemblance to Lucia was an inducement she could never have anticipated. And this young woman paid such close attention, seemed so eager to hear whatever Anne might choose to say. She'd never had an opportunity quite like this not only to express herself but to have so willing an audience who might have been Lucia herself.

Jo felt the woman's hesitation and said, "Go on, please."

"Yes. Well, as fate would have it, Bertie left early that evening with one of her famous headaches—Jimmy later told me she developed either headaches or food allergies in order to avoid people or menus she didn't care for—and the upshot of the evening was our creeping away together. I left first and waited at a designated corner, then he came along fifteen or twenty minutes later." She smiled, caught up again in the vivid details of that night. "We walked, talking, for hours. Then we ducked into dark

corners, doorways, alleys, to touch one another, to kiss. We made arrangements to meet again, and he went home to Bertie, and I to Cadogan
Square. It was all terribly intense, and we weren't as discreet as we could
have been. Although, looking back, I can't see where discretion might
have entered into it. It wasn't something I, at eighteen, had any interest
in or knowledge of.

"It's odd, you know, but I couldn't possibly have put into words what it
was I was after all those years ago. I didn't know until I first saw Jimmy,
until we touched one another. And then I knew without question what
I'd always wanted, and nothing could have prevented me having it. In a
very real sense, we invented each other. He'd been married for six years,
as I've said, but he knew nothing, *nothing*. Which could only be a comment on the lamentable terms of that marriage. And I'd certainly never
been married, and had almost no experience whatever. But together we
discovered ourselves, and nothing and no one else mattered. Reckless."
She shook her head over the antics of the girl she'd been. "I found I was
pregnant. Jimmy was ecstatic and at once started divorce proceedings.
What a scandal, my dear! We were only slightly less of an outrage than
Edward and Wallis. We were utterly determined, however, and succeeded
in overcoming the many obstacles just six weeks before Terence was
born. Our 'honeymoon' on the Orient-Express actually took place three
months after Terry's birth.

"So," she sighed, "you can see that I wasn't without sympathy for
Lucia. After all, I'd played actively at rebellion once upon a time myself
and it cost the families involved very dearly. But no matter how hard I
tried, I simply could not communicate with her."

"It must have been awful," Jo commiserated.

"It was about to become a great deal worse. She asked to go to boarding
school, and we agreed. It was a dreadful mistake, dreadful! Somehow, it
was at that school where she first began taking drugs. And once she'd
started, we went with her down a long, terrifying road of threats and
reprisals and pleas and promises. On and on.

"The problem, you see, was Lucia had her own money, inherited when
she was eighteen. We couldn't control her assets, therefore we couldn't
control her addiction or her access to drugs. It destroyed Jimmy. He gave
up his career—something he hadn't wanted in the first place, but which
he'd grown to tolerate—and spent most of his time trying to find someone
who'd help Lucia; some program, some doctor, someone with knowledge
and experience who would tell us how to proceed.

"And then she died. They found her in a London hotel room with the
needle still in her arm. She'd been dead for more than thirty hours when
they found her. And when they rang to tell us, it came as no surprise.
We'd been expecting that telephone call for a very long time. We claimed

Lucia's poor ruined body, and once the inquiry and the funeral were over, we were able to begin living our lives again. Tragic, but that's what it had come to. Jimmy returned to his interest in painting. He'd always wanted to be an artist, you see, but his parents had refused to allow him to study. He did architecture instead, and spent his professional life designing blocks of flats, offices, buildings about which he cared very little. The only design he's ever pointed to with pride is our home. All the others could've been destroyed at any time and he wouldn't have cared.

"He's quite happy now. At seventy-nine he's finally free to do what he wanted all along: to immerse himself in the works of other artists, and try his hand at his own."

"And what about you?" Jo asked.

"Me?" Anne took a moment to think about that. "I am free, I suppose, to . . ." For a few seconds she looked positively stricken, her eyes round as she surveyed the landscape for possibilities.

"To do anything you want," Jo offered, anxious to rescue her. "Absolutely anything."

With visible gratitude, Anne latched on to this. "Yes," she agreed. "Anything." For a second time, she extinguished a burnt-out cigarette. Jo thought that if they hadn't been on the train she'd have put her arms around this woman. But if they hadn't been on the train, they'd never have met. So she did the next best thing. She reached across the table and took hold of Anne's hand, and kept on holding it as they searched each other's eyes.

"My mother died two years ago," Jo told her. "I was trying to tell Lucienne a bit about it last night, and she made some very sensible comments that I've been thinking about. While you and I have been talking, I couldn't help realizing how much I miss being Lily's daughter. I miss that feeling I always had when I was with her of being somebody's little girl, no matter how frustrating it was or how old I got to be. And I miss the part where it started turning around so that sometimes I played mother to my mother." The hand she held was dry and cool, the skin silken. It had the thinned-down flesh and prominent bones of someone whose youth was long since gone. It also had the ability to communicate, through its grasp, all the emotions that had remained unstated. Jo now held that hand against her cheek and closed her eyes at the influx of those emotions. As she had in the kitchen with Henry, she simply opened and allowed herself to receive everything, feeling it swell her veins, pumping along in crowded communion with her blood. She didn't stop to consider how her gesture might be received, or if anyone else might see. She was fully aware of the honor Anne had bestowed upon her in divulging so much of the family's history, and she wanted more than anything else to prove herself worthy of the woman's trust. For one of the very few times in her life, she surrendered to her instincts, and accepted into herself another mother's caring.

For Anne, it was an epiphany. On the occasion of her fiftieth anniversary, long past the time when she'd believed any such thing could be possible, she was allowed to know what it might have been like to have a loving daughter. Yes, her sons had been good, devoted boys, and most rewarding. But she'd gone on hoping for too many years that she and Lucia would somehow one day be close. It never came to pass, so Anne could never be certain that the memories of the small girl she'd held so precious were accurate and not colored by her own longings. Now this young woman who too strongly bore a likeness to Lucia had appeared in her life to offer the empathy and understanding and even the overt affection that Lucia had withheld for a lifetime. Anne simply couldn't take her eyes off Jo, and had no wish to break the intense communion. For however long it lasted, she wanted to cherish the opportunity to feel valuable and loved as a mother.

It was overwhelming, she thought, utterly overwhelming. She could feel Jo's breath on the back of her captive hand, could feel the young woman's pulse beating in syncopation with her own. She felt as if she'd been drowning, but at the crucial moment had been towed to shore. And not only had she been saved, she was being transfused with some substance almost as vital as blood. If she never again saw this young woman, she'd remember her always because of these minutes when Jo held her hand pressed to her smooth, firm cheek.

At last Jo opened her eyes to look at her companion, their hands still joined. She took a somewhat ragged breath, unsure of her ability to speak over the top of the clot of emotion in her throat, and said, "It wasn't your fault. I hope you know that. Nothing you ever did made things turn out the way they did."

Did things like this actually happen? Anne wondered, gauging the depths of Jo's eyes. Or was she a foolish and gullible old woman asking for and receiving something purely synthetic? But no. Those eyes couldn't lie. They were the eyes of a believer, of a seeker—like herself—of kindred warmth, of truth, of acceptance. Everyone paid in some way or another for their snippets of truth, their nuggets of unblemished affection. She had paid, and so had this dear young woman.

"One tells oneself that," Anne said. "But between the telling and the belief is a gap of unthinkable proportions. Thank you for the absolution. It isn't something one is able to give oneself with any real degree of success."

"I owe it," Jo tried to explain, the hand secure within hers growing warmer. "There are all kinds of debts. My mother wanted a conversation, but the timing was wrong. I was completely wrapped up in my work, too busy; and it wasn't until it was too late that I saw I'd never given her a chance to say what she'd wanted. The thing is, I asked her for an explanation of her life when I was six years old. I think she wanted to give me that explanation twenty-eight years later, but I was too preoccupied to recognize what she was offering. I thought there'd be more time, later on. But there was no later on. She died and took all the answers with her." The face opposite had grown very familiar and inestimably dear to her, and she wanted to tell this woman that she loved her, but couldn't think of any way to utter the words without sounding insincere. How did you tell someone you'd only known for a matter of hours that she'd become very important to you? She could feel it all right, but she couldn't say the words. So she closed her hand more firmly around Anne's and told her through the connection.

"I thought I'd show you the photograph. I didn't intend . . ."

"I know," Jo cut in. "It would sound crazy if either one of us tried to explain this to anyone else. But that doesn't matter. I'm *glad* you told me. I want you to know that. It means a great deal to me." She allowed her fingers to open, and the hand slowly slid away.

"I'd best go look in on Jimmy," Anne said. "And you will be with us this evening for dinner, won't you?"

"Nothing could keep me away."

Anne got up and stood with her hand on the back of the seat as she looked one long last time at Jo. "I am glad, too," she said softly, then moved off.

A few minutes later, Luke came to offer Jo fresh coffee. Distractedly, she thanked him and, sipping at the hot drink, turned to stare unseeing out the window. All of a sudden, she wanted badly to talk to Henry.

Jimmy was sleeping soundly. Anne withdrew, closing the door quietly, then stood outside in the corridor, trying to think where to go. Straightening her shoulders, she turned and walked back along the corridor to the lavatory. Once inside, with the door locked, she wrapped her arms around herself, sagged against the wall, and allowed herself to go to pieces.

Lucienne took three aspirin, then sat with her arms holding her knees tight to her chest, head bent, willing the pain away. It refused to go. Her body, like a cage of bone, contained the snarling, raging savage. Inside, behind the trap of her pelvic structure, it dug its long talons into the defenseless tissues of her deteriorating organs, into the helpless purse of her womanhood. Its fury was vicious and unrelenting. Sweat streamed down her sides, between her breasts, behind her ears. Her eyes screwed shut, her hands laced together, she pulled her knees closer, harder against her body and prayed for the blood to move, to flow, to carry away with it some portion of the pain. She could smell herself, the stink of perfume and sweat and deodorant, and was filled with disgust for her weakness. Come! she insisted. Move!

There was a tentative, reluctant, easing inside. Feeling it, she allowed her grip on her knees to ease fractionally, paying extreme attention. An interior expanding, as if the savage was growing wearied of the battle. More, then more. She allowed her arms to fall to her sides, her legs to extend themselves. A sudden cramping, then release. She opened her eyes, her head falling back against the seat; her limbs throbbed from the loss of tension. Wetting her lips, her hands twitching at her sides, she tracked the passage of the relief-giving blood, almost able to visualize its route through her system. She would have four or five days of freedom before the savage collected its strength and began again its assault on her body.

After a time, wearied, her hand rose to unfasten the shirt buttons, then the trousers. She felt bruised, fragile as she stood to remove the damp clothes, then bathed herself at the basin, stopping for a moment to study the blood-stained washcloth. Her blood, proof of her identity as a woman, evidence of a body still intact.

Jo returned to her compartment. Mark asked if she cared to have afternoon tea. She declined politely, then looked at the scenery, which had changed as the train moved now through Italy: terraced farms reaching upward along steep hillsides; fields of grapevines; pink stuccoed houses with terra-cotta-tiled roofs; stately rows of streets; once grand, now crumbling houses with green-painted shutters hanging askew; bits of rubble on the sides of the track.

And then the train very slowly came to a halt. Silence. The air conditioning went off. People came out into the corridors to stand by the open windows, talking quietly.

Lethargically, feeling grubby, Jo went to the door to look out. She was in time to see Mark pleading with the small Japanese woman and her round little boy, who was trying to climb up the wall, one hand fastened to the lowered window.

"Please, Madame," he was begging. "It's very dangerous. You must not allow him to do that."

"He wants picture," the mother explained, smiling precisely the way her son did, so that her eyes all but disappeared into the surrounding flesh. "You go, you take?" She pointed, indicating she wanted the steward to go outside the train to take a picture of herself and her son at the window.

He muttered under his breath, looked up and down the corridor as if for help, then said, "All right. But he must not climb up. You lift him." He mimed, and she nodded her comprehension. Then he raced to the end of the carriage with the boy's camera in his hand, opened the door, jumped to the trackbed, ran along to beneath the window, aimed the camera, took the picture, then tore back to climb inside.

"We thank, we thank," the woman said several times.

"You're welcome," he told her, and again mimed, this time to make sure she understood to keep the boy away from the open window.

"Bloody hell!" he said under his breath as he breezed past Jo.

"You should be getting danger pay," she whispered.

He laughed. "Too bloody true!"

The train continued to sit on the track. Jo moved to the window in the corridor. The sun cast a glaze over everything. There seemed to be no breeze at all.

Returning a few minutes later, Mark stopped to say, "There's some sort of electrical problem ahead. I'm afraid we'll be a while."

"Oh!" she said. "Thank you."

She decided she'd go visit with Lucienne, and made her way along the now-congested corridors.

Lucienne had changed clothes, and was sitting writing a letter. Upon seeing Jo, she broke into a welcoming smile and said, "Ah, good. I am very bored. Come sit! You are so good to visit. Hot, eh?"

"I don't mind. It's kind of a relief after the air conditioning."

"Soon you will mind. If we sit for long, it will get very hot."

"Has this happened before when you've been on the train?"

"One time." She gave one of her shrugs. "It makes no difference to me. I don't see Paolo for three days. He is away to Florence for business with the family money. And since we are to dine with your royal family and they are here also waiting, there is no reason to be bothered." She folded the letter, or whatever it was she'd been writing, and tucked it into her purse. "So! What have you done this afternoon? You have five hundred more photographs?"

"Maybe only a hundred."

"Wait until you see Venice! You won't have enough film, Mignon. Sometimes I think when I am old I will come to live in Venice."

"But I thought you were coming to live here now."

"Oh, no!" Lucienne said sharply. "Only to be married. We go back to Paris to live. This is the agreement. I have not consented to give up Chez Lucienne. I am not ready to do such a thing."

"I see." Jo thought this marriage seemed to have a lot of strikes against it before it had even begun.

"Did you notice?" Lucienne asked. "In all other countries, we go fast.

Comes the officials, the engineer, the train goes fast-fast-fast. We come to Italy, everything is slow, slow. The officials, the engineers, they come with families, with pizza; they make a picnic." She laughed. *"Bienvenu à l'Italie,* Mignon."

Thirteen

SHE STAYED CHATTING WITH LUCIENNE FOR HALF AN HOUR. THEN, ALL at once, she knew if she didn't get up and leave she was going to start to cry. She was suddenly overcome by emotion and fatigue, and needed some time alone.

"I think I'll head back to my compartment," she told Lucienne.

"You are all right, Mignon?" Lucienne asked, her brows drawing inward.

"Oh, sure. I'm just tired. I didn't get much sleep last night."

"Wait for me when we have arrived. We will travel together to the hotel, eh?"

"That'll be great."

Back in her compartment, she sat and fanned herself with the cabin-service menu. The heat was growing intense. She sat, fanning the air, and worked to bring her emotions into check as she watched the steady stream of people passing her open door: the three entertaining American women; the French family, the parents arguing in quiet but bitterly fierce tones, with the son trailing after looking disenchanted; the round little Japanese boy streaking past with amazing speed and followed, moments later, by his harried mother; the two American men who'd spent most of the trip with their heads bent over their portable backgammon set; the handsome young British honeymooners.

Then, slowly, the train began to move. Relieved, Jo got up and went again into the corridor to stand by the open window, glad of the breeze.

Mark came by to return her passport. She tucked it into her pocket, her spirits steadily climbing as the track approached an open expanse of water. Buildings backed right up to it; a variety of boats were tethered at the shoreline. The sky was pale at the horizon and filled directly above with striated clouds.

In the remaining half-hour before the end of the line, she hurried to give tips to Giuseppe and to the waiters, to Luke in the bar, and, finally, as she was queueing up to leave the train, to Mark, the cabin steward.

She had no idea where the baggage claim area was or what the protocol might be, and followed along after the other passengers, arriving at the head of the platform to see the chef, Giuseppe, and two of the chief stewards standing in a row to say goodbye. She took a couple of quick shots of them and of curious onlookers who were there to see the train and its occupants.

A roped-off area to the left, outside the VS-O-E office, was filled with luggage, the bulk of which consisted of identical pieces of Louis Vuitton. Inside this area, several uniformed female VS-O-E employees were frowning as they attempted to match passengers to their luggage.

Lucienne appeared at Jo's side, saying, "I have arranged our transportation."

"Oh, that's good. I was beginning to wonder what I'd do if I didn't find you."

"You shouldn't worry," Lucienne said, and then laughed. "This is very amusing, eh? So many people all with the same baggage; they will break into fighting maybe."

Inside the roped-off area, the women were struggling with heavy bags, hefting them over to anxiously waiting passengers.

"I would've thought they'd have men to do this," Jo said, "the way they did in London."

"You would think," Lucienne agreed. "Me, I wait. At the end, it is not so difficult to find the luggage."

She was right. Ten minutes, and they had their bags and were turning them over to a porter Lucienne had summoned.

"Oh, brother!" Jo exclaimed. "Can you wait just a minute? I'm supposed to confirm with somebody here about going to the depot tomorrow to see the train being serviced."

"Go," Lucienne told her. "We wait."

Luckily, Antoine, the train manager, was in the area trying to sort out a mix-up in the bags. He heard her out, then said, "I knew of this. Please, I will have someone telephone to you at the Cipriani." Apologetically, he added, "You can see it is most difficult now. But the arrangements are in order. If there is any problem, here is my card. You can telephone to me."

She thanked him and rushed off in the direction Lucienne had gone, emerging from the station to find all kinds of boats traveling past the foot of the steps. Transported, she hurried down to the launch where

Lucienne was waiting, climbed aboard, and at once the boat veered away from the station and into the center of the canal.

Jo sat with Lucienne inside the enclosed area for a minute or two, turning this way and that in an effort to see as much as possible. Finally, she said, "I just have to have a better view," and went to the rear to stand in the open air, awestruck. The evening light gave the buildings a peachy hue: domes and spires, arches and porticoes; mosaics and statuary. It was like moving at high speed past a series of paintings.

She kept turning, so immediately and totally taken by the city that she regretted her prior commitment to go to the depot in the morning. She'd have to spend several hours making notes, taking photographs, learning all there was to know about the train, instead of being free to wander through the streets with her camera.

From inside the boat, Lucienne was smiling at her. "You like it, eh?"

"God! It's fabulous!" Jo ducked down, shouting over the engine's roar. "No wonder you like to come here all the time. I have a hunch after this trip I'm going to spend the rest of my life figuring out ways to get back here."

"You are like a child," Lucienne said fondly.

How, Jo wondered, was she ever going to be able to identify all these buildings? She'd have to buy every guidebook going and make note of the places she photographed. With the air whipping her hair around, and spray coating her skin, she was made dizzy by the spectacle. Facing forward, she saw they were cutting across the canal to Giudecca, nearing the hotel. She ducked back inside and dropped down on the bench beside Lucienne. "I love it," she said breathlessly. "I just flat out love it!"

There was a hotel employee waiting on the small dock to assist the women from the motor launch. Jo reached for her purse, but Lucienne insisted on paying the fare. And then they walked along the winding front path toward the hotel entrance. Trees, beds of flowers, grassy areas; the pink-painted facade of the hotel with balconies running the length of the top floor; a terrace over there facing the open water.

Inside the foyer a crowd was waiting to check in. Jimmy and Anne were at the desk signing the register. A pair of porters then led them off. The line moved forward. More recent arrivals tried to work around the perimeter of the crowd but were efficiently ignored by the preoccupied staff. In the office behind the check-in desk, a number of people moved quickly, pulling reservations, reviewing telexes, making telephone calls.

"Very busy," Lucienne observed. "But it will not take long. Many people from the train."

"Quite a few," Jo agreed, recognizing the still-embattled French family, as well as the Texas quartet. The frowzy daughter was chattering away nonstop in her high, penetrating voice. Her parents and husband appeared to take no notice of her, as if they'd long since grown acclimated to her ceaseless monologue.

Lucienne was recognized by the staff, warmly greeted and in a matter of minutes had registered and was on her way to her room. "One-three-zero," she called to Jo. "I will meet with you before dinner."

Then it was Jo's turn. As she was about to identify herself, an angry middle-aged man smacked his hand on the countertop demanding attention.

"Pardon," the assistant manager said to Jo, and turned to the man who wanted currency changed.

"I am sorry," the assistant said, "but we are not able to do this now." With extended hands, he indicated the people waiting to check in. "In one hour, sir, please." He turned back to Jo, saying again, "I am sorry," took her name, and stepped back into the office area. A moment or two, and then he returned. "Signorina James, we are expecting you. Everything is arranged. You will be going to Scomenzera in the morning. A launch will come at ten to take you. Also our public relations director will meet with you for lunch, when you return." He asked her to register, then summoned a porter to show her to her room.

The first thing she saw upon entering were the flowers, two arrangements. One was from the hotel manager, Dr. Rusconi, "with best compliments," the other was from Henry. The card read, "Hotel Hart is exceedingly vacant. We eagerly await your return. Your hotelier in good faith, Henry." His card in hand, she looked around: twin beds side by side on a carpeted platform, with what looked like space command modules on either side; ranks of buttons, telephones, lights. In the center of the huge room was a console concealing a television set, on its top a ceramic ashtray. On the wall facing the bed, a refrigerator-bar, a desk, a settee and coffee table, a pair of armchairs, a side table, two standing lamps. Facing the door, floor-to-ceiling windows with sliding doors opening on to a terrace only a matter of feet from the pool. In an alcove to the left of the bed, an antique writing desk with folders of stationery, a room-service menu, a box of wrapped candies, chocolate, a ceramic penholder and pen, several brochures. Shades of cocoa and beige decor, thick carpet. To the right as one entered was a door that opened to reveal the toilet and bidet, an oval mirror on the wall with a marble shelf beneath. And to the left, the bathroom.

It was Wonderland, Jo decided, stepping into the marble bathroom to see the round sunken tub behind which was a window covered by a shade that could be opened should you wish the occupants of the bed-sitting room to witness your frolicking in the tub. Thick white towels on a heated rack, a separate shower enclosure, double sinks set in a marble countertop, built-in ultramodern hair dryer, a basket containing Emilio Pucci hand soaps, bath soap, shampoo. The bathroom wall also had a rank of buttons, with line drawings on each to signify the valet, the maid, the light for the shower stall.

On either side of the door to the bathroom were built-in closets, and in the main room, another closet, with a drawer unit that locked. She promptly placed her valuables and passport in the top drawer, locked it, and dropped the key into her purse. A few minutes, and her clothes were hung away, her suitcase stowed. Then the telephone rang.

It was Anne, to say, "Since we've arrived so late, we've put dinner back an hour to give everyone time to refresh themselves. I hope this won't affect your joining us."

"Oh, no," Jo assured her. "That's just fine."

"Good. I've told your friend as well. So we'll meet with you in the dining room at nine."

With an extra hour free, Jo got the hotel operator, gave her Henry's number, and sat on the side of the bed to wait for the call to go through.

When the phone rang, she jumped and snatched up the receiver.

"We are ready with your call," the operator said. "Please go ahead."

"Henry?" Jo spoke over the crackling line.

"Jo," he laughed. "I take it you've arrived safely."

"Henry, I love the flowers. Thank you."

"Think nothing of it. Just a token of my affection."

"Henry, there's something I want to ask you. Do you know Stanleigh Dunn?"

"Do I know her? Of course I do," he answered, sounding bemused. "You know we have an agency contract with Miles Dearborn. Why?"

"Did you know they live together?"

"Yes, I know that. Why . . .—? Oh!" There was a pause, then he said, "Are you suggesting the establishment of a trend, Jo?"

"I don't know if I'm suggesting anything, Henry. All I know is that I've thought about you a lot during the last thirty-odd hours. And I wanted to call you now, because I'm going to be up to my ears for the rest of the time I'm here. I—uh—God, Henry! Say something important!"

"What am I supposed to say?" he wanted to know, sounding suddenly distraught, even angry. "What about Tyler Emmons?"

"God! I don't know, Henry. What *about* him?"

"This isn't possible over the telephone," he protested. "I'm not sure what it is you want me to say, what you want to hear."

He was right. It was impossible. "Never mind," she said. "I just wanted to thank you for the flowers."

"How was your trip?" he asked.

"Wonderful," she said without inflection. "I met a lot of really terrific people. In fact, I'm about to go have dinner with some of them. Thanks again for the flowers, Henry. I'll see you in a week." She said goodbye, and hung up to find her hands were shaking. "Shit!" She threw off her clothes and went to take a shower.

Angry, she scrubbed her body, reapplied her makeup, pulled on a white linen pantsuit with a white cotton shirt, picked up her bag and key, and went in search of Lucienne's room. It turned out to be on the floor above and was starkly modern, with skylights at each end, and desk and storage units tucked under the eaves.

"Not too much time, eh?" Lucienne said, stepping into her shoes.

"How do you *do* that?" Jo was once again amazed at the transformation the woman had managed to achieve in about half an hour. She was dressed now in a perfectly tailored pale pink suit with hand-stitching around the notched collar, and white patent high heels.

"I am used to having very little time," she said nonchalantly.

"You look wonderful."

"You also look very fine. Come."

As they descended the stairs, Lucienne said, "You are sad again, as before, eh?"

"Pardon?"

"When the train is stopped and we sit together, I think you are sad then. Now, you are sad again."

"You don't miss much, do you?" Jo said as they went along the marble hallway toward the dining room.

"Not so very much. I think you listen to everyone, but you don't say so very much about yourself. I am here to listen if you have a wish to talk."

"Oh, it's nothing in particular. Back on the train, I got a little weepy. You know how that is. And I guess I was just feeling it again. It's lack of sleep."

"If you say," Lucienne said skeptically, stopping her before the entrance. "But perhaps you will change your mind, and then we will talk."

"Thank you."

Jimmy and Anne greeted them with affection, as if they hadn't seen one another in a long time. Anne embraced Jo, and held her for a moment, saying, "This is very good of you."

Jo hugged her, whispering, "No, it isn't. I think it's sheer necessity."

Lucienne kissed Anne on both cheeks and then, to Jimmy's delight, greeted him in the same fashion.

"What could be more perfect," he exclaimed once they were all seated, "than the company of three beautiful women!" He asked the headwaiter to recommend the wine, then sat back to look at each woman in turn. "Quite a place this, isn't it!" he said expansively. "Fifty years ago we stayed at the Hotel des Bains on the Lido."

"That's the hotel where *Death in Venice* was set," Jo said. "I'm not sure if it was in the movie, but if it was it looked fabulous."

"It was lovely," Anne said. "I'm familiar with Mann's book, but I'm afraid I didn't see the film."

"So boring," Lucienne put in. "Very beautiful, the images of Venice, but so tiresome to sit for hours watching an old man looking at a young man."

"What a pity," Anne said. "I'm fond of Mann's work, and that is one of my favorites. Some books really cannot be made into films."

"I thought it was a metaphor," Jo said. "I mean, it was celebrated as a gay movie, you know. But I didn't think it was. I thought it was an old man wooing the lost youth the young boy represented. Of course," she wound down, "I didn't read the book."

The wine was poured, and Lucienne lifted her glass in a toast. "To new friends," she said, which got Jo choked up again. The first swallow of wine washed her throat clear, and she was able to smile at everyone while mentally berating herself for being a fool on the telephone with Henry. Why the hell had she called? And why had she said all that stupid stuff? God! The man sends her flowers and she begs him to say something of monumental importance to her over the telephone. *God!*

"You like carpaccio?" Lucienne asked her.

"I've never had it."

"You like smoked salmon?"

"Sure."

"This is the same, only beef. Very good. You must try this."

"If you're going to order it," Jo hit quickly on a compromise solution, "why don't I have a taste of yours?"

"But of course," Lucienne agreed.

There were so many selections, Jo was having trouble deciding. After going back and forth over the four pages of the menu, she settled on the Insalata Shirley—a salad described as mixed sharp and bitter baby lettuce, foie gras, and truffles—and grilled scampi.

After they'd given their choices to the waiter, Lucienne turned to Jo, saying, "Your salad, you know what this is? This is created by Shirley Sherwood, wife of the man who makes the train."

"Indeed!" Jimmy said. "I'll have to try that." He stopped the waiter to change his order, then said, "If the salad's half as good as the train, I'm in for a treat."

"Jimmy likes continuity," Anne explained. "If one thing ties to something else, he wants it to succeed. So, you see, if the salad's a great success, he'll believe forever that the two things—the train and the appetizer—are inextricably related."

"Makes me sound a bit of an idiot," he complained to his wife.

"You are a bit." She gave him a sweet smile. "It's why I've always adored you."

Lucienne lit a cigarette, then tasted the wine. "This is very good. I must remember to ask the sommelier for the name."

"I understand you have a restaurant in Paris," Jimmy said.

"Yes. I will give you my card. When you come to Paris, I will give you dinner Chez Lucienne."

"And you're getting married," Anne said. "Congratulations."

"I am, yes. In five days."

"Will you be living here in Venice?" Anne asked.

"Oh, no! We go back to Paris. I love very much Venice, but I love Paris more. It is my home almost twenty years."

"Lucienne's from Canada," Jo clarified, and was rewarded with a smile from Lucienne.

The other three began to talk of Canada, and Jo sipped her wine, telling herself to go slowly with it. It was heightening both her fatigue and her irritation with herself. Why, *why* had she called Henry? Well, she'd done it, so she was wasting her energy being mad at herself.

Setting down her glass, she looked at Anne, admiring her gray silk dress, the long rope of slightly pink pearls around her neck, the hair brushed softly around her face. She was still a beautiful woman. And Jimmy could well have been a Malaysian planter, in his cream-colored suit, fresh white shirt, and another Liberty cotton floral tie.

Everything about this couple was of the best quality, from their clothing to their impeccable manners. And all who came into contact with them seemed to sense they were in the presence of special people. It wasn't just that Jimmy was titled. It had to do, so far as Jo was able to see, with the bond of caring between them.

After fifty years together, and much pain, they'd grown so secure in their knowledge of each other, so comfortable with one another's quirks and habits, that they were free in ways most people seldom, if ever, were to be open to others. And those who came near served in some way to reflect to Jimmy and Anne externalized images of their better selves. Jo wanted very much to photograph them, to capture their pain and dignity, their exceptional bearing, their regard for one another. She wanted to show the experience etched into the fine lines on their faces; she wanted to capture the look of Anne's hands and the subtle softening in Jimmy's eyes whenever they fixed on his wife.

"Where have you gone, Mignon?" Lucienne was tapping a long, polished fingernail on the back of Jo's hand. "Are you dreaming? Are you in love, *chérie?*"

"I'm sorry," Jo apologized to the table. "I didn't sleep too well on the train. I'm afraid it's starting to catch up with me."

"Nor did I," Anne said. "Jimmy slept like a baby. I've been convinced for years he could sleep absolutely anywhere."

"Me, also, I sleep very well on the train. I like so much the music of the train in the night, the turning of the wheels on the tracks."

"As do I," Jimmy agreed wholeheartedly. "Nothing quite like it. Minute I board a train, I'm ready to sleep."

Jo thought about the work she'd have to do the next morning, and tried to estimate what time she'd have to get up to be ready for the boat at ten. At some point she was also going to have to go through the hotel and take pictures. She'd have given anything not to have placed that embarrassing telephone call. Imagine asking Henry if he knew one of his own authors!

"I believe," Lucienne said, again tapping Jo on the back of the hand, "Mignon must be in love. This is what I think. You are in love, eh?"

Jo's face went hot, and she smiled sheepishly. "I'm trying to keep track of everything I've got to do. And I shouldn't even be thinking of that now. I really am sorry."

"Ah, well," Anne said, "you *are* working, after all. We must try to remember that." Beneath the table she took hold of Jo's hand and gave it a squeeze. Jo held on. She'd have liked to throw her arms around Anne at that moment, because the covert gesture was confirmation of their ongoing closeness.

The appetizers came. Anne smiled encouragingly, and gave Jo's hand a final squeeze before releasing it.

"One would think," Jimmy said, gazing at his plate, "after all we've eaten on the train, it wouldn't be possible to eat a single bite more. But there you are! I'm famished, and this looks most promising."

The Insalata Shirley was an inspired combination of tastes; the foie gras, rich and savory, was balanced nicely by the crisp, slightly bitter, subtly dressed lettuce. And the scampi, when they came, were large and succulently sweet, liberally basted with butter. Jimmy ordered more wine; everyone commented happily on the food. The headwaiter deferentially asked if he might suggest the dessert, and then served up a chocolate soufflé with bitter chocolate ice cream that had them all but moaning with pleasure. Espressos for Lucienne and Jimmy; Jo and Anne had cappuccinos. Then, with a meaningful look at her husband, Anne opened her bag for a cigarette. He rolled his eyes as if to say, See what I have to put up with! but gallantly struck a match and lit her cigarette.

Then the dinner was over and the four walked from the dining room together. Lucienne and Jo thanked the older couple for their hospitality. They all promised to meet, perhaps for drinks, the next evening.

Lucienne said, "I know you must work in the morning. But perhaps in the afternoon you will come with me to help buy shoes."

"Sure. I don't think I'll be back any later than one. I've got a lunch meeting with the hotel's PR director, and I should be free by two-thirty."

"Good." Lucienne hesitated, then said, "Mignon, I think perhaps I make you upset with my small joke of being in love."

"Oh, no," Jo quickly assured her.

"You are certain?"

"Honest to God!"

"*Bon!* I would not like to make you hurt with me." She gave Jo kisses on each cheek. "We are friends, eh?"

"Yes, we are."

"Good," Lucienne said, then went off up the stairs to her room.

Jo was too worn out to do more then get her clothes off and set her traveling clock before crawling into bed and plunging at once into a deep and dreamless sleep.

Fourteen

THE MORNING LIGHT WAS BRILLIANT, THE SKY CLOUDLESS AS JO stood looking out through the sliding doors at a gardener collecting leaves that had blown down in the night. No one else was around. It was one of those mornings when she'd awakened in much the same mood she'd had the night before. She was still bothered by having called Henry, and by an image she couldn't shake of someone with her face lying dead in a hotel room with a needle jammed into her vein. She didn't feel like working; she didn't even feel like moving. She had the arbitrary notion that if she just kept standing there, thinking hard, everything would suddenly make sense to her. Since her conversations on the train with Lucienne and Anne, she'd had the feeling that with a bit of time to concentrate, everything that had been bothering her for the past year or so would fall into a pattern she'd be able to interpret. But she simply wasn't free to take the time.

Hefting the Lowe-pro and her purse, she left the room and went along the empty hallway and through the gallery that faced onto the pool, stopping for a moment to admire the way the sun shone in on the enormous potted ficus trees placed at intervals the length of the area. The windows were a series of glassed archways with swagged draperies of rich brown. And on square columns between each arch sat terra cotta pots of healthy palms. The walls and ceilings were painted pale cocoa, with white trim.

To the right at the end of the gallery was a boutique, not yet open for the day, filled with VS-O-E gift items including packets of postcards— reproductions of six posters by Pierre Fix-Masseau in a bold Art Deco style with primary colors. Making a mental note to come back for the

405

postcards, Jo proceeded to the terrace, where the maître d' greeted her by name and led her to a table overlooking the canal. It was sheltered by a white umbrella with brown trim, one of a number positioned to keep the sun from those tables out in the open.

She asked the waiter for coffee, then went to help herself from the buffet where croissants and brioches were being kept warm in an acrylic bin. A long table bore big round bowls of several kinds of dry cereal and fresh fruit. A cooler at the end of the table held yogurt and a large pitcher of cream. She took a croissant, a brioche, and an apple and returned to the table. While she waited for the coffee, she got out the Pentax and took half a dozen wide-angle shots of the area, noticing as she did that the needle on the built-in light meter wasn't holding steady. Odd, she thought, aiming at the sky to check the meter's reaction. Okay. But when she pointed down again, the needle didn't move. What the hell?! She gave the camera a shake, looked again, and the needle had dropped. Relieved, she put the KX aside.

As she ate, she spotted a number of people from the train, including the Texas foursome at a table to her right. The parents and husband of the frizzy-haired, overweight blonde were eating mechanically while she read aloud in a singsong voice from what was evidently a pop-psychology book. The mother looked up every so often to nod and smile, while the father and husband worked diligently at their food as if the grinding of their jaws might drown out the sound of her voice. The woman set the book face down and began to elaborate on one of the points she'd just read. "See," she said, "what y'all gotta get from this is a sense of how important it is for y'all to express what y'all *feel*. This here book's sayin' it's bad to *repress* your true feelin's, but it's good to speak out 'n' say what y'all're thinkin'. Get it?" The mother and father nodded obediently. The woman's husband looked at her, his mouth slightly open, as if on the verge of declaring his true feelings. Then, as if deciding that was a lousy idea, he blinked and went back to his food. His wife picked up the book and read on.

At a table to Jo's left a bearded, badly-dressed American of about thirty-five was talking loudly about the art in Venice and how disappointed he was after all the build-up. He had a flat New York accent and was talking at a couple who sat and stared at him as he ranted. "It's all dark and decadent!" he insisted, while the woman stared, her face revealing no reaction whatever, and the man with her gazed at the speaker with an expression of utter disbelief. He looked ready to leap to his feet and knock the younger man right out of his chair.

Meanwhile, an astonishing cross section of people made their way past the buffet. A second bearded man, this one with wild shoulder-length hair, was sitting alone across the way writing furiously in a notebook. Another writer? Jo wondered. Maybe, but definitely not a journalist.

A young English couple fed huge strawberries to their baby in a highchair, laughing softly as the child gobbled up the fruit. The French couple from the train were seated at the far end of the terrace, glaring at each other as they ate in silence. Their son looked back and forth at each of them, his expression both confused and resigned. Jo watched the boy with a sense of recognition, not of him but of what he was feeling. It brought back an evening—she couldn't have been more than eight or nine—when she'd sat with Beamer and her parents at the dining table listening to her parents' conversation but unable to follow it.

"You make pronouncements," her father had been saying. "You're like some kind of household oracle with your goddamned declarations, Lily. But in view of your critically limited exposure to the kind of reality the rest of us confront daily, I'd be fascinated to know just what it is you base this knowledge on."

"You don't think my life is every bit as real as yours?" Lily had challenged him. "You don't think I know what the world's all about just because you commute into the city and I stay out here? Who ever told you that the inside of an *office* is reality? You live in your microcosm and I live in mine, but you'd like to believe that because your microcosm produces a regular check it's more valid than mine. Doesn't that strike you as just a little arrogant?"

"What's a microcosm?" Beamer had asked Jo in an undertone.

"I don't know. Something little, I think."

"What's a microcosm, Mom?" Beamer had asked loudly.

"What?" Her brow furrowed, Lily had directed her eyes to her son.

"Be quiet, Beam," Jo had whispered.

Looking now at his father, he'd asked, "Dad?"

"This is an adult conversation, Beamer," his father had said.

"Then why're you having it when we're here?" Beamer had displayed his ever-present logic.

"Ask your mother!"

"Oh, that's brilliant!" Lily had snapped. "Dump it all in *my* lap!"

"You're the one who had to bring it up now, so you answer the boy."

Jo had followed this, her head turning back and forth, feeling dizzy as she tried to comprehend what was being said. She couldn't. All she knew was that the two of them were mad at each other and if she and Beamer weren't careful they'd wind up being yelled at. It had happened a couple of times before, and she and Beam had been sent to bed way before bedtime. She didn't want to get sent to bed early tonight because she hadn't finished her school project, a topographical map she was making of American mountain ranges for geography class.

"That's okay" Beamer had said. "I don't need to know. Never mind." But it was too late.

"Don't try to sidetrack me with the children!" Lily's voice had risen. "I spend every day of my life with those two. I know them better than you ever will." Suddenly, as if the truth of her words had managed to penetrate her anger, she'd turned to look first at Beamer, then at Jo. She'd looked so unhappy Jo had wanted to cry. "This is a travesty," Lily said thickly. "If you're finished, go to your rooms. Your father and I want to talk."

"I'm not finished," Beamer had protested.

"Take your plate to the kitchen," Lily told him.

"Come on, Beam." Jo picked up his plate and pushed through the door to the kitchen, then turned to watch Beamer follow a moment later.

"How old d'you have to be to be a mother?" Beamer had asked, settling in at the kitchen table.

"I don't know. Why?"

"Are you old enough to be my mother?"

Jo had laughed, tickled by the idea. "No, I'm not. I'm just a little kid, Beam. I think you have to be way older, maybe twenty-five. Why?"

"Just wondered." He'd stabbed his fork into the mashed potatoes, then poked the meat with the tip of his knife. After staring at the plate for a few more seconds, he abandoned the utensils and picked up a piece of meat with his fingers, eyeing his sister as he did.

"I don't care," she'd said. "But you better not let Mom catch you."

Later, when they'd gone upstairs and Beamer was sitting playing with a tennis ball while he watched Jo on her hands and knees on the floor carefully painting her flour-and-water mountain ranges with green poster paint, they'd heard their parents coming up the stairs. Jo had sat back on her knees, paintbrush poised, and Beamer dropped the tennis ball, his eyes on the door. The footsteps went past, down the hall, and then the bedroom door had closed.

Beamer had looked over at Jo and said, "They were naughty so they sent themselves to bed early." He'd nodded to himself with sober satisfaction. "Good!"

Jo poured more coffee into her cup, noticing an American family midway along the terrace in the throes of a quiet but intense argument. The parents were both in tennis clothes. The daughter, about sixteen, slouched in her chair looking peevish; the son, ten or eleven, was trying to interrupt the father, who was saying to the daughter, "We didn't come all the way here to spend entire days sitting at the pool. Now your mother and I have a game in fifteen minutes, and then we thought we'd go into town."

"Dad, I want to go now," the boy broke in. "I don't care about tennis or the stupid pool. This is *Venice*, for God's sake!"

"I *said* we'll have our game and then we'll—"

"*No way* I'm going!" the daughter interjected. "I'm staying here to work on my tan."

"Great!" the boy snapped. "Just great! I'm supposed to sit around here doing dick while you guys play tennis and Wonder Dummy soaks up rays! Terrific! If I'd known we were coming all the way here to sit around while you guys do the same dumb stuff you do at home, I wouldn't've come. I could've gone to Outward Bound. I could've done something that requires a little intelligence. This is a total, complete, absolute, colossal waste of my time, you guys!"

Jo thought the kid was bang-on. He was also very cute. Unfortunately, he lost the argument. At least it looked that way to her as she left to go to the landing stage to wait for the launch.

When it came, she went directly to the rear of the boat where she could stand and survey the view as they zipped along the canals. She had no idea what the buildings were, or what the names of the churches they passed might be; she just shot film, overcome by the magnificent architecture, by the beauty of the morning and the light that lay so gently over every surface, and by the warmth of the sun on the top of her head and on her bare arms.

As they neared the depot, Jo spotted a woman waiting by the water's edge, and waved. The woman waved back as Jo fumbled in her bag for some lire to tip the driver. He said, *"Grazie, grazie, Signora,"* gave her a hand out of the boat, then returned to the wheel and swung away.

"Hi, I'm Jo." She offered her hand.

"I am Giovanna." Her handshake was good and firm, her smile open. She looked to be in her early thirties, with short sun-streaked hair, a friendly face, and an easy manner. She was wearing a sleeveless turquoise jump suit with a white cotton cardigan. Slim and casual, she gave the impression of being accustomed to dealing with a wide variety of people. "We go around here," she told Jo, and they started off around the side of the depot to the entrance fronting on the tracks. "This is where we have our offices," she explained. "You would like some coffee?"

"I'd love some." Jo followed Giovanna up a flight of stairs to her second-floor office, which was large and airy and had all kinds of Italian-designed items Jo found most attractive: ultramodern telephones, shelf units with slick lines, an espresso machine, even good-looking wastebaskets.

Giovanna introduced Jo to another young woman, with long dark hair, who smiled warmly while Giovanna encouraged Jo to have a seat. "I make the coffee," she said, and busied herself with the espresso. Both women watched Jo openly, with frank curiosity. For a few moments, Jo felt like someone from outer space who was being given a friendly but bewildered reception.

"You enjoyed your journey?" Giovanna asked from across the room.

"It was fantastic. Absolutely fantastic. You've got a great train."

The two women laughed. Giovanna came to perch on the edge of the desk. "They don't say what it is you wish to see."

"Everything!"

"Okay." Giovanna smiled as she lit a cigarette. "We show you everything. You like sugar with your coffee?"

"Yes, please."

The second woman leaned on her elbows on her desk, asking, "You are writing for a magazine?"

"That's right."

"And you take the pictures, too, yes?"

"Right."

"You do this all the time, write for magazines and take pictures? This is your job?"

"Uh-huh."

"This bag you have is all cameras?"

"It has different lenses, this and that."

"Much equipment. You do this a long time?"

"Quite a long time, uh-huh."

The woman was about to ask another question, but the telephone rang and she turned to answer it.

Giovanna brought Jo a demitasse and sat again on the edge of the desk with her own cup. "Did you arrange to meet Renato and see the kitchen? You like the coffee?"

"It's delicious, thank you. I do want to see the kitchen, but I wasn't sure how to go about it."

"We do it for you." She spoke in Italian to the second woman, who covered the mouthpiece of the receiver as she listened, then went back to her call. "It is good if you go today or tomorrow," she told Jo. "She will speak with the kitchen, tell them you come. Okay?"

"Good. What exactly is it you do?" Jo asked, envying the woman's relaxed manner. There was nothing contrived about her, no concealing shadows thrown by the brim of a professional hat.

"I am the operations supervisor."

"God, that's terrific! You're in charge of all of it?"

"All." Giovanna seemed a bit taken aback by Jo's reaction. "This is unusual to you?"

"I guess I just assumed operations would be run by a man. I mean, there are no female employees on the train itself. But I like it that a woman's got the job. It says something good about the company."

"This is unusual?" Giovanna asked again.

"I think it is."

The other woman completed her second call and said, "Okay. They know you will come."

"Good, thanks a lot."

"I think," Giovanna said with a wry smile, "that the journalists, the *paparazzi* are all men, huh?"

"I know," Jo conceded. "Why is it women always assume men do everything?"

"I don't know, but this is true what we think."

Jo drank the last of her coffee, and Giovanna said, "We go now and you see everything."

Out again in the glaring sunshine, Giovanna put on a pair of mirrored sunglasses, fished a pack of cigarettes from the pocket of her cardigan, and lit one. Jo looked around at the various detached carriages here and there on the sidings. As they walked along the platform, headed for a short flight of steps leading down to the tracks, a man in an undershirt and blue overalls came riding up on a yellow bicycle, calling out, "*Ciao*, Giovanna!" Seeing Jo lift the camera, he obliged by holding still, gave her a beaming smile, then pushed the bicycle off around the side of the building.

Several tracks over, a woman in a pink smock was pulling a trolley laden with cleaning gear.

"This is one of the cleaners," Giovanna said, following Jo's eyes.

"They all wear pink smocks?"

"Yes."

"Are some of these extra carriages?" Jo asked, looking at the blue cars baking in the sun.

"Extra, yes. I think maybe you will want to see this." Giovanna pointed ahead to where a cluster of men were at work, using some sort of bright orange wheeled contraption.

"What're they doing?"

"They wash the carriages. You will see."

"Your English is very good. Where did you study?"

"You think so?" Giovanna looked pleased. "I studied here, at school. I don't get to speak it very much, so you are good practice for me."

"D'you do this often, take journalists around?"

"Never. You are my first."

Well, that explained their curiosity about her. "I would've thought you'd have them coming all the time."

"Not ever. Arrangements get made in London. When the journalists come to Venice, someone will meet with them, usually Laura at the Cipriani. You are the only one to come to Scomenzera. You have met with Laura?"

"Not yet. Boy, that's really odd. You'd think if people wanted to know the ins and outs of the train, this is where they'd come to find out. I mean, the first thing I asked was to come to the depot. What *is* that thing, anyway?" she asked of the orange machine. It had a platform upon which a man was standing, and fastened to its base was an immense roller brush that ran along the side of the carriage, spraying out water as it went.

"This is how they clean the outside. The carriages are uncoupled in pairs, then they are pulled over to this—tank? This is the word?"

"Tank, right."

"If you look under, you will see."

Jo bent down to see a cement pit filled with dirty, sudsy water. "What's that for?" she asked, straightening.

"The water from the washing is collected here. Then, once a week a special truck comes to vacuum up the water and carry it away for disposal. It used to go into the canal, but now because of the pollution laws it must be taken away. I don't know to where. When they have finished one side," Giovanna said, watching from a respectful distance as Jo took pictures, "they do the other. Then the carriages are moved, and two more come." When Jo had finished, she asked, "There is something special you would like to see?"

"Is the Lalique car here? I'd really love to see that."

"You can see, but it is very hot inside now, from the sun."

"That's okay. I don't mind."

"Hard work to get the pictures, huh?" Giovanna observed as they moved toward a carriage standing directly in front of the depot.

"I honestly don't even think about it, unless there's some problem with the equipment. Sometimes, like today, you crawl around where it's a hundred and ten degrees. Other times, you stand outside shivering, trying to keep snow off the lenses. I've been doing it for so long it's become second nature."

Jo stopped to take shots of details from several cars: the gold crest on the side of one; the words CARROZZA–PULLMAN NO. 4141 on another; then SCHLAFWAGEN NO. 3425 on a third. She also took a shot of two men laboring on an air-conditioning unit beneath a carriage, and a couple of Giovanna, who laughed for the camera.

"You put me into your story?"

"I might. It's a good angle, and I'd really like to show people the woman who's in charge of the train. Do the men give you a hard time?"

Giovanna paused to consider that. "A little," she said, "at the begin-ning, but not now."

"Do you feel you're the same person at home as you are at work?"

Giovanna's brows drew together. "I don't understand."

"When you come here in the morning," Jo rephrased the question, "do you feel you have to change yourself in any way to do the job, to deal with the men?"

"It's all the same," Giovanna answered, still somewhat mystified. "Are you different when you take the photographs?"

"Depending on the circumstances, I think I am," Jo said truthfully. "If I'm uncomfortable, if I'm dealing with people who put me on edge for one reason or another, then I fall back on being professional. It helps me deal with the situation."

"But it's still the same" Giovanna insisted. "It's you, the same."

"It's me, but different parts of me."

"This is confusing," Giovanna said. "Everyone has many different parts."

"I'm sorry. I didn't mean to confuse you."

"No, it is interesting," Giovanna persisted. "You are not happy with the parts?"

"I'm trying to get to the point where I *am* happy with the parts."

"Aaah! I see. I warn you it's very hot inside," Giovanna said, stepping from the platform into the carriage.

She wasn't exaggerating. Entering the car was like pushing one's way into warm Jell-O. Giovanna drew back the curtains to let in some light, and Jo sighed with pleasure at the sight of the lustrous mahogany panel-ing and Lalique glass inserts in single panels and in groupings of three. Each was of a bacchanalian nude set against a background of grape clus-ters and swirls, and above and below were pairs of smaller panels of grape clusters. She'd expected them to be quite large, but the panels were only eighteen or twenty inches high. To set them off there was a frosty bluish-gray upholstery on the chairs and silver-gray curtains that went well with the milky, faintly blue caste to the glass. At the far end was a bar, with a large plate glass window behind it; to the left of that was a single female Lalique nude and beyond that an oval frosted window the center of which was amber stained glass.

"It doesn't look the same as it did in the movie," Jo said.

"No. It is quite a story," Giovanna explained as Jo started setting up her equipment. "The Lalique panels were removed when the carriage was to be refurbished. They were stored in a shed, and the majority were stolen. So only a few panels were put into the carriage when it was finished, and the Lalique Glass Company made molds from one original to make new panels. If you look up close, you can see that the old panels are a little yellow in color."

"They never found the stolen ones?" Jo asked, unable to get a light reading from the camera.

"Never."

"That's rotten." Sweating, she got out her pocket meter, attached the cable release to the KX, which she'd mounted on the minitripod atop the bar, adjusted for a long exposure, and, praying to God nothing else was wrong, squeezed off the shot. She was suddenly nervous as hell.

"My camera's acting up," she told Giovanna, who, with a display of exceptional patience, stood calmly smoking a cigarette. "If this film's no good, I won't have any shots of this car."

"You have only the one camera?"

"Usually I carry a spare body, but I knew I'd be on foot while I'm here and I didn't want to have the extra weight, so I only brought this one." And why had she brought it? she wondered. She'd been influenced by some vague nostalgic idea that because she'd taken so many photographs of her family with this camera she might somehow forge connecting links by bringing it along. She'd been thinking about Lily when she'd packed the camera gear. Obviously, it had been a mistake.

"This carriage might be on when you travel Saturday," Giovanna said. "Then you would have time to take more pictures."

"That'd be a break. I know there are file photos, but I really prefer to take my own pictures. If you want to wait outside, I'll try not to be too long. It really is incredibly hot in here."

"It's okay. I like to watch."

"You're a good sport," Jo said apologetically.

"It's okay," Giovanna said again. "You never get to meet a woman who is operations supervisor. I never get to meet a woman who writes stories and makes photographs."

"It'd be a hell of a lot more interesting, and faster, if this camera was working properly. You see, I have to set everything manually because the built-in light meter's out of whack, and that takes longer."

"You can make pictures when it is so dark in here?"

"There's a fair amount of light coming through the panels, and that helps."

While she worked, removing the camera from the tripod to take hand-held shots of details of the interior, she wondered what Henry would think if he could see her on the job in conditions like this, with perspiration running down her ribs and soaking the hair at the back of her neck. He wouldn't think anything, she told herself. What's your problem? It didn't matter to Henry how she worked, or where. He liked the end product, and he understood there was a degree of physical labor involved.

Of course he understood that! After all, Henry got out there in the garden every weekend on his hands and knees. He knew about putting an effort into the achievement of satisfactory results. Unlike Tyler, Henry had seen her with and without hats, not to mention with and without clothes.

It actually felt cool outside in the shade of the depot. Both women stood breathing deeply, blotting their faces.

"Could you give me a rundown on the schedule?" Jo asked, getting out her notebook. "I know there are two northbound departures weekly, Wednesday and Saturday. What happens in between?"

"Okay. Today, as you see, the carriages are cleaned. The dirty linens are taken off. While the outside gets washed, the inside also is done. But before the washing, the undercarriages are checked. Every four months a car must go off for one week of complete service. It is lifted off the ground with hydraulic jacks and everything is examined."

"Are there the same number of carriages each trip?"

"The computer in London takes the reservations. Then they are telexed to here, giving the number of passengers. When we have this number, we know how many cars. If there will be more than one hundred forty passengers, there will be three restaurant cars. If less, only two. The French Pullman that you love," she smiled, "becomes the third restaurant. But since it has no kitchen, it is placed between the other two and shares the kitchens.

"Later today, the coal and wood will be loaded, also the linen supply and the requisitions for the restaurant cars and the stewards' supplies. The train staff make requisition forms and these are filled here. Come, I show you the storerooms."

Inside, Giovanna gave her a tour. One room contained coffee, tea, jams, cleaning products; another had linens, blankets, pillows, and silverware.

"What about the china?" Jo asked.

"At the beginning it was Limoges, but there was too much theft and breakage, too expensive. Now it is the same design but made in Portugal, not so very expensive."

"What's the one thing people steal most often?"

Giovanna laughed, color rising in her face. "The toilet brushes," she replied.

"You're kidding! The *toilet brushes*? That is totally disgusting! Can you *imagine* hiding a toilet brush in your luggage? I mean, picture it!" Jo exclaimed, using her hands for emphasis. "You've got your handmade beaded evening dress with matching silk shoes, your outfits for the two days on board, not to mention your underwear, cosmetics, and all the rest of it. And you put a *used* toilet brush in there, too? God! I thought you'd say the silverware or something. The toilet brush? It makes me want to heave my heart out."

Giovanna laughed harder. "I think the same," she said, mopping her eyes. "You are very funny."

"*I'm* not funny!" Jo howled. "*They're* funny, the ones stealing the toilet brushes. People are absolutely *amazing*!"

"Yes, I think so" Giovanna agreed, blotting her eyes on her cardigan sleeve.

"Toilet brushes! I can't get over it. What's next?"

"Okay, we go on. Wednesday morning, at seven, the food comes by boat from the Cipriani. At eight comes the staff to load supplies, prepare the tables, get extras if anything is needed. At nine-fifteen comes a diesel engine to take the train to Santa Lucia Station. By nine-thirty the train is in the station, and by ten-forty the passengers are boarding."

There were more storerooms: one where spare basins were kept; another for various mechanical parts, including a large supply of heavy springs; an area with rolls of carpet to replace worn or damaged sections in any of the carriages; a room with bins of glass of various shapes and sizes, as well as mirrors. And outside, in an open-ended roofed area, great stacks of wood and sacks of charcoal.

"Everything's very well organized, amazingly clean and neat," Jo noted.

"You think so? Good. Thank you."

"Thank *you*. You've been incredibly patient, and I've taken up a lot of your time. I should start back to the hotel."

"I'll take you to where you can get a boat," Giovanna offered, lighting a fresh cigarette as they picked their way over the stony track bed.

"Have you been with the company long?"

"Since the beginning, in nineteen eighty-two."

"And you like it, right?"

"Yes. This is heavy, the bag with the camera?"

"I'm used to it."

"You like it, huh?"

"Yup." Jo looked over and they smiled at each other. "You're terrific," she told Giovanna. "I *still* can't get over the toilet brushes."

"You make me see everything as if for the first time," Giovanna said. "It's good." She stopped to talk to a group of men who were seated together at the water's edge, eating their lunch. The men exchanged looks, and one of them nodded and began folding the paper over his food before getting to his feet.

"He will take you back," Giovanna told Jo.

Jo gave her a kiss on the cheek, and said, "It's been a pleasure meeting you."

"For me, too. *Ciao*."

Jo climbed on board and went to sit at the rear of the boat, at once dragging out the KX to examine it and swearing under her breath as the light-meter needle fluctuated erratically. The only way to find out if the roll she'd shot was salvageable would be to have it processed. And she'd have to buy another body, because with a broken-down camera the assignment would be a write-off. What the hell, she asked herself, had she been thinking of when she'd packed this goddamned dud?

Fifteen

WITH ABOUT TEN MINUTES TO SPARE BEFORE HER MEETING WITH the hotel's PR director, Jo rushed to her room to freshen up. The air conditioning was a relief after the heat of the depot, and she thought how nice it would be to sit for a while on the sofa and cool down. But there wasn't time. And the problems with the Pentax were nagging at her. She washed her face and neck, brushed her hair, and flew back to poolside where lunch was being served.

The maître d' showed her to a table, saying, "Signora Abruzzi asks you please to wait. She is delayed by a telephone call."

Jo thanked him and sat back, glad of a chance to collect herself. Never before had she worked on a feature in such an addled state. First there was the business with Tyler and Henry; now she had a crippled camera. She felt impaired, and jittery.

A tall, lean, smartly suited woman came toward the table, extending her hand. "I am Laura. I am sorry to be late." She pulled out a chair, asked, "You will have a drink?" and turned to summon a waiter.

"Some mineral water, please."

Laura ordered white wine and Jo's water, glanced at her wristwatch, then looked over at Jo. Almost as an afterthought, she smiled. "Everything is to your satisfaction?"

"Oh, yes. Very much so."

Laura had the air of someone permanently preoccupied with the pressures of her job. Her manner was one of extreme competence that was constantly being tested, and the slight lag—in her speech, her gestures, and her smiles—seemed a result of being forced repeatedly to decide if

418

her time was being wasted. In her mid-to-late forties, she had short gray-ing hair brushed back from an attractive face with wide-set, somewhat slanted brown eyes. She was, Jo guessed, a woman who was overbooked and knew it, a woman who didn't suffer fools gladly. Her efficiency and busyness seemed designed to conceal a certain sadness her eyes couldn't quite hide. Jo made the decision to win her over, in the hope of getting past Laura's obvious professionalism.

"I have taken the liberty of making some arrangements for you," Laura began. "Tomorrow evening there is a meeting of the Venice Restoration Society, with a slide show and cocktails after. I thought this might be of interest to you. If you have made no other arrangements, I hope you will join me. Unfortunately, I have an engagement for dinner, so I will have to leave you after the cocktails. Then on Thursday there is a dinner spon-sored by the Venice Tourist Board. I have your invitation here." She laid an envelope on the table between them. "The dinners are held twice weekly, always in fine palazzi, for perhaps twenty, two guests from each of ten hotels. This dinner on Thursday is to be held at the Malipiero Trevisan Palace, which I am told is very beautiful. The guests will meet at seven-thirty at the Caffè Florian for drinks, and then the group will be escorted to the palazzo. Since they are most anxious to have travel agents and journalists in their groups, I took the liberty of recommending you for this evening. Also I have spoken with Renato and he will be happy if you wish to come to the kitchens tomorrow or the day after. So," she wound down with a tentative smile and wary eyes, "how was your visit to Scomenzera? You have seen all you wish to see?"

"Even some things I didn't think I'd see," Jo laughed. "It was very worthwhile, and Giovanna couldn't have been nicer. But I do have a bit of a problem and I hope you'll be able to help. My camera's broken down, and I need two things: a camera store, and a place that will process my film quickly so I'll know if I have to reshoot."

"This is serious," Laura said. "I think it best to talk with the concierge. He will know. We do this after lunch, okay? For now, we will be relaxed." Again she looked at her watch.

If this was her relaxed mode, Jo thought, her active mode had to be nothing short of dizzying. "I get the impression they keep you running here," Jo ventured. Not only could she see Laura's professional hat, she had the sense that it was slipping regularly.

Laura stared at her for a moment, then laughed quite heartily. "You get the correct impression," she said. "The summer is our most busy time, always too much to be done."

"I'm sure," Jo sympathized, wondering if the impression she gave was anything like Laura's.

After the waiter had brought their drinks, Laura asked, "You have seen the buffet? Or would you prefer something from the kitchen, some pasta perhaps? We make fresh pasta every day."

"I think I'll try the buffet. Have you worked here long?"

"A few years," Laura replied, sliding back into the public relations officer role.

"Have you always worked in hotels, doing PR?"

"No. I worked at this first when I lived for several years in America. Before, I was in management."

"But don't you think what you do now is a form of management? I mean, I've always thought it's the PR people who pretty well run the show. If they're no good at the job, they can really mess up a place. And you seem to be right on top of things."

"Why do you say this?" Her expression was guarded, as if fearful Jo might become critical.

God! Jo thought. This was tricky. "Only because," she answered, "of the trouble you've taken to arrange things for me, and to keep track of my comings and goings. Usually, I have to chase around, setting things up on my own. You're making my job a lot easier, and that's not only very nice, it's a major change. The attitude I get most of the time is: 'Oh, no! We've got another damned journalist on our hands.' You're also the second woman I've met today who has an important position and is right on top of it."

"You are a feminist?" Laura asked her, still wary.

"I'm a person, that's all. But I do like to see women getting ahead. Why not? We're just as capable as men. Let me give you an example," Jo said, warming to the subject. "You're one of the very few PR people who's ever taken the time to sit down for lunch with me, never mind making arrangements to take me to a slide show because it might have something to do with the feature I'm working on."

"This is true?" Her caution was clearly ebbing.

"I swear it."

"Hmmm." Laura drank some of her white wine, then set her glass on the table with care. "I have seen some of your work," she said. "We receive many travel journals, to clip pieces on the Cipriani. I liked very much the story you wrote about Jerusalem." She admitted this rather shyly, as someone who rarely offered personal opinions.

"You saw that?"

"It was very"—Laura searched for a word—"personal. I thought from what you wrote that you would be someone interesting to know. Also I liked the photographs, in particular the one on the roof over the market."

"That's one of my favorites," Jo said eagerly. "I wouldn't have known about the roofs, but there was this darling man who had a pottery shop in the Arab section of the market in the old city, and we got to talking—he'd been a teacher, and his English was perfect—and he took me outside and up some stairs to show me the view. You could see for miles from up there. You could also look down through arches and air vents into different parts of the market. The thing that struck me was all the TV antennas, hundreds of them. Anyway, it's exciting when you find a new view of something most people have already seen."

"You liked it there?" Laura asked, her guardedness replaced by interest.

"It was a beautiful and fascinating country, but it scared the hell out of me. I'd be walking around the city, and all of a sudden there'd be some kid of about eighteen in a uniform with a submachine gun. It was like constantly being jolted awake. You know? It seemed as if the minute you relaxed, a tank or some soldiers would go by to remind you where you were. I think the most moving thing I saw was the afternoon I went to the Wailing Wall, and there were all these notes tucked into the crevices between the stones. The whole lower portion of the wall was crowded with them. Like letters to God. It was very humbling.

"Then, you'd go out a ways into the newer areas, and there was all this ultramodern housing in a kind of golden stone. All the complexes had solar heating, and special window shades to keep out the sun but allow the breeze in. It was very energy-consciousness-raising. I mean, I live in a condominium in Connecticut, and the gas bills every winter are astronomical, and getting higher every year. We could save ourselves a fortune if we got together and installed solar heating systems. But I think we've grown lazy, and things always seem more trouble than they're worth. Oh, I'm as guilty of that as any of my neighbors, but after that trip to Israel, I couldn't help feeling our lethargy might one day bankrupt us. God, listen to me! I'm sorry. I didn't mean to give a lecture."

"No. It is very interesting," Laura told her. "I was almost four years in America, and I liked it very much. But I saw this laziness also. It is here, too; it is everywhere in Europe. And you are right: It will ruin us. We have forgotten how to work hard. Please, go ahead to the buffet. I will have some pasta. I have my main meal at midday, and something small in the evening." She signaled again to the waiter as Jo got up to go to the buffet.

There were at least three or four different kinds of zucchini or eggplant dishes, as well as combinations of vegetables with shrimp; baby squid; mozzarella and tomatoes; rice-and-crab salad; fresh tuna; and traditional salads. She filled her plate, then returned into the sunshine.

People were sunbathing on lounge chairs by the pool; a few kids were splashing around in the water. A steady light wind lifted the scalloped edges of the umbrellas and the tablecloths. A variety of boats traveled past the hotel—motor launches, water taxis, fishing vessels, yachts. The

Texas foursome were standing at the end of the path waiting for the hotel launch to take them across to the Piazza San Marco. The daughter was still going on about the theories put forth in her pop-psychology book. The other three were looking around, trying not to hear her.

Remembering the American family from the morning, Jo looked back at the pool area and spotted the teenage daughter alone at the far end. In a skimpy bikini, her skin shiny with tanning oil, she lay unmoving, her eyes shielded by a pair of plastic goggles, and a thick coating of zinc ointment covered her nose. Jo wondered where the young brother was, and if he'd finally gone off to tour the city with his parents.

Laura encouraged her to go ahead with her meal. "The pasta will take only a few minutes," she told Jo, stealing another look at her watch. "I am," she apologized, "in the habit of eating very quickly."

Again Jo wondered what the woman's haste and time awareness was hiding. She seemed able to relax only for minutes at a time before snapping back into hyperalertness. She certainly didn't misrepresent, however. Although her pasta arrived when Jo was halfway through her plate of salads, they finished together. Then Laura said, "If you come with me, I will ask the concierge if he knows of a camera store." Seeing Jo look around for the waiter, she said, "It isn't necessary. You enjoyed the food?"

"Very much. Thank you. If I may, I'll leave a tip for the waiter."

Laura nodded approvingly and waited—all but tapping her foot—while Jo opened her bag to find some lire.

In the foyer Laura explained Jo's problem to one of the concierges. He listened closely, then in English asked Jo if she would kindly wait while he made a telephone call to a store he knew.

"I will leave you now," Laura said. "If you have need of anything, please let me know. I look forward to seeing you tomorrow evening. We will meet here at five."

"That'll be fine. Thank you very much for the lunch."

"I enjoyed it." Laura gave one of her infrequent but sunny smiles. "Perhaps we will talk more tomorrow."

"I'd like that."

"Good!" Laura said, her body already turning away. "Good," she said again, and was off, back to her office.

The concierge spoke for a few minutes, then held his hand over the mouthpiece to ask Jo, "What is it that you are needing?"

"A body compatible with Pentax lenses, K-mounting."

The concierge repeated this in Italian into the telephone, then listened for another minute before again covering the mouthpiece to say, "He has this, Signorina, but it is very expensive. I try to make him give to you a discount."

"Thank you." She noticed the long-haired man from breakfast, sitting at the far end of the lobby, writing in his notebook. He couldn't be another journalist, she reasoned. Otherwise Laura would have stopped to talk to him. Was he working on a book?

The call completed, the concierge wrote out the name of the shop, pulled a small map from beneath the desk, and with a marker indicated the shop's location. "They will also do one-hour service for film," he told her. "You will go to see the camera. If it is suitable, the owner promises a discount. I hope this is what you need. If not, you come to me again; I make more telephone calls."

She thanked him, shook his hand, then went to get her camera bag before heading upstairs to Lucienne's room.

Lucienne came to the door saying, "I am on the telephone, Mignon. Sit, please. I will not be long."

Jo sat on the sofa at the bottom end of the room as Lucienne returned to the telephone on the bedside table and her conversation in both Italian and French. She sounded very angry, and Jo tried not to listen, even though she understood only the odd word here and there. A copy of the Orient-Express magazine was on the coffee table, and Jo leafed through it, looking up at the skylight as the first drops of rain began to fall. The sky had gone a dull gray, and the rain was coming down hard, making a lot of noise as it hit the glass. She swore under her breath, growing agitated as Lucienne's call went on and on, and the rain drummed down on the skylights at either end of the room. She had to get over to the camera store, no matter what. If Lucienne's call went on much longer, she'd leave her a note and go. She had a small folding umbrella and a light-weight raincoat in her room. She'd get them and head off.

Looking over, she saw Lucienne was seated now on the side of the bed, lighting a cigarette as she listened impatiently to the voice on the other end of the line. As if sensing Jo's eyes, she turned and signaled her inability to end the call, then barked into the receiver. Finally, after another seven or eight minutes, she slammed down the phone and stood up. *"Merde!"* she exclaimed, crushing out her most recently lit cigarette. "I am sorry, Joanna." She came down the length of the room, looked up at the skylight, then at Jo, and said, "We go anyway, eh?"

"I thought I'd stop on the way and get my raincoat and umbrella."

"I have nothing," Lucienne said furiously. *"Stupide!"*

"No problem. You can have the umbrella and I'll wear the raincoat."

"But you'll get very wet, Mignon."

"I'll dry out. Look, do you mind coming with me to a camera store? I have to buy another camera. Mine's had a nervous breakdown. Just what I needed."

"This is bad, eh?"

"It's death," Jo said flatly.

"I will come, maybe bargain for you."

"It's all arranged. The owner's going to give me a discount."

Even in the downpour, the Piazza San Marco was beautiful. And deserted. Jo and Lucienne ran, sloshing through puddles, to the far side of the square and along a narrow street to a small store that had a display of cameras and lenses in the window, as well as along the rear inside wall and within a small showcase that also served as a counter area. A young man was busy with a processing and printing machine that took up better than a quarter of the available space; an older man sat on a stool behind the counter.

When Jo announced herself, the old man smiled sadly and held up a hand to stop her, miming that he didn't speak English, and called to his son.

"The concierge of the Cipriani telephoned," she explained.

"Ah, yes. I have only one camera that will work with the Pentax lenses," the son said, reaching for a box in the rear display. "It is a good camera." He showed her an Exakta, a name with which she was only vaguely familiar. "You know this camera?" he asked.

"Not really. I know it's German, but that's about all."

"It is quite good," he said critically, removing it from the box to demonstrate its features. "Self-timer, built-in light meter, flash setting at 125, shutterspeed up to 2000. You have your lenses?"

"Yes, I do." She put the Lowe-pro down on the counter and pulled out the wide-angle. The lens snapped securely into place, and she removed the cap to have a look. The TTL meter was on the right-hand side, the opposite of the Pentax. That would take some getting used to. On the plus side, the body was lightweight and compact. She asked the price, then held her breath as the young man launched into a lengthy explanation of the normal price versus the one he would give her. When he at last named an amount, it sounded to Jo like a fortune, and she turned to Lucienne to enlist her help. All the while, the father looked on with interest.

"How much is that, do you know?"

"I know only in francs," Lucienne said. "But it is quite a lot, I think."

The father paused in lighting a cigarette to offer his package to Jo and Lucienne. Jo said thank you, but no. Lucienne gave the man a smile and took one of his cigarettes. He gazed at her lovingly, as if she were a minor miracle that had occurred in his small store.

"In dollars, it is this," the young man was saying, punching out a series of numbers on a pocket calculator, and holding it out to show her. Almost $250, a hell of a lot in terms of what that amount would buy in New York.

"That's very expensive," she protested.

"I am giving to you at a discount," he said sadly. "Three hundred thousand lire; I ask only two hundred forty-five thousand."

The father, who'd torn his attention from Lucienne to follow this exchange now said, *"Scusi, Signorina, scusi,"* and held a hurried discussion with his son.

Jo stepped away from the counter to confer with Lucienne. "What're they saying?"

"The father says to lower the price more. The son refuses. The father insists. I think they will make a compromise. The father seems to like you."

"The father," Jo corrected her, "seems to like *you.*"

"That's okay," Lucienne said coolly.

The compromise consisted of an offer to process both her roll of print film and the roll of slides at no charge. Since this would have cost at least an additional twenty-five or thirty dollars, Jo gave in, turned over the two rolls of film and her American Express card, and, with a sigh, signed the charge slip.

"You come back in one hour, the prints will be ready. The slide film I give to a very good technician. He will make ready for tomorrow afternoon."

"Could you make double prints?" Jo asked.

The father wanted a translation. The son explained. The father smiled at both women and said, "Okay, okay."

"Great!" She turned to Lucienne. "Thank you for being beautiful. I'd like to have you around whenever I go shopping. We can go get your shoes now."

"First we have a drink. Okay?"

"Sure, fine."

"There is a place I know very near."

They stepped out into the still-heavy rain. The additional weight of the new camera body in Jo's bag bore down on her shoulder as she trailed Lucienne to an unprepossessing café that was, as promised, only yards from the camera store. Except for the staff, the place was empty.

Lucienne ordered a glass of red wine. Jo asked for water. Lighting a cigarette, Lucienne said, "Why is it you drink so much water?"

"When I was little, my grandmother told me if I drank at least six glasses a day, I'd always be healthy."

"And this works, eh? You are healthy?"

"Very. I don't know that it has a thing to do with the water, but I've been doing it for so long now, I think I'm almost superstitious about it."

Lucienne appeared to have stopped listening halfway through Jo's explanation. She smoked her cigarette, gazing down at the tabletop, tapping her long fingernails on the edge of the table.

"Is something the matter?" Jo asked, as the aproned waiter came with their drinks.

"This telephone call," Lucienne said. "It was with Paolo I was speaking. There are difficulties with arrangements for the marriage. It is very boring."

"What difficulties?"

Lucienne lifted her glass, her expression going hard. "His family wants an important ceremony. Church, and a priest, many guests. I have planned it will be small and private, only me and Paolo, with witnesses. He wishes to satisfy the family. I say, to hell with his family. I would be a spectacle, eh? Forty years old in a bridal gown, with my little boy, in the church? It is *dismal*. I refuse. He declares I am impossible. I tell him I do not marry the family. Ridiculous! Absurd!" She took a long swallow of the wine, then puffed away on her cigarette.

"So what'll you do?"

"You know what I hate? I hate when I say I will do this thing or that thing not to do what I have said."

"I'm the same way. D'you mind if I ask you something?"

"I don't mind. Ask me anything," Lucienne said disgustedly.

"It seems to me you don't really want to go ahead with this, with getting married, I mean. Maybe I'm reading it all wrong, but that's really how it seems. And if you don't want to do it, then don't! I'm one to talk, I know. But people are forever coming along after the fact to tell you they knew all the time you shouldn't do something. And you always wonder where the hell those people were before you went ahead with it—whatever it was. So what I'm saying is, if you've changed your mind, say no and forget it. Don't do it if it doesn't feel right to you."

Lucienne smoked her cigarette and stared through the smoke at Jo for quite some time. Jo wondered if she'd gone too far. What business did she have giving out with her opinions? Who was she to this woman, anyway?

Finally, Lucienne reached for her glass and looked at the wine that remained before drinking it down. The waiter came over the moment she set the glass back on the table to ask if she cared for more. When Lucienne shook her head, he retreated.

"I was thinking," Jo said, "if you like, I could call my friend Sally in New York and find out the name of the pills she took. You might be able to get a doctor here, or back in Paris, to prescribe them for you." God, why did I say anything? she asked herself. Lucienne looked ready to blow her stack.

"You take big chances, eh, Joanna?" Lucienne said hotly. "You say how you see things, what you think."

"If I'm out of line, I'm sorry," Jo said hastily.

"I don't *know* if you are out of line. I am thinking. Most people, they talk only because they have a wish to hear what they are thinking, not because they have any desire to hear the opinions of others. With you, I am not so sure. You are this way with everyone, saying what you are thinking?"

"Don't I wish!" Jo said with feeling. "I wish to God I had the guts to say what I think and how I feel, but I hardly ever do. I mean, I actually blew up at my agent, Henry, last week. But it's one of the few times I've done it. No. It's just that, from everything you've said about this Paolo and his family, it doesn't sound as if getting married is what you really want. And is it possible," she asked, treading in dangerous territory, "that you've been talking to hear your own thinking on the subject?"

"It is possible," Lucienne allowed with a sigh, unable to sustain her anger with this woman. It was so clear that Joanna was being brave, trying to be good. She was swayed by the fact that Joanna had given so much thought to all that had been said. "The difficulty is I have no wish to lose him."

"Oh, brother! If you say no, if you say you've changed your mind, what's the worst thing that'll happen?"

"He will finish with me. *Comme ça.*" She snapped her fingers.

"Then he's a jerk, Lucienne! If he'd break up with you because you've changed your mind, then maybe that'd be the best thing that could happen. I mean, would you rather break up now, or would you prefer to spend the next five or ten years being miserable because you went ahead and got married in spite of your reservations? I'll tell you something. I slept with two different men last week. Nothing planned. It just happened. Both of them are decent guys, but I've got reservations up to my hairline. Whatever happens—and God must know, because I sure as hell don't—I'm not about to let myself be talked into anything unless I'm one hundred percent sure. I want the satisfaction of knowing that whatever I do, even if it's not one damned thing, it was my decision."

"I decided this for myself," Lucienne took the defensive.

"Sure you did. And you can undecide too, if you want. God, Lucienne! You're not exactly a weakling who can't fend for herself. I mean, running away at sixteen to work in a bowling alley, starting your own restaurant and making a huge success of it. You're someone with accomplishments, someone who stops traffic, and charms little old men into giving your friends discounts. You're not exactly a woman with nothing to recommend her. Do you *want* to be pushed into a marriage you're not sure about just because—" She stopped. "I'm sorry. All of a sudden, I don't know if I'm talking about you or about myself."

Lucienne laughed. "I think maybe you talk about all women, Mignon. We are very clever, but also very stupid. I have been feeling afraid because I am not so sure as I was many months ago when I said, 'Yes, in

July,' to Paolo. But for you, it is different, eh? Two men," she said with a sly smile. "This is *formidable*."

Jo flushed. "I can't believe I just blurted that out."

"Why not?" Lucienne said. "You listen to all I say, and tell too little of yourself. This is important information."

"More like confusing information."

Lucienne reached over the table to cover Jo's hand with her own. "We give to each other much to think about. I thank you for speaking the truth. And now," she said, pulling back her hand, "we go shopping, eh?" Taking some money from her bag she put it down on the table before looking out through the open door at the rainy street. Turning back, she asked, "You have plans for dinner?"

She *is* lonely, Jo realized. "Why don't we eat together at the hotel?"

At once Lucienne grew lively. "Perfect! Now, we spend money. It is good for the spirit, eh?"

Sixteen

SHE GOT TO THE HOTEL BOUTIQUE JUST BEFORE IT CLOSED, AND bought three packages of the Fix-Masseau postcards. Then, back in her room, she sorted through her purchases—Fendi wallets for Beamer and her father, a gauzy blue and white Max Mara shirt for herself, and a pair of Italian-version white leather Topsiders to replace her old ones, which went directly into the trash. Then she hung away the dry cleaning and laundry that had been returned to the room in her absence, before closing herself into the shower stall.

A good forty minutes ahead of the appointed meeting time, Jo positioned herself at a small corner table in the bar to write up her notes and to take a look at the prints she'd collected from the camera shop before they'd returned to the hotel. She smiled at the images of Florella and Mai-Ling, and the shots of the train and the staff.

A good-looking man was playing quiet jazz on a grand piano at the far end of the bar. A few couples were having drinks. Outside, the rain pelted down on the terrace. A waiter came over, and she asked him what it was everyone in the bar seemed to be drinking.

"This is a Bellini," he told her. "Fresh peach juice with sparkling white wine."

"That sounds wonderful. I'll have one."

There were four small bowls on the table: one with pistachios, one with shelled hazelnuts, one with large green olives, and one with small ripe black olives. She took a black olive as she got out her address book and two packs of postcards. She wrote quickly, intermittently sipping at the drink, which was rich with the scent and taste of peaches and was a lovely pink color.

The cards done, she got out her notebook.

"Tuesday, clear in the a.m. and brilliant, hot, then rain in the afternoon; everyone huddled in sheltered parts of the piazza. Front of church w/ scaffolding; repairs. Lunch, tables set out on patio near pool; buffet. Guests either very well dressed or very odd/unchic. At depot, pallet loaded with cases of Krug champagne; complete booze storeroom; special vegetarian food for passengers on request. Must ask for Cipriani menus; see VS-O-E kitchen Wed. or Thurs.; get photos of rooms, also exterior, din. rm., bar, etc. Laura says meals outside on terrace in good weather, only lunch served by pool, not dinner; chef decides daily on buffet selections. (Pick up slides Wed. aft. Maybe Thurs. for kitchen; three days prep for each trip, better Thurs. to see from start.) Told L. about H.& T., then felt stupid. Managed not to think of either one for most of day. I wish . . ."

A hand lightly touched her shoulder, and Anne said, "Good evening, my dear."

Jo got up to kiss the woman's cheek, saying, "Hi. Will you sit with me? Did the rain ruin your day?"

"Oh, not at all. Jimmy's just having a chat with Dr. Rusconi. I'm not interrupting, am I? I see you're busy with your notes."

"I was finished." Jo swept up everything and dumped it in her bag. "Did you go to a lot of churches?"

"Several. Luckily, we got an early start. By the time the rain came I think Jimmy was secretly glad of it. He doesn't have the energy he used to. He was quite happy to come back and have his afternoon lie-down."

"Is the city the way you remember it?"

"It's far better. Certainly cleaner. And so many of the buildings have been restored. Jimmy's so keen on the restorations we're going to a slide show tomorrow evening, sponsored by the restoration society."

"I'm going, too. With Laura from the hotel."

"How splendid! Perhaps you'll come to dinner with us after."

"I would love that."

Jimmy appeared at the entrance to the bar, spotted his wife, and came over to say hello to Jo, then said to Anne, "It would seem we're to dine with Dr. Rusconi. He insists."

"That's good of him," Anne said.

"Very decent chap." He pulled out a chair and sat down. "Have you been to the depot?" he asked Jo.

"I went this morning. I'm rapidly becoming something of an expert on the train. It was just fascinating."

"Wouldn't have minded seeing that myself," he said. "You're not on your own for the evening, are you? We can't have you dining in solitary splendor. That wouldn't do at all."

Jo smiled at him. "I'm waiting for Lucienne. I came down early to write up my notes. And," she confided, lowering her voice, "to check out the guests. Did you *see* that woman in the black minidress with no back?"

"My dear!" Anne gave a little laugh. "I thought Jimmy was going to chase her down the corridor. But isn't it the most appalling garment you've ever seen? Horrid of me, but it truly is quite ugly."

"If you looked up ugly in the dictionary, you'd find a picture of that dress," Jo said.

Jimmy blinked, then burst out laughing. "That's very good!" he declared. "Oh, that *is* good! I really must remember that."

"He has a wicked sense of humor," Anne told Jo. "Perhaps we'll see you later on."

"Have a turn round the dance floor," Jimmy put in. "You do dance? I don't mean all that convulsive, contortionist nonsense, but actual dancing."

"I do a passable box step," Jo answered. "Enjoy your dinner," she said as they went off, then finished her Bellini and checked the time. Lucienne was late.

She was deliberating whether or not to call up to the room when Lucienne came striding into the bar, her angry energy galvanizing everyone into a sudden, brief silence. She paused for a moment, looking around, and everyone including Jo stared at her.

She was wearing a marvellous dress of white dotted Swiss cotton with a square-cut neckline, a close-fitting bodice, and a skirt that flared with yards of material. The sleeves were short and puffed exaggeratedly, and as she spotted Jo and came toward the table, Jo saw she was wearing a crinoline underneath. She grabbed a chair, sat down, crossed her legs, and thereby revealed layer upon layer of lace-trimmed netting. Her high heels were white leather, cut very low in the front.

"I am late! I am sorry!" She at once opened her bag for a cigarette. "What is that?" she asked of Jo's empty glass.

"A Bellini."

"Wonderful! We will have two," she told the waiter, who listened, gaping, then simply backed away.

"Your dress is heavenly."

"Thank you. I will commit a murder, or I will get drunk. I have not yet decided."

"What happened?"

Lucienne wrapped her hand around Jo's wrist, leaned across the table, and said "First, I drink, then I will talk with you. Okay?"

"Sure, fine."

Jo sat quietly, respectful of Lucienne's palpable anger, and watched people pass by in the corridor on their way to the dining room. The

American family with the sunbathing daughter and frustrated young son straggled past, the boy saying, ". . . the whole morning. And then finally, *finally*, we're going to go, but it rains so you won't. I want my own table for dinner. I really do."

At the bar sat the woman in the backless dress. She was extremely tall; several inches over six feet, fairly young, and not unattractive. But her body, which consisted of straight uninterrupted lines from shoulders to hips, was misplaced sadly in the dress. The man with her, however, seemed to like the garment, or rather, its absence. His hand stroked up and down her defenseless spine as he leaned with one elbow on the bar and spoke to her in low, insidious tones.

The Texas quartet went past, the daughter in a becomingly frilly dress that managed to disguise her bulk. "We just bought out the stores," she was saying. "Wasn't a soul around, and we had ourselves a spree. I'm goin' back tomorrow."

Beside Jo, Lucienne gulped down the Bellini, then asked the waiter for a double vodka, no ice. She lit a fresh cigarette, drew hard on it, and looked at this small American woman with her pretty doll's face—very large dark eyes; the skin of an infant, with a shine to it and genuine color in her cheeks; the mouth of a cupid; and thick dark hair cut in the style of a Dutch boy with a fringe across her forehead that tended to flow like heavy liquid back and forth from her face when she moved. At some moments she was very young; and then, most unexpectedly, she would grow serious and demonstrate a strong intelligence. She had an appreciation for clothes, Lucienne thought, but not for her own body. And so she wore the garments without certainty, as if unaware that she was nicely formed. Quite a diffident, complicated woman, yet Lucienne had confided more to her than she had to anyone in many years; they had formed a friendship, but it would come to an end Saturday when Joanna returned to London on the train. It didn't seem right, or fair, and she wondered if Joanna also had a sense of the unfairness of making a friendship with a limited future. Perhaps she had chosen to confide in her because of this limit. It was possible. Still, with the exchange of thoughts and confidences had come an understanding and even a caring that was rewarding. She wondered if Joanna had any sense of her own appeal. She had a lovely face, a sweet face, one that was like a book anyone could read. Lucienne could understand why men would wish to possess her. They would want to read themselves in her face; they would wish to make amusing remarks in order to hear her laughter, which was sweet like her face, and quite irresistible; they would be filled with desire for the very size of her—so small, but so very female. She was most American in her directness, yet not American in her openness and concern for others.

"Your grandmother, the one of the drinking water," Lucienne asked, "she was American?"

Jo pushed her hair back behind her ears. "No, she was Irish."

Look! Lucienne thought. The ears of a doll, too. "I knew it! And you were very close with her, yes?"

"Very. Why?"

"I am thinking of the ways you are American, but not. In the ways that are most important to me—I intend no insult, eh?—you are not American. And this must be because you have had an Irish grandmother."

"Could be," Jo allowed. "I've never given it much thought."

She looked again at Joanna, strongly taken by the notion that this woman was somehow half in shadow—not actually, but in spirit. She had not yet become entirely real to herself, and this was why she carried herself without pride; it was why she responded with such surprise to other people's displays of interest in her; it was perhaps also why she seemed so very young. But what a gentle person she was! And how good to look upon! If I were a man, she thought, it might be too simple to be deceived by the face into believing I could have this woman. And I would have her only to discover that this face misleads; it conceals much fear, and wisdom, and a capability of great passion. But a passion more of the mind than of the body, because Joanna has not found the connection between heart and mind.

This seemed so major a realization that Lucienne was tempted to comment on it, then thought better of it. For a woman still half in shadow, to make such an observation might cause her to return entirely into the dark. Joanna was in the process of finding her place in her own mind. And it was unwise to disturb anyone engaged in such a process. But how odd it was, she thought, that women came at different times to the finding of themselves. For herself, she had always known. For Joanna, it was coming now. It made Lucienne feel even more drawn to her, and also most protective of her.

"When do you come to Paris?" Lucienne wanted to know.

"It depends on the assignments. I don't get that many in France. But that doesn't matter. I was thinking I'd like to come visit anyway. I mean, I'd like us to stay in touch."

"I would like this, too, Mignon. It is the truth. I am just now thinking I wish to keep our friendship. So you will come to visit with me, eh?"

"Definitely."

"I have had a disastrous argument on the telephone with Paolo. He is returning immediately from Florence."

"Why?"

Lucienne drank some of the vodka, her eyes widening as the liquid flowed like clear fire down her throat. "I have told him I will *not* marry in the church with the priest and the bridal gown and the invited guests. I wish to keep the plans as we have made them. He says it is an offense to his family. I say to him I do not marry his family. He says I *do* marry his family. I say he is a child and ridiculous. He says I am stubborn and too accustomed to having my own way. I agree, and say this is so. He says he cannot have this discussion over the telephone when I am being selfish and stubborn, so he will drive from Florence immediately to speak with me in person and make me see he cannot distress the family by refusing to honor their wishes. I say he has no need to do that because I will not change my thinking. I also say that his mother and sisters deplore this marriage and believe he has gone mad to wish to marry me, and why doesn't he see this when it is the truth. He says I am hysterical because it is the wrong time of the month. And I go absolutely crazy and tell him he is a pretty little pig and if I am bleeding or not it has nothing to do with my brain. We scream at each other. And now he is returning to Venice. I will kill him! At this moment, I despise him. If he comes here, I will be out. I will not see him. I have tried to telephone to my friend in Portofino, thinking I will go there to visit for a few days, but my friend is not at home. So I will have to stay here to argue more with Paolo. And then I will kill him."

"Oh, boy," Jo said softly.

"Yes, oh, boy," Lucienne muttered. "You are quite right, Joanna, when you say what you do this afternoon. It is a mistake to marry the little boy. I was dreaming. I was not in my right head, only thinking I am tired of being alone. Imagine saying to me I must be deranged in my thinking because I have a period! Only a man would say something so stupid, so insulting! I am going to have to meet with him, and I dread it. It is unbelievable that I would dread seeing Paolo when yesterday I was going to marry him."

"You might feel differently when you see him."

"But of course I will. Because when I see him, I will like the look of him, and he will persuade me, and I will wish to make love with him because he is Italian, after all, and very handsome. I should have re-mained in Paris."

"Maybe I shouldn't have said anything," Jo said guiltily.

"This is not your fault!" Lucienne said sharply. "You spoke the truth, but *you* don't decide for me. You help me to decide for myself. I am *grateful* for this. I don't *blame* you."

"I still feel guilty."

Lucienne shook her head, her eyes filling. "No. Don't feel this way." She blinked away the tears, grabbed her glass and drank down the vodka in one gulp.

"Jesus!" Jo said. "How can you *do* that?"

"Because I am a crazy, hysterical woman who bleeds with her brain!" she said, then laughed "How ridiculous! How absolutely ridiculous!"

"We should go eat," Jo suggested, catching the waiter's eye and gesturing for the tab.

"It is *so* insulting," Lucienne persevered. "It is the greatest insult, don't you think?"

"Are you kidding? I'd murder a guy who made a dumb-ass remark like that."

"So you agree with me?" she asked in almost pleading fashion.

"Damned right, I agree with you. It takes guts to do what you did, Lucienne." The waiter brought the check and Jo signed it, adding in a tip. Lucienne was so distraught she didn't notice. "I made us a reservation," Jo told her. "And you should eat something."

"Joanna," Lucienne said quietly, her awareness returning, "I have not made a fool of myself here, have I?"

"No way! I'll tell you something my Irish grandmother used to say to me. She told me there was never any point in worrying about what other people might think of you because other people were always way too busy worrying about what *you* might think of *them*."

"I like your grandmother," Lucienne said with a watery smile.

"You'd have loved her. Let's go eat now. That's also good for the spirit."

"You were worried I would get drunk, eh, Mignon?" Lucienne said after dinner. They'd chosen to sit near the piano player, who shifted after the cocktail hour from the small bar adjoining the dining room to this larger one down the hall. "I think this makes you nervous."

"When people drink, I'm always afraid they're going to hurt themselves. Or that they're going to drink so much they change character and become someone I don't know."

"This has happened?"

"A few times. There was this once, when I was about fourteen. I came home from a date one night, and my mother was sitting in the dark in the living room with a full glass in her hand. I let myself into the house and jumped a mile at the sound of Lily's voice coming at me from out of the silence of this pitch-dark room. She told me not to turn on the lights. 'You can sit down and keep me company for a minute if you like, but I don't want you to see me,' she said. It gave me chills, but I went to sit on the edge of the sofa, listening very intently as if to compensate for being unable to see much more than shadows, and hearing only the clink of ice cubes as Lily drank. We didn't talk. I just sat there, waiting. And after a while Lily started to cry. I didn't know what to do, so I sat there while the

minutes ticked off on this four-hundred-day clock on the mantel, and my
mother drank and wept. I felt like the guardian of Lily's secret misery,
and I was determined to stay there in case she needed me. But finally, as
she stumbled over to the bar to refill her glass, she spoke to me in this
hoarse, totally unfamiliar voice. 'Go to bed, Joey,' she said. 'Nothing's
going to happen.' And I said, 'No, that's okay. I'll just sit here.' I was
convinced she'd need me. But she said, 'Go to bed, Joanna! Everyone has
the right to be disgustingly self-pitying once in a while. Nothing's going
to happen, so go to bed. I'll see you in the morning.' I asked her if
anything had happened. 'Where's Dad?' I asked. And in this very harsh
voice, she said, 'Don't be tedious! I want to indulge myself without being
obliged to explain. *Please!* Go to bed!' So, feeling rebuked, I said okay and
got up, and as if it was any other night, I said, 'Goodnight, Mom.' And,
amazingly, sounding normal, she said, 'Goodnight, Joey. Sleep tight.' In
the morning, when I came downstairs, there wasn't the slightest bit of
evidence that the scene the night before had actually happened. Even
bombed, Lily cleaned up after herself."

"I am a good drinker," Lucienne said. "I don't drink too much, and I
don't change. So there is no need to be worried, okay?"

"Okay."

Jimmy and Anne came in. Jimmy marched directly up to Lucienne and,
with a bit of a bow, said, "A dance, Mademoiselle?"

"I would love it," Lucienne responded gaily.

Anne slipped into Lucienne's place beside Jo, and the two of them
watched Jimmy and Lucienne dance.

"He's terrific," Jo said, noting the grace and control with which he
directed Lucienne around the floor, her skirt lifting to reveal the lacy
crinoline.

"A lovely dancer," Anne agreed. "And so is your friend. When I was
young, I'd have resented her," she said frankly. "Her beauty and her
effortless charm would have undone me. One of the good things about
age is the perspective one gains, and the tolerance we develop toward
those we see as more appealing than ourselves."

"I'll bet you were every bit as beautiful as she is. And I can't honestly
imagine you resenting anyone."

"Don't paint me in too saintly colors, my dear," Anne cautioned.
"We're all human and plagued by small personal demons." She looked
again at her husband and Lucienne, then in an undertone said, "She's not
well, is she?"

"What makes you say that?"

"She carries herself with extreme care. I think I must have appeared
very much as she does just before I had surgery many years ago. I went
about for months with the sense that any sudden motion would create

chaos inside me, everything would be jarred loose. It was," she explained, "an ectopic pregnancy. I was forty-four and had no idea I was pregnant. It simply didn't seem possible. I thought I was premenopausal, and there I was pregnant. In any case, it was most painful. I do hope she's looking after herself."

"I'm working on her, nagging a lot."

"Good for you! What a kind girl you are!"

"I don't know about that. It just doesn't make sense to ignore a physical problem."

The little American boy poked his head around the doorway, spotted the pianist, and stood listening. He looked small and lonely and bored, and Jo felt sorry for him. He was having a rotten vacation. With a glance around to see if he was being observed, he slid inside and sat down at the table nearest the door, his fingers beating out the tempo on the table-top.

"That poor kid's having such a lousy time," Jo said, pointing him out to Anne. "Nobody in his family wants to do anything but hang around the pool or play tennis. And all he wants is to get into the city and see everything."

"Seems a terrible waste, doesn't it, to come all this way and not see the city? Dear, cheeky little face he has, don't you think?"

"He's adorable," Jo agreed. "I feel like adopting him."

"He'd probably like to be adopted. Although more than once I've come across children who deserved far better than the families they had only to have the children defend those families quite violently."

"I know what you mean." She was about to wonder aloud where his family might be when they stepped into the doorway. The father made an angry jerking motion with his arm, and with a show of reluctance the boy got up and, after a last look at the piano player, went off with his family. Both parents could be heard berating the boy as they traveled down the corridor.

"Would you like to have children?" Anne asked.

"I've never thought so," Jo admitted, "but sometimes I see babies—at the supermarket, or being pushed around in a stroller—and I get this awful kind of aching feeling, and I want to pick them up and hold them. I probably won't have any." She smiled at Anne. "You need a man around, if only to get a baby started."

At that moment Lucienne and Jimmy returned to the table.

"Will you dance, darling?" Jimmy asked his wife.

"In a bit. Why not have your cognac now?"

"Good idea," he said and, breathing heavily, sank into his chair.

Mysteriously, Anne took hold of Jo's hand under the table and gave it a gentle squeeze.

Seventeen

ER DREAMS THAT NIGHT WERE MUDDLED AND UPSETTING, AND RE-
volved around Henry. In various scenarios that took place in his house,
yet didn't look at all like it, they talked and talked without arriving at any
agreement. At one point she curled up comfortably on Henry's bed, her
arms wrapped around a heavy comforter, and dozed while Henry laughed
and told her he'd better take her home. Her dream self managed to get
her eyes open and to protest that she'd been waiting for ages and had no
intention of going home now when they'd been planning this evening for
weeks. He'd already canceled out several times, she reminded him, and
then when they'd finally set a date, he'd kept her waiting for so long that
she'd fallen asleep. He laughed again and said he was merely testing her
interest. She kept her eyes closed while he talked, sensing his approach.
He plucked the comforter from her arms and kissed her closed eyes
before fitting his body against hers. The strength of her reservations and
her awareness of underlying motives on both their parts distressed her,
and she struggled lethargically under the weight of his body. Yet even
while she pushed at him, he made her laugh, and she had to wonder how
she could laugh when he made her uncomfortable in so many ways.

The alarm went off at six. She got up, still caught in the muddled mood
of her dreams, plugged in the Melitta, and went to shower while the water
dripped through the coffee in the paper cone. She hadn't thought to ask
for a newspaper and didn't feel like reading either of the novels she'd
brought along, so she slid open the doors and sat out on the shrub-
enclosed patio to write a couple of notes—one to Laura saying she'd go
see the kitchens tomorrow, and one for Lucienne telling her she'd be
spending the day looking around before returning to dress for the slide

438

show in the evening. The notes done, she sipped at the coffee and examined the differences between herself, Giovanna, and Laura. They were all on the job, yet of the three of them Laura was the one most outwardly role-playing, Giovanna the least. She herself was somewhere in the middle, tending to drift occasionally toward either pole. Did people actually see her change, she wondered, the way she'd seen Laura change? Did it matter if they did? And why was she all at once so obsessed with the issue?

All those years ago Lily had put a camera into her hands and said, "This is who you are." And because she'd wanted to please her mother, even to emulate her, she'd accepted the camera and the career that eventually went with it. Undeniably, she was someone who saw the world best and most clearly through a lens. But was that the sum total of Joanna James? Who the hell was she when she wasn't on the job? Was she really someone Henry could fall in love with? Was that what she wanted? The only answer she had was the regular little interior surge she felt now every time she thought of him. But did a small surge constitute the basis for caring in the long term? Who's Joanna anyway? she wondered. She's this woman who falls for babies in strollers; a woman who'd sleep with two men she likes and then run away from both of them; a woman who wasted four years of her life on a guy like Greg, waiting for the approval he was never going to give her, because he was too much like Lily on that score: incapable of demonstrating either love or approval in any overt way. God! Was that the truth?

She sat forward in the chair, both hands holding the coffee cup as, eyes on the patio flagstones, she closely examined this possibility. She was what Lily had told her to be, but Lily had never once come right out and said it was good or bad. And she'd played for a time at actually *being* Lily by burying herself in a hole with Greg. He'd never have married her although she'd always thought it was a possible option; he'd never have been willing to give her even that much approval. So she'd not only played at being Lily by involving herself in a hopeless affair, she'd compounded the game by selecting someone with whom to become involved who was a strong Lily type—with unfocused talent, with a deficient ego, and with a limitless well of resentment.

I'm not Lily! she told herself angrily. I tried it once and it didn't work. And since she died, I've been stumbling around, lost without my role model. Hell, I don't *want* to be Lily! I'm me. And just lately I've started getting close to knowing who I am. That's what's been happening; that's what the invisibility's been about. Well, okay! she thought, feeling strengthened. *Okay!*

By eight she was on her way to the lobby where she left the notes for Laura and Lucienne. The only other person waiting for the hotel motor launch was the young American boy, who said, "Hi. The boat ought to be here any minute. I just missed it before, so I've been hanging around waiting."

"Hi. Going over to have a look around?"

"Better believe it." He looked at the camera around her neck and the Lowe-pro over her shoulder and asked, "You gonna take pictures?"

"I sure am." She gave him a smile. "It's my first chance since I got here."

"Yeah, mine too. You professional?"

"Uh-huh."

"Going anywhere in particular?" He leaned comfortably against the wrought-iron gate, one Nike-shod foot propped on the other.

"Nope. Just where my feet take me, starting on the far side of the piazza."

"Me, too," he said, eyes scanning the water.

He was a very cute kid, she thought. Sandy blond hair, big round long-lashed brown eyes, freckle-splashed tidy nose, and a wide smile over teeth in the process of being straightened. He was wearing a short-sleeved white cotton shirt, Levi's, sweat socks, and the Nikes.

"Where are you from?" she asked him, thinking she couldn't possibly find a more perfect companion for the day. She had a need all at once to spend some time with someone whose view of the world was still form-ing, and whose opinions would be fresh. Since her conversation with herself on the patio, she'd been feeling lighter and younger and filled with curiosity about herself. With this boy she'd have no need of hats of any kind. She'd be able to be whoever she was and possibly get a fix on Lily's daughter now that she'd finally reconciled herself to the fact that Lily was gone for all time. Poor unhappy Lily with her needlepoint, her uncontrollable husband, and her compulsive cleaning.

"Indianapolis. Where're you from?"

"Connecticut."

"I've been there. We went with my dad for his twentieth reunion at Yale. You been to Yale?"

"I've seen it."

"It was cool. I think I'll probably go there when I graduate."

"Really? What grade are you in?"

"Going into tenth in September," he answered. "Surprised, right? Thought I was maybe in seventh or eighth. Right?"

"Right."

"Wrong. I know I look about eight, but I'm fourteen. Probably have arrested hormones or something. Pediatrician's been telling my mother forever that I'll have like this big growth spurt any time now. It worries the hell out of her that I'm a notch away from being a midget." He gave a little laugh. "Myself, I figure there are lots worse things than being short."

"Of course there are," Jo agreed. "And you're not *that* short."

"Right. But it's like this really major thing with her, you know? The way she sees it, my getting good grades and having a pretty decent bunch of friends are just kind of compensations. Like I'm an overachiever, and the guys I hang around with feel sorry for me. What crap! She likes to have something to worry about, so I let her believe all that stuff."

"Are you one of those brains who never studies and always pulls straight A's?"

"Oh, I study all right. Not like all the time or anything, but I put in the hours. How long've you been a professional?"

"I sold my first photographs when I was seventeen. In terms of a career, it's about fourteen years."

"Seventeen, huh?"

"Yup. Sold some stuff to the local newspaper. It was great."

"What kind of stuff?"

"Snow scenes. We had a big storm on the East Coast that year. I went out with my little brother and took pictures of frozen wires, abandoned cars, Beamer—that's my brother—making snow angels, all kinds of stuff. The paper used three of the shots in its front-page feature about the storm. Paid me a hundred and fifty dollars, which was a fortune back then. The only snag was I didn't know anything, and I let them buy the copyrights. Still, it was a big thrill. I used the money to buy an enlarger, so I could have my own darkroom in the basement."

"What does that mean, about the copyrights?"

"It meant the paper owned the rights, so I couldn't sell the pictures anywhere else. And the thing is, one of the shots got picked up by a wire service and went national. I figure the paper made a nice little profit on that deal, even if I did get the exposure. Since they owned the copyrights, they didn't even have to give me the credit, but they did. They were being kind, I guess, because I was just a kid."

"Must've been a good picture."

"Must've been. See, the thing is it's very hard to shoot in snow, because of the light. If you don't get the exposure just right, all you come out with is a dark blob and some glare."

"No kidding."

"Uh-huh."

"I never knew that. I always thought you just point the camera and take the picture."

"That's about what most people think. And with the automatic cameras, that's pretty well what happens. Except that even with the automatics, the built-in light meters take a reading that'll be accurate in the normal situation. But in a high-light situation, those TTL meters go crazy.''

''What's TTL?''

''Through the lens. It's another way of saying built-in.''

''Oh. Hey! Here comes the boat.'' He pushed away from the gate and looked away over the water. ''It's about time,'' he said, turning back to her. ''Fourteen years. How old're you, anyway? You look about twenty-five, maybe.''

She smiled. ''Thirty-six.''

''No way! My mom's only five years older than you.''

''Pretty old, huh?''

''You don't look that old at all. What's your name? I'm Jackie Watts, by the way.'' He wiped his open palm on his Levi's before offering his hand.

''Joanna James. Call me Jo.''

He gave her hand a hearty shake and said, ''Hi. It's really nice to meet you.''

''It's really nice to meet you, too. Would you be interested in coming along with me? I mean, since neither of us has a set destination, we might as well head off together.''

''Great! I can watch you take your pictures. Maybe I'll learn a few things. Blow Dad's brain when I tell him how to improve his stuff. He's got one of those little Minolta jobs. It even loads the film. All he has to do is drop it into the back of the camera, and the thing starts to click and whirr. Amazing.''

Once in the boat, Jo automatically moved to stand at the rear, and Jackie followed suit.

''Isn't it great!'' he said over the noise of the motor. ''I've never *seen* such a great place! I read all about it when Dad said we were going to come, got a zillion books from the library and read up on the floods in 'sixty-six and 'sixty-seven, and all the restoration and preservation work they've been doing since then; all about the carnival, and the algae problems in the lagoons. Did you know that Venice is probably the safest city in the whole of Italy? They've never even had one case of kidnapping. Nobody gets mugged. Hardly any crime here at all. And the real estate's worth an absolute fortune. There's also a ghetto. Did you know that?''

''No, I didn't.'' She turned to look at him. ''We should definitely go see that.''

''Definitely. Except I don't know where it is, and I forgot to bring my map.''

''No problem. I've got one in my purse.''

''Great! This is going to be great!'' He was practically dancing with excitement.

She swung around and took a shot of him, then lowered the camera with a smile.

"Hey! You took my picture. Are you going to put me in a book or something?"

"I'm not doing a book, just a feature on the Orient-Express, and the hotel."

"They're owned by the same company, aren't they? Have you been on the train?"

"I came to Venice on it, and I'll be going back to London on the train Saturday morning."

"Is it sensational? What's it like?"

"It's fabulous. And the food is beyond belief. You'd love it."

"I *begged* my mom and dad to ride that train. But no. We're *flying* to London from here. It takes too long, my dad said. Not 'It costs too much,' because he couldn't get away with that one. I mean, figure what four first-class tickets round-trip have to cost from Indy to New York to Venice, Venice to London, London to home. A fortune. We could've gone economy or even business class and had a ride on the train. But no, it would take too long. These people have no sense of adventure. I mean *none*. I mapped out this entire trip, right, with side trips to Florence and Rome; then a ride on the train to Paris; then a boat over to England, and a ride on an English train to London. I mean, think of all the stuff you could see. And what does he do? He says, 'That's nice, Jackie,' then gets this travel agent who books all his business trips, right? And she has no goddamned imagination. Four first-class tickets with as few stopovers as possible. Because he's this busy executive who doesn't want to waste any time. It's such bullshit. We've got an entire *month*. And one week's already shot with the two of them playing tennis and Wonder Dummy out by the pool defying the holes in the ozone layer. I mean, that girl uses *cooking oil*, for chrissake! She'll probably croak from massive skin cancers before she's twenty. Seriously! She wants to go home with this major tan to wow her girlfriends. Like a *Venetian tan*! Get it? I can't believe I was actually *born* into this family! No shit! They're time-sharing a brain, but they can never remember whose day it is."

Jo burst out laughing, then apologized. "I'm sorry. I'm sure it's sheer hell for you, but you've got a very funny way of expressing yourself."

"Oh, that's okay." He grinned at her, revealing two rows of metal braces. "I know. If you don't laugh, you could get ulcers."

He scampered off the boat and then, with a touching display of gallantry, turned and held out his hand to assist her ashore.

"Will you *look* at this!" he crowed. "You could break down and cry over a place that looks like this, no shit. What should we do first?"

"I think we should get some breakfast. By the time we've eaten, things should be open. You haven't eaten yet, have you?"

"Nope."

"Do you see any restaurants that look open?"

"Bound to be some on the other side of the square." He started off, then turned back and said, "Listen, you want me to carry any of that stuff for you?"

Her first instinct was to say no, but he seemed so anxious to help that she swung the camera bag off her shoulder and let him take it.

"What's in here?" he asked as they crossed the square.

"Lenses, film, filters. I'll tell you what," she said, inspired. "I'll show you the different lenses and you can hand them to me when I need them. I'll teach you how to clean them, too."

"Okay, cool."

"There's a place just up here where we had drinks yesterday. Maybe it's open."

"I thought you said this was your first chance to look around."

"It is. I had to come over yesterday afternoon to buy a new camera. My other one had a nervous breakdown and died."

He chuckled and patted the side of the Lowe-pro. "Pretty funny yourself, Joey old girl."

She mussed his hair saying, "All my best friends call me Joey automatically. So I guess you're going to be one of my new best friends, Jackie old boy."

"Fine by me. What magazine's your story gonna be in?"

"A trade publication called *Travelogue*. Make sure you give me your address, and I'll have the magazine send you a copy."

"When's it coming out?"

"I'm not sure, probably February or March."

"This place isn't open yet." Jackie rattled the doorknob. "Guess we'll have to keep on looking. D'you *believe* how amazing this place is?" he asked, craning to look at the upper levels of the buildings they passed. "The trick is to follow the yellow guide signs. I read that you absolutely can't get lost if you follow the arrows. See!" He pointed out one of the signs appended to the wall of a building they were approaching. "That way to the Rialto. Wanna go that way?"

"Sure."

"Great!"

After several turnings they came to an open restaurant. They stopped to look at the menu posted outside.

"What d'you think that means?" she asked Jackie. "The exact same things on both sides of the menu, but two different prices."

"Oh, that's easy. The lower price is what you pay if you eat standing up. The higher price is if you want to sit down."

"Are you sure?"

"Positive. I'm telling you, I read *everything*. This is my first trip to Europe, you know."

"Is that so?"

"Yup. And next time I'm coming alone, without Wonder Dummy and the Two Stooges."

"You shouldn't talk about your family that way," she laughed.

"Keeps 'em humble. If you want to sit down, I don't mind. It's up to you."

"How about if we sit down, but we eat quickly? Sound fair?"

"Sure. That's fair."

They entered the restaurant and looked at the cheeses and cold cuts and breads and prepared sandwiches, trying to decide.

"I think I'm going to have one of those sandwiches," Jackie said. "And some espresso. I love those little cups."

"Makes you feel seriously mature, right?"

"Believe it. I've got this like major caffeine addiction. I *love* coffee. Especially first thing in the morning. I drink a couple of cups, then go stand outside to wait for the schoolbus, and I'm like *vibrating*. No kidding. All the guys I know are drinking Cokes, right, and I'm having coffee. They think I'm mondo weird, right, but I don't care. It gets me really revved, and I like it. These are the same guys, you know, who think it's major cool to drink their parents' booze and smoke J's. Then they spend the next three hours doing the old technicolor yawn. Dorks. Me, I have a couple of coffees and I'm set. Can't stand smoking; dope makes me heave. I don't mind a beer. Beer's okay, if it's good stuff and not the shit you buy at the supermarket. I mean, *imported* stuff like Tuborg, or Kronenbourg. Course I have to yack it up with old Dad and pretend we're into all this manly macho crap so he'll break into his supply and let me have one of his beers.

"Lemme ask you something. How come people grow up and turn so goddamned stupid? I mean, okay, not everybody comes out brain-damaged. You're not; you're really all right. But you should check out my family. My dad was Phi Beta Kappa at Yale. Meet him and you wouldn't buy that on a dare; you sure as hell wouldn't buy shoelaces from him. This is the same guy who, as a teenager, invested in Xerox in 1964. Feature it, *Xerox*. He totally cleaned up. Can you imagine that? This is the same guy who has conversations with my mom or with Wonder Dummy you wouldn't credit. I mean, he sounds like Eddie Murphy doing Mr. Rogers. I want to hire people to come check up on me in twenty years, and if I'm all vegged out and worrying about shit like snowblowers and Toro lawn mowers, they've got to bounce my head off a wall a couple or three times to get me straight. You know?"

"I know."

The aproned man behind the counter went to make Jackie's espresso and Jo's cappuccino while a waitress brought over their sandwiches and two thin paper napkins. She smiled, as if in recognition, and Jo understood that the woman thought Jackie was her son. Jo liked it; it occurred to her that she wouldn't mind being mother to a boy like this. He was bright and funny and terrifically alive.

"I'll bet your folks are crazy about you."

"Why d'you say that?" he asked, looking suspiciously at his sandwich before picking up half.

"Because if I was your mother, I would be."

"Oh, yeah, but that's because you don't have to live with me. If you lived with me, you probably wouldn't see me or hear me, just the way she doesn't. I mean, they're not bad people or anything," he qualified. "I don't want to give the wrong impression. It's just that the stuff that's really important to them is totally inconsequential." He took a tentative bite of the sandwich, chewed, swallowed, said, "This is good," and proceeded to wolf down the rest while Jo watched. "I'm gonna get another one," he announced, then got up and walked with a springy step over to the counter where, with a big smile, he asked politely for another of the same. "I'm usually very fussy about what I eat," he told her, returning to the table. "When we all go to like McDonald's or Burger King, I eat the salads. I wouldn't touch a Big Mac or a Whopper if you paid me. I'll bet you the next report from the surgeon general's gonna tell us junk food causes cancer."

"Everything does, from the sound of it."

"Right. So I'm very careful about my food. Which is probably why I'm not six two like my Dad. He grew up on Wonder Bread and Twinkies. Stuff's probably loaded with steroids. I mean, feature it." He started to laugh. "If he didn't eat all that processed crap when he was growing up, he'd probably be a dwarf like me. Hey! Great title, right? *Dwarf Like Me*— the chilling sequel to *Short Like Me*."

"You're not a dwarf, for God's sake."

"Okay, short."

"Maybe a little. D'you hate it?" she asked him.

"Not hate. I'm just tired of hearing about it, so you get into the joke routines, you know."

The waitress returned to the table with the coffees, and Jo indicated which went where.

Jackie said, *"Grazie, Signora,"* and the waitress pinched his cheek and said something endearing in Italian. Jackie blushed and pinched the waitress's cheek. The woman laughed loudly and went off behind the counter, telling the counterman in Italian about what had happened.

"Great people!" Jackie said, starting on the second sandwich. "I'm having the best goddamned time. Aren't you going to eat that?"

"Yes, I am." Jo picked up her sandwich, which was a rich white cheese on bread with green and black olives baked into it.

"What is that?" Jackie asked, looking suspicious again.

"I think it's fontina cheese. And the bread is heaven, with olives baked in. Want to taste?"

"No, thanks. Too much salt in olives. It's bad for you, causes hardening of the arteries and makes you retain water."

"I'll take my chances."

"Well, maybe just a little taste."

"Go ahead." She pushed the plate with the second half of the sandwich across the table.

"It *is* good," he said, returning the plate. "But it's still not good for you."

"If you worry so much about things when you're only fourteen, maybe you'll be so worried by the time you're thirty you won't be able to have any fun anymore."

He paused in his chewing to stare at her. "Jesus! You think so?"

"It's a possibility."

"Boy, that's scary! I'd hate that."

"Kids're supposed to eat junk and drink their parents' booze and then throw up. They're supposed to sneak cigarettes and then cough their hearts out. I did all that stuff and it didn't wreck me."

"Yeah?"

"Sure. You know how tiny babies can survive diseases and illnesses that would kill adults? It's because they have special built-in genetic protection. And I think it's the same for teenagers. I used to smoke with my girlfriends, but I never got into the habit. And I definitely used to raid the booze supply when my folks were out. But I didn't turn out to be an alcoholic. I don't know about the Big Macs and Twinkies, but that's only because when I was little my granny always told me never to eat hamburgers in restaurants. She implied it was seriously dangerous, and I believed her. So the only burgers I ever ate were ones my father barbecued, or that I made myself when I was a student. Now, I hardly ever eat red meat. The thing is, it's experimentation, Jackie, that's all."

"You're pretty sharp," he said. "I kind of thought so yesterday when you were taking pictures of everybody at breakfast. I made up this whole story about how you were like from the *National Enquirer*, getting the scoop on the guests."

"The *Enquirer*? God! Do you *read* that?"

"Are you kidding? Every time I go to the supermarket with my mom, while she's in the check-out line, I head right for the rag racks they have by the cash registers and check out the Werewolf Family, and the movie-star anorexic who stabbed her manager in the hand with a pair of scissors, and the latest on Joan Collins, and all those rubes who've gone for rides in UFOs. It's the best, the absolutely best in comedy. They should have like special awards for the year's weirdest as-told-to stories, not to mention all those features about miracle diets where some totally obese guy lost four hundred pounds. Now he's down to only eight hundred and twenty." He started to laugh, his face twisting. "Boy!" he chortled, slapping his hand on the tabletop. "I *love* that stuff, love it!"

"You're terrific," she told him. "We're going to have ourselves a truly great day."

"Count on it! Are you going to eat the other half of that?"

In answer she pushed the plate back across the table to him. She'd been right, she congratulated herself as she watched him eat. She'd picked someone to spend the day with who was exactly the companion she needed. She felt real and visible and happy, and closer to an insight into her own identity than she'd ever been.

"I wish I'd known you when I was fourteen, Jackie."

"Oh, yeah?"

"Honestly. We'd have had a lot of fun."

"Yeah," he agreed. "Except that girls who look like you all hang out with jocks, not with the twerp brigade."

"Not all of us."

"Hey!" he exclaimed. "Keep that up and next thing you know you'll be giving me like serious hope for the future."

"Well, you should have. You're a seriously terrific guy."

"Maybe I'll get into a thing for older women." He did a Groucho bit with his eyebrows, one finger laid across his upper lip. "Say the magic word, sister, and the duck'll lay a hundred on you."

She laughed and went back to her half sandwich.

Eighteen

THE TRAFFIC THROUGH THE DOGE'S PALACE WAS STRICTLY ONE-way, with rope barriers and arrows to point out the route. This early in the day there weren't many people, so Jo was able to stop at the top of the stairs to shoot the gilt latticework above and the stonework and painted panels of the ceiling over the stairwell. Marble columns and lintels supporting statuary; ceilings thickly crusted with gilded stucco work in elaborate classical designs surrounding painted panels of religious significance; vast windows opening onto courtyards and affording unimpaired views of the canal and of the piazza; the great echoey cavern of the Sala del Maggior Consiglio with Tintoretto's *Il Paradiso* occupying an entire wall at the far end.

"It's the largest oil painting in the world," Jackie told her. "Cool, huh?"

When the guards weren't looking, Jo leaned far out one of the windows to take a picture of the Bridge of Sighs connecting the palace to the dungeons. Then they continued on through the unfurnished rooms, down stone steps into the dungeons.

"This is creepy," Jackie said quietly, with his hand to his head, measuring the low height of the heavy cell doors. "Short people. You could like *never* break out of this place." Tentatively, he touched the iron grillwork over the cell windows, then peered in to study the writing on the walls.

It was a relief to emerge into the sunlight of the courtyard, where he watched as she took close-ups of the stonework and the clockface, then they both stood looking up, turning slowly to take it all in: domes, more statuary perched improbably upon pointed spires; arches and decorative stonework at the roof, rainspouts; and boarded-off areas where restoration work was underway.

Back in the piazza people were milling about, snapping each other's pictures in the center, posing for one of the street photographers, or buying Venezia T-shirts and tacky souvenirs from the vendors.

"It's the most beautiful city I've ever seen," Jo said in reverent tones.

"We can get a vaporetto that'll take us to the ghetto. Then we could walk back from there. I'm not sure of the number of the boat, but there's a ticket place where we could ask."

Jo agreed, and they walked back to the canal. Again, very politely, Jackie asked his questions, bought their tickets, then told her, "He says to wait right here. Are you having a great time? I am. This is *so* cool. My folks never do anything spontaneous."

"I am having a fine time," she assured him, turning to take a shot of one of the exquisite lamp standards with its four lilac-tinted glass globes. Removing the telephoto, she handed it to him. Treating it respectfully, he replaced the lens cap, stowed it in the bag, and gave her the 50-mm.

"You learn fast," she complimented him.

"Easy as pie." He gave the side of the bag a pat. "Makes me feel kind of—official."

"Well, you are. You're my official lens handler."

"All right!" he laughed.

Once on board the vaporetto, she remained standing in order to get shots of the boats on the canal and the buildings lining either side. Efficiently, Jackie dealt with the lenses, cleaning them before replacing the caps, watching her all the while, intrigued.

"Boy," he said as they left the boat, "you see everything. I mean everything. All the other people, they're walking along looking left and right, but you, you're looking up, down, sideways, and close up. Oh, boy! Here it is."

An oblong yellow sign in Hebrew and Italian was fixed to the wall over a low square stone archway. Another sign beside it read HOSPEDALE PEDIA-TRICO.

"Well, that's good," Jackie said. "If I get sick, you can just drop me at the children's hospital on the way."

They went through the dark tunnel and along a walkway, emerging into a small square. To the left was a very tall building with few areas of plaster remaining on its facade; the red brick beneath was exposed, and the shutters stood open on most of the windows. Two of the second-floor windows had boxes filled with healthy red geraniums. A lone blue shirt hung on a clothesline. It was a sad-looking building, and Jo backed away to take a wide-angle shot that included the capped wellhead in the center of the square.

Following the arrows, they passed more neglected buildings that nevertheless had a certain grim beauty.

"It's one of the poorest areas of Venice," Jackie informed her, looking around. "Only about eight hundred Jewish people still live here. According to the stuff I read, the word 'ghetto' comes from the Italian *getto* which means to cast metals. See, there was a foundry here where they made cannons, right. Then, I think it was like the fourteenth century, they gave the Jews permission to live here, and they called it the 'ghetto.' It was the very first ghetto in the entire world. Did you know that?"

"No," she said, impressed by the amount of reading and research he'd done, "I didn't know any of that."

"Yeah, well, this is it." Eyes narrowed, he said, "Pretty depressing place. They had gates over those archways there, so people couldn't leave. And there's a wall around here somewhere with inscriptions. Supposedly, it's just outside, so I guess if we keep going that way"—he pointed across the square they'd just entered—"it'll be over there."

As they came out on the far side, Jackie said, "Here it is! I told you!" and ran over to the wall.

Jo followed, and looked first at the seven bronze bas-relief panels on the exposed-brick wall, and then at the two panels of writing on the same wall just beyond a wood and ornamental iron gateway. The larger of the two panels was in French, Italian, and English and read:

MEN, WOMEN, CHILDREN, MASSES FOR THE GAS CHAMBERS
ADVANCING TOWARD HORROR BENEATH THE WHIP OF THE EXECUTIONER.
YOUR SAD HOLOCAUST IS ENGRAVED IN HISTORY
AND NOTHING SHALL PURGE YOUR DEATHS FROM OUR MEMORIES.
FOR OUR MEMORIES ARE YOUR ONLY GRAVE.

The smaller plaque, also in three languages, read:

THE CITY OF VENICE REMEMBERS THE VENETIAN JEWS WHO WERE DEPORTED TO THE NAZI CONCENTRATION CAMPS ON DECEMBER 5TH, 1943, AND AUGUST 17TH, 1944.

The pictorial plaques were impressionistic depictions of massed bodies; a sole naked figure standing before an overcoated firing squad; crucified figures.

Backing away, she lifted the camera only to find herself unable to see. Tears ran from her eyes, warping the view.

"You okay?" Jackie put his hand on her arm.

She nodded, reaching into her purse for a tissue.

"Pretty goddamned terrible, huh?" he said, his hand still on her arm, his eyes on the wall.

Her voice thick, she said, "It makes me so furious when I think there are morons who go public saying none of it ever happened, that it's all propaganda."

"You kidding?"

"I'm *not* kidding," she said hotly. "Assholes who say nobody ever got gassed in a shower, or cremated, or thrown into a mass grave. God, but it makes me mad!" She raised the camera again and took shots of the whole wall, then close-ups. Then, shaking her head, she said, "I've had enough. What about you?"

"Yeah, me too."

As they were strolling along in the hot sun, she said, "I'm sorry about that."

"Oh, that's okay. It got to me, too. I felt like crying myself."

She put her arm around his shoulders and hugged him against her side. "You're one swell kid."

"So're you." He put his arm around her waist and gave her a squeeze, which made her laugh. "I'll bet you go home and you never have even one picture that has you in it. Right?"

"Right."

"Why don't you show me what to do, and I'll take your photograph?"

"God, I look terrible in pictures."

"Be real!" he argued. "Come on. Stand right here and let me do it."

"Okay," she gave in. "I'll set everything so all you have to do is turn the focusing ring here until what you're seeing is clear. Have a look." She gave him the camera. "Focus on that guy sitting outside that shop there."

He did as she said, then exclaimed, "This is really cool! Okay. Stand where you are and give me a big veggieburger."

She smiled. He made the exposure, then returned the camera. "I could really get into this," he said, jamming his hands into his back pockets. "Maybe I'll sign up for the camera club this year, buy myself a camera and start snapping away. It's even worth extra credit if you take it as an option course. I could cash in a couple of my bonds, get set up. I might just do that."

"You have bonds?"

"Oh, sure. So does Wonder Dummy. We got them for being born. I come from a family that believes heavily in liquidity, kiddo. You're nothing if you don't have tangible assets. Wonder Dummy's already used up most of her money on clothes but I've still got almost all of mine."

They went on, following the yellow signs, occasionally ducking down laneways that dead-ended at canals, then doubling back to continue on while she photographed a pair of doorbells that had been built into the mouths of two tiny brass lions' heads; gracious balconied dwellings with boats moored outside; a picture of the Virgin in a flower-decked niche behind an ornamental grille; an ornate antique watering trough that was still functioning; a bricked-in doorway at the end of an extremely narrow passage; dozens of noble stone heads positioned at the apex of archways or the undersides of windows; squares with newspaper kiosks, and squares with displays of fresh flowers in buckets, and squares with outdoor cafés; a pair of exquisite gondolas with armchairs and pillows, the pair tethered to the underside of a bridge; a restaurant situated on a bridge over a secondary canal, with yellow and white striped umbrellas protecting the diners from the midday sun; lines of washing suspended between buildings; a pair of straw-hatted gondoliers leaning against the railing on a bridge, halting their conversation to offer their services; sheets and towels draped over a balcony railing to air out in the sun; an elegant old building that turned out to be a bank, with burnt-umber walls and marble supporting corner columns; restored palazzi next to ancient churches in disrepair; thoughtful statues in the center of squares with tourists sitting on the steps at their bases feeding crumbs to the pigeons; a small-scale yacht docked between two huge houses; a row of new windows all standing open in a building whose exterior was crumbling; pointed arches over tunnels leading from a landing stage to an adjoining street; variations of the classic lamp standard with one, two, three, or four lilac globes; more gondolas, these with carvings and carpets and highly-polished bits of brass trim.

"Are you hungry?" Jackie asked her after a time. "I'm starving. I could probably eat a small whale."

"Then we'd better eat."

They sat at an aluminum table out of doors and ate thick slabs of cheese and salami on crusty bread, and drank Cokes.

"Better not breathe on anyone for several days," Jo warned him with a laugh.

"Nobody gets close enough anyway. Normally, you know, I wouldn't drink one of these if I were dying of thirst. But I'm too hot to rev up on a cup of the old caffeine right now. Maybe for dessert."

"Personally, I love Coca-Cola. It's the one American thing you can buy anywhere in the world. I wouldn't admit this to just anyone, but seeing as how you're my official lens handler and all, I'm confiding in you."

"You're putting me on."

"Yeah, I am."

"That's what I thought." He wiped crumbs from his face with the back of his hand. "It's okay being American, for the most part. But some of our foreign policy really sucks. And most of those guys in Washington make me like *very* nervous."

"You know who makes *me* really nervous?"

"Who, aside from the guys who say the Holocaust never happened?"

"All those people who take so-called moral stances on things, the ones who have whole organizations that're supposed to be religious but who're lobbying politically. They scare the hell out of me. Any group that says it's right, regardless of the issue, and thinks because it's right it can blow places up, kill people, picket and harass anybody who doesn't agree with them."

"Okay," he said, thinking. "But that's one of the good things about our country: that you're free to think what you want."

"Oh, I want people to be free, Jackie. I just don't want them trying to force *me* to believe what *they* believe. That isn't freedom; it's coercion; it's simply another, subtler, form of terrorism."

"I never thought of it that way, but I guess you're right."

"God!" she said. "I'm getting heavy, and this isn't the time for it."

"Why not?" he wanted to know. "I hardly ever get a chance to talk about this stuff. It's one of the major disadvantages of looking ten years old. People never get serious with you, as if your brain's the size of a peanut because you're a kid and you're short. It really pisses me off. The only time my dad ever has any kind of serious conversation is with like my uncles, or with business types. Or if I give him some kind of abstracted topic, like for an essay. Usually, he brushes me off. You know: 'I'm busy'; 'I'm tired'; 'I just got home from a rough day at the office and I'm not in the mood for this'; 'I don't have time.' Being a kid's a major pain in the ass a lot of the time, no shit."

"I know," she agreed. "Have to get all your important information from the *Enquirer*."

He smiled. "I'm really into the news, you know. I mean, Wonder Dummy'll sit there and watch reruns of 'The Partridge Family' or 'The Brady Bunch' and she thinks it's great stuff. Me, I go for CNN. I can do a couple of hours of that, then tune into Brokaw for the network poop. You've gotta know what's going on," he said earnestly. "You can't like wait until you're out of college before you start finding out what the rest of the world's doing. How come you don't like having your picture taken?"

"I'm not photogenic."

"I'll bet you are. You're really pretty." He flushed but didn't look away.

"I'm not, but thank you."

"How can you *say* that?" he asked, amazed. "You're a great-looking wench. I bet guys are all over you like a cheap suit."

She laughed. "Not quite."

"Then they're idiots! I was older, I'd be all over you. Boy," he scratched his head, confused, "I thought women all think they're great."

"God, no! There probably aren't more than two women in the entire world who think they're great. Truly. We all have something about ourselves we hate."

"Like what? What d'you hate about yourself?"

"I don't know. My nose. It's kind of lumpy."

"You're nuts! Your nose is perfect. What else?"

"I need to lose at least five pounds."

"You're *insane*! You'd be a total skeleton, you lost five pounds. What else?"

"Those are my two major bugs. D'you like everything about yourself—?" she challenged.

"Well, I'm not like in love with me or anything. But I think I'm okay. I'm short, but I'm still growing. And even if I don't grow much more, that's cool. At least my head's on right, and I'm using it. Which is more than I can say for a whole lot of people. I can't *believe* you'd say stuff like that about yourself. Your nose is great. And you're definitely not fat. If anything you're on the too-skinny side. I mean, look at your teensy little wrists." He took hold of her arm between his thumb and forefinger, and lifted it. "Look at that! *Little kids* have bigger wrists than that. This is too weird!" He let go of her arm, rolling his eyes. "Wise up, Joey old girl! You're top quality. Somebody tell you one time you had a lumpy nose?"

"No. That's just how it looks to me."

"You're a banana. It's a seriously aristocratic honker," he said, then laughed and waved to the waitress to ask for an espresso.

"I'll bet the girls are crazy about you."

"Sure. They're lining up to go out with like the second shortest guy in tenth grade."

"You don't have a girlfriend?"

"There's this girl I like, but she lives in California. We met last winter when Dad took us to Eleuthera."

"D'you stay in touch?"

"Yeah. We write, and we talk on the phone every couple of weeks. But it's losing steam, you know. It's hardly likely I'm gonna be going out to San Francisco anytime soon. And the world's not making a big rush on Indianapolis. Armpit of the goddamned universe. I definitely plan to go to Yale, get the hell out of Indy. Wonder Dummy'll probably get married before she graduates, so Dad'll save a fortune on her tuition. I just have to keep my grade-point average up, then look out! I'm gone. Off to old Eli Yale. Four years of English major and I'll go work in New York, or maybe Boston. Somewhere cool."

"Doing what?"

"I don't know. Maybe I'll work for the *Enquirer*," he chuckled. "Fix up their semiliterate prose. Or maybe I'll be Jackie Watts, ace reporter, pulling the scoop on Wall Street scams, or getting guys to give me their secret papers." He shrugged as the waitress brought his espresso. "I definitely don't want to go my Dad's route into that whole corporate thing. It's so goddamned boring, rots your brain out. He never has any good stories to tell, never meets any interesting people. I'm not putting him down or anything, but I want more than the nine rooms in the suburbs with the three-and-a-half bathrooms, the Seville, and the country club. Not to mention the wife and two kids. I mean, they've been married *forever*. They've been married so long they don't even talk to each other in full sentences. They just kind of grunt. And I'm pretty well positive they don't make it anymore. If you want to know the truth, I think Dad screws around. And I'll tell you something else: I think my Mom doesn't even care. As long as she doesn't have to know about it, as long as she's got the Buick and the club and the credit cards, that's cool."

As he spoke, she felt a chill, remembering Beamer's vow as a twelve-year-old never to marry—and for almost these exact same reasons. It was like déjà vu, but she had the power perhaps to change it this time.

"It doesn't mean they don't care about each other, Jackie."

"No," he conceded. "I guess not. The thing is, I don't get the point. I mean, if you're gonna be married, then be married. If you're gonna screw around, why be married?"

"I'd like to tell you a little story," she said so quietly that she had his immediate and complete attention. "Years ago I was in the city, in Manhattan, one afternoon. It was just before graduation, and I was going around with my portfolio, showing editors my work, trying to get assignments. Anyway, I finished my last appointment and I was heading back across town, walking to Grand Central. I'd just missed a train, so I had plenty of time before the next one. It was in the spring, May, I guess, and the weather was perfect. For a couple of weeks every year, I just love the city. Things look cleaner, fresher than at any other time, except when there's a big snowfall. It's the best time for New York, really."

Jackie nodded, listening closely.

"So anyway, there I was walking along, just coming up to the St. Regis. I'm waiting at the corner for the lights to change and I see this couple coming out of the hotel. The doorman goes to signal a taxi, and this couple are standing there waiting. A cab comes along, the doorman opens the car door, and these two people turn to each other, say something, and then they kiss; they *really* kiss. Then they separate, the woman gets into the cab, and the cab goes off. The man stands there watching until the cab's out of sight, then he tips the doorman, turns, and heads off down the street.

"People are bumping into me, calling me names, and I finally realize I'm holding up traffic at the intersection. So I start moving with the crowd, but I have no idea what I'm doing or where I'm going. It was terrible."

"It was your dad?" Jackie guessed.

"Right."

"Shit!"

"The thing is, I'd known for years that there was something going on in my house. You know? I never knew exactly what it was until that afternoon. I just knew there was *something*. When he was twelve years old, my brother Beamer said he'd never get married. He never wanted to get locked into something as messed up and confusing as our parents' marriage. At the time I told myself he'd grow out of it. But my thinking was entirely about Beamer. I wasn't really thinking how the whole thing was affecting me, probably because Beamer was outside of me, an entirely separate other person. And I could see how it all affected him, but I couldn't see that it was affecting me, too. The *really* confusing part of it was that no matter what else went on, my mother and father were devoted to each other. When my mother died, my dad totally fell apart. For an entire year he couldn't do a thing. Half the time, if you tried to talk to him, he'd start to cry. He truly loved her.

"Their marriage drove me and Beamer crazy, Jackie. Beamer's thirty-two now and he's never even come close to getting married. And to be truthful, neither have I. But you know what?"

"What?"

"I think now it's just the way things are. It's something that happens, and in a lot of ways it hardly has anything to do with the marriage. And I also think that somehow as nice as it is to be a success and have some money in the bank and a decent car, it's just not as much fun when you're all alone. Sure, you don't have to get married to have that, but it's good to have people around to make you laugh if you're bummed out, or to help you calm down when you're pissed off about something."

"You have people like that?"

"I have friends," she answered.

"Not friends. I mean like a boyfriend."

"I think maybe I do, but I don't know yet. There's someone I like an awful lot."

"Oh yeah? What's he like?"

"He's English, and very funny, and kind of sweet in a reserved British way."

"Where does he live?"

"In London."

"Yeah? You gonna move to London?"

"God knows!" she laughed.

"D'you mind if I ask you something really personal?"

"I won't know till I hear you ask it."

"D'you, um, like do it with this guy?"

To her surprise the question didn't bother her in the least. "Uh-huh," she said, "I do."

"That's what I thought. Mind if I ask you something else?"

"Go ahead."

"Is it all heavy breathing and moaning and groaning like the movies?"

"Not quite, but it's good. The thing is, it's not everything. Let me give you one big piece of advice, Jackie. Okay?"

"Sure."

"If you're ever truly interested in a girl, make sure you get to know her. Find out who she is, how she feels about things, her opinions. Do it because you like her, not because you're trying to cultivate her interest in you. If you make the effort, then making love'll be great, because people need time. All of us do. And one other thing: Don't ever make the mistake of thinking that because you're really hot for somebody that you're in love with her. Sex is definitely not love."

"Okay. I'll remember that."

"You do, and all the things that bother you now will make sense later on, I promise. And Jackie! One other thing. It's very goddamned hard sometimes to make sense out of what our parents are doing. If you understand that it's just as hard for *them* to make sense of what they're doing, if you can be a little more tolerant, life'll be easier for all of you. Don't gauge your own future on what you see of your mom and dad's marriage, because that isn't the way it has to be for you. Don't make the same mistake Beamer and I made, and mess up years of your life because your parents' marriage wasn't like 'The Brady Bunch.' The fact is, nobody has a marriage like that. *Absolutely nobody.* Okay. That's it. Ready to go?"

When he reached into his pocket for money, she said, "Listen, kiddo. You paid for breakfast, and for the vaporetto. Lunch is on me."

"Okay. Thanks."

"You're good company, Jackie."

"You, too. These have been some of the best conversations of my life. And don't ever again let me hear you say your nose is lumpy or that you need to lose weight. You're totally perfect the way you are."

She weighted the bills with one of the cups, then took his hand, saying, "So're you. And they've been some of the best conversations *I've* had, too. Don't underestimate yourself, fellow. You've got a lot to say. Now! We have at least three hours left. What say we go see the Rialto?"

"Definitely!"

Nineteen

ONE MOMENT SHE AND JACKIE WERE OUTSIDE THE HOTEL, LAUGHING as they reviewed the highlights of the day; the next moment they were in the heart of pandemonium.

Jackie went ahead, holding open the door, her camera bag still over his shoulder. Jo came after and stopped dead, watching and listening in a state of low-grade horror as Jackie's father, mother, and sister turned from the heated conversation they'd been having with an assistant manager and one of the concierges. Their faces seemed to twist and swell at the sight of Jackie, and they came charging across the lobby like deranged creatures, all shouting at once. Jo instinctively hunched into herself in an automatic lifelong response to unpleasantness of any kind.

"*One more hour and I was calling the police!*" Mr. Watts railed, red-faced. "*Where the holy hell have you been?*"

"How could you *do* this to me?" Mrs. Watts shrilled.

"*Thanks a lot for messing everything up, jerk!*" the sister bleated.

Mr. Watts grabbed Jackie by the arm and shook him so that the Lowe-pro slid from his shoulder to the bend of his elbow where it hung, dragging the boy's arm down.

"Hey, wait a minute!" Jackie protested, with his free hand trying to get hold of the bag, which was swinging back and forth between him and his father.

"*Don't you wait-a-minute me, mister!*" Watts roared. "*What kind of games d'you think you're playing here, sneaking off with nobody knowing where the hell you are. D'you have anything up there besides air?*" he demanded, rapping his knuckles hard against Jackie's temple.

Watching, unmoving, Jo told herself to do something. This wasn't right.

She couldn't just stand there and let this happen, especially not after having established the closeness she had today with this boy. Are you going to stand here and do nothing? she asked herself. This kid meant something to you today. Do people only mean something when it's convenient for you?

"Please don't hit him," she said, but so quietly no one heard her.

Mrs. Watts now had hold of Jackie's other arm and between her and her husband it seemed as if they might literally tear the boy in two. Stunned, Jackie simply looked at them as they yanked at his arms and shouted into his face. Again, Mr. Watts rapped his knuckles against the side of Jackie's head. And Jackie blinked, wincing.

"Stop that!" Jo said more loudly. "*Please!* There's no need for this."

The assistant manager and concierge both sighed audibly, as if in agreement with this lone voice of rationality. The members of the Watts family went silent and, as one, turned to look at her.

"Who the hell're you?" Watts wanted to know.

Shaky but determined, she said, "Jackie was with me all day. Helping," she added.

"Helping you do *what*?" Watts demanded.

"I left you a note," Jackie spoke finally.

"I know all about your goddamned note," Watts blustered, and then, as if pushed beyond his limits, smacked Jackie across the face, saying, "Shut up!"

Jo broke. Her hand shot out and closed around Mr. Watts' wrist. "Please stop hitting him!" she said, her voice gone breathless and low. "Whatever you think he's done wrong, you're humiliating him in front of all these people, and you're making a fool of yourself."

Watts stared hard at her for a moment, then slowly turned. A number of hotel guests had stopped at the far end of the lobby to watch the proceedings, as had most of the front office staff. They all looked uniformly aghast. There was an awful silence as Watts absorbed this, then looked back at his hand, which was still clamped to Jackie's arm. Reason returning, he released his son. Mrs. Watts took a step back. Jo let go of the man's arm.

"If you'd like to sit down quietly somewhere, I'll be glad to help try to sort this out," Jo said evenly, taking full control of the situation, and awed by her own words and actions. "Let's go to the sitting room over there."

After looking at each member of the family in turn, she took hold of Jackie's hand and led him to the sitting room which, luckily, was unoccupied. "Sit here with me," she instructed Jackie, directing him to the sofa, "and don't say anything unless I ask you to."

The rest of the family trailed suspiciously after, casting each other baffled glances that still contained a volatile residue of anger. Jo watched them sit in the armchairs, wondering just what they were so fired up about.

"Jackie," she asked him, "*did* you leave a note?"

"Sure I did," he answered. "I left it right where Wond—Nance would find it."

"Oh, I found it all right," the girl put in sarcastically. "The idiot—"

"I don't believe I asked you a question," Jo rounded on her. "Please be quiet until your input is asked for."

The girl's mouth closed, and her face creased petulantly.

"And did you say where you were going and when you'd be back?" Jo returned to Jackie.

"Sure I did. I said I was going into town and I'd be back later this afternoon."

"So," Jo turned now to the parents, "you knew where he was."

"We did *not*!" the mother insisted.

"Now you listen," the father said. "I don't know what this has to do with you—"

"It has to do with me," Jo said, furious, "because he was with me all day, because he hasn't done anything wrong, and because he doesn't deserve to be abused in a public place in front of strangers."

"What're you talking about, abuse?" Watts asked, a slight note of uncertainty creeping into his tone.

"What do *you* call it, Mr. Watts, when three people stand in the lobby of a hotel calling someone names and hitting him? *I* call it abuse."

"Well, we were *worried* about him," Mrs. Watts defended them.

"Oh! I see. You were worried about him. Funny, I don't recall any of you shouting anything about that. Do you, Jackie?" She turned to Jackie, who shook his head. "Your son wanted to see Venice," she said, controlling her voice, "which, apparently, you've traveled thousands of miles to do. He left you a note, and did precisely what he said he wanted to do. I realize I'm a complete outsider, but it seems to me he's behaved very responsibly."

"That's right," Watts said. "You *are* an outsider. What business is this of yours?"

"What is the *matter* with you people?" Jo asked hotly. "I mean, d'you behave this way all the time? If you do, maybe you should get family counseling or something." Her anger had taken her over, but she didn't care. "I've known Jackie for one day, but I'll tell you this: If he was a kid of mine, I'd be damned proud of him. He's bright, and funny, and smart. He sure as hell doesn't deserve to be hit and humiliated. God! I'm really tired of people like you. I really am. If you don't want him, if he's just some kind of whipping boy for the three of you, there are plenty of other people who'd be happy as Larry to have him. I would, and that's for damned sure." Retrieving her purse and camera bag, she got to her feet. "You've got a great kid here, and from the looks of it you're too stupid to realize it. He doesn't drink or smoke; he's a good student; he's terrific company; and he hasn't done *one thing wrong*. I think the three of you could use a few whacks across the head, maybe smarten you up." Her hands trembling from anger, she opened her purse and got out one of her cards. Giving it to Jackie, she said, "Here's my card. You feel like leaving home sometime because they're piling too much of this crap on you, call me!" Facing the other three again, she lowered her voice to say, "You ought to wise up, you people. You're taking your problems out on him, and not only does he *not* deserve it, you don't deserve *him*. You honest-to-God make me sick! It might be a good idea if you thought a bit about the scene you just put on in the lobby. This isn't some Holiday Inn, you know, bub!" she addressed Watts. "I'd be willing to bet the management won't be too eager to have you back here again. Except maybe for Jackie. He's got beautiful manners and he knows how to behave. You all owe him an apology. You, Mr. Watts, are supposedly a shrewd businessman, a Phi Beta Kappa from Yale. If you're so damned smart, how come you don't think about your public impression a little more? Just because you're a few thousand miles away from home doesn't mean you're invisible. It also doesn't mean that word doesn't travel. Sooner or later, someone in your company's going to hear you were beating up on your kid in the lobby of the Cipriani. And the next thing you know, your personal stock might start sliding. I'll say this one last time, and then I'm leaving you to sort this mess out: If you don't want him, there are plenty of people who do, and I'm sure as hell one of them." Turning to Jackie a final time, she extended her hand to him, saying, "Thank you for today. I loved being with you." Then she marched out to the foyer.

While the concierge was getting her key and handing over a message, Jackie came hurrying up. He stopped and leaned on the counter beside her for a moment, framing his words. "That was great, what you did, Joey," he said quietly. "They've been pulling that shit on me for years, and they're probably not going to stop now, but I can handle it. I'm used to it. But you're the first person who's ever stood up for me, shut them up and put them in their place." He gave a slow shake of his head. "It was great. Did you mean it?" he asked, looking at her card. "Could I call you sometime?"

"You'd better," she said with a smile. "I can't believe I just did that, but I had to. Today was wonderful, really wonderful." She glanced defiantly toward the sitting room. "And if you want to go out again with me before I leave on Saturday, I'd be delighted."

In response he gave her a hug, then stepped back, red-faced, saying, "I'd better get back. I'll see you later, okay?"

"Okay."

He ran off to the sitting room, and Jo stood for a few moments waiting for the sound of raised voices, but it didn't come. Clutching her key and message, she took the long route—avoiding the sitting room—to her room. She had about forty-five minutes before she was to meet Laura. She could have used a few hours. She felt exhausted, and sank down on the sofa, hearing herself say, "Just because you're a few thousand miles away from home doesn't mean you're invisible," and realized, with a jolt, that people had been saying the same thing to her for ages. Well, she'd certainly just proved to everyone she was anything but invisible. And not only had she proved it unequivocally, she'd also, for the second time in a week, said exactly what she thought. It hadn't seemed as if she had any choice. So she'd taken a stance; she'd defended somebody else; she'd assumed control. And she didn't regret any of it. Sure, she was still shaky, but she'd done something she was proud of. A week ago she'd have slipped away from that scene and come back to her room to brood over her failure to do what she knew to be right. A week ago she'd stood in the doorway of Henry's living room, waiting for Tyler and Henry to notice her. What the hell had she been doing all these years? she wondered. Hiding out, keeping her thoughts to herself, never taking a position, never involved or committed. She could look back to last week and view herself with a definite objectivity, as if remembering some girl from high school she'd once known, a girl who'd made her a little sad and impatient.

She became aware she was still clutching the envelope the concierge had given her, and tore it open.

JOANNA JAMES CIPRIANI VENICE. UPON CONSIDERATION IMPORTANT STATEMENT IS AS FOLLOWS. YOU ARE OF IMPORTANCE TO THE WRITER. EXTENT OF WHICH PRESENTLY UNCERTAIN BUT HAS GROWTH POTENTIAL. WRITER CONSENTS TO PORTRAIT IN GARDEN AT PHOTOGRAPHER'S CONVENIENCE. LOVE HENRY.

She read it twice, then held the telex to her breast, her eyes filling. "Oh, Henry," she whispered, "you're so goddamned sweet." She read it again, then went to shower.

"I do hope you won't mind if we dine at the hotel," Anne said. She looked over to where Jimmy was standing talking to Laura. "Jimmy's not feeling entirely well," she added in an undertone.

"If you'd rather," Jo said, "we can put it off to another night."

"Oh, no, dear." Anne took hold of Jo's hand. "We wouldn't dream of that. We've both been looking forward to this evening with you."

Jo's immediate reaction was to wonder why. Then, deciding this reaction was only worthy of last week's Joanna James, she discarded it and said, "So have I," and watched Anne slowly nod, her eyes still on her husband. Jo remained silent for a time, sensing something. It was a piece of knowledge lodged irritatingly in the corner of her mind—like a pop-corn husk wedged between two teeth—but it wouldn't come forward. All she knew was that this was another of the moments in her life when joining hands with someone else was of great significance. And it was the second time with this woman. She thought of other times—her mother's hand hard in its grip on hers near the end; Beamer's hand linked with hers throughout the funeral services; the first time Tom Harper, her first real boyfriend, had held her hand. Now she was standing, hand in hand, with Anne, both with their eyes on Jimmy, and Jo simply couldn't make the meaning of the moment come clear. Her consciousness had no words, yet it felt bulky with information.

"Come sit with me," Anne said, at last looking away from her husband. "Obviously, he's discussing something of interest with Laura."

They sat, and Anne folded her hands on top of the handbag in her lap. Jo couldn't help being aware of Anne's every move and gesture and wished she could get a clearer fix on the situation. Caught up in her speculations as well as in the thoughtful mood of her companion, she said, "I spent the day with that boy we saw in the bar last night. He's so darling, such a dear, funny boy. I loved being with him. Several times we encountered people who assumed he was my son, and neither one of us told them otherwise. It was like a little game the two of us played. And he had as much fun as I did. Then, we got back to the hotel, and his family made the most dreadful scene, shouting and hitting him. It was a night-mare."

"So I heard," Anne interjected.

"You did?"

"A noteworthy event. One of the waiters confided the details to us. Quite a little scandal. Although I'm given to understand you were the heroine of the piece. Your stock's rising hourly among the hotel staff. Our waiter described you as a cross between a Valkyrie and Saint Joan."

"My God! I had no idea . . . They were being so horrible to him, Anne. I just couldn't stand it. Something's happening to me," she admit-ted. "All my life I've been—a witness, sort of. I mean, I'm there, watch-ing things happen, but I never get involved, never put my two cents' worth in. If I don't like what's going on, I quietly disappear, go away and never come back. I've always made my 'statements' by not making them. You know? Now, all of a sudden, I've not only stopped disappearing, I've also started telling people exactly what I think. It's different and kind of scary, but it's also exciting, like I'm crashing out."

"Don't be afraid, dear," Anne said. "Speaking one's mind, provided one's mind is decently functional, is one of the great joys of life. Personally, I take a very definite delight in being regarded in some circles as opinionated and cantankerous simply because I no longer care whether or not I'm universally liked. It's a definite advantage of old age, although there are times when I simply cannot believe I'm almost seventy. My mind is sixteen and reels at the sight of this face in the mirror."

"I feel the same way," Jo said.

Anne laughed disbelievingly. "How can you possibly? You're still very young. And the face looking back at you from the mirror hasn't a line in it. Your flesh still has a close fondness for your bones." She laid her hand against Jo's cheek. "You're *very* young, Joanna. And it would appear you live a frightfully lonely life, traveling about alone from one place to the next, rarely having the time or opportunity to get to know people." She returned her hand to her lap, her eyes remaining on Jo's. "Perhaps this journey is affording you a chance to break the habits of a lifetime. And if you're not unhappy to have those habits broken, it can only be viewed as a good thing. Don't you think?"

"It does feel that way, but I can't be sure."

"Why do you doubt?" Anne asked her. "There's not a thing wrong with your powers of reasoning, or your sense of right and wrong. What you did for that boy was admirable, honorable. You know what the truth is."

"I do, but it's hard to go along with what you think is right sometimes. You get to thinking maybe your perspective is exaggerated, distorted. Something happens and you don't know what's true and what you just *want* to be true."

"Oh, you know well enough. Why do you doubt yourself—?" she asked, as if the idea of this grieved her. "Don't do that, my dear. Don't." Again she grasped Jo's hand, as her eyes sought out her husband seated across the way, still in conversation with Laura, who seemed to be enjoying his company.

Jo wanted to prolong the dialogue, to move it toward a point where she'd gain conscious understanding of that stubborn bit of knowledge still cloistered in the recesses of her mind. But the members of the panel took their seats at the front of the room just then, and the meeting began. Anne's hand slipped out of hers.

Like a small chime struck lightly and repeatedly, Jo's sense of something amiss grew during the boat ride back to the hotel. Anne seemed to be guarding her husband, not physically, but with her awareness. She kept a close watch on him, ready at any moment with words or smiles or subtle private signals. Yet for his part, Jimmy appeared oblivious to any alteration in his wife's behavior. And Jo thought she must be misreading what she was seeing. These people had grown very familiar to her—their facial expressions, their gestures and deferential displays to one another, their style of dress and manner of speaking were not only recognizable to her but somehow just as they should have been. Whether or not she wanted it, she'd very quickly become very attached to them. And so the slightest variation, every nuance, registered on her. And something was going on. It showed in the tilt of Anne's head as she listened, during the drinks before dinner, to her husband speak of the slides they'd seen of several landmark buildings in the city, before and after restoration; it showed, too, in Anne's sudden breath-held stillness when Jimmy set down his knife and fork midway through his first course and began to cough. He held a handkerchief to his mouth until the brief spasm passed, then blotted his eyes and smiled first at his wife and then at Jo, saying, "You'd think I'd have learned to swallow properly by now." Then he retrieved his utensils and went on eating.

With an impish smile, Anne said, "You've always gobbled your food. It's as if," she addressed Jo, "there's a set time allowed for each course. And if he fails to finish within that set time, a great hairy pair of arms is going to snatch away his plate."

Jimmy snorted with laughter.

Jo smiled at them both, wondering if those were really signs of strain in the lines around Anne's eyes and mouth.

"It will take decades," Jimmy was saying, "before they're able to get past all the bureaucratic rubbish and see to the work that needs doing. Their so-called Special Law from 'seventy-three has probably done more harm than good."

"Why is that?" Jo asked him.

"Ah, well. With the best intentions, of course, they set about to create a law that would guarantee protection of various and sundry buildings and so forth from pollution, floods, et cetera, in order to ensure that Venice and her environs would stay alive socially and economically. The fatal flaw in their good intentions was to involve not only city and regional delegates in this decision, but to set it down as part of the law itself that the government of Italy would have representatives in the group overseeing everything from the regulation of water levels in the canals to the restoration of buildings belonging to the state as well as to individuals. And when you have any group attempting to make decisions with wide-reaching effects, you're bound to have endless red tape to boot. From what I'm given to understand, it can take years on end simply to get permission to begin a restoration. And when one understands that the restoration itself can also take years, one is looking at vast amounts of time being wasted on bureaucratic wrangling. As I say, they meant well, but what's evolved is not ideal. Too many cooks, as it were, making a right muck-up of the broth.

"Still," he went on, "I wouldn't have minded having a hand in some of the restoration. At least I would've had the satisfaction of seeing something magnificent returned to life. Superb job they did on that spiral staircase of the Palazzo Contarini del Bovolo. One could be proud of work like that."

"There's a great deal you can be proud of," Anne reminded him. "A great deal."

He scoffed at this. "Purely functional buildings without soul."

"At least none of them has fallen down."

He gazed at Anne for a second or two, then laughed. "You should have seen this woman at eighteen," he told Jo. "The most exquisite creature I'd ever seen. Masses of jet black hair and brilliant cat's eyes that, I swear, glowed in the dark. Outrageous and willful and altogether remarkable."

"The first words he ever spoke to me," Anne confided to Jo, "were to ask if I would pose nude for him. I said I'd be delighted, and he choked on his Yorkshire pudding." She laughed.

"Not quite the *first* words," he argued.

"Indeed they were! I'm not likely to forget, ever."

"Did you do it?" Jo asked, entering into their playful mood.

"Of course I did." Anne's laughter gained in intensity.

"And there I was," Jimmy guffawed, "with no bloody paper, and not a pencil to be found anywhere."

"He didn't believe for a moment I'd actually consent," Anne put in. "Of course, I had ulterior motives."

"Immediate ones, too." Jimmy was blotting his eyes with his handkerchief.

She had to be wrong, Jo told herself. She'd been reading too much into things. These two were keenly attuned to one another, and fifty years later still found each other attractive. What did it take, she wondered, to make an affair of the heart last for fifty years? She tried to picture herself fifty years down the road with Tyler, and couldn't see it. Replacing Tyler with Henry, she was surprised to be able to see possibilities. "YOU ARE OF IMPORTANCE TO THE WRITER, . . . GROWTH POTENTIAL." In thirty-six years she'd made only one real attempt to share herself with a man, and it had been a disaster. After it was over, she'd sealed herself away. She'd crept out every so often for a kind of hit-or-miss encounter but before it had any chance to prove itself good, bad, or indifferent, she'd be off and running home, or on assignment, anywhere just so long as she didn't have to deal with the implications of involvement.

"This is too terrible of me," Lucienne said, arriving at the table. "I may please sit with you to drink a glass of wine?"

"Oh, do join us!" Jimmy got quickly to his feet, breaking into a smile at the sight of her.

"Please do," Anne said graciously. "Have you had dinner? Perhaps you'd care to have something."

"You are so very kind," Lucienne said, taking the seat beside Jo. "I thought I would take dinner in my room, but I am too *agitée*."

She was very visibly agitated. Her hands were shaking so badly that Jimmy took the lighter and lit her cigarette for her.

"What happened?" Jo asked her.

"Is something wrong?" Jimmy asked at the same moment. "I think you need something stronger than wine. A brandy, perhaps?" His upheld hand kept the waiter at attention.

"Please. I am so sorry to do this," she apologized, waving away the smoke from her cigarette before stubbing it out. "Never do I do this. But I could not stay alone in my room."

"What happened?" Jo asked again.

"Ah!" Lucienne laughed ruefully. "It does not make for dinner conversation. You forgive me?"

"There is no need to apologize," Anne said. "And if you'd care to talk about it, I know we'd all like to listen."

"It is ridiculous! When I am past the unpleasantness, I think I will be very much relieved. I am no longer to be married," she said with one of her little shrugs. The waiter went off and returned with a snifter of brandy and a menu. Without consulting the menu, she said, "I will have the tournedos, rare, please," returned the menu to the waiter, took a swallow of the brandy, then said, "We will celebrate my unattachment, eh?"

"I am sorry," Anne said.

"No! It is not to be sorry. I am saved from a big mistake." She tried for a smile that didn't quite come off, and shrugged again instead.

"I'm sure it was a most difficult decision to make," Anne said gently.

"Paolo made it quite simple. He was ugly. We spent many hours arguing. He has only now gone. And my room is very noisy still from all the shouting." She laughed suddenly, quite gleefully. "I think we make a great entertainment for the chambermaids." Her laughter escalated until the others joined in. "Absurd!" she declared. "*Ciao*, Paolo!" She raised her snifter in the direction of the door, then drank down the remainder of the brandy in one gulp.

Twenty

LUCIENNE INSISTED ON SIGNING FOR THE DINNER DESPITE JIMMY'S PRO-
tests. "Please, I will do this. I come uninvited and disarrange your evening. I will feel very much better if you will permit me to give you
dinner."

Jimmy would have gone on arguing, but Anne's hand on his arm
stopped him. A slight shake of her head put an end to all discussion.

"Thank you very much," Anne said simply.

"You will come for a drink in the bar?" Lucienne asked.

"I think not. It's been rather a long day, and I'm afraid we're both
ready for bed. Jimmy's arranged a very full schedule for tomorrow, including lunch at the Hotel des Bains, for old time's sake."

They stood to leave, and Jo got up to embrace the older woman. Anne
held her close, then released her saying, "I expect we'll see you at some
point tomorrow."

"I'm sure we'll run into each other."

"Perhaps you'd ring me," Anne said in an undertone. "Possibly before
you set off for the day."

"Sure. I'll call you after breakfast."

The four of them left the dining room together, parting at the entrance
to the bar.

Jimmy went off, cautioning them to "watch out for any stray Italian
Lotharios! Don't let yourself be plied with bonbons and amaretto!"

Lucienne and Jo waited in the corridor until the older pair were out of
sight, then Lucienne said, "You will have a drink with me, Mignon?"

Jo turned to look at her. Lucienne was wearing a simple navy cotton
suit, with a slim skirt and severely cut collarless jacket. The severity of

469

the cut was redeemed by the V neckline which revealed a respectable amount of cleavage and a strand of lustrous pearls. "Are you sure you're all right?" she asked Lucienne.

"I feel stupid," Lucienne admitted. "I am furious. I have wasted time and money and my affections. But, yes, I am all right. You have influenced me, Joanna. You know this? It is true. I have been too busy for a very long time for friends, for serious conversations. I listen to what you say, and I know you are right, eh? I think if I do not meet you, I go ahead and marry Paolo." She made a face. "This would have been tragic. So I thank you because you save me from this tragedy. And now we have champagne, to celebrate. Yes?"

"Okay, yes."

Lucienne linked her arm through Jo's and they walked into the bar, heading for a table near the piano player. Jo was aware peripherally of someone rising abruptly on the opposite side of the room but paid no attention.

"I hope you're going to invite me to join you," said a familiar voice, and Jo turned to see Tyler grinning at her.

"My God!" she exclaimed as he drew her into an embrace, then kissed her on both cheeks. As always, she was starting to pull away when he moved in with the second kiss, and she felt graceless.

"I thought I'd surprise you," he said, still grinning, "and ride back to London with you. May I join you?" He asked, looking now at Lucienne.

"Well, sure," Jo said, flustered. "This is Lucienne Denis. Tyler Emmons."

His eyes alight with appreciation, he accepted the hand Lucienne offered and, to Jo's mild dismay, kissed it. *"Enchanté,"* he said, then folded himself into one of the chairs as Jo and Lucienne took seats on the opposite side of the table. "I take it," he said, "I have indeed succeeded in surprising you?"

"More like flabbergasted," Jo said. At first sight of him everything inside of her had given a startled leap, and was just beginning to subside. Here was Tyler, in a suit, no less; a very smart one of gray summer-weight wool, with an open-necked pale blue shirt, and black Gucci loafers. He did look good.

"We will have champagne," Lucienne told the waiter. "Moët et Chandon."

"Lovely!" Tyler said. "Are we celebrating something?" He looked from one woman to the other.

"We celebrate my unattachment," Lucienne said airily, trying to interpet the looks passing between this man and Joanna. "You will celebrate with us, eh?"

"Delighted."

Lucienne lit a cigarette while Jo asked Tyler, "When did you arrive?"

"Oh, an hour or so ago. Flew down, then traveled by land and sea. How has it been? Are you having a super time? You look very well indeed."

"It's been great. Busy, you know. I've still got all kinds of work to do."

"Well, I'll do my best not to get in your way. I decided on the spur of the moment. I knew you'd be busy, but I thought I'd keep you company on the train going back. I've been wanting to ride it for ages, and this seemed as opportune a time as any." As he spoke, his eyes slid away from her to Lucienne.

God! Jo thought. Things were getting unbelievably complicated. The last thing in the world she'd imagine could ever happen, but here was Tyler. It was almost too much to absorb, particularly on top of the long list of things she had left to do. And from the way he was staring at Lucienne, he might have been struck by lightning.

"Have you two just met?" he was asking Lucienne.

"We are very old friends," Lucienne lied smoothly, giving Jo's knee a squeeze beneath the table.

"We met ages ago," Jo put in gratefully. She had no idea why, but Lucienne's decision to make their friendship long-standing was exactly what Jo needed. "When I got the assignment, we decided to take the train together."

"Funny, you never mentioned that. You live in America, do you?" he asked Lucienne.

"No. I am born in Canada. I live in Paris."

"I did a piece on Lucienne's restaurant a while back," Jo compounded the lie. "She's got a marvelous place, Chez Lucienne."

"Indeed? I'll have to look it up when I'm next in Paris. So tell me, Joanna. How was the train?"

"Great," she answered, all at once filled with dread at the prospect of his expecting to sleep with her. She didn't know what she'd do if he wanted to come to her room. She had a job to do here and she hoped he really did understand that, because not only could she not spare the time to be with him, she didn't want to take the time away from Anne and Lucienne and Jackie. And just as her thoughts turned to Jackie, he came bouncing into the bar, caught sight of her, and moved right in, saying, "Hi! Can I come sit with you for a sec?"

"Sure," she said with an effortless smile. "Come meet everyone. This is Jackie. Lucienne and Tyler."

Jackie said, "Hi," and shook hands, then exclaimed, "Wow! Champagne! Can I have a taste?"

"But of course," Lucienne said, and gave him her glass. In return Jackie gave her an admiring smile of epic proportions.

"Jackie and I spent the day together today," Jo explained as he took a sip of the wine, then returned the glass to Lucienne.

"Thank you very much," he said to Lucienne, leaning for a moment with his elbow on the table, chin in his cupped hand, gazing adoringly at her so that she simply had to smile and pinch his cheek.

"I was her official lens handler," Jackie told them, coming out of his short-lived trance. "So guess what?" he said to Jo.

"What?"

"You missed the best part. Wonder Dummy and the Two Stooges were like totally chilled out by what you said. Right? I mean, I thought my dad was going to have like cardiac arrest over that bit about word getting back to his company. I bet nobody's *ever* talked that way to old John. Anyway the deal is, I can be lens handler again tomorrow, if you want."

Jo glanced guiltily at Tyler, decided he didn't dare question her actions, and told Jackie, "Perfect. I'm doing the kitchen. It's at the near end of the gallery. Meet me there at ten. Okay?"

"Okay, great! You know what my mom said, Joey?"

"What?"

"Get this! It's too amazing. She subscribes to like about a hundred magazines, right? So when I showed her your card, she had a spaz attack and got like all nervous because she recognized your name. Then she did this major number on my dad, and she actually took my part. Can you believe it? I mean, there she was, going, 'Jackie was *helping* this woman, John.' John's what she calls my dad when it's like serious, right? 'She happens to be a well-known journalist, *John*. And you *would* go and make a *scene*! I've never *been* so embarrassed!' Then the two of them got into this major don't-you-dare-raise-your-voice-to-me type number. And Wonder Dummy wants to get into the action, but the two of them turn and they both tell her to shut up. Beautiful! Anyway, they've got this important tennis date in the morning, you know. And old Nance has to get out there to soak up more rays by the pool. So I can help you out again. Great, huh?"

"Yup." Jo smiled at him.

"My mom's impressionable," he elaborated for the benefit of the other two. "She's knocked out by celebrities. Say," he said, staring at Tyler. "Aren't you the actor? You're the guy from *Lion's Gate*, right?"

"That's right," Tyler said, amused.

"I saw the whole nine episodes on PBS. It was great! *You* were great! Say, could I have an autograph? Would that be okay?"

"I'd be delighted," Tyler said.

"I'll get some paper, okay, and be right back." Jackie pushed out of his chair and went running off, sneakers squeaking on the marble floor.

"Another old friend of yours?" Tyler asked Jo.

"New friend," she corrected him, bothered a bit by what sounded like a crack. "He's a wonderful kid. I wish he was mine, if you want to know the truth."

"I like him," Lucienne said. "A pity he is so young, eh?" She looked at Jo meaningfully, and they both laughed.

Tyler followed this exchange with the sense that the two women had tacitly agreed to join forces against him for some unknown reason. It made him feel slightly foolish, somewhat defenseless, and unreasonably, albeit mildly, angry. Their complicity created an energy that was fairly commanding. He had to wonder if coming here unannounced might not have been a tactical error. Certainly, Joanna hadn't given him quite the welcome he'd anticipated.

Jackie came skidding back to the table with a piece of hotel stationery and a pen, which he put down in front of Tyler.

"Jackie, is it?" Tyler asked, at once feeling a little guilty for being condescending to this boy, taking out his anger on a kid. He tried to compensate for it by personalizing the autograph and giving the boy a genuine smile as he handed back the paper. "There you go."

"Boy, this is great! Wonder Dummy'll have a shit fit when she sees it!" He folded the paper carefully and tucked it into his pocket. "I better be going," he said. "See you tomorrow, Joey. Nice to meet you both." Again, he shook hands all around, then took off.

Lucienne was laughing. "I like him very, very much," she told Jo. "I like also 'shit fit.' I think this is what I have before, eh?"

"Could be," Jo laughed with her.

"It is *very* good, 'shit fit.' So, you are a famous actor?"

"I wouldn't go quite that far," Tyler said, shifting sideways in his chair to recross his long legs. "I do a fair bit of work."

"Tyler acts and directs," Jo told her. "And he works *all* the time. He's been in the theater his whole life."

"Very interesting," Lucienne said. "I see very few films except late at night on the *télé*, when I am home after Chez Lucienne is closed. I am sorry I have not seen you."

"We can always remedy that," he said, then reconsidered and added, "I mean, I'll be glad to let you know when I've got something on in Paris."

Jo was intrigued to see how attracted to Lucienne Tyler was, and even more intrigued to realize she didn't mind in the least. For her part, Lucienne handled his interest with ease, but looked questioningly every few moments at Jo, as if for permission.

"I have to go to the john," Jo announced.

"Me, also. I will come with you," Lucienne said at once.

"We'll be right back, Tyler," Jo told him, feeling like an adolescent as she and Lucienne went arm in arm down the corridor, stifling giggles.

Once inside the ladies' room, Lucienne asked, "He is one of your two men?"

"God, yes! I can't believe this!" Jo held her hands to her flushed cheeks. "He can't take his eyes off you. If he had a spoon, he'd eat you up." She laughed, then clapped her hand over her mouth. Two glasses of wine with dinner and a hastily downed glass of champagne had taken their toll.

"This bothers you?"

"Not one bit. Last week it might have. But tonight it's just funny. You want him?" she asked boldly.

"He is interesting," Lucienne conceded. "Not unattractive. But he has come to see *you*, Mignon."

"He came to see my body, not me." She laughed again, and again covered her mouth. "I think I'm a bit drunk."

"I think you are a lot drunk. What will you do?"

"God! I don't know. I really do have to work; I'm completely booked up tomorrow. Friday's pretty clear. He's planning to come back on the train with me. I just don't *believe* any of this."

"I will also come back on the train Saturday," Lucienne informed her. "I have made the arrangements today."

"Before or after the fight?"

"Before."

"Well, good for you. So, we'll all go on Saturday. That was great before, the way you said we were old friends."

"If you could see your face, you would know it is not so great. I think to myself when he comes you have gone into shock."

"That's a serious understatement."

Lucienne finished lighting a cigarette and folded her arms under her breasts. "It is the other one, eh?"

"The other one what?"

"The other one you love?"

"I don't know about that, Lucienne." Jo leaned against the wall and tried to think. The alcohol had made her brain feel huge and aerated, like Swiss cheese. "I *know* Henry. I mean, we've known each other for ten years. I know he spends a lot of evenings sitting alone in his living room with a bottle of wine and the TV set for company. I know he's dedicated to his garden. You should see him! He was out there for six solid hours last Saturday, patiently pulling weeds and pruning his plants. He never says or does the things I expect him to. But he *tries*, you know? I mean, Tyler shows up, and all I could think while the waiter was pouring the champagne was I hope to God he doesn't expect to sleep with me tonight. I'm so tired of that kind of thing. You know? Men showing up, expecting things, without bothering to think about what you might expect."

"I know." Lucienne took a puff on the cigarette, keeping her arms around herself. "I know this very well."

"What's wrong?"

Lucienne didn't answer, but continued to stand with her arms wound around herself. Then, looking fearful, she dropped the cigarette, turned, bent over the basin, and threw up. Still bent forward, she reached to turn on the faucets, while her body commenced a series of painful heaves. Jo picked up the cigarette, put it in one of the ashtrays, then went to stand by Lucienne, stroking her spine as the retching went on and on. There was a lull, during which Lucienne splashed water on her face, then turned her head sideways to say, "I am so very sorry."

"Don't be silly," Jo said, wetting a towel in cold water and placing it on the nape of Lucienne's neck before continuing to stroke her back.

Lucienne started to say something, but was overtaken by another spasm. When it ended, she drank some cold water from her cupped hand. Still hanging over the basin, she said, "I think it is finished. *Merde!* This is a disgrace." She splashed more water on her face, then straightened, removing the wet towel and setting it aside as she rinsed the basin.

Jo smoothed the hair from Lucienne's face, then held the back of her hand against Lucienne's forehead. "You're hot," she said. "You should probably go to bed."

"I think you are right."

"I'll come up with you."

"But your friend . . ."

"I'll go tell him, then come back. Don't you move! Okay? I'll be two minutes."

Lucienne had turned and was staring at her reflection in the mirror with an expression of complete disgust. "Go," she said. "I'll wait."

"Tyler," Jo said, back in the bar. "Lucienne's not feeling at all well. I'm going to take her to her room, see her into bed, then I'll be back."

He simply didn't believe her. After all, he'd heard the two of them go off laughing down the corridor. Now, a matter of minutes later, she was back with this flimsy fabrication. If she wanted to be rid of him, why didn't she come right out and say so? "If you'd rather," he said, "we can call it a night. I could meet you for breakfast."

"Would you mind terribly?" she asked anxiously. "She hasn't been well since she left Paris, and I'm really pretty worried about her."

"Go ahead. I'll finish my drink and take myself off to bed."

"Oh, God!" she said, remembering. "I'd better sign for the champagne."

"Not to worry, Joanna," he said tiredly. "My treat. Tell your friend I hope she's feeling better soon."

He didn't believe her, she thought as she hurried back to the ladies' room. Did he think she and Lucienne had nothing better to do than make up stories in order to avoid him? No, wait a minute! Would she have believed it if she were in his place? She'd apologize to him in the morning. Well, maybe not apologize, but explain. Something.

Lucienne was sitting on the floor with her head down on her drawn-up knees.

"Come on," Jo said. "We'll get you to bed."

"Not for a moment, eh?" Lucienne said weakly. "I will faint if I move now."

"Shit!" Jo knelt on the floor beside her. "You have got to see a doctor. No kidding!"

"I will be all right," Lucienne murmured.

Jo got the towel, soaked it again in cold water, then placed it once more over the back of Lucienne's neck. She shivered, her head remaining on her knees. Jo sat on the floor beside her, feeling faintly queasy herself. If she hadn't performed these same actions so many times in the early stages of her mother's cancer, she'd undoubtedly have thrown up herself in sympathetic response. She held the cold towel secure with one hand and with the other smoothed her friend's hair, marveling over how they'd gone from drunken hilarity to sober seriousness in a matter of minutes. Of course Tyler hadn't believed her when she'd gone running back to say Lucienne was ill. Well, she'd clarify matters in the morning.

"I think it was a mistake to eat," Lucienne said, her voice muffled.

"I think your big mistake is *not* eating. At least, not stuff that's good for you."

"It's like the cigarettes." Lucienne experimentally lifted her head. Her face was dreadfully pale. "You say to yourself you know they will make you die, but then something happens which is bad, eh, and you think, Pah, so I will die. It is of no consequence. And it is too much difficulty to change, to give up the pleasures."

"That's crazy," Jo said softly. "You don't want to die."

"Sometimes, yes."

"But you *can't!*" Jo protested. "You've got everything going for you."

"I say this also. But just in case, eh? Things are bad, or not how you wish, so you have a cigarette and you say, Okay, I have no wish to live forever."

"God! That's terrible!" Jo said, and started to cry.

Her head propped on her hand, Lucienne looked at Jo's tear-washed face, bemused, and asked, "Why do you cry, Mignon?"

"I don't know," Jo wailed. "Everything's just so ridiculous. I mean, look at the two of us! God!"

"You care too much," Lucienne said.

"No, I don't. Most of the time, I hardly care enough. I really don't. And you make me so mad. I swear, if you don't see a doctor, I'll take you to one myself. Okay, so you're afraid. Everybody's afraid, goddamnit! But being afraid beats hell out of being dead. And I don't want you dead."

Lucienne smiled. "You have passion, Mignon," she said admiringly.

"I don't know about that. D'you think you can get up now?"

"I think so."

Jo helped her up, then dusted off her skirt.

"I am able to walk," Lucienne told her, and held herself very erect as they went through the lobby, up the stairs, and along the hallway to her room. Once inside, though, she had to sit on the edge of the bed, her arms again winding around her midriff. She swore furiously and rocked back and forth for several minutes while Jo tried to think what to do. "It would not be so bad," Lucienne said at last, "but when he was leaving, Paolo he pushed the door at me, eh? It hits me right here." She pointed to her abdomen. "*Cochon!* It hits me very hard, so I have no air."

"Come on," Jo said. "Let me help you." Getting no protest from Lucienne, she removed the suit jacket, then assisted her out of the skirt, stopping to stare at the large livid area just above her navel. "Jesus!" she whispered. "Do you know you're black and blue?"

Lucienne looked down at herself, then at Jo.

"He did *that* with the *door*? What a bastard!" Jo swore.

Lucienne stood in her filmy black brassiere and patterned panty hose, looking at herself while Jo reached for the yellow oversized T-shirt the chambermaid had arranged artfully on the bed. "Can you manage, or do you need help all the way?"

"I manage."

"I've got some Valium," Jo said, going to the coffee table for her purse. "I hate giving people stuff that was prescribed for me, but I really think you need it." She went to the bathroom for some water, then came back to the side of the bed where Lucienne was now sitting in the T-shirt. "Take this!" she ordered. Without argument, Lucienne took the tablet, then gingerly lay down. "Tomorrow, you'll go see a doctor. Please?"

"I will telephone to my doctor in Paris, make arrangements to see him when I return."

"You promise?"

"You treat me like a child," Lucienne smiled at her.

"You need it. I don't understand why you refuse to look after yourself."

"You will see: In the morning, I am fine."

Jo dropped down so they were at eye level. "Will you be able to sleep?"

"I am sure. Thank you, Mignon. I am sorry to make such a disaster of your evening."

"I don't care about the evening. I care about you. Please look after yourself." She kissed Lucienne's forehead, turned off the lamp, collected her purse from the coffee table, switched on the DO NOT DISTURB light, and opened the door. "If you need anything, call me. I'll come right away. Okay?"

"Okay."

Back in her room she sat for a time on the sofa with her feet propped on the coffee table, Henry's telex in her hand. She read it over and over until it ceased to make any sense.

It seemed as if she'd managed to get through her entire life so far without investing emotionally in anyone. Now, suddenly, like someone who'd come into an immense inheritance, she was expending her emotions on all who came near. Unaccustomed as she was to the activity, it made her nervous, and rendered her vulnerable, but she not only didn't mind, she had no desire to put an end to the spree. If anything, she wanted to perpetuate it, keep it going until she ran dry, until she'd used up every last bit of her emotional currency.

Just remember it's nighttime, she reminded herself, looking around the luxurious room. You might not feel this way come morning.

Twenty-one

". . . INSIDE PALACE, HUGE EXPANSE OF ROOM WITH TINTORETTO; J. TELLING about painting while parents allowing children to tear around, shrill cries echoing in vast chamber; creepy going through dungeons; names, dates written on dungeon walls; all roped off. City is like exotic and wonderful board game—you go forward, then double back at dead ends; mazelike; fun finding ongoing route; so much to see, J. terrific tour guide. Dinner last eve. at table at edge of terrace overlooking water with splendid bldgs. in distance; chatter from bar area adjacent; 60ish man alone 2 tables along; all manner of boats going by, endless silent traffic; pianist played theme from *Borsalino*, brought back memories so long ago when Lily had the sound-track album one year and played it nonstop; after she died, I played it all the time. Atmosphere here reminiscent of West Indies, primarily the lushness, plantings, flowers, sandy color of hotel, flagstones, pines in planters, white tables, chairs; red and pink geraniums in pots hanging from wall above terrace; French windows with wooden shutters in older part of hotel; at breakfast sm. birds come to eat off tables and flagstones, just like Indies. Venetians v. pleasant & accommodating. L. upset, came to table; she dumped the fiancé, guy sounded like real creep; T. showed up out of blue. Almost too much going on; every day more intense, more complicated. I feel as if I started out as one person who agreed to do a job, now daily evolving into a sort of distilled version of that same person; not sure anymore what Joanna James will say or do; can't count on her to be predictable; all the old rules gone. V. confusing."

She closed the notebook, finished her coffee, and checked the time. Almost seven-thirty. She'd been up since six, making notes and checking the slides she'd collected the previous afternoon. They were all properly

479

exposed. That meant she wouldn't have to reshoot anything, which was a tremendous relief. She couldn't remember when she'd been quite so tired. Just thinking of all she had to do today made her even more tired. But she had to admit she hadn't ever felt quite so fully alive.

Then there was the matter of Tyler. Without question, it was quite a gesture for him to show up the way he had. But it was an impulsive move he'd made, she was sure, without giving serious consideration to the fact that she had a job to do. Henry would never in a million years have gone charging ahead without first making sure both of his welcome and of the advisability of such a visit. Henry would be very careful about any move that might be subject to the slightest misinterpretation. He was, she thought, a lot like her in that respect. Neither of them would rush into a situation without first checking the pros and cons. And that was why he'd been unable to blurt out something "important" over the telephone when she'd asked him. She suspected Tyler would have said what he thought she wanted to hear. Not from dishonesty, but simply to please her. That was because Tyler didn't think beyond the immediate present —at least not where she was concerned. But Henry always did. Amazing, she thought, how clear things suddenly seemed to be.

Seven-forty. She returned the slides to their plastic container; notebook and pen went into her bag. Several fresh rolls of film from the minirefrigerator went into the Lowe-pro, and she was set to go.

As she passed through the gallery, she thought again of how she and Lucienne had sat on the floor in the ladies' room, and of how she'd started crying. All those months when she'd spent hour upon hour with her mother—before and after her several hospital stays—she'd never allowed herself to break down because she hadn't wanted Lily to see her go out of control. She'd had the idea that her breaking down would only make things more difficult for her mother. So she'd wept after the visits, but never during. Now she couldn't help thinking she shouldn't have worried so much about showing Lily a strong, cheerful face. Maybe she'd done them both a disservice in failing to allow either of them an opportunity to cry together over all they both were losing. It hadn't felt wrong or embarrassing to sit there and cry in front of Lucienne. It had been the most spontaneous demonstration of caring she'd ever made. Yes, she had friends at home. But since her move to Connecticut she no longer saw them as often as when she'd lived in the city. She was actually closer now to Anne and Jimmy, to Lucienne and Jackie, to Henry and even Tyler, than she was to most of her friends at home. She could live anywhere and it wouldn't affect the friendships that were already firmly established. If she lived, say, in London, she'd be able to perpetuate the new ones. She could even, possibly, stay in the house with Henry.

You're rushing ahead, she cautioned herself. You're building imaginary homes that can be knocked down by a telephone conversation or a negative reaction to something that might be said. Everything she was experiencing now was taking place in a kind of fantasy land. No one could live this way full-time. She'd leave on Saturday, arrive back in London Sunday evening, and all this would be over. It was temporary, time out of time; it didn't really count. Or did it? At the end, was she going to go back to being the Joanna James who hung back, waiting for other people to notice her? Was she going to return to being the silent witness who felt invisible most of the time? God! It was the last thing she wanted. But she wasn't sure what was needed to keep going forward as the new Jo. All she knew was that it had to do with people she'd come to know very well, very quickly; people she wanted to keep inside her life.

While she was waiting for the maître d' to return from the end of the terrace to seat her, Jackie's mother came along the corridor. In her tennis whites, ready for another few hours at the court, she smiled and came over to say, "I'm so glad to run into you. I wanted to say how sorry we are about that business yesterday. John tends to cover up with anger when he gets worried, and he also tends to get a little physical. But he'd never hurt Jackie. You know how men are," she smiled. "They're so bad with emotions. Jackie is John's hope for the future. He really is. It's just that he has a lot of trouble showing his feelings. And I guess, after all these years, some of it's rubbed off on me, too. Live with someone long enough and you start to become like one another. I just want you to know we appreciate your looking after Jackie. And if he gets to be a nuisance, you let us know."

She was a pretty woman, with a lot of frown lines baked into her skin from so much time spent on tennis courts, and a tendency to widen her eyes for effect, or emphasis. Jackie had her mouth, and the same shape of eyes. Jo could see him in his mother's face. It felt strange to be standing there, looking at her, watching the way her lips formed words and her eyes added the italics. She felt old enough to be this somewhat superficial woman's mother.

"Listen, Mrs. Watts," Jo said. "I meant everything I said yesterday. I think Jackie's a sensational kid. And if you want to know the truth, he looked out for me, and not the other way around. He's definitely not a nuisance, so don't worry about it. Okay?"

Mrs. Watts blinked and then, as if deciding she'd been indirectly complimented, said with pride, "He's got more energy than any ten boys."

"He's also," Jo said, "got beautiful manners and a very nice way with people. You've done a good job with him."

"Well, that's so nice of you to say." Mrs. Watts beamed. "By the way, I've read several of your pieces and they're awfully good. And your photographs are always lovely."

"Thank you. Excuse me." Jo turned to the maître d' and said, "There'll be two of us this morning."

"Very good, Signorina."

"Good talking with you," Jo said to Mrs. Watts.

"Right you are!" said the woman cheerily, and headed across the terrace to a table at the far end where the rest of the Watts family was well into their breakfast.

As Jo sat down, they all turned to smile and wave. Jo waved back, then grabbed the menu. She stared blankly for a moment at the left-hand side, which was in Italian, then shifted over and with relief read the English on the right.

THE CIPRIANI BREAKFAST. The Breakfast is served from 7 A.M. to 10.30 A.M. It is included in the room rate and offers: Coffee, Indian or China Tea, Hot Chocolate, Herbal Teas, Milk, Cream, Fruit Juice. Selections of Cereals with Milk, Fresh Bread, Home-made Plumcake and Croissants, Honey, Marmalade, Jams, fresh country Butter, 2 Eggs of the day (either Boiled, Scrambled, or Fried). THE BUFFET is served only in the Restaurant from 7 A.M. to 10 A.M. and offers a wider selection of assorted specialties (cheese, yogurts, Parma Ham, fresh fruit, etc.) in addition to the breakfast. Further requests will be charged a la Carter [sic]. . . .

She'd just started reading about those selections when Tyler arrived.

"Ah, Joanna, good morning." He sat down, bringing with him the powerful citrous scent of his after-shave.

"Good morning," she replied, taking him in.

Today he was dressed more like himself, in a pair of faded jeans and an open-necked short-sleeved Madras cotton shirt. Freshly shaved, his hair still damp, he looked loose-limbed and relaxed. His hands, she saw, were extremely large. Why hadn't she noticed before how large his hands were? Or how clean, yet neglected? It looked as if he'd taken one of those horrible nail clippers to his fingers, leaving the nails cut straight across and close to the quick, with sharp-pointed edges. As she studied his hands, she could almost hear the dreadful *cuh-lick* of the clippers. Greg had used them, whenever the notion had occurred to him, leaving his nail cuttings on the carpet or the bathroom floor for her to find. It was a habit that had repelled her, yet she'd never said a word about it. Just recalling it revived her anger.

"How's your friend?" Tyler asked, reaching for the menu.

"I haven't spoken to her yet this morning. I'm hoping she's better." That bruise had been awful, a desecration on that pure white delicately blue-veined skin. How could a door have done that? Jo wondered, trying to picture it. It hadn't been any goddamned door! she thought, appalled. That bastard had punched Lucienne! He'd taken his fists to her.

"Something wrong?" Tyler held aside his menu.

"What? No. Sorry. I was just thinking about something."

"Something nasty, from the look on your face."

"Sorry," she said again. "Forget it. It's nothing. Well, isn't this amazing! Here you are in Venice."

"Here I am!" he echoed. "Surprised?"

"Astonished."

"Good. What, by the way, seems to be wrong with your friend? She looked perfectly all right when the two of you went off to the loo."

She thought of how she'd planned to explain to him this morning, and she'd been intending to do that. But his manner and the way he asked put her off. She tried to think of some reply, couldn't, and just shrugged. "She wasn't feeling well. I think I'll go up to the buffet. I'm starving."

"Good idea. I'll come, too."

She took a croissant and some cheese, and returned to the table while Tyler loaded up with fruit and cereal, then asked for bacon and eggs. As she tore pieces from the croissant and ate it with bites of cheese between sips of coffee, she watched him consume an enormous amount of food. He did it neatly; no crumbs adhered to his mouth or chin, but there was something about the amount of food and the concentrated fashion in which he ate it that bothered her. She knew she was really bothered because of his negative reference to Lucienne, but it didn't reduce her annoyance. Since he didn't talk while he ate, she had the choice either of continuing to watch him or of looking around at the other guests. She chose to look at the other guests, noting that the Texas family had arrived and was sitting in gloomy silence as their waiter poured coffee. Where was the pop-psych self-help book? How come no reading aloud? Something going on there for sure. The son-in-law looked miserably uncomfortable, as if he'd sat in something wet and didn't have the heart or the courage to speak up. The frowzy daughter looked peevish and stared purposefully at her husband, as if she knew he'd sat in something wet and was daring him to say so. The mother and father glanced every so often at each other. When the waiter came for their order, the mother smiled, and Jo thought again what a fine-looking woman she was. Her smile was lovely and open, illuminating her face. And her husband seemed to think so, too, because he smiled as well, as if in response to the undiluted pleasure the sight of his wife gave him. Here were two handsome, worldly people who cared about each other and made an effort to present their best faces to the world. It must have been hell, Jo thought, having a daughter like that.

"I take it," Tyler said, interrupting her thoughts, "I'm being left to my own devices today."

"Afraid so. And this evening, too. I've got to go to a dinner sponsored by the Italian Tourist Board."

"Hmmmm." He sat away from the table, turning sideways to cross his legs. "Shame," he said. "Still, I expect I'll find something to do."

What did he want, pity? He couldn't show up out of the blue and expect to be entertained. "I'm sure you will," she said nicely.

"I was hoping to be able to spend some time with you," he said, briefly inspecting his critically clipped fingernails.

The waiter arrived with Tyler's bacon and eggs, and Tyler shifted back in to the table, eyeing the plate with satisfaction. He picked up his knife and fork, then looked over at her. "I think," he said slowly, his voice deeply musical, "you're a little pissed off at me, Joanna."

"Of course I'm not," she lied. "It's just that I *am* working, Tyler, and it seems as if you're trying to make me feel guilty because you've gone to all the trouble to come here and I can't spend very much time with you."

"Oh, dear," he said, frowning and smiling simultaneously. "I have no intention of trying to make you feel guilty," he lied. "And if that's the impression I've given, I'm sorry. Naturally, I'm disappointed. Winging my way here, I painted rather elaborate pictures of the sort of things the two of us might get up to. Forgetting completely, I admit, your obligations." He paused and looked at her, waiting to hear what she'd say. He did want her to feel guilty. After all, he *had* gone to a lot of trouble to make what he'd thought would be quite an impressive gesture. And while she'd been polite enough, and surprised, she was decidedly unimpressed. Which forced him to review his own actions, and to concede that as attracted as he was to her, he scarcely knew her. He, therefore, hadn't any right to expect her to perform flips for him. But knowing that didn't relieve him of his disappointment or of his mounting confusion. In the bright light of morning, from moment to moment, she seemed quite unrecognizable to him. So he had to wonder if he appeared equally unrecognizable to her. And if so, what on God's green earth had he been thinking of, coming here to take by surprise a woman whose body was more familiar to him than her face?

Was he playing out some role? she wondered. Did he have a script hidden away somewhere? And if he'd preassigned all the characters, what were her lines supposed to be? God! She didn't know a thing about this man, except that he was attractive and he made love with energy and panache. She'd gone along in conditioned blindness because he'd wanted her, and being wanted was a form of success, of acceptance. She hadn't exercised any discretion, or judgment, or selectivity; she hadn't even decided whether or not she wanted him.

"For God's sake, Tyler," she said angrily. "I'm thirty-six years old. Of course I've got obligations. All kinds of them. Yes, I appreciate your coming here. I *am* sorry I haven't got any free time today. And you *are* trying to make me feel guilty, but I don't, and I won't. Feel guilty, I mean. I'm free tomorrow evening, and if you'd like to have dinner with me then, that'd be great. Otherwise, I'm afraid you're going to have to amuse yourself. Okay?"

He rocked back in his chair, his eyebrows lifted. "This is an entirely new view of you, Joanna. A little out of character, perhaps."

"You don't know me, Tyler. And I don't know you." They were going to get into an argument, and she was dreading it. She loathed scenes and suddenly she was finding herself in the heart of them with alarming regularity.

"Ah, here you are, Mignon! And Monsieur Emmons!" Lucienne came drifting toward the table, having undergone another of her extraordinary recoveries. She looked healthy and chic in an ankle-length gauzy white skirt and a cherry-red overblouse with very full sleeves, belted at her slim waist by a broad woven fabric belt in red and white, with white espadrilles that had satin ribbons wound over her ankles and tied in bows at the sides. Her hair was swept back from her face and caught in a loose braid at the back of her neck. "I had hoped you would still be here. I may join you?"

"Of course," Jo said quickly. "You look sensational. One of these days you'll have to tell me how you do it."

"Pah!" Lucienne passed off the compliment. "It's nothing. You are well, *chérie*? You have a good night?" she asked Tyler.

Tyler nodded, convinced now that the two women had cooked up that story the night before. This woman looked as if she'd never had a sick day in her life.

"How are you?" Jo asked her. "Are you all right?"

"Fine, fine. Very hungry. Now you are to tell me what healthy food I must eat."

"Sure. You want me to come with you to the buffet?"

"But you must. Otherwise I will have coffee and a brioche, and this will not please my new doctor."

As they approached the buffet, Lucienne took a small package from the pocket of her voluminous skirt and slipped it to Jo, saying, "This is for you, Mignon. You will open it later, eh? From me, to say thank you. What is this you give to me, yogurt? I detest it."

"It's good for you. Thank you, but you don't have to give me anything."

"I know this. I only give what I am not expected to give. Fruit also?" She made a face. "I will grow fat."

"Not on fruit and yogurt. Don't be silly!"

"Listen, Mignon. You want me to take care of that one? I keep him occupied, out of your hair for the day?"

"He can look after himself."

"I don't mind, eh? I am going to look in shops, perhaps to have a glass of wine. I take him with me, if you have no feelings about this."

"All I have is gratitude, if you're sure you don't mind."

"He is not so bad." Lucienne looked covertly over at Tyler. "Now that I am finished with Paolo, it would be amusing."

"Be my guest. He's a nice man, but he's trying to give me the gears, laying a guilt trip on me because I have no time for him today. We don't know each other, Lucienne. It's very awkward. I told him we'd have dinner tomorrow."

"Okay," Lucienne said decisively. "Leave this to me."

Upon returning to the table, Lucienne leaned over to place her hand on Tyler's arm, saying, "Our friend is too busy today for us. You would like to come with me? I take you shopping. You will hate it."

Tyler looked first at her hand on his arm, then at her cleavage, and finally at her smiling face, and said, "Have you been assigned to distract me?" then felt like a complete shit for being so ill mannered.

"Pardon?" She withdrew her hand. "What is this?" she asked Jo.

"He wants to know if he's being set up," Jo answered her. To Tyler she said, "Lucienne's inviting you to spend the day with her. If you want to, say yes. If you don't want to, don't be rude. It's very good of her to offer. Don't behave like a jerk just because things aren't working out the way you hoped they would. Go on, Tyler." She smiled at him, suddenly understanding that he was hurt and somewhat embarrassed. "It's not every day a gorgeous woman wants to show you around Venice."

"Too bloody true," he agreed with a laugh, losing his stiffness. "I apologize to both of you for my suspicious nature." To Lucienne he said, "I'd love to hate going shopping with you."

"Eh, bon!" Lucienne picked up her spoon only to stop and gaze balefully at the yogurt. "I must eat this?" she asked plaintively.

"Go on," Jo teased. "You French eat disgusting things like snails. What's a little yogurt?"

"Snails are delicious," Lucienne said haughtily.

"And frog's legs, innards of all kinds, brains, for God's sake! Eat your yogurt."

"I'm rather partial to brains myself," Tyler put in. "In black butter. Bliss!"

"I'll include the English on my list of people who eat uneatables," Jo laughed.

"This comes," Lucienne told Tyler, "from a woman whose country makes a national specialty out of crushed meat on a bun." She shook her head and dutifully ate alternating spoonfuls of fruit and yogurt.

Everything was going to be all right, Jo thought with relief, pouring herself another cup of coffee. Jackie waved from the far end of the terrace and she waved back, then checked the time. Ten past nine. She excused herself, saying, "I've got to make a phone call," and went to the booth in the corridor to ask the operator to put her through to Anne and Jimmy's room.

Anne answered at once, her voice sounding deep and very cultured.

"Hi, it's Jo. I hope I'm not waking you."

"No, dear, not at all. I've been up for some time. I was hoping you'd ring. I don't suppose you have a few free minutes?"

"When, now?"

"If it's convenient."

"Sure. Would you like me to come to you?"

"That would be good of you."

"Okay."

"Oh, one thing. I'm on the patio, dear. Would you mind very much coming round? Just beyond the pool."

"I'll be there in five minutes."

"So good of you," Anne said, and put the phone down so quietly there was no audible disconnecting sound.

"I have an errand to do," Jo told Lucienne and Tyler. "I don't know how long I'll be, so if I don't make it back by nine-thirty, the two of you go ahead, and I'll try to check in at some point later on. Okay?"

"Go on, Mignon. I will take care of your friend."

"Yes," Tyler said, looking quite content, "I'm in very good hands." He gave her a smile with no hooks or hidden barbs, and she smiled back as she picked up her purse and the camera bag before heading across the terrace.

Twenty-two

ONCE PAST THE TERRACE, IT WAS VERY QUIET, THE SUN SLANTING AT an oblique angle through the trees. Jo walked past the pool, glancing at the rooms and patios to her left as she went, and almost passed Anne by. There was a space between the enclosing shrubberies, and Jo's eye was caught by a bit of color that caused her to back up. The color was in Anne's dress, a royal blue shirtwaist with white piping.

Stepping into the space between the bushes, Jo said, "Good morning."

Anne looked up with a smile. "Do come sit down, dear."

Jo put her bags on the flagstones and sat. On a low table near Anne was a tray with coffee, and an ashtray. The telephone was on the ground within arm's reach. Which was why, Jo thought, she'd picked up so quickly.

Looking relaxed, her legs crossed and elbows resting on the arms of the chair, Anne was smoking a cigarette. She seemed most serene, the movement of her hand with the cigarette calm and slow as her eyes rested on Jo for a time before she asked, "Would you care for some coffee?"

"No, thank you. How are you? You look wonderful."

Anne's smile returned as she reached for her coffee, then slowly faded. She sat holding the cup with both hands, the cigarette between the fingers of her right hand. "You look so very young," she said, her voice almost dreamy. "I think I've arrived at an age where almost everyone looks quite impossibly young. It makes me rather sentimental to look at you, and to remember the soaring energy I had at your age, and the sense I had then that everything was yet to come. Do you have that sense, Joanna?"

"Sometimes. And other times, I feel the way you said you do: unable to believe I'm not still sixteen. It's all completely relative, don't you think?"

"Yes, of course. But there does come a point when one is able to look back over the many stages of one's life and see how events, circumstances, shaped one. I've never minded growing older," Anne said. "I truly haven't. Upon turning thirty, I thought, 'Now, I will have some degree of credibility.' But I had scarcely more of it than I'd had at twenty-nine. Then, at forty, I thought, '*Now* my words and opinions will carry some weight.' And there was some evidence of that. At fifty, I was no longer concerned with credibility. I was utterly preoccupied with what appeared to be an endlessly unpleasant series of surprises nature had arranged for me." She laughed quietly. "I tried assiduously not to be horrified by my personal degeneration, by the too-visible alterations to a body I'd fairly much taken for granted for the first forty-odd years of my life. Quite a number of very rude surprises! Then, by sixty, I surrendered my preoccupation for a bit of private gratification at having survived both my regrettable vanity and nature's ongoing assault. Now, here I am, mere inches away from seventy, and I cannot for the life of me think why I fussed as I did over what is, after all, a perfectly natural progression. I have come, at long last, to accept the inevitability of it all." She drank some of the coffee, then returned the cup to the tray, and put out her cigarette, only to light another at once.

Jo wished she could photograph Anne in this light. Her hair was pure silver and it glistened, as did the diamond studs in her ears. She had around her neck an exquisite long gold necklace whose detailing was set in relief by the deep blue silk of the dress. This was the first time Jo was aware of Anne wearing makeup. Very little: mascara, a bit of color on her high cheekbones, and a pink-brown lipstick. With those clear, rare green eyes, she was still an arresting woman.

"I wouldn't mind being you," Jo told her, "if I ever grow up."

"Oh, my dear, I don't think I've ever really grown up. But how kind of you to be so complimentary."

"No, it's the truth," Jo said. "I've been sitting here thinking how beautiful you are. It's more than physical; it's light and bone-structure and the way I feel about you, too." As she spoke, she thought how strange it was that her hands rested comfortably in her lap; they didn't twitch with a need to pick up the camera.

"*Is* there someone you care about?" Anne asked. "I know you were rather embarrassed when Lucienne made that comment the first evening we dined together and it's intrusive of me to ask, but is there someone?"

"I don't really know. One minute I think yes. The next I'm not sure. All I do know is I seem to care more for Henry today than I thought I ever could care about anybody a week ago. I mean, there were flowers from him in my room when I arrived. And yesterday he sent a telex. I feel as if I want to see him very much. Then I tell myself not to hope for too much because I'll be disappointed. The thing is, I've always been afraid that I'd get married and be happy, then one day find out that this man I thought I knew was seeing other women, sleeping with them afternoons in hotel rooms. My father did, and I could never understand why my mother put up with it, why she didn't leave him. But she and I never talked about it. That was the conversation we were supposed to have, but it never happened. The whole time I was growing up I wanted to hear her side of it, her reasons. The part that defeated me was that they loved each other. You could *see* it. And no matter what went on, if they argued or slammed out of the house, it didn't make a difference, because the first person either of them turned to was the other. My grandmother one time got fed up with my going on and on about it, and said, 'Who ever promised you things were going to be easy? Who ever signed that in blood for you, Joanna?' God! I was so ashamed, because in a lot of ways that's exactly what it was like: as if I'd been promised all kinds of things—understanding, happiness, an easy route straight to what I wanted. And she made me see that there were things I was just too young to understand, and other things I had no right to expect. So I stopped expecting anything. And I stopped judging situations that didn't make sense to me. And I promised myself I'd have everything I ever wanted, because I'd work myself to death to get them. But nothing anybody could ever say was going to convince me to trust any man enough to want to commit myself to him. Yet, if I were going to trust anyone, it would be Henry. And I'm not even sure I could tell you why."

"It is well worth the pain and the effort," Anne said. "Oh, there are times when one is bound to wonder at the cost, naturally. But for the most part, one returns to the initial certainty, that instinct that told you you were about to lose a piece of yourself that you could never again retrieve, and, in return, you would have the benefit of all the drama and hilarity, all the infuriation and irritation, all the warmth and closeness that comes of making the effort to share yourself and your experiences."

"If you can say that after fifty years, it must be true."

"One would think so. Are you sure you won't have some coffee?"

"All right, I will, thank you. I'll get it." She went to pour herself a cup and to refill Anne's, then returned to her seat, aware of Anne's eyes following her. If it were anyone else, being so closely watched would have made her uncomfortable, but with Anne she felt quite at ease. There wasn't the faintest judgmental element in the woman's gaze.

"I think every marriage that's ever been has had some degree of dishonesty in it," Anne told her. "Oh, not necessarily infidelity per se, although it's far more common than perhaps you believe. But thoughts of others, the speculation of what some man might be like, or some woman. There's a benchmark, as it were. One arrives at a plateau in the marriage where one's partner is no longer so mysterious or so compelling as he was to you at the outset. You've been overexposed to one another; you know each other's habits and propensities; you know the surface of each other's bodies more intimately than any physician ever could. At this juncture you must decide if your knowledge is going to inspire either contempt or fondness. If that basic abiding attachment is there, it isn't too terribly difficult to find the fondness. And then, my dear, if one has faith, something quite extraordinary occurs: From the fondness comes a rekindling of the love. It's as if you've set a small fire that takes hold and burns far beyond its allotted time. And having come through all the tedious, tiresome times relatively intact, you're able to go forward together because what you had at the outset was of sufficient depth and strength to see you through.

"In the case of our marriage, I was the one who, as you put it, had rendezvous in hotel rooms. Ah, I've shocked you. It isn't shocking, really. I became involved with Jimmy when I was eighteen. For twenty-five years he was the sun and the moon. And then one morning I was forty-three and fearful that I'd lost whatever appeal I might once have had. It hadn't anything to do, actually, with Jimmy, but everything to do with me. And it's never ceased to intrigue me how attractive men seem to find women who are married. It wasn't at all difficult. It was not, however, particularly rewarding. Half a dozen tension-fraught illicit meetings on visits to London under the pretext of shopping, and then I'd had enough and put a stop to it.

"I'd satisfied my vanity, you see. I'd also broken vows that I'd taken most seriously twenty-five years before. But after all those years those vows scarcely seemed relevant. I'd come to believe that remaining sexually faithful to one person for the duration of one's life was not only unrealistic but impractical. If for no other reason than to confirm the strength of my feelings for my husband, what I did outside the marriage was of infinite value. It afforded me an opportunity to reevaluate my marriage, as well as my feelings for Jimmy. It also allowed me to see that no one else—should I care to go out looking—could ever touch me, in every way, as Jimmy did. And so I went home to my husband and never again had any interest in other men, or any serious doubts about our marriage. It took being unfaithful to make me appreciate how very, very much I cared for the man I'd married."

"Did he ever know about it?" Jo asked her.

"Oh, never! I wouldn't have dreamed of hurting him by revealing what I'd done. And he'd have been devastated, because Jimmy, like the majority of men, has always believed that a woman he loved wouldn't be capable of betraying him. They, of course, wouldn't consider it a betrayal if they did those same things. But wives, especially of my generation, were property, chattel. I cannot tell you how glad I am that all that has changed. I think I railed more against the notion of being another of Jimmy's 'holdings' than I would have done had he made love to a dozen other women. And heaven only knows, he had ample opportunity. But he never took advantage of those opportunities."

"How do you know that for sure?"

"Oh, I'd have known," she said with quiet confidence. "Poor darling never had any talent for indiscretion. He was always too basically honest." She looked over at the sliding doors to the suite, then back at Jo.

"You make it sound so possible," Jo said, feeling herself strongly swayed.

"It *is* possible. I have done it, after all. And if you'll forgive me for venturing to give an opinion where none's been requested, if you have a chance to share your life, Joanna, don't let it pass you by, whatever your reservations might be. I do, with all my heart, believe people are meant to be together, not alone, locked nightly into safe little cubicles. It's too, too sad to avoid an emotional life simply because of one or two bad experiences and a set of distorted childhood memories. Tell me about him," she invited. "Is he kind to you, this young man Henry? Does he concern himself with your well-being?"

"He's not overtly demonstrative, but I think he does care. But Anne," she protested, "for all I know, I'm imagining things. For all I know, he has no feelings for me—beyond the professional ones he has to have, because I'm a client of his, after all. I keep having the feeling that I'm making this whole thing up, that all my thoughts are slightly out of whack because of this trip, the train, this hotel, this city. And it's the kind of thing single women do, you know. I mean, we embroider mental images, these perfect pictures in our heads, right to the smallest detail. And then we end up not sure what's true and what we made up."

"He's sent you flowers and a cable, and you're of the opinion you're merely wool-gathering?" Anne's eyebrows lifted. "Surely not. It sounds as if he's making an effort to state his case. The question is whether you're making an equal effort."

"Are you trying to get me married off?" Jo asked with a little laugh. "You're sounding an awful lot like a mother."

Anne laughed with her, saying, "It's what I've been for the better part of my life, after all. And you do indulge me, so it seems perfectly legitimate for me to give voice to my motherly opinions."

"You and I have the damnedest conversations."

"We do, don't we?" Anne concurred. "I can't begin to tell you how much pleasure they give me. I wonder from moment to moment if, had things been different, I would have been able to talk this way with Lucia. But it wouldn't have been possible."

"Why not?"

Anne sighed. "For one thing, mothers and daughters seem congenitally unable to have conversations where the entire weight of their shared history doesn't come crowding in to affect the tone and the content."

"I guess you're right. Somehow, I'm always one hundred percent truthful with you; you keep me honest because I know you're being honest with me. With Lily I was always afraid something I'd say might inadvertently upset her. She was very complicated. I can see her so clearly, but it would take me years to describe how she was. I loved her; she fascinated me, but we were never close, not the way I was with Granny Emily. It was as if Lily used up the biggest part of her emotional resources on my father, and there just wasn't enough left over for Beamer and me. She was intuitive, but vague; she was talented, but undirected; she was inquisitive, but never persistent in terms of getting an answer. She was forward in her thinking, but I never saw her body until she was dying. And it mortified her to be so weak that she needed me to help her. Yet in helping her I finally saw the body that had made me. It seemed so strange to me, growing up, that she'd cover herself if I came into her bedroom when she was dressing. I thought for the longest time there was something wrong with her that she didn't want me to see. But there wasn't. Even dying she was really very lovely. I looked at her and tried to understand why she'd hidden herself from me all of my life. So much for that. Lily took most of her secrets with her when she died, and I'll probably get to be an old, old woman before I'm able to work out who she really was."

"We, all of us, appear differently to different people," Anne said, putting out her cigarette and lighting another at once. She drank some of the fresh coffee, then returned the cup to the tray. "I should hate to think we wouldn't have many more of these talks together."

"I'd hate it, too. I've been meaning to ask if you'd give me your address so I could come visit you both sometime."

"I have been hoping you'd ask."

"Oh, I'm so glad," Jo said, relieved. She'd been apprehensive for a moment, thinking perhaps she was trying to create a long-term friendship out of something meant to last only a short time. "I'll tell you something," she said, leaning closer to Anne. "I've learned something important this week. It may sound ridiculous, but I've discovered I'm not my mother. Just because I accepted her definition of me and have gone along with it for all these years doesn't mean I'm supposed to be a carbon copy of a woman I never really knew. I think I believed that if I were more like her she'd confide in me. But I couldn't be her, and now that I can see what it was I've been doing, I know I don't *want* to be her. And you're not your daughter, either. You're not Lucia; you're not responsible for the way she turned out.

"If we were allowed second chances, if God or whatever power there is said, 'Okay, you can have another one, pick anyone you'd like,' I'd choose you for my mother. I can't think of anyone else I could talk with the way I do with you; I can't think of anything that would feel better or more right than being able to come to see you. It feels as if it would be like coming home."

Anne's eyes filled, and Jo thought perhaps she might cry. But she held the cigarette to her mouth and drew on it, then exhaled and said in measured tones, "Only once before have I capitulated without question to my instincts, my dear. And that was when I met Jimmy. This is the second occasion. Initially, I was taken by your uncanny resemblance to Lucia. But what I've come to love in you is the great depths of your honesty. I believe you're incapable of deceit. I don't think you've ever in your life said or done anything that violated your integrity. I'm also impressed by the enormous untapped resource of your caring. It seems to me you've never allowed yourself or anyone else to benefit from your capacity for passionate attachment—except, possibly through your camera. And I've never witnessed anything quite like your interaction with that device. Is it possible you've substituted that visual aid for something more direct? Don't answer, just consider the possibility. More motherly advice," she said with a smile. "Don't be timid about your feelings for this young man, Joanna. Even if it doesn't work out as you'd wish, you'll have lost nothing. Perhaps because you didn't come to know your mother as you'd have liked, you feel you haven't come to know yourself. It sounds to me like a reasonable hypothesis. But perhaps your Lily never knew herself. Had you considered that? No matter. You have a unique ability to give of yourself even when you're not certain why you're doing it. Very few people are willing to give anything at all, but you do, wholeheartedly and with both hands open. Meeting you, knowing you, has been a positive blessing. And nothing would make me happier than to have you come to visit." She reached down to open the catch of her handbag, withdrew the Cartier wallet, and took out a card. "I would be so grateful if you'd ring me upon your return to London. Perhaps you might even come to see me midweek, if you're free."

"Midweek? I don't understand. Are you leaving?"

"I expect by this afternoon we'll have gone," Anne said.

"But what about Jimmy's schedule, lunch today at the Lido . . . ?"

Her voice still soft, her tone unchanged, Anne said, "Jimmy died several hours ago, Joanna. I will be taking him back to England later today."

Jo didn't think she could have heard correctly. Jimmy *died*? He was dead, and they'd been sitting out here, talking? She stared at Anne and suddenly things clicked into place: Anne's answering the telephone so quickly, her asking Jo to come around to the patio, her chainsmoking, the nature of the conversation itself. "Oh, God!" Jo whispered, profoundly shaken. "I don't—"

"It was not unexpected," Anne clarified. "I had thought there would be more time, but it was not unexpected."

Jo's immediate reaction was to offer comfort. But as she began to rise from her chair, Anne quickly said, "Please, don't, Joanna. I'd like nothing more right now than to embrace you, but if I allow myself that luxury, I will come to pieces, and I cannot do that now. There's too much to be done, and I must be all of a piece to do it. I'm sorry to put it to you so baldly, but please try not to be too upset. Jimmy was close to eighty, and he's been very happy these past few years. Most importantly, he was able to come here, to Venice, and that meant the world to him. It was a long-time dream come true, and there is a very real satisfaction to knowing he spent his final days in a place he loved." Anne looked at her watch. "It's almost ten, dear. You have an appointment to keep, and I'm afraid I have a great deal to do."

Jo wanted to stay and help, yet she could see she had no choice but to go. Feeling as if she'd just sustained a blow to the stomach, she retrieved her bags, got up, then hesitated. "I don't know what to say. I liked him so much, he was so lovable. . . . Is there anything I can do for you, anything at all? Oh, damn!" She had to stop. For Anne's sake she didn't dare let herself go.

Anne held out her hand, and Jo took hold.

"You've made this so much less difficult than it might have been," she told Jo. For a moment her eyes reflected doubt, or fear. Jo could see that she was floundering, as she had during their conversation on the train.

"I love you," Jo said inadequately. "I really do."

Anne nodded, then released her, saying, "Go along now."

"Will you be all right?"

"I am very selfish, you know. Being able to look forward to your visit will see me through what's to come. Is that unforgivable?" she wondered. "Is it too much to ask?"

"It's not nearly enough," Jo answered. "I'd be willing to do much, much more. I'll be there whenever you want me. I'll go back with you today, if it would help."

"Thank you," Anne said, her voice thinning. She drew on the cigarette, then lifted her hand to signal Jo to go. "Thank you so very much," she said in a whisper, as Jo backed through the hedges, then turned and ran off.

* * *

Jackie was leaning against the wall outside the kitchen door. Upon seeing her, he pushed away from the wall and smiled. She came over and gave him an emphatic hug. He hugged her back, then said, "Hey! What's wrong? Are you okay?"

"I'll tell you later. I don't think I can talk about it now."

"You're not sick or anything, are you?" he asked.

"No, I'm not sick."

"Is it about your friends, the English people?"

"What?"

"Everybody's talking about it. You heard, right? He died this morning."

"I heard. Everybody knows?"

"I guess. It's really too bad. He was cool. We talked for a while the other day. He was telling me about the restorations he'd seen. Anyway, they say he just went in his sleep. If it was me, that'd be the way I'd want to go."

"Yes," she said dully.

"You gonna cry, Joey?"

She shook her head.

"You want me to take off? I'll understand if you do."

"No. I'd really like your company."

"Sure. But if you change your mind, just say the word and I'm out of here."

"I won't change my mind. We'd better get going. I hate being late."

"I'll take the camera bag." He reached to remove it from her shoulder.

She watched him for a moment, then said, "You're a sensational guy. You know that?"

"Sure," he grinned. "Everybody says so."

"And so modest," she added, glad of his presence.

"Yeah, that too." He pushed open the kitchen door. "After you, kiddo."

"I don't think I'm going to be very good company today," she warned him.

"That's cool. I understand."

"You really do, don't you?"

"Well, sure," he said quietly, then exclaimed, "Check this out! Gives a whole new meaning to 'clean.'"

At his bidding she turned to look at the first of the two spotless adjoining kitchens. Work to do, she reminded herself. Then, with a sigh, she adjusted the camera strap around her neck and started toward the inner kitchen, where the chef was waiting.

Twenty-three

". . . THREE DAYS' WORK IN KITCHEN FOR EACH DEPARTURE. CHEF, RENATO Piccolotto, young, very little Eng., patient in miming explanations. Menus decided by group—chef, stewards. Seasonal menus: spring/summer; winter/fall. All written out on white board on wall far end of kitchen. 2 columns each side sep. by column for brunch—1 for lunch, 1 for dinner each direction (see negs). Renato works with 2 assts., all 3 in white w/tall pleated hats; R. wears white scarf knotted around neck, mustache & beard (like Henry's). He looks more like artist than chef. Wed.—veg. peeled & cut, ready to cook on train. Thurs.—1st meat, then fish made ready—all fresh, nothing frozen. Fri. a.m.—veg blanched & packed airtight in heavy plastic, sealed by special machine; half-cooked, finished on train; meat & fish then pkged. airtight. Sat. 6 a.m.—food loaded.

"After blanching, veg. & some sauces go into quick cooler for ½ hr., then made airtight. Cool rooms to store veg, meat, fish; food put in foil containers, plastic over top, then airtight machine. Very impressive, very modern equipment. Also Thurs. a.m., potatoes cooked, scooped, inside mixed w/egg, butter, cooked ham, returned to shell & gratinated. Fillets of beef; baby zucchinis sliced at top, tomato slices inserted, artwork.

"As much done in adv. as poss. Asst. slicing beef on butcher's block, trying not to smile when I take his ph., R. showing large tray of slivered carrots; very proud of his work; all 3 enjoying themselves. Whole time J. & I in kitchen, I was thinking of Anne talking, feeling I should've known, but didn't. Such a jolt, and the way she said it, so quietly. Want to call Henry . . ."

She looked up from her notes to see Jackie with her camera, carefully turning it this way and that, then holding it to his eye. He turned, aiming

497

the camera at her, and she waited to see what he'd do. He hesitated, his finger on the shutter release, and she said, "Go ahead. You know how it works. Don't be afraid to try it."

"You sure?"

"Yup. Just check all your settings, then ease out the winder a notch and push down lightly on the shutter release. If you get a red light on the meter, go up an F-stop. If it's green, you're all right. Check your focus and shoot. Get used to handling the camera. If you buy one for yourself, experiment. Don't be afraid to make mistakes, because you can learn a hell of a lot from the shots you mess up."

"Okay." He ran through all the steps as she'd instructed, took a shot, then replaced the lens cap and set the camera on the table, asking, "Finished?"

"Yup. I am now an authority on the Orient-Express. Ask me anything!"

"Okay." He thought for a moment. "What's the name of the engineer?"

"Which one?" she countered.

"There's more than one?"

"Yup. New ones in every country."

"Okay. Wait a minute. All right. What kind of train is it? I mean, what's the power source?"

"Electricity. All European trains are electric."

"No shit! I didn't know that."

"Well, there you go." She opened her purse to put away the notebook and pen, and saw the package Lucienne had given her that morning. "I forgot all about this."

"What is it?" he asked, leaning with both elbows on the table.

"I don't know."

"So, open it. What is it, a present? Who from, that actor?"

"I take it you don't like him."

"Do you?" he hedged.

"No, tell me, Jackie."

"I didn't *dis*like him or anything. I just didn't like the way he put me down. 'Jackie, did you say?' " he mimicked Tyler. "I hope he's not like your main squeeze or anything."

"No. He's just a friend."

"That's good, 'cause he's got the major hots for the French lady. She a friend of yours?"

"Yes."

Jackie shook his head. "That is one stupendous-looking wench! Also really cool. I mean, letting me taste her champagne."

"You liked her, huh?"

Jackie laughed. "Are you kidding? I *loved* her! I could feel myself starting to drool." He let his tongue loll out the side of his mouth while his eyes went vague.

Jo laughed. "You're a dirty little boy."

"That's cool. At least I've got good taste. So are you going to open that or what?"

"I guess I should, shouldn't I?" She undid the paper, then said, "Oh, God!"

"What?" Jackie wanted to know, craning to see. "What?"

"It's from Cartier."

"No shit! Open it!"

"I'm afraid to."

"Why?"

"Because it's too much. I can't accept something like this."

"Don't you think," he said reasonably, "you should check it out before you say you can't accept it?"

"I'm afraid to," she said again.

"Well, I'm not. You want me to open it?" When she didn't respond, he took the red box from her and opened it. "This is cool," he said, lifting out a simple gold chain bracelet. "Look!" He held it up for her, saw the tears spilling down her cheeks, and said, "You need a drink." Putting the bracelet into her hand, he went inside the café to find a waiter. Then he came hurrying back to sit close to her, pressing his handkerchief into her hand. "It's okay, Joey," he said, patting her shoulder. "It's okay."

The waiter came quickly, carrying a glass on a tray.

"Thanks a lot," Jackie said, taking the glass from him and setting it down in front of Jo. "Drink some of that," he told her.

She sniffed and wiped her face with the handkerchief. "What is it?"

"Brandy and soda. It's what my dad drinks when everything hits the fan, so I figure it must do some good."

She picked up the glass, took a swallow, then set it back on the table and ran her finger around the rim. "This has been one bitch of a day," she said, her eyes on the bracelet.

"Any good?" Jackie asked of the drink.

"I don't know. Have a taste and tell me."

He took a sip, made a face and put it down. "I'd rather have another espresso. But I think you'd better drink it."

"I'll get bombed."

"So what?"

"You're right. So what?" She took another swallow, then picked up the bracelet. "In my whole life, nobody's ever given me anything like this."

"It was me," he said wisely, "I'd be offended if you gave it back. It was me, I'd put it on right now and wear the sucker."

She looked questioningly at him, then again at the bracelet. "You're right," she decided. "You're absolutely right." She fastened it around her right wrist, then admired the way it looked. "It's beautiful, isn't it?" she said, the tears starting up again.

"Drink some more!" he advised, pushing the glass against her hand.

She wiped her eyes, then smiled at him. "One day, kiddo, you're going to make some woman very happy."

"You think so?" he asked, looking proud.

"I know it. Whatever their faults might be, your folks have raised you to be a hell of a decent guy."

"They're not so bad," he allowed, "just kind of neurotic now and then."

"The shops ought to be opening again soon. I really wanted to take a look at the masks in that shop by the Rialto. You know the place we saw yesterday?"

"Okay. Drink up and we'll go." He reached for his wallet.

"Save your money in case you see something you want to buy."

"Okay. Thanks a lot. The lunch was really good, especially the green spaghetti."

She had to laugh. "Spinach pasta. You can't go around telling people you ate green spaghetti."

"That's what it was."

"I give up." She looked at the bill, laid some notes and coins on top of it, then collected her things.

As they started off, she said, "Jackie, d'you ever get the feeling somebody else is running your show, that you're almost incidental to the things that happen?"

"All the time," he answered. "I'm a kid, don't forget. Everybody runs me. The only thing I get to do that nobody supervises is think. Oh sure, I can go out, hang out with my friends and like that, but there's a curfew, and stuff I'm supposed to do at home, all kinds of rules. Why?"

"I don't know. Here I am, thirty-six years old, and right now I feel kind of clueless. Yesterday I thought I was really getting somewhere, breaking away from years of doing dumb-ass things, behaving like a wimp. Today, I'm back to feeling like a wimp."

"You're upset, that's all."

"That's only part of it. It feels as if my whole life's been changed by this trip. I mean, I've been more in charge of myself this week than I've ever been before. I mean, everything that's happened, from the moment I got on the train, has been different. All the people I've met, the new friends I've made, this city . . . I'm not sure I can explain it. Take you, for example." She turned to him. "Aside from my brother Beamer, and my first boyfriend, Tom Harper, who was fifteen, I've never spent any time to speak of with kids. But the time I've spent with you has been so wonderful." She had to stop and clear her throat before she was able to go on. "I meant what I said to your parents. I think it would be fantastic to have a kid like you. I probably never will, but from now on I'm never again going to be irritated when I zip down to Darien to Baskin-Robbins for some ice cream and there are eighteen kids hanging around outside, leaning on their bikes, blocking the entrance."

"They do that in Connecticut, too?" he laughed. "I thought it was just us."

"Well, next time I'll pretend you're one of those kids, and be a little nicer about it when I ask them to move. You know what you said about people growing up and forgetting all the things they knew as kids? That's been me. It really has. But no more, though. I've learned a lot about myself this past week. And I'm through with letting people say things that offend the hell out of me and not saying anything, just sitting there getting madder and madder instead of telling them they're full of shit, they don't know what they're talking about. I loved that old man, Jackie. I felt as if I'd known him all my life. He brought out the best in me. They both did. I thought, somehow, they were going to be in my life from now until forever, that I'd go visit and take Jimmy books on the Venetian artists, or blocks of watercolor paper, or some sable brushes, or something. I was in love with the idea of being able to be with them, because they'd made it through fifty years of marriage and still cared for each other. Then, this morning, Anne and I talked, and she made me see that I'd set standards—for myself, and for others—that no one could ever live up to. She made me see I've spent a hell of a long time being a wimp with a serious hidden agenda. And she also made me see that if I'd only allow a bit of room for human error—mine and anyone else's—I could have a lot more of a life than I do. She sat there and told me to take chances, to have a little faith and trust; she cared enough about me to be encouraging, and *her husband had just died*. Don't you think," she asked anxiously, "if someone cares enough to tell you the truth at a time like that, you've got a moral obligation not only to listen but to try to do something about it?"

"You'd think so," he agreed.

"Right! So before I go to that dinner tonight, I'm going to try to get hold of Henry on the phone and tell him I'm willing to give it a shot."

"Who's Henry?"

"Henry," she explained, "is the guy in London; someone, I think, who loves me."

His secretary told her Henry had gone for the day. And when Jo called the house, she got his answering machine. She thought of hanging up, decided she'd have to pay for the call anyway, so she waited for the beep and said, "It's Jo. I was really hoping to talk to you. It's been a rough day. But never mind. I'll see you Sunday night when I get back."

She'd no sooner hung up than the telephone rang.

"Mignon, you are all right?" Lucienne asked. "We come back in the afternoon and we hear. It is so very sad. I like this old man very much."

"I'm all right. How about you? Has Tyler been behaving himself?"

"You mean, does he throw me down and try to make love with me in a gondola?" Lucienne laughed. "No, he is a gentleman, and he behaves very nicely. Listen, Mignon. Laura, she comes to us at the table this morning when you have left, to say the people who are to go with you tonight cannot go, eh? And so we go with you, me and Tyler. This is okay? You have objections?"

"No, none. I've been dreading going alone, spending the evening with a bunch of strangers."

"Good! So we meet with you at six-thirty, and we go together, okay?"

"Fine. Lucienne, the bracelet's beautiful. But you shouldn't have given it to me."

"Of course I should!" Lucienne disagreed. "I want you to have this. It makes me happy to give it to you."

"Well, thank you very much. I love it."

"*Et bon!* I go now for my bath. *Au 'voir, chérie.*"

"*Au 'voir, Lucienne.*"

After the call she thought again about Henry, wishing he'd been home. There was so much she wanted to say to him, and she had the feeling that if she didn't get it said very soon she might change her mind and go home to Connecticut without saying anything at all.

Since leaving Anne that morning, she'd found herself operating on a new plane. Pieces of information and knowledge seemed to home in on her at random moments, making her pause while she tried to assemble the knowledge into a recognizable whole. Everything seemed to tie into something else, yet bits hung over at the edges, dangling untidily. Now, as she went through her clothes, trying to decide what to wear, she couldn't help thinking how foolish it seemed to be fretting over what might be appropriate dress for the evening. It annoyed her to have to go through the process of selecting yet another outfit for yet another evening out. It shouldn't have mattered what she wore, but it did. Because it had been brought home to her in the strongest possible way that she *was* visible, that people *did* see her, and she'd also discovered that she wanted to be seen.

All her life she'd been buying clothes, as if in defiance of her sometime sense of invisibility. She'd taken pleasure in acquiring new things to wear, yet for the most part she'd felt something of a fraud in her clothes—as if she'd borrowed without permission items belonging to someone else that didn't quite mesh with her own personality. She'd been covering her body with garments she very much liked but which she felt were misrepresentational; she could never make the connection between the woman and her clothes. She always ended up wondering why she had so little pride in herself that even her clothes felt alien. Now she understood that with a bit of self-esteem the clothes would become secondary. And she wanted to explain this new insight to Henry. She wanted to take all the chances Anne had said she should, but it wasn't easy to break habits that had become ingrained. If only he'd been home when she'd called. The timing had been right; she'd have been able to tell him how she felt. What if she got back to London only to find she'd lost her nerve? God!

Fifteen minutes spent examining the items in the closet before selecting the short white skirt and purple-blue Claude Montana top Henry had admired; white high heels and sheer white Fogal panty hose with tiny white dots. Name brands. The shoes were Joan & David; her slip was Christian Dior. Goddamned ridiculous! she thought, laying everything out on the bed before going to take her shower. She was a mobile billboard, so she might as well use the Emilio Pucci soap, she decided, grabbing it out of the basket on the bathroom counter. One of these days, she promised herself, suddenly taken by an image of herself in Henry's garden, she was going to put on a no-name T-shirt, some good old jeans, jam her feet into a pair of ten-dollar running shoes and just be whoever the hell she was. Enough of all this brand-name consumerism.

Or did the labels mean something? They were, these quality goods, the rewards she gave herself for jobs well done. And her rewards were all over the condo, even parked outside the front door. She'd been diligently shopping, making purchases most of her adult life, in an attempt to fill a gigantic hole in her life. It was why she never said no when Gracie called to say there was another assignment. Because her work *was* her life. There was no one to come home to. It was too much trouble to stock the kitchen when she was never there long enough to eat more than a few meals. And when she did cook, she invariably wound up throwing food away. So what did she do when she was home? She rented movies and stunned her senses into obedience. Or she spent hours in the darkroom poring over the slide-and-negative files. She didn't even look after the place; the cleaning lady did that. At least Henry had the garden; he worked at it, and it was beautiful. She just sat out on her deck and watched the ducks on the pond. Some life: hanging around between jobs, waiting to get old and have the whole thing over and done with.

Well, it didn't have to be that way. Anne was right. She had choices; she could do any damned thing she wanted. And just because Henry hadn't happened to be home didn't mean she couldn't save up what she wanted to say to him for a time when he was available to hear her. One slight setback and she was ready to give up. It wasn't the only opportunity she was going to have to talk with him. It was, in fact only the first time she'd really wanted to. Someone special had died, and she'd wanted to share her feelings and thoughts about it with Henry, because she believed he'd care. He would care, too, she thought, looking at herself in the mirror. And why not? she asked her mirror image. Look at you! You are, according to the resident fourteen-year-old authority, a comely wench with an aristocratic honker.

Twenty-four

As THE MOTOR LAUNCH TRAVELED ACROSS THE CANAL FROM GIUDECCA toward the piazza, Jo thought about the scene in the movie *Don't Look Now* when the Donald Sutherland character saw his wife and the two strange sisters, all three in black, on a vaporetto heading down the Grand Canal. He'd been seeing the future, but hadn't known it. And at the end of the movie, after he'd been killed by the dwarf in the red cape (the small creature he'd thought was a child) there was Julie Christie, who'd played his wife, and the two sisters (one of them the blind psychic who'd predicted his death) on a vaporetto going down the canal. Strange and creepy. She imagined Anne on a boat with a coffin bearing Jimmy's body to its final resting place. Except that Anne had flown back to London in the afternoon, and Jimmy would be buried in the family plot.

"You are sad, eh?" Lucienne said quietly at her side.

"I am. But most of all, I'm worn out. It feels as if I've been in a week-long marathon, running nonstop. It's so beautiful, isn't it?" She looked at the apricot glow of the fading light, the facades of the buildings going dark as the sun dropped behind them.

"Oh, yes," Lucienne agreed, "very beautiful. This is a city to make you sentimental, eh?"

"Will you still come here, now that it's all over with you and Paolo?"

"But of course!" Lucienne looked surprised. "Why wouldn't I come? This city has nothing to do with Paolo. He is only an accident, an interruption. Venice is my holiday, my pleasure, my paradise. This is where I come when I have enough of Chez Lucienne and the days that begin at six in the morning and end at midnight. I would allow *nothing* to spoil this for me."

505

Jo looked over at Tyler, who was talking with the Texas couple who, for a change, were without their daughter and her husband. "I want to ask you something," Jo said, satisfied their conversation couldn't be over-heard by those at the far end of the cabin. "He hit you, didn't he? You didn't get that bruise from any door. It was Paolo, wasn't it?"

Lucienne's eyes shifted, and she turned, presenting Jo with her perfect profile as she stared off into space. She closed her eyes for a second or two, then opened them and turned back to Jo. "I refused him," she said, with a look that seemed to say she could scarcely believe any of it had happened. "He would have me anyway, because he wishes to show his power. I would not fight; I would show him nothing, no anger, no fear, so he cannot be satisfied, eh, because if I do not fight, if I show no upset, he cannot see that he hurts me. He makes a fool of himself, ruining my clothes, pulling at my hair. It is incredible to me to think I would marry this man when I don't know him. And he is completely crazy. He would rape me because I refuse him. But even that is no good, eh? No rape, but he tries. I do nothing, just watch him, and say to him to go because I am exhausted after so much fighting. Please go, I tell him, and get up to cover myself, thinking he is a pig to ruin my dress, my stockings. I don't care about him. I just wish for him to go away, so I don't have to see him and think to myself how stupid I am to believe I could make a marriage with such a crazy pig. Go away, I say to him. And then he hits me. He shouts and shouts, and I am on the floor thinking he has perhaps killed me because I cannot breathe. And finally, he grows tired of shouting and he goes away. *Finis*."

Jo put her arm around Lucienne's shoulder and rested her cheek against hers. "I'm so sorry," she said, holding her for a moment before sitting back, only to be startled when Lucienne grabbed her hand and said, "You save me from making a disaster, Joanna. What happened is *nothing*! I prefer to be hit once by a madman than to have to go live with him. I didn't *see*, eh? I am looking only at my little dreams, my little wishes, but not at the madman. You say to me you are sorry, as if you are the one who caused this man to be crazy."

"No. I'm sorry because what happened was rotten, and you didn't deserve to be treated that way."

"Yes?" Lucienne gazed at her, as if to verify the sincerity of her words. "Okay, good," she said, satisfied. "Just promise to me you will stop saying to everyone you are sorry, Mignon. Okay?" She put her hands on either side of Jo's face and kissed her lightly on the lips. "I love you very much. You are sister and mama and friend, eh? And if you are sister and mama and friend, then I can say to you that you are too smart to be so stupid sometimes." She sat away and smiled. "You must only be sorry when it is something wrong you have done. You must never be sorry because maybe in your head you *think* something wrong. There are many things you make better, Mignon. Not only for me, but for the Royal Family, and for the adorable American boy, and even for this frightened man who follows after you to Venice because he fears growing old all alone."

Jo looked over at Tyler who, at that moment, turned to smile at her. She smiled back, then looked again at Lucienne. "Did he tell you that?"

"Of course not," Lucienne replied. "People do not admit to such things. But it is very easy to see."

"If it's so goddamned easy, then how come I didn't see it?"

"I don't know. Maybe you didn't wish to see, eh, because you know you are not the answer to his prayer."

"God! Maybe that's true. But what about you?"

"What of me?" Lucienne wanted to know.

"Nothing," Jo said, thinking it would be unwise to attempt to do any matchmaking. She was the last person on earth qualified to try to bring people together, even if she was sitting between two who seemed to have similar needs.

"Ah!" Lucienne said, turning away. "We have arrived."

Tyler walked between them as they went from the Cipriani's dock toward the piazza, wondering what he'd witnessed might signify. He'd turned in time to see one woman kiss another woman on the mouth, and his first reaction was shock at the notion that the two were sexually involved. His second reaction was to dismiss the first, only to have it replaced by a kind of low-grade envy. He knew that what he'd seen had nothing to do with sex and everything to do with mutual understanding and caring. And he thought, not for the first time, how very lucky women were to be able to make the displays they did of affection. Two men kissing that way could only constitute a public declaration of preference. Unless the two in question happened to be father and son. And even then, the scene might be suspect. The friendship of these two women gave him a keen sense of the deficiency endemic to being male and heterosexual. He was destined to spend the balance of his life limiting his affectionate displays to women, but even that was proving no easy thing. He'd come all this way to see Joanna, with the hope of building something out of their two prior meetings. But it was all too evident there was nothing to build upon. And here he was, walking along between two lovely, fragrant women, all too aware of past attachments and future uncertainties. He also felt more than a bit guilty at having come chasing after Joanna only to feel thunderstruck by the mere sight of her friend. And feeling guilty, he couldn't act upon any of his impulses, not even the simple, friendly ones. He felt like one of those classically silly old sods who were forever chasing after nubile young creatures, without the faintest notion of how dismal and depressing a picture they made.

They went through the Piazza San Marco, past the many tables set out in the open, past the trio of musicians on a stage surrounded by wrought-iron planters filled with pots of coleus and geraniums. Ornate standing lamps, not yet lit, would provide illumination for the musicians after dark; the three men, in flowing white shirts and gray trousers, looked content with their lot as they played violin, bass, and grand piano.

"I can just see Katharine sitting at one of these tables," Jo told Tyler.

"Ah, yes, *Summertime*. My father worked on that production with David Lean."

"He did? Doing what?"

"Postproduction." he answered and didn't elaborate.

"Oh, you must look at the little girl with her dog," Lucienne said, pointing out a pretty blond child of seven or eight in an oversized white cotton sweater and baggy white trousers, straining to keep hold of a sad-looking hound of mixed blood on a chain lead. She was watching the musicians, smiling happily. "*Charmante*, eh?"

"She's sweet," Jo agreed.

"Why not let me carry that bag for you, Joanna?" Tyler said. "It looks very heavy."

"Thank you, Tyler."

"It *is* heavy," he said, adjusting the strap over his shoulder. "I can't think how you carry this about for hours at a stretch."

"Part of the job. You get used to it. So tell me. What did the two of you do all day?" She looked from Tyler to Lucienne.

"It was very amusing," Lucienne said. "We walk for a time, and Tyler says, 'If we get lost, we can take a taxi . . .' Then he stops very suddenly when he realizes this is Venice and there are no taxis, no automobiles."

"Felt like a bloody fool," Tyler admitted with a self-deprecating smile.

"Oh, but he was very good," Lucienne went on. "We walk, and he doesn't complain. We go to see the basilica of San Marco, and the church of San Zaccaria to see the Bellini at the second altar, and to San Francesco della Vigna to see the tomb of Andrea Gritti, and then to La Pietà where Vivaldi was violin master. I would go on, but our friend confesses he is tired, his feet are hurting, he is hungry, he is thirsty. So we must stop."

"She walked me half to death," he complained good-naturedly.

"In Venice, this is what you do," Lucienne said equally good-naturedly.

"But what about the shopping?"

"This we do after we stop to rest."

"This we do," Tyler laughed, "with a bloody vengeance. There were sales in all her favorite shops. And we hit every last one of them, from Valentino to some grotty little pottery place."

"You *loved* this pottery place!" Lucienne accused. "He buys many gifts in this shop."

"It was wonderfully whimsical stuff, all hand-turned. I couldn't resist."

"Yes, so! After we have finished, we go to Harry's bar to drink Bellinis and to eat. Then we return to the hotel."

"Is the city the way you thought it would be?" Jo asked him.

"It's better than that. I simply can't think why I didn't consider all the walking we'd have to do. Wore the wrong shoes, of course. Tomorrow I'll be better prepared."

"You plan to come in again?"

"Without question," Tyler assured her. "And you did say you might have some free time."

"For dinner. I don't know yet about during the day."

The Caffè Florian was old and elegant, with round marble tables and velvet-covered banquettes. They were greeted by a man and a young woman from the tourist board, who directed them to an inner room where the people from the other hotels had gathered.

"We wait for three more, and then we go to the palazzo," the young woman told them. "Please, sit and have some wine." She showed them to an unoccupied table, her eyes lingering admiringly for a few seconds on Lucienne before she turned to go.

Her partner from the board offered sparkling white wine in champagne flutes. Jo declined. Lucienne and Tyler each took a glass. Feeling most reluctant, and wishing she could just sit and enjoy the evening, Jo got up off the end of the banquette to take a few wide-angle shots of the group and of the interior of the café. Then she took several close-ups of Lucienne and Tyler individually and, finally, together.

As usual, Lucienne was superbly turned out, this evening in a white silk suit. The jacket was belted snugly at the waist, then flared in a peplum over her hips. The skirt was knee-length, with an alluring slit at the back. Her hair was smoothed back into a complicated chignon; her makeup was pale, with a touch of color on her cheekbones, charcoal eyeshadow, and vivid red lipstick. Large gold hoop earrings, and on her left shoulder an enameled snake brooch with goldwork around the scales and small rubies for eyes, were her only jewelry. As always, she was the focus of all eyes as she sat comfortably sipping her Asti Spumante. Tyler seemed unable to stop looking at her, his eyes straying repeatedly to the flawless column of her throat. And when Lucienne reached for a cigarette, he at once picked up a box of matches from the table to light it.

Lucienne's fingertips held his hand steady, her long lacquered nails just touching the back of his hand. She thanked him, exhaled twin plumes of smoke from her nostrils, then gave him a slow smile.

Jo turned her attention to the camera, noting the number of exposures left on the roll, then cleaned the lenses before returning them to the camera bag. She suppressed a sudden strong urge to tell the other two she thought it would be a damned good idea if they got together. It was one thing for Anne to offer her motherly advice, it was something else for Jo to start manipulating people.

"Have you taken a lot of pictures, Joanna?" Tyler asked.

"Quite a lot. About eight rolls, not counting the two I had processed when I arrived. I just wish I could've done some black and white work, too, but for that I would have needed a second camera body. Bad enough the one I brought with me went on the fritz. This is a new one," she explained to him. "It's not bad, either."

"I hope, if there's a chance, you'll show me the pictures before you leave London."

"They're slides," she said. "But sure. I'll be glad to show you."

The young woman returned with the late arrivals and announced, "If you please, we will go now."

Lucienne took time to finish both her cigarette and her wine while Jo and Tyler waited. Then the three of them joined the end of the line leaving the café and heading across the square.

"We are walking?" Lucienne said with dismay. "I did not think of this." She looked doubtfully at her black patent high heels. "I hope it is not too very far."

"I'll second that," Tyler said. "I still haven't recovered from the several hundred miles we've already walked today."

"It can't be that far," Jo reasoned. "Otherwise, we'd be going by boat."

They crossed to the right of the square, proceeding along a very cramped street and over a bridge. On the other side the street widened and they followed it through to an open square. The light was even more golden now, the air pleasantly cool. There were few people about, no traffic whatever to contend with. The man from the tourist board dropped back to say good evening and to ask, "You are from where?"

"Britain, France, and America," Tyler answered.

"And you are a journalist?"

"No, Joanna is a journalist," Tyler corrected him. "A very good, very well-known one, at that."

"Ah, yes?" The man smiled ingratiatingly at Jo. "This is very good. We are most anxious to have people who will write of Venice, speak of it."

"I'll certainly do that," Jo promised, hoping not to appear rude as she looked away from him at the dwellings they were passing. In this city even the most decrepit buildings had character and charm.

"You will wish to take photographs of the palazzo," the man told her, falling into step beside Tyler in order not to obstruct her view. "It has been home of the Malipiero family, a very important family with prelates, generals, and senators. Also three doges. The palazzo becomes the property of the Trevisan family through marriage. Both very important families to Venice."

"D'you have anything on paper you can give me?" Jo asked. "Any kind of background information?"

"Of course," he replied readily. "But it will have to come from our office. We will have it to the Cipriani tomorrow. This is good?"

"Fine. If I can work anything about the palace into my piece, I will."

"Thank you. You will excuse me, please. We arrive momentarily. The palazzo is just there." He pointed, then hurried off to have a quick word with his assistant before hurrying up the steps and across the bridge leading to the entrance of the still-handsome but badly aged and stained edifice.

"It would appear we're to wait," Tyler said. "Evidently, they're not quite ready for us."

"What did you talk about with that couple on the launch?" Jo asked him. "I've been dying to know who they are."

"They're lovely people," he said, "from Oklahoma. Tulsa, I think they said. He's chairman of the board of an oil company, and she's head legal counsel for the company. The daughter"—he made a face —"whom I encountered this morning, is presently unemployed. I gathered she's never actually *been* employed. And her husband is a football coach at some boys' school. The parents are terribly concerned because the daughter's on her second marriage to this same young man, and the trip was intended to work some sort of magic and smooth over all the rough patches. It isn't working. The young man's desperate to leave and go home. The daughter's burying her sorrow in compulsive shopping. And the two together are all but destroying the parents' holiday. They were telling me that this evening is the first chance they've had to be alone together since they left home several weeks ago. The daughter insists on having them with her constantly. The whole thing's rather sad."

"I knew it!" Jo declared. "I had almost all of it right except for where they're from—and the mother. A lawyer. I'd never have guessed she was that."

"You might be interested to know that Mrs. Holt was quite as intrigued by you as you were by them."

"Oh, really?"

"Yes, indeed. She was most anxious to know what you were doing."

"What did you tell her?"

Tyler laughed wickedly. "I told her you were Mandy Rice-Davies, in your new incarnation as a journalist."

"Are you kidding? You didn't actually *say* that?"

He kissed her on the forehead and said, "No, I didn't. I simply told her you were doing a story on the Orient-Express."

"Why do they keep us waiting?" Lucienne wondered, moving away from the group to have a cigarette.

"They haven't finished laying the tables or some such," Tyler said, hurrying to light her cigarette.

Jo had lifted the camera and was slowly scanning the scene through the lens, her eyes and the camera traveling around the square, then across the fronts of the buildings. She pressed the shutter release and cried out simultaneously at the sight of smoke drifting from two pairs of French doors giving on to a minuscule second-floor balcony. "There's a fire!" she cried, pointing wildly. She looked around, but no one appeared to have heard her. Tyler and Lucienne were some eight or ten feet away, talking. The rest of the group was clustered at the foot of the steps to the palace's bridge. People drifted over the public bridge next to it to traverse the close-walled street separating the palace from the building with the smoke wafting from the second-floor doors.

"There's a fire!" Jo cried more loudly, her pointing finger beginning to tremble.

At this, quite a number of people turned to look at her, then to where she was pointing. Seeing the smoke, which was growing thicker and darker, Tyler ran across the bridge and vanished from sight.

"Someone should call the fire department!" Jo called out to no one in particular.

Lucienne came to her side and stood looking at the windows.

"Oh, God! What if someone's in there!" Jo worried aloud, her throat going dry. "God! I hope no one's in there!"

As she and Lucienne watched, the balcony doors were suddenly, loudly, slammed shut. A crowd was collecting in the square while pedestrians coming from the other direction started across the bridge, saw the crowd, then turned to gaze up at the smoke. Heads tilted back, they continued on over the bridge, stopping to join those in the square.

"It's going on too long!" Jo said. "Every minute in the life of a fire is a very long time. And someone's in there. Whoever it is just closed the windows." Lucienne had moved nearer. Jo could smell her perfume mingling with the acrid odor of the smoke that was now pushing around the edges of the balcony doors. "Where's the damned fire department? I hope somebody's called them."

Lucienne was about to put a comforting hand on Jo's arm, when Jo abruptly moved away, the camera clicking, her hands automatically changing lenses, winding the film, clicking, clicking. She seemed, Lucienne thought, completely unaware of herself. Moving forward to keep Joanna in sight, Lucienne watched as she hurried to the edge of the canal to look both ways before pointing her camera up at the building. On the balcony of the palazzo a number of people, including a chef in white, had come out to see what all the commotion was about, and were leaning forward on the balustrade, pointing and commenting.

Tyler came pushing through the crowd and arrived at Lucienne's side, asking, "Where is Joanna?"

"She is there," Lucienne told him. "Look at her! Something is very wrong with her, eh? See how she shakes! I am afraid she will fall into the canal."

"You wait here! I'll fetch her back." He skirted the clusters of people watching the progress of the fire and went toward the railing where Jo had positioned herself. Just as he reached her, there was the sound of sirens, and a fire patrol boat came gliding along the canal, pulling to a stop directly below where Jo was standing. Half a dozen men in bright orange coats and yellow-banded black hats scrambled out of the boat carrying axes and slinging yellow oxygen tanks over their shoulders. Tyler put both hands on her shoulders and drew Jo back, out of the way of the firemen. He could feel her quaking quite violently under his hands, yet she continued to hold the camera to her eye, taking one shot after another. "Joanna," he said directly into her ear, "what are you doing?"

"There are people in there!" she wailed, her eyes never leaving the building, the camera never leaving her eyes. "They're trapped in there!"

"Joanna," he said firmly, "there is no one in there."

"But you don't know that, you can't be sure."

"I *am* sure," he told her. "I was just in there. I closed the windows, to cut off the air so it wouldn't feed the fire."

"You were in there?" At last, she lowered the camera and looked at him. She could smell the smoke in his clothes, and there were sooty smudges on his face and hands. "There's no one in there? You're absolutely positive?"

"Positive," he told her. "The fire seems to have started in a television set."

"A television set?" She turned and looked again to the second floor, where the balcony doors were now open and two of the orange-coated firemen were signaling an all clear to the men still in the boat below. "Did you check the bathroom, Tyler? Did you? There could have been someone in there. It's important to check."

"I went through every room, Joanna. *There is no one in there.*"

"They could be pounding on the walls or the floor, and if you don't hear them—"

"*Joanna!*" he said sharply, forcing her to look at him. "*The flat is empty!*" He spoke slowly and clearly, alarmed by her eyes, which were wide and unblinking. "What is the matter?" he asked her. "You're not listening to me. *Everything*," he said even more slowly and clearly, "*is all right.*"

Her eyes stayed on him, uncomprehending, and he felt himself starting to sweat. "Joanna? Do you hear me?" He held fast to her shoulders, not allowing her to turn away. And all at once understanding seemed to penetrate. Her eyes changed, focusing. She wet her lips, said, "I thought . . . ," stopped and tried to begin again. He put his arms around her, trying to calm her and stop her quite terrible trembling.

"I thought it was all over," she cried, "that I was over it. Oh, God! I'm *not* over it. Maybe you *never* get over it. I'm so *scared*."

"None of that," he said quietly, "prevented you from taking a whole roll of film."

She stood away from him. "What?"

He took hold of her hand, uncurled her fingers to reveal the spool of exposed film she'd been clutching. She looked at the film, then at the camera. She'd shot an entire roll and even reloaded without being cognizant of her own actions. In fact, she'd watched all of it through the lens of the Exakta. More than forty exposures—the proof was in her hand, and on the camera's counter. She stared at the spool sitting on the palm of her hand, then looked up at Tyler. She was crying, he thought, like a small child, with little hiccoughing sobs, eyes and nose streaming. He brought out his handkerchief and gently blotted her cheeks, then held the handkerchief to her nose and said, "Blow." And like a child, she did, her eyes now fixed on him as if the answers to all her questions resided in him.

"Will you be all right now?" he asked her. "It looks as if they're ready for us to go inside, and we should both find somewhere to have a quick wash."

Lucienne took hold of Jo's arm saying, "I will stay with her. Go ahead, Tyler. We will come soon."

Jo was staring at the roll of film in disbelief. "How could I *do* that? I didn't even *know* I was doing it." She turned to look at the firemen removing their orange coats, loading equipment back into the boat.

"Joanna," Lucienne said, "what is the matter?"

"I was in a fire," she explained, the residual fear thudding through her arteries. "I nearly died. It was such a long time ago. I thought I was over it. I mean, most of the time I've stopped worrying, stopped thinking I smell smoke all the time. But that's not it!" Her tears started anew. "What's so goddamned scary is the way I was shooting film, as if my brain is separate from the rest of me, as if I'm some sick kind of robot."

"But this is what you do," Lucienne said sensibly. "You make photographs. I have seen this from the beginning. Why is this so terrible?"

"It's terrible because—because it's ghoulish. I mean, here I am terrified somebody might be trapped in there, but taking pictures anyway, like a visual vampire or something. God! How could I *do* that? How could I?"

"Pay attention to me!" Lucienne said sternly. "You are being hysterical, and there is no need for this. *Listen!*" She tightened her grip on Jo's arm. "I have a restaurant, eh? Six nights of every week I greet the people who come to dine in my restaurant. I smile, I talk with these people, I ask after their children, their families. Often, I will sit to have a glass of wine with clients I have had for many years. But all the while I am smiling and talking and asking about the families, I am watching the staff, and the doors to the kitchen, and I make note of how much time passes before people are presented with their food. I look to see how well or how badly the people are responding to the staff, to the food, to the *ambiance*, to everything. It is necessary; it is part of what I do, what must be done. You are a woman who makes pictures. And while you make the pictures, you smile and you talk and you observe how things are done. It is necessary; it is part of what you do. Why do you talk of yourself so badly now because you see something which distresses you but which also you have a wish to photograph? It is part of what you do, eh? Me, I don't think this is so terrible. No one is the one thing or the other thing altogether. We are each many things. And this is okay, Mignon. *You* are okay. People who love you, they know this is how you are, what you do, and it is of no consequence. Now come. We will fix the face and the hair."

Upon entering the palace, Lucienne stopped to ask the young woman from the tourist board where there was a bathroom. The young woman showed the way, Lucienne thanked her, then directed Jo along the hallway. Inside the large marbled bathroom she seated Jo on the side of the tub, then opened Jo's bag, found a hairbrush, a compact, and some tissues. As if in a trance, Jo sat, trying to apply like a poultice Lucienne's logical words and common sense to her tangled feelings.

"That fire changed everything," she tried to explain. "Afterward, my whole life was different. *I* was different."

"But you didn't die. This is all that matters. So there is no need to be afraid now. And Tyler, he was very good, eh, to go into the fire? I am very impressed how he does this. And he has much fondness for you, Mignon. *Très gentil*, the way he speaks with you, and makes you to blow your nose, *comme une enfant*. For this, I like him very, very much."

"I'm fond of him, too," Jo said, feeling she could curl up in the bathtub and go to sleep. "I'm just not in love with him."

"We have a good time today," Lucienne said, powdering Jo's nose, then studying her for a moment before closing the compact. "You don't mind this?"

"I don't say one thing and mean something else. I think the two of you are a good match, if you want to know the truth. He's always made me kind of nervous because he seems to know what he wants and he's already going after it while I'm still trying to figure out where to sit."

Lucienne laughed and handed her the hairbrush saying, "Fix your hair," then lit a cigarette while Jo got up from the tub and went to stand before the mirror.

"You don't need my permission, that's for damned sure," she told Lucienne's reflection. "And you have my blessing. I just made a complete asshole of myself, and the two of you are being very decent about it. More than decent. And what you said about doing things that are necessary makes a lot of sense. It really does." She turned from the mirror and leaned against the basin. "You are one very smart woman."

"Not so very smart. Otherwise I would not come so close to making a marriage with a man who argues with his fists."

"You'd never have gone through with it," Jo said. "I could tell that from the way you talked about it at dinner the first night on the train."

"Maybe so. We must join with the others now, Mignon."

"Right." Jo returned the hairbrush and compact to her bag, picked up the camera and examined it for a few seconds, then said, "Thank you for helping me make sense of all that."

"Pah!" Lucienne laughed. "It is a fair trade, eh? I give to you advice, you give to me your attractive friend. I think this is very good. I think also you need to have more sleep."

"As soon as this dinner's over, I'm going back to the hotel to collapse. Maybe I'll even sleep late for a change."

"Maybe," Lucienne suggested shrewdly, "you should telephone to the other one, make yourself happy."

"I already tried that. He wasn't home."

"Ahh," Lucienne commiserated. "Too bad. But you will try again."

"Yeah," Jo managed a smile. "I'll try again."

Twenty-five

BY NINE FORTY-FIVE THEY WERE ON THEIR WAY BACK TO THE CIPRIANI, having been presented with a five-course meal and a hefty sales pitch on the city by the man from the tourist board. Jo had been shown only three of the rooms of the palace, the young hostess explaining rather sadly that there was a family in residence and only the dining and sitting rooms had been made available to the board for the evening. "But I show to you the bedroom," she'd said, and had, while the others were moving to the sitting room for coffee, whisked Jo down the hall to show her an enormous room to which the bed was purely incidental. Silk-shaded standing lamps, worn thin but still-regal Persian carpets, clusters of original oils on the walls, armchairs, and a rococco desk. Jo took a number of shots of the room, several more of the beamed ceiling and fabulously ornate chandeliers in the hallway, and several of the sitting room with its broad expanse of highly polished planked floors, twinned groupings of settee and armchairs, and candelabrae affixed to the walls. Then, having fulfilled her professional responsibilities, Jo had sat and tried to pay attention to a California couple who exclaimed over the palace, the dinner, and the wonders of Venice. The events of the day—beginning with Anne's disclosure of Jimmy's death and culminating in the fire—had left her in a state of exhaustion from which she had repeatedly to rouse herself in order not to offend either her hosts or the other guests. When Tyler had sympathetically suggested it was perhaps time to leave, she was deeply grateful.

"It was very interesting, eh?" Lucienne was saying. "Too much food, but not so very bad."

"Three courses with bivalves," Jo said, "is more than I can handle."

"What is this, bivalves?"

"Food that comes with shells. You know: oysters, clams, mussels."

"Ah! Yes, I think this, too. I don't mind the fish as an entrée. But also pasta with mussels, no."

"I quite enjoyed it," Tyler contributed. "Of course, we British thrive on *bivalves*." He smiled over at Jo. "And other oddities of the sea—pickled eel, and so forth. We are, as my sainted grandmother used to say, an island, after all."

"When does she say this, your sainted grandmother?" Lucienne wanted to know.

"For the last five years of her life, she said it several dozen times daily. Went a bit dotty, poor Gran did. Perfectly healthy in every regard, but she took to repeating certain key expressions sometimes five or six times in the course of a single conversation. At the start we found it rather annoying. But at the last it amused the Emmons children no end. We'd manipulate conversations to get her going. Then she'd be off, and she'd take great umbrage when we'd roll about laughing."

"I think this is cruel," Lucienne said.

"Perhaps. But we were children, and children are, for the most part, oblivious to their cruelty. They are the center of their small universes and believe devoutly that only they are capable of feeling hurt. My son is a perfect example. He has little time for the things his mother or I say to him, and goes into a huff when we fail to pay him what he believes is his due portion of attention."

"And how old is your son?" she asked him.

"Twelve, nearly thirteen."

Jo walked along mechanically, tuning in and out of their conversation, listening to the sound of their footsteps on the paving stones, and smiling at passers-by who nodded and said, *"Buona sera."* They'd reached the canal, and the light shone gently through the lovely tinted-glass lamps she'd previously seen only in daylight. The air smelled of salt and the sea, with wisps of Lucienne's perfume and lemony tendrils of Tyler's aftershave. She felt as if she were sleepwalking; her ability to concentrate was down almost to zero. All she wanted was to get back to the hotel and into her bed.

"Look," Lucienne said to Tyler. "She goes in a dream."

"Joanna!" Tyler laughed. "The boat is back here."

Jo stopped, turned, and saw she'd gone some twenty yards beyond the hotel's dock. She'd probably have kept on going if they hadn't stopped her. She went back, following after them along the wooden walkway to the motor launch.

In the hotel lobby, while Jo was getting her key and several messages from the concierge, Tyler suggested going to the bar for a drink.

"I just couldn't," Jo told him. "I've got to go to bed. I'm only barely conscious."

"I go as well," Lucienne announced.

"Well," Tyler said, "I'll see you to your room, Joanna."

"Your eyes are closing, Mignon." Lucienne drew her close. "We will meet for breakfast?"

"Absolutely. Is eight-thirty too early?"

"It is perfect. Sleep well." She kissed Jo on both cheeks, released her, and then turned to say *au 'voir* to Tyler.

"It was a pleasure having your company today," he said to her. "Perhaps I'll have that pleasure again tomorrow."

"Perhaps. I have made no plans. Take care of *ma petite* Joanna."

"Night, Lucienne," Jo said, then allowed Tyler to direct her to her room.

She got the door open and reached inside to turn on the lights, saying, "Come in for a minute, Tyler." Inside, she stepped out of her shoes and proceeded to the sofa, dropping the key and her messages on the coffee table.

Tyler closed the door and held out the Lowe-pro, asking, "Where do you want this?"

"Anywhere."

He put it beside the other things on the coffee table, then came around to sit with her on the sofa.

"There's something I want to say to you," she said, stifling a yawn.

"And what might that be?" he asked pleasantly.

"What I said this morning is true, Tyler. You and I hardly know each other. I do like you a lot, and your coming here was a wonderful thing to do. You were heroic this evening, running into that place the way you did."

"Oh, I don't know about that. In some circles that act might be construed as sheer lunacy."

"Well, I don't think so. And you were very nice to me while I was having what Jackie would call a spaz attack. The thing is, I want us to be friends. I really do, if that's possible. It's just that, well, you've met Henry, and I think something's happening, if you know what I mean."

"There's no need to explain, Joanna. I understand."

"You do?"

"I think so. And I can't see any reason why we can't be good friends."

"Good. I'm glad. Because you are a nice man and I like you."

"Joanna, it's time for you to go to bed, luv. Your eyes actually are closing, so I'll leave you to it and, if I may, I'll join you for breakfast in the morning."

"Okay."

He got up and walked around the coffee table, on his way to the door. She trailed after, colliding with him when he stopped and turned.

He laughed and reached to stroke her hair. "I do think you're a dear little person. You're not still bothered about the fire, are you?"

She shook her head. "I'm okay. I'm sorry to have behaved like such a crazy person."

"Not at all. Good night, Joanna." He gave her kisses on both cheeks, then opened the door. "Sleep well," he said, and went off down the hall.

"Night," she said, and closed the door.

He stood in the lobby debating whether or not to go to the bar, decided he would, started on his way, and found himself swinging in the opposite direction, climbing the stairs to the second floor. His footsteps were inaudible as he walked along the carpeted hallway, halted, and knocked at the door. A few seconds, the door opened, and a bare arm reached out, took hold of the front of his jacket, and pulled him inside to the sound of laughter.

The only light came from the bathroom, and it took a few moments for his eyes to adjust. During those few moments Lucienne said, "I knew you would come," looped her arms around his neck, and kissed him on the mouth.

"You did, did you?"

"But of course."

Her hair was hanging free and she was wearing some kind of sleep shirt. He put his hands on her hips and she came closer.

"I thought you might change your mind and come for a drink," he said, bending to breathe in the scent of her hair, touching his lips to her temple.

"I have no wish for a drink," she said, her hips subtly shifting under his hands as she lifted her mouth again to his, biting lightly on his lower lip.

The kiss evolved as if in stages so that it seemed to last a very long time. She tasted of mint and tobacco, and her hipbones were prominent against his hands.

"I knew also you would be good to kiss," she said, unwinding her arms from his neck and placing them around his waist.

"Quite a lot you seem to know," he said, as his hands searched for the bottom of the shirt, found it, and slipped underneath. Starting at the tops of her thighs, he drew his hands upward slowly until they covered her breasts, his thumbs pressing into her nipples.

"I knew you would have very good hands," she told him. "I have watched how you use them."

"*I* knew how you'd feel," he countered, pulling the shirt off over her head and letting it drop to the floor. Her hips shifted again and she pressed into him.

"You like me, eh?" she asked, taking hold of his hands, holding first the left and then the right one to her mouth.

"I more than like you." He freed one hand and placed it against the small of her back as he lowered his head to her throat, breathing deeply of her perfume as he left a trail of kisses along her shoulder, partway down her arm, and across to her breast.

She sighed, an appreciative sound, as her hand went over the back of his head, holding him to her. "Come, take these off," she whispered. And he straightened while she busied herself with the buttons on his shirt and he struggled out of the jacket. Then she moved away, into the deeper darkness of the room, whispering, "Come here!" and laughed again. "*Vite!*"

He had a moment of complete paranoia standing there in the dark with his clothes off, wondering if the two women had cooked up some grotesque scheme to humiliate him. Then he told himself not to be such a bloody fool, and followed the sound of her voice to the bed. This simply had to happen, he thought with slight desperation. As they had discussed earlier, he truly believed only children were intentionally cruel. He lay down at her side and threaded his fingers through the silky abundance of her hair. "Am I really so predictable?" he asked her.

"Ah, no! It is only that I can see you wish to make love with me. And so now we do. Come!" she urged, and stretched briefly against the length of his body before rising over top of him to kiss his forehead, his nose, and then his mouth. "It is a long time since I make love with a man who loves women. And you love women, don't you, Monsieur?"

"Oh, yes I do. Particularly exotic French women with ebony hair and fine long legs and impertinent breasts."

"What is this 'impertinent'?"

"It means perfect and proud."

She laughed and drew her nails lightly down the length of his inner arms, giving him goose bumps. "I like English men with not enough flesh and big hands and very little hair at all." She swayed above him so that her breasts just touched against his chest, then she ducked her head and her hair tickled across his ribs, down his belly. "You are very nice," she said after a moment, her hand playing over him, then she ducked her head again.

He could scarcely believe they'd moved so quickly, with no preamble, to so intense an intimacy. A minute or two, then he sat up, took hold of her, turned her and put her belly-down on the bed so that he could take his hands and mouth on a slow tour from the nape of her neck down the length of her body to her feet before turning her over in order to repeat this investigation with even more deliberation.

"I love this," she murmured. "This is wonderful, wonderful."

"Is there a need for precautions?" he asked, his mouth against hers.

"No need."

"Lovely." Wrapping her in his arms, they rolled over so that she lay above him.

She raised herself up and sat astride his hips, guiding him inside her. "Just touch me here, *chéri*. Ah, yes."

Her body a curved-back arc, she lifted and fell sinuously, knowingly, reading the pressure of his hands and the thrust of his body, gradually increasing the tempo until she froze, her fingers digging into his flesh as she drew at him, deep interior waves he found irresistible. And then she came toppling down on his chest to bury her face in the side of his neck, laughing softly.

"I knew you would be good," she told him with a kiss.

"You are beyond my wildest, Mademoiselle."

"Ah, yes?"

"Oh, yes, indeed."

"There is much to say for older women, eh?"

"Very definitely. You are a wonder."

"You also are a wonder," she said, and eased away from him to reach for her cigarettes, then changed her mind and settled her head on the pillow.

"You prefer the dark, do you?"

"Only sometimes."

"That's good, because I'd like to be able to see you next time."

She didn't respond, but he thought nothing of it, and folded his arms under his head, temporarily sated and very happy. He was aware of her moving beside him and assumed she was making herself comfortable. Then she groaned, and the sound was so unmistakably one of pain that the hair rose on his arms and he asked, "Are you all right, Lucienne?" When she failed to answer, he felt for the switch on the bedside lamp, found it, and turned on the light to see her wound into a knot, her forehead on her knees, her arms locked tightly around her drawn-up legs. "What is it?" he asked anxiously, watching her rock from side to side in obvious and terrible pain. "Jesus Christ! You really were ill last evening."

"You didn't believe this?" She raised her head slightly to look at him, and he was shocked by the waxy look of her skin and the beads of perspiration gathering at her hairline.

"What can I do?" he asked, on his knees beside her. "Perhaps I should fetch Joanna—"

"No!" she got out, then groaned again, shutting her eyes tightly.

"The hotel doctor, then."

"*No!*"

"Well, at least tell me what it is, if you know, so I can try to be of some help here. I can't just sit and *watch*. Let me help."

"It is endo—in the womb," she gasped.

"Right!" he said decisively, and sprang into action. In the bathroom he turned on the cold-water faucet, snatched up one of the hand towels, then tested the water. Tepid. "Bloody hell!" He turned off the faucet and went to the small refrigerator, relieved to find two full trays of ice. He pulled one of the plastic dry-cleaning bags from a hanger in the closet, then carried the plastic and the two trays of ice back to the bed. "First thing, you've got to lie back, straighten out."

"I cannot!"

"You're going to have to." Putting everything down on the floor, he sat beside her and began trying to get her to unwind her arms and legs. "You must try," he said. "I'm sure it comforts you to fold yourself into a knot, but it can only heighten the pain. Come on now." Keeping his voice low, he encouraged her to lie back. "Please trust me," he said, his eyes on the terrible bruise above her navel as he laid the plastic across her midriff, then emptied the ice from both trays on top of it. Centering the ice, he closed the sides of the plastic bag over the cubes, then held his hand flat on top of the package he'd created. "In a minute or two, you'll feel much better," he promised.

"If I do not," she said between her teeth, "I will die."

"What a thing to say!" he chided with a smile. "Try to untense your muscles," he instructed, caressing her brow with his free hand. "I know it's dreadful, but you must try. The more tense you are, trying to fight it, the more painful it's going to be."

"How do you know this?" she challenged, starting to feel the cold penetrating her abdomen.

"In my long-departed youth I put in my time with the National Service. Conscription," he explained. "I did my stint with a medical corps. Learned quite a few useful things. This is one of them. Any better?"

"A little."

"You see," he smiled again. "I'm more than just another pretty face, my lovely. How did you get that nasty bruise?"

"Some other time I will tell you."

"Fair enough. Have you seen a doctor about this problem?"

"I have."

"And nothing was prescribed?"

"I refused."

"What did you refuse?"

"Everything."

"I see. You prefer pain to some sort of remedy?"

"Please!"

"You'll forgive me, I hope, if I suggest you should see another doctor?"

"I have made an appointment. I go Monday."

"I see. And how long has this been going on?" he asked, checking to make sure the ice wasn't leaking.

"Some time."

"Some time," he repeated. "I'm beginning to acquire some skill at translating your cryptic answers. Some time undoutedly means *quite* some time."

"I detest doctors!"

"That's sensible."

"You make fun of me!" she accused.

"Only a bit. You really should have this seen to, you know."

"I am seeing to it. On Monday."

"You know what I think? I think if you're feeling reasonably well come Monday you won't bother to keep that appointment. And I suspect that if you don't keep the appointment, you're going to end up in a lot of trouble. So I think it might be a good idea if someone came along to make sure you do keep the appointment."

"What are you saying?"

"I'm saying, I'll go with you, hold your hand should it prove necessary."

"Why would you do this?"

"I suppose because I like you. Better, isn't it?"

She nodded, her features slowly relaxing, her eyelids beginning to droop.

"We'll give it a few more minutes, then tuck you up."

"I want a cigarette," she said, moving to reach for the pack on the bedside table.

"I'll get it. You stay still." He lit a cigarette, handed it to her, then placed an ashtray close by.

"You are very kind," she said. "Men are not usually good with illness."

"I wouldn't say I was good with it. It just doesn't frighten me. And I've got some interest in your well-being. I'd like to think we'd see one another again."

"You would like this, eh?" She managed a smile.

"Wouldn't you?"

"Yes, I would like this. You make good love."

"I was inspired. I think you should put that cigarette out and try to get some sleep. I'll get rid of the ice, then make sure you're settled for the night."

Returning from the bathroom, he plucked the cigarette from her fingers, surprised her by taking a puff and inhaling deeply, then put it out.

"You are going now?" she asked.

"Well, I thought . . ."

"Stay," she said, then added, "Please."

"Mademoiselle says stay, therefore I must stay." He climbed into the bed, gathered her up as if she were weightless, and cradled her in his arms like a child, his hands smoothing and stroking as he said, "Go to sleep now. I'll stay for a bit."

"A kiss?"

He kissed her softly, then eased her back against his chest. "Pain gone?"

"Tyler, I like you very much. Thank you for caring for me."

It was a matter of semantics, of course. What she meant was "Thank you for looking after me." But he much preferred her words, finding in them a somewhat ironic potential.

"Thank *you*, Mademoiselle, for a most memorable experience. It is my great pleasure and privilege to care for you."

"You are so English," she said sleepily.

"And you are so deliciously French. Sleep now."

Twenty-six

J O WAS JUST ABOUT TO GO TO BREAKFAST WHEN SHE REMEMBERED THE messages she'd collected the night before. One was from Laura, asking her to stop by her office in the morning. Another was from Jackie, saying he'd finally managed to convince his family to spend a few hours away from the hotel, and he hoped maybe to see her at dinner. The third was a telex from Henry that had obviously been sent before she'd left her message on his machine. PLEASE RING ME AT OFFICE FRIDAY. HENRY.

From the brevity and terseness it seemed likely it was business he wanted to discuss with her. She'd call after breakfast, and no doubt he'd be every bit as brief and terse as his telex. Talking to Henry in person was one thing; talking to him over the telephone quite another. Over the telephone he usually sounded somewhat irritable and even unfriendly. In the years that she'd known him, she'd come to accept that telephones and Henry were not compatible. Yet she'd been hoping—foolishly, she now told herself—that this would change because of last week's events. As she headed for the terrace, she was gearing up for what she believed was bound to be a not especially heartwarming telephone conversation, and wondered, too, why, just because her feelings had undergone a change, she thought that Henry's would as well. She hadn't actually declared herself to him.

Tyler was already there. She went directly to his table, saying, "Hi. You're early. I was thinking I'd have some coffee and get my notes done before you came."

"Joanna." He half stood as she pulled out a chair, then sank back into his seat. He looked frazzled, although he was freshly shaved and smelled nicely of his lemony after-shave.

526

The waiter came, she asked for coffee, then turned back to Tyler, who was sitting with his hands laced together on the tabletop.

"You look worn out, Tyler. Didn't you sleep well?"

"I scarcely slept at all. Look, Joanna. This is rather awkward, and I hope you won't misunderstand."

"Don't confess, okay?" she said with a smile. "Whatever you do on your own time is none of my business, and it's not up to me to judge it one way or another."

"That does make it a bit easier. You see, I didn't believe you the other evening, about Lucienne's being ill. And I apologize for that, because there's no question that she is. I spent much of the night trying to help her with the pain. Unfortunately, as you undoubtedly know already, she has a complete and, to me, bewildering aversion to the medical profession."

"I know how she is."

"Yes, well. I finally succeeded in convincing her at four this morning that she really must see someone, and soon. I rang her doctor in Paris. Luckily, he speaks quite good English. And after explaining the situation, he said he'd see her later this afternoon. So I've booked tickets on the first available flight, and I'm taking her back to Paris. All the arrangements have been made, and a water taxi's coming in half an hour."

"My God!" Jo exclaimed. "How bad is it? Where is she?"

"It's pretty bloody bad. She's just organizing the last of her bits and pieces, then she'll join us. The thing is, I felt if I didn't escort her, she simply wouldn't go."

"I think you're right about that."

He looked at his hands, and unlaced his fingers. "I didn't want you to think I was jumping from one woman to another, that sort of thing. I truly did, and do, feel something needed to be done. She's really very ill, Joanna."

"Did you think I was going to be mad, or jealous, or something?" she asked him. "And why would I be? I mean, I know she's not well. And if you've managed to talk her into seeing a doctor, then good for you. The fact that you'd take her personally is very goddamned impressive, Tyler."

"The last thing I imagined, when I set out on this trip, was that I'd be accompanying a woman I've only just met to a hospital in Paris."

"You're taking her to a *hospital*? And she agreed?"

"I omitted some of the details. I simply said her doctor would see her. I had the decided impression that if I mentioned the word 'hospital' she'd refuse in no uncertain terms. Given the struggle I had to get her permission to ring the doctor in the first place, I hardly thought it wise to say more than was needed."

"Why are you doing this, Tyler?"

"Haven't the faintest," he admitted. "It needs to be done, and there isn't anyone else. You're not available; you have commitments. Although I'm sure you'd chuck it all and go with her. But my time happens to be free at the moment, and it seems the only decent thing to do. Being truthful, I have to tell you I was frightened for her."

"She's terrified they'll insist on her having surgery of some kind, even a hysterectomy."

"From what her doctor told me, I gather she may not have a choice in the matter. She's left it a very long time. He first saw her for the problem close to three years ago. I'm ignorant on the subject, suffice it to say, but I am able to recognize great pain when I see it, and she's in absolute bloody agony. It's nothing short of amazing that she's managed to function at all in her condition, let alone turn herself out as she does to such dazzling effect.

"I know it sounds unlikely," he said, his eyes on hers, "but I've come to care rather a lot for her in a very short period of time." He emitted a grim laugh. "Last night was like being in the trenches together—a great deal compressed into a very short time. We talked for hours, or rather, I talked, trying to distract her. I admitted things out loud I've never admitted to anyone, not even to myself. Especially not to myself. It may not lead anywhere, but I feel obliged to see this through." He glanced away, then dropped his voice to say, "Don't say anything to her, please. She's coming now."

Even if he hadn't warned her, Jo would have known. Lucienne looked unwell, even with the artful application of makeup. Her eyes were sunken and there was a tightness around her mouth as she sat down and said a subdued good morning.

"Tyler says you're leaving," Jo said cheerily, "the two of you running off together. Very nice."

"Does he tell you how I have disgraced myself?" Lucienne asked, looking at Tyler. "Has he told you he has become my nurse?"

"No," Jo lied, also looking at Tyler. "He hasn't said a thing."

"Well, it is true. I am falling in pieces and he is very kind to stay with me."

"Tyler's a very kind man," Jo said.

"Mignon, this looks bad," she said, taking hold of Jo's hand. "Please don't be angry."

"Why would I be angry?" Jo asked with genuine candor. "If anything, I'm glad somebody's finally looking after you, because you sure as hell aren't doing much of a job of looking after yourself. I just want the two of you to promise you'll call me and let me know how it goes."

"Oh, of course!" Tyler said quickly. "I intended all along to do that."

"Are you going to have something to eat before you go?" Jo asked, "Is there time?"

"I will have coffee with you," Lucienne said, her hand very tight around Jo's. "And this man is complaining of hunger for hours. Eat!" she told Tyler. "I will not run away."

The moment he was out of earshot at the buffet, Lucienne whispered, "I thought it would be a diversion, eh? But he has been so good, and I am very afraid. You think I am bad to allow him to come with me? I am thinking only weak women, silly women, fall on men this way."

"You're not weak or silly. And maybe *he* needs to do this," Jo told her.

"I know they will cut me, Joanna; they will take everything away, and I am very much afraid."

"Tyler will stay with you. He'll make sure you're all right."

"He will stay, but he cannot make sure I am all right," she said sagely. "And he cannot take away the fear. But I am so grateful that he would do this for me. And I am sad to leave you. You will telephone to me, come to see me?"

"You know I will," Jo assured her.

"He makes me to care for him, eh? Big surprise. If it was Paolo and I was sick, he would run away. But this man, he is like my papa. He holds me like a baby, and he *sings* to me." She smiled and shook her head.

"He sang to you?"

"Unbelievable, eh? He rocks me, and he sings, and I am able to sleep."

"God, Lucienne. Maybe the two of you have found what you've both been needing."

"I do not need," Lucienne declared.

"Oh, *please*! We all need, Lucienne. Every last one of us wants to be special to somebody else. And I'll tell you one thing I know for sure: Tyler's not some half-assed jerk who's going to belt you around if you say or do something he doesn't like."

Lucienne's grip was suddenly fierce, her cheeks sucked in, her eyes clamped shut.

"God, it's really bad, isn't it?" Jo said worriedly. "Let me give you another one of my Valium. Maybe it'll help."

"Please," Lucienne whispered. "I will take anything now to help with the pain."

Jo freed her hand to open her bag. She gave Lucienne a tablet, then poured some water for her.

"How is it that you have these?" Lucienne asked after she'd swallowed the tablet.

"They're muscle relaxants, for my neck and shoulder. Listen, even if it turns out you do have to have surgery, at least you won't suffer anymore.

You'll be able to enjoy your life again. And if you change your mind and decide sometime you want to have a child, there are lots of kids waiting to be adopted. Your life is important. It's important to me. I don't want to lose you."

Tyler came back to the table with a heaped plate. "I know it's obscene, but I'm ravenous."

"He eats everything they put into the room—the chocolate, and the crackers, the sweets, all," Lucienne told Jo. "When we are home, I will have to feed him."

Around a mouthful of cereal Tyler said, "She's going to give me my very own table Chez Lucienne."

"I have not said I would do this."

"You'll have to," he grinned at her. "It's my nursing fee. And cheap at half the price."

"You are not eating, Mignon?"

"I'll see you two off first. God, I'm going to miss you both. My last day in Venice, and no one to play with."

"Pah! You will go out and take hundreds of pictures. And tomorrow you will go on the train and make many new friends."

"Maybe," Jo said, doubting this. "It won't be the same without you. And I'm getting a little tired of looking at everything through the camera. I might just give myself and my eyes a break and go sightseeing empty-handed."

"Impossible," Tyler said. "Joanna without her camera is like a vase without flowers."

"What?" Jo laughed.

"It's part of you. Surely you accept that," he told her.

"I do, but that doesn't mean I can't get tired of it."

"True," he conceded. "But it's also probably your very dearest friend, and you take it with you for company and protection, even consolation."

"Very profound, Tyler."

"Profound and true. I envy you your camera and your lenses and your built-in armor. Most of us go about with no protection at all."

"It's too early in the morning for this," she said. "Give me a break and just eat."

At that moment one of the assistant managers came to the table to say, "Signor Emmons, your water taxi is come."

"Thank you. Would you tell him we'll be just a few minutes?"

"Very good."

"Bloody hell!" Tyler groused. "I haven't finished."

"Take your croissants with you," Jo said, "and eat them in the taxi."

"Brilliant. You *are* clever!" He scooped up the last of the yogurt, wiped his mouth, plonked the napkin on the table, and said to Lucienne, *"Mademoiselle, nous départons."*

Lucienne shook her head. "His French is deplorable."

Jo told the waiter she'd be returning, then walked with Tyler and Lucienne to the landing stage. At the foot of the walkway, Lucienne turned abruptly and embraced Jo, fervently whispering, "Don't forget me, Mignon."

"Never! Take care of yourself, and be well. I'll be thinking about you."

Her arms still around Jo, Lucienne leaned away to say, "Only good things have happened since I meet you, Mignon. *I* will not lose *you* now, eh? You will telephone to me, come to visit?"

"I will, I promise."

"Bon!" She kissed Jo on both cheeks, then turned and allowed the boatman to assist her into the water taxi.

"I'll ring you first chance I have," Tyler told Jo.

"Please do. I'm so worried about her."

"So am I," he confessed, then gave her a pair of kisses, and followed Lucienne into the boat.

Jo's hands went automatically to the camera. She lifted it and took a few shots of the two of them standing in the taxi, then lowered the camera and waved until they were out of sight. And once they were gone, she let out her breath slowly before turning to go back to the terrace.

While she tore a croissant into small pieces, she tried to write up her notes, but couldn't begin. All she could think about was Jimmy's death and Lucienne's illness. The pleasure she'd experienced on this trip was suddenly overshadowed by sadness and by a feeling of aloneness. There was no one on the terrace she recognized, and the people she'd come to know so well since leaving London had all gone. She gave up on the notes and was tucking the book into her bag when Laura came over and stood with her hands on the back of one of the chairs. "Good morning, Joanna. How are you?"

"Oh, I'm fine. I was about to come to see you."

"Yes? Good. I am free today," she said. "I thought you might like to come with me to see some of Venice you would perhaps not have a chance to see otherwise."

"I'd love that. I've just been sitting here trying not to feel sorry for myself."

"Your friends have had bad luck," she said. "Everyone is sad about Sir James. And now Lucienne goes. Always she is so much fun."

"I take it you know her from her previous visits."

"Oh, yes," Laura said brightly. "And I have been to her restaurant in Paris. You have been?"

"Not yet, but I hope to get there soon."

"It is very special. And the food is magnificent. But the people, they come because of Lucienne. She is most charming, *molto bella*. Such clothes, uh?"

"Fabulous," Jo agreed. "I'm really going to hate to leave here, you know. Everybody's been so nice, all the Orient-Express people, and the hotel staff."

"They like you," Laura said simply. "You show you are pleased, so we all wish to please you more. Now! I have some little work to do in my office, then we go. Yes?"

"Great. By the way, do you think I could have a couple of the menus to refer to for my piece?"

"I will make a package," Laura told her, and went off.

Jo returned to her room to put in a call to Henry. As she waited for the operator to ring her back, she drummed her fingers on her thighs, hoping his call to her had been personal and not about business.

When he came on the line, he sounded very cheerful. "How are you?" he asked. "I did get your message last evening. Seems we crossed wires," he chuckled, and there was the slightest edge to the sound.

"I'm kind of blue, Henry. Tell me about you, about what you've been doing."

"Oh, the usual, you know. The garden's doing beautifully. Weather's still glorious. And have you had a smashing time?"

"Yup, smashing. Do you miss me, Henry?"

A pause. Then, "Yes, I do, actually."

"Look, I know you're at the office, and I know you hate taking personal calls at the office; furthermore, I'm beginning to realize you hate telephone calls in general. But will you, just this once, please, try to overcome your hatred and say something nice to me? I feel really shaky right now—I'll explain why when I see you. But if you'll humor me, I'll say something nice to you."

Another pause. Then: "I was thinking there's ample room below stairs for a darkroom. I went down the other evening to have a look round, and thought it would do rather nicely. There's access to running water and, all in all, it's not bad. I've never done anything about it, you see, and there's quite a lot of usable space."

"Ah," she said. "That's nice, but it's not *nice*."

"Sorry you don't think so," he said curtly. "You're quite correct in assuming this is not my favorite pastime."

"You're definitely not a star on the telephone, that's for sure."

"*One* does *one's* best," he said. "And having done it, I do believe you are now obliged to say something nice to me."

"Are you kidding?" she laughed.

"No, I am not. And I've another call waiting, so hurry it along. I mean, really, Jo! First, it's 'important,' now it's 'nice.' What, *one* wonders, will be next?"

"I don't know. I'm not there yet."

"Come along. I did do my best, and it's now your turn."

"Okay, here goes. I want to stay," she said, then quickly added, "another week. At least. Would that be okay?"

"Not much of a star turn yourself, Jo dear. But yes, naturally, it's okay."

"Thank you."

"I am still waiting to hear your something 'nice,' " he reminded her.

"Okay. Henry?"

"Yes, Jo?"

She gulped down some air, said, "I think I love you," then slammed down the receiver and sat staring at it, her heart pounding. "Jesus H. Christ!" she said to the telephone. *"Christ!"* She sat for a few moments, then thought he might call her back, so she jumped up, snatched her things, and went to find Laura.

The sadness hit her again late that afternoon while she packed. She'd bought gifts the day before for Tyler and Lucienne, but hadn't had a chance to give them. Now they sat, wrapped and set aside, somehow reproaching her for her forgetfulness. Then she wondered about the mask she'd bought for Henry, a pale Pierrot's face with burgundy lips and eye slits decorated in such a way as to make the mask appear to be shedding tears. It was a beautiful creation, with black satin ribbons, that she'd selected because she could visualize it on Henry's living room wall. And maybe, she thought, that was presumptuous. Oh, no more presumptuous than blurting out what she had over the telephone before severing the connection in order not to have to hear his response. But she wasn't sorry she'd said it. It was how she seemed to feel, so she'd told him. It was now up to him to show her, one way or another, if it was what he'd wanted to hear.

The bulk of her packing completed, she looked at her luggage and then at the room, sadder still at the knowledge that it was over. She'd have dinner now, come back here to sleep one last time, and then, in the morning, climb on board the train. She didn't want to leave Venice. Who knew what Henry might have to say to her? There was a fair degree of uncertainty facing her, yet she had to go. All journeys had to come to an end. She'd already shot the train, so she'd be free, if she wished, to sit in her compartment and stare out the window at the scenery. If she wanted, she could go sit in the bar car and have a drink and listen to the piano music. She almost wished the Pentax had failed on the southbound trip so that she'd be forced to pay as close attention to details as she had on the way out. The need to work would again lend purpose and meaning to her presence on the train.

In the shower she told herself none of it mattered. She'd get back to London to find Gracie had lined up five more jobs, and she'd have to be in Montana a week from Wednesday, or in Auckland two weeks from tomorrow to cover some goddamned kiwi festival or something. Then she'd be bitching and groaning about that. You chose it, kiddo! You were the one who said you'd be glad to travel on assignment; you were the one who could see money, and success, and potential, in going to twenty different places in any given year. But what'll you do when you're fifty, huh? Are you still going to be hopping on planes with the camera bag, rushing to meet some magazine's deadline because you've got no personal deadline of your own? Is this what you're going to do until you're too old, or too wrecked from dragging the equipment around, to go on the road anymore? Or do you want to follow through, find out what Henry's got in mind?

I want Henry! she thought, and felt a jolt of something awfully like dread at the idea that she was putting so much store in the events of so short a period of time. But he was so goddamned sweet—the way he'd put her to bed that first night in London; the way he'd looked on his knees in the garden; the way he'd pleaded his case on the bench in the park. No. If she had a choice, and everyone insisted that she did, then she'd choose Henry, take her chances with Henry. She'd still be hopping on planes, and dragging equipment around, but someone would be waiting for her. The only question was: Would Henry choose her? Did saying some space would make a good darkroom constitute any kind of commitment?

The maître d' gave her a table at the edge of the terrace, from which she could look out at the Canale San Giorgio and watch the water traffic. As she ate the fresh spinach pasta in a basil-and-tomato sauce, and the salad nutty with arugula, which the waiter had made for her from the cart, she watched ominous clouds gather over the city in the distance, and sizzling streaks of lightning illuminate the buildings. A rising breeze lifted the tablecloths and turned the pages of her notebook on the table. She was the only guest seated out in the open. Everyone else had been placed beneath the canopy extending from the hotel wall. She didn't mind. From this vantage point, she was able to view the tremendous storm as it slowly approached over the canal. She ate slowly, winding the pasta around her fork the way the Italians did, the way she'd seen Laura do it at lunch. A glass of crisp white wine to wash it down, then a mouthful of the best salad she'd ever had.

The boom of thunder was coming closer, the breeze increasing to a wind. She felt quite bold, out there unprotected from the elements. She was determined to stay until the storm was ready to break directly overhead, and she wouldn't move a moment sooner. She hadn't watched a storm this way since that summer years and years ago when her parents had rented a house on Fishers Island, and she and Beamer had crouched on the balcony outside her bedroom to exclaim over a ferocious storm they could see across Hay Harbor. She'd never forgotten the excitement of being secure and sheltered while the sky was split by zagging streaks of lightning and the house behind them seemed to shake with the thunder. She'd held Beamer's hand, and the two of them had laughed, pointing and shouting, "Look over there! Oh, over there! Look!" until her mother had come to stand at the door behind them saying, "Are the two of you aware that it's three in the morning, and some people are trying to sleep? Could you possibly try not to shriek?" And then she'd stood behind them to watch, so silent, so wonderfully fragrant, that it was quite some time before they realized she was no longer there. Now, she was gone forever. *Goodbye, Lily. Be happy, Mom.*

She was finishing her coffee when the storm broke overhead and one of the concierges came to the table to say, "Signorina James, a telephone call, please."

She picked up her bag, stood, and began moving toward the door just as the rain came cascading down. Perfect timing, she congratulated herself, and went to the booth in the hall.

"Joanna, it's Tyler."

"Tyler! How is everything? How is Lucienne?"

He sighed tiredly. "It's been quite a day, Joanna. As we both knew she would, she got quite hysterical when she saw I was taking her to the hospital and not to the doctor's office. The only way I could induce her to go through the front door was to promise I'd stay with her, no matter what. I have *never* seen anyone so cataleptically terrified of a *place*. But I gave her my word I would stay, and I did. I had to hold her hand through the examination, and she refused to allow me to leave for so much as a minute, so the doctor—a very decent chap, by the way, and most tolerant, under the circumstances—had to give us both the news. Which was that she was in fairly desperate condition and he wanted to perform emergency surgery, which, he said, was the only chance she was going to have, very literally, to save her life. Then, it took the two of us the better part of an hour to convince her her life was worth saving and that a short period under anesthetic wasn't the torture she somehow imagined it to be. And, of course, the only way she could be persuaded to sign the consent form was if I swore to her I would go with her right into the operating theater.

You can well imagine the doctor's delight at this. But he was so concerned, and so determined, that he agreed."

"My God, Tyler! It sounds awful."

"You haven't heard the worst. We had to get a nurse to stay with her, to talk to her and hold her hand while the doctor went off to prepare for the surgery and I got rigged out in surgical gear. Anyway," he sighed again, "half an hour later there we were in the operating theater. And while they were getting everything ready, she clung to my hand and, convinced, utterly convinced, she wouldn't survive the procedure, told me why she was so afraid. It seems that her parents had, when she was nine years old, placed her in the care of a young nephew in order that she could have her tonsils removed at a Montreal hospital. The nephew was apparently perfectly charming to the parents, and acted the soul of discretion during her overnight stay at the hospital. However, upon taking her home with him where she was to recuperate for a week before a checkup with the doctor followed by her return home, the son of a bitch proceeded to rape her. And not just once, but repeatedly. Then, after threatening to find her and kill her if she told anyone, he took her home.

"Somehow, in the years after, she substituted her hospital stay for the events that came after, and associated hospitals in general with gross abuse. Hence her terror. Hence her soliciting my promise not only to remain with her but to be there when she came round from the anesthetic. I could hardly refuse," he said, his voice starting to break.

"Joanna, it was a horror show! They had to double the normal dosage of anesthetic because she struggled so hard against it that the doctor had already started the incision and she was still awake."

"Oh, my God!"

"It was dreadful, dreadful," he said, starting to weep in noisy sobs. "I'm sorry," he apologized. "Just one moment."

She could hear him put the telephone down, then he blew his nose, coughed, and came back on the line.

"Sorry," he said again. "The doctor," he continued, "as if to prove to me how urgent the need was for the surgery, was good enough to show me, in an enamel basin, the condition of the organs he removed from her body. As if I were another doctor, or someone accustomed to the sight of such things. Christ! They were literally, and I mean literally, disintegrating. He touched an instrument to them, to illustrate, and they simply came apart. I very nearly passed out, and one of the nurses had to give me a whiff of ammonia. Anyway, after telling me she was very fortunate to have come in when she did, he sent the lot off for biopsy, sewed her back up, and said she'd be right as rain in a matter of weeks. Provided, of course, the biopsy came back negative. Which, thank God, it did."

"Poor you," Jo said. "Poor Lucienne. How is she now?"

"She's sleeping. They've shot her full of all sorts of drugs, and she's out of the recovery ward and into a regular room. I'm stopping the night with her."

"You sound so worn out. Are you all right?"

"Never mind me!" he said impatiently. "I want to fly to Canada, find the child-raping son of a bitch, and strangle him with my bare hands. I have *never* felt such helpless, overwhelming rage. I want to *do* something, but there's nothing I can do," he ranted. "I want to put my fist through a wall, kill someone. I've never *been* so angry."

"You *are* doing something," she told him. "You've done it, Tyler. There isn't anything else."

"Christ!" he cried. "While she was on that table, Joanna, I stood there and I prayed. I didn't know what I'd do if she didn't come round. I imagined her dead, and was suddenly terrified that I'd never see her laugh, or hear her voice again, have her tease me the way she does, taking the Mickey. Am I mad?" he asked. "Have I lost my senses? I'm here in a hospital in Paris with a woman I've known for what, three days, four? And if anything happens to her, I simply don't know what I'll do."

"Is there something wrong with that?" she asked him. "Do you have some objection to caring?" Listen to me! she thought. I sound like Anne. "Life's too goddamned short, Tyler. *It is too goddamned short.*"

"It is," he said, sounding less frenzied. "You're right, it is. We've been through so much. It feels as if it's been going on for weeks, months. I've known her all my life, and I can't possibly let go now."

"Then don't. It isn't written anywhere that you have to."

"I must get back," he said suddenly, "in case she awakens and I'm not there."

"When she does wake up, tell her I love her. And I'll be coming to see her. Both of you, if you're still there."

"I think I'll be here, Joanna. I think I'm going to be here for quite some time."

"That's good, Tyler. It really is. And I love you for seeing her through this."

"Thank you for letting me rant and rave. I know it wasn't quite what any of us had in mind."

"*Please don't thank me*, Tyler. Will you keep me posted?"

"My word on it. Good night, Jo."

"Bye, Tyler. Don't forget to give her my love. And try to get some rest."

The air inside the booth had grown very warm and stuffy, and it was a relief to open the door and step outside. She was far too distressed by what Tyler had told her to go back to her room for the early night's sleep she'd planned. So she went along to the bar. And on her way inside she stopped to place some lire on the piano top, and asked the pianist to play the theme from *Borsalino*.

Twenty-seven

AFTER TWO BELLINIS IN THE BAR, A STOP AT THE CONCIERGE'S DESK TO order a water taxi to take her to the station in the morning and to pick up the envelope left for her by the tourist board with information on the Malipiero Trevisan Palace, she returned to her room and stood for a long time at the patio doors watching the storm whipping the trees at the front of the hotel. Then she went to bed and had anxiety-ridden dreams of death and diseased organs and angry confrontations. She saw her dream self sitting with a bottle of gin in the dark of Henry's living room, telling a small child, who was also her, to go away. Lucienne stood naked in a boat, a gaping hole beneath her ribs and her spinal column visible. Tyler shouted down the length of an ornate and gleaming coffin whose top sat open to reveal Anne's corpse, while Jimmy pushed at him, asking him please to be a little more respectful.

Twice in the night she got up to go to the bathroom, where she drank several glasses of water, then stood holding the glass, gazing at her fuzzy reflection while she waited for the latest dream siege to recede.

By six she was sitting in her nightgown on the sofa with her notebook, writing about what she'd seen on her two-hour tour with Laura the day before. The time constraints had been considerable, since everything closed at noon, and she'd chased after Laura from one place to the next, taking pictures on the run and hoping she'd be able to find guide books that would tell her where she'd been.

Now all she could recall were random details—a miniature statue of some saint; a haunting triptych of religious significance; glass cases of hand-embroidered antique religious garments; a darkened vestry with a window in one corner through which light fell like an ax, cutting the room into two separate segments.

By seven-fifteen she was in the dining room—it had stopped raining, but the outdoor furniture was still wet—helping herself to croissants from the acrylic warming bin. There were few people about this early; the dining room was very quiet. The terrace bore a litter of stripped leaves, broken blossoms, and evaporating puddles of rain water. She ate, feeling drugged and sluggish—the cumulative effects of more than a week with little sleep making themselves felt. She checked to make sure she'd put the Dramamine pills in her purse. If she spent one more sleepless night, especially on the train, she'd collapse. And she couldn't afford the luxury of taking to her bed for a few days, not with a visit promised to Anne, and one certain trip to see Lucienne in Paris. And then, of course, there was Henry. So she'd take some Dramamine and knock herself out on the train in order to have the energy she'd need.

After breakfast she went to give the concierge his tip along with the equivalent of fifty dollars and the name of Lucienne's hospital, and received his solemn guarantee that he would make all the arrangements for flowers to be sent in her name. Then she stopped in the kitchen to shake hands with and say goodbye to Renato and his assistants.

As she double-checked the drawers and closets of her room, she wondered where Jackie was. She hoped to be able to say goodbye to him, but just in case he wasn't around, she wrote a note saying how much she'd enjoyed their time together and asking him to stay in touch.

She cleaned the portable Melitta and packed it into a corner of the Hartmann. She made sure she put the Walkman and the microspeakers into her carry-on bag. And then the concierge rang to say her water taxi had arrived. She asked for a porter to come for her luggage, laid some lire on the TV console where the maid would be sure to find it, then followed the porter to the lobby, where a small group had assembled to see her off: Laura, Jackie, the concierge who'd arranged her camera purchase, and the maître d'. The concierge and the maître d' expressed their pleasure at meeting her, then excused themselves to return to work. Jackie and Laura walked with her to the landing stage.

"Come back again very soon," Laura said, giving her a hug before presenting her with a gift-wrapped package. "Something to remember us by."

"Thank you for everything," Jo told her.

"Don't forget to send me some pictures," Jackie said, also giving her a wrapped package. "And thanks a lot for taking me around, and for showing me how to take pictures, Joey. You're really cool."

Jo hugged him and mussed his hair, saying with a smile, "You've given me hope for the future, Jackie old boy. If the other kids turn out half as terrific as you, we're looking pretty good."

"Wait till I start sending you *my* pictures," he threatened. "Maybe you'll change your mind."

"No, I won't," she told him. "I'll just write back with helpful hints. Seriously, Jackie," she said, taking his hand, "I had some of the best times of my life with you. Just eat some junk every now and then. It's good for you."

He laughed and said, "The minute you're gone, I'll order a burger and fries."

"Right!" She climbed into the boat and waved to Laura and Jackie until she could no longer see them. Then she went to the rear of the taxi for her last look at the city.

When she arrived at Santa Lucia, a stocky man wearing a CIGA Hotels badge came racing down the steps to the taxi. "Signorina James? I am asked by the Cipriani to assist you in checking in."

"That's great," she said, glad not to have to cope alone with her bags as well as with the crush of people in the station. "Thank you." She paid the boatman, then had to rush to keep up with the CIGA representative, who'd taken the Hartmann as well as her carry-on bag and was racing back up the steps and into the station.

At the VS-O-E check-in, he left her, apologizing for his haste, and explaining, "I have other boats I must meet. *Scusi, scusi.*"

She pulled out some money to tip him, but he held up his hands, shaking his head and smiling, then tore off.

"*Ciao*, Joanna!"

Jo turned to see Giovanna and said, "Hi! How are you? It's great to see you."

"I come to see you off," she said. "Also, the Lalique carriage is on today and I thought if your pictures are not good, maybe you like to take more."

"They're okay, but I wouldn't mind taking a few more."

"Okay. We check your bag, and I take you on."

As they were walking down the platform, Giovanna said, "I have told them to put you into a different carriage, so you are not freezing this time with the air conditioning."

"Bless your heart."

"So now first we put away your bag, then we go to see the Lalique. Okay?"

"Great. This is so sweet of you."

"I wanted to see you to say goodbye. You have a good time in Venice?"

"The best. I have enough material for about five features."

"Maybe you should make a book. Here is your carriage."

Giovanna stayed until Jo had had a chance to admire the Lalique carriage in full sunlight with the curtains open and everything freshly cleaned and polished. Then she said that she had to get back to the depot, and Jo descended onto the platform with her to exchange hugs and say goodbye.

"Have a good trip, Joanna," Giovanna said. "You come back, huh?"

Jo stayed on the platform to get some shots of the arriving passengers and the stewards with their clipboards waiting to direct them to their compartments. Then she went back on board to unpack her clothes for the evening and the next day. That done, she set up the Walkman and the speakers, popped in the sound track of *Manhattan*—Gershwin music that felt most appropriate for the train—and sat down to open her gifts. Laura had given her a journal with painted scenes of Venice at the top of every page. And Jackie's gift was a pointy-headed pottery Viking, complete with spear. A note inside said, "He's also a whistle. You can blow his head, if you'll excuse the expression. Love, Jackie."

Just as the train began to move, a handsome young man knocked at her open door and introduced himself as Adrian, the chief steward. "Is there anything you need? I've been told I'm to look after you." He said it with a smile that dimpled his cheeks.

"I can't think of a thing," she smiled back at him. "But if I do, I'll let you know."

"Be sure you do," he said, and went on his way.

All the staff she'd met on the southbound journey greeted her effusively, and were most appreciative of the prints she'd brought for them. Luke, the waiter from the bar, beamed at her; Gian Paolo, the waiter with the memorabilia collection thanked her shyly but profusely; Giuseppe welcomed her with a deep bow. It made her feel as if she belonged to an elite minority of people privy to the innermost workings of the train. She felt proud and quite humbled at being on her second trip on this extraordinary vehicle and wished she could, as Lucienne did, ride it whenever she was in need of cosseting or diversion.

To give herself courage at dinner, because she was not only eating alone but also didn't have a camera with her, she ordered a half-bottle of St. Émilion to drink with the salad she had in lieu of St. Peter's fish steamed with carrots and zucchini, and the roast duckling breast and duck liver sautéed in muscat wine, with mange-tout peas, thin-sliced pan-fried potatoes, and the brie she selected in preference to the caramelized walnut sponge cake listed on the menu. By the time her coffee came, she was having trouble staying awake. She took two Dramamine, paid in sterling for the wine, and headed along to the bar car to see what was going on.

There were perhaps two dozen people in evening dress having aperitifs before the second dinner sitting. The atmosphere in the car was subdued, and the pianist's rendering of a Viennese waltz seemed to be making people comatose. Luke greeted her happily, asking if she was going to stay for a drink or some coffee, but she told him she was off to bed and would see him in the morning. She wasn't up to sitting alone in the bar car.

Again she had to undress in stages, noting as she did how small the compartment felt in its nighttime configuration. But at least this time she wasn't cold, and she'd sleep, thanks to the Dramamine. By the time she'd bathed at the basin and packed away the clothes she'd just removed, her mouth had gone into the familiar dry stage the pills always created before they knocked her out.

She lay down, settled the blankets around herself, closed her eyes, and at once fell asleep.

The steward's knock awakened her at eight-thirty, and she sat up to let him in, thanked him, then raised the shades to see that it was raining as they passed through the French countryside. Another half-hour and they'd be in Paris. While she ate, she toyed briefly with the idea of dressing quickly and leaving the train in Paris to go to see Lucienne. Impossible. Even as she was considering the idea, the train was speeding through the outlying areas of the city. At just before one in the afternoon they'd get to Boulogne and transfer to the Sealink. Venice was a day and a night behind her. London, and Henry, were ahead.

God! she thought, pausing with a half-dipped fragment of croissant poised over her coffee cup. What if his primary reaction to her abrupt declaration was discomfort? Oh, come *on*, Joanna! Two telexes, flowers, and the phone calls proved his interest. And Anne was right. She had to take this chance because she really didn't want to get to be a fifty-year-old photographer running around the world because there was no one to come home to. The photographer part was fine, but the rest of it wasn't.

Don't let me down, Henry! If this whole thing's only in my head, I'm going to feel like the biggest fool of all time.

There were eighty-seven passengers on this northbound journey, and better than a third of them left the train in Paris, while only twelve got on for the ride to London. Hence the bar car was very quiet. And the brunch —she simply couldn't believe how consistently hungry she was on the train—was also quiet.

She tried not to wolf down the scrambled-eggs-with-smoked-salmon appetizer, followed by broiled lobster in butter sauce accompanied by one of the baked, stuffed potatoes she'd watched Renato prepare. The caramelized apple tartlets were heavenly. She drank two cups of coffee, then

tipped the dining car staff and Giuseppe before returning to her compartment to prepare for their arrival in Boulogne. The time had flown by. It
seemed as if she'd only just climbed on board and already she was following the others to the ferry. And as on her previous crossing, she was lulled
to sleep by the all but unnoticeable motion of the ship as it surged across
the Channel.

One of the lounge staff came to tap her on the shoulder, saying, "We've
arrived at Folkestone. We'll be leaving the ship momentarily."

Jo sat up, her mouth still dry from last night's Dramamine, and collected her belongings. She made a mental note to mention somewhere in
her article something about arriving to ride the train in a well-rested state.
It was all too easy to sleep the trip away.

The cream and brown British Pullmans were waiting. And once the
passengers were settled in the coaches, the white-suited waiters at once
began serving an afternoon tea of dainty finger sandwiches, scones with
clotted cream and strawberry jam, chocolate shortbread, and Ceylon tea.
She ate yet again, wondering what it was about train travel that provoked
such enormous hunger. She could see herself dieting for the next six
months as a result of this sustained gluttony. And no sooner had she
finished the last of her tea than she fell asleep, only to jerk awake as the
train rounded a bend in the tracks. She looked around guiltily, hoping no
one had seen her asleep with her mouth hanging open. She was turning
into a gorging narcoleptic, she thought, staring out the window as the train
brought her closer by the minute to London.

Undoubtedly, Henry would have left dozens of Post-its appended to
every available surface. Eat-me chicken, and chocolate biccies, and cream
in fridge. Henry Hart, Hotelier with the three-piece suits and the Vandyke beard, who looked so dear when he slept.

They were slowing to pull into Victoria, the rails branching to reach the
many platforms. An hour, perhaps, and she'd be at the house in Chelsea.
She checked herself in her compact mirror, put on fresh lipstick, then got
out money to tip the waiters. She was back. It was over. She took a long
last look around the magnificent parlor car and prepared to leave the train.

After so many hours in motion it felt odd to walk on firm ground. She
started down the long platform, bags in both hands, moving carefully until
she could get used to the lack of sway. She looked up to see how much
farther it was to where they were off-loading the luggage, and there was
Henry, one hand raised to catch her attention. Suddenly, she was smiling
so hard it made her cheeks ache, while he worked his way among the
passengers and threw his arms wide as he came toward her. She put her
things down on the platform and walked right into his embrace.

After a moment she said, "God, Henry! I was worried you'd think I was
crazy or something."

"I am well aware that you're crazy."

"That's nice, thank you. Give me a kiss."

He held her away to have a look at her, saying, "You look well, but a bit tired."

"All I did on the way back here is sleep. Give me a kiss, Henry, or I'll stop asking."

"Don't do that," he said, and kissed her. Then he said, "An entire week you've been putting me through my paces."

"You know what I think? I think you liked it," she said, her nose touching his. "And you like me, too, don't you, Henry?"

"Of course I like you. Although I do believe you're even crazier than I thought."

"But do you really, honestly, like me?"

"Don't be a ninny, Jo. I've always liked you. In fact," he said a bit slyly, "I *think* I love you."

"Henry!" She laughed and hugged him again. His neck was smooth and soft; he smelled wonderful. "I can hardly believe it," she said. "Here you are, in one of your famous three-piece suits, Henry Hart, Hotelier."

"Hardly famous. You do realize people are bestowing slightly fatuous, rather doting smiles upon us?"

"I don't care. Do you care?"

"Not if you don't. You're getting me to do things I'd never do for another living soul."

"Such as?"

"Making me say 'nice' things, 'important' things. Do you put everyone through such rigorous testing, Jo dear?"

"Is that what you think I was doing?"

"Wasn't it?"

"No. I just wanted to know where I stood. So! What do we do now?"

"First things first. We'll collect the rest of your luggage. Then we'll go out and get a taxi."

"What if I never want to leave, Henry?" she asked, as he picked up her carry-on bag.

"Were you planning to? I mean to say, I've already been onto the chap who did the work on the house, and he's drawing up an estimate for your darkroom. I've also been making inquiries about a work permit for you."

"You're kidding!" she said as they moved several yards along the platform, then stopped. You care about me, she thought; you're concerned with my well-being.

"Of course I'm not kidding. Do you honestly think I'd joke about taking time away from the office, from my many other clients?"

"Oh, good heavens, no!" she quipped. "Seriously. Why would you do all that?"

"Well," he shot her a grin, "it isn't every day someone rings me from Venice to say she *thinks* she loves me."

"No, I suppose not."

"From Leeds perhaps, or even Manchester. But never from Venice."

She hooked her arm around his neck and kissed him once more. "You know what, Henry?"

"What, Jo?"

"I think it's taken me too damned long to figure things out."

"Ah, well. I'm noted for my patience. And better late, as they say, than never."

"There are some people I really want you to meet, Henry."

"I always enjoy meeting new people."

"You'll love them."

"I will, will I?" He ran his hand over her hair.

"You know what I mean."

"Yes, I do. Before we do anything, however, you simply must see the astonishing new improvements to the kitchen."

"Oh, yeah? Like what?"

"Super things: cushions on the countertops, scented candles, incense, that sort of thing."

She laughed loudly. "Can't wait to check it all out!"

"I'm sure you'll find everything to your satisfaction."

"I'm sure I will," she murmured into his neck.

"We should look for your bag," he said.

"It'll wait another moment. Say something significant, Henry."

"I knew it! Didn't I just know it!" He held her away again. "Let me take you home now, Jo. I'd really hate to go to the trouble of dragging you into one of those empty carriages and risk having some waiter come upon us in the fragrant delicious."

"In the *what*?" she roared with laughter.

"You heard me."

"Yup, I did."

"You seem quite—different, somehow; changed."

"Yes, I am. Say, 'Thank you, Train.' "

"I beg your pardon?"

"Nothing." She kissed him on the tip of the nose, then turned inside the circle of his arm to point, saying, "That's my bag right over there. Let's grab it and go."

"Don't you want to hear my 'significant' something?"

"I already heard." She smiled at him. "Every single word. Now come on. Take me home, Henry."

Night Magic

I am indebted and grateful to Claire Smith for her unfailing support, and to my friends Nina Ring Aamundsen, Philamena Stevanovic, Gloria Goodman, and Dina Watson for their wholehearted enthusiasm.

"Only try to find me out, no matter how I may be disguised, as I love you dearly, and in making me happy you will find your own happiness. Be as true-hearted as you are beautiful, and we shall have nothing left to wish for."

"What can I do, Prince, to make you happy?" said Beauty.

Beauty and the Beast
(La Belle et la bête)
Madame de Villeneuve

"Love me and you shall see! All I wanted was to be loved for myself. If you loved me, I shall be gentle as a lamb; and you could do anything with me that you pleased."

The Phantom of the Opera
(Le Fantôme de l'opéra)
Gaston Leroux

1968–1987

One

ON HER THIRTEENTH BIRTHDAY, MARISA'S FATHER TOLD HER THAT being her parent was the single most challenging and rewarding experience of his life.

"I had my doubts, you know, Keed," he admitted that day. "The last thing I thought would happen would be my raising you alone. Scared the living hell out of me—more than anything else ever did, I promise you. But you were my girl. We wanted you, Rebecca and I, and I just couldn't turn you over full-time to a nanny and go on about my business, pretending I was doing my best by you. It felt like I was on my knees when she died." He looked off into the corner of the dining room, his voice dropping. "I just couldn't believe it, couldn't believe anyone could die that way at the age of twenty-four. Twenty-four," he repeated, with fresh disbelief. "We were such wise-asses, Risa; we thought we were going to live forever. I at least should've known better. I mean, I was older. But your mother . . . she was still a kid. She was so young . . ." His eyes returned to her. "I remember sitting on the landing staring out the window, with the feeling there was this tremendously heavy *thing* weighing me down. I couldn't move, the weight of it was so enormous. And then I heard you come running down the hall and I turned to watch you, with your arms held out and your little legs pumping away. Laughing. How could you be laughing? I asked myself. And then I realized death wasn't something that could possibly be real to you, not the way it was to me. You were only a baby, two years old. What could death mean to you? I remember that moment in every detail, remember understanding I had a choice: I could call for Sarah to come get you, or I could open my arms and catch you when you came running. I could make something of what your mother and I had created."

"So you caught me." Risa smiled.

"Damned right, I did! You weren't some accident that happened to us, Keed. You were someone we wanted, someone we'd planned for. And now, here you are, a teenager. I'd sure as hell like to know how that happened, when a few minutes ago you were this titch I could pick up with one hand."

"You'd get a hernia if you tried picking me up now with both!" She laughed.

"To say the least."

"You always go all mushy on my birthdays," she said fondly.

"I thought that's what birthdays are for," he replied, fixing an ingenuous expression on his face.

"Naturally," she agreed. "And I hoped you'd go so mushy this year you'd maybe break down and let me have a dog."

"You are one relentless kid," he told her with a smile. "The answer's the same as it's always been: no. I've explained this to you maybe three or four hundred times. Dogs make me nervous, Risa. I can't live with one. I'm sorry. You're going to have to wait until you're an adult, with a place of your own. Then you can have eight or ten dogs, if you want them."

"Okay," she backed down. "But I had to try."

"Do me a favor, Keed, and give it up. You've 'had to try' one time too many."

"All right, Dad. I'm sorry."

That evening at dinner he gave her the tortoise-shell combs that had belonged to her mother. She only wore them at home, fearful of losing or having them stolen at school. She intended someday to give the combs and other items of her mother's to her own daughter. And she'd given them in just the way her father had given them to her: on each birthday, to celebrate the occasion.

Over the years he told her he wanted her to have a sense of occasion, to know that some times were more meaningful than others. "You have to earn what you most want, Risa. Otherwise, you'll have shoddy values. And you have to know that things can never be as important as people, or occasions." He paused, then said, "I hate the idea I might be spoiling you."

"I'm not spoiled, Dad," she said very seriously.

"No, you're not," he concurred, proud of her.

He hadn't ever segregated her out of the company of his friends because of her youth; he'd encouraged her to speak her thoughts; he'd tried to teach her to be as thoughtful of his employees as she was of him and of her friends; he'd insisted she believe in her worthiness as a person. He'd worked hard to be sensitive to her needs, to be open and accessible the way he imagined Rebecca would have been to their daughter. He took time away from his business in order to be at home with Risa or to take her away on holidays; they played one-on-one basketball together, and raced each other the length of the driveway. It was all by ear, as he liked to say, all from instinct tempered by good judgment. And she wasn't spoiled. Which had to mean he was succeeding as a parent. She did have a tendency to get hold of an idea and pursue it—like the business of wanting a dog, despite his repeated explanations—but he quite admired her tenacity.

The ongoing, concerted effort he put into guiding Risa through her childhood had an unexpected and gratifying reward in his dealings with the women he saw from time to time. He found himself more attuned to their words and moods, and was able as a result to enjoy their company more. He even, early on, considered remarrying. But in the end he managed to find reasons why it would be unwise to upset the status quo. He couldn't stand the thought of anyone or anything detracting from the closeness he felt to his child. He did study the issue closely, to determine if he was behaving too selfishly, and decided that if his devotion to Risa could be deemed selfish, then he'd live with the consequences. He was happy to watch her evolve and grow. As the years passed, it seemed he required little more than this.

On the evening before her sixteenth birthday, he announced, "It's time for some renovation, Keed. This place is starting to fall down around our ears."

"What renovation?"

"I don't know exactly. The kitchen, primarily, which is driving Kitty crazy. She says if we don't get some decent appliances, she may have to resort to dire action. And you know Kitty. That could be anything from serving up nothing but macaroni every night until we beg for mercy, to leaving us altogether. And we don't want to lose her. Plus, my bathroom plumbing's a disaster. I'm tired of having to shower down the hall. So, I guess, mostly it's a complete overhaul for the kitchen—expanding it, bringing it into the twentieth century. And redoing a couple of the bathrooms. I've got someone coming to look things over—as a personal favor to me, you understand."

"One guy's gonna do the whole thing?" She looked around the room as if trying to gauge the scope of the work.

"Not quite. And this 'one guy' isn't just 'one guy.' I've actually persuaded Erik D'Anton to consider doing the renovation. It's not the kind of thing he'd normally do."

"*Persuaded* him to *consider* it? Who *is* he, anyway?"

"A genius," Cameron Crane answered simply.

Risa rolled her eyes and made a face.

"He's stopping by tonight to have a look at the house."

"Why tonight? Why not during the day when he can really see everything?"

"Erik doesn't do business during the day."

"Why not? What is he, a vampire?" She laughed.

"You'll understand when you meet him."

"You're being very mysterious," she accused.

"I'm really not. You'll understand," he said again, "when you meet him."

"Okay. But this is weird."

"I cannot tell you how pleased I'm going to be when that word finally vanishes from your lexicon."

She got up and went behind her father's chair to press her cheek against the top of his head. "No, I'm not going to ask for a dog," she said with a soft laugh. "So don't get nervous." After a moment, she asked, "How do you do business with someone who only works at night?"

"Quite easily, all things considered." He shifted to pat her arm, then got to his feet. "I've got to dig out the original plans for the house. They're in one of the boxes in the cellar, and I want to do it before Erik arrives."

"Okay. Do I get to sit in on the meeting?"

"Of course, if you want to. He'll be here in about an hour."

"Boy, maybe I should go check to see if there's a full moon."

Instead of laughter, her father frowned. "Go easy, Risa. Erik isn't like anyone else you've ever met."

Sobered, she said, "All right, Dad."

Upstairs in her room she looked at the homework waiting to be done. She didn't feel like working and instead turned on the radio before stretching out on the bed with her arms folded under her head. Three more months until school ended. Then, next year, she'd be a senior and they'd really start putting on the pressure for her to decide what she wanted to do after graduation. The problem was she didn't know. There were so many things she thought she might like to do: art college, to study either painting and drawing or fashion design; a music school to pursue her singing seriously; theater school to study acting, or maybe set or costume design. Why did people expect you to know so young what you wanted to do with the rest of your entire life?

Cousin Brucie was raving away on WABC, going at his usual hundred and fifty words per second. She tuned him out, waiting to hear what they'd play. Most of the time she preferred the stations that played jazz or stuff from the twenties and thirties. It was a song by Bread. "(I'd Like to) Make It with You." She liked the song, mostly because David Gates had a decent voice. But she had to wonder about the time and energy, the books and movies and records all dedicated to the theme of love and sex and romance. The only boys who ever asked her out were the mental midgets, the jocks who thought being seen with her would score points for them. She couldn't stand those guys. The one boy she'd decided to go out with was Hardy Belmont, who'd used up all his courage just phoning to ask her. When they were finally in his car on their way to the movies in Westport, he was so nervous he couldn't talk. He'd kept staring over at her and gulping a lot. She'd felt sorry for him, and to help him out she'd started this totally one-sided conversation that she thought made her sound like a complete moron. Poor Hardy. He had the highest grades in the school, but when it came down to it he was exactly like the rest of them. He'd only asked her out because of the way she looked and not because he really wanted to get to know her.

She couldn't figure out why people got so worked up about the way she looked. For years now she'd been staring at herself in various mirrors, trying to see what people saw when they looked at her. All she could see was that her nose was too short and her forehead too high, and her ears were kind of long, and so was her neck. She was way too tall—by the time she started eighth grade she was already five feet ten—and had practically nothing in the chest department, not to mention arms and legs that would've been better suited to an ape. The only things she liked about herself were her hair, which was long and black and wavy like her mother's, and her eyes, which she thought were a good shape and an interesting amber color. Her skin was white as paste, and ten minutes in the sun turned her into glowing neon. She also had this weird pale line that ran from her navel all the way down her belly, as if she'd been made in two pieces and this line was the seam where they'd joined the parts of her. She was positive nobody else had a seam like hers, and thought she was probably a freak altogether, what with her skinny ankles and wrists, and that line bisecting her dead-white body. Yet the jocks were forever calling her up, chuckling and snorting over the phone. And the girls never wanted to be friends. Except for Meggie. God, but she missed Meggie!

All her life Meggie had lived in the house next door. Then, just like that, she was gone, the family moved to Boston. Sure, they still talked on the phone and wrote letters back and forth, but it wasn't the same. Meggie was already writing about the new friends she'd made and how much better Boston was than Darien. And Risa had no one. The weekends lasted forever; the summer would be endless.

She looked over toward the window, thinking of how, for years, she and Meggie had gone creeping around the old house on Contentment Island, believing it was haunted, terrified the ghostly occupants would come shrieking out at them. They'd crawled around the perimeter of the house on their bellies, trying to get a look inside through the filthy basement windows. Then something would always happen to scare them off and they'd go running, fearfully laughing and breathless, back up the driveway to where they'd hidden their bikes in the bushes, and pedal off back to Meggie's house, or here, to sit huffing on the front steps, laughing and red in the face, exclaiming over their adventure.

A car door slammed. She got up and went to the window to see a tall figure striding toward the front door. Was the man actually wearing a *cape?* Was that what geniuses wore? She wished she could see his face, but a broad-brimmed hat concealed his features. The car was fantastic, sleek and foreign and black, something like a Maserati or a Lamborghini. This was going to be interesting, she thought, hurriedly switching off the radio and straightening her clothes before going to the dressing table for her mother's combs. She'd wear them for luck, although she wasn't sure why. There was a kind of security in the combs, a part of her history tucked snugly against her scalp and holding the hair away from her face.

"Here's Marisa!" her father announced, and she came across the living room with her hand outstretched, a smile on her face, to meet this night-caller, who was standing with his back to her and who began to turn so slowly that it seemed he emerged from the shadows in degrees. It took eons for that turn to be completed, so that her arm grew tired from being extended, and her smile felt exaggerated and unnatural; her entire body ached from the suspense of waiting. The man turned and turned, gradually committing himself to the available light, and in that time Risa was aware of her father watching, and of her inability to look anywhere but at the face being revealed to her. She experienced an odd hesitation in her heart, as if she'd suffered a physical blow, and felt sorrow, terrible sorrow —her own? this man's? She didn't know. She was smiling still. So was her father. But their breathing seemed to have been suspended, as were their thoughts. This man didn't smile, however. His gravity was so pronounced, so habitual, it was like an additional garment he wore.

"Marisa, meet Erik," her father said at last as her hand continued on its route toward the stranger. "Erik, my daughter Marisa," her father said, as her hand was engulfed and held in so fearful and tentative a grip that she could feel the foreign blood pulsing against her fingertips in confirmation of this man's life and reality. Her eyes, she knew, were unblinking as she took in the details of the face before her.

Only his eyes were intact, undamaged. Deep and black, they held her, filled with such a wealth of messages and emotions she couldn't begin to separate and interpret them. In the briefest fragment of time she recognized fear and great intelligence and even, surprisingly, humor. But above all, she saw the sorrow, as dense and impenetrable as something constructed of lead. Around those eyes, which sat behind heavily rimmed spectacles that seemed to be of clear glass, were overlapping ridges of scar tissue, and multi-toned areas of shiny flesh. His face appeared to have been sewn from many tattered patches of flesh. He had no eyebrows, no facial hair. His mouth too was intact but for a deep scar that began at the left corner and ran in an arbitrary path toward his hairline. Yet the eyelashes behind the lenses were quite luxurious, lending a certain innocence to his gaze. There was something about his nose, something to do with the glasses, but she hadn't enough time to figure it out. She was too mesmerized by the face and by the many faded and tortuous trails intersecting the swaths of polished skin. His hair, as if in defiance of the face it might have concealed, was cut short and brushed straight back from his high, rounded forehead. And it *was* a cape he'd been wearing, she saw when she'd regained herself sufficiently to glance away from his ruined face.

"I'm happy to meet you," she said, her hand still joined to this man's.

He nodded as if unable to speak, his fingers gently closed around her long pale hand.

"A drink, Erik?" Cameron asked, bemused by the silent interchange between his daughter and his friend.

"Thank you," Erik spoke at last, simultaneously releasing Risa's hand.

His voice was deep and very soft, no more than a whisper, so that she instinctively leaned closer to hear his words. "Cognac, if you have it, please," he said, his words lent musicality by an English accent, his eyes on Risa.

She couldn't stop staring, at the same time struggling against an impulse to lift her hands to touch that face. She managed a smile, and stood with her fingers laced together in front of her.

Stupidly, Erik wanted to ask Cameron why he'd failed to speak of his daughter's beauty. She was so young. Her bones were only just emerging from behind the protective cushion of youthful flesh. His hands curled into themselves at his sides and he forced himself to turn away at last from the painful radiance of this child and take the seat his host had offered him upon his arrival. To his consternation the girl came to sit in the companion chair that was positioned at an angle to his, and with her arms crossed on her knees, her body bent toward him, she asked in hushed tones, "What happened to you?"

"Risa!" her father exclaimed, handing Erik a snifter of Armagnac.

"Twenty-four years ago," Erik told the girl in a flat, expressionless whisper, "my parents and I set out for a drive in the car one Sunday afternoon. They died. I didn't."

Risa shook her head and sat back, only to lean forward again after a moment. She could see now that he was wearing a sort of mask. It was formed of the glasses and what had to be a false nose, with flesh-colored extensions on either side that partially hid his cheeks. He'd seated himself deep in the wing chair so that the wings cast shadows over his face.

"I didn't mean to be rude," she said, noticing that his hands were magnificent; elegant and graceful, they moved as if independent of his mental commands. One was curved around the balloon of glass, the other lay on the arm of the chair like some resting but ever-vigilant creature. Each time he spoke his hands came to life, gesturing to underscore his whispered words.

"Of course not," Erik said, assaulted by the very sight of her. Refuse this job! he told himself. It wasn't the sort of work he normally accepted, but Cameron was as close to a friend as Erik allowed anyone to be. He had enormous respect for Cameron—for his energy, integrity, and business acumen. But even so, it would be torture to have to return here and encounter this exquisite child with her curious eyes and direct questions. He'd at last constructed his life so that forays outside his house were at a minimum, because it grew progressively more difficult with the passing of the years to deal with the reactions generated in others by the sight of his obscene face. Cameron was one of the few who were willing to deal with the admitted eccentricity of his terms, of night meetings and business transacted primarily by letter or telephone. Erik accepted work nowadays only to prove to himself that his skills were in no way diminished. He had no need of the money, nor of the acclaim his buildings would have brought had he been inclined to accept it. He had no need of anyone or anything. He had his house, his music, the plans he prepared of fantastic buildings no one would ever see. Why add more horrified portraits to those already lining the walls of his memory? No. He would never again take another risk, he vowed, confronting the eyes of this breathtaking girl, whose beauty was more intimidating than anything else he could imagine. It would be so easy, too easy, to fall prey to those dreams of love, of possession, of heat and bodies and minds in concert were he to subject himself to further exposure. But he would do this job, if only for the chance of seeing her one more time. He'd held her hand for those few seconds, and he did not regret that. Marisa. Even her name had a special taste on his tongue. So very young, and possessed of such daunting beauty. Marisa. He felt like weeping at the wrenching pleasure he derived from studying the fall of her hair, the sweet bow of her upper lip, the fullness of her cheek. Marisa.

Two

O NCE THE PLANS HAD BEEN APPROVED AND THE WORK WAS UNDER-
way, Risa anticipated Erik's return to the house. Surely, she reasoned,
he'd have to come to verify that the workmen were proceeding as they
should. But if he did come, it must have been in the dead of night and in
secret because neither she nor her father saw him.

"We're in touch by phone," Cameron told her. "It isn't necessary for
him to make daily site calls."

"But how does he know everything's being done right?"

"He knows because I tell him so, and because he's made a couple of
inspections."

"When?"

"I honestly don't know."

"So he's never going to come back to see how it all turns out?"

Cameron set aside the newspaper he'd been reading to look at his
daughter. "Aren't you happy with the changes, Risa?"

"Oh, sure I am. I mean, the kitchen already looks way better. And the
sliding glass doors are really neat. I like the glassed-in breakfast area a lot.
It's going to be great, like eating in the trees. I just thought," she wound
down, "that he'd be around all the time."

"Are you displaying morbid curiosity, Marisa?"

"I don't know if I know what that means."

"It means: Are you anxious to have another look at him because you
can hardly believe what you saw?"

She pushed her head against the wing of the chair—the chair in which
Erik had sat that night and toward which she'd gravitated nightly ever
since—to consider this question.

"He was so sad," she said, as if his unhappiness had infected her. "He was the saddest human being I've ever met. I mean, I can understand why, but it made me feel so awful, Dad. Really awful. Have you ever seen him smile?"

Cameron shook his head.

"See! That's what I mean. It's so sad."

"And that's why you'd like to see him again, because it's all so sad?"

"Sort of. I can't really explain."

"He wouldn't appreciate being invited here to be stared at, Risa. That would hardly be a kindness."

"But he must be so lonely. Maybe he'd like to come and have dinner with us. Maybe he'd even smile."

"You want to make him smile?" Cameron was having difficulty following his daughter's logic.

"Maybe I do. It's weird, you know, but I keep thinking about him. Like all the time. Really. I'll be in the middle of math or something and I'll start thinking about him, wondering where he lives, and if somebody looks after him. Does he do his own laundry? And what does he do if something needs dry-cleaning? Who does his grocery shopping? Can you imagine him at Palmer's Market?" She gave a bark of laughter, then clapped her hand over her mouth, appalled at herself. "I didn't mean that. I'm really sorry. But you know what I'm saying."

"I'm not sure I do, Keed."

"Why don't you invite him to dinner, Dad?"

"He wouldn't come."

"I bet he'd come if *I* asked him."

Again, Cameron paused and stared at her. Then he said, "Don't make a contest out of this, Risa. A lot of what you kids think is funny is downright cruel. And it's very goddamned cruel to make fun of a man like Erik."

"I'd *never* do anything like that!" she protested.

"Then why all this business about inviting him to dinner?"

"I liked him," she said quietly.

"What, precisely, did you like?"

"Dad, I don't know! Couldn't you pick up the phone and ask him?"

"If you say or do anything . . ."

"You *know* I never would! God! You're making me sound like one of the stone idiots from school. Go on. Call and ask him. I'll bet if you say it's my idea he'll come."

With his hand on the receiver, Cameron wondered if it was possible that his sixteen-year-old daughter had a crush on a brilliant, disfigured man of thirty-one. And if that was the case, how did he, Cameron, feel about that? Certainly he'd never imagined anyone less than intact for

Risa. Did he have the right to make emotional judgment calls for her? Hadn't he always insisted she follow the dictates of her own heart? And besides, she was only sixteen and probably just trying to demonstrate a little kindness. He lifted the receiver, and Risa said, "Tell him if he'll come, I'll cook the entire meal myself."

"Dear God!" Cameron made a face, then smiled and with a shrug picked up the receiver.

Raskin answered the telephone, asked who was calling, then put Mr. Crane on hold while he buzzed the music room on the intercom.

As was his habit, Erik simply picked up the receiver and listened.

"Mr. Crane's on line one," Raskin told him.

Erik remained silent, deliberating, then said, "I'll speak with him," and punched the button for line one.

"Cameron," said Erik, "is there some problem?"

"None at all," Cameron answered, rattled as always by the knowledge that one never opened a conversation with Erik in the traditional way by inquiring after his health. A "how are you" was met with no response at all. One was expected to swing directly into conversation. "Actually, Risa and I are sitting here and she's been after me to invite you to dinner. She's asked me to tell you that if you'll agree to come, she'll cook the entire meal herself."

Erik sharply drew in his breath and held the telephone away from his ear. His free hand fluttered like a startled butterfly, then settled firmly on the edge of the table. He wanted to say no, to say he couldn't possibly subject himself to the agony of swallowing food in front of witnesses. But, closing his eyes for a moment, he could too easily see her exceptional face and her tall, as yet unfinished form, and he felt himself being drawn irreclaimably toward the prospect of seeing her one more time. So dangerous, he warned himself. Too dangerous. A beautiful child, she'll destroy you. And you have no skills for dealing with what you most crave and admire.

"What day, what time?" he asked.

"Let me consult the chef," Cameron said with a laugh, breaking off to speak to his daughter.

Erik could hear her answering voice, the clear treble notes of her reply, and felt himself lurching, sinking, all the hundreds of thousands of tiny cells comprising his being sent into uncertainty by a schoolgirl's few words.

"Friday evening at nine? Would that be convenient?" Cameron wanted to know.

"At nine," Erik confirmed, and with a trembling hand put down the instrument. He couldn't possibly return to his music now. He was too distraught. He called Raskin on the intercom to say, "I'll eat in my room. I won't need you anymore this evening."

"Okay, Erik. I'll make up a tray. I'm not going out, so if you need anything, I'll be around."

Thank God for Raskin, Erik thought, pacing the room, the music now silenced. Poor alienated, shattered Raskin. Who else but I would find him ideally suited for employment? A veteran of an unethical war who screams in his sleep and goes on night maneuvers in a sleeping Connecticut commuter town. A man of vast intelligence, the best education, and keeper of a thousand personal horrors, who can cook and clean, who can type and answer telephones, who has a master's in engineering from Yale to put to good use, who appears perfectly intact and even handsome in the eyes of some, but who cannot function in any effective way in "normal" society. I even envy Raskin, he thought miserably. For all the cracks in his foundation, Raskin is able to deal with the many women who respond eagerly to his bald proposals tendered in bars and other local establishments. Quite often the telephone rings for Raskin and it is some woman with a wish to position herself in open receptivity beneath Raskin's shrapnel-torn body in the hope of pleasure and disclosures. Raskin is most dispassionate in the telling of some of his less salacious conquests. He has an artist's eye for details, a musician's feel for the rhythm of encounter, and a madman's obsession for detachment. How, Erik wondered, would Raskin respond to Marisa?

An interesting proposition, that. Perhaps her curiosity would be such that she'd be eager to see this house and know the lengths to which he'd gone to secure his privacy.

He turned to survey the room, alarmingly able to visualize Marisa in one of the black upholstered chairs with graceful gilt legs and rounded backs that so reminded him of the chests of pouter pigeons. The contrast of her, the very black and white of her, would be sublime in this room. Perhaps she'd even sing for him. Hadn't Cameron said his daughter had quite a wonderful voice, and that she sang frequently for their guests? Cameron's pride in the girl was boundless. Did his indulgence of her run to humiliating business associates for sport? The very notion caused Erik's hands to shape themselves into fists. A mistake, mistake, mistake. Accepting an invitation to dinner as if he were the eligible bachelor in the neighborhood and not a freak who hid behind eight-foot-high stockade fencing topped with barbed wire; a chimera who protected himself with the very latest in security measures that ran to electric eyes and heat sensors, not to mention television monitors and cameras placed everywhere on the property; a miscreation who so mistrusted everyone that even his own home was honeycombed with hidden doorways and listening devices because anyone, even Raskin, might be tempted to sell him out for some obscure or arcane reason.

It was so difficult not to succumb entirely to what he knew to be utter paranoia, but it was right, entirely right, to exercise every possible caution because people would harm you if they could. They didn't see that beneath the harrowing surface lived someone not so very dissimilar to them. No. They believed that the face mirrored a ravaged soul. And perhaps it did. But he had proof of his onetime humanity. He had the photographs of that child, proof of the early ages, the progress he'd made from birth through to the age of seven when—he could still see it, could still hear the smashing, grinding impact roaring in his ears—they'd been crushed, ground to nothing human by a runaway lorry; when the little boy who'd always liked to stand on the back seat as they took their Sunday drives through the countryside so he'd be able to see everything, the full three hundred and sixty degrees of everything, when that little boy ricocheted from window to window like some bit of weightless debris that ended at last flung over the ruined bodies of his parents, the parts of his parents that had, in death, tried to claim him with clutching hands and leaking blood, to drag him down with them into the steaming horror of their irredeemably shattered beings. He could remember how he'd screamed, the cries breaking his chest as he'd begged not to go with them, *Don't take me with you!* he'd implored them, fighting to break free of lifeless curling fingers and lethal bone shards and wetness he knew had been contained within them, those people so giddy and pleased with the lives they wore like expensive clothing. They were the only ones who'd ever loved him, who'd ever truly cared, who'd called him Darling Boy and spun him in dizzying circles from one to the other, always catching him before he fell, always so pleased by their Clever Boy, their Darling Erik, who lived now in a cage of his own constructing, tenanted only by himself and a man others knew only to fear but who, to Erik, made better than perfect sense. If you've viewed the wreckage, if you've been there first-hand to see the meaningless losses, you will only make sense to those others who recognize and empathize with your vision.

And now he was daring to go out, to sit and try to eat while his eyes ravished this child who, all unknowingly, was picking at his exposed innards with her dainty, clear-polished fingertips.

Risa pored through cookbooks, planning the dinner. On Wednesday after school she went to three different markets to get the ingredients, and on Thursday morning she advised her father of the menu and asked if he'd buy appropriate wines. She took Friday off from school and claimed the kitchen immediately after breakfast.

"This is new and fascinatin'," Kitty observed, sitting in the newly created breakfast area finishing a cigarette and her coffee. "Since when d'you have an overwhelmin' interest in cookin'?"

"Since now," Risa answered, glancing back and forth at the index recipe cards she'd prepared while she assembled ingredients.

"Why?" Kitty asked, exhaling a plume of smoke that drifted upward through her tightly permed, carrot-colored hair. "I've known you most all your life and I never once have seen you show the least bit of interest in cookin' anything more complicated than popcorn."

"You're forgetting that whole year I made chocolate-chip cookies," Risa reminded her. "And eighth grade when I tried practically every recipe in that casserole cookbook."

"That's one very long time between drinks," Kitty said, putting out the cigarette in the new white ashtray—one of four Erik had ordered for the kitchen, along with a service for twelve of white Wedgwood porcelain."

"This is important," Risa told her, impatient with the conversation. She was truly fond of Kitty; she even loved her, but she wanted to concentrate on getting everything right for that night.

"I didn't know better," Kitty said with a knowing smile, "I'd say you were in love."

"Oh, definitely!" Risa snapped back. "Absolutely. He's a hundred years older than me, for heaven's sake."

"Never stopped nobody before." Kitty gulped down the last of her coffee, got up and carried the white cup and saucer to the sink. "I'm not sure I'm that hot about all this white stuff," she said, rinsing the dishes before popping them into the dishwasher. "You sure you don't want me to help?"

"Positive. You go off and have a swell time with Freda. What're you going to do, anyway?"

"Goin' into the city, do a little shoppin', lunch, this 'n' that. Macy's has a sale on. Might pick up some new sheets. We could do with some."

"Well, you have a nice time."

"You sure about all this?" Kitty looked doubtfully at the crowded top of the new center island. "I don't mind givin' you a hand. We're just playin' it by ear, me 'n' Freed."

"I'm sure I'm sure. You're distracting me, Kitty. I almost forgot the chives."

"Chives, yet. Okay. I'm goin'." She came over, reached into her dress pocket, pulled out a rubber band, and in several quick motions fixed Risa's hair into a pony tail, patting it affectionately. "So you can see what-all you're doin'," she said. "Hope it turns out fine. You get in trouble, I'll be at Freed's for another hour or so. You can call me."

"I won't get in trouble."

"I'd sure like to see this fella you're doin' all this for."

"Good-bye, Kitty. Have a terrific day in the city, Kitty."

Kitty laughed, picked up her handbag from the counter by the door, and, with a skeptical shake of her head, went clicking off down the hallway on the three-inch-high stiletto heels she wore day and night. Some twenty-odd years earlier, a young man Kitty had been dating had so extravagantly admired the look of her legs and slender ankles in her high-heeled shoes that she'd not only made love to him with the shoes on but she'd never once, since then, considered any other footwear. Even her slippers were mules with heels, and decorated in front with bits of mara-bou that wafted in her wake as she traveled about the house of an eve-ning. Her shoes had been a source of amusement to Cameron from the outset, and he'd occasionally stoop to catch one of those drifting feathery bits on the tip of a moistened finger and smile and make some whimsical remark about bordellos.

With Kitty gone, and everything assembled, Risa took a deep breath and sat down for a few minutes to review the index cards one last time before she actually began creating the meal. For appetizers there'd be a tray with a good ripe Brie and imported crackers, as well as a crystal dish of carrot and celery sticks. Then, while her father and Erik finished their drinks, she'd set out the vichyssoise—one of her all-time personal favor-ites. After the soup, she'd bring out the main course: breasts of chicken with shallots and mushrooms in a heavy cream-and-cognac sauce, rice, and French beans. This would be followed by the salad of Boston lettuce, endive, and watercress with a chive dressing. And for dessert, a chocolate mousse, followed by espresso she'd serve in the new white demitasses, with neat little snippets of lemon rind tucked next to the cup. Erik would have to like it. Everybody liked chicken. But what if he didn't like mushrooms? God! She hadn't even thought of that. Meggie, for one, loathed and despised mushrooms. Of course Meggie also loathed and despised books of any kind on any subject, the Beatles, one-on-one bas-ketball, and all classical music. Well, if Erik didn't like them he could push them aside.

Looking up from the cards, she sighed. Food everywhere. Maybe Kitty was right; maybe she did need help. But no! She'd promised to cook the dinner, and she'd do every last bit of it herself. It would be perfect, and he'd smile and compliment her.

Momentarily forgetting the work to be done and the cards in her hand, she thought about poor Erik and his ruined face, and wondered how he looked under the mask. She decided it must be very bad, especially in view of the condition of those areas that showed. Again, she felt that desire to place her hands on his face, to touch those shiny patches of skin.

They'd be soft and cool. His eyes were so grief-stricken, so uncertain. It made her throat constrict and her heart hurt to think of him. Imagine Kitty saying she was in love! It was all Kitty ever thought about, what with her romance novels and her soap operas and her movie-star heroes. Kitty professed to know all about love, claimed to have tried it all, done everything, and had, at the age of forty-one, long since satisfied her curiosity. She knew everything she needed to know about men, thank you very much, she said. And one thing she knew for sure was that there weren't but a handful, Mr. Crane included, of course, worth the powder to blow them away.

Risa thought she probably said stuff like that because no man had ever wanted to marry Kitty, so she was letdown by the way things had turned out in her life. After all, it was only logical that a woman so old who didn't have a husband would be a little bitter on the subject of men. Although, according to her father, when Kitty had first come to them fourteen years before to look after the widower and his baby, every time he'd gone out to the kitchen there'd be some man sitting at the table with a cup of coffee and his eyes on Kitty as she bustled around, flashing her legs in her outrageous high heels.

Kitty was very pretty, although the permanent had been an admitted mistake. "They went 'n' gave me an Afro!" she'd railed upon her return from the hairdresser. "All I wanted was some body, and look what that fool woman went and did!" She'd taken herself off to her room and spent three hours under the shower, shampooing her hair over and over, trying to get rid of some of the curl. She ran the hot water tank dry and her hair came out almost exactly the same. "It'll just have to grow out," she'd said with a sigh. "But, Lord, that tees me off! White people don't look good with Afros. And will you look at this color! Be six or eight weeks at least before this tones down some. I *love* goin' around havin' people think I *chose* to look this way!" She slammed around the kitchen for a few days, then gradually calmed down, only occasionally pausing to put one carefully manicured hand to her hair and mutter, "Still tight as bedsprings, damn it!"

Taking a deep breath, Risa got up and went to the closet for Kitty's apron. As she tied it on she wished fervently that she had a proud full chest, like Kitty's. Kitty really did have a terrific figure, although she wore her clothes way too long, insisting, "Women my age look plain foolish in these mini things. Bad enough I got me an Orphan Annie hairdo!"

Risa couldn't help thinking it would make all the difference if she, too, had a terrific figure. But she wasn't sure how, or why, or to what.

Three

CAMERON WAS BOTH AMUSED AND PUZZLED BY HIS DAUGHTER'S BEHAVior. By eight-fifteen on Friday evening she'd posted herself by the living-room windows, and turned every few moments to look out. In between times she dashed to the kitchen to check the various pots on the stove. Back at her post by the windows, she absently smoothed the skirt of her dress—one Cameron couldn't recall having seen before. It was an unexpectedly somber garment of lightweight black wool with long sleeves and a full skirt, relieved by a round white collar. Her hair was parted in the middle and held back from her face by Rebecca's tortoise-shell combs. She looked pale, yet had a flush to her cheeks as she stood chewing on her lower lip for a moment before suddenly darting across the room to start a record going on the stereo.

"If I'd known this was going to make you so nervous, I wouldn't have agreed to it," Cameron said after half an hour of this performance. "You look on the verge of collapse."

"I'm fine. There's just a lot to think about," she said, again going to the window. "I honestly don't know how Kitty does it, getting it so everything's finished at the same time."

"It's only a meal, Risa, not a career. If it doesn't come together perfectly, no one's going to condemn you. Why don't you sit down for a few minutes, try to relax?"

"I can't. I've got too much to do."

"Well, standing there isn't going to make him arrive any sooner. If Erik said nine, he'll arrive on the button, not a minute before or a minute after. He's almost frighteningly punctual."

"What do you know about him?" she asked with sudden eagerness. "Do you know anything about him?"

"Not a whole lot. He was recommended to me for a job by an old friend of mine who taught Erik at Princeton. That was about six years ago. He was damned good, so I recommended him to a few other people. We've stayed in touch. He'd call to thank me for the referrals, that sort of thing. I know he lives here in town. He has a local number. But I couldn't tell you where. He has a post-office box and his mail goes there. He has an assistant, man named Raskin, who does the fetching and carrying, handles the correspondence, the telephones and so forth. He's also Erik's professional associate. As for Erik, his work is inspired and unique; his jobs are always completed exactly to specification, on time, and on budget. Beyond that, I know very little."

"But you must know more than that. Where does he come from?"

"I believe he grew up in England, although I don't think his parents were English. His degrees are from Princeton, so I'd imagined he lived for some time in New Jersey. French, I think, his parents were. I recall hearing somewhere that his father was a brilliant violinist, but I'm not up on classical music, so I couldn't swear to that. I know Erik plays some instrument, piano perhaps."

"Maybe he'd play for us."

"Don't ask him!" her father said quickly.

"Why not?"

"Just, please, don't! I have a suspicion that simply coming here tonight is as much as he can handle."

"You'd think he'd get bored," she said, almost to herself, once more looking out the window. "Only going out at night, never seeing anyone. It must be awful." As she gazed out at the driveway, she heard an echo of Erik's soft compelling voice saying, "They died. I didn't." She shivered and rubbed her hands up and down her arms. Eight fifty-five. Her stomach was kind of shaky, unsettled, and she thought she probably wouldn't be able to eat. Her whole body was stiff. She wished he'd get there. He'd smile for her; she was certain he would. And she knew he'd be someone else altogether when he did.

"Was his throat, his voice box, you know, injured in the accident? Is that why he whispers?"

"So far as I know, there's not a thing wrong with his larynx. Listen, Keed, I want your promise you're not going to hold an inquisition when the man gets here."

"I'm only curious," she defended herself.

"I hadn't noticed." He laughed and held his hand out to her. "Come here a minute, Risa; talk to me."

She placed her hand in his and stood looking down at him.

"Your hand's like ice." He gave it a squeeze. "Marisa, maybe I'm being a silly old fart, but you've got the symptoms, you know."

"What symptoms?" she asked, resisting the urge to turn toward the windows.

"You're acting like someone in love."

"Oh, crap, Dad!" She laughed, her color heightening. "That's what Kitty said. The both of you have been single too long. You two have one-track minds."

"That's what Kitty said, huh? No flies on our Kitty. Well, maybe that's true and we're looking too closely. But go carefully, Risa. I think you've got a crush on this man, and it's only going to make you unhappy."

"Supposing that was true, why would it make me unhappy?"

"Because nobody at sixteen knows her own mind. You're a long package of exploding hormones and sudden impulses. And neither of those things has anything to do with good judgment. Erik's a grown man with a strange life and a lot of problems. He's not about to take up with a teenager."

At that moment there came the sound of tires on the gravel and Cameron released her hand to look at his watch. "On the dot," he said, sounding pleased. "I'd dearly love to know how he does that."

When he looked up again it was to see that Risa seemed fixed in place, on her face an expression bordering on agony. She appeared on the verge of tears. Then, in an instant, she drew a deep breath, turned and ran off to the kitchen, calling over her shoulder, "Don't forget to turn the record over when it gets to the end of the side. I'll be in in a couple of minutes."

In the kitchen she splashed cold water on her face, then hung over the sink wondering if she was going to be sick. She felt nauseated and strangely afraid. The water she drank from her cupped hands seemed to calm her stomach and she dried herself with a towel before turning her attention to the stove. As she turned the heat off under the rice she had an overpowering desire to run up to her room, hide under the bedclothes, and cry. Her emotions were so tangled, so unfathomable that she wished she'd never instigated any of this.

Her father was showing Erik into the foyer as she returned to the living room to position herself near the fireplace. She was perspiring and her stomach had started dancing again. Erik was there! In his broad-brimmed hat and flowing cape he came over the threshold into the living room, his movements balletic. She hadn't before noticed the way he moved, the sinuous extension of his legs as they drew his torso forward. He was a tall, muscular man who gave the impression of great power. His face was not so startling to her this time, yet his graveness had precisely the same impact as it had at their first meeting. His eyes settled on her and she couldn't look away. They had the effect his hands might have had had he placed them on her body. Wide behind the heavy-rimmed glasses, they held her, unblinking and black. And then his hands rose from beneath the protective cover of the cape and she laughed in delight at the appearance of the pink roses in a paper cone that seemed to materialize in the space between them.

"For you," he said, in that voice that pushed so gently and pleasurably against her ears.

"Thank you." She stepped forward to accept the roses and stood admiring their still-damp color. "I've never been given flowers before," she told him. "I'd better go put them in water."

How splendid she was, pellucid skin and golden eyes, abundant black hair slipping forward as she bent to inhale the bouquet of the just-maturing blossoms. She moved before him like the slowly unspooling frames of a film, indelible impressions, each a minute shock to the system; low-voltage spasms of electric gratification generated by the engine of his impossible longing. For a few moments, he yearned to envelop her, to absorb her into his very cells. Madness! He shook off the cape and surrendered it into Cameron's waiting hands before accepting his host's offer of a drink. As he seated himself in the wing chair and watched Cameron fill glasses, he thought how ridiculous this was, how truly ridiculous. He was playing out a role, acting out some part they'd assigned to him—the visiting business associate; as if he were ordinary, undamaged, a man to whom they were well accustomed.

"It's good of you to come, Erik. I know you rarely socialize."

"I never socialize," Erik answered, more abruptly than he intended. He had, after all, a certain fondness for this man; a fondness that had grown considerably since meeting Marisa. He took a sip of the neat Glenfiddich, allowing it to slide over his tongue and ease its way down his throat. Setting the heavy-bottomed crystal glass down with care, he tried to think of something he might say to soften his remark. "Your daughter," he began, then shifted direction slightly. "It's generous of you to invite me."

"Had I thought for a moment you'd come, I'd have invited you a lot sooner." Cameron gave his guest an open, honest smile. Erik nodded, his hands poised *en pointe* on the arms of the chair. He breathed cautiously, traces of Marisa's faint fragrance tingling in his nostrils as he had a fleeting vision of placing his lips in the curve of her neck while her body flowed like a river into his. The vision created a sudden constriction in his lungs and he reached again for his drink. His free hand reassured itself by stroking briefly the pocket flap of his black cashmere jacket.

"Okay!" Marisa said with an edgy little laugh, coming to sit in the companion chair beside Erik. "Ten minutes until dinner. What're you drinking?" she asked of both men.

"Glenfiddich," her father answered, noticing she'd grown animated and less pale with Erik's arrival.

"Can I have a taste?" she asked Erik, holding her hand out for his glass.

Erik looked inquiringly to her father, who said, "I have no objections. Risa's been tasting my drinks since she was about three."

Erik gave her the glass and watched as she held it to her mouth, took a swallow, then looked at the ceiling while she decided whether or not she cared for the taste.

"It's interesting. Thank you." She returned the glass to Erik. "I'd rather have wine. Have you actually seen the work they've done on the house?"

"I have," Erik told her, his eyes on the impression her lips had left on the rim of his glass, his entire body surging in response. Looking up at her, he lifted the glass in such a way that he was able to drink from precisely the same spot. Foolish, but it thrilled him; a cool kiss.

"Are you pleased?" she asked him.

"Are you?" his deep whisper inquired.

"Yes. Yes, I am," she said decisively. "Every time I sit down for breakfast, I feel great knowing nobody else has a room anything like it. It's like being right outside and yet completely protected."

Again Erik nodded.

"It's a treat being able to use my own bathroom again," Cameron put in, feeling as if he were eavesdropping. There was a silent communication taking place between these two that excluded him utterly. It both fascinated and discomfited him. After all, this was his daughter, his baby, not some woman he scarcely knew. And that, he realized all at once, was a substantial part of what so discomfited him: the understanding that Risa had attained womanhood, but he hadn't noticed until this moment. Yes, she was still shedding the last soft vestiges of her childhood, but she had a woman's height and grace and lure. He was able to see, with quite alarming clarity, how another man—this man, this one man most certainly— might find her highly appealing.

She got up to turn over the record—one of the Mozart piano concertos, Cameron could never remember them by number—and both men watched her lift the cover on the turntable and with the very edges of her fingers take the LP by its outer rim and deftly flip it over.

"I'll organize the first course now," she announced, "if you'd like to come to the table."

"We haven't finished our drinks yet, Risa," Cameron pointed out.

"Bring them with you," she said airily, as if she'd done this dozens of times before. "It'll be another minute or two before we're ready to start."

"Then why," suggested her father indulgently, "don't we just sit here and enjoy our Glenfiddich until those two minutes are up?"

"Oh, Dad!" She was reassuringly childlike again as she capitulated. "All right. But have some of the Brie, then." She dropped to her knees beside the coffee table to cut the cheese, then offered the tray to Erik.

He thought he'd choke if he tried to swallow any food. Yet how could he refuse anything she offered? She smiled at him as he took one of the pieces she'd cut, and he felt the powdery surface of the cheese between his fingers as he noted the golden clarity of her eyes and the all but invisible down on her cheeks. His eyes wanted to close; too much, this proximity. Why had he come here? Why was he subjecting himself to this socialized torture? And how could she look at him that way, so unflinchingly, as if he were someone other than Erik D'Anton, social pariah? He couldn't eat. How could he? But he had to. He could scarcely return this yielding overripe morsel to the tray, or push it down between the cushions and the side of his chair. As she held the tray out to her father, he slipped the cheese into his mouth, bit into its melting, faintly acrid core, chewed quickly, then swallowed. At once he drank the last of the Scotch, allowing it to carry away all the remnants of the unwanted tidbit. There was an entire meal still to come. He might very well asphyxiate in an effort to appease this determined child.

"Okay!" she said. "Now you have to come to the table." She rose and went to push apart the doors to the dining room, standing aside in order that they might appreciate her artful table arrangement: Erik's white porcelain and Dansk stainless-steel cutlery set on white linen, Rebecca's bridal-gift Waterford goblets fracturing the light, and in the center an arrangement of still-green forsythia branches and tall white candles in polished silver candelabra. She'd placed one of Erik's pink roses diagonally across each of the plates.

Erik's hands drew together in a devotional attitude inspired by appreciation of her work. "Lovely!" He turned to look at her with approving eyes.

She waited a moment, hoping he might smile. But he didn't. She seated them, then went to the kitchen for the tray with the vichyssoise. "So far, so good," she said to herself before pushing through from the kitchen.

It all went far more easily than she'd imagined. Somehow, incredibly, everything came together, and she didn't drop anything in her lap or, more importantly, on her father or Erik.

"This is wonderful, Risa." Her father beamed at her. "I'm proud of you, Keed."

"It's splendid," Erik told her across the table, although he could do no more than sample each dish. He was so moved—by her, by the effort she'd made in preparing this sumptuous meal, and by her very presence so close by—he was incapable of ingesting more than a few bites. He drank the wine gratefully and watched her as she ate, and as she glanced over to smile at her father, or even better, at him. He couldn't think what to do. There was no point to promising himself he'd never return here. The thought of her would bring him back if other invitations were not forthcoming. A mistake, mistake, mistake.

But if he were to leave here and not return, he had to know before he left if she could sing. He felt a spark of hope. If she sang and was no better than mediocre, he'd have some hook upon which to hang his departure. He'd be able to discount or discredit her. And so, as she was shepherding them back to the living room for coffee, he ventured to say, "I understand you sing rather well. Would you sing for me?"

Her face creased becomingly with indecision. "Dad's always bragging about me. I'm nowhere near as good as he says. You really don't want to hear me sing."

"Yes," Erik said firmly. "I do."

"Honestly?" Her luminous eyes questioned him.

"Yes."

"Well, okay, if you're sure. Let me just go get the coffee. You two sit down and make yourselves comfortable."

Comfortable? Erik repeated the word to himself as he resumed the wing chair. It was a concept almost entirely alien to him. The only times he felt even remotely close to comfortable were when he worked, or when he involved himself with his music.

After serving the espresso, she went to the grand piano—Rebecca's Steinway—and sat down, at once turning with a self-deprecating grin to say, "Remember, you asked for this." She stared at the keyboard for several moments, rubbing her knuckles as she decided which number to do. Then she spread her fingers over the opening chords of "Sweet and Lovely."

Erik's hands pushed themselves between his knees, which in turn locked tightly, almost painfully, against them, as her wondrous voice oozed over him like warm lotion. Rich as Cornish cream in the low register, clear as early morning air to the E above high C, with quirky phrasing and powerfully intimate intonation, she was a natural. Perfectly pitched, she did admirably eccentric things with the melody line, sang a chorus and a half of good jazz over a perfunctory rendering of the piano chords, and stopped.

Risa turned to acknowledge the applause her father always offered, then looked to see Erik's response. He stood suddenly and took several steps forward, halted, then continued across the room until he was standing directly in front of her. Uncertainly, she held still, for a second wondering if he was going to strike her as his hand, the fingers slightly spread, approached the side of her face. The hand brushed against the hair falling over her shoulders, then pulled back and, with a flourish, he revealed to her the silver dollar standing upright between the first two fingers of his left hand.

Enchanted, she accepted the coin. "You do *magic!*" she laughed. "How terrific!"

"No," he corrected her, grave as ever, "*you* do magic. May I?" he asked, indicating the piano bench.

"Sure." She shifted to the far end of the bench, curious to know what he'd do.

His majestic hands lowered themselves to the keyboard where they lingered for a moment before bearing down to produce the chords that simply had to accompany her.

"Oh, that's wonderful!" she sighed, watching his effortless fingering, the great span and agility of his left hand.

"You come in here," he said, leading out of the introduction and offering her a slight pause in which to insinuate herself into the music. She slid in on cue, his sweet complicitous partner, and sang the song again, even more fluently now that she no longer needed to bother with the accompaniment.

Cameron sat listening to the two of them, watching the way Erik seemed to be breathing in time with Risa, as if he'd achieved something of lifelong importance, and experienced a unique gratification when Erik actually smiled. It seemed an entirely involuntary gesture, perhaps even one of which Erik was unaware. And dear Risa, who'd planned this evening with the hope in mind of making this very thing happen, missed it. She was so lost to the music that she failed to see the transformation she effected in Erik. For several long moments, he was a young, happy man. Then the music was ended and Erik was getting up, saying, "I must go," as he rushed toward the foyer to throw open the closet door and retrieve his hat and cape.

Taken aback by the swiftness of this departure, Risa and Cameron followed after him.

"You don't have to go yet," she protested. "It's still early. And I don't have school tomorrow."

Erik paused in his flight, the cape over his arm, hat in hand. "I must go," he whispered urgently, and looked at Cameron as if for assistance.

"Say good night, Risa," Cameron told his daughter, automatically draping his arm across her shoulders.

"I wish you didn't have to go," she told Erik. "I love the way you play; I loved singing with you. I know tons of other old songs. Maybe you could come again, we could . . ." She trailed off, knowing nothing she could say or do would prevent his leaving.

"Good of you to come, Erik." Cameron shook the man's hand.

"Please come again," Risa said. Then, impulsively, she took a step forward, put a hand on Erik's shoulders, and kissed his cheek.

He reacted as if she'd struck him. His hand went at once to his cheek. He turned, flung open the door, and in seconds was in the sleek black car, driving away.

Risa stood in the open doorway with her father watching the taillights of the car disappear down the driveway, saying, "He didn't have a good time."

Again Cameron put his arm around her shoulders. "He had a great time," he said consolingly. "Probably one of the best times of his life. C'mon, Keed. I'll help you clear up." He closed the door.

"Dad, I feel so *bad*," she said, her face twisting. "He didn't have a great time at all. You're just trying to make me feel better."

"No, I'm not. He smiled, Risa; a great big happy smile."

Her eyes went wide, "He did? When? Where was I?"

"You were singing."

"He did, honestly and truly?"

"Smiled his heart out."

"He smiled and I didn't *see* it? Oh, damn! You promise?"

"Cross my heart."

"D'you think I sang all right?"

"As good as Sarah Vaughan."

"Did you *hear* the way he played? *God!* Wasn't he *great?*"

"You were both great. The dishes're waiting, Risa."

"Okay. I'll be right there. I have to get the coffee cups."

She went into the living room, collected the cups, then stood looking at the piano. He'd sat so close to her their bodies had touched; he'd been so close she'd been able to smell his many aromas—soap, and shampoo, a hint of tobacco. And his clothes had been so soft; the brush of his sleeve against her bare hand had been like a caress. They'd sat right there together on that bench. He'd smiled, but she hadn't seen it. She'd kissed his cheek and it had been as soft and as cool as she'd known it would be. If only he'd stayed a little while longer.

She felt somewhat queasy with mixed disappointment and elation.

Erik picked up the intercom and waited for Raskin to answer.

"Yes, Erik?" came Raskin's even-toned, very Eastern voice.

"Raskin," said Erik, "tell me about your evening with the insurance secretary."

"The one last December?"

"Yes."

"All of it, or just the key parts?"

"The key parts."

"Okay. Let me grab a cigarette. Hold on a minute."

While he waited, Erik settled on the floor with his back against the wall, positioned so he had a full view of his entire bedroom.

"I'm back. Okay. After we left the bar we went in my car and I took her home to her place. She lived in one of those condos in Stamford on Strawberry Hill. We had another drink in the living room, a quick one, then we went into her bedroom . . ."

As Raskin's voice buzzed in his ear, Erik touched his hand to his cheek and mentally transposed the players so that it was he, not Raskin, and it was lovely Marisa, not some nondescript secretary, who came together skin to skin on the cool sheets. Her hair was liquid ebony pouring through his fingers; her mouth opened to emit loving murmurs; her long limbs enclosed him. Marisa, angel. She'd touched her precious mouth to his cheek. She'd kissed him. Marisa.

Four

OR DAYS ERIK'S FACE BURNED WITH THE IMPRINT OF HER KISS. HIS HAND
lifted repeatedly, his fingers gingerly examining the area. He remained
for long hours at a stretch in the music room, the speakers throbbing from
the powerful thrust of Corelli and Vivaldi, Mozart and Handel, Beethoven
and Chopin. When he grew weary of the confining legitimacies of the
classical compositions, he switched to lengthy periods of Bill Evans or
Charlie Parker, Wes Montgomery or Oscar Peterson, Dizzy Gillespie or
Charlie Byrd. He walked the room from side to side, corner to corner, in a
turmoil. His brain seething, he waged war against the instinct that urged
him to return to that house to see the child again. His eyes haunted by too
many images of her, he fought his terrible need, his impossible longings.
The flames of the candles dimmed as his frantic passage created drafts in
the vast underfurnished room.

Pausing for moments, his eyes searching the deeper darkness of the
perimeter, he'd imagine the door opening to reveal her figure on the
threshold, and the potential for all but fatal joy promoted by his imaginings destroyed his taste for food and drink. The trays Raskin brought
remained untouched, and silently Raskin removed them after a time, only
to replace them later with fresh offerings.

Back and forth, back and forth, he paced out the nights, music howling
in his ears and candle wax dripping silently to form unheeded sculptures.
Once when a tape ended, he sat down at the piano and spread his hands
over the keys, but couldn't begin to play. The sound of his yearning had
no melodic line. He was helpless in the face of what he craved, yet
powerless to give it meter and rhyme. Another time, determined, he was
able to play four bars of introduction and opened his mouth to sing, but

had no voice. She'd come to stand between his intent and his ability to make good on that intent. How could he push whispered words into the tallow-scented air when all he truly wished to hear was the schoolgirl's self-taught brilliance? If only she'd been ordinary! If only, when she'd emitted her first notes, they'd been slightly less than true, even a little less felt. But no. She sang with divine purity, unimpeachable clarity.

What should he do? None of Raskin's stories contained clues that might assist him. And there was no one to whom he could speak of his heart's folly. He'd been rendered voiceless and heartsick by a child who could be harmed, it seemed, simply by the admission of his hopeless passion for her. She might, yes, be able to look at him without evincing horror; she could even place her acid kiss upon his patchwork cheek, but she could never respond with anything less than outraged contempt to an invitation to enter the inner sanctum of his life and feelings.

And why should she respond otherwise? What, after all, did he truly know? His experience of women was predicated completely on hearsay. He was the invisible partner in Raskin's conquests, the uninvited third party whose unseen presence and weightless flesh followed in Raskin's wake. Through his compliant employee he'd gained access to the world of erotic pleasures, to acquiescent limbs, billowy breasts, and moistly yielding chasms. But he could stake no claim on any direct contact, ever, with the exception of one child's lips grazing his startled cheek. And it burned, it scalded, it seared. His hands groped the smoky air, his fingers spread wide to catch any stray wisp of possibility. Nothing. Opening, closing, his pathetic hands searched the limited atmosphere, settling at last on the hated face where they pulled and punished the dismal ruin that was all that remained of Darling Erik's childhood beauty. The mask set aside, his fingers probed the bony mass and puckered ridges of what had, long ago, been a young child's promising future.

I *can't* go back! I must *never* go back! he roared inside the cavern of his skull. Kindness and pity and the sudden laughter of a beautiful young girl were not the guaranteed precursors of love. He would never be granted access to the resilient sweep of her embrace. No one so beautiful could ever conceive of leaving the daylight world to which she had a natural claim in order to be smothered by the midnight secrecy of his illicit caress.

Oh, but to see her again! To note the way the flesh dimpled and acceded to the flexing of her lissome limbs; to hear her draw in breath and see the rise and fall of her chest as it filled, then expelled exotic sounds that caused his skin to swell and shudder as if it might burst from the effort to contain such undeserved pleasure. What could he do? he asked the walls, the ceiling, the floor. What should he do? he asked Rachmaninoff, Respighi, Poulenc. One way or another, he'd die from this breach of common sense. Either she'd murder him with her young girl's good intentions, or he'd expire from the mammoth effort of attempting to suppress more emotion than he'd ever thought to feel.

He could not go back; he dared not go back. He'd held so long, so tenaciously to this life he was doomed to live, he couldn't now surrender it for the sake of these unworthy and adolescent yearnings for a girl half his age. She had smiled for him; she'd cooked and sung for him; she'd made it seem she sincerely wished to have more of his company; and she'd kissed him. With her eyes fully open, her hand placed trustingly on his shoulder, she'd leaned across the abyss to press her lips to his noisome face. It was once; it was done; he would not go back.

Four days of intermittent sleep, four endless nights of parading back and forth before the arras he'd embroidered with the silken threads of his besotted longings, and the need was beaten down to a manageable level. Leaving the music room, he walked through the dark house, breathing the refreshing air through nostrils still thick with the scent of the girl, to climb the stairs to his room. Throwing off his clothes, he closed himself into the unlit bathroom to sink into soothing hot water and soak away the countless coils of tension. He could not go back.

Days, then weeks, passed and the anticipated telephone call didn't come. Risa couldn't understand it. She'd been so positive, so utterly convinced he'd call. But he didn't. And she tried to imagine why not. Perhaps the meal hadn't been the success she'd thought; or her singing had been too amateurish; she shouldn't have given in to her impulse to kiss him. She'd never forget his reaction, the way he'd looked—as if she'd struck him. He'd fled from her, roaring away in that unearthly black vehicle, its taillights like spots of blood on black velvet. There were too many things she could see now she shouldn't have done. Yet she'd been so certain he liked her. Her father assured her Erik had actually smiled. But she hadn't seen it for herself, and her father had always made his best effort to ensure her happiness. Her father was prejudiced in her favor, blind to her many faults and shortcomings. God! She couldn't believe Erik didn't intend to call, and couldn't bear the idea, rapidly becoming a conviction, that he wouldn't.

"Daddy, phone him," she asked Cameron one night just before school ended for the year. "Or give me the number and let me phone him."

"What for?"

"We'll ask him to dinner again. You said he enjoyed himself. Maybe he's embarrassed or something to call us, so we'll have to call him."

"Risa, what's the point of this? You can't force people to do things just because you want them to."

"But he wants to come back. I know he does."

She was, her father thought, inches away from hysteria. If one telephone call would keep her from going over the edge, what harm could there be to it? "All right, Risa. I'll call him."

"Oh, thank you." She sat down at his feet as Cameron reached for the telephone after looking up the number in his address book.

Raskin asked who was calling, then went off the line for quite some time.

"What's happening?" Risa asked, tugging at her father's trouser cuff.

"Nothing. I'm on hold."

At last Raskin came back on the line. "I'm sorry, Mr. Crane. Erik says if there's any problem with the billing for the job, don't pay it. He's not available just now to talk."

"It's not about the bill. There's no problem with that. I was calling to ask if he'd care to come to dinner."

"Erik isn't seeing anyone at the moment, Mr. Crane, but I'll give him the message. Anything else?"

"I don't think so. Thank you."

"Good-bye, Mr. Crane."

Cameron hung up and turned to Risa.

"Well?" she wanted to know. "What?"

"Erik isn't seeing anyone at the moment."

"What does that mean?"

"I think it's fairly clear."

"But did you *talk* to him? Did he actually *say* that *himself?*"

"I spoke to Raskin. I have no reason to believe he'd lie to me, Risa."

"Oh!" She lowered her head and sat looking at the carpet. "Did he say how long it was going to be before Erik was seeing people again?"

"I didn't ask, and he didn't say. You really should forget about this," he said gently. "I told you at the outset Erik isn't like other people."

"I know," she said dully, still looking at the carpet. "Thanks for trying," she said after a time. "I guess I'll go to bed now."

She got up and kissed him good night then trudged upstairs to her room. Erik didn't want to see her. That's what Raskin had really been saying. Something she'd said or done had offended Erik, and now he never wanted to see her again. But what had she done? If only she knew that, she might be able to fix it, smooth things over. It made her frantic to think she'd messed up without even being aware of it. How could she have been so stupid? And that's what she was all right: stupid. She hated herself for thinking she was so clever when all the time she'd been an idiot, a stupid idiot. All at once she disliked herself so intensely, so violently she felt like doing something wild, something painful to punish the idiot inside her. She yanked at her hair but the pain was tolerable. She pinched her arm but that, too, was tolerable. Whirling around, she tried to think what she might do to herself that would be commensurate to the degree of hate she felt. Nothing. What could she do? She could drown herself in the bathtub, or swallow an entire bottle of aspirin. But then she'd be dead, and if she were dead there'd be no chance, ever, of seeing Erik again.

Why, she wondered, did that strike her as such a terrifyingly empty prospect? She scarcely knew him. But, oh God, all she had to do was think about how it had felt to sit beside him on the piano bench, his thigh hard against hers, his broad long-fingered hands pressing into the keyboard, his elbow just touching her wrist, and she could barely breathe. Did love feel this way? Was it something so immense and painful that it made you think about things like failure and death? Did people in love go around suffering all the time? She'd always believed love was something light, the consistency of beaten egg white, the weight of one of Kitty's bits of marabou. Love was something that made you feel good, not stupid. So how could this possibly be love? No, no. She'd liked him because he'd brought her pink roses—she'd pressed two of them between the pages of Anne Sexton's *Love Poems*, with the collected works of Shakespeare on top to weight them down—and he'd played for her while she sang; and he'd made a silver dollar appear in her hair. She'd liked him because his sensuous whisper made the muscles in her belly contract, and because he moved like someone in a dream, and because she'd believed with every ounce of her being that she was the one person in the entire world who could somehow make him smile. What an idiot! Who did she think she was, anyway? He probably thought she was just some smart-ass kid, too tall, with no chest, and delusions about her abilities and power.

But she missed him, and she thought about him even more now than before. Just this morning at breakfast, after her father left for the office, Kitty had come to sit with her in the lovely breakfast area Erik had created, and said, "Reese, you're really draggin' yourself around here these days. You feelin' okay, hon?"

"I'm just tired. Too much studying for the finals."

Kitty had shaken her head. "That's crap. You could ace them exams without ever crackin' a book, and you and I both know it. It's that fella, right, the one you turned the kitchen into a disaster area for?"

"What is it with you and my father? The two of you are forever on my case about Erik. I've met the man exactly twice in my whole life."

"Once can sometimes be enough to do it."

"Do what?"

Kitty finished lighting a cigarette before answering. "To turn on all your electric lights and charge up the batteries real good."

"What?"

"Look," Kitty said, taking hold of Risa's hand. "I'm gonna say this one thing, then I won't go bringin' the subject up again. If you get to the point where you're considerin' gettin' seriously involved, you come to me and we'll have us a talk about it, make sure you know what's what and how to protect yourself."

Risa stared at her, then slowly pulled her hand free. "You'll be the *first* to know," she said angrily. "And thanks a lot for this heart-warming little chat."

"Don't be bitchy!" Kitty cautioned. "You got more goin' on inside your head right now than you know how to handle. And I can surely sympathize with that. But don't chew me out just 'cause I care enough about you to want to be sure you know which end is up."

"I'm sorry, Kitty," she said tearfully. "I didn't mean it."

"Yeah, you did," Kitty said, her eyes narrowed against the smoke. "But I can take it. You better get goin' now. You're gonna be late."

"I really am sorry," Risa insisted.

Kitty softened. "You'll miss the bus. Scram on outta here."

"Your hair's looking good again," Risa said by way of additional apology.

"Yeah," Kitty agreed. "And about goddamned time, too."

Sitting now on the side of her bed, gazing down at her shoes, Risa reviewed that morning's conversation and the grinding embarrassment she'd felt. Kitty had been talking about sex, for heaven's sake; about her, Risa, getting into bed with some man. Not some man. Erik. Her face went hot, but the idea held a very definite appeal, and she thought her father and Kitty and Meggie would have screaming fits if they knew she could picture herself taking her clothes off for Erik, of all people. Yet why not Erik? The way he played . . . She let her head fall to one side and closed her eyes, seeing and hearing once more the marvelous music he'd made—for her. How could he do that and not want to see her again? It didn't make sense. But obviously he wasn't going to phone or come back. It felt like a death, as if someone she loved with all her heart—her father, for example—had suddenly died. The ache inside was paralyzing in its enormity. It made her eyes fill and created spontaneous sobs she tried to stop by covering her mouth with her hands. She was such a moron! she told herself, furious. Why was she carrying on this way? She'd have to stop or her father and Kitty would decide to do something about her, like sending her to a psychiatrist, or having her locked up in some place like Silver Hill or something. And no doubt a psychiatrist would confirm her incredible capacity for sheer outrageous stupidity.

She told herself she'd have to stop thinking about him. Yet even as she thought it, she couldn't imagine how she'd do it. It was as if Erik had taken control of her brain, as if it were *his* voice and not her own that narrated her thoughts as they sped past the receptors that translated some items into action and others into immobility. And when she slept, things happened that made her waking self giddy with shame as well as with a small perverse pride in the accomplishments of her sleeping self. Because in her dreams she marched through the front door of Erik's house— wherever it was—and claimed him, in clearly stated terms demanding that he capitulate to what they both knew to be the truth. And he ac- ceded, his magical hands creating brilliant effects. He revealed himself to her, then deluged her with a pleasure that swamped her senses and left her weakly subservient to his desires, and her own. In her dreams their conversations underscored their every action as he whispered into her ear the tragic tales of his lifetime and his unabridged aspirations for the future they'd have together. "Help me," he whispered. "Save me," he begged. She held him secure in the anchor of her arms, and without pain found herself the able channel through which he might pass to safe harbor. In these dreams they were both rescued by the truth, which—as only hap- pens in dreams—was effortlessly acknowledged. "I do love you," she told his astonished eyes. "I love you," her body insisted to his. "I don't care about the way your look or about the need to live a life of nights with no end. Let me be with you and I'll never again ask for sunlight. I'll swim with you in tidal pools at midnight. I'll sing all the songs I ever knew, for you. I will be your home, your shelter, your haven. You're all I want, all I will ever want."

She fell asleep finally with her clothes on, and had to hurry the next morning not to miss the bus. Somehow she got through the last days of school, and somehow she wrote the exams, although afterward she couldn't remember even one of the questions. Then summer spread itself before her in all its heated lassitude and she lay on a chaise out on the back lawn, blinking at the sunlight glinting off the waters of the Sound while she allowed the brutal sun to punish her hapless flesh for her many and critical inadequacies. She burned herself day after day until her skin cracked and split, and finally Kitty came marching out the back door to drag her physically off the chaise and into the house.

"I don't know what-all you think you're doin'," Kitty ranted, "but if you think I'm gonna sit by and watch you tryin' to incinerate yourself, you're plain crazy. Now you get up to your room and take a long cool shower. After that, you put on plenty of Noxzema. If you don't come down here with a good thick layer of that glop all over you from head to toe, I'll come up there and do it myself. And if I catch you outside there one more goddamned time, I'll take my belt to you like maybe somebody shoulda done a long time ago. Now you git!"

Risa just stood there, radiating heat and giving off a faint smell of burned flesh. Her visible grief undid Kitty, who gathered the girl into her arms and stroked her overhot naked spine as she murmured, "It'll be okay, Reese. You'll see. Everything's gonna be okay."

Risa nodded dumbly and bent her head to the smaller woman's shoulder. "I feel so bad, Kitty," she confessed. "Nothing I do will make it stop."

"Time'll see to you," Kitty crooned. "You need to find something to do with yourself, something to take your mind off what's troublin' you."

"I've tried! I've tried everything I can think of, but nothing works. I feel as if I want to die."

"I don't want to *hear* that!" Kitty said sharply, taking hold of Risa's upper arms. "I don't *ever* want to hear that! Maybe you don't think of me as much more than the hired help around here, but I'm kind of possessive about you, girl. And I care one whole lot about your life. It's all out there in front of you, and there's nothing that's happened that's so bad it should make you want to think about dying." She paused, then asked, "Is there?"

Risa had to admit she was right.

"Well, all right then," Kitty said, greatly relieved. "Git on upstairs and do like I told you. When you come down, you'll have some nice fresh lemonade and we'll watch the soaps. That'll keep your mind off what's distressin' you so."

Risa gave her a shaky smile and went off to do as she'd been told. But while she stood under the shower, she couldn't help thinking she'd be happy again if only Erik would call or come to visit. It wasn't such a lot to ask, was it?

Five

ERIK HAD ONE LAST PROJECT TO WHICH HE WAS COMMITTED. HIS DECISION was to finish this job and refuse all future offers. The making of this decision and the recognition of his final existing responsibility allowed him to take up work again at the drafting table in the attic office.

Almost the first thing he'd done upon purchasing this house was to gut the entire area under the eaves and redo it according to his needs. The only items he'd left intact were the two round stained-glass windows set at either end, facing north and south. The Victorian caprice of installing two very fine windows in an area where they'd never be appreciated, and the excellent quality of the glass itself, prompted him to respect the original builder's intent—whatever that might have been. Since these windows were placed high in the end walls, and were comprised of cut pieces of deep hue—a blood red, an emerald green, an eggyolk yellow, and a royal blue—they admitted little direct light but did, in the early morning and late afternoon, project wheels of color that were kaleidoscopically pleasing to his eye.

He and Raskin had undertaken to do the work themselves, and had placed fiberglass insulation between the ceiling joists, then a layer of soundproofing and, at last, covered everything over with Sheetrock, which they'd spackled and seamed for hours on end until their arms quivered from strain and their necks were stiff and kinked from work done entirely above their heads. The walls were given a similar treatment. Wearing face masks, they sanded the wide-board pine floors, then coughed for days afterward in spite of their precautions. With the floors stripped and the Sheetrock joints sanded smooth, Raskin spray-painted the room a matte black, per Erik's instructions. The floor was given three coats of the darkest stain, then sealed.

When Erik was satisfied with the results, the drafting table and file cabinets, Raskin's typewriter, the Xerox copier, and the telephones were put into place. A handsome old Oriental carpet in predominantly navy tones with hints of red was laid in the center of the floor; overhead fans were installed to assist the new central air-conditioning that operated through the existing floor ducts; and then Erik positioned the high adjustable stool upon which he sat to do his work so that his back would be to the room.

With the office completed, Erik next went to work on the remaining two floors and the cellar. The six original bedrooms were restructured into three; the three upper bathrooms were gutted and done over with new fixtures and fittings. On the main floor the old parlor and sitting room were merged to form one very large room. The several pantries were eliminated to create the huge kitchen where Raskin prepared the meals. The dining room, paneled in gleaming mahogany, was left intact with its brass wall sconces and crystal chandelier. The front hall was done away with altogether, the walls taken down so that the front door opened directly into the living room, which was painted charcoal gray and outfitted with two custom-made sofas upholstered in black glove leather. The only adornment anywhere in the house consisted of the two portraits in the living room that hung on either side of the fireplace: the one of his parents, and the one of Erik and his mother, done when he was five.

Everything in the house was in shades of black or gray, so that no matter where Erik might choose to stand or sit, he could effectively disappear into the background or upholstery. Only the Oriental carpet in the office, the stained-glass windows, and the kitchen appliances had any color. And one corner of the kitchen was the sole area where direct light was allowed to enter. Erik didn't question Raskin's choice of color in bed linens, but his own were navy—the darkest shade available.

The cellar now housed the music room, which ran beneath better than half the ground floor. Beyond it was a tidy area where the washer and dryer, a large freezer, the hot-water tank and furnace were situated. The oil tank was buried in the ground at the side of the house, and the air-conditioning units were concealed behind shrubs planted exclusively for that purpose.

There were speakers and intercoms throughout the house, even in the bathrooms, so that Erik could summon Raskin, or listen in on him, should he care to, or have music instantly if he felt the need. As well as all this, there were several concealed doors and passages of which Raskin was unaware; one Erik had devised that led from the music room along an old tunnel he'd discovered during the renovations. It ended at the tumbledown boathouse—about which he intended to do nothing at all, since it was structurally sound despite its ramshackle appearance—and allowed him to go late at night to sit and gaze at the moon or the water, or to get into the boat moored in clement weather to the rickety dock. He did install an electric winching system that made it possible to shift the boat easily and quickly, so that if he felt a sudden need to be out on the Sound, it could be accomplished in minutes.

Sometimes, deep in the night, with the motor barely ticking over, he'd tour the waterfront, gazing at the houses along the shore, occasionally seeing figures pass before lighted windows. And once, he'd had the rare opportunity of watching a nude woman standing on the balcony outside her bedroom, backlit as she slowly drew a brush through her hair.

Another of his doors lay beneath the carpet in the office. Should he care to, he could flip back the end of the carpet, open the trap door, pull the carpet back into place above him, and vanish down the narrow ladderlike stairs that brought him to a sliding panel at the rear of the walk-in cupboard on the landing.

The third door was at the side of the closet in his bedroom. By pulling forward a piece of the molding, he could open the door to enter the secret room he'd created during the initial stages of the renovation. Six feet wide by ten feet long, with an air vent cut into the floor, this was where Erik frequently spent the night when he couldn't sleep. There was a deep armchair, a small table, and several items of extreme importance to him: his mother's photograph album, his father's violin and mother-of-pearl dress studs, his books on magic, his props, and a gun. He never touched the gun. It remained in its box, positioned precisely at the far right-hand corner of the table, beside a supply of bullets. Periodically, he'd raise the lid to look at its gray, oiled and loaded, finality. Then he'd close the box and return to practicing his sleight of hand. He worked with coins, and flowers, and silk scarves. Card tricks bored him. He preferred to make things appear and disappear, and could spend four or five hours at a time moving coins between his fingers, or stuffing his curled hand full of varicolored squares of silk that were gone when he flung his opened palm into the air.

Often, when restlessness overcame him, he'd strip off his clothes and in the dim candlelight work his body through a rigorous series of exercises that maintained both his flexibility and his strength and muscle tone. He'd subject his body to an hour or two of calisthenics, of bends and stretches and twists; of handstands, shoulder presses, and leg lifts that left him trembling and sufficiently exhausted to sleep.

At times he would simply sit in the chair with the photograph album in his lap, one hand flat over its leather cover, the other moving back and forth with a cigarette from his mouth to the ashtray at the front of the table. When he did dare to look at the pictures it was invariably an act of self-punishment. He'd be contained initially as he admired the lovely child his mother had been, as he examined his parents' laughing faces in their wedding portraits. Then he'd come to those first shots of the infant Erik and he'd begin to seize up inside, so that by the time he got to the candid and posed shots of the small boy in short pants cavorting on the front lawn or clinging to his doting mother, he'd be in a state of fulminating rage. None of this was directed toward the innocent trio who played for all eternity on the fraying pages, but rather toward the ogre he'd grown to be.

He couldn't think now how he'd managed to survive his university years and the feigned acceptance of some of his classmates. He'd believed then, and still did now, that the most honest of those young people had been the ones who'd let their horror show, who'd covered their mouths or clutched their chests at the sight of him. But he'd been younger then and still knotted in the last skeins of his unfeasible optimism, his ill-founded hope that someone, somewhere, one day, would be blessed with eyes that saw beyond the surface of things. Time had proved him wrong and had rotted the optimism, crushed the hope. The last brave thing he'd done had been placing the advertisement in the "Help Wanted" section of the New York *Times*. There'd been a deluge of responses, and he'd sifted through them, discarding the majority at once. But Raskin's letter had been unlike any of the others. It was one written by a man Erik recognized, a letter penned from desperation, and without pretense. "I need a job," Raskin had written. "I've got a master's degree in engineering from Yale. I'm a Vietnam vet. I don't care where I live, so relocating's no problem. But I prefer to work in quiet surroundings, with only one person to answer to. I can cook and type. I can drive anything that has four wheels and a motor. I'm single and intend to stay that way. I'll do anything reasonable for fair pay, and I'm free to start right away."

Erik had telephoned and asked him to come to the old Riverside house for an interview. Raskin seemed unfazed by the front door that clicked open to admit him, or by following instructions issued over the speaker to seat himself in the living room. He'd sat with a cigarette and calmly answered Erik's questions, unconcerned by the television camera in the corner of the ceiling or by the heavily draped interior of the house. Erik knew, watching and listening to the then twenty-eight-year-old Raskin, that luck had provided him with someone ideally suited to his many needs. When Erik has asked, "Have you any questions?" Raskin had looked directly into the camera and asked, "Do I ever get to see you? Or do you have a real problem with that?"

"You may see me," Erik had replied, and descended the stairs to enter the room, halting just inside the doorway.

Raskin's expression had remained unchanged. "That's what I figured," he'd said. "The war?"

"No."

"No problem. Do I get the job?"

He got the job, and for over two years now Raskin had been his cushion against the world, his bearer of news to and from the outside, and his personal raconteur. Upon seeing Erik enter the office and go to his desk now, Raskin's only comment was, "I was starting to think I'd have to do this job without you."

Erik drew over the plans, seated himself on his stool, referred to the specifications, then set to work; his back, as ever, to Raskin, his face to the wall.

Somehow Risa managed to get through the summer and returned to start her senior year at the high school, grateful for the daily distraction of other faces and voices, and facts to be studied and remembered. The days passed with relative ease; the evenings remained as difficult as before.

While the autumn weather held warm in the evenings, she'd walk the length of the back garden after dinner to stand for a time where the land left off some eight or ten feet above the water. She'd then sit on the dock with her legs dangling and watch sailboats returning to shore. An occasional motorboat would roughen up the water and send choppy waves splashing against the pilings beneath her. Sea gulls complained like hungry babies as they swooped and soared, scouring the surface of the Sound for food of any kind.

Often she'd look across the inlet to the old house on Contentment Island, which appeared now to be lived in. Sometime in the course of the past eighteen months, someone had bought the house and fixed it up before installing high fencing that blocked all but the upper stories from view. As the evenings grew chill, she'd see smoke rising from one or two of the several chimneys. People not only lived there, they used the fireplaces and even kept a good-sized motor launch tied up outside the old boathouse. In a way, she was glad about the house. Despite the games she and Meggie had played as children, scaring themselves witless, she'd always thought it was a fine, dignified house, and she'd never understood why people hadn't seen its potential. Well, someone finally had, and although she couldn't help smiling when she thought of the way she and Meggie had gone creeping around over there looking for ghosts and terrified of encountering any, she was pleased to see the place returned to life.

For the most part, as she sat nightly on the dock, she wondered about Erik—not so urgently or despairingly as she had, but with an ongoing hurt at her very core that felt as if it would never diminish. Every time the telephone rang, she thought it might be him. Each day's mail was liable to bring some message. A knock at the front door could signal his arrival. But his silence remained absolute. She'd said or done something to wound or offend him, and he'd decided never to see her again. The feeling she had when she thought this bordered on agony. It came accompanied by a squeezing sensation in her chest that made it hard for her to breathe and equally as hard to sleep.

Her nights had grown long and noisy with the imagined dialogues she held with Erik. When she did sleep, it was only for an hour or two before something, some thought or idea, awakened her. Restless, she took to late-night rambles through the house, often sitting in the dark living room or in the moonlit breakfast area. She'd go from room to room, familiar with the various settling creaks and tiny shifts of the house, the noises of the furnace and refrigerator. She was comforted in a minimal way by her unlimited access to the house, to its sleeping cadence, its particular smells.

In early December, in the course of one of her nocturnal strolls, she came across her father's address book open on his desk in the den. Grabbing a pencil and a piece of notepaper from the drawer, she flipped through the pages, found Erik's name and number and made note of them. Then she carefully folded the paper and tucked it into the pocket of her robe where her fingers toyed with it ceaselessly as she continued on her way to her frequent night post in the kitchen.

She was there at the kitchen table, staring up through the denuded branches of the chestnut tree one night in early January, when she decided she simply had to talk about what was happening to her. And the one person she could talk to was Kitty. It was almost one-fifteen, but Kitty regularly stayed up late to watch the Carson show or some old movie with Clark Gable or Spencer Tracy. Risa pushed silently away from the table and went along the hallway at the rear of the house to where Kitty had her rooms.

As she came down the hallway she was relieved to see Kitty's door ajar and an orange slice of light falling through from inside. Risa went toward the light and was about to tap lightly on the door when caution took hold, prompting her to lean forward and look inside through the gap of some six or so inches. Inside, a scarf draped over the bedside lamp was responsible for the orange-tinted light that fell in an appealing crescent over half the bed. And there in that crescent lay Kitty and Risa's father. They were talking quietly. Cameron's head rested against one of Kitty's ample breasts, his hand idly stroking the other. It was, in an instant, manifestly clear to Risa that this was only a part of a long-ongoing conversation the two of them in the bedroom had been having for years.

She backed away and returned upstairs to her room, wondering why she hadn't figured out the situation ages ago. Her father's good-natured bordello comments, his indulgence of Kitty, which had prompted the remodeling of the kitchen, which was, in turn, directly responsible for the advent of Erik into Risa's life. She was neither upset nor angry. She merely wished they'd told her about this, let her in on the fact that neither one of them was so lonely or love-starved as Risa had imagined them to be. In fact, when she thought about it, it made a good deal of sense that her father would spend his nights with Kitty. After all, she was right there, and familiar; she was pretty, and sexy too, in a kind of no-nonsense way. And she was, as she said herself, very involved with this family. The thing was, she was a whole lot more involved than anyone had ever let on. But that was okay. She was really, honestly, glad the two of them had each other. What moved her to tears was the understanding that she was on the outside of just about everything. Cameron had Kitty to talk to; the two of them had been talking about her, Risa, for years and years, obviously; both of them had discussed her stupid behavior, the weird way she'd been carrying on for all these months. That part was unfair. She should have been informed that there was one voice speaking in the household, and not two as she'd thought.

Curling up on her bed, she held the worn-smooth paper with Erik's number in the palm of her hand. No matter what happened, she had to hear him tell her personally that he didn't want to know about her, that he didn't care.

The next afternoon she got off the school bus at the end of Tokeneke Road and went into the variety store near the corner of the Post Road to use the pay phone. Her mouth dry, lips parched, she dialed the number, then waited with her heart thumping as the ringing on the other end began. When a man's voice answered, she said, "Is this Mr. Raskin?"

"Yes, it is."

"This is Marisa Crane. Could I speak to Erik, please?"

"Please hold, Miss Crane," he said, and went off the line.

She waited, sweating, repeatedly moistening her lips. He *had* to talk to her. She didn't know what she'd do if Raskin came back to say Erik wouldn't accept her call. He was gone for ages, and her hand grew slick around the receiver as she glanced about, hoping to God nobody else would decide to want to use the telephone.

There was a click, and then he was there. "What is it?" came Erik's peremptory whisper.

"Erik," she said, hunching closer to the mouthpiece of the wall-mounted phone, "what did I do wrong? Why don't you want to come back? Do you hate me?"

A pause. And then there was the sound of laughter devoid of any humor, laughter bitter and disbelieving and breathless; it went on for several merciless seconds. Ashamed, Risa's eyes filled as she listened to the cruel sounds he made. When a lull came, she said quickly, "I'm sorry. I shouldn't have called. I'm sorry," and hung up.

Clutching her books, she tore out of the store and started running toward home. A stitch in her side, she slowed to a fast walk as she got past the entrance to the turnpike. Blind to everything but her self-inflicted humiliation, she fled toward home, down Old Far Road, slipping on the icy road, oblivious to the bitter cold. All she wanted was to get into her room and turn on the radio really loud to some acid-rock station to drown out the hateful echo of her pathetic little voice asking, "What did I do wrong?" She wanted to die, and wished it were something that could be accomplished just by willing it to happen.

She knew she'd never be able to face Kitty or her father over dinner. They'd guess from looking at her that she'd done something truly idiotic. God! *Why* had she done it? What on earth had made her think she could do a thing like that? The way he'd laughed, the breathy hollowness of the sound rushed inside her head. Maybe she'd go ahead after all and take a whole bottle of aspirin. Or better still, she'd sneak into her father's bathroom and steal all his prescription bottles. He had things in there like Percodan and Nembutal. Pills like that could put you to sleep forever.

"My stomach's upset," she told Kitty upon reaching home. "I'm going to skip dinner, just do my homework and go straight to bed."

"You comin' down with something?" Kitty asked, touching the back of her hand to Risa's forehead, which was cold and clammy.

Without knowing in advance she was going to do it, Risa looked into the older woman's bright-blue eyes and said, "Kitty, how come neither one of you ever bothered to tell me? Did you think I'd mind, or that I'd make a fuss? Is that why?"

"What . . . ?"

"I know about you and Dad," Risa said unemotionally. "I don't mind a bit, honestly. I only wish the two of you trusted me enough, thought I was intelligent enough, to be told."

"Oh, hell!" Kitty exclaimed and grabbed for a cigarette. As she held it to her lighter, her eyes on Risa, she asked, "Is that why you're not coming down to dinner tonight?"

"That has nothing to do with anything. I don't feel like eating."

"Are you telling the truth, Reese? Or are you tryin' to make the best of things?"

Standing there, holding her schoolbooks to her chest, Risa began to cry.

"It's the truth, honest to God. If you want to know, I'm glad the two of you aren't alone. I always worried about Dad being on his own." She bent her head over her books and started to go, then turned back and lifted her head. "I've always loved you, Kitty. It's okay, really." She swung around then and made good her escape.

Dumping her books on the desk, still in her coat, she sat down in the slipper chair by the window. To hell with it! she thought. She'd go clean out her Dad's medicine chest right now and, with luck, she'd be dead before dinner. She was on the verge of getting up when the telephone in her room rang and she turned to stare at it. Her father had arranged for her to have her own line years ago, believing that all teenagers tied up telephones for hours on end. But in her case the only person who'd regularly called her unlisted number had been Meggie. And since the start of this school year, not even the jocks were bothering anymore. So who could be calling? Another ring. She put out her hand and, puzzled, picked up the receiver.

"Be on your dock at eleven," Erik instructed. "I will come for you." There was a click, and then buzzing. He was gone.

Six

*E*RIK, WHAT DID *I* DO WRONG *?* WHY DON'T YOU WANT TO COME BACK *?* Do you hate me?

Hate you? Hate *you?* It had never occurred to him that she'd construe his determination to remain away in those terms. It had never occurred to him that she might call, or that the sound of her name on Raskin's tongue could send him into such an immediate state of distress; it had never occurred to him that she might actually care, or take it personally, that he hadn't responded to their second invitation to dinner. And his shock was such that his only immediate reaction was the hurtful laughter that—he'd heard it in her sad, injured voice—had spewed so automatically, so laden with irony, from his mouth.

She'd spoken softly, asking her questions timidly, directly into his ear, causing shock waves to travel through his body, and he'd rewarded her with mocking laughter. For close to ten months he'd managed to survive without the sight or sound of her, although he hadn't for a moment ceased thinking of her. He had even, at last, been able to return to the piano and his music; he'd been able to sing in the secret seclusion of the music room. He'd been well on the road to learning to live again his peculiar brooding life of solitude. And then she'd come seeking him, wanting absolution or explanation. He'd laughed, and she'd flown away.

What did this girl *want* from him? he asked the curtained walls of his lightless bedroom, where he'd come to speak in private over the telephone, away from Raskin's hearing. Why was she pursuing him? What did she hope to achieve with her schoolgirl's persistence?

His hands smoothed his hair, ground together briefly, then flew, spread-fingered, to reassure himself that the mask was in place, that he was fully clothed, everything properly buttoned and fastened.

He'd made her weep, he was sure of it. There'd been such a telltale catch in her voice as she'd made her small forlorn apology. She'd gone off shedding tears because of his unfeeling spontaneous reaction to the absurdity of her innocent questions. Do I hate you, Marisa? Hate? I adore you, revere you. I would drop my life down at your feet and allow you to dance upon it, if the fancy took you. I want you as I've wanted nothing else, nor will I ever want again. You're in my mouth, my ears and eyes and throat. My hands crave your hair, the bends of your elbows, the acquaintanceship of your flesh and the bones it conceals. Just your name, the sound of your voice in my ear, and control is lost. I am rendered deaf and blind, dumb and senseless with the pleasure your very voice gives to me. You're the living embodiment of every lovely thing ever created. And you ask do I hate you. I could *never* hate you, dearest child. It's me. I'm the one toward whom I direct my considerable hatred. This face, this grim joke of fate, is what I hate. But you? Not ever, never you. If I die as a result of loving you, I will never be capable of bearing you the least malice.

It was all in aid of very little, this additional period of excoriating deliberation because he was, and had been, a victim of her youth and beauty and piercing sweetness from the moment his eyes had initially focused upon her. He'd separated himself for months on end from the one person, the knowledge of whose very existence renewed his hopes and revived his near-dead spirit. Life until first sight of her had been a tedious, sometimes self-indulgent, routine through which he was obliged, by the sheer questionable tenacity of his instincts, to travel. From the night they'd met he'd been fueled by emotions more powerful, more consuming even than the loathing he felt for the boy who'd fought against being a fellow traveler on the long black journey embarked upon by his mother and father those many years ago; emotions more potent than the contempt he had for that feckless child who'd fought to retain his life without the least notion of what that life would come to mean.

She might very well cast him aside, abandon him, once her girlish curiosity had been satisfied. But there'd never been a question of choice. She had the power to turn him any way she chose, to deprive him of all rational thought. She turned him into a creature made entirely of nameless and dimensionless need simply by her being alive in the world, and within his grasp. He could only surrender to something greater than his fear; could only close his eyes and submit himself to the boundless depths of his incapacitating need for her.

So he capitulated, as he'd known all along he would, and called Raskin on the intercom.

"Is the shoreline accessible?"

"There's no ice," Raskin answered. "Do you want to take the boat out tonight?"

"Have it ready, please."

"Okay, Erik."

She was able, after all, to dine with her father that evening. As they ate, she was overtaken by a keen sense of finality. She might eat in this room, at this table, with her father, another ten thousand times in the days and years to come, but the Marisa who came to sit with him would be someone else. Everyone in the household would, from now on, have some secret to withhold. She was prepared to do anything, anything at all, should Erik ask it of her. She hadn't understood that a few hours earlier when she'd climbed off the school bus to go to the telephone at the variety store, but she could see now that she'd already pledged herself to whatever was to happen when she'd picked up the receiver and asked for Erik.

As she smiled across the table at her father, and answered his questions about her day, and chatted easily about inconsequentials, she wondered if there was any way he could possibly divine that he was seeing the Marisa he'd always known for the last time. The Marisa who returned to eat with him at breakfast and again at dinner tomorrow, and all the tomorrows thereafter, would be altered irrevocably. Just how, precisely, she didn't know. But she would be changed. For the first time in her nearly seventeen years of life she'd seen what she wanted and she'd undertaken the initiative to have it. She felt aged at having been bold enough to make her wishes known, and too lacking in knowledge of the world and its esoteric inner workings to be able to gauge the full extent of the possible consequences. All she knew was that she would be at the water's edge at eleven, and that nothing whatever could prevent it. Were she suddenly taken seriously ill, were her father and Kitty to learn of her plans and lock her up somewhere, she'd still find some way to be waiting for Erik when he came for her.

Picturing his hands, those masterful, free-sweeping birds of fancy that acted out what the man could not or dared not say, she felt herself loosening, softening, her flesh accumulating new texture and density. Anything! He could do anything, and she would offer no protest. Her eyelids started to lower in anticipation of the many possible outcomes this meeting might have.

"You look sleepy, Keed," her father said. "You're not getting enough rest."

"I'm not tired," she told him. "I don't need a lot of sleep. I was just thinking, that's all."

"Thinking about sleep, from the looks of it." He laughed, then cleared his throat. Solemn all at once, he said, "Kitty told me about the conversation the two of you had."

"And?" She looked at him, thinking how familiar he was and yet how many areas of his life there were about which she knew almost nothing. She knew that face, clean-shaven and appealing, with its enviably arched eyebrows and its gray-green eyes, its squared chin and slanted jawline; she knew the kindness and concern that glowed out at her in all its parental benevolence.

"And? You tell me," he said, a bit fearfully.

"I told Kitty, and now I'll tell you: I wish you'd had enough respect for my native intelligence to let me know about it. I mean, Dad. What did you think I'd do, throw a fit or something, insist you drive her out into the snow?" She laughed indulgently. "I'm not a little kid. I'm almost seventeen, for heaven's sake. I know what's what. And anyway," she wound down, "I like Kitty. Are you going to marry her or anything?"

He had to chuckle at the way she put the question. "I don't think so. Neither one of us is interested in that. We're friends, Risa. That's really what it comes down to. I have no real say in her life, and she has none in mine. From time to time, when there's a need, Kitty and I spend a few hours together and talk—for the most part. If it bothers you in any way, it can be over, just like that." He snapped his fingers.

"Why should you give up something you enjoy for me?" she asked earnestly. "I don't know if I'd be willing to do that for you, Dad."

"Wow!" He rocked back in his chair, his eyes appraising. "That's getting pretty deep."

"I'm trying to be truthful, and that's as truthful as I know how to be. I think that's the way things are, the way people are, when it comes right down to making choices. Nobody really decides for anybody else. I mean, you're a grown man. You're fifty-one years old, Dad. Are you going to start letting me make your decisions for you? Are you going to invite me to sit behind your desk at the office and start running your business? I don't think so. Oh, sure, you'd try to do something about the situation if I made a fuss. But that would just make you ticked off at me, and make me feel guilty. I don't want either of those things to happen."

"Risa," he said, "when did you get so smart?"

"I don't know about smart. I mean, I read about what's happening in the world, about the way women are starting to demand equal rights, and I agree with that. The thing is, I know how I'd feel if it was me we were talking about, and not you."

"Still," he said, thinking it through, "this does change things."

"Not so far as I'm concerned. If you want to come down to talk to Kitty at midnight, it doesn't have a thing to do with me. Not one single thing. I mean, you've gone to all this trouble for a pretty long time to keep me from knowing. Just because I know now doesn't mean the two of you are going to start carrying on in public, does it?"

"And would it bother you if Kitty and I *were* seen together in public?"

"Would it bother *you?*" she asked calmly.

"Oh, brother!" he said slowly. "You've got me every way to Sunday on this one. I don't know the answer to that, Marisa. For better than thirteen years Kitty's been a damned good friend. We've had an understanding that what goes on inside this house doesn't necessarily have anything to do with what goes on outside. She and I have both seen other people. Somehow we always manage to wind up back together. If anyone had told me years ago that I'd come to admire and care very much for an opinionated, stubborn yet flighty, hard-soft Southern woman who dotes on daytime television programs and who likes to do crossword puzzles in bed, I'd have laughed myself silly. But here we are, and I'm fonder of her than I can say. She makes me laugh, Risa. And she's got more common sense than most people I could name. She listens well, and she *hears*. And, most important of all, she cares about *you*. It's one of the major attractions she has for me. To be truthful, there are plenty of willing women around. But there's only one I know who cares for you almost as much as I do. It's reassuring to know that, God forbid, should anything ever happen to me, Kitty would be here to look after you."

"I hardly need looking after, you know. I mean, I'm not eight years old."

"In the eyes of the law, you're still a child for a while yet. It'd be irresponsible of me, Risa, if I didn't consider your well-being in all eventualities. I told you: We wanted you, Rebecca and I. I made a promise a long time ago that I'd be your father to the best of my abilities. That includes considering the future."

"Okay. But nothing's going to happen to you. And I'm not a little kid. So don't worry about it. Okay?"

"Have I ever told you how much I like you, Marisa?"

"Only six or seven million times." She smiled.

"Well, don't ever forget that I do. I like the hell out of you."

"Me, too, you, Dad. Why don't you pretend I never found out?"

"That's easier said than done. But I appreciate your understanding. I truly do."

"Oh, Dad," she said, starting to choke up. "Don't *thank* me. You're my *father*. I love you. I'm going up to do my homework. Okay?"

"Sure. Don't stay up too late, though, Risa. You really do look kind of worn out."

"I feel fine." She stopped behind his chair to kiss the top of his head, then stood for a few seconds with her hand on his shoulder, feeling grieved, as if she were in some way saying good-bye.

She'd taken a very hot bath, washed and dried her hair, and then dressed herself in everyday clothes when she realized that if she encountered her father or Kitty on her passage either into or out of the house, she'd have to explain being fully dressed at that hour of the night. So she removed her day clothes and pulled on a freshly laundered soft flannel nightgown, a long one with buttons down the front and ruffles at the cuffs, in white with a pattern of sprinkled violets. Over this she put her robe. Before leaving the house, she pulled on her coat, wound a scarf around her neck, stepped barefoot into her boots, then slipped out the kitchen door. The night was cold but very clear and she stood on the dock with her hands in her coat pockets, her face uplifted to a sky alive with stars, and waited.

It was only minutes before a boat slid alongside, and there was Erik, one gloved hand holding fast to the dock to steady the boat, the other assisting her over the side. Without a word he returned to the wheel, the noise of the motor gained in volume, and the boat swept in a slow half-circle away from the house. The wind clawed at her face, making her eyes water, but she stood where he'd left her, waiting to see where they'd go. Not far. Just across the inlet to the old boathouse where he cut the motor, tied the boat secure, then nimbly hoisted himself up and turned, his hands reaching for her.

As if she weighed nothing at all, he drew her up, then turned away, expecting her to follow. He opened a trap door at the far end of the boathouse and she went with him, scarcely able to see in the disc of light cast by a flashlight he held out in front of him. Frightened and exhilarated, with the sense that she was trailing some mythical figure and not anyone real, she hurried after him along a damp narrow tunnel that went for quite some distance. Then he opened another door, stepped inside, and waited for her to enter.

Accustomed now to the darkness, she moved into the huge candlelit room, slowly turning to take stock of her surroundings while Erik closed and bolted the door through which they'd come. This had to be the cellar of the old haunted house, she thought, and yet it didn't seem possible. There, positioned close to the far wall, was a gleaming black grand piano. And over there, along the near wall, were shelves filled with all sorts of equipment: tape decks, tuners, amplifiers, and other electronic items she couldn't identify. Speakers were mounted on the walls in all four corners of the room. There were two lonely yet elegant antique chairs, a single small table, and the candles—dozens of them, some massed in candelabra atop the piano, some on the shelves housing the equipment, others placed at random on the floor near the walls. The light from the many flames created an underwater, rippling effect with their slow-waltz motion. The silence was so complete she could hear Erik's quick breathing, and her own, as he removed his hat and cape, then came to her side indicating that she should give him her coat and remove her boots. Obediently, she took off the coat and scarf, then set her bare feet down into the surprising warmth of luxurious carpeting.

"Where are we? Is this your house?" she asked.

"This is my music room," his deep tuneful whisper informed her as he draped her coat and his cape across one of the chairs.

"It's wonderful," she said inadequately, aware of the pulse beating strongly in her throat as he straightened from his brief domestic chore to stand gazing at her.

He was dressed in black again, perhaps the same suit or its twin. His shirt front was so white it seemed to glow in the uneven illumination of the room. With exquisite slowness he began to peel off his gloves. His every move seemed choreographed as part of some never-ending ballet; even the slightest gesture had an impressive grandeur. She felt imperiled, yet reckless, and drew deep breaths as if about to take a plunge into cold dark water.

He dropped the gloves on top of his cape, then moved toward her to stop perhaps a foot away, his head tilting slightly to one side as he looked at her, his eyes large and inner-lit behind the heavily framed glasses.

"Sing for me," he whispered, and held out his hand to lead her over to the piano.

Her hand again caught in his tender yet tentative grip, she allowed herself to be directed, and sat at his side on the bench where he turned once more to say to her, "Anything at all. The music will be there."

She took him at his word, certain in this mystical environment that she could do anything, no matter how improbable. Without pausing to consider if he'd derive some personal thinly coded message from her choice, she began "Mean to Me." Why must you be? and he was already there underscoring her voice, her life, with chords of an unearthly force and lyricism that compelled her to open her throat more, to place even more of her lungs' accumulated power into the words, their sound and meaning. In perfect synchroneity they became the embodiment of the music.

At the end, with Erik's graceful fingers still poised over the keys, she allowed her head to come to rest on his shoulder, content. And as if they'd been together this way a hundred times before—she with her head on his shoulder, he with his hands on the piano—his fingers bore down to make more music, and he opened his mouth to sing for her, a song of his own composing, with a voice so pure and refined, so intimate and meaningful, that she had to close her eyes in order to appreciate it fully: a ballad built on the dreams of a lifetime, filled with vivid images that told her everything about his naked, barren existence. He sang for her his lullaby, his slumber song, his night music, and she absorbed his warmth and his fragrance as his arm moved against her side making melodies, and his voice delved into the deepest recesses of her mind and thoughts, possessing her.

I love you, Erik, she thought, wanting never to have to leave here. *I'll never in my life love anyone else the way I love you.*

The song at an end, he sat feeling the dear weight of her head on his shoulder, wishing he were an ordinary man so that he might take her in his arms and claim her as his own. Here she was, beautiful Marisa, with her hair falling over his arm, her long pale hands folded serenely in her lap; so very close, yet separated from him forever by his accursed and pernicious disfigurement.

"Come," he said at last. "I must take you home."

In one sudden motion he was gone from her, gathering their outer clothes from the chair before enfolding her in her coat. His cape slicing the air like that of a matador, it settled around his shoulders as he pulled on his gloves, then pushed back the bolt of the door to the tunnel and drew her into it.

Before leaving her on the dock, he kept hold of her hand for a moment, whispering, "Tomorrow," and then the boat turned and cut away back across the inlet. "Tomorrow," whispered in her ears as, in a trance, she made her way across the snow-glazed lawn to the house.

Seven

IGHTLY HE CAME FOR HER, EITHER IN THE BOAT OR, WHEN THE shoreline was ice-encrusted and inaccessible, in the otherworldly sleek black car. Nightly they sat together at the piano and made music. And nightly, after an hour or two, he returned her to her home before dissolving into the darkness and leaving her to wonder if all this was nothing more than some fabulous extended dream.

Week after week, through the end of January, past February, and into early March, they managed to steal time together in the subterranean music room. For Marisa, the expense of so much energy and the withholding of so much more, combined with the lack of sleep and her general disinterest in food, finally took its toll. She simply slid out of her seat in English class one afternoon, and when she regained consciousness she was tucked in bed in a private room in Greenwich Hospital, being fed intravenously.

She lost track of time. People came and went—nurses, doctors, her father and Kitty. She slept for the most part, able, it seemed, to stay awake only for minutes at a time. She was fairly sure it was real and not a dream when her father sat on the side of her bed holding her hand and telling her, "We have to take better care of you from now on, Marisa. I had no idea you were so run down. Anemia combined with malnutrition's no laughing matter, Keed. You're going to start getting a lot more rest, and paying more attention to your poor tired body."

She seemed to remember promising him she'd be good from now on, and she would take the pills and anything else they wanted her to do. But she slept for such long periods of time, and so deeply, that everything had an unreal quality.

* * *

The first night Erik drove to the top of the driveway on Butlers Island to discover Marisa wasn't there waiting, he experienced such a spasm of dread he could scarcely think. When there was no word from her the next day or the one after that, he got Raskin on the intercom and said, "I need you to go to the Crane house and find out in whatever way you can what's become of Marisa."

Raskin said, "Sure, no problem," and reported back later that evening that the girl was ill and in the hospital.

Profoundly frightened and guilt-ridden, positive he was responsible for whatever illness Marisa might have, he climbed that night into the Lamborghini and went streaking off down I-95 to Greenwich. Making his way through back doors and fire exits, he located her room and went to stand at the side of the bed gazing down at his beautiful child in the slim strips of light entering through the gaps between the curtains. His fear for her well-being and his dreadful guilt reduced him to tears. He stood and wept silently over her, praying for her recovery, and cursing himself. She was a child and needed her rest, yet he'd deprived her of it for months for his own selfish purposes. And if she should die he'd be entirely to blame.

"Don't die!" His lips shaded the soundless words. "Please, don't die."

She was so pale, so utterly without color, so still she scarcely seemed to be breathing. And then, stunningly, her eyes opened. She looked at him and smiled, and with agonizing slowness lifted her arms to him, whispering, "Erik!"

How could he help himself? He bent into the circle of her arms, to breathe his abject apologies into her ear, to press his lips lightly against the frail flutter of the pulse in her temple. "I love you, love you," he whispered, his tears dropping into her hair. "More than life, I love you." But her arms had gone limp; she'd returned to her deep-dreaming sleep. With the greatest of care, he disentangled himself, stood a moment more gazing down at her, then turned and left that place of acute angles and antiseptic odors and echoing corridors.

He was killing her, he told himself as he took the car speeding over the highway toward home. His love had never been intended to harm her. They could not go on as they had been. He was draining the life out of her body with his unquenchable thirst to have her near him. He had no right to harm her; he had no wish to do so. In order to save her, he had to allow her to return to the normalcy of her life before him. The only way he could do that was to remove himself altogether from the arena of temptation.

"Pack!" he told Raskin over the intercom. "We are leaving at once!"

"To go where?" Raskin asked equably.

Where? Erik asked himself, trying to think. "London," he said. "Make arrangements, book passage on one of the Cunard ships. We'll leave for New York tonight. We must be on a ship tomorrow.''

"I'll take care of it," Raskin assured him. And true to his word, by late morning of the following day he and Erik were installed in adjoining staterooms on a Norwegian ship—no Cunard sailings being available— bound for Southampton.

Throughout the voyage, Erik remained in his stateroom, pacing its abbreviated length and alternately grating his hands together or tugging at his face, in a state of sorrow and renewed self-hatred.

On the day before they landed, when he came to bring Erik's dinner tray—Erik refused to permit a deck steward to enter the stateroom— Raskin ventured to say, "I know I'm out of line, Erik, but it's not your fault the girl is sick.''

"How would you know that?" Erik rounded on him, his whisper razor-edged.

"I know that," Raskin said, cool as ever, "because, number one, that girl wanted to be with you. She *chose* to be, whether you believe that or not. And, number two, people get sick sometimes, Erik. It's not neces-sarily anyone's fault. It just happens. And lastly, number three, I think you're making a mistake running away. I know my opinions probably don't interest you one bit, but that girl cares about you. And your running off this way can only hurt both of you.''

"Leave me alone!" Erik said irritably. "And take that with you!" He pointed at the tray. "Just leave me alone!''

"No offense intended," Raskin said, retrieving the tray.

"None taken," Erik relented. "Just, please, leave me alone.''

"I'm right next door if you need anything.''

"I need nothing," Erik declared flatly. "Nothing!''

The first thing Marisa did upon returning home from the hospital was to call Erik's number. A woman answered, saying, "Answering service," and for a moment Risa couldn't think what to say. She'd been so geared for the sound of Raskin's voice that she was totally thrown.

"Is Mr. D'Anton available?" she asked at last in her most grown-up voice.

"Mr. D'Anton is in Europe," the operator told her.

"For how long?''

"Indefinitely. But we are taking messages.''

"Oh.''

"Is there a message?" the woman asked rather impatiently.

"Yes," Risa told her, angry that Erik could have gone away without letting her know. "Tell him Marisa Crane called and that I said he should come back *at once!*''

She put down the phone and stood looking at her outheld hands, which were trembling quite violently. How could he *do* that? How could he leave without so much as a word? Was it some game he'd been playing with her throughout the winter? God! She was furious. Well, to hell with him! she told herself, going to her desk to look over the pages and pages of assignments she'd have to complete in order to catch up on the three weeks of school she'd missed. *Go to hell, Erik! You can stay away forever, for all I care!*

Pulling the chair out from the desk with an angry yank, she sat down and started in to work.

For two weeks, every time her thoughts started to shift toward Erik, she'd swear under her breath and refuse to allow it. She would *not* think about him. She'd do her work, get through the rest of the year until graduation. She couldn't think beyond that point, but concentrated instead on the immediate present.

Her dreams, however, were something else altogether. Each night while she slept the hours were crowded with endless and overlapping scenes with Erik. And once—a dream she had great difficulty shaking in her waking hours—she opened her eyes to see him at the foot of her bed, a tall silent shape somewhat darker than the surrounding darkness. He came around the side of the bed and lifted away the blankets, revealing her nakedness, and stood for a very long time staring at her. Then he laid himself over top of her, his weight no burden at all. Reverentially, she held him, deeply elated by his presence in her arms. Scarcely moving, they joined together, his body merging with hers, and her flesh grew molten and swollen, before she was overtaken by a lengthy series of downflowing inner waves accompanied by her whispered outpouring of affection for him. He gave her unimaginable pleasure, then began to lose substance in her arms. She tried, but could do nothing to prevent his leaving her. In the end she was alone, naked and very cold on her bed, weeping with confusion and frustration.

The other dream that returned to her waking self was the one in which she was sitting at her desk, working on a trigonometry assignment when she heard the door open, and turned to see Erik entering. He came to stand halfway between her desk and the door and, his eyes riveted to hers, his hand lifted to remove the mask. She knew what was coming and steeled herself, prepared to show no reaction to what she was about to see. The mask was taken away to show a livid configuration of scars down the center of his face in the area where his nose should have been but where there were only two skeletal holes concealed by a vestigial trace of elevated flesh.

"It's not so bad, Erik," her dreamself told him. "I don't mind, honestly."

The Erik of her dreams elected not to believe her and with a cry of mingled pain and fury he spun about and vanished.

"*Don't go!*" she called after him. But it was too late, and she was left to wish she'd thought to say words other than the ones she'd chosen.

Maybe, she thought, during the few minutes when she looked up from her schoolwork to permit herself to think about him, nothing she could ever say or do would either be completely satisfactory to Erik or guarantee he'd stop running away from her. What did she actually know about him? Almost nothing. But that wasn't true. She knew everything she needed to know, everything he required her to know. Hadn't they used music to effect their communication? Hadn't he told her through his many compositions all he wished her to know? And hadn't she responded in kind with renditions of songs that spoke for her? What more did he want? She'd offered everything she had, but it hadn't been enough. She couldn't do more.

The net effect of all this was to make her feel aged, and a little jaded, and determined to preserve herself at all costs. That, of course, was her waking philosophy. The Marisa who dreamed had another agenda entirely. That Marisa sensed she was temporarily powerless to do anything and so must bide her time. Eventually she'd be able to do the one thing that would put a stop forever to his doubts, to his need periodically to flee from her: She would, upon his return, give to him one ultimate gift. She would give him her body. It was, she believed, a gift of such scope and immensity that he couldn't afterward possibly harbor any doubts about her love. Luckily, her two selves were unaware of their separate pacts and so she was able to go about her daily business; she was able to talk with her father and with Kitty, to eat with them and even to be present when her father's business associates and their wives came to dinner. She played hostess to her father's friends and marveled over her newfound maturity. Yet, every so often, something nagged at the edge of her attention; something having to do with her stay in the hospital, and the strong impression she had that Erik had come to her in the night and told her he loved her. But that was impossible. It couldn't have happened. It had to have been something she'd imagined in her delirium. Yet it had seemed so real. She could almost feel again his substance, could almost smell him and feel the dampness of the tears that had fallen into her hair; she could swear she'd heard him whisper, "I love you." But it must have been some dream manufactured by her ludicrous and childish longings.

Erik did nothing in London. He remained secluded in the suite at Claridges, picking at the room-service food Raskin regularly arranged to have delivered and staring sightlessly at the television set he kept on almost constantly. He sat in one of the armchairs, or paced the length of the sitting room, or threw himself face-down on the bed, where he lay for hours at a time, not asleep, but reviewing his near-disastrous acts and berating himself for the inimical behavior inspired by his affliction. His accursed face, his long years of living behind a mask that only partially shielded him from the probing eyes of strangers, had taken him far beyond the bounds of reasonable thought and decorum. The loathing he felt at being trapped behind an image in no way representative of the man he truly was threatened to devour him. And as he lay prone on the hotel bed, his fingers clawed at the bedding and the mattress beneath, as if hoping to dig their way to freedom so that his hands—these two independent and resourceful entities—might find some better life, free of the six-foot-three-inch appendage they were presently obliged to carry about with them.

"There are messages," Raskin said one evening, sitting himself down in one of the chairs. "Are you interested? I checked in with the answering service."

"I am not interested," Erik said, his voice muffled by the pillows banked around his head.

"There's one I think you might want to know about."

"What?" Erik asked, his body almost vibrating in its attempt to stifle his raging self-loathing.

"Marisa Crane called almost two weeks ago. She said to tell you you should come home at once." Raskin sat with the piece of hotel stationery upon which he'd noted the message, waiting.

First, Erik's body seemed to go very still. Then his arms, which had been at his sides, began to extend outward from his body to the perimeters of the bed. They traveled upward until they were stretched parallel to his torso, his fingers hooked over the edge of the mattress as if, at any moment, the entire bed might levitate and he wished to save himself from falling.

"Everything else is routine," Raskin went on after a time. "Business mainly. Nothing I can't handle with a couple of calls."

Erik remained unmoving, his hands still clinging to the top of the bed, his body a long arrow.

"Personally," Raskin said conversationally, as if having a pleasant chat with someone in full control, "I've had a nifty time, what with seeing the shows and several of the more interesting female employees of this establishment. You, on the other hand, are having what I would say has to be one of the worst times known in the history of mankind. What the fuck are you doing, Erik?" A note of exasperation sounded clearly in his voice. "D'you need an engraved invitation? Or do you want me to haul my ass out of here and stop volunteering my impressions?"

When Erik failed to answer, Raskin said, "I know my own feelings on the subject of women and attachments. But that's me, and I'm not you. You've got a chance to have something you seem to want. Why not have it?"

With a roar, Erik leaped from the bed, tearing off the mask. Pushing his face against Raskin's, his whisper a maniacal shriek, he demanded, "*Who could want to see this? Who?*"

Without losing a beat, Raskin calmly said, "I've seen worse. I've seen guys with their eyes hanging out of their sockets and their faces half shot away. I've seen guys with their arms and legs blown off, with their guts piled in their laps. I've seen them without ears or noses, or mouths, Erik. I've seen little kids incinerated, and grandmothers eviscerated. I've seen paraplegics and quadriplegics. I've seen guys who scream nonstop, and other guys who're quiet as can be right up to the moment they go out with a gun and start shooting pedestrians. You can't show me one fucking thing I haven't seen a thousand times before and don't see most every night of my life in my sleep. You're worse-looking than some, and not as bad as others. This whole thing is bullshit. Either go crazy once and for all, or go home and take this girl off the hook. But don't leave both of you suspended in mid-air. It's not decent. I may be a lot of things, and crazy's definitely one of them, but I'm not stupid, Erik. I have all kinds of respect for you, for your work, for your music, too. This whole scene's not worthy of you. So your face got wrecked. Too bad. You want to let it wreck your head, too, that's your choice. Personally, I think it's a waste." He got up and said, "Let me know what you want to do. I'll be in my room."

"*How dare you!*" Erik thundered at Raskin's retreating back. "How dare you presume to equate me with some filthy unethical war?"

"Because," Raskin said without inflection, turning back, "you *are* a war, Erik; an entire one-man war of epic proportions. You've got more dead and wounded inside you than any six battalions. Inside, outside, it's all the same. War's war. One way or the other, everybody gets fucked up. Or dead." With that, Raskin continued on his way to his bedroom, leaving Erik stranded with his rage and bewilderment.

Unable to leave it at that, Erik stormed after his employee, heaving open the bedroom door to demand, "Why are you saying these things to me?" Quivering, he hung in the doorway with his clenched fists held in front of his chest.

"Because," Raskin said, "believe it or not, I like you, Erik. Now what're you gonna do, try to beat up on me?"

Erik was defeated. Gradually, his fists unclenched; then his arm fell to his sides; his outraged energy drained away and he sagged against the doorframe.

"I'm your friend, whether you like it or not," Raskin told him. "And as long as you've got work for me to do, I'll stick around. I know a few things," he said without cockiness. "Not a hell of a lot, but a few things. And I know you're crazy for this girl. She wants you back, Erik. Don't be an asshole. Let's go home. I hate the fucking weather here. And half the time I can't understand what these English girls are saying. The accent throws me." He offered Erik a conciliatory smile.

Erik suffered through this proclamation of friendship. He was so accustomed to rejection he wasn't sure how to handle a straightforward declaration of caring. *No one liked him.* People never had. Certainly not the aunt who'd undertaken his guardianship after the death of his parents. She'd been unable to look at him once the surgeons had stated they could do nothing more to improve his appearance. She'd shipped him off to boarding school where he'd suffered a thousand indignities at the hands of "well-bred" little boys who found him a suitable object for their hostility and humor. There'd been no one for more than twenty-five years who'd wished to be seen in public with him, and most definitely no one, except for Raskin, who'd been at ease in private with him. Except for Marisa. Marisa whom he'd almost killed with only a small measure of the enormous love he had for her. Marisa who'd left an imperative message, insisting he come back to her at once.

And here was Raskin saying he cared, giving advice, being a friend and telling him he had every right to care and be cared for by others. Could this be real? Would it actually be all right for him to return home and dare to open his heart to this girl?

"Tell me about your night with the waitress while we pack," Erik said finally.

"Sure," Raskin said. "Let me just grab a cigarette."

Eight

B Y THE END OF HER SECOND WEEK AT HOME, MARISA WAS IRATE. SHE was so angry with Erik that she thought if she ever did see him again she might just kill him. She wanted to hurt him, to go at him with her fists and beat him bloody. *Why* was he doing this to her? She'd done nothing to him, not a single thing. And was she out of her mind or hadn't they sat side by side nightly for months, touching but not touching as their voices blended and they told each other of their autobiographies through music? She got sick and he ran away. It made no sense. Unless, she thought slowly, he'd decided for some reason that it was his fault she got sick. Could that be it? Could he really have pushed and pulled at the facts, distorting them to make them suit his reasoning? With a terrible need to know, she went downstairs one evening to talk with Kitty.

She related to Kitty the hypothetical scenario of a story she was supposedly writing for English class.

"Oh sure," Kitty said knowingly, puffing away at a cigarette. "Some men'd do exactly that. Most men can't deal with it if a woman gets sick. They come unglued. They're rotten with physical things, men. Most of them expect a woman to be a hundred percent all the time. The least little thing goes wrong and they either assume it's their fault, or they head for the hills so they won't have to deal with it. Not a lot of really grown-up men in the world, Reese. Mostly, they only play at it. What kinda story you writin', anyhow? Doesn't sound like the sort of theme I used to get handed in high school."

"It's out choice of topic," Risa lied easily. "I thought this might be kind of interesting.

"Well, it's different, that's for sure. You finally gettin' interested in the opposite sex?" Kitty teased.

"Maybe. And maybe not. It's only a story, Kitty. No big deal."

"I wonder," Kitty speculated. "You're different lately. Nothin' I can put my finger on. Just different."

"I'm older, that's all."

"Hmmn. So you say."

"Kitty," Risa changed the subject, "how'd you ever come to be a housekeeper? Surely that wasn't what you set out to be."

Kitty gave an amused laugh and ran her hand through her now grown-in hair that was back to its normal light-brown color. "Hell, no!" she replied. "Way back, I was gonna be a movie star. That didn't last too long, thank the Lord. Then, for a time, I was mighty taken with the notion of nursin'. You know, tendin' some grateful young man who'd reward me with marriage and a life of luxury. But when I thought on, considerin' blood and bedpans and bedsores, I decided I didn't have the stomach for it. At which point, I thought it might be okay to be somebody's secretary, 'cept that I couldn't learn to type to save my life, and I figured an office job'd be too borin' for words. Then, I went and got married when I was nineteen and figured I wouldn't have to give it another thought."

"I never knew you'd been married!" Risa exclaimed.

"You never asked. Sure, I been married. I figured everything was settled and I'd be right where I was for the rest of my days. 'Cept that after a year or so, we couldn't hardly stand the sight of each other. We went ahead and stuck it out for another year. Savin' face, you know. But it wasn't ever gonna work, so we moved apart easy as pie and I got a job waitressin' for a time. This 'n' that, gettin' through, livin' a not bad life, when there was this ad one day in the paper—I always liked to read the ads to see what was bein' offered—put in by this man with an invalid wife, needin' somebody to come cook and clean and help out. It raised my curiosity. I don't know why, but I went ahead and answered that ad, got the job, and decided it suited me down to the ground. I could run the whole house with none of the grief of ownership, and still had me plenty of free time for socializin'. So I stayed with them, the Wendells, for near on four years, until she died, poor thing. And then I was sittin' one night, lookin' through Mr. Wendell's alumni magazine—used to tickle me, those things—and there was your father's ad. Widower with baby girl, needs carin' woman to tend to house and child. Kinda got to my heart, and I thought, what the hell! So here we are."

"That's what it said? 'Widower with baby girl, needs caring woman to tend to house and child'?"

"Word for word," Kitty confirmed. "Touched me, that did. I had this picture of some poor young man, left helpless with this needy infant. It wasn't quite like that. Your daddy was older'n I thought he'd be, for one thing, but it wasn't too far off, neither. I liked the man right away. And I took one look at you and thought, I'll have my hands full, but it'll be okay. And it was. You were way easier than most kids, no trouble at all, 'cept when you got hold of the notion there was somethin' you wanted and you wouldn't turn that notion loose no way. But I've always admired folks with gumption, and you were a tyke with plenty of that, for sure. Your daddy and I kind of drifted together natural-like after about a year or so. It bother you, my sayin' that?"

"No. It doesn't bother me a bit. I'm glad you answered that ad, Kitty. And thanks for helping with my theme."

"Anytime," she said. "I like havin' my opinion solicited. Makes me feel right important."

"I bet Freed asks your opinion all the time."

"Oh, sure. Half the world's lined up wantin' to know what I think about this and that." Kitty laughed and put out her cigarette. "You want anything? Some tea, a Coke?"

"Nothing, thanks. I want to get back and finish writing this thing."

"Come on down anytime," Kitty invited.

"You're great," Risa told her, and gave her a kiss. "I don't know what I'd do without you."

"It's what everybody says," Kitty joked to hide her delight.

Risa returned to her desk having almost managed to convince herself there actually was an English composition waiting to be written. It took her a few moments to remember that she'd gone down to Kitty seeking confirmation of her sudden insight. And she'd received it. She had no doubt now that Erik had fled either from guilt or from fear, but in no way from a lack of affection for her or from some inclination to play bizarre games. He'd run away because he cared too much. Believing this, she was comforted. All she had to do was wait for his return. She knew exactly what the next step would have to be.

She hadn't long to wait.

The next day, she'd been home from school less than an hour when her private telephone began to ring. Instantly excited, she raced over to hear Erik's voice whisper, "Tonight at eleven. I will come for you with the car."

She was ecstatic. She'd been right. He did care; he did want to see her; he wasn't able to stay away. She'd never been happier, more filled with elation at the prospect of seeing anyone.

It was difficult for her to contain herself during dinner. Her father was in a mood to talk. She tried to accommodate him, but was so preoccupied with thoughts of her forthcoming reunion with Erik she could barely pay attention to the conversation. She absolutely couldn't eat, and merely pushed the food around her plate until she'd put in enough time at the table and excused herself on the pretext of having to finish her homework.

Upstairs, she took a long time bathing, washing and drying her hair before selecting a long pink silk nightgown with hand embroidery on the front panels and a high neckline. Over this she put on her new white dressing gown, then stood before the full-length mirror to study the results. She thought she looked too young but acceptable, and wished again that she had a more voluptuous body. Her feet were too big, too white and bony. Perhaps Erik wouldn't notice, she thought, as she placed dots of perfume behind each ear and at the base of her throat.

At last it was time. Stealthily, she crept through the house in her coat and boots, let herself out, and walked up the driveway to discover the car was already there. Like a resting panther it sat quietly rumbling, its lights off. As she approached, the door opened and she climbed into the passenger seat. At once the headlights went on, Erik put the car into gear and they raced toward his house. Neither of them spoke. She sat back and breathed in his enticing scent, holding her hands together in her lap.

Upon arriving at his house, he flew from the car to open her door, offering his hand. She placed her hand in his and was drawn into the interior of the house, along unlit corridors, down to the music room. Once inside, with the door bolted, he took her coat, mutely urged her to remove her boots, then came to stand nearby, his hands attempting to convey with their silent language what he couldn't bring himself to say. They stirred in the air between them, approaching then retreating, until she reached to take hold of them, stilling their distressed communication.

Holding fast to his hands, confronting his apprehensive eyes, she asked, "Why did you go?"

He couldn't reply; he could only turn his face away as his shoulders rose helplessly.

"I didn't get sick because of anything you did, Erik. But you thought it was your fault, didn't you?"

"I asked too much of you," he said, plainly angry with himself, his face still averted.

"Look at me," she said softly, and waited for him to do so. When he turned back to her, she said, "You haven't asked a thing of me. You could've asked for whatever you wanted anywhere along the line and I would've given it to you. Don't you know that?"

He shook his head, but his hands took a firmer grip on hers.

"Don't you want me, Erik?" she asked him bluntly.

He responded by throwing back his head and making an anguished sound low in his throat.

"Don't you?" she asked again, uncertainly.

His hands freed themselves and he shifted away, presenting his back to her.

"Erik?" She put her hand on his shoulder, and when he refused to turn, she stepped around in front of him. His head at once lowered self-defensively. "Erik?" She stepped closer.

With another of those eerie cries, his arms opened and wound themselves around her, to hold her pressed to his chest. She sighed and rested inside his embrace, feeling the heat of his body and hearing the ragged unevenness of his breathing as he kept her face hidden from his against his shoulder.

For many minutes he held her captive, not daring to demonstrate his ineptitude. Everything he wanted stood within his grasp but he lacked the courage to take it. She might express willingness now, but revealing his features would put an end to this closeness. And he had no alternative but to reveal himself. It was one of the last barriers remaining between them. Once he'd shown himself, she would either leave him for all time, or she would stay. It was that elemental, that simple. He believed she would leave him, and he was using these minutes to brace himself for that parting.

At last, he opened his arms and backed away from her. Then, as she watched, his hands went to his face and removed the mask. Not daring to breathe, he stood waiting for her reaction.

She looked at him and felt the pain begin in her belly and rise, spreading to fill her. "I love you," she whispered, distraught. "I've seen your face in my dreams and it didn't frighten me." Words, just words, she thought. Not enough. More was needed. She placed her hands on his poor dear face and kissed his mouth, then looked at him again. More, she thought. And put her lips to his damp eyes, to his temples, to his cheeks and chin, to the deep scar that commenced at the corner of his mouth, and then, once again, to his lips. "I want to make love with you, Erik," she whispered.

"*I can't!*" he cried, his hands on her shoulders, attempting to hold her away. "*I can't!*"

"Why not?" she asked. "Is it because I'm too thin and bony?"

"You're perfect, *perfect!*" he cried, his arms how winding protectively over his face.

"I know I'm not," she said unhappily. "I don't have much of a chest, and my neck's too long; my feet are too big. Is it because you think I'm too young? I'm not, really. Lots of girls at school have been doing it for ages. I hear them talking about it. Compared to them . . ."

"No!" He put a stop to her litany of doubts, his arms flinging themselves wide, one hand still clutching the mask. "It has nothing to do with *you*," he whispered fiercely. "Nothing! It's *me*. Don't you understand? I can't! I don't know *how*."

"Oh!" She paused to think about that, then said, "It doesn't matter to me. I don't know how, either. But don't you *want* to?" She was beginning to feel embarrassed at pushing the issue. "All you have to do is say so, if you don't want to."

He answered by pulling her forward to kiss her, tasting the minty interior of her lips and tongue; kissing her until her arms had gone tight around his neck and her long body was pressing urgently into his. They were generating a heat that threatened to incinerate both of them. But he couldn't get past either his reservations or his conviction that it would be wrong, morally and in every other way, to inflict his unskilled body on her. His hands explored the length and breadth of her back, the nape of her neck, her arms, as he drew air into the starving lungs before again seeking the eager welcome of her mouth. How did he dare to know such pleasure? he wondered. How could she give of herself this way to him? How could she, with such satisfied sighs, surrender to his hands' investigation and his mouth's ravening appetite? How was it she didn't pull away when he ventured to kiss the delicate column of her throat, or the supple curve of her neck? Why did she tolerate his hands as they traced the embroidered patterns that lay over her small round breasts? Yet she did surrender; she didn't pull away; she not only tolerated his hands but reached to loosen the robe and undo the several buttons at the neck of her nightgown in order to offer her naked flesh into his disbelieving hands. Trembling, he was granted access to her breasts, to the delectable weight of them on his palms. Exalted, he found the courage to look at her, to touch with hesitant fingertips the exquisite buds that sought to blossom against his inquisitive hands. She held her hand over the back of his head as he bent to pay homage, as he rested his cheek against the gentle rise of her tremulous breasts, hearing the steady thudding of her heart beneath his ear. Could this be? he wondered, daring to place careful kisses on her bared breasts. Was this actually happening? Was this miraculous child offering her naked self to his close scrutiny, and behaving as if the gesture not only pleased her but was also pleasurable? Did she actually emit soft sighs and shiver responsively to his tongue touching the stiffened tips of her nipples? She made no move to run from him, but remained as if rooted in place, prepared to accept whatever he might offer. It brought him to his knees before her. With his face pressed into the slight swell of her belly, he thought he might literally die from the munificence, the enormity of this gift. He could reach down and stroke her elegantly arched foot, learning the circumference of her ankle, its bony prominence, the silken rise of the underside of the arch, the spaces between her strong, well-formed toes. His hands could rise slowly up the length of her legs, curtained in silk, discovering the rounded thrust of her knees and, higher, the gradual alteration in the texture of the skin as knees gave way to thighs. And, beyond, the bones of her hips jutted hard against his palms, her belly warm and fresh as milk under his cheek, against his lips.

When he simply had to know, beyond any point of resisting, all of her, and allowed his questing hand to shape themselves to her shape, molding themselves to her haunches, he was moved beyond measure to feel her yielding more, then more, beneath his hands. She touched his face, his neck and shoulders. Pliant, she was opening like the sky at sunrise, offering him the definitive gift of knowledge and experience. Hesitantly, yet unable to deny his need, he delved between her thighs to find the sleek moist core of her body. At this, the message she delivered to his head and shoulder grew more urgent. It could only mean she had no objection to the progress he was making in charting the topography of her physical landscape. It had to mean she approved of his preliminary incursions. And, as if to ease any lingering doubts he might have had, she hoarsely whispered his name while her hands clutched at his shoulders and he stooped to kiss her ankles, her knees, her thighs and hips, her belly from side to side, while his fingertips went on with their investigation of her most secret self. Stirred beyond his wildest conceiving, he was lost to sensation.

It was she who, as if caught finally in the heart of an inferno and consumed by the flames, tore off her robe and nightgown, to stand completely naked to his searching hands and mouth. With her eyes closed and her senses wide open, she encouraged his voyage of discovery. He remained kneeling before her as his hands swept back and forth, touching, seeking, testing, while he attempted to taste every area of her body, his teeth at one moment grazing her hipbone and, in the next, closing with extreme caution over her nipple. He immersed himself in her body with a dedicated fascination that erased from her mind everything but the idea of perpetuating, perhaps forever, this immensely arousing assault.

It was also she who, finding it near impossible to remain upright for very much longer—her knees kept seeking to buckle beneath the pleasure—began to grope for access to his body, finding buttons that opened to admit her hand to an expanse of broad, muscled chest; finding the means with which to remove him from the clothes concealing his upper body so that she had the warmth of his smooth skin to savor, and was able for some time to content herself by feeling through the sensitized skin of her fingertips his every reaction to her slightest inquiring touch.

When she was very nearly mad with a need to bear the weight of his body upon her own, it was she who finally whispered, "Erik, I have to see you. I want to. Please, let me see you."

Which put an end to the first part of their mutual investigation and led to the next.

Nine

HE WAS DEEPLY RELUCTANT, RETURNED TO HIS SENSES BOTH BY her overt and perplexing interest and by his instinctive timidity and countless qualms. The fact of his face was one matter, the reality of his body another. He couldn't accept the validity of her claim to want to see him. Nowhere in his imaginings had his nakedness played a part; and the niceties of disrobing had never been detailed in any of Raskin's chronicles. His body was scarred too, though not as terribly. To show himself, even when nearing the pinnacle of the greatest pleasure he'd ever envisaged, seemed exceptionally risky.

"Don't be afraid, Erik," she encouraged him. "I'm not."

And that not only appeared to be the truth, it also struck him as phenomenal. She was fearless, his heavenly child. She was predisposed to all eventualities. She shamed him with her courage. So, there in the candlelit music room, he tacitly agreed to meet her display of fortitude with one of his own. Separating himself from his entranced involvement with her succulent body, he got to his feet and turned his back to shed the last of his clothes with unsteady hands.

"Don't turn away from me," she entreated him. "If you do, I'll be afraid again."

"Were you afraid?" he asked, turning in surprise.

"Of course I was," she admitted. "I've never done any of this before either, don't forget."

He'd neglected to give this fact due consideration. He was actively engaged in the process of deflowering a virgin. That he, too, was a virgin seemed scarcely relevant. He was, after all, a grown man of thirty-two and had, for several years now, listened avidly to Raskin's recountings of his dissolute activities. Nevertheless, he was daunted by the passage of her eyes over his body. Chagrined at being seen in so enflamed a state, he covered himself with his hands. Where her eyes touched him, he burned, with both desire and agonized embarrassment.

"No, let me see you," she said softly, moving his hands aside.

Then, to his delirious stupefaction, she put her hand on him. His own hands, startled starlings, beat against the air for a moment before coming to rest in her luxuriant hair.

The feel of him was unexpected, wonderfully silken and smooth. Her awareness of his vulnerability overjoyed and frightened her. This was undeniably real, inescapably real. She was wholly involved in something about which she knew nothing at all, and could only rely on instinct to guide her. Her instinct told her that he was as frightened as she. And she could see it in the way he tolerated yet appeared to relish her caress like some great barely tamed animal holding still out of sheer blind faith in her unspoken promise not to harm him.

Suffering the almost insupportable exhilaration of her touch, he forced himself to be brave, to allow this to occur, and worked to keep his eyes open, despite their need to shut down his sight. Twenty-five years before, his mother had scooped him up to kiss him on the top of his nose before depositing him on the back seat of the automobile. It had been his last close contact with the body and flesh of another. Now he was being rewarded—for no reason he could think of—by this gracious child, this indulgent, loving child.

Looking into her eyes, searching for signs, he could find only caring. There was no hint of anything but welling fondness in eyes that gazed unswerving into his. His fear began very slowly to lessen.

"I think you're beautiful," she said, and held her arms open to him.

In one sweep, he held her clasped to the length of his body, experiencing for the first time the heady power that came with learning the symmetry, the inescapable logic of why their bodies had been made as they had. She fit to him as if she were the missing other half of his person. He hadn't known until this moment that a woman's body could be such a source of completion, that the texture of her skin, her contours, and hollows, might have been created solely for the purpose of filling all the empty spaces in him that had craved substance for so many years.

"You feel so good," she sighed, fitting herself even more closely to him. "I never thought it would feel as wonderful as it does."

Freed finally of everything that might have held him back, he lowered her to the carpet in order to trace the length of the veins running from her wrists to her shoulders and across her upper chest, to warm his knuckles in the shallow caves beneath her arms; to enclose with his two hands her ribcage and then her waist; to rest each cheek and then each finger in turn against the tightened tips of her breasts, lost to her softness and increasing warmth. It was a miracle; she was his miracle, this long lovely creature with her newly acquired skills of kissing and stroking, with her satiny limbs and beguiling inner heat.

She set about her own exploration, intrigued by the way her slightest caress caused his muscles to bunch reflexively. His body was hard everywhere, arms, chest, shoulders, buttocks, thighs, hard hard. His belly jerked against her palm as if flinching, but she soothed him, gentled him, understanding that she had the ability to do this, to calm his fears so that she might, again, hold him between her hands, wondering if it really could be possible for him to place himself inside her. She doubted that her body could contain him entirely. But she had to know, had to see to completion what they'd begun. It would be the final proof of her love for him, the very essence of the gift she'd planned to give to him. The more he fondled her, the proportionately stronger her need and determination · became to fit him within her. Yet he seemed so engaged with the other parts of her she feared distracting or accidentally upsetting him.

"Erik," she whispered, her hands closed around him, "put yourself inside me."

His eyelids lowered, he shook his head in agitation. "I'm afraid to hurt you, Marisa. I can't bear to hurt you."

"It doesn't matter," she insisted, spreading herself beneath him. "It doesn't matter." What she couldn't speak of, because she wasn't sure she understood it, was a mounting kind of craziness she was feeling that would only be quelled by the kind of hurt he was so fearful of causing her. She thought perhaps she was losing her mind. Her body had taken charge, moving with independent rhythms, opening in readiness for a satisfying attack. She directed him forward, her eyes holding his, and then lifted to meet him. She'd never dreamed it could be possible to be this naked or this vulnerable. And perhaps it wasn't possible after all, she thought, her fear returning. She could feel him hesitating, could read the misgivings in his eyes. "Don't be afraid, Erik," she insisted. "I want to love you. You have to do it."

His eyes half closed, he collected himself, drawing upon her plentiful reserve of courage, and pushed cautiously against her, his slight effort aided by her heated moisture.

She knew at once the truth of his fears. It would hurt; it did. He withdrew, then slowly pushed forward again. More hurt.

"Oh, God!" she whispered, feeling deficient, defective.

At once he withdrew, his eyes flying open.

"No! Go on!" she urged. "We have to go on!"

Holding still for this, keeping herself receptive in mind and body, was far more difficult than she'd imagined. The pain seemed to return her to sanity, and to separate her from Erik. It appeared that in order to join with him she first had to suffer through yet another separation, one that would occur even while she was as close to him as it was possible to be. She was all at once chilled, but her body was growing wet with the perspiration generated by their slow exertions. Once more he approached her. She held her hands to his hips and watched him closely as he made progress inside her, on and on, never ending, as sweat rolled down the sides of her face and a groan gathered strength in her throat, but she labored to suppress any expression of the pain she underwent. At last, it seemed they'd succeeded. She'd managed to bring him entirely inside her. And there he rested, pulsing within, surrounded by the flesh she knew he'd torn in his entry. They were separate, but joined. She lay beneath him thinking nothing could ever hurt more than this, and fearing there might be additional pain still to come. Why had she ever thought love to be painless? Why had she daydreamed of lightness and feathery things when the reality was of a transition made with tearing and with blood?

He leaned on his elbows, his body astonishingly embedded deep within hers, and looked at her exquisite face, searching for a way to bring her back from the torture he knew—could feel in every part of him, and in her—he'd inflicted upon her.

"I love you so," he confessed, humbled. "If you live a thousand years, you will never outlive my love for you. Do you want this to end? Tell me what I must do, Marisa?"

It brought her back to him. This was Erik, dear gentle Erik, who'd choose to put his hands in fire before he'd knowingly, intentionally, hurt her. This was Erik, and she had a peculiar need to revolve somehow around the center of his being. Her muscles inside clenched involuntarily and Erik's face was illuminated by the surprise of heightened sensation. Abandoning words, he sought her mouth as he began to move resolutely within her.

There was no further pain. Relieved and grateful, she held him as he rocked against her, witnessing the emergence of another Erik. His features cleansed, his expression beatific, he strove toward the conclusion his body indicated was expected and necessary. In the arms of his beloved child, aware of every aspect of her being—the shift of her hips, the tightening musculature of her arms and thighs—he labored to get to the end of something close within his reach. And then, in a dizzying explosion of interior lights, with a heart out of control and love beyond all bounds, he lost himself finally and forever in the darkness of this womanchild's body.

For many minutes he went away to a place he hadn't known existed but to which he was destined to want to return daily, nightly for the remainder of his life. Deadened, yet not unaware, he dragged his weight somewhat to one side in order not to crush his darling Marisa while he regained control of his breathing and of his senses. Then, concerned for her welfare, he hastened to ask, "Are you all right? Have I hurt you?" He stroked her forehead and cheeks, desperate for her reassurance.

"It did hurt," she admitted, and then smiled for him. "We did it!" she laughed, and hugged him in congratulation. "We *did* it, Erik!"

"But I hurt you," he persisted.

"I'm pretty sure," she said with newfound confidence, "that it only hurts that way once. Next time'll be fine."

"Next time," he repeated, awed. She would not flee from him, from his abusive body, but would return to bestow more gifts upon him. "You'll come back?"

"Well, of course I will. What did you think?" she wanted to know, holding his face between her hands. "Did you think I'd run away and never come back? You did, didn't you? That's just what you thought. Don't you *believe* me, Erik? *I love you!*"

"How can you?" he asked, curious to understand this magical circumstance. "How can you possibly?"

"Because you're good and kind, because you brought me pink roses and made a silver dollar come out of my hair. Because you write wonderful music, and I adore the sound of your voice. And *now*," she added momentously, "I know I love the way you touch me."

"You do?" He seemed like a small boy who'd been given a present beyond his comprehending when it wasn't even a holiday or a special occasion.

"I do," she declared. "But I think I need to move. My legs are going all pins and needles."

At once, and again with great care, he withdrew from her. She gave a startled cry, unprepared for the final pain, and they both looked at the blood streaking her thighs.

"I am so sorry," he cried, his hands hovering over her, "so terribly sorry."

"It's all right, but I think maybe we need a towel."

"Don't move! I'll fetch something."

He disappeared into the shadows and in a few moments returned with a small white linen napkin. Kneeling between her legs, he applied the hastily dampened cloth to her skin, cleaning away the evidence of their communion.

He sat back on his heels holding the cloth in both hands, looking at its stained surface with renewed horror. He'd given her unthinkable pain and here was the proof. How could she tolerate this? How was she able to speak of returning to him, of doing that again?

"Erik," she said quietly, watching him, "you're supposed to be feeling terrific, not unhappy."

"Is that how you feel?" he asked, unable to fathom her ongoing display of fondness.

"Well, I'm definitely not unhappy. Give me that," she said, holding out her hand for the napkin. "It's on you, too," she said, and began sponging him clean.

Amazed by the intimacy they'd achieved, as well by her lack of self-consciousness, he allowed her to tend to him while a disbelieving tape rolled inside his brain, insisting that none of this could be real. It struck him then that if he spent every minute of every hour of every day for the rest of his life working at it, he'd never fully comprehend another person; he'd never be able to predict with any real accuracy the things that person might say or do or feel. Certainly, he doubted—although he did intend to try—he'd ever know this girl's mind as well as he'd know her body. Were he never to see or touch her again, he'd remember every line of her, every slope and curve; he'd be able to summon instantly the fragrance of her, the heft of her hair as it slipped through his fingers, the faint down on the lobes of her ears, the set of her shoulders, the knobs of her spine, even the shape of her toes.

Risa studied him as he sat on his haunches in front of her, his gravity in no way diminished. If anything, it seemed more pronounced in the aftermath of their awkward lovemaking. All she'd ever wanted, from their first meeting, had been to make him smile, to see him show some sign of happiness. She'd believed the experience they'd just shared was bound to achieve that. She'd been mistaken. In all the time they'd spent together she'd never seen him quite so shrouded in the darkness of his thoughts and feelings as he was at that moment.

"Do you feel happy, Erik?" she asked, her own mood rapidly descending to match what seemed to be his.

He raised his eyes to her as if puzzled by the question. "Happy?" The word had no meaning for him. "Happy" belonged to the realm of small children and those beyond the points of thought or caring. "Happy" lived in storybooks and silly films. "Happy" wasn't a state of existence one could realistically think to achieve within one's lifetime in a world full of cringing strangers. And yet what was this odd emotion staking its claim on him? It lacked the bulk and urgency of his other emotions; it felt cloud-like and pastel-tinted and terribly frangible, as if the slightest negative occurrence might cause it to shatter. Could that be happiness? he wondered. Or could it be the influx of excruciating tenderness that overwhelmed him every time his eyes came to rest on this glorious, generous girl?

"I don't know that I believe in happiness," he confided, scarcely able to credit that, without benefit of clothing, they were actually conversing.

"I believe in it. I know I feel it now. Don't you feel good?"

"I don't have words for what I feel," his mellow whisper conceded.

"But it's not bad, is it?"

"No, not that. We must dress. I must return you home."

"Wait!" The flat of her hand on his chest stopped him. "Don't rush me away, Erik, please. I want to be with you a little while longer."

"Why?" He understood none of this.

"Because no matter how much time I get to spend with you, I always want more. That's the way I think it is when you care about someone. Don't you agree?"

His head gave a slow shake. It saddened her. "Poor Erik," she crooned, and sat up on her knees to embrace him. "That's the way it is for me, anyway. Wouldn't you like to be with me all the time?"

"I would like to keep you here forever," he said, again inundated by multiple sensations at having her skin-to-skin with him.

"And what would we do?" she asked playfully, her face in his neck.

"I don't know," he told her.

"We could sing together," she prompted.

"Yes. But for now you must finish school, complete your education."

"School's boring," she protested. "Maybe I'll just get through to graduation in June, then come live here with you."

"You're too young to think in those terms."

"What terms? I want to *be* with you."

"Perhaps someday that will come to pass."

She yawned against his shoulder and he sat smoothing her hair for a minute or two, then said, "I must take you home now, Marisa. It's very late."

Sleepy, she stopped resisting and put on her nightgown and robe, then watched him conceal himself once again in his clothes. As she dressed, she wondered if it would always be this way, that they'd be profoundly close for long moments, then entirely distant for hours and days. And even in the same room together, only a few feet apart, they were somehow disconnected. "It's weird to think I have to go to school in the morning," she said lazily. "I feel way too old to be someone who's still in high school."

Holding her coat in his hand, his mask back in place, he turned and came toward her. Getting to her feet, she reached to hold his face in her hands, her heart suddenly lifting. "Erik!" she exclaimed. "You're *smiling.* You *are* happy! I made you smile."

Wrapping her in her coat, shy again with these new emotions, he had to have her in his arms one last time.

"You are so dear, Marisa, so very amusing. Come now." He unbolted the door and led her by the hand to the front of the house and out to the car.

In minutes they were at the top of the driveway and he was hurrying to open the passenger door for her.

"Tomorrow?" she asked, offering him a final kiss, drugged by the softness and warmth of his lips.

"Tomorrow," he agreed. And then he was gone.

Instead of going to school the next day, she took herself off to the Family Planning Clinic in Stamford where she took another irrevocable step into adulthood.

Returning home with her newly filled prescription and the flat packet of birth-control pills, she was so looking forward to nightfall she was unaware of anything but her own anticipation. To be with Erik, to have his hands on her, to talk with him and, perhaps, see him smile again was all she wanted. She ate hugely at dinner—everything looked good, smelled better, and tasted terrific—which prompted her father to say, "I can't believe you're the same kid who sat here last night and played hide and seek with the peas and made castles out of her mashed potatoes."

"I'm hungry." She laughed.

"More like ravenous. Looks as if you're trying to make up for years with one meal."

"Not exactly, but maybe."

"I've been giving some thought to the summer, Risa," he began. "I was thinking since you're graduating we ought to do something to celebrate, take a trip maybe, or a cruise. What would you think of that?"

Her chewing slowed and she tried to answer carefully. "What did you have in mind?"

"I don't know. Europe? We haven't been for a few years. Or a Mediterranean cruise, something along those lines. Maybe you'd like to go to southeast Asia, Hong Kong."

"You're talking about a long vacation."

"Three weeks, a month. You don't like the idea?"

"Oh, I do. It's just that I hadn't thought about being away. I mean . . . I . . ."

"What?" He asked, sensing she was trying to spare his feelings.

"I want to stay here for the summer, Dad."

"Every summer of your life you've complained nonstop of boredom. Now, I'm offering you a change to get away and you want to stay here. Why? What's going on, Risa? Something's definitely up. I'm getting it in bits and pieces. First you don't eat at all and you're moping around here like somebody died. Then you're high as a kite and eating everything but the tablecloth and the cutlery. Would you care to enlighten me?"

She put down her knife and fork, debating telling the truth. If she did, she'd get Erik in trouble. No matter how tolerant her father might be in most cases, she knew he still thought of her as his little girl, and finding out that she was in love with Erik would probably send him into fits. She hated to lie to him, so she did the next best thing. She sculpted the truth somewhat, to make it fit her needs.

"Erik's been giving me music lessons," she told him. "It's going really well, and I'd hate to have to interrupt it at this point."

"Erik's been giving you music lessons," he repeated doubtfully. "Since when? For how long? And when exactly do the two of you get together?"

"I thought you'd be mad or say no, so I didn't say anything. It's been a while now. I go to his house almost every night. He picks me up and then he brings me home."

"Every night? Well, now that explains quite a few things. I'm not sure I care for this, Marisa. I don't know that I like the idea of a young girl alone every night with a man so much older."

"Dad, you said yourself Erik isn't like other people. I mean, can you see him coming here in the afternoons, or me going there? He doesn't do things in the daytime. You know that. And he'd never harm a hair on my head. You know that, too."

"I think I'm going to have to have a chat with him," her father said.

"You don't believe me? You don't trust me?" she demanded, getting red in the face.

"Now, calm down. I didn't say either of those things. I'd just like to talk to Erik."

"Dad," she said evenly, "if you upset him and he stops my lessons, I'll never forgive you. I mean that with all my heart. I will absolutely never, as long as I live, forgive you."

He abruptly sat back in his chair, shocked by the passion of her outburst. "Since when did music lessons become so important to you?" he wanted to know.

"Since Erik said I was good." Her defiant tone giving way to one of pleading, she said, "Please, don't call and upset him, Dad. Please?"

"Marisa, you are sure that's *all* that's going on?"

"What else could there be?"

"I don't know, but I don't think I care for this. I don't like the idea of my daughter sneaking out of the house at night for so-called music lessons."

"Are you saying I'm *lying?*"

"I'm not saying that at all. I just don't think I'm hearing the whole truth."

"Then you *are* calling me a liar. I've never once in my entire life lied to you. Why would you think I'd start now?"

"Because you've never before in your entire life done anything like this—sneaking out every night for God knows how long to be with a man almost old enough to be your father."

"He is not! And besides, that has nothing to do with anything!" God! She wished she hadn't said a word. But he'd forced her into it. What else could she have said to get out of being away from Erik for maybe as long as a month? "Why are you *being* this way?"

"If it's what you say it is, neither one of you should be in the least upset by my having a talk about it with Erik."

"I don't mind your talking to him. I just don't want you accusing him, the way you've been accusing me."

"I've accused you of nothing," Cameron said heatedly. "I'm merely trying to get to the truth."

"I've *told* you the truth!"

"And *I've* told *you* I have misgivings."

"Why? About what?"

"I've told you that, too: about your spending hours every night alone with a man so much older than you."

"What d'you think he's going to *do* to me?" she challenged him. "And how d'you know I'm not the one who might be up to something? Why do you automatically assume the worst about Erik? I'll tell you why!" she stormed. "Because of the way he looks! Because you think he's a freak, that's why! If he looked like everyone else you wouldn't mind one bit."

"That is not true!" Cameron defended his position. "That is not only not true, it's unfair and insulting. I have no objections to Erik, on any grounds. What I do object to is the secrecy of this whole business, the underhanded way the two of you have agreed to get together without my knowledge or consent."

"You seem to forget I'm not a child anymore. I'm perfectly capable of making my own decisions."

"I don't deny that. But you're also very impulsive, and inexperienced in the ways of the world."

"Well, if I have to come to you for permission every time I get an idea, how am I going to *get* any experience? I can't believe you're talking to me this way, as if I'm stupid, as if I haven't got a brain in my head."

"You are not stupid; you have a very fine brain. What I'm trying to get across is that you haven't lived long enough to know that people sometimes have hidden reasons for the things they do."

"And which one of us is supposed to have those, me or Erik?"

"Christ!" he sighed, wearied by the argument. It was so rare an incident and so unexpected that he found himself halfway willing to surrender and halfway determined to exert the full strength of his parental authority. "What the hell kind of father d'you think I'd be if I just smiled and said yes to every goddamned notion that comes into your head? It's like that damned dog business all over again that you kept on at me for years about. Marisa"—he softened his voice—"this has to be discussed by all the parties concerned. Since I suspect you'll head directly to the telephone to tell Erik what's transpired here, I suggest you ask him to come over tonight so we can thrash this out. In fact, I'd like you to do that now, if you would."

"He's only going to tell you the same things I have."

"Good. Then I'll be satisfied."

"Shit!" she muttered under her breath as she dutifully went upstairs to call Erik.

Ten

ERIK FELT REMARKABLY WELL. HE'D SLEPT FOR FIVE HOURS, A SLEEP SO deep and so crowded with sensation and dreams of Marisa that he'd awakened in the early morning brimming with renewed energy and rekindled optimism. He was also taken, immediately upon waking, with the idea of buying for Marisa something as rare and marvelous as she herself was.

After he'd bathed, reluctantly washing her scent from his skin, he dressed, then got on the intercom to Raskin.

"I would like you to do an errand for me."

"Sure. What?"

"I want you to drive into the city and buy something at Cartier. A necklace, I think. In gold, a fine chain, with a small pendant. Diamond. A good size, but not too large. Nothing ostentatious."

"No problem. You want me to go now?"

"If you wouldn't mind."

"I'm on my way." Raskin hung up, smiling to himself.

Alone in the house, Erik ate some bread and butter standing by the counter in the kitchen while he watched the sunlight that, through the filter of the tree branches outside, darted by inches back and forth across the far corner of the room. Like something alive but penned by the dark boundaries of the kitchen, the light hesitated, then shifted, hesitated once more, then held still. Fascinated, Erik watched as he drank his coffee. Then he poured himself another cup and carried it up to the office where he had to stop to admire the brilliant primary-colored reflections thrown across the walls and floor by the sun insistently cutting its way through the stained-glass window. Altogether, he felt most unusual. And

633

touching his fingers to his face, he found his mouth upturned into what Marisa had called a smile. Odd, yet today everything seemed to please him. The coffee tasted exceptionally flavorful; the light seemed less menacing; and his facial muscles were creating peculiar effects. He lit a cigarette and that, too, had a better than usual taste. Most peculiar of all, the problem that had been so irksome regarding the cement-canopied entryway to the office building in Greenwich appeared suddenly solvable. All that was needed to accommodate both his client's preferences and his own dissatisfaction with the concept of a covered entrance was to arch the canopy somewhat higher and extend its perimeters no more than a foot on either side. Simple. Yet he'd been unable to see it before, and had been stalled on the design for quite some time. Now it was viable. And his inspiration had come somehow as a result of studying the trapped light in the corner of the kitchen. Structurally, he could see the change represented no difficulty. And aesthetically the building was now all of a piece.

Quickly he sketched new front and side views of the entry, noting the dimensions and calculating the stress factors created by the additional weight of concrete. Extra steel rods at either end would secure the castings. So simple. Having penciled the details in the margins, he set the views aside for Raskin to copy to scale. All that remained were the electrical, mechanical, and heating/ventilating requirements for a building of this size: boiler capacity, ductwork estimates, the usual gutworks. Once Raskin drafted the last of the views, the project could go to the modelmaker. Then the client would see the plans, the model, and go over the presentation with Raskin, who did this part of every job for Erik. A client knew in advance all queries and problems would travel with Raskin back to Erik, who would either settle them—usually by telephone—or alter the design to suit, although he required a good reason to doctor his designs. ·

But this was, as he'd promised himself, the last project. It had become yearly more difficult to deal with referrals who didn't understand the special circumstances under which he'd agree to work. He detested having to explain himself, and seldom did. Raskin undertook to inform potential clients of the terms, and if they agreed, initial contact was made. But there were clients who'd been known to grow peevish at having to deal with their architect secondhand, who felt if they were spending the money to have a building designed it was their right to have direct communication.

Erik loved the work, loved the challenge of creating buildings to suit the needs of different people. But the contact, however minimal, with querulous, demanding businessmen with no comprehension of the fine points either of architecture or engineering, made his work difficult and robbed it of pleasure. So much of the time what was wanted by these men was a monument to their personal potency, the bigger the better, good taste not an issue. There was no shortage of potential clients. His designs were successful and much admired. His buildings were of clean lines and pleasing angles, with their interior square footage used to provide the most natural light and warmth. He thought it highly ironic that his best concepts made the most use of the sun—including two Connecticut low-rise office buildings predominantly fueled by solar energy—when there was nothing he could think of that would draw him out of doors before sundown.

The sun was his enemy, daylight his torment. He was imperiled in the light of day, put at risk by the exposure of his gruesome features. He had once—and still shuddered to recall it—caused a serious but fortunately not fatal accident on the turnpike when, driving home from an unavoidable meeting in Stamford with the banker and lawyer who were the executors of his parents' estate, he'd moved into the outside lane to pass a slow-moving car driven by a young woman with long blond hair accompanied by a young man also with long blond hair. The young man saw Erik and began wildly gesticulating and yattering at the young woman, who looked to her left to see what he was raving about. Upon seeing him—Erik had felt the peripheral scorching her eyes caused his flesh—she'd evidently forgotten she was in a moving vehicle and plowed into the car ahead of her. The resulting crash involved some four or five cars, so far as Erik could determine in his rearview mirror as he swung back into the center lane and kept going. As he left the turnpike at the Darien exit, he hoped no one had been badly injured. Then he'd amended that, hoping the stupid young blonde and her hippie boyfriend had been ground to mush in the collision. He despised them for their ignorance, their lack of sensitivity and so revised his wish for their death to the hope that they'd both been left with injuries that would result in their spending the remainder of their days with disfigured faces. It would be, either way, a very long time before they were quite so quick to point and gape.

Daylight was his nemesis, his undoing, but his respect for its power was limitless. And, he thought with a pang, his Marisa lived in the light. She was a child of the sun; her skin was fragrant with it even now, in the last of winter. Her voice, when she sang or spoke, was redolent of daytime. It contained the sounds of birds, of the breeze, of sun-dappled water washing over smooth rocks. It was the whish of leaves lightly brushing together, the diffusion of sunrays through cumulus cloud clusters, the push of a bird's wings against the oppressing air. She was all that was good of the daylight world. So how could he dare to imagine having her near him always in the protective penumbra of the exclusive little world he'd constructed with such obsessive care?

Ah, but he did imagine it. Descending to the music room, where he lifted a tape from the shelf and fitted it to the reel-to-reel player, he not only imagined it, he craved it as he'd never before craved anything. With her voice and his music emerging from the four speakers, he sat in one of the black-and-gilt chairs and shut his eyes to appreciate the sound. He did so admire her natural interpretative skills, her instinctive inclination to sing slowly, hauntingly, a song traditionally chanted up-tempo. Her rich lower register gave new resonance to a song he'd previously considered trivial. I want to be happy. I won't be happy till I make you happy too.

With her voice surrounding him, with the feeling he was somehow contained by her sound as he'd in actuality been contained by her demonstrative limbs, he permitted himself to dream. And what he dreamed was of a new life, a life infinitely improved and made more tolerable by her presence within it. He visualized her moving through the rooms of his house, pictured her taking possession of the house the way she'd assumed ownership of his heart. Knowing it was foolish and likely improbable, he saw himself drawing perfumed baths for her, then being accorded the privilege of sitting close by to watch as she immersed herself in the steaming scented water; he saw the two of them eating together beneath the tinkling crystals of the dining-room chandelier; he followed after her as she traveled from room to room, subtly altering forever his perception of his home by leaving faint traces of herself everywhere; he felt her by his side at the piano, and even at the drawing board and, most significantly, he saw himself standing guard over her sleep, vigilant in his love.

It electrified him to review what she'd given him and to absorb its enormity. He'd been accorded the unprecedented privilege of becoming her lover. His entire body suffered a frisson at the recollection of the feel of her beneath his hands, the taste of her on his tongue. She had actually allowed him to penetrate the interior of her body, allowed him to divest himself of a lifetime's longing while, in the process, consigning himself to a lifetime's caring. It had been real, oh yes. She had offered, and he had dared, to immerse himself in sensation. So real had it been that even now, with his eyes closed and her voice in his ears, he could feel again the impossibly deep inward sweep of her waist, the taut thrust of her breasts, the tight heat of that yielding interior corridor. Real! Dear God, too real! So real that just recalling it filled him with the need to hold her again, to touch and taste and feel her again; to know her better, deeper, and to find ways in which to return to her some measure of the stunning pleasure she'd so liberally given to him. He knew, from years of Raskin's uninflected tales, the ways in which love could be made. And while before he'd been nothing more than an unseen specter at the proceedings, he had now an opportunity to be an active participant, an eager accomplice in the act of making love. He couldn't think how he'd get through the hours until he could see her again. There were so many things he wished, all at once, to say to her, so many long-suppressed thoughts and memories he might at last share.

He wanted to give her everything within his power to give: knowledge and music and diamonds, secrets and stories and love. Love. Was he a fool? he wondered, suddenly opening his eyes to the realization that the tape had come to an end and so had his fevered conjecturing. Was he placing far too much store in the as-yet-untried emotions of a schoolgirl? Perhaps he was nothing more than a convenient means by which a head-strong girl had chosen to rid herself of her tedious virginity. No. That was not Marisa. She was different; she knew her own mind. And, heaven only knew why, but she'd chosen him. It was scarcely credible, but she had chosen him.

When Marisa telephoned that evening and said, "My father would like you to come over, Erik. He wants to talk to you," Erik's hand closed tightly around the red-and-gold Cartier box in a reaction of complete and immediate fear.

"Why?" he asked, his body coated with sudden perspiration.

"He was suggesting he and I go away to Europe this summer and I had to give him some reason why I didn't want to go. So I told him you've been giving me music lessons. It was the only thing I could think of in a hurry, Erik. I haven't told him anything really, and I won't. But I had to say *something*. Now he's furious with me and wants to talk to you. I'm sure it'll be all right, and I'm really sorry to drag you into it, but I couldn't think of anything else to say. Are you mad at me?"

His fear abating somewhat, he answered, "No."

"You are. I can tell."

"I am not angry with you," he said stiffly. "Tell your father I will come at ten."

"Please don't be mad at me!" she implored him. "I love you so much, Erik. I couldn't go away and leave you for three weeks or a month. I *had* to say what I did."

"I understand," he told her, and hung up.

He was filled with apprehension, all but drowning in it. Cameron had it within his power to separate them forever if he chose. Marisa was a child, an underage child. Her father could dictate the course of her life with impunity. The man could do anything he wished with regard to his child, and Erik would have no way or any right to stop him. Please don't take her away from me! he thought desperately. I will do anything you ask, but please don't take her away.

He had to forearm himself, had to think of what he would say. Pacing back and forth the length of his bedroom, he tried to calm himself enough —the red box still in his tight grip—to think clearly. Cameron was bound to want to know why, if Erik had consented to giving his child music lessons, he hadn't bothered to confer with Cameron on the matter. What to say? It simply happened. He hadn't thought any harm would come of it, but of course he'd been completely in the wrong and did apologize most humbly for causing any distress. Obsequious, toadying, but appropriate. He would prostate himself, if necessary; he would pave entire city blocks with apologies, and promise anything at all if Cameron would only forgive this breach of manners and custom.

He longed to be able to approach the man and say, Sir, I love your daughter. I would marry her tomorrow were that within the bounds of acceptability. I would give up my life for her. And, sir, I believe with every fiber of my being that your daughter reciprocates that love. Please don't act rashly and sever something that represents my very ability to continue living. For a few hours I was permitted to feel complete, unimpaired in any way. It was a gift, sir, of such magnitude I haven't the words to articulate for you its scope. For a brief time I was a normal man, an ordinary man, able to give and receive love. Don't take that away. Don't deprive me of the only possibility for peace I've ever known.

So rattled and fearful was he that he decided to confide in Raskin.

"What should I do?" he asked over the intercom, the red box turning, turning in his fingers.

"That's a tough one," Raskin replied. "I think the only thing you can do is wait and find out what the man wants to hear, then say it. Don't volunteer anything. He'll let you know what he wants you to say. Just be cool, Erik. Say too much, and you'll blow it."

"Thank you," Erik whispered fervently. "That is good advice. Thank you."

"The necklace what you wanted?"

"It's exactly right. Thank you." Erik put down the phone and at last gave up his hold on the Cartier box. Setting it on the chest of drawers, he backed away to stand staring at the box as if his entire future hinged on the successful giving of this diamond token. The meeting with Cameron Crane would, in fact, determine his future. Of that he had no doubt. And should the meeting go well, Marisa would soon have in her hands the first of many tangible offerings Erik hoped to make to her.

Marisa came running up as he pulled into the driveway.

"I've been waiting for you," she said, the wind driving the hair across her face. "Don't worry. I'm sure everything will be all right."

He was too fearful to speak, and so afraid of losing her that he simply had to hold her for a moment, hoarding her embraces so that their recollection might sustain him in desolate days to come.

His fear was so palpable she couldn't help being aware of it. "It'll be all right, Erik," she promised, pressing quick kisses on his face. "Let's go in."

Taking his hand, she towed him inside, pausing to turn off the overhead light in the foyer, a gesture that touched him deeply. She was real; she was his; she was concerned for his comfort. She even knew to release his hand once inside, and stood waiting like a well-trained hostess to take his cape. He gave it into her hands, then turned, squared his shoulders, and entered the living room.

Cameron got to his feet, offering his hand and a drink.

"Cognac?" he asked Erik.

"Please."

"Relax," Cameron said. "Have a seat."

Erik forced himself to sit down in the wing chair. He was sweating again. His hands went at once to the arms of the chair and waited there like sentries.

"Here you go!" Cameron gave Erik his cognac, then went to his usual chair. Both men tasted their drinks, their eyes on each other. Then Cameron said, "Risa tells me you've been giving her music lessons."

Erik nodded, concentrating on Raskin's advice: Volunteer nothing.

"I have to tell you," Cameron continued, "not only did I have no idea of Risa's interest in furthering her music studies, I was also completely unaware these lessons were taking place."

Again Erik nodded. Risa came in to sit in the companion chair.

"Suffice it to say, I'm angry with Risa for neglecting to apprise me of the situation. I can understand why you'd choose to give these lessons at night, given the circumstances. What I really can't fathom is why neither one of you thought to tell me. Unless"—he directed his eyes to Risa—"you were under the impression that I did, in fact, know."

"He thought you knew, Dad," Risa put in. "It's totally my fault."

"Is that true, Erik?" Cameron asked him.

"No," Erik replied in his alluring whisper. "We didn't discuss it. I was remiss, and for that I apologize."

It was Cameron's turn to nod. "I'm sure you can appreciate my concern, Erik. A young girl going alone nightly to the home of a grown man, a home whose address I don't even know."

"I will rectify that at once," Erik volunteered, his hands flying to his inner jacket pocket for the notebook and gold fountain pen he always carried. Setting the notebook on the arm of the chair, he quickly printed out the address in his draftsman's lettering, then tore the page from the book and handed it to Cameron.

Cameron looked at what Erik had written, then began to laugh. "I'll be a son of a bitch!" he chortled. "You bought the old Terwilliger place across the way. *You're* the one who finally rescued the poor old ruin."

Unutterably relieved, albeit still on his guard, Erik's facial muscles relaxed some and he said, "Yes."

"Well, if that doesn't beat all," Cameron crowed. "And here I was worrying that Risa here was going off every night into the sticks somewhere, when all the time she was right next door. Why the hell didn't you tell me that, Risa?"

"You didn't ask." She smiled at her father, then turned to look at Erik.

"My God, that place had to be empty a good ten years. You had your work cut out for you there."

"It took some time," Erik allowed. "Five months."

"Well, I'll be," Cameron said, taking a last look at the page before folding it away into his pocket. "Just do me a favor, the two of you. See if you can't hold these lessons at a more reasonable hour, say nine o'clock. Risa's only got a few more months of school, and then you can sing all night, if you want. But for now, let's agree to an eleven-thirty curfew. Okay?"

"Sure," Risa said at once, looking to Erik.

"Of course," Erik agreed. "And I do apologize for the misunderstanding."

"Not at all. Let's forget the whole thing. Now, tell me. I understand you've submitted a plan for Farrell's new building."

It *was* going to be all right. Erik's loss of tension was so great it left him feeling sleepy, barely able to pay attention to the ensuing conversation. Risa sat back in her chair, crossed her legs, and let one foot swing lazily back and forth as she listened. Riveted to the sight of her schoolgirl's knee socks and bare knees, Erik responded to Cameron's questions, not daring to look at her face. He knew if he did he'd give the game away; his feelings were bound to transmit themselves to her father. And he couldn't do anything to jeopardize their now-sanctioned visits.

He stayed just over an hour, then excused himself on the pretext of work waiting to be done.

"I'll walk Erik to his car, Dad," Risa said, and contained herself until they were well beyond her father's seeing or hearing before winding her arms around Erik's neck, whispering, "I was looking forward all day to making love with you tonight. It was all I thought about the whole day long. Now it'll have to wait until tomorrow."

"Marisa, there are things to consider . . ."

"I've taken care of those things," she interjected. "I cut school today and went to the Family Planning Clinic."

"You did what?"

"I went and got birth control pills. Now we don't have a thing in the world to worry about. Unless I got pregnant last night."

He was jolted. "I never gave it a thought," he reproached himself aloud. It was something Raskin hadn't ever covered in any of his tales. As far as he knew, neither Raskin nor his women ever took any precautionary measures. Erik's only knowledge of their necessity was derived from his reading.

"Well, why would you? It's not as if it's something you've ever had to think about before, is it?"

"No," he replied honestly.

"So, okay. *I* thought about it, and it's taken care of." She held her mouth to his to be kissed and he somewhat distractedly obliged her. Then he pulled away. "You must go back inside, Marisa. It's too cold to be out here without a coat."

Her response to this was to pull his cape open and enclose herself within it. "Do you feel me trembling?" she asked him. "I wish I could come home with you now. I was a little sore this morning, but I kind of liked feeling it. All day I kept thinking about the way you touched me. I'd go off into these little dreams and start remembering everything we did, and I'd get this jumpy feeling in the pit of my stomach. I want you to touch me again. I love you so much."

"Perhaps," he ventured, "it's only making love you love."

"Don't say that!" she told him, stung. "It's *you* I love. I know the difference. Thinking about you today," she whispered against his ear, "I could hardly sit still, Erik. It made me all wet."

"Christ!" he exclaimed, automatically holding her closer while his own body rose in response.

"Give me another kiss and then I'd better go."

He touched his mouth to hers, then shifted out of her reach. "Please, hurry back inside. I will come for you tomorrow at nine."

"Say you love me, Erik."

Ah, he thought, she was capable of subtle torment. "I love you" came his whisper. And then he was driving away and she was running back to the house.

Eleven

WITH RASKIN OUT FOR THE EVENING, ERIK BROUGHT RISA IN through the front door and invited her to view the house. As she inspected each room, he drank in whatever praise she offered. When she commented on the softness of the leather covering the living-room sofas he felt much as he did when she placed her hands on his face. When she appeared not in the least bothered by the funereal lack of color, but opted instead to admire the dining-room chandelier and the spaciousness and clever planning of the kitchen, he was humbled. And when at last they stood together in his bedroom, having completed their tour of inspection, she pronounced his room "Sensational. It feels like sleep, like the way it is when you're tired beyond belief and all you want is to sink into bed, and you do, and it's just the best thing ever," it was the highest praise he'd ever received.

There she stood in her student's clothing—white button-down shirt, Shetland cardigan, short pleated skirt, knee socks and Bass loafers—looking at his bed, saying, "It's the biggest bed I've ever seen. Did you buy it so there'd be room for me?" She smiled so lovingly, holding out her arms to be embraced, that he could no more have resisted her than give up breathing.

"You're quite sure about this?" He had never taken anything for granted and was not about to begin now.

In answer, she took off the cardigan, then her hands went to the buttons on her blouse. But he stopped her, asking, "May I do that?"

"Yes, you may," she replied and stood in place while his eager hands tried to contain their excitement, flexing then curling several times before commencing the delicious task of baring her body to his eyes. "But," she added after a moment, "only if I get to do the same."

"Wicked girl!" came his whisper.

"Wicked you!" she returned happily.

He couldn't help wondering as he slowly opened the front of her blouse why he'd never considered that intimacy, in particular physical intimacy, could be sufficiently elastic to contain humor and conversation. All he'd learned from Raskin was of the act itself, its variables and permutations. He'd heard everything about the graphics, but nothing of the freedom, the euphoric loss of restraint. Perhaps, he realized with a sympathetic pang, it was because Raskin knew nothing of these things. Raskin either feared closeness or failed to hope for it, for he'd never once referred in the telling of his many encounters to anything beyond perfunctory conversation between perfunctory drinks followed by businesslike lovemaking. His tales lacked emotion, Erik now saw; they were titillating only by dint of their aspects of conquest and sportsmanship and athleticism. Poor Raskin, Erik thought, reclining on the bed beside his adorable lover. Fortunate Erik.

As before, he was drawn into a prolonged and extravagantly pleasurable minute examination of her flawless body. In the faint light from two thick candles placed on the dresser top, he watched the way her nipples tightened and elongated at his touch; he studied her face as his cautious fingers made her writhe and reach for him. His actions upon her affected her breathing and her body temperature; they turned her moist, especially when he touched her just there. At this point, just here, his seeking fingers created a visible and quite violent reaction in her. And this in turn created a matching response within him that prompted him to learn to what extent he might augment and prolong this reaction of hers. It had to be possible, he reasoned, to take her to a place parallel to the one he'd discovered in their first encounter. And the route to that unthinkable ecstasy was precisely here. How astonishing to find himself possessed of the ability to please her, when the process itself so thrilled him! He could close his eyes and lose himself to her taste and texture, drinking from her as if from some jeweled chalice, greedy yet never incautious in the pursuit of a no longer elusive secret.

If someone had suggested to her, even three days ago, that she might one night lie naked on a bed while a man she felt she loved more with each passing moment kissed her between the legs the way he'd kissed her mouth, she'd have laughed and declared it was the most ridiculous thing she'd ever heard. But it was happening, and it wasn't in the least ridiculous. It was terribly serious, and she liked it so much she thought she might very well have some sort of seizure. Her hands of their own accord held Erik's head close to her as he delivered this lengthy kiss, and her eyes rolled closed in order that nothing should distract her from her pinpoint focus on the flame he'd lit and was now stoking to a bonfire at the very center of her being. Her knees, independent and determined, bent and parted; her belly quivered; her entire body quaked, her chest and neck now caught fire; and her breathing apparatus had gone completely haywire so that she could only draw in occasional sips of air that were exhaled on encouraging murmurs over which she had no control. His hands continued to search her flesh like homeless creatures seeking to nest, examining every part of her, challenging its potential as a new dwelling. She abandoned herself to him, entrusting her very soul into his keeping.

The longer it went on, the more her body responded and the more heated it became; the more sensitive to touch and pressure. Until, all at once, there was an utter interior silence, a space in which all thought and movement ceased. Then Erik delivered the final spark that set her ablaze. She went rocketing, selfless, into the heart of the conflagration, gasping with shock as a tide of exultation capsized the vessel that had always contained her.

Erik was awed by their achievement, by the visibility of the pleasure he'd managed to give her. He lay with his arms wrapped around her hips, his face hidden against her belly, feeling the love she transmitted through the hand that stroked his head. In this lull, he had a sudden and dire insight. Marisa was taming him, crashing through the defenses he'd spent so long structuring. With her love, she was domesticating him, bringing him in from the wild. And out of his love for her, he was going docilely, albeit guardedly. He was so undone by his feelings for her that he could no longer maintain the barricades with which he'd secured himself for so long. She loved him, and one day she would leave him. When that happened, when he found himself armorless and alone, he would die. He'd have nothing left to protect himself from marauding strangers, no means of escape. And he'd have no Marisa. He wouldn't wish to live without her.

"What's the matter, Erik?" Her hand now lay on his shoulder. "What's wrong?"

He had no words for the vast emptiness of the horizon he'd glimpsed off in the future. He could only succumb to his horror of that eventual day.

"Erik." She slid down through the loop of his arms to cradle his head against her breast. "Tell me what's wrong."

Ashamed of his weakness—he'd fought most of his life against his easy inclination to tears—he sat away from her, rubbing his fists into his eyes.

"Is it me?" she asked. "Did I do something wrong?"

He couldn't speak of his feelings for fear of appearing an ingrate or a fool. "It's just that I care so very much for you," he was able to say.

"And that makes you cry? Come here." She pulled him back into her arms and caressed his patchwork face. "Be happy, Erik. I care just as much for you. I may be young, but that doesn't mean I don't know what I want or how I feel. I want to spend my whole life with you."

"You can't know now what you'll want for all of your life," he told her, pressing his lips to the alabaster mound of her shoulder. "You may think now it's what you want, but one cannot guarantee anything, especially not emotions."

"*I* can," she insisted with the charming arrogance of her youth. "I know I want to be with you forever. If I could, I'd marry you tomorrow. And if the other night did get me pregnant, I'd be glad."

To her dismay, he cried, "*No!* Don't *say* that! It was imbecilic of me to take such a risk with you. We'll have to pray you don't become pregnant as a result of my ignorance."

"But why?" she wanted to know, cowed by his adamance.

"I will *never* put a child into this world to know the humiliation and horrors I've known."

"But, Erik, a child of ours wouldn't have to grow up the way you did—however that was. I know so little about you, about your life."

"Please, I'd prefer not to discuss it."

"It's all so weird," she said, half to herself, drawing up her knees and winding her arms around them, her eyes on his brawny back. "One minute we're so close, and the next we couldn't be farther apart. I wish I could understand how this happens. Sometimes, I feel so lonely with you. I don't know why that is."

He peered over his shoulder at her to see that she did, indeed, look forlorn. At once, he melted.

"I'm sorry." He placed his hands on either side of her face and raised her head in order to look into her eyes. "I am most truly sorry. I have no right to burden you with my thoughts, my fears."

"But you *do*," she said ardently. "Love gives you that right, Erik. It's not a burden. It's an honor. If you hold back on your feelings, then I'll have to do the same. And neither one of us will have anyone to tell our true feelings to, so we'll both be lonely."

"Oh, my sweet girl, dear little girl, I don't want you to be lonely." His facial muscles made their smiling contractions again, and he was rewarded by the sight of a smile lifting the corners of her delectable mouth. "My angel," he crooned in his low whisper. "My lovely Marisa."

"I love the way you say my name," she told him, falling back against the pillows. "And I *love* what you just did. It was like holding a prism up to the sun right in front of your face so that all the rainbows fall in your eyes. Is that how you feel when you shudder inside me? Is it like rainbows in your eyes?"

"It's rather more like *being* the rainbow," he said, straightening her legs before bending to touch his cheek against her instep. "So very lovely," he sighed, his hands reverently skimming over her knees and up the length of her thighs, then reaching beneath her to turn her over onto her belly so that he could dip his tongue into the twin indentations at the base of her spine while his hands, uncontrollable scavengers, went seeking treasure underneath. These two eager explorers roved over her body, locating new areas of reaction, ways of probing and teasing that had Marisa lifting and pushing back into him. The more overt her reactions, the more potent he became. He hadn't ever felt quite so powerful or so aware of his physical strength and the need to be gentle. He vowed he would never hurt her in any way, and kept this firmly in mind as she moved against him, her arms spread to the sides of the bed. She repeated his name over and over, nearing another peak. Sensing this, he turned her again, lifted her easily and brought her down in his lap with her legs on either side of him.

With an instinct and intent that galvanized him, she reached to guide him as he lifted her forward. "It doesn't hurt," she reassured him, before opening her mouth over his, all eagerness and heat.

Locked together, he held her to his chest, amazed by her resiliency and zeal. There was nothing, it seemed, she couldn't do, his brilliant womanchild; nothing she wouldn't do. Unlocking her legs from around him, he eased her down again, maintaining the heartening connection. Then, fluidly, he swung to one side so that she lay above him, her knees tight against the outer sides of his. "How does it feel?" he asked, monumentally concerned.

"Wonderful." She raised herself to smile down at him, then playfully tilted her head so that her hair fell across his chest. "How does it feel?"

"Wonderful," he echoed, his hands on her hips holding her steady as he rose higher into the liquid core of her body. "And how does this feel?" he asked, watching her face closely as he slipped his hand between their bodies to press cautiously against her.

In response her muscles clamped around him inside; her face cleared as all thoughts fled from her mind and she rose and fell to perpetuate the feeling, to commence a ride that at each descent stabbed her with pleasure. Lowering the upper half of her body to his chest, her fingers interlaced with his, she kissed his forehead, his eyes, and then his mouth, deeper and deeper, accelerating the motion until she felt, in an instant of separation and awareness, his body being overtaken by spasms as it completed its journey within her. Only a moment and then she was paralyzed, trusting him to know she needed him to pull her with him over the edge.

"Please, Erik!" she cried, lost to dependency. And he climbed to meet her, keeping her oscillating on the brink for perilous seconds before hurling her off into space.

He returned to himself slowly, opening his eyes to find Marisa sharing his pillow, her eyes gazing into his.

"I was watching you sleep," she said, tracing the outline of his lips with the tip of her forefinger. "You sleep so nicely, like a little boy. I looked at you all over," she said with bold impishness. "I love looking at you. Tell me all the things you like to do."

"I don't understand." His forehead furrowed.

"Well." She smiled, the eternally patient teacher. "Do you like to swim? Or play basketball? Do you dance? I love dancing."

"I don't know how to dance."

She sat up and gaped at him. "You don't know how to *dance?* I don't believe it! You have to know! You move like a ballet dancer, for heaven's sake!"

He laughed. A pure stream of untainted laughter gushed from his throat.

She punched him lightly on the arm, asking, "Why're you laughing?"

"A ballet dancer," he scoffed. "It's too absurd."

"But it's true. I've never seen anyone move the way you do. Your beautiful hands, and the way you seem to drift from one place to the next. I know absolutely you can dance."

"No, I cannot."

"Then I'll teach you. There has to be a radio or something in here." She jumped off the bed and stood peering into the shadows.

"There is a switch on the wall to one side of the dresser," he told her, amused and curious to see what she'd do. "Push it and a panel will slide back. There is a radio behind the panel."

She did as he said, then stood fiddling with the tuning dial, found a station and turned, beckoning to him. "Come on, Erik. I'm going to prove to you you can dance."

He got up good-naturedly and went to stand in front of her.

"Okay. Now put this arm around my waist, and hold my hand with this hand. Great. Bend your elbow a little. Perfect. Now, on the beat all you have to do is step forward, toward me, then to the side, then back, then to the side again." Following her instructions, they moved through the four steps. "Just don't look down," she said. "Hold me closer and put your cheek against mine, and we'll do it again."

It was easy. After eight bars, he attempted a turn, completed it successfully and received her effusive congratulations. "Didn't I *tell* you? *Of course* you can dance. You've got that perfectly. Okay. Now don't move!

Let me find a different station, and I'll teach you something else." She fussed with the tuning dial until she found a station playing what sounded like a Strauss waltz. "You can do this, for sure," she promised him. "It's just one-two-three, one-two-three." She started out leading, then stopped to say, "We can't do a waltz cheek-to-cheek. This one we do at arm's length, looking deeply into each other's eyes." Again, he laughed, but gamely submitted himself to her instructions. In a minute or two, he'd taken the lead and was waltzing her around the room, dancing as if he'd been doing it all his life. And laughing completely spontaneously.

"This is great!" she exclaimed. "Every night when I come I'll teach you a new dance. I *love* dancing, don't you?"

"I love *you*. And I must take you home. It's eleven-twenty."

"I wish I could stay and sleep beside you, wake up early and watch you sleep. I wish I *never* had to go home, or go back to school. I learn so much more from you than I do at school. I'm so happy with you."

"I wish you could stay, too," he said, gathering her clothes and his own from the floor. "But for now, we must get you home."

"Why do you whisper, Erik?" she asked, pulling on her undergarments.

He stopped dressing and looked over at her. The air was suddenly filled with tension and static. "Would you speak loudly if you were trapped behind this face?"

"Oh, Erik!" At once distressed and apologetic, she went to put her arms around him. "I'm sorry. I only thought it might have been because of the accident. I'm sorry."

"It's of no importance. I must learn not to foist my bitterness on you."

"I understand." She kissed his shoulder, then went back to her dressing. "I really do understand, you know."

He didn't reply, and she had the wits not to force it. Privately she believed she truly did understand. And she'd make it up to him for all the awful things that had happened in his life. She'd make him forget he'd ever been unhappy.

Before they left the room, he went to turn off the radio, then picked up the Cartier box from the dresser. He studied the box thoughtfully for a moment, then held it out saying, "This is for you, Marisa."

"You bought me a present?" Her eyes were wide. "You really do love me, don't you?"

"Yes."

"Oh, my God! It's a diamond. Erik!" Her widened eyes filled with tears. "I wish I could wear it," she said mournfully. "But I'd never be able to explain this to my father."

"You'll wear it when you come here," he suggested.

"Yes, I will. Thank you." She flung her arms about him and hugged him hard, then went to put the box back on top of the dresser. Returning to take hold of his hand, she said, "I can make you happy, Erik. I can show you what it is. It's not very hard. You'll see."

He held her hand to his mouth, then whispered, "Come now. It's late."

Twelve

JUST OVER TWO WEEKS AFTER THEIR INITIAL LOVEMAKING, RISA GOT her period. It saddened her because despite Erik's protestations she'd secretly hoped she'd get pregnant. Now that wasn't going to happen and it meant she'd lost the opportunity to prove to him that a child of his could have a full and happy childhood. It also meant they could not make love.

When she explained this to him he looked at her in something like wonderment. Whatever basic knowledge he had of women came from books he'd read. To have this living, breathing, healthy young woman tell him matter-of-factly that her body was in the process of renewing itself was a revelation and a furthering of their already intense intimacy.

"Do you feel ill?" he asked her. "Shall I take you home?"

"I feel fine. We could go to the music room, if you like."

"Yes," he agreed, and gingerly took her hand to direct her downstairs.

As in the early months of their nightly visits, they sat together at the piano.

"Sing for me," he whispered.

"What would you like to hear?"

"Anything at all."

"I'm in a silly mood, Erik," she cautioned him. "Can we do silly songs?"

"Is this what happens to women?" he wondered quite seriously.

She laughed, delighted, and said, "No, not at all. I'm just in a happy, silly mood. Okay?"

"Yes, of course."

She sang "Shuffle off to Buffalo" and "Yes, We Have No Bananas" and "Abba Dabba Honeymoon," then said, "I want to ask you something."

His head tilted to one side.

"I'm afraid I'll make you mad."

"Perhaps you will," he said. "But ask."

Turning more toward him on the bench, she held her open hand gently to his face. "It's funny," she said softly, "but I know your face. I mean, when I look at you what I see is the face you were meant to have. I know how you look. Your eyebrows are kind of feathery, and your beard isn't heavy, not the kind you'd have to shave twice a day the way Dad does. Your nose is straight and not too long, and there's a very nice little groove here"—she touched the space between the bottom of the mask and the top of his upper lip—"and your chin is strong and a bit square." She paused. His features revealed no reaction. "I don't mean to be unkind. I just want to understand. You know?" Still he showed no emotion. "Couldn't they have done more for you, Erik? Was this the best they could do? Oh, God! Please, don't be mad at me!"

When he spoke, it was with the dispassion of someone highly skilled after years of lecturing on one subject. "There is," he told her, "just so much skin on the human body that can be used for grafting purposes. The only skin entirely compatible with facial skin is that which is located directly behind the ears." He turned his head and pulled his ear forward to illustrate graphically. "There is not very much of it," he explained, as she studied the stripped-looking region. "When the facial trauma is such that more grafts are required, the surgeons are obliged to raid other parts of the body. In my case," he went on, slowly turning away from her, "they had to use what skin they could. And since the grafts all came from different areas and each area has its own tone and texture, we have the resulting patchwork effect. As for the nose, it could have been reconstructed. But without natural skin or bone. *Plastic*, in essence. The chances were I'd have looked even more grotesque, so there seemed no point. Besides, I'd come to loathe those surgical procedures. A few months recuperating, then they'd bundle me off back to hospital to put me under one more time, make a few more grafts, bring me round and hold a basin in front of my mouth while I vomited blood. Twenty-two procedures in all, and then I refused to go back. I was very young." He gave one of his embittered laughs. "I thought it wouldn't matter. Because, you see"—he turned back to her—"I looked *so much better*." Another derisive laugh. "It's all a matter of comparison. This face is nowhere near the horror of the face that emerged after the collision. I find that rather amusing." Again, he turned away. "Wonderfully amusing."

"I'm sorry," she said softly, wishing she hadn't questioned him.

As if he'd failed to hear her, his fingers moving noiselessly over the keyboard, his voice lower still, he said, "Quite often it comes back to me, the terror of those few seconds, the deafening noise of the crash, the frantic weightlessness as I fly about the interior of that automobile, the screams, and the blood. So much blood, gushers of it, sheeting across the seats, spattering on the shattered glass, and over me. The *smell* of it, the slippery *ooze* of it; its sticky thickness. Mine and theirs. And I feel the demented pounding of my heart as I see them, those monsters who'd been my mother and father. Only a few seconds and my heart is trying to escape from my body, trying to escape those bodies holding me down, spilling their poisonous liquids over me, looking to take me with them to their black world, their reeking haven. But I will not go; I refuse to go; I push against them, strike them with my fists, screaming all the while my refusal to go with them." He went silent, listening to the echo of his steady heartbeat in his ears, swallowing to rid himself of the taste in his mouth so like blood. The sounds of the crash gradually diminishing, his eyes returned to the present to gaze at his fingers splayed on the keyboard. Then he lifted his heavy head to see Marisa shedding tears. She sat very still, her eyes never having left him, and wept. Still caught up in that long-ago scene, he studied her, finding it hard to connect her tears to the tale he'd just told.

At the beginning, in the immediate aftermath of the accident, the few remaining family members had wept, copiously and long, including his Aunt Dorothy. She'd believed then that members of the medical profession could work miracles and so it was bound to be only a matter of time before Erik was once again the perfectly beautiful child he'd been prior to that Sunday afternoon. But it was not to be, and Dorothy was dutiful in arranging his frequent returns to surgery. She packed his bag and saw him into the Daimler, then stood at the front door until the chauffeur had driven out of sight. And turning every time to look out the Daimler's rear window, Erik had seen his aunt make a face before going back inside the house.

It was Henry, the chauffeur, who oversaw the admitting procedures, who made sure Erik was safely installed in his hospital bed, who placed a large caring hand on the small boy's head, saying, "There's a good lad," before regretfully leaving. Only Henry had sought to offer consolation, had been in the least sympathetic to the child's undiminished fear. "You'll be right as rain in no time, and home again," Henry said every time, producing some boiled sweets from his uniform pocket before marching away in his military fashion. Erik several times heard him tell one or the other of the nursing sisters, "Look after the lad now, won't you?" or "Have a care to leave a night light for the boy. He finds the dark worrisome."

Erik had had, in those early days, a terror of darkness. Very quickly he'd discovered that it was his ally, and not something to fear. And when his body had mended, wide awake when the rest of the household lay sleeping, the boy had gone down the wide staircase to turn cartwheels on the Aubusson carpet, to walk the countertops of the kitchen barefoot, pretending they were high wires, to dance about on the wet early-morning lawn—all acts of useless defiance directed toward Aunt Dorothy who so prized her carpet, her immaculate countertops, and who railed against hapless guests who chanced to set foot upon the closely cropped grass.

Twenty-two surgical procedures in three years, and then his aunt had shipped him off to boarding school with no concern for the type of reception he might meet in this upper-class jungle of smug, vicious little members of the peerage. These future dukes and earls and lords were masters of creative cruelty, geniuses at the art of torment, and set about the task of demoralizing and victimizing the new boy, the monstrosity, with manic determination. Erik's only recourse had been to seek knowledge in the school library, reading up on ways to defend himself and strengthen his body, and perfecting his skills in the dead of night when the wearied little shits, exhausted from a day's active abuse of one small child, slept sprawled in their tidy beds. He imagined acts of vengeance, dreamed of a moment of triumph when he would make them all see how truly badly they'd behaved. But, of course, it never came. He dared not take on singlehandedly dozens of opponents who'd happily have ground him into the dust. So what he did instead was concentrate on music, picking up his instruction from the point at which his father had left off. To evade the other boys he spent hours in the music room after lessons, attempting ever more difficult pieces, practicing scales and exercises and committing to memory entire concertos, and not merely those composed for piano but ones for trumpet, or violin, or harp, as well as others intended for bassoon, or flute, or cello. So that when they found him, as they inevitably did, and began their poking and taunting and physical assaults, he played fully orchestrated suites inside his head, conducting whole orchestras while playing solo piano, or flute, or contra bassoon. The blows fell upon him but he paid them no mind, lost to the swelling crescendos only he could hear.

No one, not even the masters, had cared. Only Henry, when he came with the Daimler to collect Erik at the start of each school holiday, expressed the least interest in his well-being. And because of Henry's position as employee, Erik was not permitted to spend any of his time at home in the older man's company. Aunt Dorothy frowned on fraternization between the classes, and Erik must always remember, she told him repeatedly, that he had been born into a family of high standing and must behave accordingly. Which did not include socializing or even conversing with the chauffeur.

When, at seventeen, Erik was leaving for New Jersey to attend the American university that had been quick to accept him, Henry drove him to the airport, saw Erik's bags safely into the hands of a porter, then went with him to the check-in desk. Before leaving him at the departures lounge, Henry had taken hold of Erik's hand and held it in both his own. "I hope life is good to you, Erik," Henry had said. "God knows, you deserve it." Then he'd touched two fingers to the brim of his peaked cap, and marched out of Erik's life forever. He remained in Aunt Dorothy's employ for another six years, then retired to a small inherited cottage in Surrey, where he lived four more years before he died. Henry was the only one to whom Erik had ever written, the only one who'd remembered Erik's birthday and sent a card each year. Henry alone, with his limited contact, had provided sufficient proof of his caring to give Erik the courage to try to make a life for himself.

And now there was Marisa, this tender-hearted girl who could weep over the small fragment of his history Erik had elected to offer. This girl represented his salvation, yet he was so mired in a lifetime's anger that all he could do was hurt her repeatedly in order to prove the truth of her caring. It was wrong of him, and as cruel in its own way as the things those boys had done all those years before.

"It was hateful of me to do that to you," he said now. "Please forgive me."

"I forgive you, Erik. It wasn't hateful at all." She accepted the handkerchief he gave her and blotted her eyes. "I want you to feel you can tell me anything. I'm just sorry your life has been so unhappy."

He had to wonder how much proof he was going to require before he accepted that her caring was in no way synthetic, not generated by curiosity or, worse, by some perverse streak.

"It's something I seem unable to stop myself doing," he tried to explain.

"I know," she said. "It's hard to trust people."

She truly did understand. It staggered him. Placing his arm around her shoulders, he drew her to him, appalled at the way the past was constantly interfering with his present contentment. "I do trust you," he told her, for this evidently was the truth. "I simply have no experience of exchanging confidences, of holding extended conversations, of talking at all."

"But the best of it is the talking part, Erik. You could tell me absolutely anything and it would only make me love you more. I like to think you'd want me to come to you when there are things I need to talk about."

"I would, I do."

"I'd do anything for you, anything. I wish you'd believe that." She sat back from him, her hands fastening to his forearms. "I don't know *why* I love you, not really. I mean, I don't have just one reason, and I don't know how it happened. I only know that I do, and it's very real. When you came to dinner that first night, all I could think was: I could make you happy. And I know I could; I can. I know you wonder all the time why I would pick you to love. I know you do wonder about that, because every time we're together, I can feel you asking questions; I can almost *hear* you. But what you don't understand, what I can't make you see, is that I'm on the inside of me, too, and can't see the outside. Just the way you're on the inside of you. Nobody ever sees their own outside, Erik. That's the part *everybody else* sees. So you see me, and you have your picture of me. And I see you, and I have my picture of you. And I'd bet you anything that if we could actually have those pictures and hold them in our hands to show each other, neither one of us would believe for one single minute that that's the way either one of us actually looks. *Because we don't see ourselves!* Do you get it?"

"My God, you're incredibly bright!"

At once she smiled. "You think so?"

"I think one day you're going to be a woman to reckon with."

"Right! Whatever that means."

"You know precisely what it means."

"I guess. I *wish* we could make love."

"Is it out of the question?"

"I don't know. I don't know if people do. Have you noticed it's something they never write about in books—whether or not people do it at times like this?"

"It'll wait." He kissed her forehead.

"It's only a few days." She rested in his embrace for several long moments, thinking. Then she announced, "I have an idea, a wonderful idea. In fact, it's a sensational idea. Let's go upstairs!"

Feeling rarely childlike, caught up in her sudden enthusiasm, he let her hurry him upstairs to his room, then stood and watched, bemused, as she locked the door. Then, turning, she said, "Take off your clothes!"

"Oh, now, just . . ."

"Come on, do it." She tugged at his jacket. "You'll like this, I promise."

Doubtfully, he began to undress while she stripped down to her underpants and then folded back the bedclothes. "I love watching you undress," she said, waiting for him. "I love seeing your body, the way you move. And best of all, I love touching you. Come here and lie down with me."

He obeyed and she curled up against him, whispering, *"You're* not having a period. So *I* can make love to *you*. Now you'll know what it's like when you do this to me."

Then she gave herself over to an examination of his body that was as intense and prolonged as any he'd made of her. She took her hands and mouth over his body, kissing and stroking, probing and caressing until she was playing him in the way the boy he'd once been had, in self-defense, played entire symphonies in his head in order to save himself from going mad with loneliness and despair.

She tracked the passage of the slim raised scars that traversed his body, the one that ran horizontally across the base of his belly, another that lay across his right hip, the twins that sat precisely down the center of both thighs, the slick, slightly raised scar that began inside his left shoulder and went halfway down his back. And as she ran her tongue over the evidence of what had to have been unimaginable pain, she concentrated on healing him. Her hands and lips and tongue could erase the evidence of his torment; she could, with her personal magic, make him whole—if not in the eyes or minds of others—to himself. Can you feel how I love you? she silently intoned. Do you feel it? Can you tell? You must see it, know it! Believe in us! she willed through her ministrations.

Rapaciously she tended to him, without permitting him to touch her. She dined on him, a lavish banquet. She gorged herself on his flesh and displayed for him her newly acquired skills and some she was only just discovering. And throughout she gauged his reactions by the sound of his breathing, through the tremors that shook him. She showed him the way along a lengthy winding path toward rapture, determined he should know a happiness as great as her own. Her determination was blended with sorrow for the little boy who'd been so torn apart, so mangled, and so ultimately deprived by what had started out to be a jolly Sunday outing. She would make up for his years of hiding and isolation; she would be his deliverance. And in return, he would allow her to be with him, to hear his music, to learn the many things he had to teach her, and to sleep away her nights at his side.

When it was done, she lay with her head on his chest listening to the antic drumming of his heart, her arm possessively enclosing him, as she vowed, "I'll always love you, Erik. You'll never have to be alone again."

Decimated, he could only hold her while tears leaked from his eyes. One day, he reminded himself, just as she'd come so unexpectedly bringing with her his life, so she would leave again, taking it away. But until that day, he would treasure each moment of the time he spent with her. He would learn to trust her and to trust the part of himself that loved her, because he knew without question that it was the best part of him—the salvaged remnants of the battered boy.

For quite some time he could do no more than weave his fingers through her abundant hair while he underwent ever-milder aftershocks that at last ebbed and left him utterly at peace and even, quite possibly, happy.

Thirteen

AT THE END OF MAY MARISA BEGAN TO GET PANICKY. "I'M SO FAR behind in my work," she told Erik over the telephone. "I'll never pass my finals. And if I don't graduate, Dad'll go crazy. I haven't even looked at the last of the novels we were supposed to do for English. I'm months behind in French. And forget math."

"Bring your books," Erik told her. "Raskin can help with the mathematics. I will work with you on the French and English."

"But I don't even know Raskin," she protested. "I've never even met him."

"He'll be happy to help you."

"And how can you help with the French and English?"

"First of all, what is the novel you didn't read?"

"*Northanger Abbey*, by Jane Austen."

"Fine, bring your copy with you. I have another here somewhere."

"And what about the French?"

"I was born in France," he reminded her. "My father was French and always, in private, spoke to me in French. For the first seven years of my life, I was completely bilingual. I am still fluent."

"You honestly wouldn't mind?"

"I would be delighted and so, I'm sure, would Raskin. You may come now, if you like. I'll send Raskin to collect you."

She was about to question this when, turning the window, she saw it was still daylight. "Let me check with Dad at the office, and I'll call you right back."

Cameron had no objections. "That's very decent of Erik," he said. "Don't take advantage, Keed. And make sure you say thank you."

"No, Dad. I thought I'd spit on his shoes as I was leaving." She laughed. "I can't get over the way you think I'm such a ninny I don't even know how to say please and thank you, as if you and Kitty haven't been going, *'What do you say, Risa?'* to me my whole life long."

Cameron laughed. "Give Erik my best. And by the by, don't you think we should do a little something, make some kind of gesture to show we appreciate all the time he's devoted to you?"

"Definitely. I was planning to buy him a present."

"Well, good. For now, why don't you take one of the bottles of that Armagnac he likes?"

"Great! I will. I won't be late, I promise."

"See you later, Keed."

She called Erik back, and he said Raskin would come at once.

Five minutes later, she was waiting outside with her books in a big canvas carryall and the bottle her father had suggested. She'd long been curious about Raskin, having pictured him—based solely on their short telephone conversations—as a big, burly man with black hair and bulging biceps. She was therefore mightily surprised when a black Mercedes pulled up and a slim, good-looking, sandy-haired, hazel-eyed man jumped out and came around to open the door for her before extending his hand and saying, "Hi. It's about time we met. I'm Raskin."

"Hi." She shook his hand. "Do you have a first name?"

"Everyone does," he hedged.

"Well, if you're going to call me Risa, which you are, then I need to called you something more personal than Raskin."

He smiled at her, all but assaulted by the combination of her exceptional beauty and her warm, unassuming manner. He fully understood at first sight of her why Erik was so hopelessly in love with the girl. She had a directness and a lack of pretension that were so in contrast to what her tall, cool beauty led one to expect that it turned him somewhat tongue-tied. It was flabbergasting to think that this was the girl who loved Erik, the girl who'd left that imperious message demanding Erik return home at once, the girl who was regularly making love, and obviously liking it, with Erik. Fucking unbelievable! he thought. "Call me Hal," he told her, hefting her bag of books onto the back seat of the car.

"Hal," she repeated as he climbed into the driver's seat. "I'm happy to meet you finally. I really hope it's not an imposition, Erik's asking you to help me with my math."

"Not a bit. I minored in math, and at one point—before the war—I even thought I might prefer teaching to engineering."

"You were in Vietnam?"

He nodded, his jaw going tight, his eyes on the road.

"I'm sorry," she said inexplicably, and he glanced over to see she

actually did look sorry. For some reason, her saying these two words made
him feel absolved in a way. And he thought if she could do that for him
with just two words, she must be working miracles with Erik. Certainly
since her advent into his life Erik had changed, not in ways anyone else
might perceive, but subtly. He no longer barked commands over the
intercom, but requested that Raskin do this or that, and often thanked or
commended him on jobs well done. Erik still worked facing the wall, still
clung to darkness and almost never went outside in daylight. But his
bearing had changed; he exuded well-being. He was loved. And by this
girl. Raskin could understand Erik's reactions. He wasn't entirely sure he
understood what motivated Risa, though. But he was confident he'd
know soon enough. For one thing, Erik had to be extremely sure of her to
trust her alone with Raskin, knowing as he did Raskin's predilection for
women and his abiding determination never to become involved in any
binding fashion with one. He'd never harmed a woman physically. He
was not an abusive man. He simply felt murderous when a woman harbored expectations of him. He was incapable of forcing his attention span
to spread beyond a few hours, or a night. If you cared, you got killed.

"Is this your car?" Risa asked him.

"It's Erik's. Everything is Erik's."

"Does that bother you?" she asked incisively.

"It's the only way I'd have it. He enjoys the cars, their style, their
power. To me, they're just hunks of machinery that'll get you from point
A to point B. I'm not interested in possessions. They only bog you
down."

He pulled the car to a stop at the front of the house so that it was nose
to nose with the Lamborghini, then jumped out to give her a hand out of
the car, saying, "Erik's finishing up some work. So we'll go over the math
first, if that's okay with you. I've got fresh coffee made. We have a couple
of hours, then I'll whip up some dinner while you and Erik work on your
French and good old Jane Austen."

She made a face. "I can't even get past the first page. Her stuff's so
boring."

"Old Jane grows on you, if you let her, if you can see the humor."

"You like Jane Austen?"

"I don't hate her," he said, going ahead to carry her book bag into the
kitchen. "Will you be okay here?" he asked her. "If not, we can shift to
the library."

"I didn't know there was a library."

"Oh sure," he said, reaching for two cups. "Coffee?"

"Yes, please."

"The library's in the living room. Press a couple of buttons and the two
walls opposite the fireplace open up to show you all the books. Erik loves

gadgets. The whole house is filled with them. Buttons to open the doors by remote control, buttons to turn the appliances on or off, buttons for the telephones and intercom, buttons to switch over from heat to air-conditioning, buttons to turn on the TV or the radio or to activate a tape." He smiled like a proud father speaking of a brilliant but erratic son. "There must be a thousand miles of wiring in this house. Cream and sugar?"

"Yes, please. How long have you worked for Erik?"

"What is it, three years? About that." He carried the cups over to the table and sat down opposite her.

"Thank you," she said, her eyes on him as she tasted the coffee. "It's very good. I love coffee. It's as if you can taste the country it came from when you drink it. I imagine people in bright printed clothes in Jamaica. Or dark-skinned Italians walking between rows of coffee plants. Or maybe South Americans, Colombians, say, all in white, with white bags over their arms, picking beans."

Raskin laughed. "That's some imagination you've got."

"Yeah," she laughed with him. Then quietly she asked, "You love Erik, don't you?"

The question rocked him.

"I know you do," she went on. "I know how much you do for him, and you wouldn't do half of it if you didn't love him. I was wrong about the way I thought you'd look but I wasn't wrong about the way you are. You've been good to him."

"People should be," he said, quite dangerously moved by her and her candor. "Erik is unique and pretty amazing, all things considered."

"Yes," she agreed. "I think so, too."

Raskin smiled at her. "I know that. Now let's crack these books."

"It's social satire," Erik was explaining. "You have to take everything she says and turn it, hold it in such a way that you can see she's mirroring the manners of the time, the fads and fancies. And making mock of it all. She's painting you a portrait, then laughing and saying, 'Can you believe how ridiculous these people are, how trifling and petty their concerns?' "

"I don't get any of that. It just puts me to sleep."

"Concentrate," he insisted. "If you can write rational answers to the examination questions, you'll come through beautifully. You simply have to understand her point in writing the things she does. Satire," he said again, "subtle and devilish."

She chewed on the eraser of her pencil, listening. He was enjoying himself in his role as tutor. He'd already reviewed the French with her, and at the sound of his perfect accent, she'd fallen in love with him all over again. It seemed as if there wasn't anything he didn't know. He'd read every book ever written, studied every subject ever taught. And he was able to simplify anything in order to make it readily comprehensible to her. He'd brought her upstairs to the bedroom to work, leaving the kitchen to Raskin. They were sitting together on the floor with their backs against the end of the bed and books and notes strewn across the carpet. A cluster of candles provided the only light. Tossing aside her pencil, she suddenly lunged at him, biting his neck and laughing.

"I can't *take* anymore!" she cried. "No more Jane Austen or I'll lose my mind."

She toppled him to the floor, chewing at his lapels and growling. "No more! No more!" Snorting and tossing her hair, she flopped down on top of him, snuffling with her nose against his neck, tickling his ribs. "I never want to hear that woman's name again as long as I live! And if you don't promise right now to let me off the hook at least for the rest of tonight, I'll be forced to tickle you to death."

Laughing and trying to fend off her groping fingers, he managed to say, "No more. I promise."

"Thank God!" she groaned, and collapsed atop him, letting her arms and legs go any which way.

His laughing subsiding, he pushed the hair back from her face, then ran the tip of his finger across her eyebrow and down her nose to her lips. Lulled by her apparent torpor, he was startled when her mouth shot open and her teeth closed around his finger. She began growling again and shaking her head around his captive finger, like a puppy with a stick. Again, he began to laugh. From someplace very distant, the memory came to him of wrestling with his father in a room where sun poured in through wide-open windows, bathing them in light and warmth, and giddy laughter floated along with the dust motes caught in the light. From his remembered vantage point on the floor, he could look over and see his mother's slender legs in the doorway, and hear her contributing laughter. It was a happy memory from long ago, returned to him intact by Marisa's playfulness.

Then the playfulness took a shift, and she was drawing each of his fingers in turn into her mouth, then licking between his fingers and across the palm of his hand. Instantly, matters turned flammable. His hand closing over the back of her head, he directed her mouth to his, immediately needful. Fumbling at their clothes, they made a hurried connection, and moved in greedy haste, Erik withholding and withholding until he knew she was on the verge of leaving him for the self-contained world of her private pleasure. Then he raced to meet her, to be with her and not left behind to imagine how it must be inside Marisa's world. It was suddenly started and as suddenly completed. Then they looked at each other and laughed. They were still laughing when Raskin announced over the intercom that dinner was ready any time they cared to come down.

"Can he hear us over that thing?" Marisa wanted to know.

"I hope to God not," Erik chuckled, biting her dear cleft chin. "I like to think you're my well-kept secret."

"Don't be crazy, Erik! He knows all about us."

"Why do you say that?" he asked, at once alert to possible menace.

"Of course he does," she said reasonably. "I mean, you send him out to buy me a diamond necklace; you send him out to buy fresh flowers for me every day; you ask him to tutor me; you and I disappear into this bedroom for hours at a stretch. He knows, and he approves, too. He really cares about you, you know, Erik. He's a good friend to you. I like him."

"I suppose you're right," he said, relaxing again. "I have moments of supreme stupidity when I think I'm invisible to the world and everyone in it."

"You may be to most people, but you're certainly not to me, or to Hal."

"Hal?"

"That's his name: Hal."

"I'm well aware that's his name. I'm just rather stunned that he told it to you."

"Why?"

"Because Raskin never tells anyone his name. It's some sort of protective device. The women he sees only know him as Raskin."

"Does he see a lot of women?" she asked, looking around for her underpants.

"Legions. Quite often they ring up, asking for him when he's not in. They usually stop after a time. They always sound so hope-filled the first time they ring, asking may they speak to Raskin. And they're invariably crushed when I say he's not available. More often than not, they don't bother to ring a second time. But some few do. He never sees any woman more than once."

"That's because he's afraid," she said, smoothing down her skirt. "He doesn't want to care about anyone, not counting you. It might have been the war, but I'll bet it was something else that didn't have a thing to do with the war. That has to be it, otherwise he'd be in touch with his family at least once in a while. And he isn't, is he, in touch with them, I mean?"

"Not that I know of."

"See! Something happened. I really do like him. He kind of reminds me of this big dog Meggie's family used to have. I can't remember what kind of dog it was, but he was huge and ferocious and he'd bare his fangs and snarl when kids came over to play. And Meggie's dad was always grabbing hold of his collar and dragging Charcoal—that was his name and he was a Rottweiler, I think—off to chain him up outside. But this one time Meggie dared me to go pet Charcoal, and I was scared silly, but I thought to myself, That dog's all show. So I went and let him smell my hands and petted him a bit, and then the big stupid pooch lay down and rolled over with his legs in the air, wanting me to scratch his stomach. Wait a minute, Erik. Your shirt's caught in your zipper." She deftly corrected the problem, then said, "Hal's like Charcoal. He just wants someone he trusts to scratch his stomach."

Erik smiled and kissed the top of her head. As they started out of the room, he said, "I don't recommend you try it. Aside from the fact that I'd probably detonate from sheer jealousy, Raskin might very well stab you in the hand with a bread knife or a pair of scissors."

"Hah!" she scoffed. "You men like to think you're so complicated and hard to understand, but you're all just big stupid pooches."

"For that compliment," he said at the top of the stairs, bowing from the waist, "I thank you from the bottom of my heart."

"Yeah!" she laughed. "Let's go eat. I'm starving."

It was the first time she'd sat down to a meal in Erik's home, and the first time the three of them dined together. It was just fine. She felt safe, protected, with not one but two men to look after her. Raskin was a good cook and had prepared halibut steaks broiled with lemon and butter, new potatoes, and slivered carrots, with a green salad and garlicky hot rolls. The three of them ate in hungry silence. Then Risa set down her knife and fork and said, "That was divine!" which, for some reason, set both Erik and Raskin to laughing loudly.

"What's so funny?" she asked, but neither of them was able to answer.

"It's just funny," Raskin said after a minute or two. "You're funny." He looked to see if Erik disapproved, but Erik was laughing wholeheartedly, nodding in agreement.

"She is," Erik declared when he was able to draw a breath, *"divinely* funny." Which set them off again.

Risa sat looking at the two of them, failing to get the joke, and finally said, "You're both batshit. I'll make the coffee." And she got up to start clearing the table, leaving the two men mopping their eyes and pounding the table.

"Batty as bedbugs," she told them, taking away their plates and depositing them on the counter. "Out to lunch, mentally AWOL, looney tunes. Brother!" She shook her head in pretended disdain, perfectly happy.

Fourteen

ITH THE HELP OF ERIK AND RASKIN, RISA MANAGED TO GET through the final exams. The talk all around her at school was of the parties everyone seemed to be planning. Several of the jocks even ventured to ask if she'd care to go to one or another, but she declined. She found it singularly odd to be in the midst of so many very young people. She herself felt, in many ways, far older and infinitely more mature. She intended to go only to the graduation ceremony. Otherwise, she was glad finally to be free of high school. She was also free, at last, to spend some time looking for the perfect gift to give Erik. In view of how pleased he'd been by her father's bottle of Armagnac, he was bound to go wild over a gift she'd give him—if she could only find something wonderfully unique.

Kitty said she had no objection to Risa's taking the car for the day, but couldn't resist asking, "Don't you mean to go to any of the parties your friends're bound to be havin'?"

Risa hoisted herself up to sit on the edge of the kitchen island to finish her morning coffee, saying, "You know perfectly well I haven't had one single friend since Meggie moved away. And I hardly ever hear from her anymore."

"You're never home to hear from anyone," Kitty said mildly. "Seems like you spend every free moment with that Erik fella. He must be somethin' pretty special for you to be runnin' over there every chance you get."

Kitty was fishing, Risa knew. She'd been dropping hints about Erik since the night Risa and Cameron had argued about her purported music lessons.

For her part, having never laid eyes on the man, but well able to make a four out of two twos, Kitty had long since figured Risa and this fellow had something substantial going. Cameron was mostly closemouthed on the subject, only telling Kitty, "I trust him with Risa. He's no ordinary man."

"He's *very* special," Risa confirmed now, in part fairly desperate to discuss Erik with Kitty, who, being another woman, would understand; and in part very afraid Kitty might not understand and, because of her closeness to Cameron, might carry whatever Risa said back to him. "In fact," she continued casually, "I'm going shopping today to buy him a present for being so good to me."

"Oh?" Kitty's eyebrows lifted inquiringly, cigarette smoke hanging in a cloud around her head and shoulders.

"Your hair looks really good now," Risa said, able to see why her father would be attracted to Kitty. "I like your natural color, and this length, way better than all those little red curls."

"I always thought dirty-blond hair was a true curse." Kitty said, "but I'm fed up with payin' these women a fortune to mess it up. It'll probably go yella," she said, holding a strand out to look at it, "like my mama's before it turned pure white. I wouldn't mind the pure white, understand; it's the yella that gives me the shudders. The color of nicotine, my mama's hair was, before it finally turned." She let her hair drop and returned to the subject at hand. "So, you're off shoppin' for a gift for this special fella. And what d'you reckon you'll get him?"

"I wish I knew. Nothing ordinary, like shirts or ties or any of that boring stuff."

"How about cuff links? I always admire a man with a handsome set of cuff links."

"It's possible."

"Or maybe a cigarette lighter. Does he smoke?"

"Sometimes."

"What about cologne, or aftershave?"

"That's so boring. That's the kind of stuff you buy your father, not someone like Erik."

"Well, now," Kitty said, getting more of a picture from Risa's replies than Risa knew. "There's wallets, or key cases, or even a briefcase, if you're out to spend the money." Risa was shaking her head, so Kitty thought on aloud. "Okay, then. How about a tie clip, or maybe a money clip? Or what about . . . ?"

Kitty went on reciting suggestions, but Risa had an idea. Maybe it was vain of her, or presumptuous, but she'd latched on to the notion that Erik would really like a photograph of her. She could easily have one taken, then buy a good silver frame for it. As Kitty's voice hummed beneath her thoughts, she visualized the scene: She'd give Erik the package; he'd open it, and be totally knocked out. Or maybe he wouldn't like it at all. There were no photographs in his house, only the two portraits in the living room. What if it upset him? But why would that upset him? She knew she could never have a portrait of Erik to carry about with her, but she couldn't help believing he'd like one of her. And there was a photographer right in Darien who'd probably be able to take her picture on the spot if she walked in off the street and asked.

"You're not listenin' to a word I'm sayin'," Kitty complained, waving the smoke away from her face before putting out her cigarette.

"Sorry. I was thinking."

"Is there anything you want to tell me?" Kitty asked, folding her arms on the tabletop and looking meaningfully at Risa.

"Yeah," Risa said with a smile. "But I'm not going to. I'd better get going."

"I take it you've come up with an idea."

"I think so. I should be back in a couple of hours. You want anything while I'm out?"

"Where you gonna be?"

"Just in town."

"I'm low on cigarettes, if you wouldn't mind pickin' me up a carton. Wait and I'll fetch you some money."

"That's okay. You can pay me later." Risa was in a hurry now to get to town to see the photographer, and then go looking for the right frame.

Halfway into town, she wondered if she shouldn't go back and change clothes. She decided not to. She didn't want this photograph to be too stagey, too "dressed." A casual portrait would be better, and the cotton dress she had on would be fine.

She was in luck. The photographer had had a cancellation and could take her right away. All he had to do was set the lighting, if she didn't mind sitting on the stool in the studio for a few minutes while he did this and that, checking every so often to see how the lights were falling on her.

"I think this is going to be nice," he told her. "Just head shots, right? You sure you don't want any background?"

"Nothing."

"Okay." He spent several minutes positioning the camera, turning dials, then came over to hold a light meter in front of her face. Back behind the camera, he looked at her through the lens and said, "You're a beautiful girl. These're gonna be beautiful shots."

She smiled reflexively, ready to dispute this observation, but he said, "Hold that!" and began making exposures, telling her to turn this way, then that, until he'd shot an entire roll. "I can have contact sheets ready for you to look at by tomorrow morning," he said, removing the exposed film from the camera and giving it a toss before catching it in his hand.

"Normally, it'd be at least a week, but I'm kind of anxious to see these. I don't too often get the chance to shoot someone as photogenic as you. You don't have a single bad angle, not one," he complimented her, while she collected her shoulder bag and walked with him to the reception area. "I think you'll be very happy with these pictures."

After leaving the photographer's studio, she got into the car and began systematically visiting the antiques shops in town, in search of a frame. She found exactly what she wanted in the third place, an extravagantly ornate Victorian sterling-silver frame that would take an eight-by-ten print. She paid in cash, then waited while the proprietor lovingly wrapped the gift in several layers of tissue.

She almost forgot Kitty's cigarettes and had to go back to the variety store to get the carton of Kools. While she was waiting for her change, she noticed a row of imported cigarettes and on impulse bought a pack of Gauloises for Erik and, as an afterthought, some English Rothmans for Hal. She loved having people to buy things for. She daydreamed on the way home of someday shopping for Erik, deliberating over silk ties or dressing gowns; she even saw herself in a supermarket selecting imported cheeses or prime cuts of meat for him. She thought she could be very happy spending her days seeing to his needs, and spending her nights at his side in the music room, or in his bed. To sleep an entire night in that big bed with Erik was something she badly wanted and which she was determined to have, if she could just think of some way to work it out.

As she pulled into the driveway, the front door opened and Kitty came running out. Risa knew at once something was wrong. It showed in Kitty's face and in the graceless way she ran in her high heels over the gravel toward the car. Oh God, Risa thought, something's happened to Erik!

"What is it? What's wrong?" she asked, scrambling out of the car.

Kitty's face ashen and drawn, she dragged Risa into her arms and held her tightly to her cushiony breasts. "It's your daddy, Risa. They called right after you left. I been phonin' all over town tryin' to find you."

"What? What's wrong with him?"

Kitty's arms went even tighter around her, and she sought to free herself but Kitty held on with surprising strength. "There's no easy way to tell you," Kitty said, her lips against Risa's ear, her perfume and ciga-rette aroma rising richly into Risa's nostrils. "One of the secretaries was late gettin' to the office. She parked in the lot and was hurryin' inside when her eye was caught by your daddy's car sittin' with its motor run-nin'. And when she took herself a closer look, she saw him slumped behind the wheel. She figured somethin' was wrong and went for help, but it was too late."

"Too late?"

"He's dead, Risa. Looks like he had a heart attack and it took him." She could feel Risa's denial in the way she began to turn her head back and forth, and struggled to escape Kitty's embrace. "Don't fight against it," Kitty told her. "I know it's gonna be hard for you, but don't fight it. Your daddy loved you better than anything in this world, and you're a lucky girl in that, 'cause he showed it to you. Now you're gonna have to begin lettin' him go. But I want you to know I'm here for you if you need me. D'you hear me?"

"I have to call Erik!" she cried, and broke free to go running into the house.

Trailing after her, Kitty watched Risa fly to the telephone and dial a number, wait, then ask to speak to Erik. Shaking, all but palsied, she waited. And then, gripping the receiver with both hands, she wailed, "Erik, I *need* you!" Something was said, then Risa put down the receiver and rushed into the living room to position herself by the windows, gripping the draperies as she stared out.

Kitty backed away to stand near the dining-room doors where she lit a cigarette, her eyes never leaving the girl. She'd guessed there was strong feeling on Risa's part for this Erik fella, but she'd seriously underestimated how strong it was. And it struck her as a downright pity that she was finally going to get to meet this Erik under such tragic circumstances. She stood quietly, smoking her cigarette, until she saw Risa start, her hand pulling so hard at the curtains she nearly brought them down. Then she ran to the foyer to open the front door.

Shifting slightly, Kitty had a clear view, and watched as Risa, sobbing out, "Erik, my father's dead!" threw herself into the arms of the man who entered. He reacted overtly, seeking to shelter her with his body. Kitty let her cigarette fall into the ashtray, her eyes on the two in the foyer, unable to believe that this was the man to whom Marisa had given her heart. A pitiful-looking creature with a face you might see in some side show, or in the aftermath of a five-day drinking spree; a man who'd suffered some truly terrible accident once upon a time; a man whose eyes slowly lifted to connect with Kitty's.

She'd never forget the moment, never forget the way those eyes beseeched her, begging her to understand how powerless he was to resist the love—Kitty could almost reach out and touch it, it was so real—that he had for this girl. Maybe at some other time she'd have given in to her immediate reaction to the sight of his face. But now, because she knew she herself would grieve for a long time to come over the loss of Cam, she could only give her unspoken approval to this man who'd come at a moment's notice because Risa claimed to need him.

"I'll make some coffee," Kitty said, and left the two of them there.

In the kitchen, with the percolator plugged in, she stood with her hands braced on the counter looking down at the floor, trying to take everything in. Cameron was gone; Risa had herself a lover whose face would cause most hearts to stop for a beat or two; all kinds of changes would be coming now. And she was too old, and knew too much about too many things to make rash judgments just on account of a man's face. Because whatever he might look like, that man had a heart full of love for a seventeen-year-old girl who'd just lost her daddy.

When she returned to the living room and set down the tray of coffee things, Risa was with Erik on the sofa. Upon seeing Kitty, Risa got up to volunteer herself into Kitty's arms. "Kitty," she whispered, "please . . ."

"There, there," Kitty consoled her. "Everything's gonna be all right. I'm Kitty," she introduced herself to Erik, keeping one arm around Risa's waist. "And you're Erik. It's right decent of you to come so quick."

Erik rose to take the hand she offered, stricken with gratitude for the woman's kindness. "Please sit with us," he said in a tuneful whisper that captured Kitty's complete interest and attention.

"This is the lull before the storm," Kitty said, seating herself without thinking in Cam's favorite chair. "There's gonna be a whole lot needs doin'."

"Where is he?" Risa asked, on the sofa again close to Erik. "Can I see him?"

"They took him over to Norwalk Hospital," Kitty told her. "There's gonna have to be an autopsy so they can say the cause of death. I called his lawyer and the lawyer's tryin' to get hold of your Uncle Harmon to get permission."

"Why can't *I* give it?" Risa wanted to know.

" 'Cause you're not of age, honey."

"Well, then, why can't you give it?"

" 'Cause I'm not kin, Risa. It's gotta be a member of the family."

"I want to *see* him!" Risa reached for Erik's hand. Her grip was fierce. "I want to see my father, to say good-bye." Her voice cracked, and she broke. Erik held her while she cried, his eyes again on Kitty.

"I will help in any way I'm able," he told the woman, deeply saddened by the loss of the only man outside Raskin who'd ever treated him simply as another man.

Kitty nodded, knowing the only way Risa was going to get through the next few days was with this man's help. It was real odd about his face, Kitty thought, but the more she saw it the less it seemed to bother her. Maybe it was because there were other things about him that were downright attractive—that voice, for one, and the build on him, for another, and his hands, which were just plain beautiful. She didn't think she'd ever seen another pair of hands that were their equal. And his eyes. He had the eyes of a boy, but filled with a grown man's wisdom and apprehension. And one thing was absolutely certain: All you had to do was look at the way he sought to comfort Risa, the tender way he stroked her through her tears, and any fool could see he might not look too fine, but his feelings were all in the right place.

"I'm glad you're here for her," Kitty told him. "Have some coffee."

The church was jammed with friends and business associates who'd come, some of them, from as far away as California and Vancouver, even two from London; there were former classmates from St. Paul's, and men he'd gone to college with. His brother Harmon and his wife Tenny, along with their two sons, Harmon Junior, and Rolly, had flown in from Boston. There were two distant cousins from upstate Connecticut, and Great-Aunt Patience who, at eighty-seven, was still fit and trim but quite deaf.

An audible murmur started up at the back of the church when Risa entered on Erik's arm, with Raskin and Kitty close behind. Lost to her grief, Risa was unaware. But the other three were not. Kitty automatically drew closer to Raskin, and the two of them cast stony glances to each side, quieting the perturbed whispers.

They made it all the way to the front of the church in the ensuing silence when suddenly, loudly and very clearly, Great-Aunt Patience demanded, "Who *is* that creature?" Her question fell like a grenade into the center of the silence that held for a few seconds before the whispering started up again and people all around tried shushing the elderly woman.

Risa had stopped dead, her hand fastening around Erik's. Turning slowly, she scanned the crowd until she located the source of the disturbance. Casting a look of sheer hatred at the old woman, Risa turned back and slid into the pew. Seated, she leaned close to Erik to whisper, "I love you. *I love you!*" Then she straightened and stared straight ahead.

The morning was hot, the sky deeply blue and dotted with amorphous clouds. Risa blinked against the sun, clinging fast to Erik's hand, trying to make what was happening stay real. Things seemed to come back and forth, in and out of focus. They were putting her father in a box into the ground. He was never coming home again, never going to call her Keed, never going to argue or praise her. She'd never again sit with him to eat a meal, or race him to the end of the driveway, or leap up to knock his shots away from the hoop fixed over the garage door. Without a hint of warning, or any meaningful last words, he'd gone away for good and always. She knew it was only his body, not her actual father they were burying, and she couldn't stop wondering where he'd gone, if there was some place people went when they were finished with their lives. She knew it was infantile and stupid, but she wanted to believe he was with Rebecca, that the two of them were up there, looking down at her from the sky.

She didn't hear a word that was said, not by any of the several people who eulogized her father, or by the minister. Her only anchor was Erik's hand, which remained joined to hers throughout the entire grim event. At one point she turned to look at Erik and then at the crowd of faces, all of which, she saw, were directed towards them. Her hand going tighter around Erik's, she realized what an enormous act of courage he had undertaken in escorting her on this day. He'd come out into the merciless glare of morning, subjecting himself to the eyes of dozens, solely for her sake. And she was infuriated by these so-called friends of her father's who were paying no attention to his last rites but were instead gawking at the man she loved. How dare they? she wondered, enraged. Her anger robbed her of her tears. Lifting her chin, straightening her spine, she sat staring them down, her hand linked with Erik's, and wished them all in hell.

After the service, the crowd evaporated. Only the minister and Uncle Harmon came to talk with her, to express their condolences. Not even Aunt Tenny or her cousins came near. Raskin and Kitty stood a little ways off, smoking and talking quietly.

"We've got to get back to Boston," her Uncle Harmon said apologetically. "If there's anything at all you need, Marisa, please call me."

"There's nothing I need, Uncle Harm. Thank you for coming."

Her uncle offered his hand to Erik, then turned to go. Touched by his humanity, Risa ran after him to give him a hug. "I'm glad you came, Uncle Harm. My dad always thought the world of his little brother."

"He was a good man," Harmon told her. "I loved him and I'll miss him."

And then it was over. Raskin and Kitty returned to the house with Erik and Risa. The two of them went off to the kitchen to put together some lunch, leaving Erik with Risa in the living room.

"What you did today was wonderful, Erik. I'll never forget it. I know it was awful for you. And I hate those people, those idiots!"

"They couldn't help it," he said, trying to be charitable, but still feeling flayed by the hundreds of eyes that had picked over him like vultures on a carcass.

"Oh yes, they could," she disagreed heatedly. "I hate them all, every last one of them, including that senile idiot, Aunt Patience. God!" she said, forgetting her anger as she looked around the room. "What am I going to do, Erik? What am I going to *do?*"

"Things will sort themselves out," he promised. "For now, take one step at a time."

"I keep thinking I'm so lucky to have you, then I get scared something's going to happen to you, too, and I won't have anyone."

"Nothing's going to happen to me," he said, holding her.

"I feel so *guilty*, Erik. When Kitty came running out the other day, the only thing in my mind was: 'Something's happened to Erik.' I never once thought it could be Dad. As if he wasn't even important enough for me to think about."

"You know that's not the truth, Marisa. You loved your father, and he knew it."

"You think so?" She searched his eyes. "D'you honestly think so?"

"I know it. There's no need for you to feel guilty."

"Erik, would you ever marry me?"

"This is not the time to discuss something like that."

"I'm not saying tomorrow. I'm asking would you?"

He lifted the hair back from her face, then with one finger caught the tear that spilled from her eye. "Oh yes," he said very softly, "I would."

Fifteen

T HREE DAYS AFTER THE FUNERAL, AND AFTER THREE NIGHTS OF sleeping alone in her room because Erik insisted it would be most disrespectful to her father if she failed to observe a proper period of mourning, Risa and Kitty drove to the lawyer's office in Greenwich for a reading of her father's will.

The lawyer, Archie Henderson, an old friend of Cameron's who had been to the house for dinner many times with his wife, greeted Risa by saying, "I can't believe he's gone. It must be tough on you, Marisa. I want you to know I'm available at any time if you need help."

She thanked him politely, disinclined to be affable since he was one of the ones who'd stared so blatantly at Erik.

After offering coffee, which neither Kitty nor Risa wanted, Henderson sat down behind his polished desk and opened a file. "Your father," he began, "made some changes in his will only a few weeks before he died." He paused to look at both women above the tops of his reading glasses. "He was very concerned for your future, Marisa; most concerned you be secure in the event anything untoward should happen to him. He told me he had put a lot of thought into the changes he made. I hope you agree with his thinking." Removing the blue-jacketed will from the file, he said, "I'll skip the standard boiler plate and go directly to the main points.

"First of all, since his death has occurred while you are still legally in your minority, Miss Katherine Hemmings is appointed your guardian. She is also appointed co-executor and trustee of the estate together with myself, in conjunction with the Connecticut Fidelity Bank. It was your father's wish that the ownership of the dwelling on Butlers Island in the town of Darien, county of Fairfield in the state of Connecticut, should pass into the hands of Katherine Hemmings with the proviso that the minor child reside in this dwelling for as long as she so wishes.

"There are several charitable bequests, including two to alumni associations of the schools your father attended. In addition to the foregoing, it was your father's wish that Miss Hemmings be the recipient of an annual income of twenty-five thousand dollars, this income separate from and in no way to be used for the maintenance of the minor child. Along with this, Miss Hemmings is to receive title to one vehicle, a 1969 Ford Fairlane station wagon currently registered in the name of the deceased.

"The rest, residue, and remainder of the estate is to be held in trust for Marisa, with one third of the total capital payable on her eighteenth birthday, another third payable on her twenty-first birthday, and the balance to be paid on her thirtieth birthday. Any and all expenses for the minor child shall be paid for by the trustees from the interest income earned on the capital investments, and no reasonable request by the minor child for access to the capital shall be denied by the trustees or co-executors.

"There is a final term which does not directly concern either of you," Henderson said, once more opening the file to remove a sealed envelope. "Your father asked that this letter be delivered to Mr. Erik D'Anton. I've spoken with Mr. D'Anton's assistant on the telephone and have been told it is acceptable to Mr. D'Anton that you be given this letter, Marisa, to give to him. Have you any questions?"

Studying the envelope back and front, Risa answered, "No, none."

Kitty said, "What happens if Risa doesn't want me for her guardian?"

At this, Risa's head shot up. "Of course I want you!" she exclaimed. "Did you think I wouldn't? Don't you want to?"

"Sure, I do, hon. I was just coverin' all your bets, that's all."

"My bets don't need covering," Risa said, standing. "Thank you very much, Mr. Henderson. May I have a copy of that?" She pointed to the will.

"If you wish. I can have my secretary Xerox it while you wait."

"You don't have to do that. Just mail it to me."

In the car driving home, Kitty said, "I didn't know a thing about the house or the car or the money, none of it."

"Kitty, I'm glad he did that. Don't worry about it. If he hadn't left you those things, I'd've given them to you myself out of the estate. You've been good to both of us. And you've been so nice to Erik. I love you with all my heart for that. I really do. I guess you've figured out how I feel about him."

"I guess so," Kitty agreed. "I hate to change the subject, but you and I have to do somethin' about your daddy's things. Truth to tell, I find it truly distressin' to keep comin' on things of his. I'm havin' a whole load of trouble even wearin' my mules, what with hearin' Cam make some wise-crack in my head every time I slip 'em on. The other mornin' I must've lost me an entire hour just comin' across his shirts waitin' to be ironed. I figure we should clear everything out and give it to the Goodwill or the Sally Ann. How d'you feel about that?"

"Will you help me?" Risa asked, feeling all at once too young to cope.

"Well, sure I will. We can do it this afternoon, after lunch. I already went ahead and got some boxes from the market."

"I'm not hungry."

"You're gonna eat!" Kitty said firmly. "I'm not havin' you collapsin' again, the way you did last winter when you starved yourself half to death. You think your daddy would like you to quit eatin'?"

"No."

"So, okay. We'll have us some lunch, then we'll get his room cleared out."

It started out well enough. The two of them took all the clothes from his closet and put them on the bed. Then, while Kitty removed the hangers and began folding sports jackets and trousers into the boxes, Risa started going through the chest of drawers. She dumped his underwear into a carton, followed by his socks, then returned the empty drawers to the chest. But then she came to the sweaters, some of which still bore his scent. Burying her face in Cameron's favorite cashmere pullover, Risa burst into tears almost at the same moment Kitty, holding a suit in her arms, began quietly crying.

Kitty looked over at Risa. The two of them laughed, chagrined, then cried even harder.

"This is truly the worst thing I've ever had to do," Kitty admitted. "I loved your daddy, you know, Risa. I dearly loved him."

"I know," Risa told her, gulping down sobs. "I know you did. Kitty, how're we going to live without him?"

"We'll muddle through somehow. Let's sit down here a minute." Kitty put aside the suit before taking the sweater from Risa's hands. "Set yourself down here with me and let's have us a serious talk."

Sitting on the floor surrounded by half-filled boxes, Kitty took hold of Risa's hand. "We need to have us a heart-to-heart," she said, "so we both of us know where we stand."

"Okay," Risa sniffed, mopping her face on her sleeve.

"I'm not your mama, but I'm your friend. And I want you to think of me as your friend when I ask you for a straight answer, Risa. Are you sleeping with your Erik?"

Risa flushed darkly, but replied, "Yes."

"That's what I thought. Are you takin' any precautions?"

"Yes, I am."

"Okay, that takes care of that. Now I know it's early days yet, but have you given any thought to what you're gonna do next? I know you planned to take a year off. Is that still your plan?"

"Yes, it is."

"And after that, what'll you do?"

"There won't be any 'after that,' Kitty. As soon as Erik feels the time is right, I'm going to marry him."

"You don't think you're just a tad young?"

"I'm over the age of consent, and less than a year away from majority."

"You're talkin' as if you think I'm gonna be against you, Reese. This is me, Kitty, and we're talkin' friend to friend. Remember?"

"I'm sorry."

"That's okay. Now when d'you figure Erik's gonna think the time is right?"

"I don't know. We haven't actually discussed it. I just asked him if he'd marry me, and he said he would."

"You asked him, huh?"

"Yes, I did. He would never dare ask me. He'd be too afraid. But it's what we both want."

"You sure do know your own mind, always have done. Have you thought about what kinda life the two of you're gonna have? You saw what it was like the other day. Are you gonna be able to handle that for years to come?"

"Yes! What you don't seem to understand is that Erik never goes out during the day. And what he did coming to the funeral was the bravest, most wonderful thing anybody's ever done for me—not counting you or Dad. Erik loves me, Kitty. And I love him. I don't care what other people think. I only care about Erik."

"There may come a day when you have to care, Risa. There's a lotta people in this world who're gonna wanna know why a beautiful young girl like you's throwin' herself away on a man that looks the way he does. Now before you go gettin' yourself all riled up, it's not me we're talkin' about here. Anyone with eyes could see the two of you love each other. But not everyone's *got* eyes, if you catch my meanin'. And if, as you say, the man don't go out in daylight, what kind of life d'you imagine the two of you leadin'?"

"A very happy one."

"Doin' what, exactly?"

"I don't know, Kitty. I mean, I guess I'll do things other married women do—cooking and cleaning, having babies." She spoke aloud of having babies and heard again Erik's adamant refusal even to discuss the possibility. She'd dared to mention it just last week and he'd simply turned and glared at her. His anger, when roused, was formidable and frightening. She understood it but didn't wish to anger him further. She'd give him room to grow accustomed to the idea and, in time, he'd be bound to agree.

"I wonder how we're gonna work this out," Kitty mused. "I can't see you'll be spendin' a whole lotta time around here. And I sure don't much like the idea of rattlin' around alone in this big ole house."

"Why don't you get Freed to move in with you? You said she's only got a crummy little apartment in Stamford."

"Freed *loves* that crummy little apartment. No. I've been thinkin' maybe it's time for me to head back home. Oh, not right away. But if you're bound 'n' determined to marry Erik, then maybe I'll plan on goin' home. I still got some family, and you won't be needin' me."

"But I will!" Risa threw herself against Kitty. "Don't go away! Even if I do marry, Erik, I'm still going to need you. You're the only family I've got left, Kitty. I'd die without you. I'd have no one to talk to woman to woman. Please don't think about going away. You always said you hated it there. You said you wouldn't be home a week and you'd be wanting to come back here. That's what you've always said."

"I guess you're right," Kitty agreed, satisfied. She'd been wanting and needing confirmation of Risa's caring. "Don't fret yourself. I'm not gonna go off and leave you. I just want you to promise me one thing."

"What?"

"I want your word that no matter how late it gets to be, you come home nights and you sleep in your own bed. I'm not gonna interfere with the two of you, but I'm still responsible for you. And there could be trouble— I'm not sure what kind, but some trouble—if word got out I was lettin' you run wild. You can spend all the time you like over to Erik's. And he can come here any time he wants. But you've gotta promise me you'll sleep right here under your own roof, until such times as the two of you get legal."

"Get legal?" Risa smiled and wiped her eyes again on her sleeve. "God! You've got some of the corniest expressions. And," she went on, her eyes glistening, "if you're so hot on 'getting legal,' how come you didn't mind all that secret carrying-on with Dad?"

"That was different. We were both adults, with not a helluva lot to lose. But you're a young girl with her whole life yet to live, in a town that loves gossip almost as much as it loves booze, religion, and real estate, in that order. Now! What say we get on with the job at hand?"

That evening, after they'd taken the boxes to the Goodwill drop-off, and after Risa had left to spend the evening with Erik, Kitty walked slowly up the stairs and along the hallway to Cameron's bedroom. She stood for a time staring at the bed, and then at the empty closet, before going inside and through to the bathroom. She'd saved this job for last because she'd known it would be hardest of all—disposing of the very personal items Cam had touched daily.

With the wastebasket positioned on the toilet seat, she opened the medicine cabinet and one by one cleared the shelves, holding each item for a moment or two before carefully placing it in the basket. His scented shaving soap and brush, his heavy-handled blade shaver, his toothbrush, his several combs, and his nail scissors; his styptic pencils, the Ace bandage he'd used now and then for the tricky knee he'd got playing hockey back when he was a boy at St. Paul's, and his prescription pills.

It was the bottles of aftershave and cologne that finally did her in. She removed the tops of each and smelled them in turn, then replaced the tops tightly, and tearfully put the bottles into the basket.

She remembered to clear the area around the tub and to retrieve the soap from the shower stall, then went out carrying the basket. In the kitchen, she slipped the contents into a plastic trash bag, sealed the top with a twist tie, then took the bag out the rear door, headed for the garbage bin. But at the last moment she had to stop and open the bag to root around inside and find the cologne. With the bottle safely tucked into the waistband of her skirt, she resealed the bag and dropped it into the bin before returning inside.

With a glass of Cam's Glenfiddich, she sat in his chair in the living room, periodically holding her wrist to her nose, breathing in Cam's scent.

Without warning, Risa would begin to cry. She'd think of something, remember an occasion with her father, and go to pieces. She kept apologizing until Erik drew her onto his lap and held her head against his chest. "Don't go on saying you're sorry, Marisa. I'm the last person on earth who needs an explanation for the way you're feeling now. When my parents died, I was not *permitted* to grieve. Aunt Dorothy wouldn't *allow* it; it simply wasn't *done*. One was expected to get on. It never entered her mind, the hateful bitch, that I was a small boy who'd lost a great deal. I will never forgive her her cruelty. It is only fitting that you should grieve. Your father was an honorable man with great integrity. No one can ever replace him, or fill the gap he's left. You must *never* apologize, *not to anyone*, for having loved enough to feel the loss."

It was the longest speech she'd ever heard him make. Eased and thoughtful, her tears gradually subsided, leaving her so wearied she fell asleep.

He sat unmoving for hours while she slept in his lap, respectful of her sorrow. He felt an immense sense of responsibility for her, as well as a kind of fraternal kinship. They had both now lost their parents. Two orphans, one aged seventeen and the other thirty-two. It was strange to think that one could be orphaned at any age and the pain would be identical. Age wasn't the factor that determined grief. It was the knowledge of what had gone from your life forever and could never again be duplicated. He envied her her freedom to mourn. It was a necessary right that had been denied him by a mean, self-indulgent woman with entirely superficial values who'd failed to see beyond a small boy's outer injuries to the deeper, more harmful ones underneath. That she still lived, with her Aubusson carpet and immaculate countertops and untrod-upon lawns, filled him with outrage. But he buried it. He had the satisfaction of knowing she would die as she had lived: alone. And no one would mourn her passing. But he, Erik, had found someone who did care. In spite of the quite considerable odds, he'd been blessed with this dear sleeping child who claimed to want to marry him and be with him always.

Marisa slept on as if drugged and, at last, Erik lifted her and carried her out to the car. She stirred briefly when he was setting her down on the passenger seat, then sank back into sleep.

He rang the doorbell and Kitty came.

"She's quite worn out," he told her, his whisper softer than ever. "If you'd be good enough to direct me, I'll carry her up to her room."

Kitty smiled, then turned to show him the way to a bedroom that was exactly the one he'd imagined Marisa would have: with a canopied four-poster bed, swagged white curtains over the windows, and a menagerie of stuffed animals loitering on the pillows.

Easing Marisa down on her bed, Erik backed away, blinking in the offensive overhead light.

"Why not go down and fix yourself a drink?" Kitty said. "I'll get Reese squared away and be down in a tick."

He thanked her and made his way down to the bar in the living room to pour a balloon of Cameron's good Armagnac before going to the wing chair. Settled, he looked over to see the glass on the table beside the chair where Cameron had always sat. And a bottle of Royall Lyme bay rum. Noting all this, Erik sighed. More had been lost here than he'd known. This woman had loved Cameron. No wonder she was kind. Marisa's father wouldn't have cared for an unkind woman.

"We saw Cam's lawyer today," Kitty said, pausing to retrieve her Glenfiddich before resuming her seat. "Cam left a letter for you." She pulled an envelope from the waistband of her skirt and leaned forward to give it to him. "Reese was gonna give it to you, but I guess she forgot, what with one thing and another."

Erik took the envelope.

"If you want to be private when you read it, I can go make us some coffee to go with our drinks."

"No, no. Please, don't go. I would like to share this with you."

"Now why would you want to do that?"

In answer, he raised his eyes to hers, then indicated the bay rum.

They sat in silence for a time, their eyes on each other. Then Erik said, "Not long after I left Princeton, one of my professors recommended me for a job to an old friend of his. I was most apprehensive, but my professor's old friend was an exceptional man. He accepted my terms without equivocation; he accepted me without equivocation. Nothing he ever said or did was in any way judgmental or insincere. I trusted him, and in return he made further recommendations that resulted in establishing my credentials.

"Over the years, we'd talk now and then on the telephone, and he was always interested; he always had time. He was a rare man, generous and tolerant. And had I known how to go about it, we might have been friends. But I didn't know how, and so our contact was limited to occasional telephone calls. Until one day a year or so ago when he rang me to ask if I'd consider doing some minor renovations to his home. I agreed at once, and came here for the first time to discuss the matter with him." His hands lifted, signaling his inability to say more. Then he picked up the envelope.

The letter read:

Dear Erik,

I decided tonight after you came here to explain about the so-called music lessons that I've been avoiding admitting to something I've probably known since the night you came to look over the house more than a year ago. I know you love Risa, and I know she loves you. I don't have the right to make my daughter's decisions or to stand in the way of what she wants. So I thought I'd put it in writing, in case I never get around to saying it in person, although I have every intention of living to play with my grandchildren, that the two of you have my blessings. If fathers could handpick their sons-in-law, I'd have a hell of a hard time finding anyone I'd enjoy more as a son-in-law of mine. Risa's impulsive and hard-headed and stubborn sometimes, but she's funny and good-hearted and sharp as a tack. Look after her, and be happy the two of you.

With my love,
Cameron

Unable to speak, Erik handed the letter to Kitty.

Then the two of them sat and drank in the dark and shed tears for their friend.

Sixteen

THROUGHOUT THE SUMMER RISA ALTERNATED BETWEEN LOOKING forward to the future and feeling morbidly guilty about the past. She'd reached a point where she was angry with her father for abandoning her so abruptly, and angry at being saddled with the ongoing chore of making her own decisions. It had been quite all right for her to make decisions while her father was alive because, always, in the back of her mind, was the thought that she'd have him to come home to, should anything go wrong. He'd be there to support her in every way. Now he was gone, and from one day to the next she couldn't think what to do with herself. Some days she was so bogged down in anger and frustration she didn't leave her room, and consoled herself by talking to Erik on the telephone. He was endlessly patient and compassionate, which only served to compound her guilt. She was wasting his time, taking him away from the important work he had to do now that his office building in Greenwich was in the construction stage.

She had entire catalogs of doubts and misgivings and could, at any time, launch into very vocal diatribes that were in essence recitations of her many sins of omission and failings. Everyone was far too tolerant of her, she thought, growing irritated with Kitty and even with Erik for allowing her to go on and on the way she did, while one or the other or both of them sat and listened. Then she'd sink into shame, disgusted with herself for her misuse of people who loved her.

Mid-August she received a telephone call. It was the photographer.

"I came across these contact sheets and realized you never did come in for your prints. You still interested? There's some awfully nice shots here."

The call roused her from the apathy in which she'd been mired for weeks.

"I'll come right over now and have a look," she told him, then went to ask if Kitty minded her using the car.

"I don't mind. But how come you don't drive your daddy's car?"

"I'm *never* going to drive that car. We should probably sell it and get something else because I can't bring myself to go anywhere near it."

"You shoulda said so. I'll look into it." Kitty handed over the keys to the station wagon.

The photographer had gone ahead and made prints of half a dozen shots. "They were so good I couldn't resist," he told her. "Course, if you'd prefer some of the others, I'll be happy to print them."

"No, these are fine. Thank you so much." She paid him and went directly home, planning to give Erik the picture that same evening.

After a lengthy search of her room, she located the frame she'd bought in her book bag, along with the unopened envelope containing her diploma. Since her father hadn't been there to attend, there'd been no possibility of her going to the graduation exercises. The school had, in due course, sent along her final report card and the diploma. She hadn't been sufficiently interested even to look at these items. But she couldn't think why or when she'd put the envelope or the picture frame in the bag.

Pleased with the final results, she carried the framed photograph downstairs to show Kitty, who took hold of it and examined the picture asking, "You do this for Erik?"

"D'you think he'll like it?"

"Sure he will. I don't suppose you got any spares? I'd love to have me one of these."

"You would?"

"Uh-huh. Thought I'd keep it for target practice on my bedside table." Kitty laughed. "You got any more?"

"Yup. You really think he'll like it?"

"Lord, but you're thick sometimes, Reese! Course he will. That man would like anything you gave him, no matter what. And this is special, sure enough. Way better than some ole money clip."

"Great, because I'm going to give it to him tonight. In fact, I think I'll get dressed up and make it an occasion."

"You do that," Kitty encouraged her. "I'm gonna go see Freed, maybe go out for a drink or two."

Risa was quiet a moment, then said, "We're starting up again, aren't we? We're living our lives without him."

"Honey, it's supposed to be that way."

"I guess. But I keep feeling guilty."

"Well, don't! Just remind yourself your daddy wouldn't have wanted you to stop livin' because he did. And," she added, "for all you or I know, he's probably havin' a helluva good time wherever he is."

"I like to think that, too." Risa kissed Kitty's cheek before going off to her room to decide what she'd wear.

Taken by the idea of creating an occasion, she telephoned Raskin to say, "I'm going to bring over a bottle of champagne from the cellar. And I've got a present for Erik. Let's make it a little party. What d'you think?"

"Sounds good. I'll defrost some Cornish hens I've got in the freezer, and stuff their tiny bodies with a bunch of good things."

"It's going to be fun."

"I'll even wear a tie." Raskin laughed.

At nine, Erik came for her in the boat. As he pulled up to the dock, putting his hand out to assist her over the side, he said, "How very lovely you look!" and had to admire her for several moments before looping one arm around her waist and steering the boat away from the dock.

Upon arriving at the boathouse, instead of going through the tunnel to the music room, he directed her onto the grass, leading the way to the rear of the house where, on the seldom-used terrace, Raskin had set up a table and chairs. Candles had been placed here and there, and Dave Brubeck was pouring out through speakers in the kitchen.

"This is so nice," Risa said, giving Erik first the Dom Pérignon and then the gift-wrapped picture.

"What is this?" he asked of the gaily wrapped package.

"It's a present, for you."

He appeared not to understand, but stood holding the beribboned offering and staring at her.

"I'll put the champagne in the refrigerator," she said, taking it back from him. "You open your present."

Stepping inside, Risa saw Raskin, with an apron on to protect his suit, bending to check the progress of the hens in the oven. Straightening, he watched her stow the bottle in the refrigerator, saying, "You've outdone yourself. You look most elegant," and walked in a circle around her to get the full effect of the white, full-skirted dress with a square neckline, tucked bodice, and flowing sleeves she'd bought to wear to her graduation. Her only jewelry was the diamond pendant Erik had given her. She'd pinned her hair into a loosely coiled topknot from which tendrils escaped down the sides of her face and the nape of her neck. "One hundred percent," he declared. "After seeing nothing but granny dresses or half-naked females in micro-minis at the supermarket, you're a breath of fresh air from some other time and place."

"You look swell, too. A suit and tie and everything. This is going to be terrific."

"Only if you get out of here and let me attend to my hens and my wild rice and the rest of it."

Erik held one of the candles close to the photograph and gazed at Marisa's gift. There, on matte finish paper, captured for all time in her exquisite girlhood beauty, was his beloved child. It was the only gift he'd received since the age of seven, and that alone would have been sufficient to move him. But that she'd chosen to give him her image was monumentally significant. How could she have known it was the one thing he most wanted? How had she guessed that he had a need to be able to see her face when she wasn't with him?

"Do you like it?" she asked, having waited several minutes for him to say something while he stood holding the frame with one hand, the fingers of the other flitting uncertainly in the air above it like a bird before a dish of seeds, hungry but wary.

"I cannot begin to tell you what this means to me," he said at last, holding the frame before him with unsteady hands, unable to take his eyes from her portrait. "I will treasure this always."

"Oh, you wait," she said lightly. "We'll have dozens of pictures, albums full of them."

His head turned and he gazed at her, as if reminding her of the unlikelihood of that.

"I know," she said softly. "But somehow we'll figure out a way to fill a few albums. Do I get a kiss or anything? The whole point of giving people presents, you know, is that they get so excited, they're so totally blown away by them, that they want to jump up and down and kiss the giver. Things like that."

"Do you get a kiss?" he repeated, thinking he would like to be able to open his body and invite her to step inside, then magically close around her so that they need never again be apart. "I think so," he said and, still holding the frame, put one hand to her cheek while he touched his mouth to hers. "You are my miracle," he whispered, the back of his hand skimming over her cheek. "You are the dream of my lifetime. Nothing will ever be of importance unless you're with me to share it."

"I know that," she laughed. "But do you like it?"

His face made its smiling contortion, his eyes absorbing her. "I like it more than you could ever imagine. And after dinner I have something I would like to show you."

"What?"

"After dinner," he repeated.

"Erik," she said, turning inside his arm to look out at the Sound. "Will you marry me on my birthday?"

"Yes."

"Will Hal be your best man, and could we have Kitty give me away?"

"Yes."

"And will you promise to love, honor, and cherish me until death us do part?"

"Yes."

"Okay!" She laughed, turning back to him. "Could we have the honeymoon after dinner?"

"I think it could be arranged." He kissed her again. "It will be *divine,*" he whispered.

"What is this 'divine' thing?" she asked him. "Why does that word send you and Hal into silly fits?"

"I will explain after dinner."

"God! After dinner's going to last for days."

"Possibly. Any objections?"

"I've promised Kitty I'll sleep at home every night until you and I 'get legal.' That's what she calls it. Isn't that quaint?"

"I rather like it. And I'll make sure you're home before your carriage turns back into a pumpkin and the white horses devolve into scampering rodents."

Erik disappeared after dinner, telling Risa he would see her upstairs in ten minutes. Meanwhile, she sat on at the table on the terrace with Raskin finishing the last of the champagne. It had been a superb dinner and she praised Hal's culinary skills, asking, "How did you learn to cook?"

"Self-defense. Either learn or die of starvation."

"Maybe you'll teach me some of your secrets."

"I thought you already knew how. You cooked for Erik, as I recall."

"That was one time, and I nearly had a nervous breakdown over it. Would you? Teach me, I mean."

"I'd be glad to. Any time."

"You wouldn't leave if Erik and I got married, would you, Hal?"

"Not unless you or he wanted me to."

"Neither one of us would want that," she told him.

"Then, fine. Long as you're happy."

"May I ask you something?"

"You can ask. I don't promise I'll answer."

"Did you have an unhappy childhood, Hal?"

He let out a howl of laughter, then went suddenly serious and looked at her assessingly, saying, "What is it about you? There's this thing you do where you zero in on people. It could get you in trouble, kid."

"I didn't mean to pry. It's just a feeling I have about you."

He smiled wolfishly, then tapped his fingers in a tattoo on the tabletop. "You don't scare easily, do you?"

"Oh yes, I do. Very easily."

"You want to know about my childhood, Risa? I'll give you the abridged version. My father liked to beat people up. He especially liked to beat up my mother. He beat her up so well he finally killed her one night. And then I killed him. The jury decided it was justifiable homicide committed by a minor, acquitted me, and the court awarded custody of me and my older sister to our grandmother, our mother's mother. Some years later my sister got married to a man who liked to beat people up. And to save myself from killing him, I gave up my engineering career, enlisted, and was one of the first to go to Nam, to kill a whole bunch of other people instead, to get the murder out of my system. While I was in Nam, my sister hanged herself from the back porch of her house in Bridgeport. The husband took off for the hills. Five months into my tour of duty I got myself wounded, got an honorable discharge, and was shipped home. My grandmother had died, so that was the end of the family. Three months after my discharge, I came to work for Erik. End of story. Any questions?"

"How did you kill him?" she asked in a hushed voice.

"You don't want to know that. And Erik's waiting for you."

"I'm sorry, Hal."

"Yeah," he said. For the second time, he felt that odd sense of absolution. What *was* it about this girl? he wondered, watching her leave the terrace.

Erik had rigged up a small lamp and positioned it so that no light shone on him. He invited Marisa to sit with him on the bed, then he opened the photograph album across his lap.

"This is Philippe," he told her, one long finger pointing. "And this is Lavinia. And this is Erik." His finger moved over individual shots of his parents as teenagers, then turned the page to show shots of the two together. Then his fingertip moved to the picture of an infant. "Lavinia met Philippe when she was eighteen and he was twenty-two." He turned pages as he spoke. "She was in Paris on holiday with two friends from school. He was first violinist with the Paris symphony but hoped for a career as a soloist. They met through mutual friends and were immediately drawn to one another. That was in 1933. By 1935 Philippe had had a successful solo debut and he asked Lavinia to marry him. They were married in March of the following year, and in September of 1937 Erik was born." His hand slowly turned another page. "Early in 1938, Philippe began to fear there would be a war. He convinced Lavinia it would be wise for them to leave Paris and relocate in England. Since England was her home, her birthright, she readily agreed, and they left with their child.

"Philippe's career was flourishing, and by 1944, despite the war, he was performing regularly, giving concerts throughout England and making successful recordings. Things were going very well indeed.

"Then, on a Sunday afternoon in November of 1944, they died in an automobile accident. This is a photograph of Lavinia's family taken in 1932 at the family home in Gloucestershire. These are her mother and father, and *that*"—his voice quivered and his pointing finger went rigid—"is Lavinia's older sister *Dorothy*." He spoke the woman's name as if it were a poisoned pellet on his tongue.

Turning the final page, he said, "This is Lavinia and Philippe and Erik at Christmas 1943. They were very happy," he said almost inaudibly, and gently closed the book.

Risa reached to turn out the light, then sat with her head on his shoulder. "Why do things have to be so sad?" she said quietly. "It's all so unfair."

"Nothing is fair."

"Erik, I do love you—very much. I wish I knew some magic words to say that would wipe away the bad part and make you happy."

His hand lifted and moved to the side of her head, then reappeared before her holding a pink rose.

With an excited cry, she accepted the flower. "I love your magic! It's so incredible when you do things like that." Sitting up on her knees, she took the album and the rose and set them on the floor beside the bed. Then, presenting her back to him, she said, "Unzip me, please."

His hands worked the zipper, then slipped inside the loosened bodice to close over her breasts. The feel of her was a warm recurring dream, one that brought constant delirium.

Covering his hands with her own, she said, "Wait a minute! You have to tell me what that 'divine' business is all about."

With a soft laugh, Erik let his head fall forward against her bare back. "One of Raskin's women," he explained. "Everything from martinis to lovemaking is, to her, divine."

"Oh, swell! Here I am, in the ranks of Raskin's women."

"Not ever," he said, placing kisses down the length of her spine, his thumbs gently abrading her nipples.

Pulling her arms free of the dress, she swung around to clamp her mouth over his.

Seventeen

O

N HER EIGHTEENTH BIRTHDAY, THE TWENTY-SECOND OF FEBRUARY, 1970, Marisa and Erik were married, by the minister who'd conducted the service for her father, at her home on Butlers Island. The others present were Kitty and Raskin.

Risa wore the pale-pink suit Kitty had helped her select. In her hair were her mother's tortoise-shell combs, around her neck was Erik's diamond pendant, and in her pocket she carried the blue handkerchief Raskin had thought to give her just prior to the arrival of the minister.

At the appropriate moment during the ceremony, Erik and she exchanged the rings he'd designed and had made by a goldsmith in Manhattan—each band formed of two irregularly curving interlocked circles of white and yellow gold. Erik was nearly immobilized by anxiety and could scarcely utter his "I do." Risa felt dizzy and disconnected, as if this were something she was dreaming, rather than an event she'd long been anticipating.

When they'd signed the certificate, Raskin produced a bottle of champagne and Kitty brought a tray of glasses. There were toasts to the bride and groom. The minister kissed Risa's cheek and wished her well. He gave Erik's hand a hearty shake, then went on his way.

As agreed beforehand, Risa and Erik left soon after the minister to go to Erik's house on Contentment Island. Her things had been moved over during the previous week and she had, earlier that day, carried a small suitcase up to the third bedroom.

There was a note taped to the front door. It read: "Please be sure to look in the dining room, also in the refrigerator. A few surprises from Hal and Kitty."

With a laugh, Risa took Erik's hand and went running with him to the dining room. The table was set for two. In the kitchen was another note that told them at what temperature to set the oven and for how long. The refrigerator held two bottles of champagne and a pair of tulip glasses whose stems had been tied with white ribbons.

"This is great!" Risa said, relaxing for the first time in days. "I'm not hungry yet, are you?"

Erik shook his head, his eyes on his ring.

"What's the matter?" she asked, approaching him.

With his right hand he took hold of her left, so that they were side by side.

"We're married," she said. "We are actually married. I am a missus!"

"We are. You are," he said, as if numb. Despite wanting it with all his heart, and despite having achieved his greatest wish—to have her as his wife—he was stricken by a sense of foreboding so potent he could barely function. When you got all you'd ever wanted, something was bound to happen to strip you of it, to bring you to your knees and force you to rue the day you'd ever had the audacity to wish for anything. If the Fates didn't actually take away your life altogether, they'd make certain it was barely worth living. And today's ceremony, the realization of the only dream he'd ever nurtured, was tempting the Fates to the maximum. It was challenging them to wreak havoc, to whip up hurricanes or tidal waves or earthquakes.

"Erik?" She touched him lightly on the arm.

He shrugged off his foreboding and looked at her, at once and always heartened merely by the sight of her.

"My plan is that we each go now to prepare ourselves," she said. "And in thirty minutes, we will meet in your room. Do you like my plan?"

"I am captivated by the potential of your plan."

"Okay. So let's go. I've got a lot to do in half an hour." She kissed him on the chin, then went running off.

He remained where he was, battling his trepidations, telling himself that to succumb to them would taint Marisa's happiness. This nameless fear might, if he gave in to it, put down such deep roots he'd never be able to weed it out. This was the point at which he was obliged to have faith, to believe that even an ambulatory horror deserved a measure of contentment.

Squaring his shoulders, he ran his hands over his hair, took several deep breaths, then started through the house to his bedroom. He had less than half an hour to assemble everything.

With her hair protected by a plastic cap, Risa showered quickly, then placed dots of perfume behind her ears, in the bends of her elbows and knees, and between her breasts. Then she brushed out her hair and slipped on the white silk gown and robe Kitty had insisted on buying her for this night.

"You're gonna look like an angel," Kitty had said. Then with a laugh, she'd added, "You'll drive the man wild."

She and Kitty had shopped for two weeks, making several trips into Manhattan to find the many items on Risa's list. They had even, after much deliberation, ordered announcements from Tiffany's.

"You gotta do it right," Kitty had told her. "You can't make it seem like this is something you're sneakin' off to do. And, besides, wait till you see the presents that come pourin' in. Three toasters and five silver serving spoons, two irons, and heaps of mismatched towels, not to mention crap people got given and they've been dyin' to get rid of. It'll take you months to return half of it, and years to figure out what to do with the rest. You gonna buy a present for the groom?"

"No. I thought I'd steal his car and leave town. Of course I am!" Risa had said somewhat indignantly.

"You mind if I ask what you have in mind?"

"No, I don't mind. I'm going to buy him this." She pulled from her bag a page torn from a magazine.

Kitty looked at it and whistled. "That's gonna cost *thousands!*"

"It's not as if I get married every day."

"That's a good thing," Kitty teased. "It'd be very damned expensive."

Not bothering with slippers, Risa now gathered up her offerings, then went to tap on Erik's door. It clicked open and she stopped just inside the room, taking in the sight and scent of the many vases of pale-pink roses around which Erik had arranged dozens of candles. Music came from the speakers concealed in the ceiling, a violin concerto she thought was Paganini. Erik was waiting for her, his hands in the pockets of a black silk dressing gown.

"This is wonderful, Erik!"

She came toward him with her arms full of packages, the white silk swirling around her like fog, her long black hair shimmering over her shoulders as she moved. He wondered for a moment how any of this had come to be, then shoved aside his doubts and speculations, determined to savor every second of his wedding night.

"Come sit here with me so I can give you your presents." She beckoned him to join her on the end of the bed, where she let the packages fall from her arms.

"You are so beautiful," he whispered. "There are times, like now, especially now, when I have the feeling that were I to reach for you, my hands would find only empty air."

"I'm real," she laughed, and leaned forward to kiss him. "This one first." She selected a package and held it out to him.

His hands took the small square box and turned it this way and that as if performing a prelude to some conjuring trick. "I think you plan to make up for every birthday and Christmas I've ever missed."

"I intend to try. Open it. There's a lot of stuff here for you to look at and I'm dying to see how you like it all."

"You are very generous," he said hesitantly.

"Open it, Erik. The suspense is killing me."

His hands, she thought, were incapable of any hurried or ungraceful gesture. Like a surgeon's, they deftly stripped away the wrappings to reveal the box inside. He glanced up at her questioningly, then lifted the lid.

"Everything after this is sheer anticlimax." She laughed softly. "Do you like it? What do you think?"

He gazed at the gold Rolex wristwatch, then removed it from the box to hold it in his hands, turning it over and over, his fingers examining the band. "It is magnificent. I am overwhelmed. Thank you."

"If you don't like it, we can take it back and get something else."

"No, no. I like it *very* much."

"Great! Now open this one."

The second box contained a bottle of cologne. It had a gold-rimmed white label with "Erik" written by hand on it.

"I had it made for you," she told him. "Smell it."

The scent was evocative of winter and woodsmoke, with an underlying warmth of sandalwood. "You had this made?" he asked.

"Just for you. No one else anywhere has this fragrance, only you."

"Extraordinary! I like this very much, too."

The third box, large and quite heavy, held an imperial quart of Glenfiddich.

"A present," she said softly, "to you, from my dad."

The fourth, small and compact, contained a gold Dunhill cigarette lighter.

The fifth and largest of all and lined with tissue revealed six custom-made white silk shirts, with his monogram embroidered in white silk thread on the pockets.

And the last box offered up Cameron's gold-and-onyx cuff links.

"That's from Dad, too," she said. "I know he'd have wanted you to have them. I hope you don't mind."

"Mind? I am honored. These are exceptional gifts, every one of them. Thank you." He assembled the packages and discarded wrappings and shifted them from the bed to the top of the dresser. This done, he returned across the room, his hands signaling her to stand but not move. He faced her from perhaps three feet away. One hand placed itself palm outward before her eyes, then twisted from the wrist like a small acrobat and opened again with a long strand of lustrous pearls draped across his slightly spread fingers. The clasp was of platinum and diamonds, and he opened it to fasten the pearls around her neck. She was about to speak, but a finger to his lips kept her silent. Once more he held up his hands, showing them front and back before he slid them into the sides of her hair, pulling back with his fingers curled shut. Turning over slowly, his fingers uncurled one at a time to reveal a diamond earring on the palm of each hand. Another signal and she held out her hands. He turned his hands so they lay on top of hers, depositing the earrings on her outheld palms where they sat refracting the candlelight and shooting off small sparks.

Again, he motioned her to keep silent and she obeyed, captivated by this performance. His left hand danced for a moment before her eyes, then his right, the fingers opening and closing hypnotically. Then, startlingly, he clapped his hands together before folding them open to show a bracelet of small gold links each set with a diamond. Plucking the earrings from her palms, he secured the bracelet to her wrist, then dropped the earrings into the pocket of her robe.

"The show is over," he whispered, with a finger tracing a line from the underside of her chin down her throat to the hollow at its base where it remained for a moment before continuing on its way down the outside of the robe to the sash at her waist. A flick of his finger, the sash was undone and the robe fell open. She turned her shoulders, and the garment slithered away like a substanceless ghost. The violin concerto was reaching a crescendo, and she asked, "What is the music, Erik?"

"It is Paganini's Violin Concerto No. 4 in D Minor. Played by my father with the London Symphony Orchestra."

"He was wonderful, wonderful."

"He played as if God whispered in his ears. He was a genius."

"That's what my father said about you," she told him, undoing his dressing gown.

"Your father overstated my abilities." His hands at her waist, he was gathering the fabric of her nightgown under his fingers, drawing it slowly higher and higher.

"No, he didn't," she disagreed, feeling the air wind itself around her calves like a sinuous cat. "I'm very excited. I feel all shaky."

He nodded, feeling precisely the same way as he lifted the gown over her head and dropped it to one side. He paused for a moment to rid himself of his dressing gown, then, without touching her, his hands wafted over her silhouette as his eyes followed their passage. "My wife," he whispered. Such rare and gemlike words, so exceptional a concept. "My wife." Tall and proud and long of limb; passionate and funny and giving; narrow of waist and hip, with small perfect breasts and yielding thighs; fragile ankles and elegantly arched feet, finely formed toes. "Beautiful," he crooned, his hands at last closing around the supple flesh of her upper arms. "How I love you! Do you know how I adore you?"

"I know." She let him draw her closer and closer until their bodies met. Standing on her toes, extending herself fully, she pushed forward, rubbing luxuriously against the length of his broad sinewy body. Then she slipped down to rest her cheek against his belly, her hands on the backs of his thighs. She dipped her tongue into his naval, then kissed him on each hip, her hands shifting down to his knees and then up again. She was aware every time she caressed him in this fashion that it stupefied and somehow shattered him. But she had to show him in whatever way she could that however much he claimed to love her, her love for him was equal and no less deep. So it was a great pleasure and another, albeit transitory, gift she could give him to stroke and kiss him until he had to ask her hoarsely, please, to stop because she was driving him nearly mad with her devoted attentions and questing mouth.

He had to lift her onto the bed and duplicate her attentions, losing himself to her flesh while the roses exuded their perfume into the atmosphere and the candle flames darted in the sudden currents created by their shifting, sighing consummation.

Raskin looked around and said, "Let's get the hell out of here. Come on. I'll buy you dinner."

Kitty also looked around. "All right. Why not, seein's how we're all decked out in our finery."

Raskin had the Mercedes, and showed her into the car, asking, "How d'you feel about someplace with live music?"

"I feel just fine about that."

They went to a steakhouse where a trio played in the bar so that couples could dance in the small area provided. Because it was a weeknight, the dining room was only about half full and the bar was fairly well deserted. The hostess gave them a secluded table off in a corner of the dining room, then waited to take their drink orders.

After she'd gone, Kitty opened her purse for her Kools, and smiled as Raskin at once held his lighter to her cigarette.

"You're one sharp cookie." She grinned at him.

"You're pretty sharp yourself," he replied. "This is the first time I've seen you decked out in your 'finery.' You should do it more often." He gazed admiringly at her, wondering why he hadn't before noticed the size or depth of her blue eyes, or how very pretty she was, especially this evening with the hair swept back from her face and coiled into a knot at the nape of her neck.

"For who? For what?" she said matter-of-factly.

"Maybe for me."

She regarded him with raised eyebrows. "You?"

"Sure. Why not?"

She took a breath that swelled the cleavage revealed by her handsome gray suit. "Why not?" she repeated, then paused to take a puff of her Kool. "Well, how old're you, for one thing?"

"Thirty-two."

"And I'm forty-two. That alone should answer your question."

"Nope." He shook a Kent from his pack. "That's not going to do it."

"All right, then. How about this: I doubt there's a single woman in all Fairfield County who hasn't encountered you in one place or another."

"So?"

"You don't think you're spread maybe a little thin?"

"I'm not spread at all," he countered. "You don't get spread when you never spend more than one night with a woman."

"And you're thinkin' I might like to be another of those one-night women?"

"You're different."

"Maybe *I* like to think so." She smiled. "But I doubt you do."

"You have no idea what I think," he said evenly, his grayish eyes holding hers.

"Your eyes change colors," she said, distracted. "A while back, they were quite blue. Now they've gone near most gray."

"I'm a chameleon," he laughed. "Yours are always blue. Very very blue."

"I do believe you're tryin' to flatter me."

"No, just telling the truth."

The waitress came with their drinks, said she'd be back shortly to take their dinner orders, and went away.

"Why'd you want to sleep with a woman ten years older'n you?" she asked bluntly. "You got a hankerin' after saggy flesh?"

He laughed boldly. "You're not saggy. You're a lot more trim than most of the women I see. And from where I'm sitting, the view is very nice."

She looked down at her breasts, then said, "I think we've exhausted this topic. Let's see if we can't find somethin' else to talk about."

"That won't be easy. I've kind of made up my mind to talk about you."

"Well, you'll just have to change it, won't you?"

"It's going to be an awfully quiet dinner."

"You'll survive," she said. "Tell me something. How d'you figure things're gonna work out with the three of you all livin' together in the one house?"

"I figure it'll work out fine. It's a big house, plenty of room to get away from each other. Unless Erik decides otherwise, I'm satisfied with the arrangement. Risa's been halfway living there for months now. I don't see things'll change all that much now they're married."

"You like my girl?" she asked.

"You think of her as your girl?"

"I surely do. I've looked after her near all her life. She's as much mine as ever she could be."

"I like that," he said solemnly. "I like hearing you talk about her that way."

"Why?"

"I just do."

"You got any kin?" she asked. "Any people hereabouts?"

He shook his head.

"I got a few left back home. Not one I'd give you a nickel for, though."

"Back home where?"

"Memphis. I been gone so long now I can't even hardly remember the place. I left there twenty-four years ago. Better'n half my lifetime. Where-all d'you hail from?"

"Bridgeport." He smiled sardonically. "The armpit of the universe."

"As I recall, a lot of folks I once knew used to say that very same thing about Memphis. Me, I didn't mind it that much. I just didn't wanna spend my entire life there."

"Come dance with me," he invited suddenly. "I bet you're a terrific dancer."

"I don't mind," she said by way of consent.

Alone together on the dance floor, he pulled her close. She hesitated for a moment, resisting, then gave in. They danced without speaking for a time, well-matched and comfortable together. When, without breaking, the trio went into a second number, he put his lips to her ear and said, "You *are* a terrific dancer. You feel good, and you smell better."

"It's not gonna work," she told him.

"Oh, sure it is. You made up your mind about half an hour ago."

"I've been known to change my mind on a regular basis."

"But you won't."

"Now, what makes you think that?"

"Because you're lonely, too," he said simply.

That took her aback. He kissed the side of her neck, and she thought he was probably right.

"There's a condition," she said.

"Name it."

"There's gotta be a second time. After that, I don't much care one way or the other. But I'll be damned if I'm gonna get put on your list as another one-night woman."

"I might surprise you." His hand dropped down to her hip. "I've met most of them, but I haven't met you before."

"You sure do have all the lines."

"No line," he said, pulling back to look her in the eyes. "I mean it."

"My Lord!" she said softly. "I believe you do."

Eighteen

$\mathcal{E}$RIK HAD TURNED THE THIRD BEDROOM OVER TO RISA, TELLING HER TO do whatever she liked with it. Her immediate reaction was to blurt, without thinking, "It could be a nursery, Erik."

"I think not," came his frosty reply.

"Someday," she offered.

"I think not," he repeated.

"Okay," she backed down. "Don't be angry with me."

"I am not angry with you."

"You're way beyond angry. You're furious."

"Let's, please, not pursue this discussion further." He stepped out into the hallway, leaving her alone.

"Okay," she said to herself, turning to survey the room. "Okay."

Since it was the one room in the house Erik had all but ignored during the renovation, she was free to start from scratch. The walls had only been primed, and carpet had never been laid. After deliberating for a time, she decided that if she couldn't persuade him to consider the room's future use as a nursery, she'd go for vivid colors and create a room of light. She thought she might be able to tempt Erik into an appreciation of the sun. So she bought and put up herself a wallpaper with brilliant green palm fronds on a white background, and painted the wood trim a matching green. The carpet was white, as were the bed linens and the spread. She filled the room with potted plants and wicker furniture, including what she thought was an attractive, even enticing, grouping of two white wicker rockers positioned on either side of a round white table.

To open the door to this room after the darkness of the rest of the house was like entering into a cool spring morning. When it was finished, with her clothes hung away in the walk-in closet—Erik's closet being surprisingly too small to accommodate her wardrobe—she went up to the office to invite him to inspect the end result of her labors.

He actually covered his eyes when she opened the door, and she hurried to draw the curtains, but he stopped her, saying, "No, don't. Let me have a moment." When his eyes had adjusted to the assaultive light, he was most complimentary. "It's lovely, Marisa, truly lovely."

"Would you sit here with me sometimes?"

"Sometime," he said, intentionally vague. "Of course."

He kept his back to the window. She saw this and doubted he'd ever voluntarily spend any time in there with her. It crushed and defeated her. "I know you're busy," she said, swallowing her disappointment. "I just thought you'd want to see."

"Marisa," he said, well aware of her letdown, "please don't be upset. It's been too long, too many years of living the way I have to change my habits now." Reaching for her hand, he said, "There is something I'd like to discuss with you. Now might be a good time."

"Let's get out of here, then," she said, and started for the door.

"Don't!" he cautioned kindly. "Don't fly away from your charming creation simply because I don't fit in here."

"Sure you do!" she disagreed. "You fit in because I say you do, not because you say you don't."

"Please believe that it is my fondest wish to do what gives you pleasure. I'm simply not able to do all I would like. I'm not defying you. I'm engaged full-time in an effort to be worthy of you."

"You already are. You were to begin with. It *kills* me when you say things like that!" As if to illustrate, she held her fists to her chest. "Oh, hell!" she cried. "Why am I doing this to you? Come on, Erik." She grabbed his hand and began towing him to the door. "Let's talk in your room. I apologize for all that. It was stupid."

"This is *our* room," he corrected her, once they were inside and seated together.

"And so is that jungle next door. Every goddamned room in this house is *ours*. Sometimes I'm so stupid I hate myself."

"You are never stupid. You are simply very young. And that brings me to what I wanted to discuss with you." He reached into his pocket and brought out a pack of Sobranie cigarettes, taking his time to light one with the gold Dunhill. He held on to the lighter while he repositioned the ashtray. As on every other day of his life, he was wearing a black suit and a white shirt, with an immaculate dark-gray silk tie.

"In very short order," he began, "you are going to become utterly bored by spending your days and nights in this house trying to find things to do to occupy your time. Please, don't speak for a moment. Hear me out."

"Raskin and I have talked, and we've come up with an idea. If it is of interest to you, both of us will be pleased to work with you to implement the idea."

"What is it?"

"You have a talent for line drawing, and you're good at mathematics. What we are proposing is that Raskin and I teach you how to draft, with the thought in mind that eventually you will take over from him and make my presentations to prospective clients. We would, during the coming months, teach you how to read and interpret specifications and plans. Then, if you agreed, you could accompany Raskin when next he makes a presentation.

"I had planned," he went on, "to give up my work, you see. It wasn't that I dislike it. In fact, I like it tremendously. But I'm unable to deal anymore on a direct basis with the clients. With both you and Raskin to assist, I'd be free to do the work and oversee by remote control, as it were. It would also simplify matters and reduce the workload if it were divided among three. Does this appeal to you at all?"

"I don't know," she said truthfully. "I'll have to think about it."

"We all need work of some kind, Marisa. It's what, for many of us, validates our existence. I don't think you're any more capable than I of sitting idle for months on end, amusing yourself with shopping excursions or new recipes. Not that I don't very much enjoy your cooking and the things you buy. But you really should have something to do that challenges your intellect and stimulates your imagination. If you choose not to go along with this suggestion, I'd ask you to consider attending one of the colleges nearby. You're too young to immerse yourself completely in the workings of this household, with no outside interests to divert you."

"Are you trying to force me to be emancipated?" she asked with a smile. "It sounds as if I'm going to be equal whether I want to be or not."

"It's just common sense," he said, failing to see the humor.

"It was a joke, Erik," she told him, going over to kneel on the floor in front of him with her arms folded across her knees. "Joke. Funny. We all laugh. Ha ha."

He smiled at her, his hand cupping her chin. "Ha ha," he whispered. "What do you think?" he asked, turning to extinguish his cigarette.

"I'm sure you're right. Could I come up and have a look at some of what you and Hal are doing, so I can get an idea what it's all about?"

"Certainly." He returned the Dunhill to his jacket pocket. "Any time you like."

"How about now?"

"Good."

Hal showed her a set of his drawings, explaining that his specialty was mechanical engineering while Erik's degrees were in architecture and electrical engineering.

"Between us, you see, Risa, we can cover everything, including things most other architects would have to subcontract for. Another hand to help with the drafting would be very welcome, and it's not hard at all. It's just a matter of rendering to scale and being able to draw straight lines with the help of a few set or T-squares."

"It looks kind of interesting." She wandered over to look at the model on top of the drawing file cabinet. "Who does these?" she asked, put in mind of the doll's house she'd had years ago.

"A model maker in Stamford. He does good work, doesn't he?"

"It's wonderful, with the little trees and tiny cars and pushpin people."

Erik, at his drawing board, dropped his head on his arm and laughed. She marched across the room and pounded her fist on his arm. "What's so funny now?" she demanded as Raskin also started to laugh. "Is this another of those dumbass 'divine' things?"

Erik sat up and swiveled on his stool to put his arm around her waist. "Pushpin people," he said. "That's very funny, Marisa."

"Well, how'm I supposed to know what to call them?"

"Precisely! From now on they shall be termed pushpin people." He hugged her and she bent forward until her forehead was touching his and she was smiling into his face. "Don't make fun of me, buster! Not if you want me to come work for you."

"You think you'd care to try?"

"I guess. Will I get one of these nifty drafting tables for my own?"

"Oh, most assuredly. Raskin will ring up and order one for you at once."

"Yes, he will," Raskin said from across the room. "With a nice high stool of your very own, and all kinds of nifty mechanical pencils, and erasers, and everything else you want or need."

"Maybe this is a mistake," she said, looking over at Raskin, then back at Erik. "The two of you will do nothing but tease me from morning to night."

"Erik doesn't work before four in the afternoon," Raskin reminded her. "More like teasing from four till midnight. This is shift work."

"Let me make sure I've got this straight. The two of you will teach me how to draft stuff, and how to read these big thick boring-looking books. And when I've learned all that, then you'll send me out to show people your designs?"

"Something like that," Erik replied.

"And they're going to listen to someone my age tell them how my husband is going to design their building?"

"I think you'll be a bit older by then."

"Well, how long's all this going to take?"

"Perhaps two years."

"Two years?"

"Think of it as working toward a degree without the need to go to school every day with a bunch of freaked-out hippies," Raskin said. "Nobody shoving flowers up your nose, making peace signs in front of you and chanting, 'Love, love, love,' all day long."

"Yeah," she said. "Working toward a degree by coming upstairs every afternoon to sit here with a couple of weird Ivy Leaguers."

"Oh, now," Raskin said. "You really want to watch what you say, Risa. Princeton and Yale are only rivals on the football field. We might gang up on you if you impugn our establishment educations."

"I'm going down to organize dinner. Let me know when my drafting table arrives." With a kiss on Erik's chin she sailed out. At once, she popped back through the door to waggle her finger, saying, "Don't you dare start talking about me before I'm all the way downstairs." Then she laughed, and went out again.

Raskin lit a cigarette, propped it on the lip of the ashtray, then said, "What d'you think, Erik?"

"I think she'll do it and be very good at it."

"So do I."

To himself, Erik thought she'd come along to salvage his entire life, including a career he wanted badly to keep. "I'm grateful for the suggestion, Raskin."

"It was nothing. Forget it."

"She's taking to it like a duck to water," Raskin was telling Kitty. "It hasn't been six months and she can knock off a drawing in no time flat and it'll be flawless every time. She finds the specs boring, but that's understandable. She'd rather be reading a novel."

"Who wouldn't?" Kitty agreed.

"Erik's very excited about the new job. Funny, but it's about the last thing in the world I'd have thought he'd accept, let alone be excited about."

"Then you've missed the point altogether," she said tolerantly. "Designin' an office building for a group of doctors is just the kinda thing that would excite him. It gives him a chance, I'd imagine, to correct every last thing that bothered him as a child about places like that."

"Jesus! You're right. I never thought of that."

"All kinds of things you've never thought of," she said. "Like how you keep on turnin' up here, regular as a six-foot clock. I'm not sure I know what-all to make of this."

"I told you, but you didn't believe me."

"I surely didn't, and I don't know that I'm entirely happy with it."

He shot her a look, his jaw going tight.

"Don't you go gettin' mean-lookin', Harold Raskin!" She pointed a brightly polished finger at him. "I'm only speakin' the truth. And the truth is, I get the impression every so often you're tryin' to make yourself indispensable to me, the way you done with Erik."

"Are you implying I have dishonorable motives?" he asked sharply.

"I'm not implyin' diddly. I'm sayin' I don't know if I want you bein' indispensable to me. I go let myself get reliant on you, you're likely as not to up an' disappear for good 'n' always. I only slept with you that first time 'cause what you said was the truth. I was lonely, missin' Cam. Now it's gettin' on for nine months and I see more of you than I do of my girl."

"What's your point?"

"I guess I want to know where I stand."

"Right now, you're not 'standing' anywhere," he quipped.

"Don't play smart with me. I asked a question deserves a civil answer."

"What kind of answer, civil aside, d'you want me to give?"

"Well, I'll tell you," she said, reaching for her drink on the side table and recrossing her legs before returning her attention to Raskin, who was sprawled on the sofa, fully aware he was admiring her legs and watching her every move. "I'd like to know who it is I've been takin' to my bed all these months. And I'd like to know your intentions, if you got any."

"If you were a man, I'd say you were getting ready to propose." He laughed.

"Oh, fuck you, honey!" she said calmly. "You're the biggest hard-ass I ever have known. 'Ceptin' when it comes down to the crucial moment, and then you're the saddest, scaredest young fella ever did cross my threshold. You don't fool me none, Harold. I've seen you hard and I've seen you soft, and I'm still willin' to talk with you, and I haven't yet heaved you outta my bed, so don't try duckin' me. Just answer me straight."

"I like you," he said, sitting up. "You're the only woman I've ever *really* liked. If you ask a lot of questions, Kitty, you might get answers you won't care for."

"There isn't one thing you could tell me that'd come as a surprise. And that's the honest truth. I know you've done some truly terrible things in your young life."

"How do you know that?"

"You got the marks on you, and I'm not referrin' to your war injuries.

It's in the way you make yourself real gentle when you come into my bed 'cause you've got a killin' ability and it scares you. I remind you of someone, don't I? Or is it that somethin' about me makes you remember somethin' from way way back?"

"I don't suppose you'd consider coming over here?" he asked.

"I don't mind." She got up and went to sit beside him on the sofa.

"How come you're not afraid of me?"

"I'm too fond of you to be afraid. And anyway, I know you'd never harm me. There's some you would, and likely some you did. But not me. I used to wonder, you know, at your workin' and livin' with Erik the way you do. Handsome young man closed away most of the time with poor Erik. But not anymore. It makes good sense to me now. The only difference 'tween the two of you is his wounds show. Yours a person has to guess at."

"How will you feel if I leave and don't come back?"

"I reckon I'll miss you and be sad for a time. But I won't be callin' you up on the phone like them others. And I won't be waitin' home nights for you."

"I wasn't threatening you," he explained.

"I know that. It's just your way. You're not a real trustin' soul. I guess you've got cause. Lord knows, most of us do."

"I suppose it's only fair that I tell you," he said. "Mind if I put my head in your lap?"

"I don't mind."

He lay down, took hold of her hand, then told her about his family. She didn't interrupt or say a word until he was finished, but smoothed his hair throughout the telling. Then all she said was, "Don't tell me how you killed him. I don't want to know. Okay?"

"That's fine."

"Bastard deserved to die," she said feelingly. "And so did the other one." She sighed and reached for her now watery drink. "Lord, but the world treats its children badly."

"Not you, though," he said, taking the glass from her and setting it on the coffee table. "You treat all your children well."

She laughed. "You ain't no child of mine, fella!"

He ran his hand across her breasts and said, "You don't know how glad I am about that."

"So," she said, "I guess this means you'll be comin' back."

"You could say that." He sat up and turned her to face him. "I like your face," he said. "I like the way your nose tilts up at the tip. And I like your mouth."

"Don't let it go to your head," she said softly, "but I go around hot all the time, thinkin' about you."

"Come take a bath with me!"

"I don't need a bath."

"Of course you don't," he told her. "But I want to soap you with my bare hands, then rinse you off, towel you dry, then rub oil over you while you're still warm."

"Yeah," she laughed. "And after that you'll coat me with whipped cream and eat it off."

"That's not a bad idea."

"Let's skip the soapin' and rinsin' and towelin' and go direct to the main event. What say?"

"I knew there was a reason why I like you."

"Ah, Harold." She smiled and pinched his cheek. "You're such a sweet young fool. You *love* me, but it scares you to death to think it."

"You're right. It does."

"Don't worry about it none, honey. It don't scare me one little bit."

Nineteen

$\mathcal{M}$ANY NIGHTS WHEN HIS SMALL HOUSEHOLD LAY PEACEFULLY SLEEP-ing, Erik went silently down the stairs to the music room where, for hours, amid the wavering candle flames, he paced about, sometimes listening to tapes he'd made, or to albums, but as often as not accompanied only by the almost audible turning of his thoughts. His head frequently felt like an overcrowded tunnel jammed full of vehicles with racing engines and honking horns, stalled for an eternity, while their exhausts pushed out noxious fumes that threatened to smother him.

For an entire year, Marisa had lived, in apparent contentment, inside his home. She lived beside him, the evidence of her presence was every-where—a book left open face-down on one of the living-room sofas, one of her fashion magazines forgotten on the kitchen counter, her hairbrush on the rim of the bathroom sink, or some piece of her clothing draped over the arm of one of the bedroom chairs. Coming into a room soon after she'd vacated it, he'd walk unknowingly into a cloud of her fragrance and stop abruptly, his head tilting, his hands lifting open as if in the hope of collecting this cloud into a package he might carry around with him. Or he'd enter a room when she was unaware, to have the pleasure of watch-ing her unguarded actions as she lifted a pot from the stove, or sat on the kitchen counter paging through some cookbook, or being fortunate enough to see her in the midst of dressing or undressing.

All of it seemed like some fabulous film being screened exclusively for his delectation, and so gripping was it that he lost any sense of time or of himself. At moments when he heard her voice in some other room, or the echo of her laughter as she chatted with Raskin, he experienced a happiness so intense and so foreign he wasn't altogether certain it wasn't merely another, new variation of pain.

As a seven-year-old with fractured thighs and a crushed pelvis, an arm torn halfway out of its socket and a head swathed in layer upon layer of thick bandages, he'd lived for some months in a cocoon of drug-induced amnesia, where only occasionally did either memory or physical pain intrude. He recalled those months as a time memorable solely for its absence of externalized events. Faces and voices drifted to and fro, hands were gentle, and ghostly nursing sisters were kindly emissaries from heaven. He was obliged to do nothing, only to rest and regain his strength while his sturdy little bones knitted themselves back together with the help of splints and pins and pounds of plaster and contraptions that elevated some parts of his body but not others; all of this in a small white room, in a narrow white-sheeted bed, while light gushed in through an elongated window from which he instinctively averted his eyes.

On subsequent return visits, alone in the night before his scheduled surgery, he'd lie in the dark and sing to keep the phantoms at bay, to keep himself safe from harm. Through the nights, while his fingers plucked at the bedclothes and his restless body shifted this way or that, the small boy sang every song he'd ever known, and some he'd never known. Music was all that stood between him and a world of sharp-bladed instruments, all evil-smelling anesthetics, and the blinding overhead lights of the operating theater.

Now it was many years later and he hoped he wasn't behaving as that child had, instinctively averting his eyes from the things he ought to be seeing. But as difficult as his life had been until the day Marisa entered it, it was a hundred times more difficult now because his desire to keep her happy at all costs required him to think and to do things that did not come naturally. He was obliged to pay close attention to her every word and facial expression in order to satisfy himself that she was saying what she meant; he was constantly evaluating his own behavior in order to be sure he gave her nothing less than everything within his means. And even making love to her, a glorious experience that each time surpassed his most spectacular dreams, he was watching and listening and taking care to ensure that nothing went unnoticed, no word unheard. His vigilance, while entirely voluntary, was nonetheless exhausting. Perhaps he was trying too hard. Perhaps he wasn't trying hard enough. To be wedded, to have put into writing one's commitment to love another, was an all-consuming, ceaseless enterprise. There wasn't a day when he didn't wonder if he'd answered too abruptly or too slowly some question she'd asked, when he didn't fret over the possibility that he and Raskin were pushing her into a career when she'd have been quite satisfied to continue as before, with her visits to Kitty, her shopping trips into Manhattan, and her foraging expeditions through the local supermarkets. The logistics of the life-style he and Raskin had long since established sometimes defeated her. Who made his suits, his shirts? Where did he get his shoes? How did the laundry get his shirts so white? But if he had a tailor, didn't he have to go there at least once, sometime, to be fitted? And the same for the shirts and the shoes. He'd had to sit down with her to explain that there had been legendary agoraphobics who'd lived for years on end without ever leaving their homes while managing to dress and eat and survive quite nicely. He, at least, did leave the house. He simply didn't do it, unless it was unavoidable, during the day. And the tailor came to the house; so did the man who made his shoes. Wasn't she aware of the convenience money could buy? He was touched by how unspoiled she was, by how much she was of the world he'd long ago rejected. She'd never thought to connect money with power, never realized you could pay people to do practically anything.

"I don't know why," she confessed one night, "but I saw the two of us together, shopping for things. Anything. Just together. And I thought perhaps we might sometime go dancing. I'd really love to do that. But you're right," she said bravely. "I wasn't thinking clearly. And I'm happy to dance with you here, in the music room. I don't mind. I really don't."

It was one of those times—his eyes felt like camera lenses, recording the little facial tics that betrayed her—when her mouth put out words that directly contradicted what her eyes, and cheeks, and chin, said. His daylight child wanted and needed light. Could he not bear it for her sake? Didn't he owe her at least a few excursions into the outside world? He could, to secure her happiness, do that much. Couldn't he?

Couldn't he? Dear God! The thought alone of that funeral and the dozens of Cameron's friends willing him dead and gone with their eyes, as dead and gone as poor dear Cameron, without even so much as speaking to him, let alone making any effort to discover whether or not he was indeed human. *Who is that creature?* Why did they hate him so? Total strangers, supposedly educated people, they despised him and wished him erased from the face of the earth—because he no longer looked human. Had he grown up safe and sound with Philippe and Lavinia, had he known the luxury of a social life with girls and dating in his teens, to arrive at his manhood intact, would he have wished some other benighted bastard dead, gone, and, above all, out of his sight? Possibly. But *he* was the benighted bastard, and the others who'd socialized and dated and married their childhood sweethearts sought to cover their women's eyes, pulling away in revulsion as if he were evil incarnate. He had dared to come out into the heartless blood-heating light, and they wanted him gone from their sight, removed from the immediate arena of their sensibilities because he was the living embodiment of their every secret fear.

Yet his wife, this child he'd so recklessly taken to his heart, longed to go out with him in public. For all her sympathy and understanding she had no true notion, no innate comprehension of how trifling, how truly paltry, was the hatred of strangers when compared to his own. For this *face*, this grotesque mockery of a human face.

Every day, on her behalf, he surrendered a little more of himself. What would happen when he'd grown tame and unprotected? Would he feel scooped clean, gutted like some fresh-caught fish with the hook still implanted in his cheek? Would he feel, constantly and never-endingly, the lance of happiness piercing the chambers of his heart with its purifying thrust? Or would he, blind and defenseless, be led by the hand by this child only to find himself abandoned in the desert without water?

She was so much a part of him it felt she'd passed into his very veins and arteries, where she swam in happy communion with the platelets and red and white cells. She was his life, its meaning. Could he venture beyond the walls of this house? Was he willing, for the sake of Marisa's profound belief in a state of ongoing happiness, to subject himself to the unwarranted hatred of strangers?

He prayed for the courage to walk through crowds with his wife.

Just over a year after she'd started carrying specifications about with her to read in her spare time, Erik was asked to submit drawings for a proposed condominium complex in Southport, and she was able to go with Raskin to assist, and to learn the fine points of a presentation. She enjoyed it, and was determined to be the one who'd oversee the next submission.

But it took far longer than she'd imagined. The condo project was a big one, on a fairly lavish scale, that kept them busy for more than two years. Erik had, through Raskin, to do battle during the entire construction phase, closely supervising the primary contractor to keep him from skimping on costs by using materials other than those specified. Halfway through, with nine of the twenty units completed, Erik was forced to fire the contractor for installing substandard furnaces and for failing to make the upgrade changes requested and paid for by individual owners. This necessitated not only many conversations with the builder but also entailed bringing in bids from other construction companies that were interested in seeing the project to completion.

Night after night, Erik and Raskin drove off to make site inspections, to be sure the new contractor was following the specifications to the letter. By the time the two men returned home, Risa, having spent the evening either alone or with Kitty, would be asleep. She'd get up to wander through the house in the mornings, or to sit outside on the terrace while she waited for the men to appear and for the work to continue.

During the morning hours she spent on her own, she thought about having a child. She thought about it, too, every time she went to the supermarket and encountered either pregnant women or those with infants in carry seats propped in their shopping carts. She couldn't resist the babies, and made such a fuss over them, she wondered if the women didn't think she was a bit crazy. They seemed tolerant and even pleased by her one-sided conversations with their offspring, and usually smiled at her as they pushed their carts off down another aisle. Risa watched them go, keenly envious.

She was working herself up to another discussion with Erik when he announced he'd been asked to submit drawings for a new project. "And you will present this one," he told her. "You'll be involved in this from the outset so that by the time we're ready to show the design, you'll know it as well as I do. We'll work together on this job."

She sat beside him and watched the building take shape beneath his hands. It impressed her mightily that he could visualize something in its entirety and then reproduce his vision on paper so quickly and with such ease. He'd been asked to design a private residence on an outcropping of land situated on the Sound in Westport. The owner of this land was a young Wall Street wizard with a wife and three small children who wanted light, airy open spaces in an all but indestructible dwelling.

Erik created a splendid environment, with rounded exterior walls and a two-story living room with an outside deck cantilevered over the rear lawn, which sloped down to the Sound. The design incorporated six bedrooms, a playroom for the children, an enormous kitchen with both eating and sitting areas, as well as another deck, and fireplaces in the living room, master suite, and den. It also took advantage of the setting by offering Sound views from most of the rooms and using the existing trees to provide summer shade. The budget was immense; the client wanted the best of everything, including a sauna and five bathrooms, three with built-in Jacuzzis; he also wanted a suite for the maid and live-in nanny and garage space for four cars. He was prepared to spend at least two million dollars. He'd seen several of Erik's buildings, and wasn't at all bothered by the idea of an architect he'd never meet, just so long as this particular architect, who'd been written up in Ada Louise Huxtable's column in *The New York Times*, was the one who designed the house.

Raskin went along with Risa to meet the client and to provide moral support and backup should she need it.

"If I start repeating myself," she said en route to the city, "jump in and save me. Okay?"

"It'll be a piece of cake, Risa. The guy's already made up his mind. At most, he might want modifications here or there. Just go nice and slow and cover everything point by point."

"What if he takes one look at me and decides I'm too young and couldn't possibly know what I'm talking about?"

"Never happen. I told you: This one's in the bag." Besides, Raskin thought, the client would likely be so busy staring at the architect's wife he wouldn't even notice the drawings. He'd be so impressed by the fact of Erik's having such a beautiful young wife he'd okay the job just for the sake of running into her again, maybe, at the site.

"You think I'm dressed all right?" she asked nervously. "Maybe I shouldn't have worn a dress. A suit would've been better."

"You look fine. Stop worrying."

"Easy for you to say. You could do this in your sleep, but if I screw it up, I'll never forgive myself."

"You're not going to screw it up. Guaranteed."

They were shown at once into the client's office, and the young man shot to his feet as Risa came in carrying her portfolio, with Raskin behind her.

"I'm Marisa D'Anton," she introduced herself, shaking the man's hand. "And I'd like you to meet Hal Raskin, my husband's associate."

As Raskin had predicted, the man was so bowled over by the sight of Risa he scarcely glanced at the drawings. "It looks great!" he said several times. "Exactly what we want. Great!"

Risa couldn't persuade him to look at the budget.

"Leave it with me. I'm sure it's in order. All I need is a starting date and an occupancy date. The rest is up to you . . . to Erik." He went behind his desk, pulled a checkbook from one of the drawers, and dashed off a check, saying, "This'll get things rolling," and handed it over to Marisa as if he thought she'd go directly from there to Bergdorf's to spend the money on furs and evening clothes. Which he wouldn't have minded at all.

As they were driving out of the city, Risa exploded. "That man has no idea what he's buying. None. How can he say it's great when he didn't even *look* at Erik's drawings?"

"So, he's a schmuck," Raskin said. "Don't worry about it. What counts is the project, the house. And he'll be happy as all get out with it."

"I don't know if I want to do this again," she said, in no way mollified. "I felt like some idiot Barbie Doll, for God's sake! Like one of those dumb-ass girls on TV who do the weather and are forever waving their pointers at Seattle when they're talking about the weather in D.C."

Raskin laughed. "You ought to feel complimented, not angry. If I had the effect on women that you had on that guy, I'd be set for life."

"What're you *talking* about? You *do* have that effect. Or you used to, anyway, before you went goofy for Kitty."

"Goofy?" He shot a look at her.

"Well, what d'*you* call it? We never have to wonder where you are anymore because you're always over there."

"You sound pissed off about it."

"I don't know about that. I love Kitty, you know, and I hate the idea you're going to dump her one day because you decide it's getting too heavy."

"Is that something you've heard from her?"

"No. I'm telling you my personal feelings."

"You must think I'm a complete shit."

"No, I don't, Hal. I just think you could do something like that. You wouldn't do it intending to be mean or anything. You'd do it because maybe people were seeing you out with her too often or something."

"And what if I tell you you're dead wrong?"

"Am I?" she challenged.

"I don't know."

"Kitty and I have never discussed you, Hal. She's not someone who'd do that. She and my father were involved for *thirteen years* before I knew a thing about it. And I only found out by sheer accident. I'm not saying you're a bad person, because I don't think that. I guess I'm asking you please not to hurt her."

"How did we manage to get from the client to Kitty without missing a beat?"

"Because I'm a good dancer," she answered obliquely, which made him laugh.

"Listen," he said, a cigarette clamped between his teeth while he pushed in the lighter on the dashboard. "It's not my plan to hurt Kitty or anyone else. I'm not in the habit of explaining myself, and I don't enjoy it. I know how you feel about Kitty. But you don't have a clue how *I* feel about her. And I'm not about to discuss it with you. The truth is, it's none of your business, Risa. I like you a hell of a lot, but every so often you want to get into things that don't concern you. This is one of those times. For the record, so you know there's no hard feelings, I'm happy with Kitty. I trust her. And that's a hell of a lot more than I've ever felt for any woman. So, do us all a favor and leave this alone."

"Fine!" she snapped. "Then you do *me* a favor. Don't tell me it's nothing, it's unimportant that some sexist jerk pays more attention to me than he does to something Erik slaved away at for weeks! So the guy thinks I'm good-looking. Big goddamned deal, Hal! My looks don't have a thing to do with Erik's design, and I'm offended by what that jerk did. Okay? I worked for over three years, closer to three and a half, to be able to make that presentation, and all that asshole did was make goo-goo eyes at me. I'm not just a goddamned *face!* I'm a person who went there to do business, not some bimbo my husband sent out on an errand because I'm cute! And furthermore, when you pat me on the head and patronize me and tell me it's no big deal, you're being as much of a sexist chauvinist asshole as that guy!''

There was a silence while Raskin got his cigarette lit, then returned the lighter to the dashboard. Finally, he said, "I'm sorry, Risa. You're right. He *was* a moron. You *did* work damned hard. And it was a put-down—by both of us. I wasn't seeing it from your point of view."

"I'm sorry too," she said. "I was interfering."

"None of it happened. Agreed?"

"Agreed. But I think Erik should turn the job down, send that fool back his check."

"I think you're right. You want to tell Erik that?"

"Damned right I do!"

"I'll back you up all the way."

"Thank you. God, Hal! How am I going to *explain* this to him?"

"He'll understand."

"Maybe. But he wanted this job, and in a way it's my fault he's going to have to pass."

"Nope. It's the moron's fault. Not yours."

"Shit!" she sighed. "Are we friends again?"

"We never stopped."

Twenty

ERIK LISTENED CLOSELY TO WHAT RISA HAD TO SAY, AND TO RASKIN WHO supported her every word and even assumed some of the responsibility by admitting to the sexist attitudes he'd espoused. When they'd both finished speaking there was a lengthy silence while Erik sat motionless, his eyes on the portfolio Risa had placed on his drawing board along with the check.

He'd temporarily forgotten them as he pictured the scene, imagining some moneyed cretin salivating over Marisa while ignoring altogether the work they'd so carefully prepared. His lungs began to heave. With a cry, he jumped off the stool, took hold of it with both hands and sent it crashing through the stained-glass window at the near end of the room. The blood was roaring so deafeningly inside his head that he failed to hear Marisa's scream, or to feel Raskin's hands on his arm. He wanted to drive into the city and kill the man, beat him senseless with his fists, for defiling both his wife and his work.

"Erik!" Risa put her hands on his face, seeking to bring him back.

Raskin decided the smartest thing he could do was to go to the liquor cabinet for a glass of something that would calm Erik down before he did any more damage.

"Erik!" Risa cried more loudly, alarmed by this new view of her husband. "It doesn't matter," she said ineffectually.

"Of course it matters!" he ranted. *"You know it does!"* His fists clenched and unclenched. The muscles in his arms and shoulders bulged against his sleeves. Some fool slobbering over Marisa, ogling her while she forged ahead with the presentation. He'd destroy him, pulverize him. His eyes seemed filled with blood.

"I had to tell you, Erik. I didn't want you to waste a wonderful design on someone like that. He didn't deserve to live in that house."

"Don't you think I *know* that?" he said, glaring at her.

"What should I do?" she asked helplessly. "I was only trying to do what was best for all of us." She turned to look at the fragments of colored glass strewn across the floor, seeing again the way he'd lifted the stool to fling it through the window. She hadn't known he was capable of such rage. "Perhaps," she said quietly, "you'd like to throw me through the window, too."

He gazed at her tapering back, at last realizing she'd thought his behavior, his anger had been directed toward her.

"I'm not angry with you," he said in a more temperate tone. "Do you think I blame you?"

She turned to look over her shoulder at him, gave a little shrug, then stooped to pick up some of the larger pieces of glass. She wasn't being as careful as she should have, too upset to pay close attention. And suddenly blood was welling from a gash across her palm and, seeing this, Erik dropped to his knees at her side and wrapped his handkerchief around her hand. He was recognizably Erik once again, and she touched her free hand to his cheek, saying, "I'd give anything if it hadn't happened. I know how much you were looking forward to this job. But, Erik, I resent being treated that way. And I resent having your hard work ignored. Am I supposed to go along with people like that, with situations like that? I can't. I don't know how."

"There are dozens of jobs, hundreds. I couldn't cope with the idea . . ."

"Why even think about it? He made me mad, Erik, but he wasn't worth any of this." She looked over at the ruined window. "We'll never be able to replace that, and it was so lovely."

"Come, let me tend to your hand."

He lifted the pieces of glass from her lap and dropped them in the wastebasket.

"You wanted to kill him, didn't you, Erik? Because of me, or because he didn't pay attention to your work?"

"Both," he said fervently. "Both."

"It's not worth your energy. I'm not harmed. And there'll be someone else for that design."

"When someone diminishes you, he diminishes me, Marisa. Perhaps I was wrong to ask this of you."

"You weren't wrong!" she argued. "I *wanted* to do it, and I still do. God! I never dreamed it would blow sky-high this way. I suppose everything would be fine if I didn't have a brain. Then some asshole like that could make goo-goo eyes and I wouldn't even notice. I'm not sure if anything's worth all this."

"Please, let me look after your hand!" he begged, seeing the blood saturating the handkerchief.

She let him take her downstairs to the master bedroom where he sat her on the edge of the tub while he opened the medicine cabinet for disinfectant and some bandages. She sat holding her dripping hand over the tub, watching the way his concern for her turned his movements concentrated.

"Erik," she said very low, feeling dizzy, "you really frightened me, the way you did that. I've never seen anyone get so angry."

Assembling his equipment on the counter beside the basin, he said, "I apologize. It was not my intention to frighten you."

"What was your intention?"

"I didn't have one. I was simply furious."

"I wish you could know how frightening it was, Erik. It makes me hope to God I never inadvertently do anything to make you furious."

"I cannot conceive of anything you could do that would."

She almost said, *I can*, but thought better of it.

"I've made us all good stiff drinks!" Raskin called from the hallway, on his way up to the office with the stool he'd retrieved from the lawn.

Risa called back, "Thank you. We'll be down in a few minutes," then turned to Erik, who had her hand under the cold-water faucet and was sluicing out the gash.

"This is nasty," he said. "You might need stitches."

"Just tape it up. It'll be fine."

He knew from her tone the discussion was not yet over. She was apprehensive and angry now herself.

Turning off the faucet, he bathed the cut in disinfectant, then began winding gauze around her hand. "There is nothing," he said, "not a thing in this world you could ever do that would inspire that sort of anger in me, Marisa. It was an ungoverned moment, not the first, but I will endeavor to make it one of the last. I am truly sorry."

Stroking his hair, she said, "I sometimes wonder if I'll ever see you happy, Erik. We go for days and weeks, we have our routines, the things we do every day, every night, and you seem so glad of our life together. Then something happens, like today, and I can't help thinking maybe I'm deluding myself, that I don't have any special talent for making people happy, for making *you* happy. We've been married almost four years, and it's gone by so fast, with both of us busy, each inside our own heads, me worrying about you, and you worrying about me. When do we stop being separate?"

"Don't give up on me!" he implored her, as suddenly abject as he'd turned wild. "I am trying so very hard."

"I know you are," she said, drawing his head against her breast. "I know. And I love you more every day, because I do know. I just want us to be at a point where there are no more questions. But maybe that's kid stuff, storybook stuff. Maybe nobody ever gets to that point. I know how hard you try, Erik. And I know you were upset. It's all over now. We'll forget about it."

The events of that day so impressed themselves upon her that she put aside the idea of discussing their having a child. She dreaded ever doing anything to reawaken Erik's formidable anger. In spite of what he'd said, she felt it could be triggered by some less than well-thought-out comment or suggestion of hers. Not that he'd ever harm her. He was incapable of that. She simply hated the thought of ever again seeing him go so out of control. And, besides, the incident notwithstanding, she loved their life together.

When they weren't working, the two of them would spend hours at the piano in the music room, or listening to music together. They might sit quietly for a time, then rise precisely at the same moment and, with a laugh, begin to dance. There were evenings when they lit a fire in the living room and sat with books, glancing over at one another every so often to smile. There were all kinds of books and authors Erik recommended to her, dozens of performers he wanted her to hear. He'd often look up from the tiny circle of light cast on his book by the Tensor light he used for reading and say, "You must hear this," then read a line of poetry, or a paragraph from some book.

They cooked together, sometimes with Hal and Kitty, too. Some evenings Kitty telephoned to announce they were all expected on Butlers Island for dinner. And sometimes Risa and Kitty went off to the movies together, or into the city for a day's shopping. The cleaning was done by a team that came twice a week and went through the house from top to bottom—except for the office, where Erik remained with the door locked until they left. Hal took in and picked up the dry cleaning, and saw to the servicing of the cars. Risa did the grocery shopping, the laundry, and tended to her houseplants. And every day there was work to be done in the office.

There were new clients, and Risa went on to present Erik's work without further incident. Then, on the eve of her twenty-fourth birthday and their sixth anniversary, Erik told her he'd made reservations for a dinner out. With Kitty and Raskin they went to a local steakhouse and had a genuinely festive evening. Their waitress was a young woman of about Risa's age who didn't turn a hair at first sight of Erik but pleasantly took his drink order and gave them exemplary service throughout the evening.

Before shifting to the lounge to dance, Risa and Kitty set off for the ladies' room and encountered the young waitress in the reception area. She stepped forward to put a hand on Risa's arm and said, "My younger brother Tony had to have a lot of grafts, too. I really admire your husband's guts. It's been twelve years now and Tony, he's twenty-two, he won't set foot out of the house. I hope you're having a real nice evening."

Dumbfounded, Risa thanked her.

"Do you think I should mention that to Erik?" she asked Kitty in the ladies' room.

"No, I do not," Kitty replied. "Erik knows what tonight means for all concerned. Keep lettin' him go at his own pace, Risa. Don't start pushin'."

Risa found this evening out very encouraging because it meant Erik might be losing some of his resistance to a number of things, including the idea of a baby. She thought she'd wait for exactly the right moment before mentioning it again.

The moment she chose was late Christmas Eve after Raskin had gone to escort Kitty home. Raskin's use of the word "escort" was his way of telling them he'd be spending the night with Kitty. After they had gone, Risa and Erik sat in front of the fire in the living room admiring the tree they'd decorated with red and silver bows. She sat on the floor between his legs with her back to his chest and his arms around her and said, "Erik, this would be so wonderful to share with a child."

Instantly she knew she shouldn't have introduced the subject. He tensed. His breathing underwent an audible change. His voice pitched deadly deep, he said, "Can you imagine an infant gazing up from its crib into this face? Can you imagine a child of yours doing battle every day to defend a parent with *this face?*"

Shifting toward him, she said, "Actually, I can imagine all those things. Erik, you'd be its *father*. That child would *love* you. To that child, you'd be beautiful, the way you are to me." She wondered why she was debating the issue when she knew she'd already lost. "I want us to make something out of the love we have for each other, Erik. There has to be someone to come after us. There has to be a point to our having been alive in the world."

"I thought there was a point," he said in that ominous voice. "I thought the point was our being together."

"A baby wouldn't change that."

"You would have a child, and you would have no qualms about raising it in this house, this dwelling that has precisely one 'normal' room in it?

You would give birth to an infant and put it into my arms to teach it fear at an early age? You would expect a child to comprehend our somewhat bizarre domestic arrangement?"

"Yes, yes, yes, to all of it. A child of ours would understand. An infant in your arms would only know its father. And there's nothing abnormal about this house, Erik. It's a fine house, with fine things in it. And the people who live here love each other."

"I've failed, haven't I?" he said, his tone shifting to one of defeat. "I thought I was making progress, but I haven't succeeded. I'm not enough. I should have known I couldn't be enough for you."

"Of course you are. I love you with all my heart. You've done wonderful things for me. I'm *very* happy with you. I just want to share what we have with a child. I want to have your baby. I want to be someone's mother, Erik. And I want you to be the father."

"With Raskin and Kitty as nursemaids, no doubt."

"Don't be that way! This has to do with me and you, and the feeling I have every time I see some woman's newborn. Or I take the train into the city and I see pregnant women walking around, and I want to be one of them. I want everyone to know how much I love you, how proud I am to be your wife."

"There's nothing I could ever deny you, Marisa. But I cannot do that. If you could even begin to conceive . . . I can't! Please don't ask for the one thing I can't give you. I'm not able to contemplate the horror I might see on the face of a child of mine. Please, don't ask me! *Please!*"

To her sorrow, he crossed his arms over his face and began to weep. Slowly, keeping his face hidden, he fell back to the floor.

"I thought you might have changed your mind," she said, devastated by his tears. "I had no idea you were so . . . that you had such strong feelings on the subject. It doesn't matter, Erik. I'll never mention it again. You have my word. We'll go on as we have been, and nothing will change." For the first time she didn't rush to comfort him, but sat on her heels watching and waiting as his tears subsided. She was almost twenty-five. She'd lived this long without a child. Undoubtedly she'd survive another twenty-five years without one, and, with luck, twenty-five more after that. By which time, she'd be far too old even to remember having wanted to hold a baby in her arms.

At last, she bent to tug his arms away from his face. Then she dried his tears. "We'll never talk about it again. I hate to see you suffer this way, Erik. I hate the times when something separates us and it feels as if we'll never be able to bridge the sudden terrible distance between us."

Still choked, he drew her down on his chest and held her, mortified by his weakness and by the spectacle he'd made of himself.

"Don't be angry with yourself," she said presciently. "I know you couldn't help it, any more than I could help saying what was on my mind. I'm sorry you feel that way. I wish to God you didn't, but I do understand."

"They stripped me of my clothes, then stood in a circle laughing and pointing," he whispered. "They threw pebbles and small stones and called me names, as if I were the village idiot. They shouted obscenities about my parents, who had to be monsters too. Then, when one of the masters came to break it up, he treated me as if it were all my fault. He collected my clothes from the grass and threw the lot at me, saying, '*Get dressed*,' in a voice clotted with contempt, and an expression on his face of sheer repugnance.

"There was no one to tell, no one who wished to hear, except for Henry, to whom I was forbidden to speak because he was merely a servant. And when I came to America, I thought perhaps it would be different—a new life in a new country. It was no different, only subtler. College students don't strip one naked in the quadrangle and pelt one with stones. They simply cross over the grass if they happen to see one coming along the path. They exclude one from their groups, and pretend one is invisible in their classes. Yes, there are people here and there—you and your father, Raskin and Kitty are examples, as was that waitress— who go on about their business and have no difficulty allowing one to go about his. But in the end, it's infinitely less painful and humiliating simply to do one's business in the darkened privacy of one's home.

"I wish I could be strong enough, or hard enough, or sufficiently thick-skinned to go out with you and not give a damn, Marisa. I wish I could take the hatred and the stares in stride, but I can't. I wish I could say to hell with the rest of the world, you and I will do as we choose. But can you picture the scene, visualize the reaction of the hospital staff were I to take you in for the delivery of a child? Likely as not, they'd be so involved with the horror of their fascination they'd forget you altogether. I wish love were enough to work the miracles you so want to believe it can. It's not the way reality operates, Marisa. It's not the way *I* operate. I need you to forgive me for my cowardice, and not despise me for being unable to give you something you want."

"You break my heart every time you describe one of those scenes, Erik. There's nothing to forgive, and I could never despise you. No matter what happens, I'm always going to love you. Do you believe that?"

"Yes."

"Then please, stop making yourself miserable. When you suffer this way, I suffer with you. Do you know that?"

"You're angry."

"No, I'm not angry. I'm tired. Let's go to bed."

Panic sent adrenaline surging through his system. She was growing tired of him, tired of his lengthy tedious explanations and his irrational behavior.

"I will try harder," he told her. "We will go out more."

"Erik"—she sat up and pushed her hair back over her shoulders—"stop beating yourself up. I'm here because I want to be, because you matter more to me than anyone else. You even matter more to me, Erik, than I do to myself. *I* wish you'd finally believe that. I'll know it when it happens, you know. You won't have to say a word or do anything. I'll just know. Now, let's please go to bed. Come keep me company, talk to me while I have my bath."

He went along after her, convinced he'd not only made a complete fool of himself but that he'd created a small but permanent rift between them.

Twenty-one

THERE WAS NO OBVIOUS ALTERATION IN RISA'S BEHAVIOR TOWARD him. She was as loving and giving as she'd ever been, but there were nuances, slight hints of her mounting dissatisfaction. Erik could see it in the way she'd sometimes pause and sit chewing on her pencil, gazing at the replacement stained-glass window he'd had made and installed in the near office wall. He could tell from the fractionally inward curve of her shoulders and the angle of her head that she'd gone away from him, and was continuing daily on that voyage. He feared that unless he did something to halt her progress, she'd eventually slip away from him altogether.

Inspiration came to him as her twenty-sixth birthday was approaching. He and Raskin and Kitty made the arrangements. And on the morning of her birthday, Erik roused her to say, "There's someone I want you to meet."

Groggy, she pushed the hair out of her eyes. "Who?"

"Come downstairs, and you'll see."

"Let me just go to the bathroom, then I'll be down."

He watched her get up and walk across the room, admiring the flex of her long thigh muscles and the shift of her buttocks as she went. She'd stopped wearing nightgowns soon after they'd married and often moved about their bedroom nude and apparently comfortable, perhaps unaware of the ongoing effect the sight of her had on him. He was incapable of not watching her when they were in the same room together, driven to study her in all her aspects. He lived in a state of perpetual fascination, never finding her anything less than astonishing. At moments, with his eyes on her, he'd think, My wife, and feel an overpowering sense of pride.

He tried never to be obvious about watching her, correctly suspecting that it could be cause for tension. Clearly, if he so loathed the weight of others' eyes, it was only logical and reasonable that to some lesser degree others, and in particular Marisa, would find it stressful to be constantly observed.

She came out of the bathroom tying on her robe, asking, "Who'd come here first thing in the morning? Why do I have the impression you're up to something?" She stood smiling at him from the foot of the bed, then launched herself, landing on top of him with a triumphant little exclamation. "What're you up to?" she asked, brandishing her hands before his eyes in mock menace. "I can tickle it out of you if I have to."

All pretended innocence, he replied, "I am up to nothing. You have a suspicious mind."

"Me? Never. Who's this person I have to meet?"

"Come along downstairs and find out."

"This better be good," she warned, pinching both his cheeks before giving him a minty kiss.

"I hope so."

She went with him down the stairs, certain he and Raskin and Kitty had cooked something up for her birthday and their anniversary. No one but Kitty would dare to come to this house first thing in the morning. As it was, the only people who came at all were service people of one variety or another: Erik's tailor, his shoemaker, the blind man who tuned the piano, the gardener who never actually entered the house but simply toiled patiently on the grounds, the crew of men who came to collect the trash, and the cleaning people.

Raskin was standing by the kitchen counter, and turned when he heard them coming.

Erik said, "I would like to introduce you to Prince William," and Raskin put the six-week-old cocker spaniel into Risa's arms.

She held the silken, curious puppy, looked into its liquid brown eyes and felt something overturn inside her. She laughed softly, bent to put her cheek to the puppy's golden coat, and burst into tears.

For a moment, Erik was terribly afraid he'd done the wrong thing. Instead of taking her mind off her longing for a child as he'd hoped, he'd offered a poor substitute and she was in tears over the transparency and imbecility of this sophomoric attempt to placate her.

But she hooked an arm around his neck, the other arm holding the dog secure, and said, "I love him, Erik! This is so wonderful. I've wanted a dog all my life. Dad would never agree because he was bitten once when he was a small boy and was afraid of them after that. He's so adorable. Are you hungry, Prince William, or have they remembered to feed you?"

"He's been fed," Raskin told her. "And so will you two be in about ten minutes. I'm waiting for the bacon to finish, then I'll be dishing up the celebration breakfast in the dining room, if you and the pooch would care to relocate there. I would like to point out, by the way, that he's not one hundred percent housebroken and has a tendency in moments of extreme excitement to let loose wherever he happens to be. You might want to take along some newspaper."

Risa carried the spaniel to the living room, where she sat with him on the sofa, positioning him in her lap so she could pet him with both hands, then picked him up to receive his eager kisses. "You are totally adorable, Willie. I know you're royalty, but I hope you won't mind if I call you Willie. Do you mind? No, I knew you wouldn't."

Relieved to see her so immediately taken with the puppy, Erik sat on the facing sofa and watched her play with it.

"There isn't anything you could've given me I'd like more," she said happily. "Come sit over here with me and get to know him. He's so sweet, Erik. Here"—she put the puppy into his arms, exactly, he thought, the way she'd have presented him with a baby—"see how darling he is."

Timidly he accepted the animal, as she said, "Don't be afraid of him, Erik. He only wants to love you."

"I, too, have never had a pet," he confided, tentatively holding the puppy in the air. All trusting, the dog held Erik's eyes, waiting to be returned to safety. He let the dog settle in his lap, where it wound itself at once into a small furry knot and went to sleep.

Risa leaned over to kiss him. "You are the cleverest man alive. I absolutely love him. Maybe this afternoon I'll go to the pet shop in town and get him a bed and some toys."

"Actually, we did get a bed, as well as a blanket and some rawhide strips. I didn't do anything about a doghouse. I wasn't sure what you'd want to do."

"I don't know. Do dogs prefer living indoors? Or are they happier outside?"

"We'll play it by ear, shall we?" he said, somewhat thrown by the unconsidered aspects of pet ownership. "As long as you're pleased."

"I am, very very pleased." She tucked her legs under her and rested against his arm, running her fingers over the sleeping puppy's pelt. "At night, when I take him out for a walk, you can come with me. It'll be our nightly outing—the D'Antons taking their constitutional."

"Frightfully domestic."

"Thank you, Erik." She wrapped her arms around his arm. "I'm afraid my gift to you is very mundane, even boring after this. God! I can't wait for Kitty to see him! She'll probably go mad over Willie."

"They've already met. She and Raskin went together to the breeder to pick him out."

"You're all so secretive. I had no idea, none. I was actually trying to figure out who'd be coming here at eight-thirty in the morning. What a bunch of sneaks you all are!"

"I prefer to think of us as devious. Sneaky has such nasty implications."

She laughed and pulled his head toward her to kiss him.

"Breakfast is served," Raskin announced, coming in to scoop Prince William from Erik's lap. "The prince can sleep in his bed while we chow down."

Risa got up to kiss Raskin's cheek. "Thank you for going to so much trouble. This is one of the best birthdays ever. What's for breakfast?"

"Broiled sheep's eyes and sautéed lizard entrails."

"Oh, yummy! My favorites!"

Laughing, the three of them went into the dining room. Erik, bringing up the rear, felt his lungs expanding with relief; even his hands twitched with the loss of his many reservations. He'd done something right. Marisa was positively aglow with happiness.

Risa fell into the habit of walking Prince William in the early morning, most days making her way to Butlers Island to have coffee with Kitty before returning home to start the day. Perhaps because of the early hour, or perhaps because their prior mother-daughter-like relationship had evolved into a close bond between two grown women, their conversations had new dimension and maturity.

During these visits, while they sat in the breakfast area Erik had created years before, they confided to one another the intimate details of their lives. While the dog dozed in the sunlight, or chewed at a bone or a piece of meat Kitty had set aside for him, Risa allowed herself the luxury of giving voice to some of her most private thoughts. Her greatest concern, aside from her secret ongoing desire for a child, was what she perceived to be her failure to make Erik completely happy.

With surprising heat and energy, Kitty defended him. "You can't expect the man to change the habits and fears of a lifetime just like that, Reese. You can't expect him suddenly to go round smilin' all the day long. That's not the way things work. These things happen gradual-like. And you've worked wonders with him. Think about how he is now, and the way he was back when he first came here."

"I know that. It's just that I wonder how long it's going to take before he trusts me enough to . . . relax, I guess."

"Some people never do, you know. Some people live out their entire lives on the wire. I'd rather have someone like that than some fella asleep at the switch half the time. Try not to dwell on it," she counseled. "I never in my life saw anyone try harder to please someone than Erik works to please you."

Risa looked away, unable to explain the uneasiness she felt. "It's hard sometimes, Kitty, having someone pay such close attention, work so hard to do things to please you. It feels, every so often, as if I'm on a slide under a microscope. I get so self-conscious. It's inhibiting. At first, at the beginning, it was incredibly exciting to have him watch so closely, take such care. Lately, it's been starting to feel . . . I don't know . . . claustrophobic." Looking back, she said, "That's partly what I mean about getting him to relax, to trust me, so he'll lie back and close his eyes and not worry that I won't be there when he opens them again."

"It'll come," Kitty said. "Besides, it's not like he's doin' it for reasons you don't know about, not like he's spyin' on you."

"No. It's more like he's taking a doctoral degree in Risa Behavioral Theory."

Kitty laughed. "We should all be so lucky. Most men're far more interested in bein' the object of attention. You don't wanna let anybody hear you complainin' your husband loves you too much, Reese. You might get yourself murdered your next trip to the supermarket."

"I guess." Risa smiled, then asked, "Did you ever want to have a child, Kitty?"

Kitty took a long draw on her Kool before answering. "I grew up thinkin' I'd be somebody's mama, you know. And when I got married, I figured it'd be the next step in the proceedin's. But I married a child. You understand? A sweet fella, but a child. So when I got pregnant, I thought a good long time about what I'd do. Did I want to get tied to this fella for life because of a baby? Or was I gonna be movin' on, the way I knew I'd have to almost from the day we married? And I knew I could never do it. So I went to this woman I'd heard tell of who got rid of babies on her kitchen table if you had the hundred dollars to pay her. I took my savins' and laid myself down on that table and looked at the flypaper hangin' from the ceilin' while she took away the baby.

"It went bad, and I ended up in the 'mergency room of the hospital, with Billy there scared silly, not knowin' what I'd done. When they took me inside, I begged the doctor not to tell Billy the real reason I was hemorrhaging. He was a decent man, told me I was a foolish girl to do what I had, but no, he wouldn't go tellin' Billy. Then they put me under and tried to fix me up, gave me a lot of blood and so forth. When I came to he told me the woman had stuck her knittin' needle, or whatever it was she used—I never did see, I kept my eyes on that flypaper—she'd gone and put it right through my uterus, ripped it up good. So all's he could do was take it out. But I'd be good as new, 'ceptin' I wouldn't be gettin' pregnant no more.

"It's kind of why your daddy's ad reached me the way it did. I thought if I couldn't have a child of my own, I'd have me second best and do right by some other poor woman's baby. And I like to think I've done a first-class job with you. You turned out to be a woman any mother'd be proud to call her own."

"You've been a first-class mother," Risa said feelingly. "Kitty, I feel so . . . I don't know . . . strange. I'm twenty-eight years old. I've been taking those pills for more than ten years and now, all of a sudden, things seem to be happening. I've got these brown marks on my face and neck. I'm all swollen and I've gone up an entire bra size."

"You better make yourself an appointment to see your gynecologist. I've been reading how it's no good to take those pills for years on end. They can cause strokes and Lord knows what else."

"What if taking them all this time has done something so I can't ever have a baby?"

"Oh, I'm sure nothin' like that would happen. And besides, I thought you told me the two of you've agreed you're not gonna have any kids."

"Erik doesn't want one, but I do. I can't stop thinking about it, can't stop hoping he'll change his mind."

"Listen to me, Risa! I can understand how you feel, and I can sympathize. But have you ever thought that maybe it really is askin' too much? Before you came along, that man had nothin' to lose. He had his life and he had things sorted out so he was gettin' by. Then you come along and you turn him on his ear and all of a sudden he's got plenty to lose. I'm willin' to wager there's not a day of the world when he's not scared half to death he'll lose you. You have a baby, and there'll be somethin' more he's got to fear losin'. Some people just can't take risks, and he's one of them. Riskiest thing he ever did was stakin' his claim on you."

"But he's not going to lose me," Risa argued. "And a baby would guarantee that once and for all."

"You're a smart woman, but not so smart as you could be. Try to see it from his side, Reese. He managed, in spite of everything, to get himself a beautiful young wife. The man's forty-three years old and you're expectin' him to change in big ways for you. It's not gonna happen. And maybe it's not fair of you to be hopin' for it. You can't agree to somethin', girl, while you're holdin' your fingers crossed behind your back like a child, intendin' to do some serious mind-changin' on the man later on. You can't go askin' for more than people are capable of givin'. And the most he can give to anyone he's givin' to you."

"I know," Risa said quietly. "I do know that."

"Then deal truthfully—with him and with yourself, and stop pinin' away for somethin' that can't happen. You got a whole helluva lot more than most women ever get. And if I had someone who loves me the way Erik loves you, I'd thank the Lord every night before I went to sleep; I'd count my blessin's, and I'd shut the hell up."

"Hal loves you."

"Hal would eat ground glass 'fore he'd ever admit to lovin' anyone," Kitty stated. "That man knows he's his father's son, and if you think Erik's got fears, they're nothin' compared to how truly terrified Harold is that he might one day haul off and start poundin' on me with his fists."

"But he'd never do that."

"Yeah, well. You know that, and I know that, but I doubt anything's ever gonna convince Harold of that. To his mind, love equates to killing. You figure that one out and I'll see to it you get the Nobel Prize. He's got a lifelong anger, and all kinds of fear. All kinds of it."

"So why do you keep on with him?"

Kitty gave a sheepish little laugh. "It's real funny how things work out," she said, pouring them both fresh coffee. "Seems I've grown attached to the man. I'm used to the way he comes and goes, prowlin' around like a hound sniffin' out some small animal. But he's gentle as can be when he comes to my bed. I kinda like the contrast."

The gynecologist said, "These are common reactions to prolonged use of the pill. I think it's time we took you off it."

"But what will I do for birth control?"

"We'll fit you for a diaphragm. We can do it right now, if you like."

"I guess we'd better."

He gave her a brief show-and-tell lecture, inserted the diaphragm, then suggested she go into the changing room and try inserting it herself. It was, she thought, like trying to fold a small greased basketball hoop and then force it inside herself. Chuckling, she succeeded in positioning the rubber shield, and returned to the examining table so the doctor could check to make sure she'd done it properly.

He said, "Good girl!" and patted her on the knee. It irked her.

"I am not a *girl*," she told him. "I am a grown woman with a small basketball hoop inside me."

He laughed hugely. "Get dressed and I'll see you in my office, give you a prescription."

She stopped at the pharmacy on her way home and emerged with a large brown paper bag filled with supplies. It seemed like an enormous amount of gear, and she couldn't imagine how she'd be able to deal with the jelly and the powder and maintaining the diaphragm, let alone stopping in the midst of lovemaking, or having to hold Erik off should he spontaneously approach her as he so often did, while she took herself off to the bathroom to insert the thing. But she was determined, and spent close to twenty minutes in the bathroom that night before finally climbing into bed.

"Are you all right?" Erik asked. "You were gone for quite some time."

She explained to him about the side effects of the pill and about the diaphragm and he grew progressively more concerned as she spoke. "I'll get the hang of it," she told him. "Don't worry."

But when they began to make love, she found that it hurt. Erik's body seemed to be forcing the rim of the diaphragm higher and harder into her. She tried to ignore the discomfort, but couldn't. Finally, she confessed, "Erik, it hurts."

Instantly he stopped and, distressed, sought to console her. "Perhaps," he said, "I should look into having a vasectomy."

"No!" she cried, horrified by the prospect. "I won't let you do that! I'll find something else. I'll call and make another appointment, get an IUD or something. But I want you intact! You have to promise me you'll never, ever again, even consider such a thing!"

"Of course I promise, if you feel so strongly on the matter."

"I do! I feel *very* strongly. I don't want you mutilated."

He had to laugh. "In view of everything else, it's hardly mutilation."

"No! Just no, okay?"

"Yes." He backed down in the face of her strenuous objections. "All right."

The following day she returned to the gynecologist for an IUD.

"This should take care of everything," the doctor assured her. "I'm sorry the diaphragm didn't work out. It's the perfect solution for a lot of women."

"Oh, that's okay," she said with grim humor. "I'm thinking of buying a hamster, and the hamster can use it for a trampoline."

"The pigmentation blotches should fade pretty fast," he said. "A couple of months and they'll be gone. You might have a little staining for a few days, but it's nothing to worry about."

She thanked him and went home to Erik. "Everything's taken care of," she announced. "We've gone from trampolines to fishhooks."

Twenty-two

F OR QUITE SOME TIME, LIFE WAS SETTLED, HARMONIOUS, AND PRO-
ductive. Work got done in the attic office. Risa and Raskin oversaw the
running of the household. The dog got walked twice a day. And Erik
gradually drew ever deeper breaths, the passage of time convincing him
as nothing else could that he'd managed to escape notice by the Fates.
They were occupied elsewhere, and paying little attention to the goings-
on inside the house on Contentment Island.

To celebrate Risa's thirtieth birthday and their twelfth anniversary,
Raskin and Kitty took over the kitchen, telling Erik and Risa to stay away
until eight o'clock that evening.

"That's cute," Risa said. "We're supposed to walk Willie for two or
three hours."

"We will have pre-celebration festivities in the music room," Erik told
her. "This is an important birthday."

"It's an important anniversary."

"Is it?"

"I think so. Twelve years of wedded bliss."

"Are you being sarcastic?" he asked, unsure.

"It's been sheer agony. I've hated every moment of it. I don't know
how I'll survive the next twelve. God!" She laughed, winding her arms
around his neck. "*When* are you going to believe I like it here, that I
intend to stay, that I don't have a full set of bags packed and ready to go
hidden at the back of my closet? Sometimes, you're such a dolt."

"One must never take anything for granted," he said, only half
joking.

"You've never taken anything for granted in your life. Why would you start now?"

"I wouldn't."

"Right! Now come downstairs and sing some of those songs you wrote ages ago, when I used to sneak over here every night. You hardly ever sing for me anymore."

"I thought perhaps you'd grown bored . . ."

"When you sing," she said, her arms going tighter around him, "I think God whispers in *your* ear. Do you know that? Sometimes, when you're upstairs working with Hal, or I go down to the music room early in the morning while you're still sleeping, I put on one of your tapes. I play it at top volume and it feels as if I'm inside your mouth, as if I'm in this huge cavern, but it's your throat. I sit and listen and my entire body turns to jelly. I listen and tell myself, That's Erik. That is my husband, Erik. I play it so loud I can hear every breath you take, and it makes my hair stand on end when you drop your voice very low for a phrase, and then, suddenly, you're shooting up to a note I can't believe you can reach, let alone sustain. But you do. You take the words and the music and you make them so personal, you fill them with so much hope and pain and meaning, that I drown in you. There I am, sitting perfectly still, but sinking lower and lower into this deep warm pool. I'm drowning, and I'm glad. It makes me want you every time. I have to force myself to stay where I am and let you sleep, because I want to come up here to wake you, so I can touch you, hold you. I could *never* be bored by anything about you. My God! I don't know how you could think that. If I happen to be feeling blue, you come along and make silver dollars appear in my hair, or you pull fifty silk scarves out of the air and make a rainbow. I love you, Erik."

"Then, of course, I must sing for you. Come with me."

He took her hand and for a moment she felt as she had years before when he'd come for her in the boat and, pulling alongside the dock, he'd held his hand out to her. She'd gone with him every time full of a sense of dangerous excitement. She felt it again strongly now as they hurried down the stairs.

The candles were already lit. A bottle of burgundy and two goblets sat on a tray between the two black-and-gilt chairs. On top of the piano was a gift-wrapped package.

"How is it you manage to surprise me every time?" she asked him upon entering, as he turned to bolt the door. "I'm never prepared, never expect it, when you do things like this."

"That is why I do them. Shall we have the wine first, before you open your gift?"

"No. Sing for me."

"As you wish."

They sat together on the bench and he asked, "What would you like to hear?"

"Anything."

"Ah, anything." His fingers extended themselves over the keyboard, whispering over the keys before the left hand lowered itself to begin. He sang *"La Vie en Rose"* in French. She sat with her head on his shoulder, her eyes closed, feeling the side of his thigh against hers as he worked the pedals, his arms grazing her side. And she sighed, thinking how perfect it was, how utterly perfect to be with him, to be engulfed in his music, to be the focus of his considerable love. When he'd finished, she remained where she was for a few moments longer, then got up and went to put on a cassette.

Erik shifted on the bench to watch her, galvanized when she turned and began to undress. As if she'd forgotten him, she attended to the removal of her clothes. And then, when she'd dispensed with everything, even her jewelry, to stand wearing only her wedding ring, she at last looked at him. With the Haydn cello concerto sobbing into the room, she came back to stand in front of him.

"This is what I want for my birthday," she said, her hands on his face as she climbed into his lap. "Everything else, my dear, is icing."

His appetite for her in no way diminished either by time or familiarity, he was wildly excited by her accessibility. No matter how many times they made love, he invariably wanted her more. She fascinated him endlessly. And each time they touched was, for him, as thrilling as the first time.

"This may be your birthday present," he told her, reveling in the slippery softness of her flesh, "but I consider it my anniversary gift."

"Just a part of it. There's more to come. Let's get you out of these clothes," she said, unknotting his tie.

He stood up holding her and slowly turned in a circle so that her hair swung out in a graceful arc. She laughed softly, saying, "You make feel like a little girl, as if I'm not more than eight or nine and weigh about sixty pounds."

"You weigh scarcely more than that."

"I weigh a great deal more than that. But of course to a man who can lift grand pianos, what's the weight of one oversized woman?"

"Oversized? Never."

"Take your clothes off, Erik." She began undoing his shirt buttons, then slipped her hand inside. "I'm getting dizzy."

Keeping hold of her, he bent lower and lower until she was on the floor.

Then, like one of his sleights of hand, he vanished for a moment into the shadows and returned undressed.

"Come here." She held her arms out to him, and he descended into her embrace like someone dreaming.

After, they lay naked together on the carpet and drank the wine. Finally, she went for the box on the piano top. Inside, delving past layers of tissue, she found a set of keys.

"What is this?" she asked, dangling the keys in front of him.

"They will unlock your gift, which, at this very moment, is waiting out of doors."

She began to laugh, and he wanted to know what she found so amusing. Knee-walking over to the pile of her discarded clothes, she fished in the pocket of her skirt and came out with an envelope.

"The driveway must look like a supermarket parking lot," she laughed, giving him the envelope, which he opened to reveal another set of keys.

"What is this?" he asked, holding the keys in front of her nose.

"It's too silly!" she declared. "I think we'd better get dressed and go take a look."

Facing each other on the circular driveway were a new Mercedes 380 SL and a new black Rolls-Royce Silver Wraith. Erik and Risa looked at each other and laughed.

"You see me as more sedate in my middle age?" he asked her.

"I was thinking more of my comfort. I'm getting a little tired of riding along feeling as if I'm only three inches above the road. And what about you? Are you trying to encourage me to start speeding?"

"Not at all. It's a wonderfully engineered automobile with a certain rather racy appeal to it." He looked at the Rolls. "Marisa, that's a great deal of money to spend on a gift."

"You should talk!" she countered. "And you didn't get a seven-figure check today."

"Oh, of course. The balance of your father's estate."

"Henderson went to great pains to point out my father's farsightedness and acumen when it came to the market. He told me more than anyone could ever want to know about Dad's cleverness in buying Xerox and IBM and GE and half a dozen other stocks. I figured we might as well spend some of it, rather than have it sit in a bank getting dusty."

Raskin and Kitty were standing in the doorway grinning.

"I gave Raskin last year's sedan," Erik said.

"I gave Kitty the Buick."

"It's everyone's party!" Kitty called. "Come on in, you two, and eat. It's perishin' out here."

They'd cooked up a fabulous dinner, starting with Scottish smoked salmon, a main course of brandied duck, and a dessert of a three-layer chocolate cake festooned with candles. After the meal, they retired to the living room for coffee and Armagnac, all complaining they'd eaten far too much.

Raskin looked at his watch just before twelve-thirty and said, "Come on, Kitty. Let's throw everything in the dishwasher, then go for a spin in one of our new cars."

"Leave it," Risa said. "We'll clean up. After all, you two did all the work."

"That's right," Kitty said. "We did. So we're goin' for a ride in Harold's smart new vee-hicle."

They left and Risa said to Erik, "I'll make you a deal. Take Willie out for his walk while I clean up. Then we'll go upstairs and make love for three or four hours. I'm not the least bit tired."

"Three or four hours," he repeated. "I'll be dust and ashes if we keep on at this rate. I'm not sure I care for being used in this callous fashion."

"Oh, sure," she scoffed, laughing.

"I'm also not sure I enjoy being quite so predictable," he sniffed.

"You are the least predictable human being I've ever known. Now, go walk Willie before his bladder explodes."

"A very pretty image!" he said, going for the leash.

They hadn't been in the car for five minutes, heading down Tokeneke Road into the center of town, when they heard the whine of a siren and behind them came the flashing lights of a police cruiser.

Raskin muttered, "Shit! I'm not five miles over the limit."

"Just be calm, Harold," Kitty said. "Don't go arguin' with the man. Take the ticket and say thank you very much."

"Right!" He pulled over to the side of the road and reached for his wallet as the police officer approached the car. Raskin pressed the button on the center console to open the window on the driver's side as the officer put one hand on the side of the car, leaned down and said, "Good evening. May I see your license, please, sir?"

Raskin removed it from his wallet and passed it out through the window.

"And your registration, too, please?"

"I've only got a temporary," Raskin explained, opening the glove compartment, knowing it wasn't in there. It was back at the house on the kitchen counter. "I must've left it at home."

"Just a moment, please," the officer said, and went back to his cruiser.

"It'll be fine, Harold," Kitty said, her hand on Raskin's thigh. "It's only a speedin' ticket, no big deal."

"If it's no big deal, maybe you can explain what's taking him so long?" Raskin looked into the rearview mirror to see the policeman talking into his radio.

"You know how they do it," she said, wondering about that herself, but determined to keep Harold calm. "They gotta call it in to the computer to see if you're a wanted man."

"Don't joke about it!" he barked. "I've got a criminal record."

"What's that got to do with anything?"

"You'd be very goddamned surprised."

The officer returned to the car, one hand on his holster. Standing a good six feet away, he said, "Will you get out of the car, please, sir?"

"Fuck!" Raskin muttered.

"You, too, please, ma'am."

Kitty got out to see the officer slam Harold against the side of the car, turn him around, frisk him, then begin handcuffing him.

"What're you doin'?" Kitty demanded. "Why're you doin' that to him?"

"Now, ma'am, you stay right where you are." When he finished with Raskin, he reached into the Mercedes, turned off the lights, pulled the keys from the ignition, then locked the car. "Right this way, please," he said, pushing Harold from behind and taking Kitty by the upper arm toward the cruiser.

"I do not believe you can do this!" Kitty protested. "You cannot pull people outta their cars without an explanation and put them in handcuffs."

"Get in, please, and watch your head."

Once they were in the back of the car, separated from the officer by a mesh grille, trapped inside by doors without handles, the officer made a jargon-filled call on the radio, then started up the car.

Upon arriving at the station they were herded into a small room where Raskin's handcuffs were removed and they were told to wait.

"Just one damn minute!" Kitty said, becoming very angry. "You have no right to be doin' any of this!"

"Yes, ma'am, we do," the officer assured her, and went out, locking the door behind him.

"What the *hell* is going on?" Kitty wondered aloud.

Raskin lit a cigarette, took a hard drag on it, then said, "This happens every so often, Kitty. I'm sorry."

"How come you've never once mentioned it?"

"Maybe four times in the last fifteen years they've stopped me for some asinine traffic violation, like going two miles over the limit. And when they run me through the computer, they come up with a flag or some fucking thing on my MVD record. Then they accuse me of every unsolved crime for the last fifty years, push me around some, then finally turn me loose. This time, they'll probably try to make me for stealing the car. No registration, see."

"Surely to God it's not their right to do that," she said angrily.

"They think it is. I have to work hard to keep cool, because I'd like to beat the shit out of these arrogant assholes who think they're superior because they're fucking cops."

"But, Harold, you were acquitted of that crime. Why're they still holding it against you?"

"I was convicted with suspended sentences two other times," he admitted. "Assault, and assault and battery. Both when I was twenty-six. There were extenuating circumstances, but the judge said if he ever saw me again in his court he'd make sure I did hard time. So I enlisted to save us all the trouble. But I've got a record. I guess I should've told you."

"I guess you should've. But I still don't see why things that happened years ago should keep interferin' in your life now."

He shrugged. "That's the way it goes."

The door opened and a plainclothes officer came in. A tired-looking man in an ugly green polyester suit, he identified himself as Detective Raines and asked, "Either of you want some god-awful station-house coffee?"

Both declined, and he said, "Smart," as he pulled over a chair, turned it backward, then straddled it. "Who belongs to the car, Harold?"

"I do. It was transferred to me yesterday."

"Who by?"

"My employer."

"Where's the temporary reg?"

"At home on the kitchen counter."

"Your employer gonna verify that, Harold? Or did you help yourself to the vehicle?"

"For Chrissake! Why don't you have one of your flunkies drive me home. I'll show him the registration and we can get this crap over and done with."

"No can do, Harold. We're gonna have to have your employer vouch for you. You wanna give us a name and number?"

Raskin didn't want to do it. Seeing this, Kitty said, "Erik D'Anton," and rhymed off the number, facing down Raskin's glare, saying, "Don't be a fool. Erik will be glad to vouch for you."

"I'll be back." Raines got up and went out, locking the door again.

"Why the *fuck* did you do that?" Raskin rounded on Kitty.

"Why shouldn't I?"

"Because they'll make Erik come down here to ID me and the car, that's why not."

"Oh, hell!" Kitty said softly. "I'm sorry. I never thought of that."

"If you'd stayed out of it, they'd have taken me to the house, I'd have shown them the temporary registration, and that would've been the end of it. Fuck!"

"I'm sorry," Kitty apologized again and opened her bag for a Kool. "Damn! I'm really sorry, Harold. I just wasn't thinkin'."

"Never mind," Raskin relented. "How were you to know?"

"I wasn't, I guess. Damn!"

Marisa answered, then said, "Erik, it's for you. A Detective Raines."

Erik took the receiver and said, "Erik D'Anton. What is it?" then listened. Risa jumped up, convinced there'd been an accident. The moment the call ended she asked, "What? What happened?"

"They seem to think Raskin's stolen the Mercedes. They want me to bring the registration and identify him."

"Where's Kitty?"

"They're holding both of them."

"Erik, let *me* go."

"You can't. I must go in person."

"Then I'll come with you. Why would they think that?" she asked, going next door for some clothes.

"Because Raskin has a record. He doesn't know I'm aware of it, but this has happened several times over the years. They've telephoned me to confirm his identity and employment. I've asked them each time not to inform him they've contacted me. This is the first time I've been requested to come to the station."

"What kind of record?" she wanted to know, pulling on a pair of jeans as she came back into the room, a sweater tucked under her arm.

"He was involved in some brawls when he was in his mid-twenties. He broke one young man's arm and gave another several broken bones as well as a concussion. The fights were a result of Raskin's taking exception to the treatment young women were receiving—once in a bar, and once, apparently, in the back of a parked car."

"Poor Hal." She dragged the sweater over her head. "He must be so upset that they'd call and ask you to come down there."

"Yes," Erik said slowly. "I suppose so."

Without even glancing at the two new sports cars standing in the driveway, they automatically climbed into the Lamborghini. As they were heading along Tokeneke Road, Risa spotted the Mercedes.

"Have you got the spare key, Erik?"

"It's on the ring."

"Let me have it. I'll hop out and follow you, so Hal and Kitty'll be able to get home."

"Good idea."

They entered the station and went to the desk where Erik said, "Your Detective Raines rang and asked me to come down. My name's D'Anton."

The duty officer raised his head, looked at Erik and blinked rapidly several times. His mouth opened and closed but no sound emerged.

"Excuse me," Risa said to the man, who now turned to stare blankly at her. *"Hello?"* She rapped her knuckles on the top of the counter. "Anyone home? We want Detective Raines."

Without a word, the officer picked up the telephone, dialed a single digit, then said, "People out here for Raines."

"Let's wait over there," Risa put her arm through Erik's and drew him away from the desk. She could feel her anger building.

Raines came out from an inner office, saw Risa and started toward her with a smile forming on his lips. Risa tugged at Erik's sleeve, and Erik turned, causing Raines to halt in his tracks. Recovering himself, he advanced, saying, "Mr. D'Anton?" and looked up at Erik with a not-quite-formed expression that was somewhere between defensiveness and belligerence.

"Yes," answered Erik.

Raines decided to opt for belligerence. "You wanna show me some ID?" he asked. The sight of this D'Anton's face made his insides twist in anger.

"What for?"

" 'Cause I asked is what for." That face offended the hell out of him.

"Just a min—" Risa began, but Erik's hand on her arm stopped her.

"Where is Mr. Raskin?" Erik asked. "And why have you detained him and Miss Hemmings?"

"He's driving an unregistered vehicle." Who the hell did this guy think he was?"

"That is not so. I'm certain Mr. Raskin explained that the registration was changed yesterday morning."

"You got the paper?" Raines couldn't meet the man's blazing black eyes.

Erik was losing his temper. "Of course I do! I think it would be wise of you to get Mr. Raskin and Miss Hemmings now." He stared at Raines, and the smaller man was suddenly overheated and a little nervous. Undergoing a change of attitude, he said, "I'll get them," and went back through the door he'd come from.

In less than a minute, he returned, pushing Raskin ahead of him. Grimfaced and furious, Kitty followed. Raskin looked both humiliated and outraged. He moved toward Erik, set to apologize, but Erik silenced him with an upheld hand.

"You wanna ID this guy?" Raines asked, less cocky now.

"Why did you push him?" Erik asked tonelessly.

"Pardon?" Like a small child, Raines knew all at once he was in trouble.

"I asked you why you pushed Mr. Raskin."

"Oh, I . . . uhm. Look, can we just get on with this?"

"We've already done it. Very obviously, this man is who both he and I have said he is."

"Okay, okay. Show me the papers!" He made one last stab at authority.

Risa felt the air between her and Erik suddenly fill with vibrations. Moving very deliberately, Erik reached into his jacket pocket and brought out the temporary registration form. Raines took it, gave it a glance, then waved it in the air, waiting for Erik to take it back. With the tips of two fingers, Erik removed the paper from the man's hand and returned it to his pocket.

"Okay, you can clear on out of here," Raines told Raskin, then turned to go. His hands were wet and his mouth was dry. He knew he'd gone too far.

"*Raines!*" Erik said in a sharp whisper that stopped the man cold. He turned back. "Have you ever heard of harassment, Raines? Or perhaps malicious persecution? Have you ever heard of good manners, Raines, or politeness? If any of your officers ever again subject my colleague to this sort of humiliation, I shall institute a lawsuit against this station and its employees that will cost every last one of you your jobs, not to mention personal injury suits against each of you individually that will ensure you end your days as welfare recipients. Do I make myself perfectly clear?"

Eyes wide, Raines nodded. If he wasn't very careful, this guy would kill him.

"You will now apologize to Mr. Raskin and to Miss Hemmings. You will also tell the officer who perpetrated this travesty to present himself at once so that he, too, may make his apologies."

Raines nodded again, then mumbled barely audible apologies to Kitty and Raskin before rushing off to get the young officer. The man was arguing with Raines as he came through the door but went silent at the sight of Erik. He hitched up his uniform trousers, and said, "You got some problem?"

"No," Erik said. "You have a problem, as does your associate."

"I think you're mistaken, sir."

"No, I think *you're* mistaken. I suggest you go home and read up on the law. You will discover you have no grounds whatever for the actions you've taken tonight. My wife and I"—he reached for Risa's hand—"do not appreciate being pulled from our bed in the middle of the night in order to come here and be bullied. And my friends have done nothing that warrants the treatment to which you've submitted them. I have told Raines, and now I will tell you." Erik's whisper turned lacerating. "You will cease and desist your harassment of my colleague, and you will advise each of your associates of that. I will see to clearing the Motor Vehicle Department computer. Now, I believe you have something to say to Mr. Raskin and Miss Hemmings."

"I, uhm, my mistake. Sorry." He glanced at Erik who, still not satisfied, and in the grip of outrage, as well as suffering under the fluorescent station-house lights, stepped close to the young officer to say, "You're playing games with the lives of people I care about. If you want a future, of any kind, I suggest you give it up. Do you understand?"

"Yes, sir."

"Good!" With that Erik turned to Raskin and Kitty to say, "We've brought the car for you."

Outside, Kitty moved to speak to Risa as Raskin went over to Erik who, still caught in his anger, was visibly trembling. Both women turned to watch.

"Erik," Raskin began. "I can't tell you . . . Shit!" He threw his arms around Erik and hugged him, murmuring, "Thank you," then broke away, grabbed Kitty's hand and hurried her into the Mercedes.

"You were . . . I'm so proud of you," Risa said to a now stupefied Erik, who was watching Raskin drive off. "Why are you so surprised, Erik?" she asked, threading her fingers through his. "Did you think he didn't care? You're his mother, father, and brother all rolled into one. And you fought for him. Probably nobody else ever has. God!" she exhaled tremulously. "That was horrible. Are you okay?"

"Not really," he admitted as they climbed into the Lamborghini. He held his hands out to show her. They were shaking badly.

Risa took hold of them. "What you did was wonderful," she declared.

He shook his head. "I so dislike the world out here," he whispered, gazing through the windshield. Slowly he pulled his hands free in order to start the car. "It is so filled with fools."

"It's all right," she said. "Let's go home now."

As they headed down the Post Road, he said, "I wanted to destroy that place and those people. I wanted to bring it crashing down on them. I hate feeling that way."

"It's all right," she said again. "You handled it perfectly."

"You honestly think that?" He glanced over at her.

"Yes, honestly. Sometimes, you know, Erik, anger's a damned good thing."

"It didn't frighten you?"

"No." She smiled at him. "This time it only frightened you. Let's get home and finish what we started. 'My wife and I do not appreciate being pulled from our bed.' " she quoted, and then laughed. "You were magnificent!"

Somewhat shyly, he turned to smile at her.

Twenty-three

HEN SHE'D FIRST STARTED TAKING THE BIRTH-CONTROL PILLS, Risa felt she had some direct control over her life and her body. It was up to her to remember to take the pills; a conscious daily decision that compounded her commitment to Erik. But with the IUD in place killing off any possibility of a baby without her actively having to do anything, she began to feel she'd allocated control of her body to others—to the gynecologist, and to Erik. No matter how she tried to reason it through, no matter how well she understood Erik's fears, she couldn't make herself stop wanting a child. If anything, she wanted one more daily. She'd dream she was giving birth, clinging to the sides of a delivery-room table while her body split like an overripe melon, and with no pain whatever, there'd be her child. In her dreams she repeatedly delivered babies, then nursed them at her breasts; she held their small sweet bodies in her arms and felt an extraordinary well-being. But nowhere did Erik figure in these dreams. She was always alone giving birth and, afterward alone with the infant. She'd look around the vast white emptiness of the birthing place of her dreams and wonder where he was, why he didn't come to see the beautiful child they'd made.

Her dreams were so real they seemed to transcend into her waking world, leaving her with empty arms and a belly that, despite its so-recent swelling, was remarkably flat. She'd go about for hours after rising with a sense of loss so acute, a feeling of emptiness so profound she didn't think she'd survive without locating the child she'd somehow misplaced. It had to be somewhere, but she couldn't remember where she'd left it.

She had dreams where she ran through endless empty rooms, following an infant's wail, drawn forward by the cry of the child she knew wanted

742

its mother. She ran, doors slamming shut behind her, growing weary, knowing she'd never get to the place where the baby lay crying. And she never did. These nightly marathons ruined her rest; she awakened feeling drugged and enervated, as if she'd actually spent the seven or eight hours of the night sprinting along some country track.

As a result, even her emotions seemed no longer to be entirely under her control. One night at the climactic point of her lovemaking with Erik she began sobbing and couldn't stop, nor could she offer him an explanation.

"There must be something," he insisted, holding her while she wept. "Is it something I've done? Something that's happened? Please tell me. I can't bear to see you this way."

What could she say? The truth, she knew, would start *him* weeping. All she'd accomplish by telling him was to upset him. So she kept repeating, "It's nothing, nothing," and at last she was able to stop. But she could see Erik had serious misgivings. She knew he was reviewing every last thing he'd said or done for months in an attempt to pinpoint the problem. It revived her claustrophobia and made her want to scream at him. This was one of the times when she hated that feeling of being on a slide beneath a microscope into which Erik was peering.

"Erik," she said, suppressing her sudden and considerable anger with him, "why do you *do* that? You're lying here trying to figure out what sin you've committed. I don't think you realize that everybody, every last living one of us, is locked up with our own thoughts, *just the way you are.* I'm as trapped as you by what I think and feel. You are not the only one who wishes he could read minds and thoughts. I wish I could, too. I'm not some perfect toy without a brain, Erik. I've been working all these years, just as you have, to know and to understand and to care about and to anticipate the things that'll make you happy or that'll upset you. You are not the only one who *feels*, Erik! I'm up here"—she pressed the heel of her hand against her temple—"imprisoned up here, *just like you!*"

"But I know . . ."

"Sometimes I don't think you *do* know. And sometimes the things I feel have nothing to do with you; they have to do with me. But sometimes, *sometimes* you're so involved in your pain and fears and the stuff inside your head that you forget I've got all those emotions, too. Just because I'm not you and don't reveal myself the way you do, you think nothing's going on in my brain."

"What have I done to make you so angry?" he asked.

"Nothing! You haven't done anything!"

"But you're simply livid, and since there's no one else in the room, what am I to think but that you're angry with me? I'm confused," he confessed, his hands agitating as if with a need to take flight.

"I'm not livid. I know you're confused." She took hold of his hands, willing both of them to calm down. "I'm sorry. I'm getter older very damned fast," she said, her voice reedy with emotion. "Time's flying away from us, and soon it'll be too late. I'll be past the point where I'm able, should you ever change your mind."

"Ah!" he said, at last understanding. "We are discussing babies again."

"No. Yes. Yes! You want the truth, I'll tell you. I can't stop the wanting, Erik. I've tried everything, but it won't go away. I know it can never be but I want that baby just as badly as you want the face you should've had. I mean, it's positively amusing in this age of female emancipation that all I can think about is being a goddamned mother, but there you have it. It's never going to happen, but by Christ I think about it. I don't blame you. I understand your feelings, and I don't want to change you. I love you the way you are. I always have and I always will. I've just got to figure out some way to stop wanting. It's taking me longer than I thought it would, that's all. I know it hurts you," she said sadly, "and I'm sorry. I hate hurting you. But I'm tired of walking around with this need festering inside me; I'm tired of dreaming of babies every night. I know, I know! We thrashed this out a long time ago, and I accepted the terms. I still do. I do," she wound down. "I'm sorry."

"You're unhappy." He looked mortally wounded.

"No, I'm not," she said, beyond upset now and primed to feel guilty. "I love my life with you. I love you."

"But you would love me more if I consented to a baby."

"No. Maybe. I don't think I *could* love you more. It's different, Erik. It's something else, something maybe only women feel."

"You know if I could possibly face it I would do this for you, Marisa."

"I do know that," she said, saddened as she put her arms around him. "I know you'd do anything for me. That's what makes it so damned hard."

"Do you want to be free of me?" he asked, terrified that she'd say yes.

"No. And don't make it sound as if you're holding me captive. I *want* to be here with you."

"I wish . . ."

"Don't say it! I know how you feel, Erik. I do!" She put a hasty end to the conversation by engaging him in a long searching kiss, suddenly frantic to lose herself in lovemaking. She had to use her body to distract both of them from an unresolvable issue. And she succeeded.

For Erik, however, from that night in January a few weeks prior to her thirty-second birthday, the countdown had begun. Somewhere, a huge clock had begun ticking. And there was rarely a day when he didn't all but hear the grinding of its massive wheels and feel the push of its inexorably moving giant hands. He could do nothing to stop it.

* * *

"I think your girl's gonna crack up," Raskin told Kitty.

"What's that mean?"

"It means what I said. She's showing serious signs of wear and tear."

"Why? How?"

"Why I can't say. You'd probably know that better than me. How? I'll give you an example or two. The other day I'm driving her over to pick up her car from being serviced, and we're talking, you know. And out of nowhere she starts asking about my family, what were they like, did I have brothers or sisters. Kitty, she knows all about my family and has for years."

"Maybe she forgot."

"Not likely, but I'll give that one the benefit of the doubt. Here's another. She's coming back one morning last week from walking Willie. I'm in the kitchen making coffee and she climbs up to sit on the counter the way she always does and starts in on this big plan she has to breed Willie with another spaniel so she can have the pick of the litter. There's only one small problem: Willie was spayed six months after she got him. You want more examples?"

"No," she said, going to the bar to refill her glass.

"It's kind of obvious to me, to be truthful," he said. "Is it as obvious to you?"

"I guess so," she said, returning to her chair. "I'd been hopin' all that was settled long ago."

"Well, it isn't, not by a long shot."

"What about Erik?" she asked.

"What about him?"

"Has he noticed? How's he behavin'?"

"Has he *noticed?*" Raskin laughed dryly. "Erik's behaving like that guy in Greek mythology chained to a rock while the buzzards come every day and tear out his liver. I think you should talk to her, Kitty. On the surface, everything's the same as always. But underneath, things are simmering. I don't blame either of them and I wish to hell there was something I could do. But I can't do one damned thing except watch it happen."

"Harold," she said, "d'you ever wonder how all this came to be? I mean, I sure never thought when I answered that ad years back I'd be takin' on a child for life. I don't mind, understand. It just strikes me strange, every once in a while. And you. Did you think you'd be signin' on for life when you came to work for Erik?"

"I didn't think about it," he answered honestly. "I'm not sorry."

"D'you ever miss all them women?"

"D'you ever miss those guys you used to pick up, you and Freed?"

"Don't you try makin' out like I was your female counterpart, Harold.

If I live to be two hundred and forty, I'll never get through as many men as you did women. And besides, I didn't sleep with 'em all like you did."

"What if I told you I never slept with any of them?"

"I beg your pardon? Are you telling me none of those stories was true?"

"No, I'm asking you if you'd believe that."

"Frankly, I would not believe that."

"Well, it's true."

"I do not believe you, Harold."

"I don't care if you do. Yes, I used to hang out in bars most nights. And yes, I used to leave with women most nights. But I'd just walk them to their cars, or give them a ride home, or sit and talk with them somewhere."

"But what about all those stories you told me you used to tell Erik?"

"I made them up. He needed to hear, and I suppose I needed to tell them. Mostly, it was just one story with hundreds of variations. There were a few women I saw when I was at Yale, but I could never connect. I'd go out nights and have a few drinks, eat the free peanuts or popcorn or whatever, and talk to whoever was nearby. I never met so many lonely people as I did in those bars. And I saw the same ones over and over."

"That don't explain all those women phonin' up for you all the time," she said, her eyes narrowed.

"Sure it does, Kitty. I was nice to them. They liked me. They wanted to get something going."

"Why're you tellin' me this now?" she wanted to know.

"I don't know. I guess because I'm going to be forty-seven years old in a few weeks and it's time to come clean. Or maybe I'm tired of trying to live up to those old stories. I didn't lie to you that night when I said we were both lonely. It was the God's honest truth. And I'd never met anyone else who didn't either bore me stupid or irritate the hell out of me. I liked you. You were sharp and sexy, good-hearted and good to look at."

"You just liked my chest, you liar."

"That, too." He smiled.

"It's a real shame it's fallin' into my lap these days."

"Horseshit."

"You always did make me feel real good about myself." She smiled over at him. "How're you gonna feel in a few years' time bein' out with a sixty-year-old woman?"

"Probably the same way I feel now: just fine, thank you. You're the best-looking old lady I know. And you don't look a day over forty."

"Lord, what a sweet liar you are!"

"Nope. Truth."

"You don't aim to make any changes, huh?"

"Nope. Do you?"

"A bit late for that, wouldn't you say?"

"I'd say that. Talk to Risa, Kitty. I'm worried about both of them."

"Come walk Willie by here and have coffee with me," Kitty said. "I've been missin' you lately."

"Okay, in the morning."

"You okay, Reese?"

Risa sighed. "I'm fine, just tired. We've been working like crazy to get the specs and drawings finished for this new job."

"You get a good sleep and I'll have the coffee ready when you come by."

Kitty didn't even have to ask. Risa turned Willie loose to roam about the back lawn, let herself in, sat down by the table, lit one of Kitty's Kools, then put her head down on the table, and began to cry.

"I don't know what to do, Kitty. I can't let it go. All I think about day in and day out is having a baby. I'm harming Erik. He's starting to go back to the way he was when we met. He's unhappy, and I can feel it, touch it even, but I can't make myself stop. I keep thinking maybe I should go away somewhere, be miserable by myself."

"You gotta pull yourself together," Kitty said, picking up the cigarette Risa had lit and left to smolder in the ashtray. "You're gonna wreck the only good marriage I've ever known about."

"I don't *want* to go anywhere, except maybe to the doctor's office to have this goddamned IUD taken out."

"You plan to trick Erik, get yourself pregnant, then surprise him with it?"

"I couldn't do that. I want him to want it, Kitty. Why can't he want it?"

"I'm sure you know all his reasons."

"I know every last one of them."

"So, then, why're you askin' me?"

"Because I can't ask him. It's a dead-end street, and I'm in this car going a hundred miles an hour headed right for the brick wall at the end, but I don't know how to stop."

"Turn off the ignition," Kitty suggested.

"What?" Risa sat up and stared at her.

"You hear me. Just turn it off. You can't have a baby. The man you love can't deal with one. You haven't the heart to trick him. So turn it off, Risa, before you wreck somethin' beautiful. Let me tell you somethin': You've got yourself a first-class, grade-A, champeen obsession, fixation, whatever you want to name it. There's not a reason in this world why you can't be happy with what you've got—which, I'll remind you, is about a thousand times more than most other women've got. But you've fixed your brain on this one thing and you're lettin' it rule your life. It's the very same way it was years back when you nagged and nagged at your daddy, wantin' him to get you a dog. It was all you ever talked about. You went bringin' up the subject every chance you got until you near drove the poor man crazy. There wasn't one occasion for years when you didn't make him feel like the meanest bastard on earth 'cause he didn't give you that dog you were so set on for your birthday, or for Christmas. And now, here you are, doin' the same damn thing again, this time to Erik. Truth to tell, it's wearin' a little thin. Years now, you've been goin' on about babies. Grow up, Risa! Every last one of us makes compromises, but you're actin' as if you think you're exempt. I've got news for you, girl. You're not. Seems to me lately Erik's the one been doin' all the work in this marriage, and you've been settin' back lettin' him do it, punishin' him for not givin' you that baby you want. Just like you did with your daddy. I gotta tell you, I thought you were bigger than that. I thought you cared more for Erik than that. I love you better'n anyone, Reese, but you're actin' a fool over this baby business. You had your answer to this question about fifteen years ago when you married Erik and the two of you discussed it then. You keep wonderin' when he's finally gonna trust you the way you want him to. Well, I'll tell you when that'll be: when you grow up and disabuse yourself of the notion you can have somethin' you just can't have. I'd be perfectly happy to have had your life, and that's the truth. Because to be loved the way Erik loves you is a rare and special thing. *You can't have it all*, Risa. You just can't. I'm sorry to take such a hard line with you, but maybe I've been wrong to let you go on for so long without sayin' what I been thinkin'."

"You think I'm spoiled and selfish. You think I always have been."

"No. I think you're fixated, and it's ruinin' everything. Is that what you want?"

"Why is it wrong of me to want a baby?" Risa asked her.

"It's not wrong to want a baby, Risa. It's wrong to want somethin' just 'cause you know you can't have it. I'd bet anythin' you'd care to name if Erik had started out from day one sayin', 'Let's have us six kids,' you'd have made one hell of a fuss. Give it up!" she repeated.

"I can't!"

"Then you'll destroy the marriage. And you'll kill Erik."

"You're overstating things."

"Honey," Kitty said quietly. "I'm *under*stating things. You go ahead and keep on with this and you'll kill him sure enough."

"How can you *say* such a cruel thing?" Risa began crying again.

" 'Cause it's the truth, and you toyed with it yourself a while back when you got here and set yourself down and started moanin' about babies. Either go home and let him live in peace, or keep on the way you are and you'll have the pleasure of watchin' him die. And he will, you know, Risa. He'll die. You can't come into the life of a man like Erik and then, when he's placed his heart and soul in your keepin', try to cut them out with your fingernails 'cause he can't give you the one thing you've decided you have to have. I'll say it one more time: The only reason you're carryin' on this way is 'cause you know it's impossible. You want the man to be Christ on the cross for you. And I think what you're doin' is the true cruelty."

"Oh, God! Is that what you really think?"

"Sure looks that way to me."

"I have to stop," Risa said feverishly. "I have to. I wouldn't want a life without Erik in it. I wouldn't want to live if anything happened to him."

"You think about that the next time you're tempted to punish him a little more by draggin' your butt around the house, or mopin' in front of the window where you're sure he can see you."

"Now I feel even worse than I did before."

"Good! Maybe it'll smarten you up some. And in case you start forgettin', just think how well you managed to live most of your whole life without a goddamned dog."

"I have to put things back together." She reached for the Kools again, but Kitty slapped her hand away, saying, "You don't smoke. Stop messing with my cigarettes. Blow your nose, and drink your coffee. Then you get Willie and go on home to your husband."

"Has it really showed?"

"Yeah, it's really showed."

"*God!* You're right. I'm so ashamed." She reached over to the table to squeeze Kitty's hand. "Thank you for telling me. I'll get it right. I'll start paying more attention to Erik, put everything else out of my mind."

"You do that."

"I think I'll go home right now and have my coffee with him."

"Nice idea." Kitty smiled. "Go on ahead."

Risa stood up, feeling suddenly better and lighter than she had in a very long time. Giving Kitty a hug, she thanked her again, then picked up the leash and went out the back door calling for Willie.

Twenty-four

SHE HURRIED UPSTAIRS CARRYING TWO MUGS OF COFFEE, BUT WHEN SHE opened the bedroom door and looked inside, it was to see that the bed was empty. Erik was in the bathroom; she could hear the shower going. Setting the mugs down on the dresser, she quickly shed her clothes, then tiptoed over to the door to stand on the threshold for a moment allowing her eyes to become accustomed to the dark. Erik never turned lights on in any room except the office, where he was forced to use the angled lamp clipped to his drafting table.

Steam was billowing out the top of the shower enclosure. She darted forward, pulled open the stall door and was inside in a moment, with the door closed behind her. Erik started in surprise. Whirling about, he automatically took a step back. She closed the small space between them and leaned against him, feeling a powerful resurgence of her caring for him. As he'd automatically stepped back in an instinctively self-defensive move, he now just as automatically brought his arms around her. She could feel his heart pounding from the fright she'd given him. There were times, like now, when she knew how totally the man he'd grown to be had been shaped by the boy he'd once been; a damaged, frightened, neglected, and abused boy. Even after all these years, a part of him still expected to find himself in the midst of a stone-throwing crowd.

She knew him. She knew his past and his present, and the majority of his fears. She also knew the broad breadth of his chest and the tapering of his hips, the hard solidity of his thighs and upper arms. She knew the smooth hairless expanse of his chest and belly, the touch of each of the fingers and both thumbs of the two hands that enclosed her with perennial care as if fearful of holding her too tightly or too long. She knew the

750

sturdy column of his neck and the bones of his jaw, the taste and texture of his lips and tongue, even the ridges of his teeth and the sweet interior of his mouth. Her fingers were well acquainted with the varying textures of the skin behind his ears and at the back of his neck and along his shoulders; the flesh over the wide cage of his chest, even the darker, responsive tissue at his nipples. She was most familiar with the flat planes of his haunches and the inward curve at the top of the backs of his thighs. She knew the length and depth of the scar that started at the corner of his mouth. Her tongue traced its length to the rim of his ear. She knew the sound of his accelerating breathing, and best of all, most reassuring and always exciting, was the rise of his body into her hands. She knew he would respond to her with immediacy and pulsing pleasure.

She'd come back to him. Standing there with the water beating down on them, he could feel right through to his marrow that she'd returned, that she'd reconciled her differences, settled matters to her satisfaction; she was home. No need for fear, no need to contemplate a vast desolate future. He could open the doors of his mind and let it all leave him, like starlings taking flight from a disused belfry. He embraced her, his relieved tears concealed by the downpouring water.

Standing with her, both of them wrapped in one bath sheet, he laid his cheek against the top of her head, so grateful to have her back again—he could feel the completeness of her homecoming and its lack of reservations—that he offered up silent prayers to thank the Fates for this reprieve. Then the towel fell away and he carried her, with her arms and legs wound around him like a child's, to their bed.

"I came to have coffee with you, but I was too late. You were already up."

"I'm glad," he said. "I'm very glad."

"Erik, I'm sorry. I've been awful. We'll start again as if the last few months never happened."

"They never happened," he echoed, crouched over her.

"I love you. You're all I want."

"I love you. You're all I want," he parroted.

"Stop that." She smiled up at him.

"I have stopped." He gave her a smile of beatific radiance. It reinforced everything Kitty had said. She had no right to take chances with Erik, to treat him as if he were ordinary and therefore subject to pressures like an ordinary man. This was Erik, the man who lived in shadows, the dark side of her star, and she'd loved him on sight. It was unfair, wrong of her to try in any fashion to manipulate him. It was neither something he was equipped to comprehend nor that he deserved.

"Erik, I don't want to do the presentation tomorrow. Let Hal go. I want to stay home with you."

"If you'd rather not, of course."

"Touch me," she whispered, her hands in the small of his back urging him down to her.

His hands went to her waist as her legs rose on either side of him.

"I'll keep you locked inside me forever," she said. "I'll never let you go."

She directed his mouth to hers, at the same time lifting to pull him deeper, then deeper, until there was no space left, even for thought.

Of course Kitty was right, she marveled. Why had she been making herself and Erik miserable for so long? They had no need for anything more. They required only each other. Wasn't Erik's immediate retreat from beneath that shroud of sadness that had started slowly settling back around his shoulders proof of that? It was time for her to demonstrate in no uncertain terms that he was what she wanted, that this was where she wanted to be. The first thing she planned to do something about was her room and the environment she'd created with the idea of inducing Erik to grow accustomed to the light in her company.

With her hair tied up in a scarf, wearing an old shirt of Erik's, a pair of jeans, and sneakers, she closed herself into the room and began stripping the paper from the walls. Then she ripped out the carpet, rolled it up, tied it with a rope, and got Hal to help cart it downstairs to be picked up by the Goodwill truck. Then she went off to order new wallpaper, a copy of a Victorian print with small red flowers on a charcoal background, and carpeting so dark a red it was almost black. While she waited for the paper to arrive, she painted over the bright green trim with glossy black, and removed the plants to a corner of the kitchen, where they'd get the morning sun.

Out went the white linens and wicker furniture. In came low sleek Italian furniture in black lacquer with gold trim, and two very modern armchairs with appealing rounded lines upholstered in soft dark-gray wool. She had glossy black vertical blinds made for the three windows, and then set to work putting up the wallpaper prior to the arrival and installation of the carpet.

When the room was done, she closed the shades and stood barefoot on the new carpet, admiring her handiwork. Then she went up to the office to get Erik.

"You have to close your eyes," she told him, "and keep them closed until I say so."

He obeyed and she led him by the hand into the room, closed the door, then said, "Okay. Now look."

He opened his eyes to take in the details of the room, which she'd illuminated with tall black candles in heavy brass candlesticks. "It's superb," he said, "simply superb."

"Now we can sit here together. This will be our new den."

"I'll bring up some of my books," he said, and eagerly went off to do that at once.

It seemed to her highly symbolic: There were now no unused, meaningless rooms in their home. And it had taken very little to set everything to rights.

"Perhaps," Erik said, "you might be interested in doing some volunteer work."

"What?" Risa looked up from her book.

"Greenwich Hospital needs volunteers. I thought that might possibly be of interest to you."

"Why would you think that?" she asked, setting her book aside.

"It's merely a thought, in the event there isn't enough to occupy you here."

"Are you trying to get rid of me?" she teased. "Are you trying to clear the decks so you can sneak other women in while I'm out?"

"Ah, you've caught me. And I thought I was being so very clever."

She laughed as he performed a brief pantomime of hiding behind his hands only to have the hands pushed away by a powerful unseen force, revealing a guilty expression.

"No, seriously," she said, scooting over to his chair to straddle his lap. "Do I seem bored? Do I appear to be dragging?"

"Not in the least. We'll forget it. It was a bad idea."

"Yes, we will. You know what I wish?"

"What do you wish?" His hands enclosed her hips.

"I wish we could go away somewhere together."

"We could take a cruise," he said, remembering the crossing he'd made years ago with Raskin when he'd remained inside his stateroom throughout the entire trip.

"Erik! That would be wonderful! I haven't been to Europe since I was fourteen, when Dad took me along on a business trip to London. I spent most of the time waiting in offices with the secretaries of the men he was meeting. But we did go to the theater, and to Kew Gardens. And we took a terrific boat ride down the Thames to Hampton Court. There are so many places we could go, all kinds of places I'd like to see. Venice. Scotland. So many places."

"I'll tell you what. After the presentation in July, we'll take a holiday."

"You'd do it?"

"I won't promise I'll play shuffleboard, or spend my afternoons in a deck chair, but I think I could manage it."

"We'll make it your fiftieth-birthday celebration."

"Good God! Don't rush me! That's not until September."

"Okay, but the point is, I'll take you. This will be my advance birthday present to you for attaining the incredibly advanced age of fifty."

He groaned and let his head fall back against the sofa. "Entering my decline," he said dramatically. "Starting the grand slide toward oblivion."

"That's right. And when we get home, I'll have a wheelchair and a walker for you. What else? Maybe some of those smart diapers you old people have to wear because the bladder control goes."

He snorted with laughter. "Might as well have me fitted for a truss while you're at it."

"We could take Hal and Kitty with us. What d'you think?"

"It sounds delightful. They can help carry my wheelchair and the walker."

"God! It'll be so great. Will you dance with me on board?"

"Quite possibly, provided the light level is reasonable."

"Will you stroll around the deck with me after dinner?"

"Only provided my diapers aren't slipping."

She laughed and punched him on the arm. "Be serious for a minute. You know it's going to mean meeting people in the daytime here and there."

"I am aware of that. We'll try to hold it to a minimum."

"You're absolutely sure?" she asked.

"I believe so."

"Fantastic!" She gave him a kiss, then said, "I'm going to call Kitty right now. This is wonderful!"

A week before the presentation was due and three weeks before they were scheduled to sail from New York, some kids decided to investigate the potential for mischief on Contentment Island. It was just after ten, and Risa had let Willie out prior to their nightly walk. Erik had gone back up to the office directly after dinner. Raskin and Risa had finished clearing the kitchen when they heard Willie barking, followed by a muffled bang, then the spinning of tires on the gravel accompanied by a loud engine roar as a car went speeding off up the driveway.

Raskin and Risa glanced at each other, then ran through the house and out the front door. Raskin pressed the remote control to open the gates and Risa ran ahead. When he caught up to her, she was lifting the whimpering, injured dog into her arms.

"They blew up the mailbox and ran over Willie!" she cried. "We've got to get him to the vet right away!"

"I'll get the car. You wait!"

Erik came running up, asking, "What is it? What's happened?"

"They ran over Willie!" she wept, holding the bleeding spaniel tighter to her chest. "He's suffering. It's awful, Erik. He's badly hurt. Hal's getting the car. We'll take him to the vet."

"I'll come with you," he offered.

"No, you go back. We'll take care of it. I'll call and let you know how it goes."

Raskin brought the car, jumped out to open the rear door and Risa slid into the back with Willie. As Hal was getting back in, he said, "Call the police, Erik; report this. They blew up the goddamned mailbox with a cherry bomb, then backed their fucking car over the dog."

Erik nodded and Raskin sped off.

The policeman to whom Erik spoke said, "We've had half a dozen complaints already tonight. We've got cruisers out all over town. We'll catch 'em. You gonna press charges, if we do?"

"I will. They've badly injured our dog."

"That's rough. I'll keep you posted, Mr. D'Anton."

Less than an hour later, Risa telephoned to say, "They had to put him down, Erik. Willie's dead. We're coming home now."

Erik had coffee and brandy ready when they arrived. Risa came in, her face blood- and dirt- and tear-stained, her clothes saturated with blood.

"Come, I'll draw a bath for you," he said, taking her hand. "I've made coffee," he told Raskin. "Everything's on a tray in the kitchen."

"I need it. Thanks."

Like a zombie, Risa let Erik lead her upstairs to the bathroom where she stood dully waiting while he started the bath water running. She couldn't seem to assist when he began stripping her out of her ruined clothes.

"Those bastards ran him down on purpose," she said wretchedly as he pulled the combs from her hair. "He was barking. They heard him. It wasn't enough fun to blow up our mailbox. They had to kill our dog to make their evening complete. Erik, it was so horrible. The vet just looked at poor Willie and shook his head. Hal said, 'Willie isn't going to make it, Risa,' and I knew it was true, but I couldn't believe it. The vet let me stay while he gave him the shot. It only took a few seconds and it was over. I *loved* that dog, Erik."

"I know. I'm terribly sorry. You're cold. Get into the tub."

She looked at the bath, then at Erik. "Why would they *do* that to a lovely little dog? Why?"

"I don't know. It defies explanation."

At last, like someone of greatly advanced age, she slowly climbed into the tub and lay back with her head resting on the rim. "Did you say you'd made coffee?"

"Shall I fetch you some?"

"Please? I've got the shakes and it must be eighty degrees outside."

"Shock," he explained. "I'll just be a moment."

When he'd gone, she squinted at the heap of clothing on the floor. In the dark she couldn't see the blood. Knowing Erik, the clothes would be gone before she emerged from the bath. Just like Willie. Gone, her dear sweet Prince. For nine years he'd been her constant companion, there day or night to play with or take for walks or merely to cuddle. She'd never dreamed he would die—especially not in so cruel and painful a fashion.

"I thought he'd never die," she told Erik when he returned with two cups of coffee; one he set on the side of the tub for her, the other he held in both hands as he sat on the floor with his back against the wall.

"He was a fine animal with many years left, and I was very fond of him. It's most unfair."

"I've never felt so awful. When my father died that was . . . different. This was murder. They *murdered* Willie, Erik."

"They'll be caught and punished."

"A slap on the hand and a warning," she said bitterly.

"More than that, I should think. I was told they'd done a great deal of damage tonight."

"That's an understatement if ever I heard one." She took a sip of her coffee, then looked over at Erik. "I don't think I'm going to be in the mood for a vacation."

"Let's wait and see, shall we? You may find it's just what you need. We still have a few weeks."

"I'm not going to want to go, Erik. Maybe we should let Hal and Kitty go on their own."

"We'll wait," he said judiciously. "Now is not the time to make any decisions, not so soon after such an upsetting experience."

"Are you as calm as you seem?" she asked him.

"Not in the least. I simply don't know what to do, except be with you, talk about it. There are certain situations for which I have no precedents. This is one of them. Is there anything you'd like me to do for you?"

"Yeah," she said softly. "Tell me you love me, and promise me you'll never even *think* of buying me another dog."

"I love you very much, and you have my promise."

She put her head down on her knees and wept.

Three days later, although she'd finished a period less than two weeks before, she started bleeding. Only a little, but it was bright-red, not menstrual, blood. And it scared her. She called the gynecologist's office and got an emergency appointment for the following day.

"It has to come out," the doctor told her. "This happens sometimes, especially with women who haven't had children. These devices seem to work best with women who've had successful deliveries."

"I can't use the diaphragm, and now you've got to take the IUD out. What am I supposed to do about birth control?"

"You've got a number of alternatives, everything from vaginal suppositories to sponges, to a tubal ligation, if you want to be done with the problem once and for all."

"What happens with a tubal ligation?"

"Very simple. It's done through the navel, a short procedure under a general anesthetic. The tubes are tied off. You can do it as an outpatient, come in in the morning and be home by afternoon."

"Well, maybe that's what I'll do."

"We can have Liz set up an appointment before you leave. For now, let's take care of this."

She made an appointment to have the procedure in a week's time. That way, she'd have a week or so to recuperate before she and Erik left for their vacation. Not, they'd assured her, that she'd be incapacitated in any serious way. Just a little groggy from the anesthetic, and a bit swollen in the abdomen for a day or two. Then she'd be able to get up and go on about her business.

She planned to tell Erik about the removal of the IUD and her scheduled surgery, but by the time she got home she was so tired—still in the aftermath shock from Willie's death—that all she wanted was a nap. Erik and Hal were upstairs in the office, so she thought she'd lie down for an hour or two and at some point during the evening she'd let Erik know her news.

It was one of those occasions when he popped down to the bedroom to get something, saw her asleep, and couldn't resist lying down beside her. She came awake to his touch, gave him a sleepy smile, and opened her arms to him. Slowly, without haste, the embrace changed shape, acquired heat and rhythm. It wasn't until the moment when Erik shuddered in her arms, inside her, that she realized it was the second time ever that they'd made love without any precautions. She was so stunned, and so immediately guilty, as well as fearful of the anger with which he might respond, that she simply couldn't bring herself to tell him.

Holding him, she promised herself she'd explain everything after dinner, or perhaps in the morning. But what if seeds were joining together inside her at that very moment and the damage was already done? *God!* Without intending to, she'd done the one thing she'd sworn never to do. Guilt fell over her like a gauzy curtain.

Erik dozed at her side and she tried to think of ways to tell him, rejecting each one. It wouldn't matter, she decided finally. In a week's time she'd be neutered, rendered sterile for all time. Even if by some chance seeds were dividing and multiplying, the finished product would never see the light of day.

She had the presentation to do in the city in a couple of days. And then, next week, she'd go down to the hospital for the day and when she came home the question of babies would have been answered once and for all. But still she felt acutely, sickeningly guilty. It hadn't been planned; it hadn't been intentional. But it had happened. And maybe the surgery would be too late. They'd tie her tubes only to find out after the fact that they'd neutered someone who was already pregnant.

She told herself to wake Erik and confess, but she couldn't do it.

And, finally, she fell asleep again, her thighs sticky with the evidence of her inadvertent betrayal.

Twenty-five

SHE COULD NOT COMPREHEND HOW SHE'D MANAGED TO GET SO THOR-oughly trapped in her dishonesty. She was positively imprisoned in it, and wanted to get free, but she kept finding illogical reasons why the time wasn't yet right to reveal to Erik not only what she'd already done but also about the surgery she intended to have in less than a week's time. Repeatedly she asked herself what she was waiting for. Repeatedly she failed to find an answer. And to compound both her offense against Erik and her mounting guilt, she made love with him several more times during the next few days.

All at once he was like some narcotic she craved. As it had been at the very beginning, she was again stricken by a ravening sexual need she could barely contain. She thought hungrily, constantly, of his caress, of his broad powerful white body that had never known exposure to the sun. She was so single-mindedly obsessed with her need that she actually wondered if it might not be possible to expire simply from the heat of her ongoing lust for him. And Erik responded, as he always did, with an intensity that matched and even surpassed her own. She drew him into her arms, into the churning interior of her body in a desperate frenzy. And he too willingly submitted himself to the perpetual astonishment and exultation she inspired in him.

What was she doing? she wondered, appalled by her silence and by her actions. This had to stop; she had to tell him. But every time she opened her mouth to speak, she kissed him instead, or lay mutely wanton be-neath him, in the grip of something she neither understood nor was able to control.

In the car, headed for the turnpike, on the day she was to make the presentation, she vowed she'd confess to Erik that evening. She loathed feeling as guilty and deceitful as she did. And if she was pregnant as a result of these few days of obsessive lovemaking, she'd do the honorable thing and abort the child. Having at last arrived at a decision, she felt a bit better.

The weather was unbearable. They were in the middle of a heat wave, into the eleventh day of temperatures in the upper nineties, and it was predicted that it would be at least another week, mid-July, before anyone could hope for some relief. As she drove along, she imagined the clogged streets of the city, and the half-hour or so it would take her to get across town to the client's office, as well as the additional time she'd spend looking for somewhere to park the car. The thought of all that traffic and hassling in the overwhelming heat and humidity was suddenly more than she could handle. She'd leave the car in the lot at the Darien station and catch the 10:45 train.

She had ten minutes to spare after buying her ticket, and went to stand on the shaded part of the platform, surprised at how many other people were waiting. She thought quite a number of them had probably had the same idea: to leave the car and avoid the traffic jams and frayed tempers this kind of heat provoked.

Standing on the platform, she planned how she'd confide everything to Erik as soon as she arrived home that evening. He'd understand. He'd believe she hadn't set out intentionally to trick him. He was bound to be convinced of her sincerity when he learned of the surgery she'd have in the coming week. The procedure would eliminate this contentious issue from their lives forever. Then, after that they'd be going off together for the first time on a splendid holiday. Nothing she'd done was so extreme that it couldn't be remedied.

When it finally came, the train was ten minutes behind schedule and packed full, with people standing in the aisles and entryways. Carrying her portfolio, she made her way to the front, to stand beside the engineer's compartment where she could look out the window. It made her feel like a child again, to gaze out at the tracks as they rushed down the line toward Noroton Heights, where more people pushed on board, and then on to Stamford, which would be the last stop before 125th Street.

Putting the portfolio down so that it rested between her knees and the outside wall of the train, she looked out, pleased with this singular opportunity to watch their progress as they sped toward the city. And she was relieved in advance at the prospect of telling Erik the truth. He'd forgive her. He wouldn't be angry; he wouldn't fling some piece of furniture through the nearest window. He'd listen, and forgive. Then they'd go off as planned. He'd been wise to discourage her from canceling their reservations. The trip would take her mind off everything, especially Willie and his piteous cries as they'd placed him on the vet's examining table.

The train hadn't reached top speed. It was going perhaps only thirty miles an hour as it approached the station at Port Chester. Risa looked out at the people waiting on the platform for the local that would be along in a few minutes. The majority were clustered in the shade of the overhang in the center of the platform. But ahead, at the extreme far end, a man stood alone. There was something odd about that. It didn't feel right to her, for some reason. She kept her eyes on him as the train proceeded through the station, and then, as they were nearing the end of the platform, the man stepped to the edge. She opened her mouth, her hands going to the glass separating her from the outside. She cried, *"No!"* as the man jumped, collided with the front of the train—collided somehow with her—before falling beneath the wheels. There was a monstrous crunching noise as the carriage went over him; then the train came to a sudden stop. Swallowing the rush of acrid fluid in her mouth, she shut her eyes and sagged against the window, hearing again that noise. "Oh God, oh God!" she whispered, under her breath, seeing him jump, watching him fall, hearing that *sound* over and over like a short loop fixed instantly in her brain.

The door to her right opened. The engineer peered around the edge to look at her. His face was filled with horror and disbelief, glazed with perspiration, as he whispered, "You saw!"

She nodded, then covered her eyes with her hand, concentrating on not being sick. "We're gonna be here for a while," he said, placing his hand on her arm in a gesture of commiseration and fellow-feeling. "Damnedest thing, huh?" he murmured. "Goddamnedest thing."

Again she nodded, keeping her eyes concealed.

He swore softly, almost reverently, under his breath, then ducked back into his compartment.

She could hear people talking, speculating on why the train had stopped, but all she could see and hear was that man leaping from the platform and the snapping of his bones beneath the wheels. Images of Erik kept getting mixed in with that recurring scene. She'd push one away, the other would come back. "God God!" she whispered. What would make someone so miserable, so desperate for an end, that he'd wait at the end of a platform for a train that was already late, in order to put a stop to his life in such a hideous and violent fashion? Her shoulders turned inward. The sound of it! The nightmare *sound*. And the look of determination on his face as he'd taken flight from the platform. *Why?* Had he set off intending to go to his job in the city and decided upon arriving at the station that there was no point to living anymore? He'd shaved that morning, dressed himself with care; he'd put on a clean shirt and carefully knotted his tie, all for the purpose of ending his life. He had to have felt the pain, the unthinkable agony on impact; the severing of his limbs . . . She winced, shivering, her ears hurting from the looping sound track, her eyes unable to shut out the inescapable visuals. She'd see it and hear it for the rest of her life. She'd feel her body pressing forward, her mouth opening to cry out as a stranger's life ended inches away from her. She'd wanted to stop him; she'd put her hands out instinctively to stop him; she'd cried out to stop him. But he'd jumped.

She wiped her face with unsteady hands and stood with her back to the other passengers, partially concealed by the open door to the engineer's compartment. More than anything, she wanted to get off this train. But her car was parked back at the station. The clients were waiting in Manhattan, and she wasn't going to make it. The train might be stopped here for hours while the police investigation got underway and statements were taken. The clients wouldn't know what had happened to her. They'd call the house when it got past the scheduled meeting time. And Erik would be frantic, because everyone believed she was driving into the city. But she'd decided to take the train, this one time, something she rarely did, and now a man was dead, and her eyes were filled with the image of his blank eyes and his grimly set mouth and his determined look as he threw himself out in front of her—an instant of concussion when he'd been held like a magnet on the other side of the glass, and her hands had tried to keep him safely in place there—and then he was gone. Why did Erik keep sliding between these images, confusing and alarming her, tricking her into feeling somehow that it was Erik who'd surrendered his life, Erik who'd lost his urge to live, Erik who'd gone from her?

"Are you all right?" someone asked.

She'd lied; she'd had every opportunity to tell the truth, but she hadn't. She'd dishonored both of them. If he never forgave her he'd be well within his rights. She knew his feelings on the matter; knew his feelings on all matters; knew how readily he was moved to tears and how this fact distressed him because he viewed tears as a sign of weakness.

"Are you all right?"

She opened her eyes, but couldn't speak. Just then a voice came over the Public Address system to say, "Uhm, ladies and gentlemen, we're sorry to say this train is going to be delayed indefinitely. We uhm . . . Unfortunately someone jumped in front of the train. We'll keep you posted."

Shocked murmurs raced through the car, strangers turning toward one another to comment. Some stayed concealed behind their *New York Times*, or paid especially close attention to their paperback novels or magazines, or the crossword puzzles they were having trouble working.

"Sit down here," the voice said, and at last she looked to see who was expressing such concern.

The voice belonged to a tall man in his late thirties, with the most beautiful face she'd ever seen. His hair was thick and Scandinavian blond; his eyes were the same shifting blue-green as sea water; his features were so perfect they might have been sculpted from the finest Italian marble; the planes and dimensions of nose, cheekbones, mouth and jaw were the living embodiment of clean-lined symmetry.

"Take my seat," he told her. "Sit down. You've had a hell of a shock." His hands propelled her into his aisle seat. Then he squatted in the aisle at her side, saying, "You look as if you're going to faint. Better put your head down."

She did as he said, grateful to have someone take charge. But the instant she closed her eyes and lowered her head, it all happened again, and she began to quake, trying to push away the images by shaking her head free of them. *Why* hadn't she told Erik the truth? What was wrong with her?

The man in the aisle didn't say anything more for a time, but remained by her side with his hand over the back of her neck, keeping her head down. She felt alternatingly cold, then hot; she had to keep swallowing the bitter fluid that filled her mouth. She held her hands together over the handbag in her lap while she tried not to see or hear. Perhaps ten minutes later one of the doors slid open and a uniformed Metro North officer climbed into the car, followed by a Port Chester policeman.

The two spoke first in undertones to the engineer, then wanted to talk to Risa, seeking confirmation of the engineer's report. She was able to lift her head and answer their questions in a barely audible whisper. "He was waiting at the end of the platform. I thought it was odd that he was standing alone so far away from everyone else. As we got to the end of the platform, he threw out his arms"—She had to stop to catch her breath, gasping for air. "He threw out his arms, and he jumped. *He jumped.*" She shook her head again, trying to escape that dismembering sound.

The officers apologetically asked for her name, address, and telephone number, and she recited them mechanically. It didn't occur to her to open her bag and give them one of the business cards Erik had made up for her. She could scarcely think, but concentrated on answering their questions. At last, they solemnly thanked her, said they were very sorry, and left the train.

For an hour and ten minutes the train sat on the track while officials climbed on and off, and several of the conductors came through to talk to the engineer who, at one point, declared in a voice shot with distress, "I told them I wouldn't move this train until the local police give their okay, and that's the way it's gonna be." His eyes were round with shock, his skin waxy.

At last another announcement was made. "Ladies and gentlemen, we apologize again for this unfortunate delay. We're going to back the train up to the station, where you'll be able to leave through the rear carriage. For those of you continuing on to Grand Central, there's another train waiting."

"It's going to take a while for all these people to get off," her companion told Risa as he got to his feet, his hand on her shoulder keeping her in the seat. The other passengers began folding their newspapers, closing their books and magazines, preparing to disembark. There was talk about missed meetings, and of forgetting about going into the city altogether because the day was blown, but little or no mention of the reason for this unscheduled stop.

"They don't care," Risa said, looking up at the man who'd befriended her. "They're pretending it didn't happen."

"They don't know what else to do," he said, "so they're doing ordinary things to make themselves feel better."

People left their seats and began crowding into the aisles, anxious to get off the train. The man who'd been sitting beside Risa said, " 'Scuse me," and climbed past her to join the crowd in the aisle. Risa moved over to make room, and her companion sat down.

He said, "I heard you give them your name. I'm Stefan. It's too ironic, you know. I never take the train, but I had to come into town today for a meeting and to pick up my car."

"I hardly ever take the train either," she said dully. "And I've missed a very important meeting."

"Luckily," he said, "mine's not until two-thirty."

Erik would be so terribly worried. He was fearful every time she set off in the car to go anywhere; he worried if she was merely out of his sight. No matter what else he might be doing, he was always thinking about her, wondering about her, living his life through her, tormented by the idea that some misfortune might befall her. Was this why she kept seeing him leap from the platform instead of that other man, the one in the gray pinstripe suit? She knew that at that very moment Erik would be pacing back and forth in the office, or the bedroom, or in the music room, fretting over her failure to show up at the meeting. His big body shoving the air aside, his hands sending their silent cries into the atmosphere, he'd be barely breathing as he enumerated his fears, as he anxiously contemplated any harm coming to her. All at once she felt suffocated by the sheer enormity of her obligation to him. She was back to being the specimen on the slide beneath the microscope, with not one but three sets of eyes examining her. Hal would've been the one to take the call from the client. And after telling Erik that she hadn't shown up, Hal would immediately phone Kitty to let her know, too. God! She had to get to a telephone and let them know she was okay to free herself from the claustrophobic sense she had of being too closely watched—especially now when she was so guilty of dishonesty.

"They'll understand when you explain why you're late," Stefan was saying when she tuned back in to him.

"I'll have to call the client from the station, tell him I'm on my way." The client would then call the house and Erik would know everything was all right. Except that nothing was all right. She felt as if she were coming apart, small pieces of her falling on all sides every time she made the slightest move.

Stefan laughed, drawing her attention back to him. "They'll be lined up from here to next Saturday waiting to use the platform pay phones. You'll do just as well to call from Grand Central. Otherwise, you'll miss the train that's waiting."

"Yes," she agreed, her face contorting as it all rushed back at her again. Her stomach was lurching; her hands were cold and stiff, her fingers rigid like frost-bitten twigs. She looked down at her hands, recoiling from the sight of them.

Finally there was movement as the other passengers began filing out through the far door of the car. She got up to go. Stefan hurried after her, saying, "Hey! You've forgotten this!" and she turned to see him holding her portfolio.

She thanked him and started off again. He came right along behind her, saying, "I think you need someone to look after you today."

She had nothing to say to that, but doggedly kept going forward, absently noticing the empty coffee containers and abandoned newspapers littering the floor. She stepped from the air-conditioned train into the stupefying heat of the platform, her feet and legs moving with their own impetus, taking her through the crowd. Then, without thinking, she glanced to her right, only to see the body on the tracks; part of it concealed by a gray blanket, a severed arm not quite covered by a piece of cardboard.

She gasped and averted her eyes, holding her right hand like a blinder to shield her from the grisly sight, staggering as, yet again, she saw the man fly from the platform, and she heard that sickening sound.

"Come on." Stefan took her arm to lead her onto the ramp that had been set up to allow passengers to board the train on the outside track. "In here." He directed her to a seat in the first car.

She leaned heavily against the sun-warmed window, closed her eyes and hid them with her hand. A bunch of reckless children in a souped-up car had murdered poor Willie. She'd held him in her arms while his life had drained away, pouring out in sticky streams over her chest and arms. She'd five times made love with her husband without benefit of protection, and had failed to inform him of this fact. Something that might seem inconsequential to anyone else but which, to her husband, would constitute an immense transgression. And now! Now, a desperate man had chosen to end his life in the most hideous possible way. How badly he'd wanted to die! How he had to have lusted after it—just as she'd lusted after Erik's engorged flesh. That wretched man had so yearned for his death; he'd courted and wooed it like a lover. He'd wanted to be absolutely certain there was no possibility of surviving. And he'd succeeded.

She pictured a cruiser pulling into the driveway of a pleasant-looking house; she saw two officers climbing from the car and going up the walk to knock at the door. The door opened and a smiling woman stared inquisitively at those two young men, wondering what on earth they could want. Perhaps they were collecting for the Benevolent Association, or selling tickets to some raffle. And they had to tell her then, stumbling over the words, that her husband was strewn in pieces all over the tracks at the Port Chester station, where an assembly of ghouls stood gaping down at his remains. The woman shrank, her hands flying up as if to fend off this unbelievable tale delivered by two strangers. Then she went past denial into belief, on to horror at the knowledge that the man she'd lived with, likely for some years, had secretly harbored an immense and terrible love for something other than her or their children. He'd had an ongoing, clandestine date with death. Was it because of something she'd said or done, or failed to say or do? She'd probably never know. She'd live out her life periodically tortured by questions to which there could be no answers.

And there sat Risa, with the blazing sun beating in on her through the glass, on her way to an already late meeting in the city. There she sat with Erik's seeds swimming inside her receptive body, while she had an appointment already made for voluntary neutering. Willie was dead; a man lay dismembered on the tracks. Were these omens? Was there something she was failing to see? She glanced at her watch, her eyes widening. It wasn't running. It had stopped at 11:07, the precise time that profoundly despondent man had stepped out into space.

"My watch stopped," she said with fear, looking into the sea-water eyes of the man beside her. "It stopped at the precise moment it happened."

"No kidding!" He took hold of her wrist, looked at the face of the watch, then tapped it with his finger. At once, the second hand began its sweep around the numerals. She looked at the watch, then at his finger, and finally at the man. How had he done that? Was this, too, an omen?

"Look," he said. "Why don't you let me give you a ride back from the city? You'll go to your meeting; I'll go to mine. Then I'll grab a cab uptown to the garage, pick up the car, and meet you wherever you like."

"That's very kind of you," she said, intrigued by the way his lips moved when he spoke. It was like seeing a painting come to life, a work by some massively talented Old Master. "I don't think I'd be able to ride the train again today."

"Okay, then." He smiled and showed her his even white teeth. "Tell me where and when."

She couldn't think, and looked again at her watch.

"You'd better set that to the correct time," he told her, and consulted his own watch. "It's twelve-forty now."

"Twelve-forty," she repeated, and adjusted the Piaget wristwatch Erik had given her one Christmas; she couldn't recall what year. When had it been? God! Why couldn't she remember?

"Now, where and when?" he prompted.

"Yes. Four o'clock? I should be finished by then, if I can reschedule the meeting. Where?" *Why* couldn't she think? "At Grand Central?" she asked, unable to come up with anyplace else. "At the driveway on Vanderbilt?"

"Fine. I'll be there at four."

"It's very kind of you," she said again, drawn once more to look at his remarkable blue-green eyes and at his well-shaped mouth, which was, for some reason, smiling at her.

"That was the client," Raskin said. "Risa didn't show up for the meeting."

Erik slowly turned, putting down his pencil.

"They were wondering if there'd been some change of plans," Raskin went on.

"But she left here at twenty past ten. She couldn't possibly have been caught in a traffic jam for more than two and a half hours."

"I'll make a few calls, see if I can find out anything."

Erik turned back to his drafting table. There was a low humming in his ears, and his hands were writhing about together on the table in front of him. He prayed nothing had happened to her. Please, let her be safe! He stared at his anguished hands while, behind him, Raskin called the state police.

Twenty-six

S HE FLEW FROM THE TRAIN, THE PORTFOLIO SNUGLY TUCKED UNDER her arm. She'd go directly to the client's office, not stop to call. She didn't want to waste any more time. She was an hour and fifty minutes late, but perhaps the client would still be there. If he wasn't, she'd explain to someone on his staff, and then ask to use a telephone to call home and talk to Erik.

At the receptionist's desk, breathless and soaked through with perspiration, she said, "I'm Marisa D'Anton. I had an appointment at twelve, but I took the train this morning, and someone jumped in front of it. We sat on the track for over an hour. There was no way I could let you know. Is it still possible to see Mr. Simmonds?"

"You poor dear!" the receptionist said. "That's awful! Let me call through and see."

Risa paced back and forth in front of the desk, the air-conditioning raising goose bumps on her wet skin.

"You're in luck," the receptionist told her. "He'll see you in a few minutes."

"Thank you. D'you think I could use this phone?" Risa asked of the extension in the waiting area.

"Sure. Just dial 9 for an outside line."

"It's long distance, but I'll use my credit card."

"No problem."

She sat on the edge of the sofa and picked up the phone.

"It's me," she said when Raskin answered. "I've only got a minute."

"Hold on," he said, picking up on her urgency.

Erik came on, asking, "Marisa, what's happened?"

"I decided at the last minute to take the train, not bother with the car. Erik," she lowered her voice, cradling the receiver with both hands, "I was standing right at the front and as we were going through the station, a man jumped. It was so awful."

"You *saw* it?"

"Everything. I can't talk now. I'm at the client's. He's going to see me in a minute. I know you were worried and I'm sorry. I'll be home late. We'll talk then. I have to go now." She hung up as a secretary came over to show her into Simmonds' office.

"I'm terribly sorry about this," she told the woman, following her down the carpeted corridor.

Simmonds looked angry.

Risa went directly over to him with her hand out, saying, "I am most terribly sorry, Mr. Simmonds. I took the train, and as we were going through Port Chester a man threw himself in front of it."

Simmonds was at once sympathetic. "Please get Mrs. D'Anton a drink," he told his secretary. "Some brandy, I think. Do, please, sit down. You actually saw it?" he asked, echoing Erik.

She nodded, wondering if she looked as decimated as she felt. "There was no way to contact you. I do apologize. I know how valuable your time is, and I have everything prepared."

"Just relax a minute. You'll have your drink, then I'll get Trudy to order some lunch. As luck would have it, my afternoon's free. I've got plenty of time to see the renderings. Christ! What a thing to have happen."

"I keep hearing it," she confided. "It was the most nightmarish sound."

Trudy brought Risa a large glass with a fair amount of brandy and gave it to her with a kind smile.

"Trudy, be a sweetheart and order something up from the dining room for Mrs. D'Anton."

"Certainly," said Trudy and went off to her outer office.

Risa took a sip of the brandy. At once she felt the burn of the alcohol, then its spreading warmth. "Thank you," she said to Simmonds. "That helps." The man was watching her closely, as if he could see she might disintegrate in front of him. "I'll be all right. It was just such a . . ." She couldn't finish. She didn't know how to describe the effects on her of the suicide; she wasn't even sure she knew what they were. Primarily, she felt disengaged and at a distance from everyone and everything. An image flashed before her of that sprawled mutilated form on the tracks and she shook her head, pushing the image away as she reached for the portfolio.

"Erik's very excited about this," she said. "We hope you will be, too."

Somehow she got through the presentation. Halfway into her description of the ways in which Erik planned to use the acreage, Trudy returned with a tray, which she put down on the coffee table. Risa dared not look at it; if she so much as smelled food she knew she'd be sick. Instead, she sipped away at the brandy and accepted one of Mr. Simmonds' cigarettes, glad to have something to do with her hands.

Simmonds loved the design, had no immediate qualms, felt the budget was definitely in line, and wanted, if that would be acceptable, to study the drawings and figures for a few days before contacting Erik with his final decision.

She said, "Of course," and got to her feet, again offering her hand. "I very much appreciate your understanding, and I'm sorry to have upset your schedule."

"Not at all," he said jovially. "*I'm* sorry you had such an unpleasant start to your day. I like the proposal very much. Please tell Erik that. And I'll be in touch shortly."

Carrying the empty portfolio, leaving behind the untouched tray of food, she left the office and got all the way to the lobby before she thought to consult her watch. Three-ten. She had almost an hour before she was to meet Stefan at Grand Central. It was far too hot for window-shopping. She definitely wasn't hungry. Another drink would be one too many. What could she do? She had an hour to kill. What was nearby? Saks. She'd wander around the store for a while. It'd be cool. And the air on the main floor was always pleasantly perfumed. She'd walk up and down the aisles and look at pretty things until it was time to go to the station.

"What happened?" Raskin wanted to know.

"Marisa took the train. She saw a man commit suicide."

"Shit! How did she sound?"

"Very upset, as one would expect."

"I'd better call Kitty, let her know everything's all right."

"Yes," Erik agreed, somewhat dazed with relief. His imagination had painted a series of pictures so bleakly detailed that their abrupt departure left him gazing inward at a glaringly blank screen. He lit a cigarette and leaned over the table, exhaling with slow gratitude. How truly frightful for Marisa to have been a witness to such a thing! She'd sounded shattered. He hoped she'd take some time after the meeting with Simmonds to do something to take her mind off the event, perhaps see a film— which she sometimes did on her afternoons in the city—or go shopping, buy something frivolous and completely removed from the horror of the morning.

Raskin completed his call to Kitty, and Erik said, "I think perhaps I'll drive over later to meet her. I don't expect she'll stay late in the city."

"Hold on a minute," Raskin said. "I've got a schedule here." He looked it over and said, "Peak trains come in at 4:59, 5:33, 5:54, 6:26, 7:09, and 7:24. She might be planning to take any one of those," Raskin said. "You could be hanging around the station for up to two and a half hours."

Erik consulted his watch. "She said she'd be late. Usually, she's back on the 3:07 out of the city when she takes the train. So I wouldn't think she'd come much before 5:54. But just in case, I'll be there to meet the one that gets in at 5:33."

"I don't mind going," Raskin offered, knowing how apprehensive Erik had to have been to be volunteering now to wait at the station.

"I'll go," Erik said decisively. "She'll be glad not to have to drive home alone."

"Okay," Raskin backed off. "Whatever you think's best."

At five-fifteen, Erik got into the Rolls and drove to the station. He found a parking place opposite the platform and backed in between a van on one side and a large station wagon on the other. From there, he'd have a clear view of the trains as they pulled in, as well as of the arriving passengers. He could also see Risa's car down at the far end of the lot. He planned to sit in the car until he saw her on the platform, then he'd get out and go across the lot to surprise her.

To have the benefit of the air-conditioning, he kept the motor running and sat back to wait with a cigarette.

At 5:35, two minutes off schedule, a train pulled in. Quickly stubbing out his second cigarette, he scanned the people on the platform. No Marisa. The platform cleared quickly. He sat back again, tuning in WJAZ in Stamford. Coltrane. Good.

At 5:58, four minutes off schedule, the next train arrived. He switched off the radio, opened the car door and stood looking up and down the platform. No Marisa. He got back into the car and turned the radio back on. Woody Herman. Not bad.

At 6:12, a white late-model Mercedes cruised into the lot. A man was driving. And in the passenger seat Marisa was pointing toward the end of the lot. Ducking down, Erik watched the car go to the far end and stop. He didn't move, except to turn his head to watch.

The two sat in the car for a few minutes, talking. Then Marisa got out carrying her portfolio and a Saks shopping bag and went over to the SL. While she busied herself opening the door, Erik put the Rolls into gear and drove directly out of the lot, racing toward home. His hands gripped the wheel so hard his arms ached. Upon arriving at the house, he went directly to the music room and bolted the door.

Raskin, on his way down from the office, saw Erik sail through the front door alone and head directly for the basement stairs. Where was Risa? Raskin wondered, opening the door to look out. The Rolls sat alone at the top of the driveway.

* * *

Erik dropped down on one of the black chairs and sat with his head in his hands for several moments. Then he got up and walked across the room, stopping a foot or so away from the piano. His hands plucked at his trousers, at the lapels of his jacket, and, finally, at the mask. He removed it and allowed his fists to grind into his eyes. Then he went back and sat on the chair in the dark with his head in his hands. He sat motionless, yet he was sliding down a long chute, a tunnel of total darkness, slippery-sided and miles long; his descent was so rapid and so prolonged that the air howled against his ears and his hands flailed uselessly, searching for something to catch on to, something that might slow this sickening downward plunge.

As she was running along Forty-ninth Street, ten minutes late, she realized she was a little drunk from the brandy she'd had in Simmonds' office. Things seemed to spin outward from her field of vision, so that everything she saw was distorted, as if viewed through a fish-eye lens. Running in the high heels she'd never have worn if she'd known she was going to take the train and therefore do a lot of walking, she felt as if she were caught inside something with the transparency and density of a paperweight. She was hurrying toward a meeting with a man she didn't know. If she slowed down and let more minutes get away, he'd give up and be gone by the time she got to the station. But she'd agreed, she'd said she'd be there. And meeting him meant she wouldn't have to ride another train today.

He was waiting and with a welcoming smile he leaned over to open the passenger door as she came running up. Apologies spilling from her lips, struggling to get herself and her things in the car, she had the strange idea that she'd been catapulted into another universe, a world that somehow traveled parallel to the one she'd always known, but one in which everyone—everything—was just the slightest bit skewed.

The cool interior of the car was shocking after the intense heat outside. It took her some moments to settle, while Stefan pulled out into the traffic and started across town. He didn't remind her to do up her seat belt —something Erik always did automatically—and it wasn't until they were crossing Second Avenue on Forty-second Street that she remembered to do it, experiencing a guilty pang as she fitted the two parts of the belt together. She hadn't said a word about this man to Erik; she'd omitted him altogether from her cursory explanation of this morning's events. Erik would assume she was planning to come home on the train. And she'd told him she'd be late. He knew she didn't like staying alone in the city after dark. That meant he expected her to be no later than nine, which was when the 8:07 got to Darien. He'd be waiting at home to hear her relate the full story of her day, and to comfort her if she required it. But his instinct to comfort her would evaporate altogether if she told him about the IUD and how she'd dishonestly made love with him for the past several days. God! Her head ached.

It occurred to her that the reason things seemed so off-kilter was because, by the standards of life she'd been living since she was sixteen, they were. She and Erik scarcely lived what could even remotely be considered a normal life. She was married to a man who found it impossible to do something as mundane as meeting her in the late afternoon outside a railroad station. For Erik this would be a major, and alarming, event. For Stefan, it was not in the least unusual and certainly in no way menacing. She'd lost touch with the everyday things other people did.

Stefan asked how her day had gone. "I hope it improved after the bad start this morning."

"Things worked out," she answered, turning to look at him. He was incredibly handsome. "This is very kind of you."

"So you keep telling me." He smiled over at her, his right hand fiddling with the radio until he found a station to his liking. Nondescript music poured from the speakers and he quickly lowered the volume. "Relax and enjoy the ride," he told her. "It's all over now, and you're on your way home."

"I do appreciate it," she said unnecessarily, and looked out at the cars keeping pace with them as they bounced over the rutted surface of the FDR Drive. It had taken them nearly an hour to get this far in the rush-hour traffic.

"What was your meeting?" he asked after a time. "Are you in business?"

"I had to make an architectural presentation."

"Oh!" His eyebrows lifted; he was all set to be impressed. "You're an architect?"

"No, I'm a draftsman." She would not and could not bring Erik into the conversation. It felt wrong to discuss him—even obliquely—with a stranger. "It worked out fine. What do you do?" she asked to deflect the conversation away from her private life.

"This and that," he said casually. "Marketing, for the most part. I'm on my own, do consulting work out of my house mainly."

They were both folding the truth into origami figures, she thought, relieved. She could keep the whole truth safely to herself, and she didn't particularly care if this man chose to do the same. After all, he was just someone she'd encountered on the train who'd opted to be concerned about her. He was easy to be with, though, and she was glad of that. She went quiet, and he allowed the silence to hold for quite some time.

"You left your car at the station, didn't you?" he asked as they were approaching Greenwich. They were now running into local rush-hour traffic.

"That's right, I did. But you can drop me anywhere in town and I'll walk over." She'd never dreamed it would take almost two hours to drive home.

"Don't be silly. It's no problem to take you to your car."

"Thank you very much," she said politely, thinking she sounded like a child out with some grown-up family friend, and wishing they could go faster.

"Would you have dinner with me?" he asked as they left the turnpike at the Darien exit.

It threw her. "Oh, I don't think so." She sat up straighter.

"Why not?" he asked pleasantly.

She couldn't think of a reason. She knew she should've been able to come up with dozens of them right off the top of her head, but all she could think was how nice he'd been. She didn't feel claustrophobic in his company; there was no need to explain her every thought and deed. And he'd been there this morning; he knew what she'd seen and how she felt about it. "I don't think it would be a good idea," she said lamely.

"I think it would be a terrific idea," he disagreed. "Let's say tomorrow night. Give you a chance to recover from today," he said as he made a turn before the railroad underpass, and drove into the station lot.

"My car's at the far end," she pointed. "The red sports coupe."

When he pulled up behind her, he reached into his pocket for a business card and a pen, to write his home address and telephone number on the back. "Let's say seven tomorrow," he said, giving her the card. "I'm a good cook. I'll fix something you'll like."

Doubtfully, she glanced at what he'd written. "I really don't . . ."

"I'll be very disappointed if you don't come." He gave her a coaxing smile.

"Yes, well, thank you again for the ride." She got the door open, climbed out, then opened the rear door to get the portfolio and the Saks bag from the back seat.

"Tomorrow at seven," he said, before she closed the door. And smiled again at her.

She hoped he wouldn't be too disappointed when she didn't show up, she thought as she fumbled in her bag for the car keys, then climbed into the SL. The car's interior was almost molten from an entire day's baking in the sun. She put the air conditioner on full blast, then started toward home, driving slowly in order to organize her thoughts. She was going to have to tell Erik about the morning, and about the meeting with Simmonds, and about everything else she'd done. But she felt too drained—

seeing that man jump again, hearing the wheels crush him—and too upset to talk to anyone about anything.

She was surprised Erik wasn't in the living room or the kitchen. Whenever she was delayed, which wasn't often, he always remained close by the door waiting for her. But not this time. Raskin was nowhere to be seen either. For a few moments she stood expecting Willie to come bounding out from the kitchen, his ears flopping and tail waving with excitement. Then she remembered Willie was gone.

With a sigh, she looked at the mail Hal had left for her on the kitchen counter. A registered envelope from the French Consulate in New York. Their passports had finally been returned, after three weeks, with the French visas. Raskin had removed his and Erik's passports, leaving hers in the envelope. She put it in her purse, glanced at the several bills and left them on the counter to be dealt with later. The house was utterly quiet. Carrying the portfolio—she'd forgotten the Saks bag in the car—she stepped out of her shoes, picked them up, and went upstairs.

She left the portfolio on the landing before going into the den to get some fresh clothes. She badly needed a shower and, possibly, another drink. She didn't know if she'd be able to eat. What she most wanted was to get into bed in the air-conditioned darkness and go to sleep. No talking, no explaining, just oblivion.

She used the shower off the den, with the light on. She'd never fully mastered the art of bathing in the dark, although she did it without hesitation for Erik's sake. Since he often came in to keep her company and to chat while she was in the bath, she usually left the lights off. But there were times when she really wanted to see herself in the mirror while she brushed her hair or toweled it dry; times when she wanted to study her full-length reflection to take note of the changes in her body. And lately the changes were becoming more obvious. Somewhere along the line, she'd lost that scrawny look she'd thought she'd have for life. She only weighed four or five pounds more than she had at sixteen, but the distribution of her weight had altered once she'd reached her thirties and she thought she looked more rounded, even possibly somewhat excessively, especially on the undersides of her arms and her inner thighs. Erik laughed when she made observations like this, insisting she had absolutely no idea how she looked. She was, to his eyes, consummately beautiful. She had no flaws. And of course she had no wrinkles. She definitely didn't look her age. If anything, he insisted, she looked seven or eight years younger. "Twenty-six or -seven at most," he said regularly. "Certainly not a woman approaching the deathly age of thirty-five."

This evening she thought she looked closer to fifty. There were dark circles around her eyes and her mouth had a stern-looking set to it. She was standing with her shoulders drawn forward like an old crone. Throwing her shoulders back, she stared at herself, seeing clearly the signs of age: the softening of her jawline, faint lines fanning out from the corners of her eyes, and parenthetical ones around her mouth. She thought of Stefan, that impossibly handsome man and wondered why he'd been so insistent on having dinner with her. She'd been at her worst, sweaty and disheveled, upset and nonconversational. It had to be, she concluded, a further demonstration of his kindness and ongoing concern for her. He'd heard it, too, that horrendous *sound*. He'd mentioned that at some point on the train, although he'd only talked about her day during the ride back from the city. He hadn't actually spoken of his own reactions to the morning's suicide. He'd been deferential. Knowing it would distress her, he'd elected to steer clear of the subject.

When she came out of the bathroom, Erik was sitting in one of the armchairs, his hands spread over the arms, legs crossed. To anyone who didn't know him, he'd have appeared quite relaxed. But she knew better. He was coiled tight as a mainspring; his hands were the giveaway. They were positioned like birds of prey, hovering, ready at a moment's notice to fly off to a kill.

She stopped, looked at him and then over to the bed, where she'd laid out fresh underwear and a loose cotton dress. She said, "Hi," and went to the bed for her underwear.

"Would you care to tell me about it?" he asked softly, his hands delving into his jacket pocket for cigarettes and the Dunhill. He held these items while he waited for an answer.

"The train was absolutely packed, people standing everywhere. So I went to the front of the first car." She pulled on silk tap pants and a matching camisole. "It was fun, like being a kid again. My dad used to take me to the first car when we went by train into the city, so I could look out the window. I was thinking what a good idea it had been not to drive, how wonderfully clever I was. No sitting for ages stuck in traffic, no endless searching for a garage. And then it happened. He waited until we were right in front of him, and he jumped." She held her hands over her ears and closed her eyes.

"Dreadful," Erik said, and lit a cigarette. Holding the filter end between his teeth, he returned the pack and the lighter to his pocket, then removed the cigarette from his mouth. "How unfortunate for you to witness such a thing."

"It was the sound of it that bothers me the most," she told him, reaching for the dress. "I keep hearing it over and over." She stood holding the dress, looking at him. He was large, solid; a powerful shadow seated before the window. They weren't touching. There had never been a time when they'd been apart that they didn't touch upon being reunited. Still holding the dress, she walked over to where he was sitting and positioned herself in his lap. With a sigh, she rested her head against his shoulder and breathed in his scent. One arm went around her, but he turned his head to take another puff of his Sobranie. Something was wrong. She knew his gestures, his reflexes and automatic moves as well as she knew her own. She kissed his cheek. He accepted it but didn't respond.

"What's wrong, Erik?"

"Not a thing," came his uninflected whisper. "I had an uneventful day. You, on the other hand, have had a truly ghastly day, and I am sorry for that."

"You seem angry with me about something." She sat away from his shoulder.

Not angry, he thought. Terror-stricken would have been a more accurate assessment. "No," he lied. "Not at all. I can't begin to imagine how you must feel having seen such a terrible thing."

"I can't begin to tell you," she said, remaining on his lap for another moment, waiting for his touch. If he embraced her, if he drew her close, she'd tell him how she'd allowed him to make love to her as if there were no risk when all the time she'd been as dangerously activated as a mine field. He drew again on his cigarette, then put it out. She got up and stepped into the dress, feeling chilled. Tell him! she told herself. Tell him about the doctor, about Stefan! Clear the air and tell him everything! She opened her mouth, prepared to do just that, when he suddenly rose from the chair and she thought arbitrarily he was the same height as Stefan, but of a considerably sturdier build. He was quite a bit older than Stefan, too, and of infinitely greater consequence. *Tell him!*

"I have some work still to do," he said, standing close to her for a moment.

She put her hand on his arm, willing the words to come, but he said, "I'll leave you to rest for a bit. I expect you're quite worn out. We'll have a late dinner." And then she was alone, slowly breathing in the fragrance he'd left behind of tobacco and of cologne with an underlying essence of sandalwood.

Twenty-seven

IMMEDIATELY AFTER DINNER, ERIK CLAIMED HE HAD MORE WORK TO DO, excused himself and returned to the office. Risa sat on at the table while Hal began clearing the dishes. There'd scarcely been any conversation during the meal. Risa had described the suicide from beginning to end, feeling no more eased by the repetition. Both Erik and Hal had listened closely, with rightful expressions of horror. Risa kept looking at Erik, but he'd seemed unwilling, for some reason, to meet her eyes.

While he was loading the dishwasher, Hal asked, "Have you talked to Kitty yet?"

"No. Why?"

"Why don't you give her a call?" he suggested. "We were all pretty worried about you today. I mean, I've filled her in vaguely, but I think she'd like to hear from you."

"I thought I'd leave it until the morning."

"Call now," he said.

"You're treating me like a child."

"Of course I'm not. I'm just saying I think you should talk to her now."

"All right," she sighed, and got up to bring the extension over to the table.

"How are you?" Kitty sounded very concerned.

"Exhausted and upset."

"Why don't you come over and talk with me awhile?" Kitty invited. "Have a drink and tell me about it."

Risa looked over at Hal who was wiping the countertop with a sponge, and said, "Okay. I'll be there in a few minutes."

She put the receiver down, her eyes still on Hal, who had his finger on the dishwasher button. He'd been waiting for her to finish her call before starting the machine. "What's going on?" she asked quietly.

"What d'you mean, what's going on? Nothing's going on."

"No," she said. "I may be the one on the slide, but I've got eyes, too. I can see everyone looking through the microscope at me."

"Pardon?" Raskin looked bewildered.

"Nothing. Never mind. I'm going to see Kitty. I won't be too long. Will you tell Erik?"

"I'll tell him."

"Okay. Thanks."

Picking up her keys, she went out to the car in the still overhot air.

"You want a drink?" Kitty asked, leading the way into the living room.

"I don't think I should. It'll put me into a coma."

"C'mon, sit down," Kitty said, dropping into Cameron's old chair.

Kitty hadn't changed a thing in the house since Cameron's death. The furniture looked shabby, the carpets were wearing out. The place was immaculate, though. And Kitty looked better than ever. Her face had thinned with age, so that her bone structure was more obvious, and her eyes seemed even larger. She still wore her high heels, and manicured her nails once a week. Nowadays, she wore her hair in a twist at the back of her neck, and it suited her, made her seem taller.

"So," Kitty said. "What's happenin'?"

"Hal told you about the suicide."

Kitty nodded.

"I can't stop thinking about it. I feel as if I'm going to be seeing and hearing it for the rest of my life."

"It'll fade in time. Tell me what's goin' on, Risa."

"I don't know what you mean."

"There's things you're not tellin'."

Guiltily, Risa stared at her. "What things?"

"I don't know. That's how come I'm askin'." Kitty kept her eyes on Risa's, waiting. Hal had telephoned her earlier to tell her how Erik had gone to the station to meet Risa, and that he'd returned home alone to lock himself into the music room. He'd only have done that if he'd seen or heard something to distress him. Obviously, Risa was unaware Erik had gone to the station to meet her.

"I have absolutely no idea what you're talking about," Risa insisted.

Kitty picked up her drink and downed half of it in one swallow before plonking the glass back on the table. "Talk to me, Reese," she begged.

"About what?"

"About what is goin' on."

"Nothing. Is. Going. On," Risa said strongly.

"Reese, you're the worst liar who ever lived. You have absolutely no talent for it. It's written all over you that you're lyin'. And I'd like to point out that if I can see it, so can Erik."

Risa wanted to scream. They were *all* doing it to her; the three of them scrutinizing her every word and move. "I haven't lied about a thing," she said, knowing whatever she said to Kitty would be communicated back to Hal, who without doubt, would report it to Erik.

"Okay," Kitty said. "Then you're *omittin'*. What's goin' on you're not admittin' to?"

"Jesus Christ!" Risa exploded. "A man kills himself right in front of me and I come back to abuse? I simply don't *believe* this!"

"Tell me what else happened." Kitty lowered her voice. "There's more and I know it. Sure as God I know it."

"Sure as God?" Risa gave a small unpleasant laugh. "Since when are you omniscient, Kitty? All-seeing, all-hearing, omniscient Kitty! I'm going home to bed. I'm tired and I'm not in the mood for an inquisition."

Kitty followed Risa to the door where she stopped her, her hand on Risa's arm. "I know I'm right," she said sadly. "Whatever it is, please don't do it. You'll destroy everything. You don't know enough about the world to play its games, Reese. You've spent your whole life sheltered from the harder truths the rest of us've had to live with. You're a baby when it comes to what's out there." She indicated the front door and what lay beyond it. "Don't be foolish, girl. You can't deal with a world you've only visited part-time. There are people here who know you and love you. Don't put it all at risk."

"Kitty, you're imagining things. And you're forgetting that I love you, too."

Kitty released Risa's arm, saying, "If you knew how badly I want to believe you. If you could know how it feels standin' on the outside. It's the same as your bein' at the front of that train and seein' that man jump. Only for me, it's more like standin' behind barbed wire watchin' you runnin' toward the edge of the world."

"It's been a long bad day and we're all tired." Risa gave Kitty a kiss. "We'll talk tomorrow and everything'll be fine. There's nothing going on, so stop fussing."

Kitty stood at the door, watching her get into the car and drive away. At last, she closed the door and went to call Hal, to say, "I'm even more worried now. She's holdin' somethin' back, somethin' important."

"Leave her be," Hal counseled. "Things'll settle down."

"Not this time, Harold," she predicted. "This time it's serious. And you know it just as surely as I do."

Risa waited until midnight for Erik to come to bed. Then she pulled on her robe and went up to the office to get him. She opened the door to see him sitting at his drafting table with his head in his hands and the work light out.

"Come to bed, Erik." She went over to put her arms around him from behind.

"I still have work to do," he said, his back unyielding. "Go ahead. I'll be down shortly."

"I want you to come with me."

He sighed and sat up, the movement forcing her to release him. He reached for the mask and fitted it on before turning to face her, taking hold of her hands. He tried to get himself to speak, but couldn't, and instead felt beneath his fingers the long bones of her hands and the pads of flesh at her palms and the tips of her fingers. He willed her to speak to him, to identify for him the man in the white Mercedes, to explain her being with him. Tell me! he pleaded mutely. When she merely stood watching him, he bent his face into her hands and remained that way for a long moment before straightening. "Go to bed, Marisa," he said. "I'll join you soon."

"All right," she agreed, too exhausted to argue. She pulled her hands slowly from his, then turned and left him.

The instant she was gone, he wrapped his arms around his chest and began to rock back and forth over the pain.

Throughout the next day she debated telephoning Stefan to say she wouldn't be coming, he shouldn't expect her or go to any trouble preparing a meal. As she stuffed clothes into the washer, as she absently wiped down the countertops, as she went downstairs to shift the wet clothes from the washer to the dryer before going back up to the kitchen to make a fresh pot of coffee, she deliberated.

Erik hadn't come to bed at all. She'd awakened in the morning to find his side of the bed undisturbed. And when she'd gone searching through the house for him, he was nowhere to be found. Hal had only said, "He can't have gone far. Both cars are still here."

"But where is he?" she asked.

Hal simply shrugged.

The music room was empty. So was the office. Where had he gone? Why was he hiding from her? He'd never before done anything like this, and it both angered and disturbed her. Just when she'd geared herself to the point where she was ready to tell him everything, he went into hiding. Nothing made sense.

Without consciously deciding, she went upstairs at five-thirty and laid out the clothes she'd wear that evening: a simple short black skirt, a smart black Emmanuelle Kahn top, and suitable lingerie. Then she closed herself into the bathroom and locked the door, fully expecting Erik to be there when she emerged. But he wasn't. Now even angrier, she marched over to flip on the ceiling light in the den before getting dressed. She returned to the bathroom to put a bit of concealing cream under her eyes and some color along her cheekbones, some lipstick and mascara, and she was done. She was about to leave when she went back to the dresser for her mother's tortoise-shell combs. She pushed her hair behind her ears, jammed in the combs, turned off the light and went downstairs to the kitchen for her purse and keys.

Hal was at the stove pouring a cup of coffee.

"If and when Erik decides to reappear, tell him I'm going to the movies in Greenwich. I need to get out for a few hours." With that, she snatched up her bag and the keys and left. She'd been through one of the worst weeks of her life, what with Willie's death, and the IUD business, the suicide, and then the disagreement with Kitty. On top of that she'd had a night when her sleep was haunted by images of men leaping before fast-moving trains. And if all that weren't enough, Erik had decided to cut himself off from her, hiding out somewhere. Everyone was behaving as if she'd done something of truly heinous dimensions. Her claustrophobia had reached unbearable proportions. She simply had to get away and spend a few pleasant hours with someone who understood what she'd been through and who was sympathetic, not to mention plainly eager for her company.

As she drove off, Erik sat up from behind the wheel of the Lamborghini and turned the key in the ignition. He waited until she reached the main road, then put the car in gear and followed, staying well behind. Over the intercom he'd heard her tell Hal she was going to the movies in Greenwich, and he hoped to God she'd been telling the truth. He promised himself that if she took the on ramp to the turnpike, he'd turn around and go home. But she drove right past it, heading through town. He amended his promise: If she got on the Merritt, he'd follow, and if she took one of the Greenwich exits, he'd turn around and go home. But she drove past the Merritt Parkway entrance on Route 124, heading into New Canaan.

She took a right turn before the center of town and he followed. She slowed, obviously looking for a number on the mailboxes, and he held back. When her indicator showed she was about to make a turn into one of the driveways, he pulled over, left the car running, jumped out, and ran through the bushes to where he'd have a clear view of her destination. She parked, got out, went to the front door of an unprepossessing ranch house, and rang the bell. After a moment, the door opened and the man Erik recognized from the white Mercedes in the parking lot stepped out, took Marisa's hand, kissed her on each cheek, then led her inside.

His heart racketing noisily, the breath leaving his mouth in a steady low whine, Erik tore back to the car, reversed into the nearest driveway, and shot off at top speed back toward Darien. His hands opened and closed in a death grip on the steering wheel and the gear shift. Taking corners and sharp curves at well over seventy miles an hour, he was home in ten minutes, flying out of the car and into the house up to the bedroom. The door closed behind him, he stood with his back to it, panting. *She'd lied!* His beloved traducer was, at this very moment, with another man; a young, *handsome* man. She'd found someone whose beauty complemented her own; someone whole and in no visible way impaired.

Falling to his knees, he bent until his forehead touched the floor, his hands knuckled against his chest in a useless attempt to beat down the pain. It wouldn't go. Wound into a knot on the floor, he wept into his fists, then tore at his face until it bled into his raging hands. And finally, gradually, he grew still. His hands, tacky with blood, twittered slowly against the air, like dying prehistoric creatures. It occurred to him as he lay on the floor that there was more to come. Perhaps this was merely the beginning of what would be a lengthy ongoing betrayal. "Why?" he asked into the deep pile of the carpet. *"Why?"*

Ah, but he knew why. He'd taken charge of a child who'd at long last discovered there was an entire world beyond the darkness of this house. And she craved its brilliance, its brightness, its garish lure. It was to be expected. She'd stayed far longer than he'd dared to hope she might. And it was ending now. That giant clock had stopped ticking. He could no longer hear the turning of its immense wheels or the insufferable shift of its razor-honed blades. All was silent.

He got up and went into the bathroom, pausing to turn on the light. Removing the mask, he approached the mirror and stared at the abhorrent blood-drenched apparition there. And then he began, quite uncontrollably, to laugh.

Risa was very nervous, and kept telling herself to turn around and go home. What on earth was she doing, going to some man's house for dinner, as if she were single and free to accept casual invitations? But she wanted to talk to Stefan about the suicide, to review it in the company of someone who'd participated in the horror. She was also curious. He seemed so very kind, so concerned about her. Besides, what harm could come of it?

What harm? Maybe she really was crazy, as Kitty had been implying. Harm of every conceivable variety could come from this. But somehow she couldn't turn around and go back. She did regret having told that silly lie about going to the movies in Greenwich. Why hadn't she told the truth? Because none of them would have understood, particularly Erik. Hal and Kitty and Erik had spent so many years with her as their focal point that they seemed to have forgotten she had a right to life and a degree of independence. But since yesterday it had felt as if they'd been trying to control even her thoughts.

Erik didn't have to know about this. One night, one small lie. She'd have dinner with Stefan, then go home. It was nothing, a couple of hours, a chance to air some of her acutely upsetting reactions to the previous morning. She'd talk with the man, eat a meal with him, then go away, and it would be forgotten.

He greeted her so effusively she was taken off-guard, especially by the kisses he placed on her cheeks, as if he'd known her for years and had long since earned the right to offer her affectionate greetings.

"I knew you'd come!" he said, and hurried her inside just as the telephone rang. He excused himself saying, "Make yourself at home. I'll get rid of whoever that is."

She stood for a minute or two in the small entryway, then ventured to look into the living room, which had obviously been decorated by a woman, with a lot of chintzy fabric and brightly colored pillows. Somewhere a stereo was playing, that same tedious middle-of-the-road music he'd tuned in on the car radio. Clearly, he knew nothing about music. But at least the place was clean and cozy. And something was cooking that didn't smell too bad. She sat on the sofa and waited for him to come back, which took almost ten minutes.

He came hurrying in, apologizing. "Sorry about that. Couldn't get them the hell off the phone. Let me get you a drink. What would you like?"

"Nothing, thank you."

"Oh, come on." He stood and smiled at her. "You look lovely, but I should've told you this would be casual."

"This is casual." She looked down at herself, and then at him. He meant she should've worn something that would've been more in keeping with his polished-cotton pants, Izod polo shirt, and Topsiders.

"What'll you have?" he persisted. "Scotch, gin, rye, vodka, what?"

"Some mineral water, if you have it. Otherwise, nothing. Thank you."

"You don't drink?" He seemed astounded by this concept.

"A little wine now and then."

"Well, you'll have some wine with dinner, won't you?"

"Sure. That'd be great."

"Let me get my drink, then we'll talk."

He went off to the kitchen and returned quickly with a half-empty glass of what looked to be Scotch. With another smile, he sank down rather too close to her on the sofa and shifted around to face her squarely. "So," he said, "what kind of lies did you have to tell to get away to-night?"

"I beg your pardon?"

In answer, he reached across to lift her left hand, pointing out her wedding band.

"Oh! I said I was going to the movies."

"And he *bought* that?" Stefan laughed. "He really must be slow."

"I think," she said, reaching for her bag, "I'd better go. This was a mistake."

"Wait a minute! Don't get offended. We'll forget I said that. Okay? It's gone; it didn't happen. Are you hungry? I'm kind of ahead of myself. Everything'll be ready in a couple of minutes. I hope you brought your appetite."

"Actually," she began just as a timer went off.

He jumped up, saying, "Back in a minute," and went off to the kitchen again.

She sat for a minute, then thought, What the hell am I doing here? I shouldn't be here. Get up and walk out the door right now, while he's gone!

She reached for her bag and was ready to get up and leave when he came back saying, "Come on. Kind of a rush job, I know, but dinner's ready, so we might as well eat."

She had no alternative, really, but to get up and go with him.

Twenty-eight

A s STEFAN WOLFED DOWN THE MEAL HE'D COOKED—A RATHER WET meat-loaf suspiciously red in the middle, with lumpy mashed potatoes, and frozen peas of an impossible emerald green—Risa toyed with the food on her plate, intrigued and repelled. She simply couldn't understand why she hadn't left. It had something to do with good manners, with the training her father and Kitty had given her from a very early age to respect others and to honor obligations and commitments. She also couldn't understand why she'd thought this man to be so beautiful. Now that she looked more closely, she could see that his eyes, although of a wonderful color, were quite bloodshot; there were blackheads around his nose; his fingernails were bitten to the quick; his eating habits appeared to have been learned at truck stops. He talked with his mouth full so that she had to look away. She told herself she was being hypercritical. He'd been kind and considerate yesterday, while almost everyone else around them had either actively ignored the situation or pretended it hadn't happened at all. How could he have displayed such positive qualities yesterday and seem so dissolute, even decadent, today? Or was it her? There was no question that her perceptions were out of kilter. She admitted that. But was there something wrong, as well, with her ability to see things clearly?

"I can't stop hearing it," she said, looking at the black wrought-iron candlestick in the center of the table. It had a thick coating of dust, and a substantial build-up of wax spills.

"Hearing what?" he asked around a mouthful of mashed potatoes.

"The sound yesterday, when the train went over him."

He paused to swallow, his eyes on her. For a very beautiful and obviously wealthy woman, she struck him, at that moment, as being almost childlike in her refusal or inability—he couldn't tell which—to let something go once she got her teeth into it. "Hey," he said. "Let's forget that, huh. File it under the heading of 'Jumping to Conclusions.' " He laughed heartily at his own macabre humor. She was quietly scandalized that he could make a joke about something tragic that had so strongly affected her. She drank a little of the not unpleasant California Cabernet Sauvignon, abandoning her attempt to eat. The sight and smell of the food was making her queasy.

"You're not going to eat that?" he asked, pointing his knife at her plate.

"I'm afraid I'm not very hungry. I'm sorry. It really is very good."

"No wonder you're so skinny," he said, scraping the contents of her plate onto his own. "What d'you do, take pills?"

"Pardon?"

"You don't eat, right? So you take pills."

"Why would I do that?"

"To stay thin," he said patiently.

Mystified, she said, "I eat. Quite often, as a matter of fact."

He found this funny, and laughed again before going back to eating at an amazing pace. She was transfixed by the sight. In only a few minutes, he'd consumed everything in sight and was lifting the bottle of wine to refill their glasses.

"We'll have coffee and dessert in a little while, okay? Take a breather now, and let things settle." He patted his stomach, then picked up both their glasses. "Come on. We'll take a break, listen to some music, talk, get to know each other."

He led the way back to the living room, where he set the wineglasses on the coffee table before going to the stereo to raise the volume. An insipid bass-heavy orchestral rendition of a Beatles song blared from the speakers at either end of the room. It made her ears throb, and she thought it was a crime that anyone would ruin a good song by stretching the melody line thin as thread and then destroy the composer's intent altogether by throwing a full string section into the background to distract the listener entirely from the theme.

"I really can't stay too long," she said as he turned from the stereo.

"What's your rush? It's early. Movies last at least a couple of hours. Sit down," he said. "Relax."

Relax? She couldn't imagine what he meant. In what way did he intend her to relax? She sat at the far end of the sofa and took a sip of her wine before carefully positioning the glass on the coffee table. She felt woefully out of place, out of her depth, and was glad to have moved from the dining room because it brought her somewhat closer to the door.

"I knew you'd make it tonight," he said with a smile, sitting down in the center of the sofa. "I would've made book on it."

"Why do you say that?"

"I'm never wrong," he said with preening self-confidence.

"About what?" The longer she spent with this man, the more convinced she became that she'd made the mistake of a lifetime in coming here. As Kitty would have said, the man was common as mud and twice as thick.

"About turned-on women," he said. "About Darien and New Canaan and Greenwich and Westport housewives who get bored and like to play away from home once in a while." He took a gulp of his wine, then returned the glass to the table. "I know all about you."

She had no idea what he was talking about, but suspected he was making veiled sexual references. It heightened her nervousness. When he slid over closer to put his hand on her shoulder, saying, "Nice top," her nervousness began edging into fear. And yet she was still very curious. It was like visiting some alien culture, one she'd never guessed existed.

She said, "Thank you," and shifted away, coming up against the arm of the sofa. She crossed her legs tightly, and tugged the skirt down over her knees.

"You're so antsy," he said, moving closer still, smiling to reveal bits of food between his teeth and at his gumline. "It's probably your first time off the ranch. Right? Relax, sweetheart. It won't be your last." His hand descended once more to her shoulder.

"I'd prefer you didn't do that," she told him.

"Do what?"

"Put your hand on my shoulder."

"Oh!" With an exaggerated movement—pretending her shoulder was hot and he'd burned himself—he held his hand to his mouth and blew on it. "Ooops! Hey! You're not drinking your wine. You don't like it?"

"No, it's very pleasant, thank you."

"Very pleasant," he repeated. "Christ, it's cute the way you talk. What were you, raised by nuns?"

"I'm not Catholic."

He laughed. "You're adorable, flat-out adorable. I could eat you up with a spoon."

She looked at her watch, then said, "I really should be going."

"Take it easy," he said, his voice dropping. "Once you get started, it'll be okay."

What *was* he talking about? She looked at him blankly, about to tell him she was leaving, when he put his hand over the back of her neck and glued his wet open mouth to hers. She jerked away from him, protesting, but he ignored her, muttering something about ". . . the ones who want to but just don't know how to get it going."

"Stop it!" she insisted, swatting at his hand, which was busy with the buttons of her top.

"Relax!" he said maddeningly, giving up on the buttons and pushing his hand down the front of her blouse over her breast.

"I *asked* you to *stop!*" she said loudly, pulling back while, with both hands, removing his hand. She was astonished that he was disregarding everything she said.

"Just be quiet now!" he told her, then fell heavily on top of her. She shoved against his chest to no avail. His tongue was worming around in her mouth, his hand over the back of her neck preventing her from escaping this obscene invasion, while his free hand pushed between her thighs. Very frightened, she clenched her fist and hit him on the temple as hard as she was able. Instantly, he went motionless. Then he smiled and said, "Like that, huh?" as his hand flew out and he hit her back, twice, very quickly. For a few seconds she was stunned by the blows and overcome by bursting panic. If she didn't get out of there, he'd beat and rape her. And she was unprotected. If he raped her, he might make her pregnant. The idea of being raped was terrifying in itself; the thought that a pregnancy could result from it sent her nearly demented. He was so involved in his determination to complete this sexual act that he scarcely seemed aware of her. Frantic, she glanced around, looking for something to use to defend herself. There were only the two wineglasses on the coffee table. He was pulling at her clothes, exposing her, his hand working its way up her thigh, and she was trying, one-handed, to fend him off. She extended her left hand, her fingertips meeting the edge of the table. He was dragging her skirt up around her hips, then ripping at her panty hose. A pause. He unzipped his fly. She wanted to scream, terror racing through her bloodstream. Her struggles of no concern to him, his knees were pushing her thighs open. Her hand closed around the stem of the glass. She overturned it, spilling the wine and shattering the glass so she was left clutching a jagged spike. He was pushing harder, higher. Getting a good grip, she drove her weapon into his upper arm. He let out a howl of pain, his left hand immediately going to his wounded right arm as he reared back in agonized surprise.

Instantly, she grabbed her bag and went running through the house and out the door toward the car, fishing for the keys as she went. She found them, got the car open, threw herself inside, pressed down the button to lock the doors, then, with a violently shaking hand, tried to jam the key into the ignition. It wouldn't go in. He came charging out of the house, blood streaming down his arm, his face contorted with rage, shouting.

"Oh God, God! Go in, go in!" She got the key into the ignition, turned it, released the hand brake, threw the shift into drive and floored the accelerator as his hand closed on the passenger-door handle. He hung on, pounding on the window with his fist, until the speed of the car threw him aside.

Quaking in the blast of the air conditioner, she drove madly back along Route 124, until she came near the entrance to the Merritt Parkway. She pulled over where the road widened before the entrance, put her head down on the steering wheel and sobbed, her chest heaving with accumulated fear and anguish. She felt sick and dirty and rabidly ashamed. Opening her bag for a tissue, she wiped her mouth over and over, trying to rid herself of his imprint while her body twisted in revulsion, feeling his hands all over her. She sat mindlessly wiping her mouth, staring blindly out the window, loathing herself and that despicable pig. How could she have gone to that place? How could she have done *any* of the insane things she'd done?

She'd lied to everyone; she'd been colossally disloyal to Erik; a strange vile man had dared to put his hands on her. He'd put his filthy fingers inside of her. She cried out and pushed her hands between her thighs, feeling as if a snake had crawled into her vagina. "Oh, God!" she moaned, unable to control her shaking. What was she going to do? She felt so dirty, so utterly, atrociously soiled. What could she do?

Slowly, a bit of reason seemed to return. She put out her unsteady hand to adjust the climate control and cut off the push of gelid air. Then she looked down at herself. He'd ripped her top, torn the strap of her camisole. Her panty hose were shredded. And there was blood all over her left hand. Crying out again, she tried wiping it off with the tissue. But it just flaked, remaining imbedded in her pores. She spit on her hand and rubbed it with the tissue. Then she opened the window and threw out the stained tissue.

What else? Her joints seized up, her muscles cramped with residual fear, she opened the lighted mirror in the sun visor to look at her face. Her entire cheek was discolored, starting to bruise. The mascara had run, leaving black rims beneath her eyes. She couldn't possibly let anyone see her looking this way, especially not Erik.

At the thought of Erik, she folded her arms over her breasts and began weeping again. He'd never want to touch her if he knew about this. He'd be as disgusted with her as she was with herself. What to do? Kitty! But, no. Kitty would tell Hal; Hal would tell Erik. And Erik must never know! God! He'd never forgive her for this. She'd been a fool, an incredible fool. She could see herself saying, "This is casual," and wanted to murder that imbecilic woman.

What was she going to do?

Run!

Where?

Her open handbag on the passenger seat caught her eye. The envelope with her passport was still in it. And the Saks bag was on the back seat. She had a wallet full of money and credit cards. She'd go away somewhere, stay away until she recovered from the self-loathing, the engulfing aversion she felt for a woman so stupid she'd go to the house of a man she didn't know, thinking he'd invited her out of sympathy and fellow-feeling. You silly pathetic bitch! She swore at her mirror image. You're too stupid to live. She shoved the mirror closed.

Run!

She'd deceived Erik; lied to him. She'd behaved badly with Kitty; she'd smugly gone out to put herself in the soiled hands of a woman-beating rapist. Kitty had been right. She was mentally and emotionally retarded when it came to the harsher realities of the outside world. What on earth had made her think she could deal with strangers, with all their unknown and inexplicable drives? She'd been vain and arrogant and, above all, extraordinarily stupid.

Run!

It was the only thing she could do.

She started up the car and followed the ramp onto the parkway, intermittently turning her head to blot her face on her sleeve. If only she'd never got on that train. She wouldn't have witnessed that poor man's death, and she would never, as a direct result, have met that beast she'd thought so handsome. All she'd done for days was tell lies and behave offensively; she'd even driven Erik to hide from her. Erik knew she'd done something; he'd always sensed her moods and thoughts and feelings. He'd hidden himself in order not to have to see or speak to her. How could she have *done* that to him? She'd broken every promise she'd ever made, dishonored everything between them.

Remembering trips years ago with her father, she automatically followed the airport signs until she found herself taking the exit for the British Airways terminal. She'd been to England several times. It seemed far enough away. She parked the car. It wasn't yet nine o'clock. They'd all hate her for the things she'd done. She'd done exactly what Kitty had said she'd do: She'd destroyed something beautiful. Now she had to go away, to hide.

Using the mirror from her purse, she cleaned her face as best she could, then tidied her clothes. She reached over the back seat for the Saks bag, took the keys and got out of the car.

"Hal, I need to talk to Erik!"

"Hold on a minute, Risa."

Hal got on the intercom to say, "Risa's on line one, Erik. Says she needs to talk to you."

Numbly, Erik said, "Yes," and pressed down the button. "Marisa?" He was very afraid of what she might say.

"Erik!" She broke into tears at the sound of his voice. "I know you'll never forgive me. I don't blame you. I'll never forgive myself. I'm sorry. I'm so sorry. I'm going away. I need time to think. I have to get away. Please, try to forgive me. The car's in the British Airways lot. You can arrange to have it picked up. I can't talk. I just wanted to tell you I'm sorry."

"Wait! Don't hang up! Where are you going?"

"Just away. I have to go!"

"Please, don't go," he pleaded. "Please don't! Let me come get you! Let me come with you!"

"I don't want you to see me, Erik. I have to go now."

"Wait!" he implored her. But she'd gone. She'd severed the connection, cut them apart.

Slowly he put down the receiver, feeling deadened. He had hoped he might have more time, another chance. But she had to get away. *Now.* So soon, with so little warning. From the start of one day to the end of the next, everything he'd loved and lived for had ended. She'd left the house yesterday morning planning to be gone for a few hours and now she would be gone from him for all time. Perhaps she was running away with that handsome young man. Perhaps it was something that had been going on for a long time, but he'd been too busy, or too preoccupied to notice. It was of no consequence, not anymore.

He picked up the photograph in the heavy silver frame and held it to his chest, his eyes closed, his impossible heart beating and beating. After a time, he returned the photograph to the dresser and walked leadenly to the closet to push aside the clothes. He entered the secret room and closed the door behind him. Going at a leisurely pace—he had all eternity now—he lit several of the candles with the gold Dunhill lighter she'd given him, then sat down and put the lighter on the table next to the candle there.

For a time he simply listened to the sound of his own breathing as he reviewed scenes of their marriage, of the many nights he'd gone hurrying to fetch her in the car or the boat just to be near her, to hear her sing, to be close enough to study the sweep of her eyelashes, the delicate tracery of veins in her eyelids, the dainty cleft in her chin.

At last, he reached for the box that had for so long sat at the back of the table, and positioned it on his knees. He drew back the lid to look at the oily gray surface of the gun. His hands removed it from the box and opened the chamber. Full. Then, keeping hold of the gun, he returned the box to the table.

Such a long lovely dream it had been, so filled with sound and sensation, so charged with emotion and quiet excitement. A dream beyond his dearest hopes, a dream of cherished moments revolving around a beautiful child who had, as he'd always feared she would, led him deep into the wasteland of his own ravaged emotions only to abandon him there. He couldn't blame her. She'd given him far more than he'd deserved. She'd sung for him; she'd taught him to dance; she'd shown him how to smile, and even to laugh. And now the time had come for her to go away. She cared enough to express sadness, even remorse, at the death of the dream; she had shed tears over its passing. And she would find consolation in other arms, another's bed. But he couldn't contemplate any of that. It revived the pain. He couldn't cope with the pain. The pain was lacerating his bowels; it was collapsing his lungs.

At last, with a deep sigh, he removed the mask and set it aside. He gazed at the gun with a certain fondness. It would save him finally, take away the pain forever. He opened his mouth and lifted the gun.

Suddenly, alarmingly, the door slid open, and Raskin cried, "Don't do it, Erik!" and dived across the few feet separating them to try to wrestle the gun from Erik's startled hands. *"Don't be a fool!"* Raskin cried as he struggled for possession of the gun.

"Get out!" Erik insisted, refusing to yield. *"Go away!"*

"I won't let you do this!" Raskin argued, grappling with the bigger, stronger man; tugging with all his strength at the weapon.

"I have to!" Erik ranted. "You can't take it from me!"

"You *don't* have to!" Raskin panted, determined not to let this happen; his determination giving him almost superhuman strength, while at the same time destroying the cool veneer that had sustained him throughout his life. *"This isn't the answer!"* he persisted, straining against Erik's mighty hold on the gun, so bent on preserving the other man's life that he was unaware of his own frustrated tears. "I *won't* let you do this!"

"I must! Leave me be! Stop this!" Erik cried, frantic as the gun began to slip from his fingers.

"I fucking won't!" Raskin shouted. *"I won't just back off and let you die!"* With a last, valiant tug, he succeeded in wrestling the gun from Erik's grip. At once, he emptied it and tossed the bullets into a corner of the room where they fell soundlessly to the carpet.

Erik sank back into the chair and buried his face in his hands.

"Weren't you *listening?*" Raskin demanded. Distraught, he tossed the gun into the opposite corner. "Didn't you *hear* what she was telling you?"

Furious at having his so-careful plans thwarted, Erik lifted his head. "Why were *you* listening?" he roared. "And what in bloody *hell* are you *doing* in here?"

Raskin laughed bitterly. "You think you're the only person in this house who knows all the hidden doors, Erik? Don't be an ass! It's my goddamned *job* to look after you."

"I am no one's *job!*" Erik barked. "And it is *not* your prerogative to eavesdrop on my telephone conversations! Damn you! *Damn* you!"

"Don't be a schmuck, Erik," Raskin said tiredly. "You didn't listen! She was saying *she* screwed up. Not *you*. Her!"

"Why is she *leaving?*" Erik asked him beseechingly, his anger departing.

"Listen to me!" Raskin dropped down in front of him. "You have a choice, Erik. You can sit here and splatter your brains all over the walls. Or you can do something about this."

"What? What should I do?"

"Go after her!"

"But she wants to be away from me."

"No, she doesn't. Something went wrong, and now she doesn't know how to face you."

"What should I do?"

"The big question is: What are you *willing* to do?"

"Anything!" he said passionately. "*Anything!* I can't be here without her."

"Okay!" Raskin got to his feet. "Okay! Leave it with me, but be prepared to go traveling."

"Just to be able to see her," Erik whispered. "That's all I ask."

"Then that's what you'll do," Raskin told him, impatiently wiping his face on his shirt sleeve. "Forget that fucking peashooter and pull yourself together. And why the hell don't you turn this goddamned room back into a closet?"

"Hal?"

Raskin stopped and turned back.

"Why are you doing this?"

"Why d'you think?" Raskin replied.

"But why should you care?"

"Oh, shit, Erik! Why the hell *shouldn't* I?" With that, Raskin went off to make some telephone calls.

Twenty-nine

"**S**HE'S ON A FLIGHT TO LONDON THAT ARRIVES EIGHT O'CLOCK TOMOR-row morning local time. I've made arrangements to have her tracked from the minute she sets foot in England. You and I will be on the Concorde flight tomorrow morning that gets in at six in the evening over there. By then, we'll know where she's staying and what she's doing. And you can decide how you want to handle it."

"I want only to be near her."

"Fine. I've arranged for a car and driver, and you can do that."

"But what about Kitty?" Erik asked.

"For now, Kitty's going to stick close to her telephone. And I've got the service set to take care of ours. They'll relay messages to us, in case Risa decides to call home. I've also arranged to have her car picked up from the BA lot. A limo'll be coming here for us at seven-thirty."

"Why," Erik wanted to know, "did you listen in on our conversation?"

"Because of the way she sounded, because I was afraid something like this was going to happen, and because I knew if it ever did, you'd get it all ass backwards exactly the way you did, and point it at yourself just like that goddamned gun."

"She saw another man," Erik confided. "He was young and very hand-some."

"He was probably a schmuck. Most of them are. Of course, she wouldn't know about that, in view of the fact that the only man she's ever known or cared about, outside of her father, is just a little bit different."

Erik smiled wryly. "You've picked an odd time to become cautious with your turns of phrase."

"Let's not play games here. I've known Risa almost as long as you

795

have. I've seen her grow up, and I've seen her change. And I'll tell you something: She's taught me a few things, fixed a few of my attitudes. I know what she's given up to make a go of your marriage. And I know what kind of work you've had to do, too. Shit, Erik! Don't you get it yet? You *did* it. You went ahead and got what you wanted and made it work, in spite of everything. There's not a fucking thing wrong with this face"— he pointed to himself with a stabbing finger—"but I've never had the guts to go after what I wanted. Now, instead of working at it a little more, for a little while longer, so you get the goddamned happy ending that comes with the fucking fairy tale, you're going to shove a gun in your mouth and blow your brains out. You can't give up just when you're winning! She loves you, stupid. The thing is, she's a kid in a lot of ways. Just the way you are. So she looked at another guy. So big deal! She gave it a try and it went sour; she didn't like it; it wasn't what she thought it'd be, wasn't what she wanted. Would you want her to blow *her* brains out if you made one mistake? Of course not. I'm like the fucking referee in this marriage, or the keeper of this particular zoo, or something. The point is, I *like* what goes on in our house. It feels like a *family,* Erik. And in view of the fact that the only family I ever had turned to ratshit, I'd kind of like to keep this one. Purely selfish, but there you are. I get to see one decent marriage, to experience it vicariously, even to be a part of it. Believe it or not, you're my goddamned role model. You set me such a good example, I've been gearing up maybe to try it myself sometime soon."

"You'd marry Kitty?"

"I'm trying to get up the nerve to let her know I care that much about her. But first we've got to get this house back in order."

"Twice now you're rescued me," Erik said humbly.

"Oh, hey! You can forget that garbage. Okay? I can't even *count* how many times you've saved my ass. Look, Erik! We're friends. We have been for a hell of a long time. But you've got this one small problem: You're even worse than I am at knowing what name to put to what situation. Risa's your wife, and that's your marriage. I'm your friend, and this is your friendship."

"Why are you shouting at the poor man?" Kitty asked, letting herself in the back door. "You leave him alone, Harold! He's had a rotten couple of days. Come here, Erik," she said, and drew him into her arms, standing on tiptoe to embrace him. Then, stepping back, she said, "The two of you better keep me posted every single day. You hear? I want to know where my girl is and what she's doin' and what condition she's in. And Erik, you listen here to me. This don't have one single thing to do with babies. Not one thing. This has to do with a bunch of hooligans runnin' down poor Willie, and then seein' a man die in front of her eyes. And I'll wager my eyeteeth it has somethin' to do with some fella standin' close by watchin' and waitin' to take advantage. Now, she's gone runnin' off, and it's likely because she learned herself a hard lesson tonight. It's only 'cause she's ashamed of herself, Erik, and can't stand to look you in the eye that she's gone off to hide and lick her wounds. You understand? That girl's loved you since the day she first set eyes on you, and as soon as she gets herself put back together she'll be callin' you up to say she wants to come home. She's gone and got herself traumatized, like they say on the TV. But she's sensible, and she's resilient. It might take her some time, but she'll come around. Now, what in heaven's name have you done to yourself?" she asked. "Lord, but you're a mess. Harold, go get me somethin' to clean up Erik's face, and some antiseptic. Erik, you sit right down here and let me tend to you. I've never *known* anyone so liked to punish himself for every little thing."

Hal went off to do as she'd asked, and Kitty pulled over a chair, pushed Erik into it, then sat down close to him, holding his hands firmly in her own. "I'm gonna give you some advice," she said. "Stay back from her, Erik. Don't go crowdin' in on her. Don't go nowhere near her until she lets you know it's time."

"Kitty, twice I saw her with another man."

"It don't mean nothin'," she said flatly. "I slept with her daddy for better'n fifteen years and I looked at plenty of other men. But I didn't go off with none of 'em because he was the one I cared for. There's no sin to lookin', Erik. It's the leavin' part that's worrisome. I have to confess I'm surprised this didn't happen a whole lot sooner. But you can't blame yourself, because it don't have a thing to do with you, and that's the truth. You're what's constant in her life, and it'll go back to bein' that way again. This was somethin' that was bound to happen, and now it's out of her system. You're a dear, sweet man, and she loves you. So I want your promise you won't go hurtin' yourself anymore. D'you promise?"

He nodded.

She leaned forward and kissed him lightly on the lips. "We all love you, Erik, especially Reese. Everything's gonna be okay. So don't you cry anymore. Everything's gonna work out fine."

The Saks bag contained two dresses she'd bought the previous afternoon. As soon after takeoff as it was allowed, Risa closed herself into one of the lavatories. She stripped naked, pushed the panty hose and the ruined clothes into the waste bin, then fastened the torn camisole strap with a safety pin. She filled the basin, took one of the small squares of soap and a washcloth from the tidy stack, and began scrubbing herself from top to bottom.

It took ages. She had to change the water four times. But at last she felt somewhat cleaner. She pulled on the camisole, stepped barefoot into her shoes, and put on one of the new dresses. Then she tried to do something about her face with the concealer stick from her makeup bag, but she couldn't camouflage the darkening bruise. The concealer only drew attention to it. She washed off the makeup, then picked up her hairbrush only to see there was just one comb in her hair. With a pang, she realized she'd lost it, perhaps in that man's house. It made her start to cry again. She stood cradling the remaining comb in her hands, convinced she'd betrayed everyone, even her long-dead mother.

She wrapped the comb in several tissues and tucked it into her purse before at last returning to her seat, undone by the loss of the comb. It struck her as so pointed an illustration of her overall stupidity that she had to wedge a fistful of tissues against her mouth in order not to make any sound that might either disturb the other half-dozen first-class passengers or call their attention to her.

She'd have given anything not to have been so supremely foolhardy, and not to have lied to Erik—about anything—or to have allowed that repugnant rapist to refer to Erik even indirectly. She'd ruined everything by not telling him about Stefan at once. It would have been so simple to tell Erik about the man on the train who'd been so kind to her. But no. She'd hoarded her experiences with that fiend like some fuddled teen-ager with a crush on a rock star. If she had mentioned him she'd never have gone to his house, and none of this nightmare would've occurred. But she had gone. And now, coupled with her recurring auditory and visual experience of the suicide, was the cringing self-hatred she felt at that man's thrusting his tongue into her mouth while his filthy hands invaded her. Squirming, she longed to bathe properly and rid herself of the impression his brutalizing hands had made on her body. She kept reliving that moment when she stabbed him, the sound of rending flesh as she'd driven the glass deep into his arm, wishing it could have been his eyes, or his heart, or his groin—someplace where the damage would have been permanent and crippling. She had visions of driving back to that dreary house and murdering him in his sleep, slashing his throat with a butcher's knife, or severing his penis with a pair of gardening shears. He'd *dared* to strike her! He'd hit her twice, hard, and she could feel the resultant swelling, the throbbing ache in her head. She could never face Erik after having done all that, and feeling, as she did now, such a raging need to commit mayhem. She could only believe Erik would be as repelled by her now as she was by herself.

Throughout the flight she reviewed the suicide, and Stefan's attack. The garlicky reek of his breath was like a foul coating on her skin and in the interior of her mouth. She dug her fingernails into her palms to keep herself from screaming as she felt again his knees forcing her legs apart, his fingers pushing up into her.

In the morning, wearing her sunglasses and carrying the Saks bag, she went through immigration and out the "Nothing to Declare" customs exit. She got into a cab and told the driver, "I need a hotel."

"What kind and where, my darlin'?" he asked over his shoulder.

"A good one, in the center of the city."

"You might like the Park Lane," he told her. "Right near Green Park, very nice it is."

"That'll be fine."

"Right you are, my lovely," he said cheerily, and they were off.

Anywhere, she thought. As long as there was a bathroom where she'd be able to begin trying to scrub herself clean.

Erik was smoking a cigarette in the narrow seat at the rear of the slim supersonic plane, with Raskin dozing beside him. So far, despite their being forced to travel during the day, the trip had been uneventful. No one at the Concorde check-in had been anything less than friendly and helpful. Luckily, there had been only a handful of other passengers waiting in the lounge, and he and Raskin had found a quiet corner at the far end of the room where they sat to drink some of the complimentary coffee while looking out the glass wall that separated them from the plane sitting on the tarmac beyond the windows.

Raskin was worn out from a sleepless night and from the many telephone calls he'd had to make in the course of it. Well before takeoff, he folded his arms across his chest, tucked the small airplane pillow between his head and his shoulder, and fell into a heavy sleep.

Erik had watched his friend sleep for a time, then lowered the window shades, and waited, holding his hands together in his lap. As soon as the "no smoking" sign went off, he lit a cigarette, and began to study the scenes that played on the screens of his closed eyes.

He could see, in vividly graphic detail, every failure of his life with Marisa, every last occasion when he'd neglected to be fully aware, to be more open to her needs. In order to win her back he had no choice but to collect what courage he had and put it to good use. His only hope was that he hadn't left it too late.

Marisa, he told her mutely, I was dishonest when I said there was nothing I wouldn't do for you. I withheld and withheld because I didn't dare believe what you insisted was true. I denied you and deprived you because my fears were greater than my love for you. Come home to me and I will make amends. I will lay myself at your feet and give you everything within my power to give. I don't care what you've done, or what you think you've done. I don't care where you went, or what was said, or to whom. None of it matters. If I must spend the rest of my life lurking in doorways only to have a glimpse of you, it will be just punishment for my errors and omissions. To be able to see you, regardless of where you are, regardless of how distant, will be enough to sustain me. There is no point to a life without you in it, without the sound of your laughter, without the feel of you next to me in the night, your head resting lightly on my shoulder as we make our music, your breath sweet and slow as you trust me to transport you to safety. Come home to me and I will devote myself to the care and shaping of your days and nights until the last breath leaves my body. Come home to me and I will try with all my heart to open doors and windows, to tolerate the bludgeoning light. Anything. Just, please, come home.

A small nattily dressed man with a fedora was waiting for them outside the arrivals area. Erik stood to one side, with his hat brim pulled low over his face, smoking yet another cigarette—he'd been chain-smoking since his confrontation with Raskin in the secret room—while Raskin conferred with the man.

"She's staying at the Park Lane," Raskin came over to report, as the small man took charge of their luggage and led the way to a vintage Bentley limousine with dark-tinted windows. "We're booked into the Ritz, just up the road. It's the closest we could get. So far, she's stayed in her room, ordered one meal from room service, and asked the switchboard about good stores nearby where she can buy some clothes. She's alone, by the way, in case you haven't figured that out. We've got it worked out so her calls are being monitored, and the staff is organized to let us know the instant she sets foot out of her room."

"It seems wrong somehow," Erik said, staring out the limousine window, "stalking her this way, invading her privacy."

"You have a better suggestion?" Raskin countered.

"No, I have not."

"Okay. When we get to the hotel, I'll order up some dinner, then we'll check to see if anything's happening. Okay?"

"Yes, fine."

"You're not starting to slip, are you, Erik?"

"No. I'm all right."

"We both need some sleep. I'm getting too old to be staying up all night."

"Yes," Erik agreed, distracted. In his head, he continued the lengthy prayer he'd started on the flight over. He had the completely irrational, and admittedly arbitrary, idea that if he kept on praying, everything would come out right.

Risa spent three hours in the bathtub after being shown to her hotel room. But upon emerging from the bath she felt scummy. That foul coating still adhered to her skin. So she turned on the shower after the bath water had drained away and rubbed her skin raw for another hour. Then she inspected herself in the mirror. Not only did she have the now purple bruise on her cheek, she had additional bruises on her breast and thighs. She'd broken three fingernails below the quick and had actually cut herself on the shattered glass. There were several small deep gashes on her left hand. It relieved her somewhat to know that the blood had been her own and not that revolting rapist's. Her face was a mess, and she had nothing in the way of makeup that would cover it. She also had no underwear, only two dresses and a pair of shoes. She was going to have to go out and buy things. She was also going to have to prevail upon the hotel to give her some cash because she had no sterling. She'd persuaded the taxi driver to accept seventy-five dollars for the ride from the airport, apologizing even after he'd agreed to take her money.

She was utterly worn out, but when she lay down on the bed to try to sleep she found herself back in the chintzy living room with that man unzipping his trousers, exposing himself to her horrified eyes while his fingers forced their way into her body like foraging animals that only lived underground and were blind in the light. It drove her almost insane with self-reproach and she raked her loathsome body with her broken fingernails, despising herself so convulsively she wished she could shred her skin right off.

She got up, turned on the television set, and sat naked in one of the chairs with her knees drawn up to her chest and her arms wrapped tightly around them, to stare at some children's program hosted by a young man and woman whose vivacious energy made her feel more exhausted. She fell asleep in the chair and woke up with a jolt as she felt herself falling. She stayed awake only long enough to relocate to the floor in front of the TV set. The nap of the carpet was rewardingly rough against her skin, and as she sank into a troubled sleep she thought approvingly that it was only right for her to pay the full premium for her exceptional stupidity. She pounded her fists on the carpet, sandpapering her body against the rough fibers, grieving for everything she'd so casually, so cavalierly, thrown away.

Thirty

FEELING LIKE A WHORE, RISA WALKED THROUGH THE LOBBY, NODDED in response to the doorman's greeting, touched a hand to her sunglasses to make sure they were in place, and went out, following the hotel operator's directions, on her way to Bond Street. She felt as if everyone were staring at her, as if it were obvious she'd managed to get herself beaten up and very nearly raped; as if it were clear she had nothing on under her dress. It was a testament to the completeness of her absorbed self-loathing that she failed to notice the limousine crawling along, keeping pace with her to the extreme irritation of other drivers.

"She'd headed up Bond Street," the driver told them. "It's one-way, I'm afraid, gentlemen. I could circle round up to the top at Oxford Street and come down."

"No!" Erik said and, in one instant, before Raskin even realized what was happening, Erik had jumped from the car and gone darting up the street.

"I'll be damned!" Raskin said to himself, then told the driver to do as he'd suggested, to go to Oxford Street and then come down Bond.

As they headed toward Albemarle Street, Raskin watched as Erik tugged his hat brim low, slowed his pace, and followed after Risa as she turned the corner into Bond Street. Erik seemed so bent on his pursuit that he appeared unaware of the several people who turned to stare after him.

" Go to it!" Raskin cheered him on, losing sight of Erik as the driver made the turn.

Risa glanced into shop windows, determined not even to consider buying any clothes before she'd found someplace to get some underwear or panty hose. She stopped in front of the window of Fogal, backed up a few steps, and went inside to buy six pairs of panty hose from the charming, if bemused, shop manager who, when Risa asked if she could put on a pair then and there said, "Oh, but of course, madame. Please, use the office."

Feeling fractionally more secure and less whorish, Risa signed the charge slip, thanked the woman, and stepped out of the store.

From his vantage point across the street and several doors down, Erik watched Marisa come out of the shop, his hands folding into fists at the sight of the large bruise that covered most of her cheek. That bastard had struck her! She was wearing dark glasses. Was that to conceal more damage? he wondered, wishing he could hurry over, take her in his arms and console her. But he heeded Kitty's advice and waited to see which way she'd go. She chose to go on in the direction she'd been heading, toward Oxford Street. He stepped out of the doorway, adjusted the brim of his hat, and went after her.

A few doors along, she stopped to look in a shop window, and he fell back to wait. After a moment, she went inside. He reached into his pocket for a cigarette, lit it, and settled in to wait again. Farther up the street, he could see the Bentley pulling up at the curb. Then Raskin got out and came strolling toward him, asking, "How's it going?"

"She's been beaten!" Erik whispered hoarsely.

"Exactly how d'you mean that?" Raskin asked.

"I mean *beaten*. I mean that son of a bitch took his *fists* to my wife!"

"Oh, shit!"

"This is very difficult," Erik admitted. "I'm having terrible trouble restraining myself."

"Smoke your cigarette and try not to think about it. You're doing what you said you wanted to do."

"I have never done anything I cared for less."

"Yeah." Raskin smiled. "But you're doing it."

"Harold," Erik said humorlessly, "there are times when your cheerleading is something of an impediment to my progress, as well as an outrage to my sensibilities."

"Oh, now it's Harold. Soon it'll be Hal and you'll be inviting me for drinks at the Princeton Club."

"I doubt it. I'm not a member."

"Here she comes," Raskin said, stepping in front of Erik to block him from her view.

"Which way is she going?" Erik asked, dropping his cigarette and grinding it out beneath his heel.

"On up the street."

"Good," Erik said, neatly sidestepping around Raskin. "I'll meet you later at the limousine. Why don't you buy yourself a new tie, or some diaries at Smythson's?" With that, he glided away off up the street.

At one-fifteen, Risa sat down at an outdoor table in front of a restaurant on South Moulton Street. Erik took himself into a jewelry shop diagonally opposite and spent some time pretending to examine the window displays while simultaneously discouraging the young saleswoman from offering assistance. He held a quite wonderful bean-shaped gold wristwatch in his hand as he watched Marisa speak to the waitress across the way. As he went on with his mock deliberation of the pros and cons of the timepiece, the waitress brought a cup of coffee and a sandwich out to Marisa, who drank the coffee and ignored the sandwich. Then to Erik's great surprise, she opened her handbag, removed a package of cigarettes, lit one, and smoked it while she drank a second cup of coffee. He couldn't have been more taken aback if she'd injected herself with heroin. In view of her strong opposition to his and Raskin's smoking, it was nothing short of astonishing to see her indulging now in something she considered not only a vice, but a lethal one. It stated categorically the high degree of her upset.

At last, in order to justify his malingering, he purchased the wristwatch. He thought perhaps Kitty might like it. While he signed the charge slip, he kept glancing out the window, and his transaction was completed just as Marisa laid some coins on the tabletop, collected her numerous bags and packages, and started on her way down to the far end of the street.

She made no further stops but returned directly to her hotel. Erik had no choice but to go back to the Ritz—Raskin and the driver having long since given up waiting—where, as promised, he put in a call to Kitty to bring her up to date before turning the telephone over to Raskin, who'd spent the previous two hours cat-napping between other telephone calls.

A short time later, the telephone rang. Raskin answered, listened, then hung up to say, "She just phoned down to ask where she could buy something to read. She's on her way to Hatchard's, a bookstore almost across the road from the Meridien in Piccadilly. I say we sit tight on this one. It's too visible."

Reluctantly, Erik accepted this, and resumed his pacing of the suite.

Another call less than an hour later confirmed she'd returned to the hotel and gone directly up to her room.

"Time to eat," Raskin announced.

Erik gave a shrug of indifference, picked up the remote control, sank into a chair and turned on the TV set. He stared at the screen while he imagined himself driving to that house in New Canaan and knocking at the door. When that handsome young bastard came out, Erik put his gun to the forehead of the odious villain and pulled the trigger. The scene provided him with a small, savage satisfaction. It also augmented his anxiety for Marisa's well-being. God only knew what else that slug had done to her! He dared not think of it. It frightened him to feel such rampant hatred.

It helped to have several changes of clothes, as well as underwear and some makeup with which to hide her bruises. But it didn't help as much as she'd have liked. She felt unworthy of the new clothes, even of the hotel room and the staff, who responded so pleasantly and quickly to her simplest requests. And nothing seemed to hold her interest—not the television set, nor the radio, nor any of the several novels she'd bought. All she could do was review, over and over again, the events of the previous few days, and her part in them. The resulting despair and disgust so filled her, it all but seeped from every pore.

When her period started early in the morning hours of the second day in London, she was both so relieved and so distraught, she thought she really might go insane. She hadn't anything to use, and the stores would not be open yet for hours. She had no choice but to fold up a wad of tissues and stuff them into her underwear, then sit on her still made-up bed with legs drawn up, her fists tucked into her armpits, and her teeth chattering as she battled down the raging revulsion she felt for every aspect of her being. She ran down a list of the possible ways she might kill herself in this rented room, thought of that man waiting so patiently, for so long, at the end of the platform, and knew she wasn't capable of taking her own life. She just wished something, or someone else, would. It would have been better if Stefan had killed her, because between his actions and her own, it didn't feel as if she'd ever be able to live her life again. And feeling this way, she couldn't possibly consider returning to Erik, or even contemplate picking up the telephone to be eased by the sound of his voice. She'd discredited the marriage, violated the trust he'd placed in her. She'd thrown it all away with a combination of deceitfulness and foolish naivety that galled her each time she thought of it. That anyone could live to be almost thirty-five and be so ignorant of the world and the people in it was dismal in the extreme. And it certainly wasn't as if she hadn't been warned. Kitty had told her she was playing on dangerous turf, but she'd refused to acknowledge that. Instead she'd treated Kitty vilely, with none of the respect she deserved.

She banged her head hard several times against the headboard, but it didn't hurt enough, so she tried the wall, and then the door. Finally, reeling, the wad of blood-soaked tissues stuffed between her legs driving her crazy, she threw herself face-down on the bed and managed to cry herself to sleep.

She was awakened by the arrival of a chambermaid who, upon seeing her, said, "Oh, I'm sorry, madame. I'll come back later."

Risa had the presence of mind to say, "Wait a minute, please," and explained her problem to the nice young woman, who said, "I'll fetch you something from housekeeping," and went off to return in less than five minutes with a box of self-adhering sanitary napkins. Risa thanked her profusely and gave her a pound, which seemed to amaze her. She crept out of the room quietly, pausing as she went to slip the "Do Not Disturb" sign over the doorknob.

When asked a short time later if she had anything to report, the young chambermaid deliberated for a moment, decided the matter was far too personal to discuss, and shook her head, saying, " 'Do Not Disturb' sign's still on 'er door, ain't it?"

Erik knew it was a terrible risk, but he had to do it. While Raskin slept, he silently left the room and flew down the street to the Park Lane, where he slowed his pace as he investigated the hotel's possibilities. Locating a staff entrance, he entered the hotel and made his way up rear stairways and along the corridor to stop outside the door to Marisa's room. Holding his breath, he put his ear to the door, to hear, too clearly, the sound of her weeping on the other side. His hands at once pressed themselves flat to the door, as he listened to the rending sounds. He stayed for less than a minute, then retraced his steps to the staff entrance and out to the street.

Once away from the hotel, he stepped into a doorway to light a Sobranie then walked slowly, heavily, back to the Ritz. He'd never imagined anything could be this terrible, or this agonizingly frustrating. But he had to trust Kitty's wisdom. She was the only woman, aside from Marisa, with whom he'd ever had any real connection. And Kitty, better than anyone else, knew Marisa's ways.

He walked along the empty two A.M. street and continued his silent incantation. Call for me and I will come to you. Just ask and I will take you home. Please, I beg you, come home.

For three days Risa failed to emerge from her room. Raskin received regular reports each time she ordered anything from room service and on the two occasions when she made outside telephone calls—one to a luggage shop to ask them to deliver a small suitcase to her COD, and another to a livery service inquiring about engaging a car and driver.

"Obviously, she's thinking of going somewhere," Raskin said. "I think you and I better get ready to take this show on the road."

"You should tell Kitty and notify the answering service."

"Yes, sir, boss." Raskin saluted and went to the telephone, saying, "I do so love these holidays abroad."

Erik turned and gave him a sharp warning look.

At once, Raskin said, "Sorry. I'm a little stir-crazy," and picked up the receiver.

Erik ignored Raskin's several calls, and sat staring at the TV screen, not seeing or hearing anything, so that Raskin had to tap him on the shoulder to get his attention.

"There's a hell of an interesting message the service took for Marisa."

"I beg your pardon?"

Raskin dropped into the chair opposite and referred to the piece of hotel stationery on which he'd made notes. "The doctor's office in Greenwich called to remind her she's scheduled for outpatient surgery in three days."

"Outpatient surgery?" Erik sat up straighter.

"I'll quote you the message. 'Mrs. D'Anton is booked at nine A.M. on the morning of the nineteenth at Greenwich Hospital for a tubal ligation.' " He looked up at Erik. "I take it this is a surprise to all of us."

"A surprise," Erik whispered. "More like a bombshell. I had no idea she'd done this, none."

"I've got a couple more calls," Raskin said tactfully. "I'll make them in the other room." He got up and left Erik to deal with his shock.

Erik used the remote control to switch off the television set, then lit a cigarette before getting up to walk the length of the room. Marisa had made arrangements to have a procedure that would sterilize her. She had taken him so literally at his word that she'd made preparations to eliminate any possibility of her ever having the child she'd so wanted.

He turned to walk the other way, pausing to tip the ash from his cigarette into the ashtray on the coffee table.

What had he done? he asked himself, flabbergasted by this additional evidence of the seriousness with which she viewed the issue of childbearing. Had he the right, he wondered, to dictate to anyone, but most especially to Marisa, the terms and conditions of her life to such an extent that she'd undergo surgery in order to satisfy those terms?

How, he thought on, would seven-year-old Erik have felt if there had been someone, regardless of what he or she looked like, who'd wanted to care for that boy? He would have loved that person wholeheartedly, gratefully, unreservedly. He would have tied himself to a lifelong bond with that person. And nothing about that person would have had meaning beyond the fact of that person's willingness to care. *I would have loved someone who loved me*, he thought, astounded by this realization. It was what Marisa had tried so hard and for so long to explain to him. It wasn't the face that mattered, but the humanity of the person to whom that face belonged. She was right, he thought, wondering why it had been so difficult for him to recognize this simple fundamental truth. I would love a child of ours. And that child would love both of us. Because we would be mother and father to someone we created out of the love we have for each other.

What a thing to come to so late in the day, and by so circuitous a route! He might have spared them both years of frustration and pain if he'd understood this sooner. It was the ultimate lesson she'd tried to teach him, and he'd failed to learn; he'd resisted learning because he'd been so mired in self-hatred that he'd been unable even to consider it. Now, suddenly, he could quite readily imagine Marisa and himself with a child. Not that he would take to sunlight all at once like some exotic plant. But so many things were possible. Why not a child? He was bound to love anything that was a part of Marisa. And what could be more intimate a part of a woman he loved than a child that came from her body? He'd been stubborn and infantile, he'd wept and carried on like someone demented at the very notion of impregnating his wife. He'd behaved like a complete madman, for no valid reason.

If she would consent to come home; if she decided she wanted to come home, he would never again deny her anything. He'd been made to see all too clearly how little time there was. He was no longer a young man, but he had a young wife who could bear children. He'd been insufferably selfish to deny her. How lucky to realize this now, before the irreparable surgery! It really wasn't too late. If she'd just ask to come home; if she'd only consider returning home.

On the morning of their sixth day in London, the telephone rang soon after seven.

"We're on our way," Raskin said. "The car she's ordered is picking her up in forty minutes. She just phoned down to ask them to get her bill ready. I'll get on the phone and tell them to do ours, then zip down and take care of it."

"No. I'll go down and do it. You ring our driver. I don't want to waste any time."

Filled with urgency and fearful of losing her for any reason, Erik went downstairs to pay the bill, ignoring the glances of the reception staff and of the several early-rising guests in the lobby. He really didn't have the time or energy to concern himself with anything but his fervent need to see Marisa, to remain as close to her as he was able.

When her car and driver pulled up in front of the Park Lane, Erik and Raskin were in the Bentley a short way ahead. Peering out through the dark-tinted rear window, they saw her come out of the hotel followed by a bellman with her suitcase. She tipped both the bellman and the doorman, who held open the door to her hired limousine, then disappeared into the rear of the Rolls.

As the liveried chauffeur cruised past them, their driver allowed two cars to get ahead of them, then swung out into the traffic to follow.

"It's a magical mystery tour," Raskin said, then waited for Erik to get angry.

Erik chose to be philosophical. "I suppose it is," he said, his eyes never leaving the car just ahead.

They drove through the day, stopping only when the Rolls did—to fill up with fuel outside Birmingham, for Marisa to go to the ladies' room once, and once mid-afternoon when her chauffeur went into one of the roadside restaurants to buy food.

Erik couldn't even think of eating, but drank several containers of not bad coffee, and smoked Sobranies until he'd given himself a headache.

"The only problem I can see we're going to have," Raskin said, "is finding accommodations when she decides to stop."

"We'll manage," Erik said, closing his eyes for a moment. "Have you any aspirin?"

"Headache?"

"Yes."

"I've got some somewhere in here," Raskin said, digging around in the leather satchel Risa had given him on his birthday a few years before. "You don't have anything to take them with."

"It doesn't matter." Erik popped the tablets into his mouth and chewed them up, then closed his eyes again.

"That," Raskin declared, "is probably the most impressive thing I've ever seen you do. How the fuck can you chew aspirin?"

"You should see me do razor blades," Erik replied. "*That* is impressive."

"Jesus! Maybe you should try to cut back a bit on the cigarettes."

Erik opened his eyes and turned to look at Raskin. "When I am sitting somewhere with Marisa and she has agreed to return home with me, I will go back to smoking the occasional cigarette. Until then, my choices consist of alcohol, cigarettes, or narcotics. Since I don't believe on principle in the use of narcotics, and since I wish to remain in full possession of my so-called faculties, I will continue to smoke."

"Right," Raskin said, and looked out the window. He hoped to hell this wasn't going to go on for too long. He and Erik would wind up at each other's throats. On top of that, he missed Kitty. This was the first time they'd been apart, and the separation pains he felt were an unpleasant surprise. He missed their telephone conversations, their arguments, and, most of all, their lovemaking. She'd started talking a lot about her age lately, the difference in their ages, and he'd been using up all his energy telling her it didn't matter a rat's ass to him how old she was. But now that they were apart, he could see he'd been less than convincing because he could never get himself to say he loved her. And she was such a proud and feisty woman she'd keep her tongue between her teeth forever rather than be the one to say it first. "What a fucking jerk!" he muttered, disgruntled.

"Are you speaking to me?" Erik asked quietly.

"No, I'm speaking to me. But you qualify, too. A pair of first-class jerks, that's what we are. You because right when you're standing at the end of the rainbow in front of the fucking pot of gold you decide maybe it's all just a sham, and me because I don't have the balls to break down and tell Kitty I love her. What the hell are we doing, Erik?"

"We are working to get my wife back," he answered. "And when we have succeeded at that, you're going to get on the telephone and tell Kitty to come—wherever we are—on the next available flight."

"Yeah!" Raskin said. "That's a damned good idea."

"And then we will have our holiday, as planned."

"You're starting to believe it'll all work out, huh?"

"I have no choice," Erik said fatalistically.

Risa's car left the M-6 fifty or so miles south of the Scottish border.

"I think we'll be stopping soon," their driver told Erik and Raskin. "It's getting late."

"We'll see where they go, then find a place nearby," Raskin told the driver, then said to Erik, "She must've made a reservation, but I'll be damned if I know how. The Park Lane switchboard didn't know a thing about where she was going or where she planned to stay."

"Perhaps," Erik offered, "she saw a travel agent and we're not aware of it."

"I'd say perhaps you're right," Raskin said.

Risa's car stopped at the Old England Hotel in Windermere. Erik and Raskin were able to obtain rooms for themselves and their driver at a smaller hotel up the road. A couple of quick calls ensured the cooperation of several staff members at the Old England, then Erik and Raskin took a short walk to stretch their legs.

"This is going to wind up costing a small fortune," Raskin said, as they looked at the choppy surface of Lake Windermere under the last of the setting sun.

"I don't care how much it costs," Erik stated. "I thought you realized that."

"Just checking. It's not my money, remember, and I've been playing fast and loose with it, paying people off right, left, and center, not to mention the agency in London and the staff at the Park Lane."

"If it costs every last penny I have, it will be well worth it. I think we should return to the hotel now, in case there's news."

* * *

After a room-service dinner at which she picked, Risa decided to take a walk through the town. She strolled out into the balmy night air, noting that a number of the shops were still open and quite a few tourists were out and about despite the lateness of the hour. Grateful for the darkness, she went along the winding streets, her hands jammed deep into the pockets of the cashmere cardigan she'd bought in London, looking down at the Ferragamo walking shoes she'd also acquired there. She felt fractionally better, less crazy, than she had even the day before. And the bruise on her face was beginning to fade.

Looking up, she wished suddenly that Erik were there with her, walking along at her side. This was such a pretty place. Had he been there, she'd have been able to point out the quaint little house across the way that leaned slightly to the left. And they might have gone inside to investigate some of the souvenir shops. She missed him suddenly, intensely, most painfully. She thought of that night he'd come to dinner, when, before he'd gone hurrying away, she'd kissed his cheek. And his shocked reaction. No one had kissed him, at that point, in twenty-five years. Thinking of it now, she felt a sharp pang, missing him so acutely she had to stop all at once and begin retracing her steps to the hotel. She couldn't bear to be out on the street, playing at being a tourist, when she'd ruined something rare and wonderful. She felt like a murderer. And, God only knew, if she'd really wanted to, she could easily have been one. All it would have taken was directing that broken wineglass to some other, more vulnerable, part of that filthy bastard's body.

Seeing her suddenly stop and turn around, Erik darted into a nearby doorway, crowding close to a rough brick wall, as, on the far side of the street, Marisa, head down, went walking quickly back in the direction of her hotel.

He watched her, a tall black-haired woman hastening toward shelter as if something he'd failed to see had menaced her. He longed to tell her not to be afraid, not to run away. He was there to see no harm would come to her.

A moment. Then he slipped back onto the street in order to keep her within his sight until the last possible moment.

Thirty-one

AFTER ONE NIGHT AT WINDERMERE, RISA WAS OFF AGAIN, THIS TIME heading north and west into Scotland.

"This could get tricky," Raskin said. "Depending on where she finally ends up, we could have serious problems getting a hotel anywhere close by."

His hunch proved right. Risa had booked herself—somehow; they still had no idea when or how she'd made her travel plans—into a very small and exclusive hotel on Loch Linnhe. There was no hotel nearer than four miles away. They had no choice but to book into that other hotel, where Raskin, struck by inspiration, at once got on the pay phone in the lobby.

"I've done it!" he told Erik excitedly. "I've hired a boat. Since there's no way we can get close to her by land, we'll do it by water."

"But how will we know her movements?"

"Easy. Our driver's already enlisted a chambermaid at her hotel, and he's talking to one of the waiters right now."

"I wonder," Erik mused, "if she can sense any of this."

Since the hotel was so small, there was no room service. Risa would have to present herself in the dining room for meals or go hungry. The only concession the hotel would make to room service was the offer of a tea tray in the afternoon in one of the two small adjoining rooms that served as lounges. Both had peat fires going that first evening, and the aroma was exquisite, as was the view from both her bedroom and the dining-room windows, of the sun setting over the loch, with the mountains beyond tangled in low-hanging gray-white clouds.

Fortunately, she was given a small window table that allowed her to sit with her back to the room and her eyes on the view. She ordered without interest, and was startled into positive response by a first course of succulent fresh langoustines, followed by a fillet of wild salmon in the best hollandaise she'd ever tasted. She wasn't able to sample the dessert offerings, having eaten far more than she'd imagined she would, but the filter coffee was dark and strong and served with heavy cream. One of the waitresses poured the coffee, then asked if Risa would care to sample the tablet, which turned out to be a sugary confection rather like fudge.

She was able to drink her coffee in the seclusion of the glass-enclosed but still chilly sitting area beyond the hotel's entryway. She wondered if the owner's wife who, she'd been told by the waitress at dinner, was also the chef and an award-winning one at that, would consider revealing the secret of her superb hollandaise. She thought Erik would adore it. Erik would love this place altogether. If she ever managed to stop hating herself, and if he could somehow forgive her, perhaps they might one day come here together. The air was crisp and bracing, and she was actually sleepy. She stayed looking out the windows for a half hour more, until the sun had long since set and the view was lost to darkness, then she rose and went up to her room.

For the first time since she'd run away, she slept through the night and awakened early the next morning feeling less frazzled, more relaxed, and even slightly optimistic. The sun was shining, she saw, looking out the window at the white Victorian cottage across the way with its splendid wildflower garden. She bathed and dressed and went down to the dining room for a breakfast of fresh-squeezed orange juice, thick savory oatmeal porridge, and several cups of the excellent coffee.

Her driver was waiting out front with the car, but she said, "I think I'll take a walk down to the port, have a look around."

"Shall I follow with the car, madame?"

"No. Why don't you wait here. Go inside and have some breakfast. I'll come back in an hour or so, then we can drive through the countryside."

"May I suggest Fort William, madame? I think you might enjoy that."

"Fine. We'll go there," she said, and set off to follow the single-lane road the quarter mile to the port.

There were all kinds of boats moored here and there. She walked out onto the long pier to stand in the wind, breathing deeply the salt fresh air. It might have been paradise, she thought, lifted by the great natural beauty of the place, by the lighthouse to the left and, beyond, in the distance, the castle standing on a small island at the far end of the loch. Fields ran on either side of the water, with bluebells, primroses, and wildflowers whose names she didn't know growing in profusion. If only Erik could see this, she thought, pushing the hair out of her eyes. There was no one about to disturb him, no one among these gentle, good-natured people who'd dream of taking pointed notice of him. She wanted so much to call him, to try to explain, but she didn't yet feel clean enough, or sure enough of her emotions to risk speaking to him.

While she stood there, she remembered the first time they'd made love, the veneration with which he'd touched her; his trepidations had moved her almost as much as his touch. He'd been so shy, so terribly fearful of showing himself to her. And she could feel even now her own fear at first sight of his naked body, the fear she'd refused to acknowledge because she'd always believed Erik would never hurt her. It had, of course, hurt. But she'd wanted that pain; she'd guided him to the apex of her thighs knowing in advance that joining with him would demonstrate as nothing else could the strength of her love for him. She'd somehow needed that pain; it was emblematic of his meaning for her. She might never deliver a child out of her body but eighteen years before she'd taken one in; she'd brought him home inside her, and had never, since that first day, even considered refusing him access to his rightful place within her. Yet just a matter of days ago she'd said and done things that had closed him out, robbed him of the home she'd vowed always to keep for him.

Erik, I'm sorry, she thought, narrowing her eyes against the sun as she gazed out at the loch. I promised never to hurt you, but it's all I've done for such a long time now. And there was never anyone who deserved less to be hurt than you, never anyone less equipped to handle the pain. Forgive me. I'm so very sorry.

From the boat anchored halfway between the pier and the lighthouse, Erik watched through binoculars as Marisa walked out onto the cement pier and stood looking around. She stayed for quite some time, not moving, just gazing soberly at the view, every so often pushing the hair out of her eyes. The binoculars brought her so close his hand actually rose to touch her. Then, catching himself, he reached for a cigarette, and went on watching.

Think of me! he willed. Wish for me! Within moments I'll be with you.

Raskin came to stand beside him. "She told her driver she'd be back in an hour. They're going to Fort William. Our waiter overheard him telling one of the waitresses. Our Ned's waiting to pick us up."

Reluctantly, Erik lowered the binoculars, saddened to have to lose sight of her again. He gave the glasses to Raskin, put out the cigarette, then picked up his hat. "We'd best be on our way," he said.

As she walked head-down back along the road toward the hotel, she stopped and turned, looking around. It wasn't possible, she knew, but she could have sworn Erik was nearby. She took a deep breath and thought there was the faintest hint of sandalwood on the breeze. She stood a moment longer, then continued on her way.

For three days they followed her about the countryside, to Fort William, where the driver showed her Glen Nevis and then Ben Nevis, and then down to Oban, where she walked along the waterfront, glancing into shops and even occasionally going inside but emerging empty-handed every time. On to Kilninver, Kilmelford, and Arduaine. She stopped now and then to drink a cup of coffee, or to look admiringly at the roughly beautiful scenery in the uniformly sunny days. Often she left the car to walk; often Erik was unable to follow and had to be content watching her through the binoculars.

On the morning of the fourth day, word came that she was on her way again, and they rushed to stay with her, heading south, back into England. The weather had turned foul overnight, and they drove throughout the day in a torrential downpour that resolved into a fine mist as they left the main highway heading—their driver guessed, and correctly—for Grasmere.

"I reckon you'll have to chance it, see if they've any rooms at The Swan, because you wouldn't want to stay anywhere else. There's too much chance of missing her if and when she takes it into her mind to leave. With luck, though, she need never know you're in the same hotel."

It was risky, but Erik wanted to try. After she'd gone inside with her chauffeur, who was carrying both their bags, they pulled into the parking area across the road from the hotel and waited half an hour before sending Ned in to ask about vacancies. The small dapper man came running back through the mist with a smile on his face to declare, "Luck's holding, gentlemen. They've had two cancellations, as fate would have it. And the lobby's empty now, it being near to dinnertime."

Raskin got them registered while Erik waited outside. Then they sprinted up to their rooms, the driver at one end of the floor, Erik and Raskin sharing another at the opposite end. Their room was immense, with a pair of double beds, a sofa, and an armchair. There were welcoming complimentary glasses of sherry on the desk, as well as a hospitality tray with coffee, tea, and hot chocolate, a small electric kettle, a teapot, and a ceramic jar containing bars of chocolate and locally made gingerbread.

Raskin went around investigating the contents of the drawers and closets, announcing, "Even hot-water bottles if our tootsies get cold! Nice place. That's another one for our Ned."

Erik wasn't listening. Marisa was so near he could feel her. He looked at the walls, then at the ceiling, cocking his head to one side as if he might hear her speak.

"I'll go arrange for some food," Raskin said, and left Erik to himself.

In the middle of undressing to take a shower before dinner, Risa stopped and stood very still. It was the oddest thing, but again she had the powerful feeling that Erik was somehow close by. Her guilt, she decided, was starting to turn her peculiar. Erik was at home in Connecticut. And as if to prove this to herself, she went to the telephone, said she wished to make a credit-card call, gave the number and waited for the operator to call her back. When the phone rang, she snatched up the receiver nervously, wetting her lips as an overseas operator said, "Your number's ringing."

It rang four times and then a woman came on saying, "Answering service," and Risa slammed the receiver down, her heart racing, to sit staring at the telephone, wondering what this could mean. The only other time Erik had resorted to using the answering service during the day—they often let the service take calls at night—was when he'd so suddenly gone away years and years ago. Had he gone away now? And if so, where? And why? Had she made such a mess of things that he'd left altogether? God! It frightened her. She put her hand out to the telephone thinking she'd call Kitty and ask her. Kitty would know. But she pulled her hand back. She couldn't do it. She didn't have the nerve to call Kitty, not yet. She didn't want to hear Kitty say Erik was gone and that no one knew when he'd be coming back, if ever.

With a final look at the telephone, she got up and went to take her shower.

"She just placed a credit-card call," Raskin said, hanging up the telephone. "Are you listening to me, Erik?"

"Sorry. What?"

"Risa just called home."

Erik's face began to brighten. "She did?"

"Yeah. But when our service answered, she hung up."

"Oh!" Erik's features drooped.

"Hey! Don't go all down in the mouth! It's a damned good sign."

"Yes." Erik looked back at the television screen.

In the dining room, she was given a booth overlooking the rain-drenched garden with its varicolored rose bushes and its thatch-roofed birdhouse. She nibbled at overdone roast lamb with bottled mint sauce and stared out at the misty hills across the way, then at the garden slowly losing its color as an unseen sun sank behind the clotted clouds.

She drank two glasses of wine with her dinner, then lingered in a corner of the lounge afterward curled up in a window seat with a cup of coffee. She smoked several cigarettes, one after another, as she continued to stare blankly out the window, completely unmindful of the cloaked figure hidden by shrubberies, who stood out in the rain and, immobile, watched as she got through her dinner and then shifted to see her inside the lounge as she drank coffee and persevered with her new cigarette habit.

He was perfectly reconciled to stand perhaps ten feet away, totally concealed, and yet with an optimum view. He stood for close to ninety minutes, his eyes on Marisa, his treacherous hands safely clasped behind his back. When she let her head come to rest against the window, he very nearly reached out to her, but he kept the control, and remained stationary. And when at last she uncurled herself and left the window seat, he remained outside another five minutes on the off chance she might come back. But she didn't. It didn't really matter. He'd been closer to her for those ninety minutes than he had in what felt like years.

By six the next morning, Erik and Raskin were back in the Bentley with Ned at the wheel, the car parked half a mile up the road at a point Risa would have to pass on her way to the M-6. They knew that she was now en route back to London because the Swan receptionist had booked a reservation for Mrs. D'Anton at the Park Lane.

Raskin wanted to know why they didn't just get a good head start and beat her back to London.

"I want to keep her in my sight," Erik said, and that ended the discussion.

By that evening, he and Raskin were again in their suite at the Ritz and, according to the Park Lane staff, Risa was ensconced in a suite of her own.

"She started to place another credit-card call," Raskin told him, "then changed her mind and canceled it."

"Did she give a number?" Erik asked, hope-filled.

"She didn't even get that far. Started reciting the credit-card number, then said, 'Never mind,' and hung up."

"Oh!"

"Don't keep deflating that way, Erik! Who the hell d'you think she'd be calling, if not you?"

"I don't dare take anything for granted."

"That's not taking for granted. That's plain logic and common sense."

"So you say," Erik said, and toyed with the remote control, flipping through the channels on the TV set. "I'm beginning to think this may take a very long time."

"Why d'you say that?"

"I'm tired, Harold. I've never felt so tired."

"Well, hell! I wonder why! Let me think. What could it be? Could it be because of the couple of hours you spent standing in the rain last night? Or could it be maybe a solid week's worth of chasing all over hell and gone, sneaking around back alleys, hiding in doorways, creeping through bushes, hiking on and off boats, in and out of limos, sneaking around hotels? What d'you think? Or maybe it could have something to do with the week *before* that, chasing all over London. D'you think that could have anything to do with why you're tired? Erik, go the hell to bed and get some sleep. Of course you're tired. I'm amazed you're still *conscious*, for Chrissake! I'll order up some food. You'll eat, grab a shower, then hit the sack."

"And what about you?" Erik wanted to know.

"I've got to talk to Kitty, bring her up to date."

"Tell her you love her, Harold. Learn something from the mistakes I've made."

"What mistakes might those be?"

"Too numerous to mention. Do it! Perhaps you should even consider going home. I know you're missing her."

"Better yet, why don't I tell her to come over? It's still early back home. If she hustled, she could get on a flight tonight and be here in the morning."

"Do that," Erik told him. "I'm going to take your suggestion and have a shower. If I'm still awake when the food arrives, come fetch me."

In the dark bathroom, Erik wearily got out of his clothes and turned on the shower. He did feel exceedingly tired. He also felt very middle-aged and somewhat flabby. His hair was thinning, he was getting jowly, too; as if his face weren't bad enough already. He needed to get reading glasses but hadn't so far summoned up the grit, or been sufficiently hampered by his increasing farsightedness to see an eye doctor. Fortunately, his teeth were still good, and his flexibility in general had diminished only slightly with age. But he was incredibly tired. He wanted Marisa to make the move that would mean he could go to her, reclaim her, take her into his arms, and return her home. He stood under the shower willing her to pick up the telephone in her room and make good on that credit-card call. Please! he urged her. It will take so very little. All you have to do is say you want me.

Risa walked back and forth through the rooms of her suite, each leg of her circuit bringing her to a halt before the telephone. She'd pause for a moment or two, then turn and start walking again. Thirteen days, thirteen nights. It was the longest period of time she'd ever spent entirely alone. It felt much longer.

For an hour she paced. Then suddenly she had to stop and stand very still. She was overcome by a driving need for Erik. It was a longing so intense it almost bent her double. She had to try; she had to hear his voice at least. She had to tell him how sad and sorry and ashamed she was.

She pounced on the telephone before she had time to change her mind, and rhymed off the credit-card and house numbers, then hung up and stood wringing her hands, waiting beside the telephone for the operator to call her back.

"Your number's ringing," the overseas operator told her.

And then the damned answering-service woman came on the line.

"I want to leave a message for Mr. D'Anton," Risa said hotly.

"Yes, ma'am?"

"Tell him Marisa wants to come home!" She recited the hotel number, then said, "Have you got that?"

"Yes, ma'am, I do."

"Good! Make sure he gets the message," she snapped, then threw down the phone. "Damn, damn, damn!" she muttered, and went back to pacing.

Erik had just fallen asleep when Raskin came bursting in, crowing, "She called! I've got a message for you, Erik!"

Erik sat up, instantly awake, his heart drumming. "What is it?"

"She said to tell you Marisa wants to come home! She called, and she wants to come home!" Raskin did a mad little dance.

"Thank you," Erik said thickly.

"You're welcome. And Kitty'll be here in the morning. If it's okay with you, I'm going to go out to Heathrow to meet her."

"Of course. Thank you," Erik said again.

Raskin stood for a moment, a bit confused by Erik's subdued reaction. Then he went out and quietly closed the door.

Erik waited alone during the morning for the call from the Park Lane. When it came, he thanked the caller, then went hurrying from the hotel.

Risa walked along, crossed Piccadilly, and strolled toward Covent Garden. She turned off into the first small street in the environs of the Garden, looking in shop windows. Cutting through smaller and smaller streets, she emerged suddenly right in the main body of the Garden. She couldn't understand why Erik hadn't responded to her message. Maybe he'd gone away somewhere. Maybe she'd screwed up so badly that he no longer cared what she did or where she went. But no. Erik cared. He had always cared. She'd been the one who'd been sidetracked for a short time. First there was that business about babies. Another subject on which Kitty had been absolutely right. She'd only carried on about it the way she had because Erik was so set against having a child. Well, that was scheduled to get taken care of. She'd missed the appointment, but she could always make another. A baby simply was no longer earth-shatteringly important to her. But Erik was.

Erik was her heartline, her source of life-sustaining nourishment. He'd married a child, and she'd stayed a child for far too long. But all that was over now. Whether she'd wanted it or not, whether she liked the form her transition into adulthood had taken or not, she was no longer a child. She'd had a large dose of the real world, as Kitty liked to call it, and it didn't taste all that good. But it hadn't killed her. And she'd taught that moron Stefan a lesson he wouldn't forget in a hurry. She was damned glad she'd stabbed him. She wondered if he had any idea how lucky he was that she hadn't killed him.

Leaving the Garden after an hour or so, having looked in most of the shops and seen nothing she cared to buy, she walked back in the direction she'd come, crossing streets to go down a meandering laneway that led to a charming restaurant with a huge skylight and dozens of thriving green plants positioned in and around the tables. It was nearly noon, and she was hungry. The hostess directed her to a table beneath the skylight and opposite the door.

She sat down, lit a cigarette, and picked up the menu, the sun pleasantly warm on her hair. As she reached to put the cigarette on the lip of the ashtray, a hand whisked it from her fingers, and it vanished. A moment, and a pink rose lay before her on the table. She looked up to see Erik seated opposite, smiling at her.

"I understand that you would like to come home, Marisa," he whispered.

"Erik!" She put her hands in his, shaking her head in wonder at the sight of him, sitting smiling in the spread of sun beneath the skylight. Her heart gave a tremendous leap against her ribs and she lowered her head for a long moment, holding fast to his hands. Then she raised her eyes to ask, "Can you forgive me?"

"Only if you forgive me," he replied, the heat from the sun soaking into the top of his head, his shoulders, his arms, scalding him. He tried to ignore it.

"There's nothing to forgive you for, Erik. I'm the one."

"There's a great deal."

"No," she disagreed. "I was a fool. I did such stupid things."

"It doesn't matter."

The waitress came to the table, looked at Erik, then looked quickly at Marisa.

Her arms still extended across the tabletop, her hands linked with Erik's, Marisa smiled at the young woman and said, "My husband and I would like to see the wine list, please." She turned, smiling, to Erik. "My husband knows a great deal about wines."

The waitress went off, craning to look back over her shoulder at the dead peculiar pair at table twelve.

Marisa had to ask, "What are you *doing* here, Erik?"

"I have been here all along," he answered, drowning in the heat and the light, but determined to withstand their effects.

"I've never been anywhere without you," she said, holding tight to his hands, unwilling to let go of him.

"Are you all right?" he asked.

"I am now. Please, could we forget the whole thing, forget any of it ever happened?"

"Forget what?" he asked, straight-faced.

Again she lowered her head, her grip going even tighter on his hands. He was so unutterably good, so very kind, so remarkably forgiving. "I'm not hungry," she said, returning her eyes to his. "Are you hungry, Erik? What I really would like is to hold you, make love. Wouldn't you much rather do that?"

"Now that you mention it, I think that's an excellent idea. Why don't we go back to your hotel?"

"What an excellent idea!" she declared, beaming at him. She released him only long enough to grab her handbag and the rose before taking hold of his hand to go rushing out of the restaurant with him. "Let's take a taxi," she said, scanning the street outside. "We'll have to make a stop at a drugstore on the way, though."

"Why?" he asked.

"Because the IUD had to be removed," she answered. "I don't know why I didn't tell you. Somehow, I just couldn't."

"Well," he said, "I'm afraid I really have no interest in making any side trips. I'd prefer to go directly back to your hotel."

She stood looking at him for a moment, then she threw her arms around him and hugged him. "Erik! I'm so happy to *see* you!"

And without giving it a thought, he held her and kissed her, right there on the street.

> "And . . . and . . . I . . . kissed her! . . .
> I! . . . I! . . . I! . . . And she did not die!"
> *The Phantom of the Opera*
> *(Le Fantôme de l'opéra)*
> Gaston Leroux

About the Author

CHARLOTTE VALE ALLEN was born in Toronto, Canada. After more than ten years as a singer, actress, and cabaret/revue performer, she began writing in 1971, and has been a full-time writer since the publication of *Love Life*, her first novel, in 1976. She has published twenty-six works of fiction, as well as the award-winning autobiographical account of incest, *Daddy's Girl*.